EMERALD

Also by Elisabeth Luard in
A COMMON READER EDITION:

The Old World Kitchen

Emerald

ELISABETH LUARD

A COMMON READER EDITION
THE AKADINE PRESS

Emerald

A COMMON READER EDITION published 1999
by The Akadine Press, Inc., by arrangement
with Transworld Publishers Ltd.

A COMMON READER EDITION and fountain colophon
are trademarks of The Akadine Press, Inc.

ISBN 1-888173-62-9

3   5   7   9   10   8   6   4   2

*For my beloved husband Nicholas, who has
been with me all the way.*

Acknowledgements

My gratitude and thanks are due to Ursula Mackenzie and Broo Doherty of Bantam Press, whose creative contributions and unflagging support made them far more than editors. To my agent, Abner Stein, who has looked after and encouraged me from the beginning, above and beyond the call of duty. To Patrick Janson-Smith, for his confidence in my ability to write a novel in the first place. To my old friend Michael Hastings, who read the first draft and laughed at my jokes. Also to the book's line-editor, Edward Leeson, for his attention to detail and patience in spotting anomalies in the text. And to my children, Caspar, Francesca, Poppy and Honey, whose love, confidence and companionship I can never repay.

1

Geneva: Friday, 3 April, 1987

The woman might have been a queen.

That, at least, was the opinion of the glittering crowd who watched her take her seat among them in the marquee which had been pitched on the shores of Lake Geneva on that bright spring day.

In the long and distinguished history of Sotheby's, the international fine arts auctioneers, no-one could remember any of its auction rooms being as crowded before.

The reason was simple. The sale of the Duchess of Windsor's jewels – 'the Wallis collection', as the Duchess had been fond of describing her Aladdin's cave of love-tokens – was a fitting memorial to a royal obsession which had captured the imagination of the world.

Edward VIII, a king by birth and by proclamation, had lost his kingdom for love of a woman he could never make his queen. He crowned her none the less – with pearly smiles and diamond tears and rubies for the heart's blood shed.

The jewels became their kingdom. For want of heirs, the kingdom came under an auctioneer's hammer.

In the thick and lavishly illustrated catalogue were prowling panthers and slippery tigers, a jungle of predatory beasts. And feathers, too, endless feathers – the emblem of a prince – superbly spread and ready for flight.

The audience – sophisticated, admitted by ticket only and linked electronically to New York, Tokyo, Paris, Riyadh and London – was greedy for drama.

Among the overdressed and heavily bejewelled crowd, the woman who had caught the crowd's attention stood out because of the sculptural elegance of her simple black dress and the absence of jewellery.

The fortune which was her passport to the gathering came not from inheritance, not even through marriage, but from her own extraordinary talents. A modern philanthropist, she wore her conscience on her sleeve – both in the conduct of her business affairs and in the way she spent her wealth.

There are some who are born to rule, and others who must earn their crown. The mystery which surrounded the woman's origins only added to her legend.

Those who wrote about her searched for clues in her physical presence. In her middle years, she had that touch of arrogance, that careless confidence which is the birthright of natural beauties, whatever their age. The bones were fine, the figure willowy, the dark hair lit with russet lights enhanced by the streak of grey. Then there was the way she moved, almost like a dancer, or perhaps a gymnast – flat-footed as a barefoot hunter, loose-hipped as a young ballerina.

But it was her eyes which caught the attention first. They were neither cornflower, nor sky, nor gentian blue. The woman had eyes of oriental amethyst – that rare variety of sapphire whose violet tint makes it the most sought-after gem of all.

There was something about the woman which in these particular surroundings jogged the memory of those who knew the previous owner of the treasure-chest.

She had already caused a minor stir earlier that afternoon. Although it was strictly forbidden, she had succeeded in persuading the stone-faced vigilantes to open the case which contained lot 159 and allow her to handle the trinket. Those nearest the woman thought they saw tears as she examined it.

At least one of the men who'd watched the woman at the private view of the Windsor jewels in Geneva's Hôtel Beaurivage knew exactly what was familiar about her. He also knew why she was interested in the trinket.

'And now to lot 159.'

The image flicked up on the screen.

'My lords, ladies and gentlemen. A keepsake locket containing three locks of hair.'

Three? The crowd murmured its surprise. Two certainly – this was the debris of an all-excluding passion – but three?

'I'll start the bidding at five thousand. Five thousand I am bid.'

The woman's black gloved hand was raised. The very observant noticed that on her wrist she wore a slender – almost childish – chain bracelet from which dangled a tiny jewelled cross. That, too, was a trademark, well chronicled. Was it a love-token? A reminder of some childhood memory? No-one knew for sure.

The locket, too, held a mystery. Three curls of hair.

'Five thousand and five.'

A rival bidder had emerged from the throng. Bid and counterbid. Ten thousand. And five. Twelve thousand. And five. Twenty thousand. Twenty-one.

The crowd craned its neck to follow the drama. The price was far too high for the little object to merit.

It was difficult to read the woman's emotions as the kid-gloved hand was raised, dropped and raised again. In her face was none of the greed, the acquisitive passion, which distinguished the bidders from the observers. The face was shuttered, sombre.

'Twenty-one at the back. Do I hear twenty-two?'

The woman's face was puzzled now. She turned her head, searching out the source of the rivalry. Suddenly her expression changed. There was anger – perhaps even fear.

The crowd stirred expectantly again.

All at once a hush fell. There was a disturbance directly under the rostrum.

An English gentleman – you could not mistake him as anything else – bespectacled, elderly and distinguished-looking, with an air of officialdom and long-exercised authority underlined by his Savile Row three-piece pinstripe, passed a visiting card up to the auctioneer.

The auctioneer studied the card, hesitated, whispered to his assistant. Finally he shrugged and nodded.

'Lot 159', he announced to the gathering, 'has been withdrawn from the sale. We now proceed to a brooch in the shape of the feathered emblem of the Prince of Wales, the brooch being set with rubies and diamonds . . .'

Reading from the catalogue, his voice ran on.

The instigator of the interruption turned and walked back towards the woman in black. The woman rose, smiled, and slipped her hand through the proffered arm. Silently the two figures made their way down the aisle towards the exit.

The crowd, intrigued, speculated momentarily on the relationship. Father and daughter perhaps? There seemed to be affection between them. Or might they be lovers? Stimulated by the trinkets on the screen, the crowd was romantically inclined. A beautiful woman kept an old man young. And a gift of jewels kept a beautiful woman by an old man's side.

Sir Anthony Anstruther, the pinstriped Englishman, would have been outraged by such a suggestion. The woman herself would have laughed – and, as now, her violet eyes would have sparkled with pleasure.

But Anthony Anstruther was not the woman's father. Nor was he her lover. He was something far more important. Anthony Anstruther was the woman's guardian angel, or devil, depending how you saw it.

2

Windsor: 27 May 1936

'Dear Alice Keppel always used to say there were only two rules for a royal mistress . . .'

Maud Cunard's San Francisco drawl curled down the corridor of Fort Belvedere, the gothic Windsor hideaway of the man who was soon to be crowned Edward VIII.

'First she should *curtsy*. And then *leap* into bed!'

Lady Cunard laughed. Tiny and perfect as a jewelled parakeet, she preferred to be known as Emerald, rather than by her given name of Maud.

Her companion, the American aviator Colonel Charles Lindberg, flinched nervously. Royal favourites were a subject which Lindberg, newly arrived from a most stimulating tour of Hitler's Germany, felt were something of a hot potato.

Maud Cunard's efforts to launch the new king's 'companion', Mrs Ernest Simpson, into London society were being rewarded with the royal favour. And the Lindbergs' invitation to spend the weekend at the Fort was a demonstration of Edward's regard for the Americans' fellow-countrywoman.

Fort Belvedere, built two centuries earlier for George II's younger son, had been the King's folly when he was Prince of Wales. Now its turrets and crenellated walls, equipped with toy cannon, provided a refuge from the affairs of state thrust on him by the death of his father, George V, four months ago.

Her eyes bright with mischief, Lady Cunard peeped round the door of the octagonal drawing-room.

The rest of the King's guests were slowly assembling for pre-dinner cocktails – to be made, they were assured, by Mrs Simpson's practised hand. Dinner, as was usual at the Fort, was not to be served before ten.

'No-one mixes a better cocktail than Wallis,' the King himself had said that afternoon while he was marshalling his guests for a little light scything and weeding in the garden. Then, with a flash of the famous boyish grin, he added one of the Americanisms which were a tribute to the influence of his new *maîtresse en titre*. 'Hot-diggety-dog! Nothing Wallis turns her hand to can be anything but just perfect!'

'Oh, sir, surely not!' Wallis laughed, her blue eyes sparkling at the flattery.

Mrs Bessie Merryman, Wallis's seventy-year-old aunt and mentor, who had driven down earlier from London with the Simpsons, glanced up sharply at the tone of the exchange.

Wallis, it seemed to her aunt, was playing a dangerous game. Particularly since her niece's second marriage to Ernest had until now been such a success. And as for His Majesty's Americanisms – they were a public declaration of an infatuation which could only lead to trouble. Why, the King even affected a slight American accent.

Yet there was no doubt, Mrs Merryman thought as she watched them walk to the window together, that the two were well matched. Wallis and the King were as like as two peas. Both were slender and perfectly groomed; at around five and a half feet tall, Edward VIII was perhaps half an inch shorter than Wallis.

The King's hair was as sleek and fair as Wallis's was dark. His was a shining gold helmet, hers she wore slicked into a gleaming ebony cap round the centre parting she had worn ever since her time in China. Both had startlingly blue eyes. Hers had always been her best feature. They were an astonishing almost violet sapphire-blue, deep and lustrous. She had the eyes of her mother, the beautiful and unlucky Alys. His Majesty, Mrs Merryman reflected, had inherited the paler blue, slightly poached look of his Hanoverian forebears.

Lunch had been light – cold game pie and salad – since the King was terrified of becoming as stout as the German princelings who were his ancestors. Afterwards, Wallis had spent the afternoon in the Fort's kitchens supervising the preparation of a surprise dinner. All day there had been comings and goings with hampers and boxes, and Bessie had watched the arrival of a great vanload of flowers from Constance Spry.

Mrs Merryman reflected that the weekends at Fort Belvedere had become increasingly Wallis's domain. One or two of the old guard were usually included among the Americans for respectability. Sometimes they were the King's cousin, Dickie Mountbatten, and his wife Edwina, or the easy-going Irishman 'Fruity' Metcalfe with his wife Lady Alexandra. Or the beautiful but scatter-brained Diana Cooper who was always put in the Pink Bedroom, which this weekend accommodated Bessie Merryman. It had pink sheets, pink towels, pink Venetian blinds, pink soap and – Bessie was delighted to find – a pink-and-white ginghamed maid who unpacked the elderly American's bags and ran the guest a pink bath.

No doubt, Mrs Merryman thought, a few of the usual old names *did* look better in the Court Circular in *The Times*.

David – Bessie Merryman had quickly learned that His Majesty preferred friends and family to use his last rather than his first given name – might not see it, but he was used to having his own way. This weekend it was Iona and Freddie Fergusson who were to be the hostages to convention. Freddie, a major in the Scots Guards, had not been able to leave his regimental duties until late on that Saturday afternoon. Iona, the hereditary Maid of Eas Forse, had just returned from some clan celebration on her impossibly distant, mist-shrouded island. The pair arrived in an open-topped Morris just as the rest of the guests were making their way inside to dress for dinner.

'What was it this time, Iona?' The King's voice was warm and teasing. 'The ancient burial rites of the Celtic Twilight? A sacred druidical bonfire?'

He bounced happily up the stairs ahead of his guests, insisting on carrying Iona's vanity case himself.

'Rather more of the last, sir,' Iona replied. 'And just as well. For without the blaze we might all have been lost in the mists – or even have frozen to death!'

Iona managed to laugh.

The reality of the visit had been somewhat different. She had, not for the first time, gone to the island to persuade her father to come south. The Laird of Eas Forse had never recovered from the death of Iona's mother five years earlier. Sunk in the misery of loneliness, he sought refuge in Scotland's favourite mist – the one which came out of a bottle. The Western Isles were damp and inhospitable in the winter, in spite of the beauty of the glittering sea and heather-clad hills. And

Forsa House, built more with an eye to repelling marauders than for comfort, was in a sorry state of disrepair, needing far more spent on it than the family coffers could provide.

Yet the old man stubbornly refused to leave his island, as his only daughter urged him, to spend the end of his days in comfort in her centrally heated London house. Not even for the pleasure of watching his three-year-old grandson Callum grow up. Old men did not like change.

'How's the Laird himself?'

'Fine, sir, thank you.' Iona's cheerful voice belied the truth. 'Sends his best wishes. Hopes to see you again before too long.'

'Good. Good.' The King's voice was vague. It had been a long time since he had stolen a week on the island with the Maid of Eas Forse.

From below Maud Cunard watched the new arrivals disappear in the King's wake. She smiled to herself.

Lady Cunard particularly liked the graceful dark-eyed Iona and her handsome soldier-husband. She had long suspected something about Iona that neither Bessie nor Wallis was aware of. The slender Maid of Eas Forse, Lady Cunard sensed, had had a brief flirtation with the 'little man' when he had still been the carefree Prince of Wales – well before the wife of Ernest Simpson cast her spell over him.

Unlike his other mistresses – including the beautiful Thelma Furness, who had introduced her friend Wallis to her Prince Charming – Iona Stuart Fergusson had not been abruptly dismissed at the end of the affair. She had remained a friend and, Lady Cunard guessed, a trusted confidante. Iona was probably closer to him than anyone alive.

'You'll have to make do with me as butler today,' the King's voice floated down over the banisters. 'Crisp's sulking. Wallis has been in his pantry all afternoon going through the silver. Something special for tonight. It's all very hush-hush.'

He stopped outside the heavy oak door and flung it open with a shout of delight.

'I've given you my brother York's room. The wallpaper is covered in the most *horrendous* birds.'

Iona walked in. The room was shrouded in the half-dusk of the short English spring day. The bay-window framed the view of the woods and lake beyond. In the twilight she could just see a couple in a rowing-boat. They had shipped the oars and were drifting quietly across the still surface of the water.

The King came over to join her. 'That's Ernest Simpson,' he said thoughtfully. 'He's taken Mary Rafferty out for a row. You'll like her,

I'm sure. Very jolly and American. She and Ernest seem to be getting on splendidly.'

Iona turned. She looked steadily at the King.

'Mr Simpson isn't married to Mary Rafferty,' she said. 'His wife is Wallis. You are playing with fire, sir.'

For a moment her ex-lover stared back at her. Then his face flushed guiltily and his eyes turned away.

'Don't lecture me, Iona! I'm very fond of Wallis. I find her stimulating and attractive. She's unlike anyone I've ever known. But if you think I'd ever do anything to threaten her marriage . . .'

He broke off and lowered his head. After a moment Iona reached out and touched his bowed shoulder.

'Oh, David,' she said sadly, 'I hope you don't. I hope to God you don't. But, if it happens, remember I'll always be here to help in any way I can.'

At that moment Freddie erupted into the room, dragging two heavily laden suitcases behind him. He dumped the cases on the floor and beamed at the two of them, his wife and the king of England.

'Just in time to change for Wallis's dinner, sir!'

Freddie began burrowing for his dinner-jacket.

3

Windsor: 27 May 1936

'Come along, Charlie.'

Maud Cunard took Charles Lindberg's arm, and pushed open the door of the hexagonal drawing-room. As they stepped inside she caught her breath.

Wallis had excelled herself.

The room had been transformed into an exotic Queen of the Fairies grotto. There were flowers everywhere: oyster-pale orchids cascaded through waterfalls of creamy lilies, drifts of fragrant white narcissus clouded sheaves of the palest of miniature daffodils. A great fire blazed in the hearth, and the air was delicious with the scent of burning pinewood. The electric wall-lights had been replaced with a forest of many-branched silver candelabra in which burned dozens of white wax candles twined with garlands of tiny-leaved ivy.

'Wallis, darling!' Lady Cunard, herself famous as an arbiter of high-society style, bubbled with admiration. 'It's quite ravishing!'

Wallis uncrossed her legs and came forward to greet the new arrivals. Charles Lindberg bowed low over her square hand. Lady Cunard was permitted to kiss Wallis's passively proffered cheek. Wallis was not given to kissing people herself these days.

She was getting, thought Maud Cunard with a wry smile, quite *regal*.

'Darling Wallis,' she repeated, 'you always look wonderful in black.'

Lady Cunard broke off abruptly, her startled gaze held not by the simple, perfect, square-necked Molyneux gown which skimmed Wallis's slender figure, but by the jewelled collar she wore. It was set with the most magnificent rubies she had ever seen. Not, she thought, the sort of gift that Ernest Simpson, however successful his business affairs, would ever be able offer to his wife. Things must be hotting up.

Wallis Simpson smiled vaguely.

'Thank you, dear. I must see if Anthony has done the placement for dinner.' She moved away.

Anthony Anstruther, son of one of the King's senior courtiers, had volunteered to lend a hand for the weekend. He was busy copying a list on to a sheet of white card.

'Will this do, Mrs S?'

The brilliant blue eyes scanned the diagram.

'Very well, Anthony. I'm glad you put Aunt Bessie next to Charles; she *so* loves flirting with him.'

Wallis laughed, the famous parrot squawk catching the attention of Ann Morrow Lindberg, elegant and cool in a knee-length powder-blue Worth dress, her graceful neck circled with a double string of pale grey pearls. She had settled on the chintz-covered sofa between Aunt Bessie and the bubbling Mary Rafferty.

In one corner, Ernest Simpson and Freddie Fergusson, trim in his tartan trews, were swapping reminiscences of guard duties at the Tower.

The King himself was resplendent in his dress kilt of the pale Balmoral tartan, a white lawn shirt with finely pleated wrist-frills and jabot in brilliant contrast to the deep-brown velvet jacket with silver buttons and the obligatory mourning band of black satin ribbon on the arm.

He had seated himself at a small Regency desk with the lanky bespectacled Walter Monckton, who had just been appointed Attorney-General to the Duchy of Cornwall, and so made responsible for the King's private revenues. Alex Hardinge, the chief Private Secretary at the Palace, leaned over the King's shoulder turning the pages of a pile of documents. Hardinge, who had arrived earlier with a couple of scarlet leather despatch-boxes, had agreed at the King's insistence to stay and make up the numbers at dinner.

'David, we *can't* have thirteen at the table. I had a coloured mammy and she made me *terribly* superstitious,' Wallis pleaded when she belatedly realized how many they were. 'Alex simply must stay. Heaven knows what might happen otherwise. He can save us from some dreadful fate.'

The King, Lady Cunard reflected, looked bored to tears by the affairs of state.

'That's it, then. Cocktails for everyone!' The King rose suddenly, scattering papers in all directions. 'No shirking tonight. Mrs Simpson has arranged for us all to make whoopee Baltimore-style.'

He surveyed the company with an approving smile. Then he clapped his hands. 'There shall be Manhattans and White Ladies.'

At the sound of clapping, the door opened to admit the recalcitrant Crisp, bearing a large silver tray loaded with half a dozen bottles, a Georgian silver ice-bucket with tongs, some short tumblers and several small cocktail shakers. A jar of maraschino cherries, a bowl of lemons, a glass juice-squeezer and a coral-handled silver knife completed the supplies.

The King dumped the scarlet despatch-boxes on the floor.

'Over here, Crisp. Mrs Simpson shall mix them, I will shake them, and you shall hand them round. Now, who is for which?'

Wallis blended the cocktails swiftly and skilfully, measuring the liquor glass by glass and pouring it over the ice in the silver cocktail-shakers. Bourbon and cherries for the Manhattan; freshly squeezed lemon juice to mix with gin and Cointreau for the White Ladies. She rinsed the tumblers round with ice to freeze them while the King, beaming happily, rattled the shakers.

'Wallis would make a wonderful professional barman. There won't be a drop too much or too little.'

Maud Cunard took a sip of her Manhattan. Then she smiled, creasing what gossipy old 'Chips' Channon had called her pretty little wrinkled Watteau face.

'Best I've had since last I was in Twenty-One,' she pronounced.

By the time dinner was announced, two more rounds had been mixed – although Mrs Simpson herself, the observant Ann Lindberg noted, drank only weak whisky and water.

'Come along, Mrs Merryman. Mustn't keep the colonies waiting!'

Bessie Merryman's cheeks flushed with pleasure as the King offered her his arm to go in to dinner.

The dining-room, too, had been transformed. The walls were swagged with loops of heavy oyster satin, held in place by posies of primroses starred with pink rosebuds. A regiment of silver candlesticks bristling with slender ivory candles marched down the centre of the white damask tablecloth. Interspersed were cut-crystal decanters each holding a perfect spray of tiny pale-green orchids. Beneath each decanter was a small round mirror, doubling the effect of the flowers and the glittering glass and the candlelight.

Wallis Simpson leaned forward when all the guests were settled. 'With your permission, sir, I must explain the menu – even though I do know it is not customary in England to talk about *cookery*.'

The King nodded. 'Go right ahead.'

Wallis smiled, the necklace of rubies flashing in the candlelight.

'My mother was a wonderful cook,' she began. 'When my father died, we were very poor – so she opened a boarding house, serving good Maryland cooking, the best in America. It didn't pay, of course – Mother would only cook the meals she enjoyed herself, so we didn't last in business very long. But I still remember the wagon driving up with the terrapins for the stew, and Mother picking out the ones she wanted, and keeping them in a burlap bag in the cellar; and I used to be sent down to fatten them up on corn meal.'

Wallis paused and glanced round the table.

Her experience of the King had taught her that the fascination royalty held for ordinary mortals was fully reciprocated by royal curiosity about those who observed them from beyond the compound. Wallis went on, sure now of the romantic effect of her simple origins on the only audience she was interested in addressing.

'So when I knew Mary was coming over from the States, I had her do the shopping for tonight. I think the captain of the *Manhattan* must have been rather surprised when she had to go on deck to feed mush to the terrapins every day. I daren't tell you what she had to give the soft-shell crabs!'

As laughter rippled round the table, Iona Fergusson kicked her husband with her toe, and nodded towards the head of the table. The King was poking gingerly at his soup-plate like a suspicious cat confronted with a half-dead mouse. Mrs Simpson leaned over and gently but firmly smacked the royal wrist.

'And that', as Maud Cunard said later, 'was not something Freda or even Thelma would ever have dared do. That was when we *knew*.'

After the dinner – which had begun with the crab, continued with a creamy terrapin stew, followed by an immense roast sirloin, underdone as the King liked it, and finished with a richly sauced chocolate cake – the King disappeared without explanation.

A few minutes later the Americans were startled to hear a distant high-pitched wail. 'For all the world,' Mary Rafferty wrote to her sister afterwards, 'as if a cellarful of cats all had their tails shut in the door at once.'

The wail reached a crescendo as it came closer, until the door was flung open to allow entrance to His Majesty, a ribboned bonnet on his head and a fully inflated set of bagpipes under his arm. The room filled with the cadences of the Highlands.

As the King marched round the room, Wallis leaned back and turned to Charles Lindberg.

'The King is playing "Majorca",' she whispered in the American aviator's ear. 'It's his own composition. He played it at Balmoral last year. Even his father said it wasn't bad.' Wallis smiled, her broad face lightening. 'David said his father added it wasn't very good, either. But, then, the old man never approved of anything David did.'

Coffee and liqueurs were served to the ladies in the octagonal drawing-room. In the dining-room there was Forgé de Sazérac brandy and Upmann cigars for the men, but not for long as the host, still magnificent in his kilt, was clearly anxious to rejoin the ladies.

'Now, sir' – Wallis stood up as the King came back into the room, 'would you mind if I played some dance music on the gramophone?'

'Go to it!'

Wallis selected a fox-trot and wound up the instrument. Then she advanced on Freddie Fergusson and held out her hand.

'Come on, Major. Let's liven things up a bit.'

Freddie kicked back the rug. Wallis was an excellent dancer, light and beautifully balanced, and the King flung himself happily down on the floor to watch her. As the record ended he sprang back to his feet.

'Absolutely high time Wallis learned a Scottish reel!' he announced. 'She'll be wonderful at it. We shall do an eightsome. Iona and I will open. Freddie can partner Wallis. Alex, persuade Mrs Merryman. And Charles and Ann will pick it up in no time.'

More of the rugs were kicked aside. With Iona humming the tune and the King calling the moves, the party flung its way through the set pattern of the dance.

For a few moments, with the King's hands gripping hers as he swung her in an exuberant finale, Iona remembered another moment – it seemed like half a century ago – when the laughing Prince of Wales had handed her a sprig of white heather and whispered an invitation in her ear.

And then the dancers collapsed in a chattering heap on the cushions, as the King released his pupils for a final glass of champagne.

Ernest Simpson was the first to go up to his room, formally asking His Majesty's permission to retire, pleading a briefcase full of work which he needed for Monday. Soon afterwards Mary Rafferty, her auburn hair glinting, slipped out, too. One by one the other guests left, until the room was shadowy and tranquil in the candlelight.

Wallis, her face pensive, was standing by the heavy silk curtains which had been parted to show a glimpse of the lake beyond in the moonlight. The King left his place by the fire and crossed the floor.

'You were looking so beautiful tonight,' he said softly behind her. 'The rubies looked magnificent. With your dark hair you might have been a Celtic queen. Morgana the sorceress.'

He slipped his arm round Wallis's shoulder.

'Look over there – across the water. Do you know the legend of King Arthur? We were brought up on it as children. The great king who saved his people – *my* people – from the forces of darkness. The king who built Camelot.' The King's voice was thoughtful. 'When I was a boy I always saw the Fort as Camelot. In the last battle, when Arthur was mortally wounded, three queens came to bear him away in a barge into the sunset.'

Neither of them had noticed Iona, curled in a chair by the side of the fire, sleepily watching the dancing light on the lilies. The Maid of Eas Forse, the last in a long line of true Celtic queens, rose and moved quietly across the room. Gently she closed the door and left the lovers alone in the flickering scented firelight.

Wallis laid her head against her king's shoulder. Her cheek, magnolia-pale even in the firelight, was velvet-soft against her lover's. Her perfume was musky and deliciously heavy; he could always tell if Wallis was in the room as soon as he entered. No other woman he had ever known wore such a sensual perfume. The King sighed. He had known a great many women, but this one was truly worth a kingdom. And a kingdom she should have, whatever the cost. Until the moment he could offer her the crown, her reign was confined to the salon, the dining-table, and the smooth linen sheets of the bower in the flower-filled bedroom within whose four walls Wallis was a peerless perfectionist.

Wallis turned her face up to her royal lover as she felt his fingers tighten on her shoulder. She smiled and laid her finger on his lips. Then she, too, slipped out of the room. She paused on the first-floor landing outside the bedroom which bore a beautifully lettered card surmounted with the Prince of Wales's feathers. The card proclaimed the weekend's occupants to be Mr and Mrs Ernest Simpson.

Quietly she opened the door of the neighbouring room, neatly labelled in sloping copperplate 'Mr Ernest Simpson's Dressing-room'.

All the Fort's dressing-rooms were equipped with single beds – ostensibly for the convenience of those gentlemen too considerate to disturb their wives' slumbers.

A most civilized habit, thought Wallis as she closed the door again, leaving behind her the slumbering figure of her husband, and one of which the flirtatious Mary Rafferty had clearly not yet taken advantage.

Satisfied, Wallis slipped into her own room.

4

Windsor: 27 May 1936

Wallis Warfield Simpson had told her personal lady's maid not to wait up to help her undress.

The monogrammed embroidered linen sheets had been turned down, and a choice of two nightdresses laid out for her. One was a slender wisp of the palest grey crêpe de Chine, demure at the front but with a deep cowled V at the back to show a creamy curve of naked skin. Beside it lay its matching négligé, a softly yoked sliver of lace and silk embroidered with the Prince of Wales's triple ostrich feathers – a delightful if rather indiscreet compliment, she had thought when she had ordered it from Diana Vreeland's little lingerie boutique in the mews off Berkeley Square.

Mrs Vreeland had told her the nuns at the Convent of the Sacred Heart in Earls Court did all the work, the exquisite tucks, the hand-rolled hems. So beautiful – and such an extraordinary occupation for the celibate sisters, brides of Christ, stitching and folding the seductive silks, the cobweb lawns which veiled other women's nakedness.

The other was pure Paris – a creation of the famous Paulette whose clients at her second-floor workshop down the rue de Rivoli included the most famous of France's courtesans. It had cost a fortune; but, as Paulette was fond of saying with her fishwife's laugh, it takes one to catch one.

Wallis slipped out of her clothes, carefully hanging up her dress, and laying the silk stockings and undergarments trimmed with Brussels lace on the chair. Over them went the embroidered chiffon coverlet which hid them from the footman's early-morning gaze when he came to open the curtains and relight the fire in the grate.

Exquisite underwear had always been her passion, a private pleasure to be savoured only by herself and her chosen lover.

She went through to the bathroom and ran herself a warm bath – just enough to soften and bring a blush to her skin. In the bath, she took time to ready her body for her lover's embrace, stroking herself and feeling the delicate folds responding to her own touch. When she was ready, she parted the lips of her vagina and slipped in the *rin-no-tama*, a pair of little hollow silver balls, one of which contained a drop of mercury, the other a tiny vibrating tongue. Every movement of her hips would now give her the most exquisitely erotic sensation, making her passionately receptive to her lover. It was a courtesan of Imperial China who had instructed the American girl from Baltimore in the craft, surprised that Western women had so little respect for the act of love that they felt no obligation to prepare themselves for their lord's pleasures. In China, the woman's essences were considered lifegiving to the male member, the *yang* nourishing the *yin:* an understanding of the art of erotic sensuality was an obligation as well as a delight.

Naked, she rubbed her slender body with almond oil, massaging herself with long gentle strokes until her skin gleamed soft and supple, pearly as kid gloves.

She slipped her feet into swansdown-trimmed satin slippers and went over to the dressing-table to apply her make-up for the demands of the rest of the night. Finally she turned her attention to the array of scent bottles lined up beside the mirror. The care she took in blending the scents was as subtle and well considered as a conductor harmonizing his orchestra.

Wallis's years in the East had also taught her the importance of the olfactory nerve – the least understood and most potent organ of all. The basic ingredients in her blend of scents were always the same; a woman's perfume, the old Chinese woman who had been her mentor had told her, should always be recognizably her own. The basics were simple enough, even if the great perfumiers who had invented them would not have approved.

With a shiver of pleasure Wallis removed the glass stopper from a flacon of Guerlain's L'Heure Bleu and poured a few drops into a small bottle. Next she added an equal quantity of Mitsouko and shook the two to mix them. Then she leaned forward and selected carefully among a half-dozen tiny phials of pure essences, weight for weight as expensive as the rubies she had earlier laid aside in their navy suede jewel-pocket.

Musk and vanilla orchid, myrrh and sandalwood, the deadly perfume of the poisonous datura, the honeyed fragrance of the tuberose, all contributed to the mystery of the woman who was preparing herself, carefully and surely, for the renewal of the spell she had cast on her royal lover.

For a moment she hesitated between the two night-garments.

Then she picked up the second sliver of silk – Paulette had spent hours draping and cutting directly on to her client's naked body – and slipped it over her head. Bias-cut pink satin bound with the palest violet skimmed her body. She went over to the full-length mirror and looked at herself.

Perfect.

Tonight she would leave the stitching nuns to their dreams. Just as Paulette had promised, the deep V of the halter flattered the long elegant neck which was her best feature. The neckline was trimmed with scallop-edged silk petals which fluttered and caressed her skin as she moved. Over the nightdress went the matching négligé, the rose petals round the edge of the full sleeves camouflaging her weakest point: her beautifully manicured but knobbly and workmanlike hands.

Now it was time to put the finishing touches to her toilette. She dabbed all the pulse points with the scent she had carefully blended – pressing the little glass stopper to the soft translucent skin veined with blue which lined her wrists, knees, the triangle at the top of her thighs, her neck and her temples.

Her work was almost complete. She walked over to her vanity case and lifted out the tray. Underneath was an elderly teddy-bear. One of its eyes was missing and the fur on its rounded tummy was worn. The toy was her secret weapon.

'Don't ask me why a teddy-bear says sex to the average Englishman, but it does,' Thelma had told Wallis on that fatal day on the quayside when David's incumbent mistress had asked her to look after her lover.

'Take care of the Little Man,' she had added.

Wallis smiled to herself. She had certainly obeyed instructions. With a last approving look at the image reflected in the mirror, Wallis picked up the bear and went out into the passage. She glanced up and down, and shut the door silently behind her. Then, sliding the catch hidden behind a window casement, she slipped through the secret door and up the narrow staircase which gave access to the King's bachelor chambers.

Iona, wakeful beside the sleeping Freddie, heard and recognized the soft click of the latch and the light tap of ascending feet. She turned over and closed her eyes, memories of what might have been flitting through her mind. It was not that she regretted her choice of the sturdy amiable soldier she had married. The Little Man, King though he might be, would not make any woman an easy husband. Certainly the adoration he had clearly laid at the feet of Mrs Simpson would not be a light burden to carry, even for a mistress. Mrs Simpson, Iona reflected, might find she had bitten off more than she could reasonably chew.

Wallis, untroubled by any such uncertainties, made her way up the dimly lit circular stair, feeling the excitement in the musky odour of her body, knowing that the smooth internal muscles – those secret caresses whose function was controlled by the daily exercises she had learned from the old courtesans in Pekin's Tartar City – would bind the King to her and her alone.

In the bedroom, as in all things, the King's mistress was a self-made woman.

If the East had refined her knowledge, Wallis had always known how to transform herself into an object of desire. Ever since, as a skinny fifteen-year-old Baltimore schoolgirl, she had persuaded her mother to take the streetcar downtown to buy her a long blue-green feather to wear in her hair at the graduation dance.

'I knew even then', she told her Aunt Bessie, 'that I mustn't dress like other young girls. I must be exotic, the siren type. Slinky. Vampish. You know, something tighter or looser, something *they* weren't wearing. And then I would be noticed. And wanted.'

As she slipped into the King's apartments, Wallis knew for a certainty that she would be wanted. The King was hooked, she was in his blood as surely as the opiates whose use the oriental seductresses understood so well. She paused for a moment at the darkened door at the top of the stairs, then slipped the latch and went into the room, the teddy-bear trailing from her silk-cocooned hand.

Her voice was soft.

'We're cold, David. Teddy and me. Eanum wuzzums wants a cuddle.' She closed the door in one swift silent movement, and hesitated, little-girl come-hither.

Then she came forward to meet him, the silk petals shimmering as she moved into his arms. Stroking moth-fingered in the flickering candlelight, she drew the King towards her, whispered in his ear the things she'd learned he loved to hear.

As he entered her, Wallis knew her power over him was absolute. So absolute, that she allowed herself to believe that one thing only was needed to bind him to her for ever. Like the beautiful Alice Keppel, that other royal mistress who had held her love till only death did part, Wallis wanted to give her king a child.

She knew the very moment, knew that if she did not take her decision then it would be too late.

For the first time in her life, Wallis made a serious mistake. The consequence of that night of passion turned out to be not only inconvenient but abominably ill-timed, making it impossible for her to be with him at the hour when he needed her the most.

Had things been different, had Mrs Simpson not been obliged to undertake her headlong flight at the exact moment she should have stood firm, perhaps the King would never have abdicated, never have chosen the path to exile. With the woman he loved by his side, he might even have had the resolve to hold fast, to see the business through.

The child might even have had a kingdom to inherit.

However, as Wallis herself remarked in the subsequent turmoil to her friend the Woolworth heir, Jimmy Donahue: 'His Royal Highness, I'm afraid, is just not heir-conditioned.'

5

South of France: 9 December 1936

'Good God, man, where the hell *are* you?'

Peregrine Francis Adelbert Cust rarely raised his voice in anger. As sixth Baron Brownlow, once comrade-in-adventure and now lord-in-waiting to His Majesty Edward VIII, he usually had no reason to. Except that today was not at all usual.

Escorting the King's 'companion', Mrs Wallis Warfield Simpson, on her headlong flight to France from the Windsor hideaway of Fort Belvedere, was not a task he would have chosen. Had it not been for his loyalty to the Little Man – and the real possibility that the Prime Minister, Stanley Baldwin, might consider the award of a dukedom adequate recompense for services to King and country, whatever the outcome of the business – he would be safely back in his comfortable bed with Kitty.

Now the whole damn business was going to hell in a handcart – and all because of that ass Goddard. Goddard's journey from London to the south of France could hardly have been less discreet if he'd been travelling with a kettleful of boiling water and a length of string for the umbilical cord.

Perry Brownlow cranked the instrument again. The line was dreadful. The French had no more idea of how to run a telephone system than they did about plumbing or soldiering.

'Janet is very upset,' he bellowed. 'She's been on to Mr James twice already.'

'Janet' and 'Mr James' were the codenames for the royal lovers – as if there was any need, given the line's ferocious atmospherics, to disguise the communications between Fort Belvedere and the Villa Lou Viei.

Theodore Goddard, fifty-four years old and a much respected City solicitor, recently entrusted with the safe conduct of the King's mistress's divorce through the King's courts, was not used to being ticked off.

He said, 'I scarcely think—'

'*Listen* to me, idiot! We've got the press corps plastered round the gates as thick as jackals round a dead elephant. Some scribbler tumbled you had Kirkwood in tow at Croydon before you even got into the air!'

Theodore Goddard swallowed audibly. 'Everyone knows I have a heart condition. It makes perfect sense that I should have my personal physician—'

'Personal physician be damned! They know the man's an obstetrician!' Brownlow was shouting now. 'What? I can't hear you through the damned line!'

'We had to land at Marseilles, Perry. We'll be with you as soon as we can.'

'Under no circumstances', Brownlow bellowed, 'are there to be *any black bags* – and that goes for satchels, briefcases, *handbags*, anything that might be even loosely misinterpreted. Is that absolutely clear?'

Perry Brownlow hung the black instrument back on its hook. He thrust his hands deep into the pockets of his check plus-fours, and walked slowly back through the dining-room, down the narrow staircase and out into the courtyard which led to the guest quarters of the borrowed villa. He would have to tell 'Janet' that Dr Kirkwood was on his way.

The colonnade of white arches which ringed the courtyard was punctuated by neatly pruned orange-trees in tubs, brought out early to bloom in the pale Riviera sunshine. Brownlow winced as the scent of the blossom reached his nostrils. Orange blossom was a little too near the knuckle for comfort.

The dukedom was receding rapidly.

Back in England at Fort Belvedere, 'Mr James' was in what his Prime Minister later described as a highly emotional state.

The pregnancy had put an end to the idea of a morganatic marriage between the King and the woman with whom he had been determined to share his throne. The British people and Parliament might just have been persuaded to accept such a union, devised as a 'left-hand marriage' between those of unequal social status, where the children cannot inherit and there is no claim on the husband's estates. But Wallis's divorce from her husband Ernest Simpson – an essential element of which was that she should be the innocent party – was not yet finalized. And the visible evidence of a wife so clearly in breach of her marriage vows would be more than the circuit judge who heard the petition – let alone the Cabinet and the Commonwealth – could be expected to stomach.

Immediately after breakfast the following day, Thursday, 10 December 1936, King Edward VIII of Great Britain, Ireland and the British Dominions beyond the Seas, King Emperor of India, having reigned for 326 days, signed the instrument of abdication.

By so doing he renounced the throne for himself and his descendants for ever. He did so on the grounds that the burdens of kingship would be too heavy without the help and support of the woman he loved.

Three months later Dr Kirkwood returned to the house hidden in the hills above Cannes.

This time he was accompanied by a brisk-mannered middle-aged woman whose passport proclaimed her a qualified midwife. The third member of the party was a nervous young man with pebble glasses, wearing a well-cut pin-striped suit. His passport named him as the Hon. Anthony Anstruther. His occupation was listed as 'attached to the British royal household'. The party arrived unannounced on the Blue Train overnight from Paris, and were installed in the villa before breakfast – thus missing the attentions of the gentlemen of the press.

The birth itself – considering, as the midwife said later, the age and delicate circumstances of the mother – went off smoothly. The doctor remained for five days to make sure there were no complications, before returning with the same discretion to his Harley Street practice.

The bespectacled young man and the middle-aged woman left, as they had arrived, very early on the morning of the birth – long before the stringer from the Beaverbrook press had returned to his post at the gates of the villa.

After a brief conversation at the highest level with an office in Paris, the party and their luggage were waved through unchecked to board a small plane that was waiting for them on the private runway of Marignane airport at Marseilles.

The baby was swaddled in so many soft shawls and blankets that nothing could be seen of her tiny scarlet face. Before the infant was taken from the villa, her mother – perhaps in a sudden access of mother-love – wrapped around the child's wrist a fine gold chain from which dangled

31

a little emerald-studded cross. Made for an adult wrist, the trinket was one of many keepsake charms – crosses for sorrow, hearts for joy – with which 'Mr James' saw fit to mark his passion for 'Janet'. Hurriedly prepared and delivered by uniformed messenger from a famous Paris jeweller, the message engraved on the reverse was written in the private language the lovers shared. That the object itself was a cross and not a heart was a distinction not lost on either the giver or the receiver.

Far too loose for that tiny wrist, the chain worked its way into the talcum-wrinkled folds and remained unnoticed until the baby was delivered and unwrapped, for all the world like a special-delivery parcel, in the attic nurseries of Iona Fergusson's tall graceful house in Notting Hill.

There the new arrival was greeted with cautious interest by Iona's four-year-old son, Callum.

Iona, picking up the wrinkled little creature in her arms, gently unwound the chain and cross, read the inscription and sighed. So little for such a little one.

After discussing the infant with her husband Freddie before he left to rejoin his regiment, Iona had the baby christened Emerald Mary in a discreet ceremony in the Guards' Chapel in London.

The first name was for Lady Cunard – 'Maud by birth, Emerald by design' as her admirer Cecil Beaton put it – who had been hastily co-opted and sworn to secrecy as the single godparent. It was fortuitous that the tiny emeralds set into the little cross wound round the child's wrist came from a legacy from the child's paternal great-grandmother, the Danish Queen Alexandra, whose dowry of cloudy green gems had been bequeathed to her favourite grandson.

The second name was for the child's grandmother, the late Queen Mary, once Princess Mary of Teck – herself the daughter of a dynasty founded on an illegitimate line.

The surname on the birth certificate was Fitzwallace. It had been suggested by the only other witness at the christening, Anthony Anstruther, the young aide-de-camp who had brought the child from France. It had been an afterthought required for the register, since only the forenames were needed for the baptism at the font. It was a nod, Anstruther explained, to the ancient tradition under which royal bastards had the designation 'Fitz' placed before their name to show they were born on the wrong side of the blanket.

Iona, *in loco parentis*, was delighted with the suggestion.

What else, she thought to herself as the regimental padre crossed the baby's forehead with holy water under the dusky battle honours won across the centuries by the sovereign's personal bodyguard, could a king's daughter be named?

When the cold droplets trickled off the priest's fingers, young Emerald Mary did not cry out as superstition required, to let the devil out. Instead the baby opened her eyes, still birth-dark but already promising to lighten to the Windsor blue, and gazed solemnly round the gathering, waving her tiny fingers, the birth-bracelet glittering in the folds of the little wrist. Even then, Anstruther was to reflect in later years, Emerald knew how to hold an audience in the palm of her hand.

Anstruther did not consider himself a romantic; but looking, as he was now, at the little scrap of new life, seemingly so self-possessed in her tucked lawn and lace, he could not help wondering what the future held in store for her. What possible place could there be for such a child in the unbending order of dynasty? If things had been different, the child would have been a royal princess – even perhaps, some day, a queen. As it was, the tiny creature had merely been bundled unceremoniously out of the way – parcelled out to the kindly Iona to await collection tomorrow, next year, or even never.

Anstruther knew his employer well enough to know the last was the most likely possibility. He clenched his jaw and kept his thoughts to himself.

After the ceremony, Iona took the baby home. She did not yet know how long the child was to remain in her nursery. With the ex-king installed in a Rothschild castle near Vienna, waiting for his mistress's decree nisi to come through, the situation was still volatile. It was not even certain that the Little Man's marriage to Wallis would happen at all.

Meanwhile Iona knew she would have to provide some story to explain the new arrival to her friends. Perhaps a German cousin, one with Jewish blood. Like most family trees in the British aristocracy, hers was capable of accommodating almost anyone. Herr Hitler's activities had already, by 1937, begun to trigger a stream of political escapees, including babes-in-arms shipped out by frightened parents, hoping their children at least might escape the attentions of the Blackshirts.

Unlike many of her friends and contemporaries, Iona had a deep and instinctive loathing of Hitler's particular brand of fascism. She and Freddie had already agreed that war was inevitable. Whatever anyone said about the Führer's good intentions, they both knew it was only a matter of time.

So it was quite in character for Iona to offer sanctuary to a tiny refugee. Her views were already well known in her own circles. Her favourite cousin had felt strongly enough to join up on the Republican side in Spain's brutal civil war – paying the price of his idealism with his life. But there were certainly many, her ex-lover included, who thought Hitler had got it about right. A little ham-fisted of execution perhaps, but more or less on the correct track.

Two years later, when war finally broke out, Anthony Anstruther – landed, through no desire of his own, with what the Private Office described as 'damage containment' – remembered to have the entry excised from the official records in Somerset House. The child's future was too uncertain to let such evidence become public property.

Evidence, however, remained. When Iona, on her return from the christening, took her new charge up to the nursery, she remembered to tuck the tiny sparkling cross in the secret drawer in the nursery bureau.

There it was to remain undisturbed for the next twenty years.

6

London: 1940

By the time the phoney war of 1939 had turned into the bloody battle-fields of 1940, Iona Stuart Fergusson had applied for and obtained a routine clerical job at the War Office.

It wasn't long before her superiors discovered Iona had much more useful talents than those of a typist. Scots girls of Iona Fergusson's background were expected to be able to speak fluent French by the time they went south to boarding school. The Auld Alliance was a reality – and Iona delighted in the fact that France had given sanctuary to one of her own ancestors, Prince Charles Edward Stuart.

Her knowledge of the language was so good, the War Office seconded Iona to the headquarters of the Free French in Buckingham Gate as a liaison officer – with, of course, a casual suggestion that she might consider that her duties included reporting back to base on the some-what unpredictable expatriates.

'These foreign Johnnies are a bit excitable. Does no harm to keep the old eye on them,' said the young major who briefed her. 'Call in here once a month. Shall we say the second Tuesday, around eleven? Just as a matter of routine, so that we know everything's running smoothly.'

The major paused and smiled. 'I'm sure you know what I mean.'

Iona did indeed.

She enjoyed her work. The subtle intellectual French suited her temperament. She even tried her best to like the tall, hook-nosed, awkward-limbed young general, Charles de Gaulle, who paced the parquet floor of his third-floor office off Buckingham Palace Road, pausing now and again to stare angrily out of the window at the horizon, as if by force of mind alone he could project his own iron will on his subjugated countrymen. The whole office was terrified of him.

He had, of course, been wonderful on the BBC Free French broadcast in June; the deep powerful voice with its characteristic pauses had given the phrases punch and aggression. 'Paysans – Patriots of France – whatever happens – the flame of the French Resistance – *must* not be extinguished – *will* never be – extinguished.'

Two months after the broadcast, the death sentence was passed on him *in absentia* by the Vichy government. The news was greeted by the Free French officers with as much delight as if their leader had been awarded the Victoria Cross.

Whatever the major in the War Office thought of him, the general's appeal for a Free French task force led to a deluge of recruits. For weeks on end Iona was kept busy until well after the streets were darkened by the blackout and London rocked to the thunder of Hitler's bombs.

Then, one Tuesday when Iona arrived at the War Office for her monthly debriefing, she found the major wasn't alone. A plump young man in a pin-striped suit was standing with his back to the room, looking out of the window across the broad sweep of St James's Park towards Buckingham Palace.

At Iona's entrance he swung back into the room. The pink, slightly sly baby-face, half-obscured by a pair of gold-rimmed spectacles, was vaguely familiar to her. She tried to place him.

'Mrs Fergusson, good to see you again.'

The young civilian came round to the front of the desk with his hand outstretched. 'You remember – Anthony Anstruther? We met at mutual friends'.' The voice was wary.

Iona, attuned by her war work to pick up such nuances, heard the warning in the voice. Many of her friends were engaged in something hush-hush. You asked no questions. Careless talk, the posters assured the nation, cost lives.

'Yes, indeed.' Iona smiled and shook the proffered hand. Now she remembered the young man. He had accompanied the nurse who had brought her little orphan back from France. He, too, had been at Emerald's christening.

Apart from his contribution to the baby's name, Iona had not paid the young man much attention, thinking him merely yet another junior

36

courtier. Studying him now, she realized there was another reason for her forgetfulness: Anthony Anstruther was not at all her type. Iona Fergusson liked something a little more . . . *rugged*. A little more like the dashing Freddie. Not that the Little Man was exactly rugged. But he had such *charm*. And – she remembered with a small smile – a neat muscular body.

Anstruther, unaware of Iona's speculations, pulled the glasses off his nose, replaced them carefully in a monogrammed leather case, and continued.

'I hope you don't mind, I asked Ronnie if I might pop in.'

He peered at the young woman for a moment. Whatever she may have thought of him, Iona Fergusson, so clear-eyed and bright-faced, so trim in her neat uniform, was definitely Anthony Anstruther's type. The trouble was he had never seemed to be able to pluck up the courage even to approach a girl like Iona.

None of these thoughts showed in his manner.

He said, almost without glancing over at the major: 'Thank you, Ronnie, I won't be a mo.'

The major got to his feet, saluted, and left the room. Iona was startled at the sudden authority the young man had displayed. If Anstruther was the major's senior officer, he must be pretty important.

As Anstruther turned his back and walked over to the window, Iona glanced round the room.

On the desk now vacated by the uniformed officer lay a gold-tooled leather folder with a familiar device stamped into the crimson morocco leather. The last time she had seen a folder like that, it had been thrown un-read on the paper-strewn writing-desk in one corner of a shadowy drawing-room, a visual reminder of soon-to-be-abandoned responsibilities.

It all seemed like a thousand years ago.

'Yes. Well.' The squeezed Etonian vowels brought her back to reality. 'We should have been in touch far earlier. Thing was, as we all know, the whole business was rather overtaken by circumstances and events. So I thought I'd better have a word.'

'About Emerald?'

Anstruther hesitated. 'Yes . . . er . . . Emerald. I am instructed to convey gratitude. From a certain person known to us both.' For once he decided on directness. 'I mean, can you cope?'

Iona said, 'Of course. Emerald's fine. She has our son Callum for company, and everyone thinks she's just another poor little refugee. I've invented an Austrian cousin—'

'Good, good. Marvellous.' Anstruther's face had gone even pinker with relief. 'No sense in disturbing the status quo then? Rocking the boat?'

Iona said, 'None at all. Cal – our son – adores her.'

It was true. She explained how Callum, nearly seven years old now, had taken charge of the bright-eyed toddler, rushing eagerly home after school to be with her. They played together for hours. Educating Emerald, Callum called it – although it was the little girl herself who decided exactly what form the education should take. Callum had just embarked on teaching her to tell the time on a cardboard clock with movable hands he had made himself in handiwork class.

Listening to her, Anstruther suddenly smiled. Iona was startled to see how the face changed: suddenly he looked almost likeable, even vulnerable – a little lost schoolboy. For a second they held each other's gaze.

At that moment Anstruther felt an unfamiliar emotion. Iona, unlike the spoilt American divorcee who had caused all the trouble, was a woman he could admire. Even, perhaps, there might be friendship.

Confused but exhilarated, he took his glasses out of the case again, and began to polish them vigorously with a large silk pocket handkerchief.

Then he leaned forward and flicked open the leather-bound folder. His face was immediately shuttered. When he spoke again, his voice was brisk, businesslike.

'Lieutenant Fergusson – Iona – I may as well tell you the Duchess doesn't seem anxious for the return of the child – and the Duke, of course, is completely obsessed by his wife. So, if it's all right with you, I think we shouldn't do anything . . . prematurely. No sense in attracting attention – particularly from the fourth estate whose enthusiasm for a story can outweigh their patriotism. I'm sure you understand. Delicate matters in which I know you have been most . . .' He hesitated again, then he finished, giving the word emphasis. *'Reliable.* The child – well, one couldn't help but be moved at the christening. She was so . . . *alive.'*

Iona looked at him. In spite of the stiff words, Anthony Anstruther was human, capable of human feelings.

Anstruther replaced his glasses and glanced back down at the file.

'Fine. Well, that about wraps it up. If there's anything urgent, about the child, you know . . .' Anstruther pushed a bit of paper across the desk. 'There's an address. It's not exactly official, just a postbox. If you want something sent on – to the parents – mark it for the attention of Mr James. It'll be forwarded – discreetly. It sounds a bit cloak-and-dagger, but we don't want any of the sort of trouble which might put anyone in an awkward position.'

Iona picked up the paper. On it was a Mayfair address. Anstruther went on: 'It's a matter of damage containment. Avoiding embarrassment.

Particularly now. With himself in Portugal, it's all a bit awkward . . .'

Anstruther caught the expression on the young woman's face and cut himself short.

'Well, I think that's it for the moment. I'll get the major. And please accept our mutual friend's gratitude. Of course, if there are any problems, you can reach me through the office.'

Anstruther hesitated, then came round to the desk and offered his hand. He held Iona's hand a little longer than necessary, pressed it a little harder than need be. Her skin was dry and warm. For a moment a thread was spun between them, a thread of complicity, or understanding, or even, as Anstruther was later to come to believe, of affection. Anstruther released the hand, turned, and was gone.

In a moment the young major reappeared, and the debriefing was conducted as usual.

It wasn't until Iona was making her way past the Guards' barracks on her way to Buckingham Palace Road that her mind turned back to the interview which had preceded the debriefing.

Anthony Anstruther was certainly an odd fish. But, then, so were most of the hereditary courtiers who had come her way during her relationship with the Little Man. She wondered how many of the younger Palace employees had made the smooth transition, as Anstruther had, to working for 'something secret' in the War Office. They were boys – boys who would never understand the complexity of women. Iona shook her head. To Iona, Scots lass that she was and as foreign in her way as the American divorcee who had captured her prince, the English were a breed apart. Her Freddie included.

7

Portugal: July 1940

'I do not need a civil servant – even if he is an old friend – to remind me of my duties, Ambassador.' The Duke of Windsor's voice was sharp with irritation. 'As far as I am aware, Sir Walford, I am not obliged to take the advice of my brother, still less of Mr Churchill, on what billet may or may not be suitable to the status and dignity of myself and my wife.'

The ex-king, dressed for the golf course in voluminous cream linen plus-sixes, a yellow check shirt with a wide pink-striped tie under a sleeveless Fair Isle pullover, swung round from the window to stare at his visitor.

Sir Walford Selby, the British Ambassador to Portugal, was not having an easy time with his old friend. David Windsor had changed over the last few months, Selby thought. There was a bitterness which had not been there before – even in Vienna after the Abdication.

'Up to a point, sir,' Selby gave the diplomat's standard reply.

The Duke and Duchess, retreating from their villa in the South of France only just ahead of the advancing German army, had arrived in neutral Portugal the previous day after an embarrassing stay in Franco's Spain, where they had been lionized by Madrid's pro-German fascists.

Unfortunately the hotel the Ambassador had chosen for his old friends had somehow managed to arrange that the Windsors should be the guests of the millionaire banker Ricardo Espirito Santo – the 'Holy Ghost' as he was known – at his house in Estoril. It was most unsuitable, considering the evidence that the banker was in direct contact with Ribbentrop, the German Foreign Minister.

'Furthermore,' the ex-king warmed to his theme, 'I want it conveyed that I will not put up with this treatment of the Duchess. Unless my wife is officially accorded the same courtesy as my brothers' wives – by that I mean the dignity of "Royal Highness" – I absolutely refuse to co-operate with anything the Government may have in mind. You'd feel the same, Walford, if your dear wife had been treated as shabbily.'

Selby sighed. He did have one card to play in this childish game, but he had rather hoped not to have to do so. Clearly the ex-king was not going to let him off lightly.

'I think you should see this. It came in from the Office this morning, sir.' The Ambassador opened his briefcase and extracted a piece of paper.

The Duke glanced at the document. Then he snapped. 'I do not intend to read any official communication which fails to address my wife by her correct title.'

'Then, with Your Royal Highness's permission, I'll read it aloud.' Selby put on his glasses and peered at the strips of text glued on to the grey paper. ' "HMG reminds HRH that as serving officer there are consequences for disobeying what is *ipso facto* military order stop. Requires he proceeds forthwith take up post Governor Bahamas stop. I most strongly urge immediate compliance with wishes of Government. Cordially, Churchill." '

'Poppycock!' Edward Windsor raised his voice. 'Threaten a royal duke – even if I am an ex-king, that at least is my right of birth – with court martial? I've a mind to resign all my military offices immediately.'

'I wouldn't do that, sir.'

The Duke snorted. 'My brother – or that plain little Scotswoman he married – would be uncommon relieved if I did.' Then he turned back to the window and the view of the green lawns of Espirito Santo's hand-watered private golf-course.

After a moment Edward Windsor continued: 'That Mr Churchill sees fit to threaten me with military discipline – even if only by implication – is, one might be tempted to say, treasonable.'

'The RAF have sent a couple of Sunderland flying boats to assure your safe passage to England, sir,' Selby said.

'The devil they have.' The Duke turned his pale blue gaze back to the Ambassador. 'Then, they can be sent right back again. *I* have a game to play, too. My host has been promised nine holes before tea.'

Edward Windsor's expression softened and he added: 'In any event, the Duchess hates flying.'

41

Selby, following his gaze, caught a glimpse of two figures on the lawn. The Portuguese banker, a bag of golf-clubs slung across his shoulder, led the way, followed by the cause of the ex-king's abrupt change of mood – an exquisitely slender figure in a bright-blue pleated silk frock with a high neck and short cuffed sleeves, a white silk parasol held open to shield her pale face against the late-afternoon sun.

There was no doubt, the Ambassador reflected, that Wallis Windsor had natural *grandeur*: she looked every inch a lady, from the sturdy lizard-skin brogues to the famous madonna parting newly softened with a fashionable perm – one might almost say queenly – whatever the style and titles she might or might not be permitted.

'She's wonderful, isn't she? So perfect.'

The ex-king's voice cut through Selby's thoughts.

Selby turned away from the window and said, 'She's looking very well, sir. I have never seen her look better.'

A broad smile of happiness spread across the Duke's face – like a young boy with his very first mistress, the Ambassador thought. Uncommon strange in a middle-aged man who had had the pick of all the women in the world, including more than his fair share of mistresses.

'Well, now, Walford, let's see what we can do.' The Duke's voice was suddenly cordial.

The diplomat waited. The Duke, he reflected, even as the young and flamboyant Prince of Wales, had always been a curious mixture of world-weariness and simple enthusiasm, of pig-headed meanness and quixotic generosity. He had all the innocence which only the shelter of privilege can preserve – a complete absence of prejudice which, though in many ways endearing, led him into dangerous waters. Selby had had trouble, he remembered, explaining to the anti-Semitic Austrians what HRH had been doing staying with a Jew – even if he was a Rothschild. And at the same time the Duke had been expressing overt sympathy for the German position.

Selby shook his head. The ex-king's volatility, as now, never failed to take him by surprise.

'There may be a bargain to be struck,' the Duke continued cheerfully. 'Let us assume the appointment proposed by Mr Churchill and endorsed by my brother, recognizes the right – *ipso facto*, as you might put it – of the Duchess to the dignity and titles which accord with her married status. Under those circumstances I may be prepared to accept the governorship, providing, of course—'

He held up his hand. 'Providing various other necessary arrangements are made. We will need at least three weeks to get the preliminaries sorted out before we can leave Europe. I will need my soldier-servants released from active duty, minor things like that. And Her Royal Highness has some business to settle in New York on the way. I can see no possible purpose in returning to England at this point. I'd be grateful if you'd convey that to Mr Churchill, Ambassador. And shut the door as you go.'

The Ambassador opened his mouth again, thought better of it, and turned to withdraw. Then the ex-king called after him.

'Sorry about all this, Walford. It's not your fault. Give my best to your lady wife; we were so pleased to see her at the wedding.'

As he drove back to Lisbon in the elderly official Bentley, Selby wondered how on earth he could possibly manage to keep the volatile Duke and his divorcee wife up to a sense of their responsibilities over a full three weeks. He would need a reliable man to keep an eye on them.

When Selby arrived at the Residence, he went straight to his study, poured himself a stiff whisky, picked up the scrambled telephone and rang the Office, as all career diplomats call the big grey building on the corner of Parliament Square.

The Foreign Office looked in its records to find a liaison officer with the necessary clearance. Anthony Anstruther was the obvious choice.

'The job's not full-time, but it needs tact and it's likely to last the duration of the war,' the briefing officer explained. 'Since you already have experience of the royal household, you'll know the kind of thing required.'

Anstruther allowed himself a small smile. He, more than anyone, knew the kind of thing required.

So it happened that the ex-courtier had been appointed liaison officer between London and the recalcitrant ex-king, somewhat against his will since the visit interrupted rather more essential work: the organization of the embryonic counter-intelligence networks in occupied Europe.

'Well, you do *know* the man, Anthony. Might be able to make him see sense. Go quietly and all that,' Anstruther's commanding officer had said.

Two days later, Anthony Anstruther, dapper in a cream linen suit, boarded a Sunderland flying boat for Portugal.

'This run's getting to be a habit,' the captain said to his navigator, as he put the floats down on the choppy water of Lisbon's outer harbour and taxied across to the shelter of the sea-wall below the statue of Prince Henry the Navigator. 'That old boy'll be saluting us soon.'

The captain cut his engines and signalled the port officials to send a launch to take off his single passenger.

Anthony Anstruther climbed down into the small boat which tied up alongside the flying machine. He had very little luggage, but tucked inside his battered leather Gladstone bag were three cylindrical tins of a hundred Craven A cork-tipped from Selfridges, as requested. Anstruther had been obliged to pay for the cigarettes himself, credit being hard to obtain in wartime.

It was not until after the war was over and the Windsors had established themselves back in the villa on the Riviera that Anstruther remembered the royal recipient had never refunded the outlay on the cigarettes. The second non-recoverable expense had been the cleaning of the sardine-encrusted linen suit after the trip in the harbourmaster's dinghy.

There was a car to collect him from the quayside and drive him out to the Windsors' villa. The Duke, scowling as he came out to greet the new arrival, cheered up as soon as he saw the cigarettes.

After a long round of golf with his newly appointed liaison officer and a short conversation with his duchess, Edward Windsor agreed to see sense and go to the Bahamas – so long as the voyage could be undertaken by sea and a stop could be made in the Duchess's native land on the way.

The next hectic few days were spent organizing passage and packing. As they left the villa, the Duke handed Anstruther a lengthy shopping-list of essential items which were to be gathered up and shipped over to the Bahamas from England. The list included a spare set of royal bagpipes and enough Scotch whisky to drown a regiment.

'We must have something to offer visitors,' the Duke explained. 'The Duchess makes a mean whisky sour.'

There would be more requirements, His Royal Highess had no doubt, just as soon as the Duchess had taken a look at the residence. By all accounts it was a disaster.

Anstruther sighed. He would have to look for space in a cargo ship. The Admiralty might not think the new Governor's requirements as essential as the Duke believed.

'And one last little thing, Anthony,' the Duke had said as Anstruther settled his charges in their stateroom in the *Excalibur*, bound for Nassau.

There was, the ex-monarch explained, an awkward little problem to be tidied up in the South of France. In their headlong flight from the Villa la Croe they had left some highly sensitive papers behind. The papers had to do with the arrangements for the fostering of the child for whom, it seemed to Anstruther, he alone was now concerned.

The documents were in a strongbox in the attic, and there simply had not been the time to pack up everything. Even the dogs, the ex-king's consort complained, had had to do without their baskets. As Anstruther left the ship, easing himself past the wall of matching cabin trunks – no doubt full of the Paris creations the Duchess considered essential for their

44

exile – he could well see that the royal couple had other priorities.

On his return to London, Anstruther set about his first task, making the necessary arrangements to have the Windsor papers recovered and destroyed. The matter was so sensitive that it could not be entrusted to strangers, certainly not to the embryonic French Resistance – at best, in Anstruther's view, a rag-tag of communists, petty criminals and surly peasants. They would be useful on the ground, of course; but the job itself had to be done by someone absolutely trustworthy.

Reflecting on the problem, he knew he really had no choice. Anstruther needed a volunteer whose French was already impeccable, whose loyalty was beyond doubt, and who already knew the score. There was one person who was not only suitable for the job, but whose insider knowledge also rendered her uniquely qualified. Iona Fergusson had already made a couple of drops into occupied France on behalf of the Free French.

In wartime, he told himself as he put the wheels in motion for Iona's briefing, one was forced to take difficult decisions – even decisions one knew one might later bitterly regret.

8

London: January 1941

The task Iona was offered was all and more she both dreaded and hoped it would be.

Long before the weekend of her briefing finished, she knew she had no choice but to accept it. The children would have to be sent somewhere out of harm's way – she had increasingly feared for their safety even when she was only on the other side of London. Now, with the new risks she was about to take, the situation had become impossible. Besides, London was already too dangerous.

Only just before Christmas, Buckingham Palace itself had been bombed, and St Paul's had received a direct hit, although the church's great dome had miraculously escaped. The home counties and anywhere near the centres of production were vulnerable to the air-raids. Coventry had just taken a terrible beating. No, she would have to make more long-term arrangements than anything she'd considered so far.

When Iona went home to Notting Hill that evening she had made up her mind. Her son would go up to Eas Forse, to the safety of her island. It would do her father good to have to care for his grandchild. It would also, she fervently hoped, keep him away from the bottle and give him something to live for.

The island had its own school. Iona herself had attended the single stone-walled classroom which overlooked the bay. If the war was not over soon, Callum would be as well taught there as anywhere. David and his duchess would simply have to face up to their responsibility. At least Emerald would spend the war well out of the war zone, in the Bahamas.

It would be a bitter blow for both the children. With Iona working, and with frequent changes of nursemaid, they were used to relying on each other's company. It was because she hadn't wanted to separate them that she had not yet sent Callum, now rising eight, away to his father's preparatory school, recently evacuated from the vulnerable Sussex coast to the Yorkshire dales. All her friends' children were sent away to board as soon as they were seven, and in wartime it could be even younger.

Closing the heavy front door behind her, Iona paused for a moment to accustom her eyes to the gloom of the unlit hall. Then she walked over to the polished mahogany hall table to flick through the small pile of correspondence in case there might be word from Freddie. He had just been promoted. Two weeks ago a friend in the War Office had told her in the strictest confidence he'd been posted to join Wavell's army in the Western Desert. It would be a month at least before she would hear from him. Even then his letter would be carefully worded to conform to the demands of the censor. No reference to geography, casualties, morale – nothing which might give 'information or comfort' to the enemy.

Iona put the papers aside and glanced up the stairwell.

She hated the blackout. The tall window with its graceful Edwardian stained glass had been blanketed with regulation purple serge. The crimson and midnight blue Venetian chandelier which in normal times flooded the hall with jewelled light now cast long shadows in the twilight. Today, in late January, the space above her was dark and cold and there was no life in the diamond droplets. A current of air brushed Iona's ankles, cutting through her thick lisle stockings. The sharp metallic scent of damp earth rose from the cellars, cleared of their racks of champagne and claret to make way for the truckle beds and cans of baked beans of a makeshift air-raid shelter.

The sound of children's laughter punctuated by squeals of protest floated down. Iona smiled. It must be hair-wash night. She took the stairs two at a time until she reached the attic nursery. She slid back the bolt of the low barred gate, walked across the landing, and entered the candlelit bathroom.

Emerald, rising four now – an enchanting child whose huge violet eyes and little heart-shaped face belied her steely will – was splashing happily in the bath under the comfortable supervision of the nursemaid.

Callum was sprawled out on the linoleum, his freckled face twisted in concentration as he studied his homework. Emerald always insisted that Callum bring his schoolwork into the bathroom while she had her bath. She didn't want to lose a moment of her time with him.

Callum, in return, adored his foster-sister. At first he had been suspicious of the scarlet-faced, open-lunged little bundle who had invaded his nursery kingdom. His reservations vanished when the baby was about six weeks old. She had suddenly stopped crying as soon as he came into the room, grabbed his cautiously proffered finger, opened her dark violet eyes and smiled at him. After that he'd been captivated.

There was nothing of the rivalry which might have been there had they been closer in age. The age gap served, it seemed, to unite rather than to divide them. When she was weaned it was Callum who would spoon her breakfast egg into her small mouth while she giggled and bubbled. It had been Callum who encouraged her first tentative steps and was endlessly patient with her early efforts to form words.

Emerald treated Callum as her most treasured possession, tugging him off to inspect her day's achievements as soon as he arrived home, trundling behind him everywhere he went, demanding her favourite games. And, Iona noted with amusement, it was usually the younger child who dictated the choice of the game.

Iona herself loved the little russet-haired girl as deeply as if she'd been her own. Sometimes she reflected on the circumstances which had brought the child to her care. Wondered about the change in her ex-lover since he had fallen for Wallis Simpson. There had once been a time when he had been a man capable of great things – a popular hero who, in the thirties when the Depression bit hard into the lives of his people, had championed the cause of the miners deprived of their livelihood, made strenuous efforts to change the lot of the unemployed and earned himself his people's affection. It seemed extraordinary that once he had fallen under the woman's spell everything had changed. Under her influence he had found himself able not only to abandon the throne, desert his duty, turn his back on family, friends and the people who had trusted him, but also to behave with such total indifference to the infant who above all needed his love and care.

It seemed doubly terrible that a child who had so effortlessly captured the hearts of her foster-family should never even have been given the opportunity to claim the love which was her birthright. It was increasingly clear that Emerald's parents had no space in their lives for anyone or anything but themselves. Wallis had quite literally unmanned him. It was a terrible legacy for a child.

'Mummy! Mummy!'

The sound of splashing had ceased in the bathroom. Emerald knew her favourite grown-up was on the way up the stairs.

As soon as Iona appeared in the doorway, Emerald bounced out of the water, held out her arms and shook herself like a wet puppy, splashing Callum's homework.

'Now look what you've done, Emmy!' Callum's voice was mock-angry.

'Sorry, Cal.' Emerald was instantly contrite. 'Nanny dry it with the towel—'

'No, she won't!' Callum was laughing now. 'I'm taking it away. I'll finish it off in peace next door. Hello, Mummy,' he added as afterthought, giving his mother a quick kiss in passing.

Iona smiled. Callum was getting very *boyish* with his mother now that he went to school.

'Now, then, young madam.' The nursemaid grabbed the wriggling pink body. 'Hold still. I have to trim your hair. You look like the wild man of Borneo.'

Emerald bounded round the bathroom, shaking her water-darkened hair until every surface was covered with spray.

'Please! Please!' Emerald's voice rose in excitement. 'I want to have it short just like Mummy's.'

'Come here, then, Emmy.' Iona went over to the bathroom cupboard to find the scissors. 'I'll do it.'

When she had snipped and bobbed to Emerald's satisfaction, Iona glanced down at the russet curls scattered across the bathroom floor. On a sudden impulse she picked one of them up and slipped it into her pocket. Then, with a surge of fear at impending loss, she gathered the child in her arms and held her close.

'Mummy?'

Emerald's violet eyes were serious as she searched her face. The little girl always knew when Iona was troubled. She had a kind of sixth sense about such matters. On Iona's island it would have been called fey – fairy-touched.

Callum, on the other hand, never noticed moods. Like his father, Callum was a sturdy pragmatist. Callum liked to know the *how* of things. The *why* could take care of itself.

'Mummy? Kiss it better?' Emerald's voice was anxious.

Iona smiled. 'It's all right, darling. Mummy's fine.'

Iona knew she had to put a brave face on it. For the children's sake. For everyone's sake.

'Come on now.' Her voice was brisk. 'Time for hot milk and storytime.'

49

'Story! Story!' Emerald was dancing round the room again. She loved stories.

Later, when the children were tucked up in their rooms, Iona went down to Callum's room.

'Read to me, Mummy. Please, Mummy. I want a story,' shouted Emerald from the next room.

Iona laughed. 'Poor Callum,' she said.

Emerald appeared in the doorway.

'Callum doesn't mind. Cal loves me,' Emerald said with satisfaction. 'Don't you, Cal?'

Iona glanced enquiringly at her son. Callum looked back at his mother with the long-suffering air of a boy bowing to the whims of a demanding sister. Then he grinned and nodded.

Iona ruffled his hair. 'All right, then.'

She followed Emerald back to her room. Sometimes the child showed flashes of her mother's determination. At others, it was her father's legendary charm which won her the prize. Either way, Iona reflected, Emerald, young as she was, knew how to get what she wanted.

'Storytime is storytime,' she said. Then she began: 'Once upon a time, in a far distant land . . .'

Emerald sighed contentedly. She *loved* fairy-stories. She particularly liked the ones where the little girl who belonged to no-one and had to tend the pigs or look after the goats, or stay by the fire when everyone else had gone to the ball, was rewarded with a handsome prince. She felt a bit like an orphan herself sometimes, even though she didn't have to tend anyone's pigs. She wouldn't have minded anyway even if she had, just so long as she could be *quite* sure the prince knew where to find her.

At other times – and they were many – when no-one came up to read to her, she would lie awake and day-dream. If she shut her eyes and wished, and if she took special care to be really good and not upset Nanny – all nannies were the same really, only some were nicer than others – and above all not to step on the cracks between the paving stones on the way to the park; then, and only then, her handsome prince would come on his white horse and take her away – far away across the sea, to his castle with its moat and its drawbridge. And the drawbridge would always be left down so she could run out into the woods and play.

'. . . and so the prince and his bride lived happily ever after.'

Emerald opened her eyes as Iona's voice drew the story to its customary satisfactory conclusion. That was the part the child liked best, the part she always waited for.

Emerald smiled and closed her eyes again, waiting for the scented cheek which would soon be laid against hers. Above all, she loved the *smell* of the woman she had come to know as her mother. Lavender and roses, it was; her mother had shown her the pictures on the bottles of scent.

Iona lifted her hand to push Emerald's hair off her forehead before she bent over to kiss her goodnight. Emerald waited hopefully. Sometimes her mother's lipstick left two little marks like crimson petals on her forehead. If that happened, Emerald would refuse to wash it off in the morning.

That was the ritual which Emerald loved, which made her feel safe. After her mother kissed her she would be gone. But tomorrow Emerald's prince would come. If she was careful with the lines and the squares. If . . .

Dimly, as the waves of sleep swept over her, she heard her mother making arrangements with Nanny to send her and Cal and Nanny away on holiday. Although Emerald loved holidays, she couldn't stay awake for long enough to hear the murmuring voices say where she and Cal were going.

It didn't matter. She'd find out tomorrow.

The following day Iona put a telephone call through to her friend Marjorie Maitland to arrange that the keys to the house would be available for Freddie if he returned unexpectedly on leave.

Iona replaced the telephone on the hook. Then she said her goodbyes to everyone in Buckingham Gate, including the tall hawk-nosed general who as usual was restlessly pacing up and down in his office overlooking the servants' entrance to the Palace.

Iona cleared her desk and went home.

Implementing her plan to evacuate the children had not been easy. Even the short voyage to Eas Forse was no longer a simple matter. The Further Isles, in common with the rest of Scotland's outlying islands, were almost inaccessible in wartime. The ferries were needed for other, more pressing duties, and it seemed impossible to ensure that the children would be on their way by the time she had to leave.

In despair she had contacted Anthony Anstruther, reaching him through the young major who debriefed her at the War Office. Fortunately he had been able to help.

In his capacity as one of the directors of SOE – the Special Operations Executive, which handled covert operations in occupied Europe – Anstruther had more serious problems on his plate than attending to the little whims of the new Governor of the Bahamas. He had at last managed to charter space for the Windsors' shopping-list in the hold of a merchantman which plied the West Indies trade out of Liverpool. The return cargo, Jamaican tobacco, Barbadian sugar and rum, were considered wartime essentials. The ship, the SS *Politician*, was scheduled to take the northern route, threading through the Western Isles off the Scottish coast before heading across the Atlantic. The captain, in common with all Britain's merchant navy officers, took wartime instructions from the Admiralty.

It would not be far out of his route to put in at Eas Forse to deliver Callum. He could then take Emerald on to her destination – delivering the child to her parents in the Bahamas. There was no other solution. David and his duchess would have no option but to accept their responsibilities.

Iona was deeply relieved.

Anstruther forbore to point out the obvious – there was no guarantee that his ex-employer, even faced with the inevitable, would accept his responsibilities. Instead, he agreed with Iona that there was no option.

'At least she'll be out of harm's way. That's the main thing.'

'Will you let them know? That she's on her way?'

Anstruther hesitated. 'It would not be . . . *wise*. Wartime regulations. The captain will be told what to do – on strictly need-to-know, naturally.'

Anstruther lied easily. He knew his ex-employer well enough not to give him a chance to sabotage Iona's plans.

'I hope . . .' Her voice trailed away.

'I know. Believe me, no-one could have done more than you.'

'It's not what I would have wanted – for any of us.' Iona's voice suddenly was passionate. 'She's very special, my daughter Emerald. And she *is* my child – make no mistake about it.'

Anstruther was silent for a moment. Then he said gently: 'It's for the best.'

'Lieutenant Anstruther – Anthony?'

'Yes, Iona?'

As he spoke her name, Anstruther felt the thread tighten on his heart.

Iona hesitated. She had one last request. No-one knew what might happen in wartime. Even those who were not on the battlefield were acutely aware that tomorrow might never dawn. You lived at the far edge.

'If anything should happen to me and to Freddie, can I have your word that you will do everything you can – for both the children? Callum has my father – but he's old and ill and as stubborn as a mule. But Emerald, my beautiful daughter, she will have no-one – outside.

No-one but you.' Iona's voice held a note of anger and hurt, not for herself but for the child orphaned not by death itself, but by the death of will.

'Promise me,' she said.

Hearing Iona's request, for a long moment Anstruther found himself unable to reply for unaccustomed emotion. He, above all, knew what Iona was asking – the risks she was about to undertake.

'I promise.' His voice was low when he at last replied, 'It would be an honour – and a privilege.'

And, he could have added, but being who he was could not bring himself to say the words, *an act of love.*

It was mid-afternoon by the time Iona got back to Notting Hill. Nanny had taken the children out for their daily walk in Kensington Gardens, and the house was quiet. The day was bright and sunny. From the high Georgian windows bright beams of winter sunshine made slanting patterns across the old polished oak floors and up the Chinese silk hangings on the walls.

As she glanced round, Iona felt a sharp pang of loneliness.

The arrangements for the children were complete. In little more than forty-eight hours neither of them would be there to tumble down and greet her on the rare occasions when she returned early from the office – not that she'd be doing that for much longer. Soon she'd be keeping a rendezvous under very different circumstances.

Iona closed her eyes and shivered.

Many things were changing; it wasn't possible to plan for all of them. But at least she was certain she'd made the right decision about the children. Anstruther might have his own reasons for not committing pen to paper; Iona had no such inhibitions – even though the letter would probably arrive after the event.

She sat down at her walnut and ormolu writing desk and unlocked one of the little drawers. Inside was the square of paper Anthony Anstruther had given her at the end of the first interview in the major's office. She studied the anonymous address once again, trying to read into it some human face and form. Number 6 Mount Street, London W1, to be marked for the attention of 'Mr James'. Then she scribbled a short note, folded it, slipped it into an envelope and put on a two-penny stamp. She copied out the Mayfair address, marking the envelope in the top left-hand corner as instructed by the bespectacled young courtier.

As she was about to seal it, Iona hesitated.

She opened the flap, felt in her pocket and slipped in the dark red-tinted curl she had saved from the trimming of Emerald's hair. She closed the envelope again, melted a blob of scarlet sealing wax, dropped it on to the flap and pressed her signet ring into the wet surface. As she walked down to the postbox at the end of the street, the first of the night's air-raid sirens wailed. Wearily she looked to the east, listening for the familiar drone of the approaching bombers.

She returned to the house, her feet heavy on the war-cracked pavement. She had one last duty to perform. The children must be told they were to be parted.

She would do it in the morning, in the cold light of day.

The following day, hearing the children's excited voices floating down the stairs, Iona, brave as she was, turned away from that ultimate betrayal.

Sorrowfully, she settled herself back at her desk. How could she explain the inexplicable? Yet the task had to be completed.

Two days later, Iona drove the excited nursemaid and the two children, each neatly labelled on the wrist with an identity-disc in accordance with government requirements for evacuees. The journey took them across the wintry fields and smoking factories of the Midlands to the busy Atlantic port of Liverpool. The boat she searched for and found in the docks was a small ocean-battered merchantman.

Iona went on board to settle the children in their cabin. Then she went up to the bridge to find the captain. The captain had been told by the harbourmaster that, on the instructions of the War Office, he would be carrying a VIP family – dropping the boy on the island and taking the little girl on to the ship's destination.

Truculent, stiff with cold, and exhausted from the endless Atlantic voyages, he'd looked up in angry resentment as Iona entered the bridge-house. An instant later his lined and grey-stubbled face cracked into a smile.

He came from the Western Isles, and he recognized her. The woman who faced him on the already-tossing deck was none other than the Maid of Eas Forse.

'It's yourself, then, Iona Stuart?' The captain's voice was gruff with pleasure. 'And me thinking it was fancy folk from London I was to transport. Och, it's no trouble. Mony's the time I've had Her Leddyship, your mother, aboard when I was running the ferry out of Oban.'

It was on the tip of his tongue to add 'and many's the dram I've had with your da', but he changed his mind. Folks said the laird had grown muckle fond of the bottle since the old lady died. The arrival of the bairn would do the laird good. A man needed a family; the captain himself had felt the sore lack of it all those years at sea.

So all he said was, 'Dinna fash yourself, Miss Iona. Your bairns will be safe with me.'

'Bless you.' To the captain's delight, Iona leaned forward and kissed his cheek. He watched her disappear down the gangway, and leaned over the rail to see her join the children and the nursemaid. She was a bonnie lass and no mistake.

Below on the deck the overexcited Emerald was tugging her tolerant brother this way and that, getting underfoot with the loading, squealing with joy at all the activity.

Emerald flung herself into Iona's arms. 'Look, Mummy. Boats. Lots of boats.'

'The boat's going soon, darling. Kiss me goodnight.'

'Mummy – come, too?'

Emerald hesitated, her violet eyes wide. Rose and lavender filled her nostrils. 'Kiss me goodnight' meant her mother was going downstairs. Except that it wasn't night, and there weren't any stairs – well, not the proper kind of stairs.

She said again: 'Mummy. Come?'

Iona shook her head. 'I can't, darling.'

Emerald's eyes filled with tears.

'Yes. Mummy – come, too.'

But Iona's face was sombre, her thoughts already busy with the mission she was about to undertake. There were no guarantees, no safety net. And the irony was that Emerald herself was the unwitting instrument of the danger.

Iona said, 'Be a good girl, darling.'

Emerald put her hand up to Iona's cheek. She had never seen tears there before. 'Mummy – don't cry.'

'No, darling, I won't cry.'

Iona held the child close. Such life and energy in such a little thing. There was no doubt Emerald was a survivor: there had been ample proof of that already.

Iona kissed the child and set her back on her feet. She had not yet told either of the children that they were to be parted. She feared that if she explained it herself, she would lose her own will to do what was right.

Instead, she had given Callum the letter for him to read to Emerald. The letter explained what was to happen to them both. It was better like that. Better that Callum should take responsibility, young as he was. It would be a link between them – and such links were doubly precious in wartime, when no-one could be sure that tomorrow would ever come.

'There. Be good.'

There were tears in her eyes as she gently disengaged the little girl's arms from her neck and put the small hand in the nursemaid's.

'Look after Nanny, too.'

Emerald was silent. She looked uncertainly from her mother to the nursemaid.

Iona turned to Callum. She put her arms round her son and hugged him to her. Callum knew that something was troubling his mother, something more than the parting itself.

'Goodbye, my darling Cal.' Iona's voice was trembling now. 'Open the letter tomorrow, and read it with Emerald. Remember I love you – both of you.'

'Don't worry, Mother. I'll look after everything. We'll all be fine.'

Callum's face was solemn, his forehead creased with the effort not to cry. With his tousled hair and his freckles he looked, Iona thought in anguish, unbearably like his father.

She said quietly: 'Be brave, my darling. Make Daddy proud of you.'

But in her heart she said, 'My beautiful son, my beloved boy – when will I see you again? When will any of us be together again?' But you did not say such things to sons in wartime – or in her generation at any time.

'I love you, Mummy.' Callum's voice was steady, but his eyes – his father's tawny eyes with the green flecks – were filled with tears.

Boys don't cry.

Iona pulled him close again. She could feel her own heart beating in time with her son's. She held him for a long moment, and then let him go. She must be brave. After all, she told herself, it wasn't as if the children were going away for ever. Not as if they were being sent away to strangers.

Iona blew her nose and straightened up. Her voice steadied.

'Look after your grandfather when you get to Eas Forse, my darling. And Emmy – if anything happens, you will have to look after her for me.'

Callum nodded, his eyes wide.

Iona said briskly: 'That's enough, then. We must *all* be very brave. You'll have a lovely time, and I'll be up very soon to see you.'

'I'll be brave, too, Mummy.' The voice was Emerald's. She looked very small standing there beside the nursemaid.

Iona smiled. 'You, too, my darling. Both my darlings.'

She embraced them both once more. Then, her eyes glistening with tears, she turned and walked resolutely off the ship.

Emerald ran over to the rail for one last glimpse, calling farewells and frantically waving her small handkerchief until Iona finally disappeared.

'Come *on*, Em.' Callum caught her flailing hand. 'Nanny wants us below.'

For once in her life Emerald obeyed, clinging tightly to Callum as he led her down the gangway. Once in the cabin, Emerald rushed into the bathroom and climbed up on to a stool to peer into the mirror, searching for the lipstick mark.

There it was right in the middle of her forehead, a bright crimson butterfly. Emerald vowed she would never wash it off. Not ever. Not even in the bath. Not even in the sea which was going to separate her from her mummy.

An hour later the SS *Politician* moved out into the crowded harbour lanes, turning her blunt nose to the north.

9

London: January 1941

The ship took the northern route as scheduled.

This meant hugging the coastline up as far as the string of silver islands, taking advantage of the captain's knowledge of the hazardous channels between the rocky headlands, reducing the likelihood of being found by enemy ships or aircraft.

The route took the ship within a mile of the island of Eas Forse.

Given fair weather, the detour would not make more than a few hours' delay. But in stormy weather it was another matter. The storms in the Western Isles whipped up fast and furious, without respect for human convenience. The captain had himself once visited the graveyard adjoining Forsa House and seen the stones which marked the last resting place of six of the old kings of Scotland – obliged by nature's mood to forgo a royal burial on the holy island of Iona, only half a day's journey beyond.

The captain knew he would not have enough draught to put into the jetty below Forsa House. The merchantman was low in the water, loaded to its gunwales. He would have to lie up at anchor in the roads and the passengers would have to be taken off by rowing boat. Later, when he was within range, the captain planned to make ship-to-shore wireless contact with the laird – making sure that the old boy was sober and capable. He had not told the mother of the bairns, the Maid, that the forecast was stormy. No sense in worrying the lassie with matters over which nor man nor beast had any control.

For the moment, the sea was calm, the weather fair. The ship made good time as it followed the coastline north. And if the weather blew up dangerously and they were forced to lie up for a while – and the captain had once had to cast anchor in a cove for a week while a Hebridean storm blew itself out – there was a bit of liquid comfort in the hold. In addition to its human cargo, the SS *Politician*'s bill of lading listed a bulk order of telephones, four boxes of axes, six trunks of assorted shoes, three crates of bicycle pedals, a crate of clay pipes, a set of bagpipes and – there was the joy of it – 264,750 bottles of good Scotch whisky. Spey Royal, no less. There was no accounting for royal whims. But the royal taste could not be faulted.

Iona drove her Austin back to London and set about closing up the now-empty house in Notting Hill.

She swathed the furniture in dustsheets, covered the beds with gingham curtaining, folded and stowed away the blankets. Finally, she lowered the Venetian chandelier onto a pile of eiderdowns on the floor of the hallway and swaddled the glittering glass with pillows. It might save something if the house was bombed. Apparently the chandeliers which crashed through the floors in the Palace had done more damage than the direct hit.

The sun was already rising over the darkened city when Iona finally locked the front door. She made her way on foot alongside the park and down Curzon Street until she reached the cavernous grey stone building in Berkeley Square where she was to have her final briefing. She had arranged to meet Marjorie Maitland for breakfast in the Lansdowne Club before she went past the discreet doorman and through the connecting underground passage into the offices which accommodated Maurice Buckmaster's French section of SOE.

The breakfast room was filling up with the early morning shift who were part of the bureaucracy that staffed the wartime ministries round the clock.

Iona was surprised to find two people waiting for her at a table in the corner. One was her school friend Marjorie. The other was a young lieutenant in the uniform of Freddie's regiment. As she walked towards them Iona checked and froze. Her happy welcoming smile for Marjorie vanished from her lips. She could see by their faces that something was wrong.

In wartime there was only one thing which could ever be really wrong.

59

Iona glanced down. The young officer was holding a telegram. His knuckles were white, and his hand was shaking. Iona took a deep breath and forced herself to walk on. Her cheeks were icy-pale but her own hand was steady as she accepted the yellow envelope stamped with the 'War Office – Urgent' classification. She knew what was inside long before she even opened it.

She read its message twice. Then she looked up. She managed a quick pale smile at Marjorie.

'I was going to give you the key to the house, darling, so you could open it for Freddie when he came home,' she said. 'That won't be necessary now.'

'I'm terribly sorry.' The young man's voice was husky. 'Your husband was my first company commander at Caterham. He was a wonderful man. If it's any consolation, he's been put forward for a DSO.' He broke off helplessly.

Iona glanced at him. 'Thank you but, no, it's no consolation,' she said crisply. She looked back at Marjorie. 'I'm still going to give you the keys, Marjorie. I may or may not be needing them again. At least one day I hope my children will. Here's a telephone number.' She scribbled a number from her address book on a piece of paper torn out of the little diary she kept in her handbag. 'Ask for Anthony Anstruther. He'll know what to do.'

Without another word Iona stood up and walked out. She had no tears left. No tears at all.

Five days later Iona was parachuted into France, into the cold winter fields north of Cannes. The ploughed earth was hard and unyielding, knocking the breath from her body. She knew she must instantly seek cover, hide the parachute, wait and watch for the rendezvous which had been arranged. For an instant her limbs would not respond, the shock of landing had been so great. She lifted her head and gazed around.

A group of figures was making its way slowly, almost leisurely towards her. As they drew closer, she realized the men were dressed not in the rough blue work-clothes of the peasant farmers she knew she was to meet, but in the knife-pleated grey uniforms and polished jackboots of the SS.

With a mounting horror, she realized she was lost.

Iona Fergusson was not the only victim of that night of fear. Long afterwards it was learned that the Resistance network she had been told would be waiting for her had been penetrated by Klaus Barbie's Lyons-based Gestapo. That night, the intelligence services lost five men. And one woman.

Iona did not have much to tell her captors. What there was she held on to for three days, just long enough for the uninfiltrated cells of the network to get clear and regroup. However, it wasn't her sparse information on the Resistance which most interested her interrogators, it was her mission itself.

Iona Stuart Fergusson, the Maid of Eas Forse, was one of the names on the infamous 'white' list, the list issued on Hitler's personal instructions to every Gestapo office in Europe. The list named all the known friends, acquaintances and associates of the former Edward VIII. Edward Windsor, Hitler believed, was the key to a secret but powerful pro-German faction in Britain which was ready to sue for peace and allow Germany to turn its uninterrupted attentions to the Soviet menace in the east.

The Gestapo officers were trained not only to listen for the information they expected, but also to pick up other small contradictions and revelations which might lead them down unexpected avenues. Since those they interrogated were not expected to survive the interrogation, results depended on timing.

The operation had to be a success before the patient died.

The young woman suffered three days of repeated beatings and three sessions of gang rape, but it was not until her tormentors had turned to their armoury of drugs, injecting her with a massive dose of an experimental hypnotic derived from mandragora, that she finally confirmed in her hallucinations what a few early slips had indicated.

Iona Stuart Fergusson was acting as foster-mother to a royal bastard. The papers which confirmed the child's existence were to be found in the attics of the Villa La Croe.

The Gestapo pored over the tapes of the interrogation, looking for the advantage to be gained.

Edward Windsor was a wild card in the German pack. The ex-king's pro-German sympathies, so well documented from his prewar days, had been reinforced by his conduct in Madrid and Lisbon. Plans had already been laid, a communication route established, to rescue the ex-monarch from the island where he was virtually an exile. Then, with the Führer's support, Edward VIII and his consort would reclaim his throne, unite the country and lead his people out of the wilderness and into the arms of their German brothers.

However, the story Iona's interrogators finally managed to wrench out of the young woman before she died did not, in the opinion of the authorities, reflect well on the man that Ribbentrop believed to be the key to bringing Britain to her senses.

But if the worst came to the worst, the child herself might be put on the throne. Among the royal houses of Europe there were plenty of precedents for inheritance of thrones by illegitimate heirs.

The papers – correspondence, documentation of the birth and much else – were duly retrieved from the chest in the attic at the villa. The matter was carefully noted in Berlin as an addendum to Foreign Policy document B15/B002635-38 and all the documents filed for possible future use as blackmail material – or, failing that, as proof of the child's identity.

On the night of Iona Fergusson's death the sky over London was lit again with the oddly beautiful tracery of dogfighting combat planes which heralded the descent of another rain of incendiary bombs on the capital. As usual, the air-raid sirens howled. As usual, the citizenry wearily climbed out of their beds and repaired to various subterranean passages to pass yet another uncomfortable night of enforced camaraderie.

The West End escaped more or less unscathed on that particular night, with the exception of an isolated stick of bombs which descended in the area of Notting Hill, causing considerable damage in the terraces of beautiful Georgian houses.

Several of the bombs scored direct hits but failed to explode, having to be laboriously and dangerously defused the following day by a sapper contingent of the Home Guard. Some of them fell in the pretty garden squares whose elegant iron railings had long been ripped out to feed the insatiable maws of the munition factories. Those bombs which buried themselves in the flowerbeds or fell on unoccupied property often remained undetected for days. Some of them were not found until long after the war itself was dead and buried.

The bomb which fell on the Fergusson family house tumbled – by some quirk of its primitive mechanism – straight down the chimney, its passage cushioned by a thick layer of ancient soot, its landing softened by a bed of soft cold ash, where it buried itself in the splintered brick of the fireplace in the attic nursery. There it remained, unexploded and undetected, for sixteen years.

Iona's death, and the posthumous award of the George Cross, was not officially confirmed until the German SS records were examined by the Foreign Office's team in 1945. Although Iona had left a will, the destruction of sections of the Public Record Office in the bombing left uncertainty over the inheritance, a confusion compounded by the near-simultaneous death of her husband in action in the Western Desert.

Iona Fergusson's personal estate consisted of a few stocks and shares and the prime property in Notting Hill. The matter came before Chancery, and the estate was placed in the hands of the Public Trustee for clarification.

The money was prudently re-invested in gilts.

The house itself remained closed and shuttered pending the outcome of the search for legitimate heirs, the crystal chandelier swaddled in its cocoon of swansdown on the floor of the hall, the attic nurseries silent.

10

The Hebrides: February 1941

The merchantman slipped through the peaceful twilight of the Sound of Mull off the west coast of Scotland.

The long sea-loch was calm, the flat grey swirls of current lightly flecked with foam. Even so, the weather report from Tiree at 1600 hours had warned of a 'bit of weather' once the *Politician* lost the protection of the Hebridean islands and embarked on the long Atlantic crossing to Newfoundland.

Narrowing his eyes to assess the clouds gathering to the north, the captain set the ship's course towards Eas Forse. He had made his calculations. The wind from the north-east was not strong enough to give his well-ballasted ship much trouble. As a near-following wind, if he pointed east-south-east it might even be an advantage. He had sailed this route since he was a cabin-boy, and there was no channel he had not navigated, no current whose pull he had not measured.

No. If there was a danger, it could only lie in delay. Naval intelligence in Liverpool had warned of a U-boat pack off the Shetlands. Lying-to for even a few hours could see the German killers scything through the shipping lanes of the north Atlantic.

The *Politician* cut steadily through the swell, a trail of herring gulls wheeling and screaming in her wake. Earlier the nursemaid had brought the two children up on deck and had allowed her young charges to work off some of their energy in the stiff salt breeze. Both of them were roped securely to the rail, but even so the nice young second mate had given them cork life-belts, wrapping them twice round the small waists and tying them with a strong sailor's knot.

'Nanny! Nanny!' Emerald shouted. 'Look at us!'

'We're *real* sailors,' Callum said proudly. 'I'm going to be a captain when I grow up.'

Callum, always practical, had begged a pair of his father's racing binoculars from his mother before they left the house in Notting Hill. Now, his face serious with concentration, he scanned the horizon, pointing out to his excited little foster-sister the guillemots and shearwaters bouncing off the crests of the long rollers.

He spotted a line of wet heads in the swell.

'Emmy! Over there!' He pulled Emerald's head round and showed her how to use the binoculars one-eyed – Emerald's eyes were still not far enough apart to let her use both eyes together – to find the seal-heads bobbing off the rocks round the little island of Ulva.

'Mermaids,' said Emerald happily. 'Lots of mermaids.'

'Not mermaids, Emmy. Seals.'

Then, as the sun stained the sea blood-red and the salt spray turned icy in the dusk, the nursemaid had shepherded her charges below. Now they were safely tucked up, although both had insisted they would not be parted from their newly.acquired badges of seamanship.

'Well, if I do let you wear them, you must shut your eyes and go to sleep at once,' the exasperated nursemaid said as she buttoned Callum's sleeping-bag. 'And no nonsense.'

'Yes, yes, Cal and me will be really good,' Emerald promised fervently.

Finally the nursemaid had been able to slip out of their cabin, down to the galley for her supper.

As the soft contours of the Inner Hebrides fell astern, the captain adjusted the course of the merchant ship for the Further Isles.

Eas Forse would pick up the signal now. It was time to call up the old laird at Forsa House. The old house, once a fortified castle, was sited on a small promontory to the south of the main island.

The link was made by radio telephone to the wireless mast at Salen, round the headland on the north of the island.

'Hello, Jimmy? Can ye read me?'

'Loud and clear, Archie.'

'Can ye make contact with the laird at Forsa?'

'I can that, if the poor old bugger is off the bottle.'

'He'll be that soon enough. I have visitors for him. Can you get him the message? I can't come in to the jetty. He'll be needing the wee boat to come out to the ship at first light.'

'Ye'll anchor in Forsa Loch, then?'

'Right, Jimmy. The bay's sheltered enough.'

' 'Tis blowing muckle hard—'

The air filled with crackling static and the radio waves went silent.

The captain tried for a few moments to confirm the message. Then, complying with wartime regulations for merchant shipping, he flicked the switch which shut down his radio receiver. Had he left it on for a moment longer he would have heard the weather station on Tiree broadcast its emergency storm warning.

The captain leaned into the wind and rested his bulk against the rail. His back was giving him trouble again. He glanced down at the deck where the young first mate was securing the anchor against the long Atlantic crossing.

The lad should find his sea-legs as soon as possible if he was going to be of any use. In wartime there was no time for fancy training. Let the boy get the feel of the wheel while the ship was still in the shelter of the islands.

He called down the gangway. 'First Mate! To the bridge!'

A second later the young seaman appeared beside him.

'Present, sir.'

The captain briefly acknowledged the salute. Then he returned to checking his instruments. Finally he glanced across at the small brass-rimmed barometer screwed alongside the porthole. The mercury was falling. He tapped the glass, shrugged, and motioned to the young man to take the wheel.

'Hold the course. Ye'll take the first watch. But keep an eye on that northern horizon. There's not been a storm warning, but I mistrust the way the waves are running on the tide. I'll be below until the second watch. We put into Eas Forse to drop the wee bairns. Pick up the lighthouse. We'll heave to by the buoy till first light.'

'Ay ay, sir.'

The captain nodded. The young man looked bright and alert. And young. For an instant the captain hesitated, his eyes shuttered again as he studied the building cumulus. Then he shook his head. He left the bridge and climbed stiffly down the gangway into the mess. He had had a long day. It would be good to get the weight off his feet and something hot in his belly.

In the second of the four passenger cabins, Callum was awake, buttoned securely into his sleeping bag in his bunk by the brassbound porthole, his precious binoculars under his pillow, reading his favourite *Swallows and Amazons* under the blanket by the light of his little torch.

In the top bunk on the other side of the teak-lined cabin, Emerald was curled up in a tight little ball, her sleeping bag fastened right over her head, dreaming of green-tressed mermaids and sleek seal-princes. The letter from her mummy, transferred to her keeping, was zipped tightly into a little pocket of the life-jacket.

The ship held her course, cutting through the lengthening Atlantic breakers, the young seaman at her helm unaware that she was heading into the worst gale to sweep the Hebrides in a hundred years.

11

Eas Forse: 5 February 1941

Margaret Mackenzie, a sturdy rosy-cheeked islander of forty summers, stood on the cliff-edge looking south towards the string of pearly islands which made up the Inner Hebrides.

Eas Forse was on the far edge of the string – the furthermost of the Further Isles. There was nothing between Eas Forse and the wide ocean which stretched all the way to the New World. Sometimes when the weather was fine it was just possible to glimpse the Scottish mainland from the cliff. Today the swiftly approaching storm had already blotted out everything within fifty yards beyond the shore.

Margaret Mackenzie had finished her day's work in Forsa House and had gone up to the cliff-top to watch for the ebb tide.

The ancient Stuart stronghold – the wary Celt who built it mindful of marauding Norsemen – stood on a small island, Forsa Isle, linked by a causeway to the main island, Eas Forse itself. The causeway, lapped on either side by the sea-loch, was only passable at low tide. On fine days, Margaret could cross dryshod.

Margaret's own croft was down the far end of the brae, the only other dwelling on the little isle. The croft had once formed part of a small crofting 'township' – four families who shared the labours of the agricultural year. Economics and the battlegrounds of Europe had finished off what the Highland Clearances – the never-forgotten tragedy that had depopulated much of the highlands and islands a century earlier – had begun. Now there was only spinster Margaret left. And the old laird at the 'Big House', of course. Even when you got to the main island of Eas Forse, there was no other neighbour for miles – or as many miles as an island only eight miles long could muster.

For some years now, since Her Ladyship had died – God rest her soul, buried in the Forsa graveyard alongside the Celtic kings – the old laird had lived on his own. Margaret, once one of half a dozen indoor servants, went in daily to clear up and do a bit of cooking, leaving a meal ready for the evening and the next day's dinner. The old laird shooed her out as soon as he could, preferring his own solitary company to Margaret's chattering. As often as not, the food had scarcely been touched when she came back. Margaret knew well enough from the shopping-list and the empties that the poor old man seemed to get all the sustenance he needed from the bottle.

The house had fallen into a sorry state since Her Ladyship had gone to her rest, with only the master bedroom and the kitchen kept habitable. Most of the good furniture and all the pictures had long gone to pay the taxes, or whatever it was that money was needed for.

The old laird was by no means penniless by island standards: he had his bit of money from his daughter in the south, and that came in once a month at the post office in Salen. The islanders managed with precious little money: crofting at least meant you could fill your belly. So Margaret would bake an extra batch of scones and bring tatties from her own patch and eggs from her own hens to stock the old laird's larder.

But from now on it would be different. The laird had greeted her that morning with a clean shirt on his back, his breeks brushed and his face alight with happiness. The grandson, young Callum Stuart Fergusson that he hadn't seen since the war began, was to be evacuated into the care of his grandfather.

The word had come on the wireless that very morning.

Margaret had spent the day cleaning the grates, laying fires and shaking out the sheets to make up the bed in the nursery. From now on there would be life in the old house again.

She would have liked to do more, but she had to catch the tide. Today was the day the postman called, today he would be bringing her the stores needed for the new arrival – or it might be more, the message hadn't been too clear – from the Salen shop cum post office. If she was not there to take it from him, the delivery would be left at the end of the causeway, and she didn't trust the hooded crows not to find it. The hoodies were terrible bold.

Margaret stood on the cliff-edge, watching the water below for the dark fringe of weed and limpets which told her the causeway would soon be passable. The island was tipped up like the prow of a boat, the cliff-edge braving the ocean, the house sheltering in the lee of the landward slope which stretched down to the causeway and the little jetty where the rowing-boat was tied up.

The tide pulled away from the sheer drop of the cliff long before it could be seen on the causeway. But today there was no sign of the water-level dropping. Beneath her the waves were rising and breaking on the rocks in angry combers of white foam. Dark storm-clouds were gathering on the horizon.

Today she would need her waterproof and wellington boots – if, that was, she could get across at all. By the look of the water she might well not be able to cross until morning brought the next ebb tide.

Margaret Mackenzie had not expected the gift to come upon her then. Usually she had some kind of warning sign – a warm breath on her cheek when the breeze was winter-cold, a movement at the edge of her sight when no living creature was near.

Today, as the wind whipped the froth from the billows, the fairies' gift came upon her suddenly, without warning, taking her breath away. To Margaret, looking out over the storm-whipped ocean, there would have been no difference if she'd been looking into the clear brilliant light of a Hebridean summer morning. Her eyes were unseeing. It always happened when the gift returned. Each time it did, she remembered the first occasion so many years ago. She had seen nothing in front of her then, only what lay beyond.

Trying to stifle the fear, she thought back to that first time. It didn't help, it had never helped, but she remembered. She wasn't known to the island folk as Margaret then. Margaret was a name for a mature grown woman – the woman she'd become. Then she was young, barely more than a child, and everyone called her Maggie.

There were many Maggies all over the Scottish highlands and islands, but she was different. Her mother was the youngest of seven, Maggie was also the youngest of seven. In the land of the Celts, to be the seventh child of a seventh child meant inevitably that she'd been born with the rare and troubling gift of second sight.

She'd known about it for as long as she could remember. Sometimes it embarrassed her; her childhood friends used to tease her at school. 'Tell us whether me da's going to find lobbies in his pots tomorrow, wee Mags!' they'd shout. She was a strong and confident child, and usually

70

she could laugh it off. 'If he doesn'a, ye'll go hungry for your tea, and that's a secret I'm keeping to meself,' she'd reply.

It had never really mattered, until the day of the Beltane fires. On the cliff-top Margaret Mackenzie shuddered. She closed her eyes and remembered.

She was standing barefoot in the clean white snow of the pass between the island's tops – the whale-back hills. The wind that blew down the pass was raw and chill. It was the first of May and it should have been the first day of spring, but the snow was lying late. The warmth of her bare feet had bitten a scallop-edge out of the snowdrift, making neat little round caverns in which her toes sat as red as rowan-berries.

The young woman glanced down at the patterned cotton of her best Sunday frock. It was sequined with ice crystals – like Cinderella's ballgown, she thought. Her dancing-pumps were tucked safely into the shoe bag that hung round her neck. Her mam would kill her if she ruined her new shoes. It was 1916, and luxuries like her shoes were almost unimaginable. A dozen eggs a week for three months they had cost – the price demanded by the puffer-man who called in at the island's necklace of rough stone jetties which serviced the isolated island communities. And he had been willing to strike a bargain only because his wife, stricken with the tuberculosis, could keep down only the most delicate of diets.

Maggie could hear the echo of her mother's voice: 'Ye keep them safe, my lass, even if ye have to go barefoot. Ye won't be seeing their like again till you are wed.'

As for a wedding, that would not be for her this year, and not for the lack of wishing, Maggie thought. She thrust her hands into the deep pockets of the greatcoat Angus had put round her shoulders as they left the Beltane circle.

There had been Donald with his accordion, and the laird's own piper, for it was still in the days when the Big House provided the patronage through which most of the island earned its small wages. And her Angus had danced the old dances with Maggie, the quick-footed matchmaking of the linked circles which delivered boy to girl, spinning her with his big rough shepherd-boy's fists until her feet just skimmed the stamped granite of the Beltane circle. Maggie's face was brighter than the flames of the Beltane fire itself. Everyone remarked on it.

Everyone except Catriona Sweeney, the beauty of the island, who tossed her head and bided her time.

Young Maggie danced round the flickering flame, her beauty shining in her Angus's eyes – Angus that Kate Sweeny thought belonged to *her* – and was not bothered by anything that evening, not even by the patient smugness in Catriona's face. She was scarcely tired at all when the piper finally ran out of wind, and the accordion player's arms ached so sore that he could no longer summon a tune.

Then the dancing had to stop and it was time for the Beltane bannock, the fat thick linked circles of salty oatcake which the older women baked on the ashes of the need-fire, with which the young girls chose their Beltane companion. The good girls put the piece under their pillows so they would dream of their future husbands. The bad girls did what they pleased. This was the one night of the year that no-one asked any questions.

Maggie took a tender leave of her Angus; he had to return to Salen in the north of the island for his family's farewells, while Maggie made her way across the high tops to her mother's croft on the southerly Forsa Isle.

Today was Angus's last on the island. As so many of the young men had done before, her sweetheart, son of the Forsa shepherd, had taken the Queen's shilling. The young men couldn't earn enough on the island to set up house. Of Maggie's own three brothers, all had gone and none had returned. One was lost at Ypres and the other two from dysentery which carried away three in every four of the casualties. But they all still went.

At eleven of the clock on the morrow her Angus would be walking down to the little jetty where the puffer-man unloaded his sacks of white wheat flour, sugar and tea for the islanders, and he would be gone.

Maggie huddled into the rough wool of the heavy shepherding coat. The Army would clothe and feed him, Angus said, so he would not be needing it until he came again. Then he would claim his Maggie and the coat together. In the pocket, she could feel the piece of bannock rough and hard under her cold fingers. Above her, rising on the thermals, a pair of buzzards wheeled and tumbled, mewling plaintive as cats, beaks held wide as parched sailors adrift. The scarlet light of dawn blooded the birds' breast-feathers.

She settled herself under the lee of Sweeney's Boulder where, a long while ago, the young ferryman and his love, a Mackenzie daughter – victims of an old inter-family feud – had hidden against the anger of her father. The lovers had been crushed by the rock's falling from the cliff above, and the place had been feared ever since.

Dawn was long and slow in the northern isles. Young Maggie watched the white-gold sun lift out of the gunmetal sea. Looking down to the shore she could even pick out the bold black and white oystercatchers flipping scarlet bills through the mussel beds. Their high-pitched cries, like keening wails for the dead, carried up on the morning current of air.

Maggie saw them then, their faces unmistakable in the ring of embers from the Beltane blaze. Angus her sweetheart and Catriona Sweeney had left the ring of fire together. Together they returned.

The coldness of Maggie's bare feet was as nothing to the cold that chilled her heart. It meant nothing, it *could* mean nothing. Angus belonged to her. They had said their farewells, and when he came back it was to her he would return.

She had meant to keep watch on the hill until Angus sailed away round the headland, past the long low island where the kings of Scotland slept under their Celtic crosses, until the very last moment, when the scarf-trail of smoke from the puffer dissolved in the cold wind from the sea. She would watch over him until he was gone. Not just to be sure he had gone alone, but because he needed her to watch over him. Because . . .

Young Maggie shivered and tucked her cold toes further into the hem of Angus's coat.

The snow was beginning to drift now, high against the rock. The jetty and the shore vanished in the white tempest. When the weather came up over the headland the air went suddenly still. Then the storm broke over the tops. By then Maggie was climbing higher.

No-one understood how it happened. How Maggie – she had known the tops since she was knee-high to a harebell – was caught in the snow.

When the storm lifted, leaving the hills blanketed with white and the air icy clear, the puffer nosed its way into the jetty. There was no Angus to meet it. When Maggie failed to return to the Big House, the young man had gone out again into the blizzard with his collie-dog and risked the climb up the sheep-track through the white tempest to find his sweetheart. That evening the collie returned alone and whimpering. Angus' body was not found until the spring thaw brought the streams rushing off the hills again.

Catriona Sweeney never spoke to Margaret Mackenzie again after that night on the hill when her sweetheart – and Angus *was* Kate's sweetheart, whatever the Beltane bannock said – walked into the blind white blizzard for the sake of Maggie Mackenzie.

As for young Maggie, she was carried down at daybreak in a shepherd's arms, her face as white as whey, her arms as blue-veined as old cheese. The girl was delirious for a month. Not all the prayers to St Columba himself could quieten her ravings or make her understand that her Angus was gone.

Ever afterwards, the islanders said Maggie Mackenzie had been with the little people when she had been in her delirium. In the islands there were plenty of precedents for such things. It was taken as the final confirmation that she possessed the gift.

To those who had it was given foreknowledge of birth and death.

It was accepted, too, and not just on Eas Forse but throughout the isles, that the night before a ship was lost on the rocks Margaret Mackenzie would see the image of it, or the real ship, whatever you believed, floating over the mist which wreathed the island whenever a storm was coming down from the north. And the next morning, sure enough, there would be the wreckage on the shore.

The night of 5 February 1941 was just such a night.

Margaret Mackenzie did not cross the causeway that afternoon. Instead, bowed down and silent with the great weight of the foreknowledge she could not lift, she helped the old laird bale out the rowing-boat and make it seaworthy.

The merchant ship with the laird's grandson aboard was on its way with its precious cargo. The captain would make the Forsa sea-loch on the neep tide and heave to until the morning. The landing's draught was too shallow for his ship, but the deeper water in the bay afforded good shelter against what promised to be a stormy dawn.

The laird satisfied himself the little clinker-built rowing-boat was sea-worthy, the oars shipped, the painter tied so that it could be loosened one-handed, a hip-flask stowed under the bows.

Then the two returned to the house.

The old laird had his bit of supper, and then went up to the fisher-man's tower to train the telescope on the sea-lane beyond the headland, hoping for a glimpse of the ship.

He often came up to the tower at night and watched the ships slip through the sea-lanes. He had the whisky-bottle handy, and it whiled away the long days and nights. In wartime, merchant ships did as much of their travelling in the darkness as they could. It made them less vulnerable to aircraft.

But the captain of the SS *Politician* had not counted on a more ancient enemy – the most implacable enemy of all. The sea churned and heaved as the storm came out of the north, sending purple towers of cloud scudding across the sky, tossing zig-zag cabers of lightning, drawing rolling thunder like tumbrils in its wake.

Down below as she rinsed the dishes and stacked them away in the cupboard, Margaret Mackenzie listened to the tempest raging. She had no need to go up to the cliff-top to watch for the ship. She knew that what was to be could not be altered by any human agency – let alone her own. It was not the business of those with the second sight to interfere. That was the most bitter knowledge of all.

So she stoked up the fire in the kitchen range, set a big pot of barley broth on the stove, and waited for what she knew must happen.

When the storm first blew up, Emerald had been dreaming of mermaids.

The mermaids were rocking her to and fro like Nanny used to do when she was a little baby, a long time ago. Emerald was big now, but she still liked being rocked. Callum said it was babyish, but Emerald liked it.

The mermaids were nice.

She knew they were mermaids because they had long green hair which was wet and cold and smelled just like the seaweed Callum had found for her on the tideline when they had gone to the seaside with Nanny. Whichever nanny it was. Nanny had rolled down her stockings and taken them off so she could take Emerald paddling.

Emerald was surprised by Nanny's legs. They were as white as rice pudding, with tiny prickly hairs sticking out of them, and you could see funny little knotted blue veins under the skin. Emerald inspected her own legs hopefully, but they were smooth and brown.

Callum had helped her make a sandcastle with a ballrun so you could roll a marble down and the marble went in and out of the little tunnels. Sometimes it got stuck and then you had to put your finger in ever so gently and push it on. Then the sea came up, all frothy and white, and ate away all the sandcastle from below, even when you dug a moat. Emerald didn't really mind, though. You could make another one.

Soon Callum would come and help her build a new one.

'Em! Emmy!' Callum was calling her. Emerald tried to run down the sand towards him, but something was dragging her back.

'Coming, Cal,' Emerald muttered. 'Wait . . .'

'Emerald! Wake up!'

Slowly she came out of sleep.

'Cal! What is it?' She sat up and rubbed her eyes.

Callum was leaning over her, shaking her. The bulk of the life-jackets they were wearing made it hard for him to reach her.

'It's a storm. There's water on the floor. I can't get up the stairs to find Nanny.' Callum's voice was steady, but Emerald could see he was white and shivering.

The little beam of his torch swung round the cabin. It was cold. Emerald was cold, and her bedclothes were wet. Mummy had told her not to cry, but she felt a bit like it. The noise was terrible –

banging and crashing as if a giant was thumping the ship with his big fist.

Emerald felt scared. She had to hold on to the bunk to keep her balance. The floor seemed to be slopping with water.

Behind Callum, Emerald could see the round porthole, the sea-window, opening its mouth at her. She knew it was not a window at all, but the mouth of an enormous sea-monster come to swallow her up.

'Cal. Look behind you! Monster!'

Emerald was really scared now.

Callum turned, the beam of his torch swinging wildly.

The ship was lurching as if she was on a gigantic seesaw. The porthole was alternately under water – when the foam frothed and swirled – and facing skyward when the water rushed away like an enormous throat opening and shutting.

Now it was creaking and shaking under the weight of the water as the ship wallowed in a deep trough.

Down, down they went. Emerald was thrown forward into Callum's arms.

'Hold on tight, Em!' Callum's voice rose over the din.

All at once the thick glass of the porthole heaved, cracked and finally, dreadfully, gave way. The water began to pour in, spitting great green globules of froth and foam.

Then the ship righted herself, poised like a dancer, riding broadside to the crest of a wave. For a moment the world held still, only to come crashing down again.

Callum was wrenched from Emerald's grasp and thrown to the far side of the cabin, the fall bringing the bunk down on top of him, trapping him beneath its beam.

Desperately Callum struggled to free himself, the water swirling around his ankles now, the drumbeat of the waves on the ship's steel plates deafening.

'Help me, Cal! Monster!' Emerald's voice scythed through the crashing and tearing of the ship. 'Monster!'

Callum heaved at the beam.

'Cal!' Emerald was really screaming now.

The monster was coming to get her. She knew it, knew it, knew it.

Sure enough, the water spewed in through the wide black gullet of the monster where the porthole had been. She could see its throat pumping and heaving. She knew that behind it were the monster's eyes, white holes centred with glittering black diamonds. The monster wanted her.

She shrank back, silent now with fear, her fingernails splintering on the cabin walls.

All at once the ship swung back, tossed high on a billow. Suddenly the monster had gone, vanished, leaving in its place the black hole of the porthole.

Emerald found her voice again. 'Callum!'

The ship swooped down into a trough, the vacuum created by its fall lifting the beam from Callum's body. Callum struggled up. The water was up to his knees now. He began to work his way round the cabin, clinging to anything his fingers could grasp.

'Emmy, hang on, I'm coming!'

At that moment the monster returned. Its mouth gaped wide. The great grey-green tongue licked out towards her. Emerald screamed again. This time the monster had come for her.

'Cal! Cal! Help me!'

'Here, Emmy, here!'

Emerald could feel Callum's hands clutching at her. But the monster was too quick for him. The monster wanted Callum, too.

'Cal!' Emerald's voice was a scream of warning.

The ship tossed herself high in the air again, and when she came down Callum was gone. Now Emerald was alone.

The monster was coming closer, closer. Emerald fought and screamed, but the monster caught her. The mouth opened wider, wider, until it had swallowed her up with all her screams still inside her.

The water rushed all around. It was wet and cold in the monster's belly. The noise had gone now, muffled by the great black throat which had sucked her in. She couldn't breathe. She opened her mouth to scream, but nothing happened, nothing except that the salt water filled her up. And everything went black. Black monster. Black as night.

12

Eas Forse: 5 February 1941

In the darkness of his castle watchtower high above the raging waves, the laird stayed his shivering with a dram. The old man huddled down into his plaid, a heavy cloak which had been his father's before him, and which would be his grandson's after him. No new-fangled tartan for him, the plaid was made of the traditional dark undyed wool from Forsa's small flock of soot-black sheep.

Overhead and all around, the sheet lightning lit up the ocean and the sky. The old man took another nip from the bottle and trained his telescope on the rolling horizon. At last he saw the ship, the ship that carried his own grandson, Iona's Callum and his only blood-heir, silhouetted against the horizon.

At first he was not even sure it was a ship at all. For an instant the old man thought he was seeing a ghost ship – an imagining born of the whisky and the wind. But then it reappeared, to be shuttlecocked from billow to billow, helpless as the puffins and razorbills taking shelter on the turbulence of the ocean's surface from the savage tumblings of the air.

The ship, the old laird knew well enough, was being pulled by the current towards the neighbouring island of Eriskay, straight on to the half-submerged boulders of St Columba's Breakwater, a line of jagged rocks which, while protecting the calm waters of the channel between the two islands, was sudden death to any ship dragged on to its spiny humpback.

Dizzy with both liquor and fear, the old man knew what he had to do. He drew his plaid tighter round him, made his way down the steep staircase, through the house, past the warm kitchen, out through the back door and down to the jetty. He climbed into the boat, threw off the rope, set his back to the sea-loch, and began to row towards its mouth as if his grandson's life depended on it. As, indeed, he knew it did.

Margaret Mackenzie heard the laird's passing, but it was not up to her to stop him. Whatever the second sight showed her, she could only be a passive observer. She went into the kitchen to wait for the dawn. Morning would bring the turning of the tide and reveal what the storm had done.

In the shelter of the sea-loch, the old man heaved on the oars and set course for the headland where he had last seen the merchantman. Even in the lee of the island, the water was as rough as he had ever known it.

He rowed with all his strength, his heart pounding with effort. He had had the old twinge many times of late, a sudden sharp pain beneath the ribs which had made him, as now, stop, ship the oars and reach for his hip-flask. He coughed once, a dry rattle, then the boat heaved and the flask slipped from his grip.

As the whisky ran out over the duckboards he cursed. He shook his head to clear the mist that blurred his sight. He peered ahead through the spray. The ship loomed larger now, pulled forward by the race of the current. He could see a gaping hole in the side, the water rushing and heaving within.

He scanned the waves. A seal-head bobbed and vanished. But the old man, whisky-confused as he was, knew the seals were far too canny to be out in this sea; they'd be safe high on the shore, waiting for the weather to pass. Except that no seal would brave those seas. It might be a buoy, or perhaps an oil-drum washed overboard.

The white mist thickened. He pulled again on the oars. The sleek shining object was real enough, and much closer now. All at once he knew with utter certainty it wasn't a buoy or a drum; it was the head of a child.

He shouted, again and again, cursing the weakness of age which left him so little strength in voice and limb.

A flash of white cheek and a faint answering cry were his reward.

He bent back to his task. The boat laboured forward, the oars bouncing off the sea's churning surface. The old man caught his breath. The pain had returned, this time as a fierce burning under his ribs. In spite of the icy salt-spray, he could feel the heat in his chest rise to choke him.

Painfully, slowly, he managed to ship the oars once more and throw out the little sea-anchor. The bobbing head was almost close enough to touch. The child was silent now, drifting helpless in the billows. The old man reached out. The small body was limp.

With the last of his strength the old man leaned down into the water, seized the rope of the life-jacket, and pulled the child on board. He took off the heavy sodden plaid and wrapped it gently round the crumpled shape. Then he took up the oars again.

The old man was tired. He was more tired than he had ever been in his life. So tired he couldn't unship the oars, let alone summon up the energy to row. His head dropped forward, and he sat slumped waiting for the exhaustion to pass. It didn't pass. Instead his throat tightened again and the pain in his chest became unbearable.

Finally he toppled over. He slipped off the cross-bench and fell into the dark pool of whisky-tainted sea-water in the bottom of the boat. Somehow he managed to put his arms round the inert bundle that was lying there and pull the child to him. Then he shuddered for the last time and was still.

The rowing boat, ballasted by the dead weight of the body over the keel, was caught by the tide. Soaring and diving from billow to billow it began to be swept back towards the shore.

Emerald opened her eyes.

The weight of the monster was pressing down on her, and she could smell its black breath. Reaching its great black tongue towards her, the monster had sucked her up.

When she opened her eyes again, a long time later, she knew the monster was crouching over her. The monster was cold, as cold as ice.

Emerald lay absolutely still in the black darkness under the monster's black shape. Something rough and hairy bristled against her cheek – it could only be the monster's skin – and she could hear the sound of water slapping round inside the monster's belly.

She waited. Soon the monster would be hungry. She moved a little, cautiously, fearful of waking the sleeping monster. Callum – where was Callum that he had not come to rescue her?

Waiting and wondering when the monster would wake and eat her, she was cross and scared – cross with Callum and scared of the monster.

Catriona Sweeney had been woken at midnight by the violence of the storm.

In the islands storms meant wrecks. She rose, pulled on an oilskin and went up to the headland, where she sheltered under the lee of the Beltane rock. Perhaps, Catriona thought, there might be a German merchantman ploughing the northern route to the Baltic ports, which had been caught up in the tempest. Or one of the wolf-pack of U-boats which patrolled the Atlantic, picking off the supply ships one by one. Or, even better, one of the supply ships itself.

There was a ship off the shore right enough. It was ploughing and heaving like a mirage in the swollen waves, although the flashes of white lightning which lit up the raging sky were too short and dazzling for her to see what it was.

Catriona waited, watching from the shelter of the rock until daylight.

There would be no school that day. If the ship went down, every able-bodied creature on the island would be down on the shore to glean.

Morning dawned clear and bright over a calm sea. The islands always looked at their best after a storm. As the pale sun lifted, wide-eyed and innocent as if nothing had happened during the night, Catriona stepped out onto the cliff which dropped to the shore.

Rainbow-flecked shafts of sunshine picked out the debris below. Heavy-shouldered black-backed gulls patrolled the tide-mark of glistening sea-weed, twisted iron and splintered wood which marked the limit of the pounding breakers. The ship she'd glimpsed must indeed have foundered in the darkness.

The tide was ebbing. It meant, Catriona thought, that the inhabitants of the nearby island of Eriskay would get most of whatever would be washed ashore. Wreckage had always been one of the few free gifts the good Lord gave the Hebrideans. Many was the time in a hard winter when congregations all over the isles would be down on their knees praying for a miracle. What the minister and his congregation well knew was that one man's miracle is another man's shipwreck.

Wartime always yielded the best wreckage, but there had never been a bounty like the Eriskay islanders found on their shores that morning.

Lord, the folk of Eas Forse often ruefully exclaimed afterwards, one little mile to the west, and it would have been their own island whose sands were left awash with the good liquor. Spey Royal, it was, worth a king's ransom and on its way to an ex-king's cellars in the Bahamas. You had to be quick in the gathering, though. Even in wartime the Excisemen had long noses.

Climbing down the winding gully of tumbled rock towards the sea, Catriona didn't know about the Duke's cargo of whisky. Nor was she aware that she was being followed. As silent and agile as a mountain goat, and keeping a cautious distance behind her, Jacob Sweeney – known as Jack – watched his great-aunt Catriona carefully. Jack knew that if his aunt – even though she was his grandfather's sister, he always called her aunt – caught him pick-poking behind her she would box his ears and send him home. As she often said in class, he was more trouble than a barrel-load of monkeys.

Jack was almost ten. He was one of the special children born nine months after the Beltane fires. It was said of Beltane children that they were fire-christened, wild, wilful, and as mischievous as Robin Goodfellow – for all the holy water that might be sprinkled on them by the minister. Even his great-aunt the schoolmistress, although she never held with the Beltane beliefs, was inclined to credit it in Jacob.

The boy's father had been an itinerant folk-singer with a guitar and an Irishman's charm, who had been island-hopping, earning his pennies in the pubs. He happened to reach Eas Forse at the time of the Beltane. For all Jacob knew, his father might have been a merman who had swum ashore, had his way with the young girl who was Jack's mother and vanished back into the spray.

The island was well used to such events, and no-one thought any the worse of what they resulted in – a small island needed all the fresh blood it could get. Births out of wedlock were commonplace, and it was quite normal for the family to bring up the illegitimate child. There was no shame in the arrangement, and no-one asked impertinent questions.

But Jack's mother had taken one look at the infant and run for dear life as soon as she had the strength to hitch up her skirts. Motherless herself and just turned eighteen, she'd emptied the biscuit tin of her widowed father's savings and hadn't stopped running until she melted into the bright lights of Glasgow.

The task of looking after the boy fell first to Catriona Sweeney's brother, whose vanished daughter had left him a widowed grandfather at just forty. Two years later he married again. Soon afterwards his new young wife produced a bairn of her own, and there was no room or time for Jack in the crofthouse.

Catriona accepted her family responsibilities and, busy as she was, she took the boy almost by default into her house. It had not been an easy decision since Jack provided a daily reminder of the Beltane fires and the loss of her own one chance of happiness.

Times were hard, and there was little enough money to go round. Catriona would send her nephew round the neighbours to collect the bits and pieces they could spare. It was fair exchange. The island's children reaped the benefit of the schoolmistress's skills. In return the parents helped with what they could – eggs and milk, a bit of crowdie and a piece of a joint when there was mutton or a pig killed. Sometimes it would be a bowl of drippings to fry the oatmeal to make skirlie, a good nourishing supper.

For some reason young Jack seemed to take charity hard, his mouth trembling when he was sent out with the empty bowl, and she would scold him a little.

' 'Tis no shame, Jack, no charity. The people give what they can. Learn to accept with grace.'

Jack's chief pleasure was when he was allowed to help his aunt in her caravan at the end of her garden, where she kept the parish records and the clippings which traced the doings of those of the islanders who'd found fame beyond its shores. He would bring her his own little items, learning the value of keeping his eyes peeled and gathering the ephemera which traced the island's life. Bird's eggs, blown and preserved in their nests, fossils set in stone - whatever he found on his scourings round the island.

The storm promised rich pickings that morning as Jack furtively tracked his aunt down the cliff.

Abruptly she vanished behind a spur of rock. Jack settled down on the cliff looking out over the bay below, waiting for Catriona to come into sight again. He waited in vain. The schoolmistress had disappeared into her own secret world.

She climbed nimbly down the rock chimney which led into the back of the *tein-eigen*, the needfire cave, as she called it for the scorch marks on a shelf of rock which told of ancient habitation. The cave was only accessible from the shore when the tide was fully out, and even then the mouth was hidden in a fold of cliff.

She was the first out this morning, but she would certainly not be the last. Half the population of Eas Forse would soon be making its way down to see what the storm had delivered. Catriona emerged into the pale light of the cave. At high tide all but the far inner chamber of the cave was sealed by the rising sea, as she'd discovered when she was the age of the small children she now taught.

Deprived of her own love through no fault of her own, Catriona, ever practical, went to Glasgow to study for her teaching diploma. She returned to the island to teach the children of others. She slipped easily into premature middle-age. On her thirtieth birthday, ten years ago to the day, she had drawn her once-admired golden tresses back into a severe bun, hidden the still sky-blue eyes behind metal-rimmed spectacles, and pulled the trappings of spinsterhood round her like a shield: her face unpainted, her clothes utilitarian, her voice authoritarian.

But in the quiet of the evening, snug in her caravan, she did the best she could with the stuff of other people's dreams. The cave had yielded rich gleanings over the years, the debris of other people's lives.

As she emerged into the inner cave, she paused for a second to let her eyes accustom themselves to the phosphorescent twilight. The tide had been higher last night than it had been in all the thirty years she had been coming to the cave. A dark scum of bladderwort washed the ledges which, for as long as she could remember, had been dusted with dry pearl-white sand. Now they glimmered black in the slanting beam of light from the cave's mouth. There was a dark bundle washed up in the weed. A dark bundle with a familiar bulk.

Human, it surely must be. Yet small enough to be a child. The sea had brought her a child. Alive or dead?

Her heart pounding, she waded through the shallow water which lapped the cave's floor. She bent over the bundle and untied the bulky cork life-jacket which must have buoyed up the body through the sea. Then she pulled back the sodden clothing.

It was a boy. The small face was puckered and tinged a chalky blue-grey with cold, but the child was still faintly, miraculously breathing. She unbuttoned her coat and her shirt, and pressed the cold limp flesh against her breasts, warming it, urging life back into it. Slowly – to Catriona it seemed to take an eternity – she transferred some of her own body-warmth into the storm's flotsam. The child's breathing steadied, the shivering stopped, and a faint colour spread over his skin.

Catriona looked at the boy again.

He was about eight or nine, she guessed, tousel-haired, sturdy, and as freckled as Angus had been all those years ago. In fact the child could almost have been of island stock himself. She pressed him to her breast again, closing her eyes and rocking him in her arms. It was years since she had held another human being close to her body. As she felt the child's heart beat against hers, a sensation of protectiveness and contentment overwhelmed her.

The sea gives and the sea takes away. The islanders had always lived by that hard implacable rule. Catriona didn't believe in miracles, any more than she believed in fairies or second sight or any of the superstitions that the folk of Eas Forse held to. Yet today she was forced to confront a miracle and accept it. The miracle was one of justice. Justice was the child she was owed and had never had. A child that no-one else knew or cared about – and, even if they did, would certainly assume to be lost at sea, yet another anonymous casualty of the murderous tides of war that were indiscriminately sweeping the world.

Catriona rocked the boy in her arms.

He would have a name; she would learn that and call him by it. She would begin bit by bit to piece together his background. She smiled to herself. The child's past was unlikely to be momentous or interesting – he was probably the son of a seaman who'd managed to get him passage in one of the merchant ships sailing for America – but at least she would try to assemble it for him.

Catriona turned. With the boy in her arms she began the long climb up the hidden passage towards the cliff-top. Below her and on the island's shores on every side, she knew the inhabitants of Eas Forse would be scouring the sands for the rest of the storm's salvage.

Catriona neither knew nor cared what they would find, just as long as it didn't threaten the miracle the sea had given her.

13

Eas Forse: 6 February 1941

On the far side of the island from the needfire cave, well away from the long sandy beach by the Salen harbour on which the islanders picked among the debris of the storm, Margaret Mackenzie waited on the rocks below Forsa House. She huddled into her heavy tweed overcoat, the same overcoat which her Angus had put round her shoulders all those years ago, the fatal night of that other storm.

Margaret knew the turning tide would bring the rowing-boat back into the sea-loch, just as surely as it had once carried home the funeral barges of the Celtic kings.

The morning had pulled a thick white mist from the sea's surface, curtaining the mouth of the loch. Margaret was not the only living creature on the promontory that wild morning. A pair of grey seals, silvery winter coats glistening in the pale light, had taken shelter from the turbulence on a ledge of rock. Now, propped up on hard-clawed flippers, they surveyed the waves from their vantage point a few yards away from where she stood.

When she had first come round the headland, scrambling over the weed-strewn rocks, the seals had turned to inspect her through huge, tranquil brown eyes.

'Well, that was a fine bit of weather,' Margaret said to the seals.

Like all those who live solitary lives, she talked to the creatures who shared her patch of earth as if they were human. And to Margaret there was no real difference. Even the red deer who came down to the shore for the salty weed and the fierce little tuft-eared wild cats all knew the sound of her voice.

Reassured by a familiar presence, the seals went back to scenting the air and scanning the horizon.

The first indication Margaret had of the little boat's return was a double splash as the big grey creatures flopped heavily into the water. Margaret swung round.

'What'll ye be after, then?'

She narrowed her eyes and peered through the mist. It was several long minutes before the dark shape of the boat drifted out through the swirling white wreaths, tugged slowly along on the current, accompanied by the inquisitive bobbing heads of the seals.

Margaret scrambled forward, careless of the icy salt water swirling over her boots and soaking the thick skirt of the overcoat. Frantically she reached for the trailing painter, her fingers clumsy with cold, her heart fiery with hope. Slowly, heaving on the rope, she pulled the boat to shore. Then, and only then, could she make out the figure half-hidden by the sodden dark wool of the plaid, slumped on the boards above the keel.

'Oh, Lord. Will you look at that? The poor old laird . . .'

Quickly Margaret made the painter fast and climbed aboard.

The old man's body was ice-cold, and no pulse was beating under the fine pale skin, clammy now and rimed with salty spray.

But underneath the plaid was a living creature.

'By all that's holy, a bairn!'

She knew it must be the grandson. Whatever the cost, the old laird had had to try to save his own.

Margaret hesitated, torn for an instant between her duty to the dead and her concern for the living. More important by far was the living child pinioned beneath the corpse.

Swiftly she pulled the body off the breathing creature beneath. The child lay curled like a half-drowned rat beneath the black plaid among the strands of kelp and bladderweed, eyes tight-shut, shivering, white faced and streak-haired. Margaret gathered the child into her arms, holding the cold little body against herself. She looked down into the child's face.

'Well, would you believe!'

It did not take an instant to realize that the child was not a boy at all, but a little girl. The storm had sent her a little girl. Her heart beat harder. Not the laird's grandson, but a little girl all of her own.

Gently she laid the limp little body across her lap and set to work to unpick the water-tightened knots of the life-jacket. It was done up firmer than a seal caught in a fisherman's net. That must have been the saving of the bairn. She worked patiently and gently, talking to herself as her fingers worked.

'Poor lambkin. Such a scrap of a bairn. And all alone on the sea with the old man dead all through the night. What must you have been dreaming, wee lambkin? All that terrible time?'

Margaret Mackenzie stroked the wet hair off the forehead and put her own soft cheek against the cold skin.

Just as she managed to get off the life-jacket, one of the sleeves caught on a metal disc, the kind used for identification in wartime. It must have been attached to the child's wrist. Although she tried to hold it, her fingers were so stiff and clumsy with the cold that it slipped away and rolled into the folds of the cloak which still shrouded the body of the laird.

No matter. She would fetch it later.

'There, my own darling,' she whispered, and held the child close, feeling the fluttering heartbeat against her own. 'Safe now, my pet.'

She wrapped the sea-chilled body in the soft blanket, rubbing the limbs to restore the circulation. Gradually the little girl's breathing quickened and she could see a patch of colour spreading over the ice-pale cheeks.

Oh, but she was a pretty one, and the sooner tucked up in the warm the better.

There were teas of wild cherry and bitter sloes to be brewed to prevent a chill, an infusion of thistle to stimulate the circulation, little gruels of egg and milk frothed up with honey and flavoured with marshwort as a tonic for the blood.

She hesitated for a moment, looking down at the death-stiffened body of the laird. There was none of her potions which would call up the dead.

'As for ye, the Stuart, God rest your soul.'

She reached over and gently closed the eyelids.

Margaret pulled the plaid over the old man's body, wrapping it round the stiff limbs, weighting the heavy cloth with stones from the shore. Once she had settled the bairn, she would go for help. She had not the strength for the task of carrying him up to the Big House on her own. Later she would wash the body with rosemary and rue, and the hereditary chieftain of the Further Isles would be laid to rest in his plot of the isle's stony earth, watched over by the runes carved round the Celtic cross.

'The Lord take ye for His care, Stuart of Clan Forsa, until you are laid to rest among your ancestors.'

She made the sign of the cross and laid two sea-shells on the old man's closed eyelids to show the mermaids he was spoken for.

Margaret Mackenzie found no incompatibility between the faith of St Columba and the wayward spirits of the green hill to whom she owed equal allegiance. Both were unpredictable, both had to be placated with gifts and flattery, both held dominion over life and death.

She looked down at the child cradled in her arms. The dead must wait for the living.

The seals bobbed out in the bay, round-eyed spectators following the progress of the bustling little human as she made her way back round the promontory and up through the matted sea-pinks and rye-grass which marked the lower limit of the meadow.

'Hush, my hen. Hushaby, my sweeting,' she sang in the soft Gaelic lilt of her own childhood.

When she reached the stone wall crowned by a fuchsia hedge that marked the edge of her little kale-yard, she paused for a moment beside the rowan tree which all the islanders planted at their entrance. The rowan was the guardian of the gate. The tree had to be shown any new arrival to the household.

'Mark her well, the bairn's my ain.'

She held out the bundle to the graceful silvery tree, its wintry branches still bare of leaves. Satisfied, she nodded and smiled. Then, her cheeks as pink as the berries the rowan would bear in summer, she carried the child indoors. For the first time Margaret could remember, she closed the door behind her. The storm-orphan would have to be kept well away from prying eyes till nightfall, just as the flotsam of the sea always had to be kept away from the curious and the covetous.

Island tradition laid down that any salvage washed up on the shore and moved by the finder above the high-tide line before sundown became the finder's property. By that token Margaret claimed the storm-orphan as her own.

Now no-one and nothing, nor fairy nor saint nor human hand, could take the bairn away from her.

Jack Sweeney was also looking for salvage round the island's storm-battered shores.

It was at the very moment that Margaret vanished into her croft and closed the door that Jack, his ten-year-old legs scarcely tired by the exertion, came out onto the stretch of hill which gave onto the sea-loch and the fortified isle.

He had soon given up looking for his Aunt Catriona on the beach below Salen. Nor did he care to join the rest of the island's inhabitants scouring the tideline. Storm salvage was a serious business in the isles, and the demarcation lines were fiercely defended. Many a young man had had his front teeth knocked out when disputing rights to some precious piece of flotsam or jetsam. Down below, he could see that a few bottles of good Scots whisky had drifted inshore. Soon the whole island would be eagerly scouring the rim of weed.

Jack had decided to try less well-gleaned shores. If his luck was in, there might be a bottle or two – even perhaps a crate – drifting round to the western shore where there was no-one but the old laird and Margaret Mackenzie to glean.

Now, after the long walk round Eas Forse's single cart-track, Jack came out on the cliff above Forsa Isle just as the grey-haired islander came up the brae. Jack had good sharp eyes – young eyes, used to searching a hillside for a lost lamb or picking out the quick flash of a herring shoal a mile away in the sea-loch. Even from where he stood, he could make out that Margaret was heavy-laden, weighed down, it appeared, with a bundle wrapped in a blanket. She had found something washed up by the tide. Whatever it was, it was clearly valuable. Jack had never known her close the door to her croft as she did now.

Maybe a whole crate of whisky? It had looked heavy.

His heart beating with excitement, Jack made his way down to the still half-submerged causeway. He slipped off his boots, knotted the laces and slung the boots round his neck. With his breeks rolled up well over his knees, he moved quickly and confidently across the stepping stones. On the far side he paused beneath the walls of Forsa House.

The castle, its blind windows dark and threatening, loomed high on the slope above the little crofthouse. Jack had never quite summoned up enough courage to slip inside and explore the echoing empty rooms of the island's only fortified dwelling. Old and liquor-sodden as the laird was, he still remained a fearsome presence to the children of Eas Forse.

Padding softly, half-scared that the laird might suddenly appear, Jack moved round the small island towards the rocks at the base of the tilted cliff. It was there that the storm was most likely to have deposited its debris, including whatever it was that Margaret Mackenzie had found.

To his surprise, the castle's rowing-boat was pulled up among the rocks beneath the promontory. On every other occasion he had visited the forbidden island, the boat was in its usual place, tied to the ring on the landing-jetty by the causeway.

Today it was in the wrong place.

A couple of hoodie crows had also come down to investigate. They were being kept at bay by a black-backed gull which had taken up a position on the prow. The great bird turned a cold glittering eye to examine the newcomer, and then swung back to the object of its curiosity inside the boat. Reluctantly, as the boy approached, the gull hunched ebony shoulders and lifted itself up on giant wings to settle again a few yards further on.

Cautiously the boy crept towards the boat until he was close enough to peer over the gunwale. Whatever had aroused the interest of the birds, they were clearly not frightened of it. An instant later he recoiled, his heart pounding.

The object the winged scavengers had found so interesting was a corpse.

Jack managed to still the tremors that swept over him. He pulled at the covering so he could see the dead man's face.

'Great scarecrows,' Jack whispered to himself. 'The old laird. Dead as a hoodie.'

Dead, indeed, the laird was. Dead as the hoodie crows the crofters hung on their fences as a warning to the scavengers who thieved eggs and mobbed the lambs.

Normally Jack was not scared of dead bodies. All the islanders were used to death. Corpses were respectfully referred to as 'the deceased', and were laid out in all their finery in the front parlour for a night and a day, while family, friends and neighbours paid their last respects.

But this was the first dead body Jack had seen in its ugly reality. This body was crumpled into a heap of bones and angular flesh, the outlines of death clearly visible under the wet dark wool of the plaid. The gull screamed, a high thin cry like a wandering ghost. Startled, Jack dropped the plaid back over the body. As he did, a round metal object rolled out from the folds and splashed into the oily black water in the keel.

Jack stared at the spot where the object had vanished.

Maybe the old laird carried golden guineas in his pockets. You never could tell. Jack rolled up his sleeve and began to explore with his fingers in the icy water. His fingertips touched metal. Eagerly he examined his find. It wasn't a coin, but a metal disc, its surface scoured with writing.

Jack had seen enough refugee children arrive on the island to know what it was. He peered at the inscription.

'Emerald,' he said to himself. 'Emerald Mary Fitzwallace.'

What kind of a name was that? Emeralds were precious stones. His aunt, the schoolmistress, had a particular interest in mineralogy, and the class was used to going for rambles to find fossils. Emerald was certainly not a name for a human child; all the islanders gave their children biblical names, like Jacob himself.

A mermaid, perhaps? He gazed out to sea, catching his breath for a moment as he noticed two sleek dark heads bobbing out in the bay. He breathed again. Much as they might look like mermen, the whiskers told him they were the pair of handsome grey seals which had set up home on the promontory.

Then he remembered the bundle Margaret Mackenzie had been carrying.

Jack Sweeney sucked in his breath.

Salvage. Not inanimate things like bottles or crates or driftwood, but *human* salvage. Jack was only ten, and this was quite simply the most exciting thing that had ever happened in all his life. And he, Jack Sweeney, had the knowledge, he had the identification-disc. A secret, a wonderful secret. He slipped the disc into his pocket.

Catriona would be pleased when he showed her what he had found. Above all things, he wanted the schoolmistress's approval. Sometimes, like the day he had found a perfect whirly-shelled ammonite – the fossil shell of a prehistoric snail – she would even ruffle his hair and smile, and call him Jack. When she was not pleased with him, she called him 'Jacob', or, if things were really bad, *young man*. 'Come here, young man, and ye'll feel the flat of my hand.'

But today she would be delighted with what he had found. He moved quietly up the slope of hill and along the brae, until he came up beneath the dry-stone wall with its sentinel rowan-tree enclosing the small garden of the little white-painted crofthouse.

The single black-framed window which pierced the three-foot thick wall gave only a narrow glimpse of the scene inside the cosy kitchen. Faintly he could hear the sound of crooning. He paused.

There was no particular mystery in that. Fairy-touched as she was, Jack knew the grey-haired island woman often muttered to herself as she went about her business feeding the hens and digging her tattie patch.

He craned his neck to peer further into the little room. Margaret Mackenzie, her back towards him, was concentrating on something out of his line of sight.

He could hear her more clearly now. She was using the Gaelic.

'Hush there, my lambkin.'

After a few moments she rose. Now Jack could see what she had been looking at: a bundle she had laid down on the cushions of the settle by the fire.

As he had guessed, the bundle was a child.

Jack drew his head back and considered. He counted on his fingers. From the birth-date on the disc the child must be nearly four years old. He could see her, limp and lying there all still and sleek as a drowned rabbit.

Even so, Jack thought, the little girl was the prettiest thing he had ever seen. All soft and doll-like even with her eyes tight shut and her small body all swaddled. The warmth of the fire was beginning to bring back a pink gleam to the transparent cheeks.

But for a few moments, it would have been Jack himself who found her. Why, he was practically her prince, like in the fairy-stories. He had her little glass slipper, dropped on the way from the shore.

Jack shrank back against the stone wall as Margaret Mackenzie came into view again. She was carrying a steaming bowl and a small horn spoon.

'Soon be ready, my lambkin.'

For the next ten minutes, the island woman patiently spooned gruel into the child's mouth. Jack could see the slender throat working, but the little girl's eyes seemed to be wide and unseeing, her face smooth and blank. After the bowl was scraped clean, Margaret Mackenzie laid the swaddled child down again among the cushions.

'There we are, my bairn.'

Jack craned his neck.

Margaret straightened up and picked up a bundle of small garments which had been drying on the polished brass rail of the black range. She went over to the dresser, opened a biscuit box with a picture of Queen Victoria's Jubilee on the lid and took out a heavy iron key. Then she went over to the oak settle which served as her store-chest.

The islanders weren't in the habit of using locks. They had no fear of thieves. There was a ritual which told the neighbours how long someone would be gone from their dwelling. When you were out for a short while, you left the broom outside the door to show you would be back soon. If you were to be away longer, then the broom was left inside the doorway.

The lock on the settle was the only padlock in the house. The key turned easily but the lid was heavy and hard to lift. Jack knew the lid was heavy because not so long ago he had wrestled with it himself. The chest was where Margaret kept her secrets.

Jack knew many things about the islanders, even more about certain parts of their lives than his Aunt Catriona knew. Of late, since he had begun to keep company with the older boys, he had begun to get bolder, peeping in drawers, slipping the catches on the cupboards, even learning how to tumble the primitive mechanism of a padlock without the key.

The boy knew the inside of Margaret Mackenzie's crofthouse like the back of his hand. His Aunt Catriona did not know of his visits because she would have been angry if she had been aware that her own flesh and blood was accustomed to begging a scone, maybe even a slice of raisin-studded cloutie-dumpling, from the woman who had been the cause of the death of her sweetheart.

A growing lad, Jack was always hungry. Margaret Mackenzie's was one of the island kitchens where Jack knew he would be sure to find a welcome.

Sometimes Margaret Mackenzie would be out when he called. The broom leant against the door-jamb told him she would be away in the big house, doing the housework for the old laird.

When that happened, Jack would set about his magpie gathering of knowledge. So he knew what she kept in the trunk. There was her father's plaid and silver-bound horn drinking-cup. A rose-patterned tea-pot which had come down from her mother. A heavy overcoat, an embroidered cotton shoe-bag with a pair of dancing-pumps. Now she slipped the small garments inside, folding up the life-jacket and slipping it right to the bottom – her glance darting round the room as if to make sure she was not observed. Jack knew that could only mean one thing: the presence of the child was a secret. That was how Jack knew he'd acquired a new and glorious bit of knowledge.

Margaret walked back across the room and bent over the settle again. Jack could see that the little girl was sleeping peacefully now.

'Bide awhile, wee bairn. I'm away to fetch help to the old laird.'

Jack's heart leaped. There would be no-one to watch the little girl. He ducked down behind the water-butt just as the door opened and Margaret Mackenzie appeared. She shut the door firmly behind her and trotted away down the slope towards the causeway.

Jack watched till she had disappeared from sight, then slipped inside the crofthouse.

He tiptoed towards the glowing hearth and the cushioned settle with its precious bundle. The little girl was breathing softly, her dark eyelashes laid on the cheek as pink now as a briar rose. He held his breath, half-frightened by the extraordinary delicacy of the little face. She was indeed the most beautiful creature he had ever seen.

He sat down on the settle and reached out his hand. The child's skin felt as soft as sun-warmed sphagnum moss. The child's hair was as fine and dark as an otter's fur, with red lights picked out by the firelight.

For a long while he looked at the little girl, drinking in her beauty. Then gently – oh so gently – he began to croon, whispering the words that children long to hear, that he had never heard. Sweetheart, dear heart, so sweet, so small. He had no lullabies to sing, no memories to draw on. Just the same he sang to her, but his songs were wordless.

He did not leave the sleeping child's side until he heard the voices which told him Margaret Mackenzie had accomplished her mission and was on her way home with the help she had sought.

Then he opened the door a crack and watched until the two figures had gone round the headland and were busy on the shore.

He smiled to himself. Margaret Mackenzie was not yet ready to share the secret in her crofthouse kitchen. He and he alone knew of the beautiful little girl.

It was a secret. A wonderful secret. In a moment he had made good his escape, crouching low behind the line of boulders, undetected.

14

Eas Forse: 6 February 1941

Margaret and Archie the postman, between the pair of them, managed to lift the stiff body of the old laird up into the castle, out of the way of the gulls and hoodies. There Margaret laid him out to rest on the big table in the cavernous hall. There were only a few mounted stags' heads to keep the vigil: the portraits of his ancestors had long gone to pay the heating bills. Tomorrow she would make the body ready for the wake. It was not the first time she had laid out a corpse, and it would surely not be the last.

After she and Archie had brought the body safely in, she had brewed up a pot of tea in the kitchen of the big house. Then she had sent Archie on his way without telling him of the storm-salvage in her croft kitchen. Time enough for that when she had worked out how to keep the bairn.

In the warm kitchen, the child lay curled up on the settle by the fire. The child's eyes were open now. But they were as dark as midnight, the pupils so wide and unseeing that it was almost impossible in the half-light to detect that they were as blue as the violets which grew round the edge of the croft's kale-patch.

Margaret kept watch over the child through the long afternoon and into the night, relying on the medicinal herbs and the sound of her own voice to bring the child's mind back to rejoin the rapidly strengthening body.

The bairn managed to swallow most of an egg whisked up with new milk sweetened with honey, but not a word had passed her lips or smile crossed her face as she passively accepted the nourishment.

Seventh child of a seventh child, Margaret Mackenzie wasn't alarmed or even surprised by the child's blind eyes and her silence. The little girl had simply retreated from the world into which the violence of the sea had thrown her. Margaret knew she had left the real world for a mirror world, a topsy-turvy dwelling-place which accommodated much older gods. From there, in her own good time, she would return.

Meanwhile Margaret had but to hold her peace until she could weave some web to explain the child's appearance under her roof. She would have to concoct some story, some tale of a long-lost niece or cousin's child. Who was there to fret over a storm-orphan in wartime? And then later – well, that would be later.

The schoolmistress was the main obstacle. She was the only islander who not only bore Margaret a grudge, but also was capable of interfering with her plans.

Catriona Sweeney must not get wind of the matter until Margaret had her story neatly thought out and ready to tell. With her lists and documents and files of records, the archivist was more than likely to come up with some official reason to deprive her old rival of the gift the sea had brought her. Margaret knew that love was more important than names on lists – and she had plenty of love to spare.

What Margaret did not yet know was that Catriona Sweeney also had a reason for not wanting official noses poked into island affairs – a reason which also had more to do with love than with lists.

For the moment at least, the storm-orphans might sleep in peace. But not for long.

No-one had given a thought to that other orphan on the island. Jack was no match for the bigger boys, well used to extracting what they wanted from those smaller and more vulnerable than themselves. He collected firewood from the shore on the way home as a special present for his Aunt Catriona.

On an island with little but peat to burn, it was always a welcome gleaning. But today the islanders had left it in preference for more valuable salvage. Twenty bottles of whisky at least had been washed up. Nothing like the bounty on the neighbouring island of Eriskay, but fine pickings none the less.

His gleaning brought him into the needfire cave, where that morning the schoolmistress had found her storm-orphan. There, glistening in the fringe of weed which rimmed the tidal shelf, was another of the identity-discs, hanging from a thick twist of string. This time it belonged to a boy. Jack counted on his fingers. The boy must be two years younger than him. His heart beat faster. The schoolmistress would be pleased with what he had found.

A little later, his sandy brows lowered over his small deep-set eyes, with the faggot of firewood slung over his shoulder and the double secret in his pocket, he joined his schoolmates on their way back up the cliff-path.

Young Marie, the innkeeper's daughter, was the first to spot him.

'Where ye been, Jack? Found anything?' she called out cheerfully.

Marie was twelve but well developed for her age, and she knew that Jack hung around with the older boys of an evening outside the pub. Marie was working her way round to fancying an older boy, and Jack was an easy way in. Jack was not really allowed to consort with the rough boys who hung around the harbour – and certainly Marie was set fair not to be good enough for him. His aunt had ambitions for him, as everyone knew.

'Mind yer own business, our Marie.'

Jack lowered his sandy brows.

Marie laughed. 'It wouldn't be *your* Marie I am, Jack.'

'Leave me be.' Jack shrugged and came to a halt.

'Any road, see if I care! My mam'll have *my* tea ready.' Marie tossed her head and ran on, throwing a parting shot over her shoulder. 'Where'll ye be getting *your* tea, our Jack?'

The mocking laughter rang in Jack's ears. Whatever his aunt's ambitions might be, they were not translated into a good hot tea.

Whenever he could persuade her to cook for him, Jack took his meals at the schoolmistress's table. Failing that, he went up the hill to the unwelcoming kitchen of his new step-grandmother.

Night was falling, and he was starving hungry.

Jack's spirits lifted. He was nearly home.

Today the schoolmistress would surely be waiting, even watching, for him to come back. She would have a hot tea ready for him. Maybe even a mutton stew – his favourite.

Jack was wrong. That evening for once his aunt wasn't at home at all, let alone watching out for his return.

Jack poked his head into the parlour, checked the kitchen and the front room. Then he went outside to see if the little square of veiled light was glowing from the caravan down the hill – the signal that told him his aunt was locked away in her private sanctuary.

Sometimes Jack was allowed inside the schoolmistress' caravan, to help her with the cutting and the pasting of her records. No-one else was allowed in Catriona's hideaway, her 'temple of knowledge' as she called it. She was fond of telling her class it was the storing of knowledge which separated man from beast.

Now, Jack thought, his aunt must be picking over whatever she had found that morning on the shore when she disappeared from his sight. Jack knew well enough the scolding he would get if he disturbed her uninvited.

Drawn back inside the cottage by the scent of food, he went into the small kitchen. On the side of the stove stood an empty pot, still warm. There was a smear of gravy in the bottom. Jack smelled it hungrily, and used his finger to scoop up the last of the rich juice. It was all that was left of the mutton stew.

As he licked his fingertips, Jack frowned. Perhaps, he thought, his aunt had guessed he'd been round the island to Margaret Mackenzie's croft and left him to go hungry to bed as a punishment.

Jack was wrong. The whereabouts of her nephew had never been further from the schoolmistress's thoughts. Inside the caravan, Catriona was fully occupied coaxing her own storm-orphan, now bathed, wrapped in dry clothes and tucked up snugly in the bunk, to swallow the last few spoonfuls of the stew.

'Come on, my lad, the broth will do ye good,' she said briskly, waving the spoon in the direction of Callum's mouth. 'Open up.'

The tousle-haired boy shook his head fiercely.

'Where's my sister? I must find my little sister.' His voice was frantic. 'Please let me get up.'

'Certainly not,' Catriona said firmly. 'I shall go myself.'

It had been a bare hour since the boy had recovered enough to find his voice. At first he had seemed delirious, crying out that he had to find the child who had, it appeared, been in his care when he was washed overboard from the ship.

Catriona soothed him as best she could, but the boy was only quietened and persuaded to eat his food when she promised to scour the shore herself. So she filled the oil-fuelled storm-lantern and prepared to go out again just as soon as the moon rose.

In fact the last creature on earth Catriona wanted to find was the boy's sister. Her blood ran cold at the thought. All her adult life she had longed for a child, the boy-child her long-ago love would have given her. Now the sea had given her a boy. If he had a sister, there would be a family not far behind. Her best hope was that the boy belonged to no-one and nobody.

As she went out into the night to search the shore again, she felt a stab of guilt. If the boy's sister had managed to survive the wreck, Catriona found herself hoping the child had drowned in the raging seas of the storm. She forced the thought from her mind and headed for the beach.

Jack waited in the shadow beside the bungalow's porch until his aunt, the flickering lantern swinging in her mittened hand, had vanished down the cliff-path.

A tiny glow from the caravan window, shrouded by the thick curtains required by the blackout, shone through the darkness.

Jack crept up under the window. What he saw made him catch his breath in surprise. Although the single pane was steamed up with the heat from the gas fire which Catriona used to warm her little sanctuary, he could just make out that there was a figure huddled on the bunk opposite. It was a boy – asleep.

Jack quietly lifted the latch, slipped in through the door of the caravan and tip-toed over to the bunk.

The storm hadn't thrown just one castaway onto the island, it had washed up two – one to a Sweeney and the other to a Mackenzie. Also, it dawned on Jack, it was more than possible that he alone of all Eas Forse's inhabitants knew of the double presence. And he and he alone knew who they were.

He did not yet know how the knowledge might benefit him.

The schoolmistress had forbidden him to visit the caravan without express permission.

'If you disobey me, young Jacob,' his aunt had said as she glared at him fiercely, 'no more hot dinners for ye in my kitchen, my lad.'

His stomach rumbled. The smell of mutton stew was rich and strong. By the empty bowl by the bedside, the boy had eaten Jack's supper.

He had meant to give his aunt both the little discs for her records. But now he was not so sure.

A girl-child in Margaret Mackenzie's crofthouse kitchen was one thing. An orphan boy in his aunt's caravan was quite another.

As yet no-one knew who the boy was, so there was just a chance he might be – like an unwanted parcel – returned to sender. Tracing addresses for the postmistress was one of the tasks his aunt undertook and with which Jack had been allowed to help her. Jack knew all about return-to-sender. If there was no return address, after a certain time you were allowed to keep the parcel. Catriona was always meticulous about the length of time which must elapse. Once he had had a brand new pair of gloves, posted up to a holidaymaker and never claimed.

He felt the two little discs in his pocket. One of them would surely send the unwanted boy back to where he came from. Jack's small blue eyes lit up at his own cleverness. It was the best idea he had had all the long exciting day.

Carefully so as not to disturb the sleeper, Jack slipped the disc back on the boy's wrist. With any luck, that would do the trick.

Return-to-sender. Jack was pleased with himself.

Now all he had to do was keep the other disc safe, and the pink-cheeked child in Margaret Mackenzie's croft would be allowed to stay. Why, she would practically belong to him.

Making good his escape, he threaded his way along the village street to his grandfather's cottage to see if he could wheedle a bowl of porridge.

His grandfather's young wife Megan greeted him with a scowl.

'If it's food ye're wanting, ye're late.'

Megan didn't care for her red-haired step-grandson. He was a constant reminder that she had had to make do with a man old enough to be her father.

'Wash your hands and set ye down,' she said, her mouth drawn into the resentful line Jack knew well. 'A dish of burstin gruel is all there is.'

Jack dipped his chapped red hands in the bucket of cold water by the sink, and slipped onto the bench behind the table. Megan ladled the thick brown porridge into a chipped enamel bowl and slid it towards him.

'Sup up and be off wi' ye,' she added curtly.

Jack was starving, and the food, a thick heavy porridge made with roasted meal, tasted almost as good as a mutton stew. Just the same, the charity stuck in his throat, as it always did.

'Wee wastrel bastard,' Megan muttered to herself as she went through to look to her own child in the cradle in the bedroom. 'No good's going to come of that one, only trouble.'

Jack didn't care what Megan thought of him. Instead he took advantage of her absence to scoop three apples from the bowl on the table into his pocket. He mopped up the last of the gruel with his fingers, washed his spoon, and went back into the night. Megan tossed her head angrily as she heard the door close; just as she'd expected, there'd been no word of thanks.

Out on the street, Jack paused for a moment. Whenever it wasn't raining, the bigger boys of the rougher sort spent their evenings hanging around outside the public house by the harbour – waiting, as it were, on the threshold of manhood.

Jack had to keep his association well away from his aunt's knowledge.

'Well, if it's not young Jack,' a voice greeted him. 'What ye got for your friends, wee Jack?'

Jack, three years younger than the youngest of the gang, was considered to be serving his apprenticeship. The gang tolerated him because he ran their errands, keeping his eyes and ears open and his mouth shut. Part of the price of their tolerance was that he brought them something as an entrance fee.

Today it was the apples he'd taken from the bowl in Megan's kitchen. But the real treasure of the day's gleaning, the metal disc, remained in his pocket.

'That all?' The older boy took the fruit. He tossed two apples to the gathering, polished one on his sleeve and took a bite.

'So, lads, what's to report?'

Inevitably all the talk that night was about the storm and the bounty the islanders of the neighbouring isle of Eriskay had trawled. Andy Cameron, the son of the island's radio operator, had the latest news.

'Whisky galore it is over there. Chrissie Macleod said her father couldn't believe his eyes. And there may still be pickings yet, me da' says.' Andy Cameron's voice was thoughtful. 'The ship passed by the Forsa sea-loch. Me da' took a message to pass on to the laird: special passengers to be taken off at first light.' Jack looked up startled.

'*Passengers?*'

'Ay. The laird's own, they were, by all accounts. And no sight nor sign of them. Me da' says it's a rum do anyway – there was na' paying passenger listed on the manifest.'

'I've a mind to borrow me da's tender,' Jimmy McCrone, the son of a trawlerman, offered. 'Wi' the full moon there's light enough for a wee run before the tide turns. Why should those daft buggers get it all?'

'I'm wi' ye.' Andy Cameron was already on his feet. 'Let's see what's for the taking.'

'Jack, ye'll cover for us.' Peter Mackay stood up. 'I want nae trouble. Anyone asks and we're awa' fishing the night tide, that's all. Understood?'

Jack nodded. 'Ay.' Then, suddenly worried at what he knew they would find, longing to keep his secret for just a moment longer, he said. 'There's nae sense going by the Big Hoose. There's nothing there.'

'How can ye know that, Jack?' Jimmy's voice was curious.

He swung round and gripped the ten-year-old's arm. Jack felt the fingers bite into his flesh. Jimmy was a strong lad, didn't know his own strength.

'What are ye telling us, wee Jack?'

The ten-year-old hesitated only for a moment.

'The old laird's deid. Drowned in the storm. I saw it.'

'Saw what?'

'The body. All stiff and black.' Jack's face screwed up into an approximation of the expression on the corpse's face.

'Ye've been holding out on us, wee Jack? What else d'ye know?'

Jimmy McCrone, the bigger boy, did not have to do anything – not even twist Jack's arm. All he had to do was lower his brows and look very hard in Jack's face for the boy to tell them everything he knew.

On an island, there was no place to hide.

So Jack told them about the sleeping boy in the bunk in the caravan. He told them about the little girl Margaret Mackenzie had laid so gently in the cradle in the croft.

Love and betrayal.

Poor Jack. He was far too young to love and betray all in the same day. Nevertheless, in that sweet time watching over the little girl in the crofthouse kitchen he had felt the glow of love for the first and only time in his short and unloved life.

15

Eas Forse: February 1941

The news flew round the island as if it had wings.

The storm had delivered two children to the islands' two rival spinsters. It was astonishing, miraculous. The islanders were in an uproar of excitement. Even the bounty which had washed onto the shores of neighbouring Eriskay had not the thrill of these live gleanings.

The island was divided in its loyalties. There were those, stern and law-abiding, who thought the children were no business of the islanders' and should be shipped back to the mainland without more ado – certainly before the two women grew attached to them. There were those of romantic persuasion who, remembering the tragedy which had befallen the women in youth, thought the spinsters had earned their good fortune.

The Lord moves in mysterious ways – or whoever it is who arranges such things for the benefit of mortals.

A haffod was declared – a gathering of all the island's elders so that they might thrash out the problem in the ceilidh-tein, the meeting-hall which housed the Beltane needfire.

The haffod dated back to the days when the inhabitants of the Further Isles governed their own affairs, and did not, as happened now, have to look to the mainland for every small decision.

The islanders were Celts, blessed with a natural unwillingness to conform to rules, inclined to common consensus rather than written laws. They looked to their own – setting aside what was needed for the support of the poor, adjudicating on the boundaries of livestock-grazing and the limits of the lobster-kreelers.

Certain social matters were considered within the competence of the haffod. It was the community's ancient responsibility to make sure that widows and fatherless bairns were fed and housed. Another of the haffod's important duties was to rule on the ownership of shore-gleaning.

It was thought the children might fall within these two categories. In which case, there was no need to refer the matter to the mainland officials.

The haffod was called for the following day but one, to allow time for Margaret Mackenzie to call in the proper spiritual authorities to complete the burial rituals for the old laird. And also to give an opportunity for Catriona to make the necessary (but discreet) official enquiries about the children, in so far as such a thing was possible in wartime.

The disc which had mysteriously reappeared on the boy's wrist was ample proof that he was indeed the old laird's grandson, even if he had not been able to speak for himself.

The little girl was still delirious, so nothing could yet be established – the schoolmistress having kept silent on the boy's claims of a sister.

What was immediately clear was that there was no-one in the Maid of Eas Forse's southern abode to take any message at all. And the Record Office had taken a direct hit in the last round of fire-bombing, so it had missing-person reports flowing out of every orifice – more than enough to occupy its energies without making enquiries into persons who were not even missing at all.

All this turmoil had the effect of joining Margaret Mackenzie and Catriona Sweeney in common cause for the first time since the terrible night of the death of young Angus, sweetheart to them both. What united them now was fear of losing the precious human salvage that the storm had tossed on the shores of Eas Forse. Catriona was most at risk. With Callum established as the old laird's grandson, Margaret Mackenzie might legitimately claim custody by default, as being the laird's housekeeper she would have had the care of the boy anyway. Equally the little girl, being apparently no kin to any islander, had no claim on the island's charity. Both women blamed Jack – snooping Jack, peeping Jack – for the premature discovery of the storm-orphans and the involvement of the whole island in what might otherwise have remained a private matter.

After the excitement which followed the discovery of the storm-orphans, the island returned to its sombre duty, the burial of the laird.

All the next day the elders of the island filed past the open coffin laid out in the front hall of Forsa House.

When the sun was at its midday height on the second day, the piper's ancient lament, the haunting pibroch, soared out over the hill, and the old man was laid to his rest in the graveyard of the Celtic kings.

Afterwards, in the bright afternoon sunshine, the procession of mourners walked slowly round the cliff road, past the harbour, and settled themselves in their mourning black, for all the world like a line of rooks on a fence, on the benches set round the walls of the ceilidh-tein.

The ceilidh-tein was a 'black-house', a smoke-crusted crofthouse without a chimney. It was the most ancient of the little township's habitations, with thick curved walls so that the wind from the sea slid round its edges. Deliberations within its walls were held to be guided by unseen influences.

The proceedings began when the two spinsters presented themselves to the haffod, already assembled in a circle round the black-house walls.

'I'm pleased to see ye all here today,' Catriona began. 'It is as well when we see to our own affairs.'

She put her case forcefully. The boy Callum Stuart Fergusson was unquestionably grandson to the old laird. He was clearly as close to an islander as anyone could possibly be without actually having been born on Eas Forse.

But the little girl . . . Well – she pursed her lips – no-one knew anything about the child. The island's records showed no trace of a girl-child born to the Maid, no granddaughter to the Stuart of Eas Forse. The child had no identity at all, so would be better off in an orphanage on the mainland.

Then Margaret Mackenzie stepped forward. Her normally round pink face was creased with anxiety, but her voice was gentle with the rhythmic cadence of the Celtic teller of tales.

Half singing, half speaking – her fingers counting the rhythm of her words – she told the story of the storm. She told of how the child had been under the laird's protection when she was found, how the laird himself had cloaked the bairn against the elements, how he had sacrificed his own life for the protection of the little girl, and how therefore the child could legitimately be said to be his own flesh in spirit, even if not in blood.

And, anyway, declared Margaret – looking severely round the crow-black circle – which of them could declare, while seated around the tein-eigen hearth which kindled the Beltane fires, that they might tell for certain who had fathered them?

There was a brief moment of silence. The Beltane children were a delicate subject. The haffod shifted nervously, twitching its funeral black.

Then everyone spoke at once.

The bairns were declared legitimate shore-gleanings, which would allow the haffod to rule on their ownership.

After further vigorous debate, the children were declared neither flotsam nor jetsam, but salvage – the property of whoever carried them over the tideline before nightfall.

The rules of salvage dictated that the children should remain with the finder. The haffod ruled that this should be so in this case.

In addition, the haffod decreed, the children must be brought up in at least some understanding of how they came to be on the island.

There was no difficulty with the boy of course. His lineage was there for all to see and read. And as for the Maid and her husband, the boy's parents – it was agreed they must have had some good reason for evacuating their son. No doubt it all would come clear in time, even if the time was the full duration of the war.

The little girl was a different problem. In her case, so little was known. Although it was agreed that Catriona should do what she could to trace her origins, it was generally felt that Margaret Mackenzie, who was of course blessed with the second sight, would be more capable of handling those particular circumstances.

'Orphan, place of birth unknown', was not something you could look up in a registry.

16

Eas Forse: 1941

It was Jack who told Callum where to find Emerald – and instantly regretted what he had done.

The two women had agreed it was better to let things settle down a bit – in case, so soon after the trauma of the shipwreck, the children were upset at being parted.

The schoolmistress had already reassured Callum that Emerald was fine, and had managed to stop him rushing out to find her immediately by explaining that the little girl was still recovering from the effects of the storm.

'All in good time,' the schoolmistress had said firmly. 'The wee bairn will need her peace and quiet for a week or so, just enough to let her get her strength back.'

Callum was bewildered. He could see no reason why he should not immediately be reunited with his beloved foster-sister. But he was not yet feeling bold enough for outright disobedience.

At first, Jack didn't tell the younger boy he knew how to find his sister. Out of everyone, he felt he had lost the most. The schoolmistress was furious with him for disobeying her, and told him he was no longer welcome in her kitchen. And Jack's own guilt at the trouble he had caused had not only kept him from the warmth of Margaret Mackenzie's crofthouse, but also deprived him of the chance to be near the bewitchingly beautiful child. Denied the food and comfort of the two spinster-women's kitchens, his belly was grumbling at the diet of porridge and burstin meal which was all his step-grandmother dished up for him. His only bargaining-counter, his chance to redeem himself, was the little disc he held tight in his fist, permanently thrust for greater safety in his pocket.

After a week, hunger and loneliness got the better of him. He decided to give up his treasure to buy himself back into his aunt's affections. Once he had decided, he risked her further displeasure and went to find her down at the caravan.

'What's that ye have there, Jacob?'

He held out his hand, beaming with pride.

'This, Aunt Catriona. I found this in the laird's boat. On the night of the storm.'

But then the schoolmistress, far from being mollified when he gave her his precious and interesting secret, had been even more annoyed with him than before.

'I'd like to know, Jacob Sweeney,' she said severely as she studied the scratched writing on the disc, 'why ye could not have saved us all a lot of trouble and brought this forward before? Emerald Mary Fitzwallace, indeed. What kind of a name is that?' She set her specs on her nose, the better to see the inscription.

After a moment she looked up. 'I'll thank ye to keep this piece of knowledge to yourself, young man. Least said, soonest mended.'

And with that she slipped the identity-disc in a brown envelope, wrote on it neatly, and locked it firmly in the little metal box where she kept her valuables.

And that was the end of that. His treasure was gone.

In revenge he told the boy where to find Emerald.

It was not a particularly good plan, but it was all he had. Return-to-sender hadn't worked at all, so now what he hoped was that Callum would run away to be with Emerald. Or he might bring Emerald home to the schoolmistress.

As far as Jack was concerned, either would do.

Emerald was confused. Confused but happy because she had found Callum again. She had thought when she opened her eyes in the little crofthouse that she had died and gone to live with whoever it was you live with when you die. This was a nice round person who smelled of lavender and roses and other things, sweet-scented things which Emerald didn't recognize at all. The lavender and roses reminded her of her mummy.

When she opened her eyes she couldn't remember who she was or what had happened to her at all. When she asked, the round person had crinkled up the edges of her eyes, picked her up and hugged her. She had told her she had been with the fairies, and to sup her barley soup like a good girl, and then she would tell her a story.

Emerald liked the stories. They were told in a sing-song voice, with the round person's little pink fingers keeping the beat. The stories were all about fairies and mermaids and sometimes they had happy endings. Not always, but mostly.

That was a week ago.

And then she found Callum. Well, to be sure, it might be truer to say that Callum found Emerald.

At first she had not known who he was. She had been confused about everything anyway. But the boy had beautiful curly hair and bright speckled eyes. And he was strong. Emerald could feel how strong he was when he picked her up and swung her round.

'Who are you, boy?' said Emerald.

Callum looked at her in astonishment.

'Callum, silly.'

'Ah,' said Emerald carefully.

'Em, don't you remember?'

'Remember what?'

'It's me. Cal. You're my little sister.'

Callum's voice was bewildered.

'What's happened, Em? Don't you remember anything?'

Emerald was more scared now. She looked at the boy, her big dark eyes round and troubled.

'No.'

'Don't you remember about the ship? The storm?'

That was when Emerald felt cold shivers run down the back of her neck, like the rainwater when it got between her collar and the bit her woolly scarf left bare.

'Storm?' she said.

She hesitated.

Then she shook her head violently – as violently as the waves which had pounded outside the mermaids' cavern all the time she was under the green sea hiding from the monster.

'No! No! No!' She started by whispering and ended by screaming. 'Don't remember anything!'

She ran away and hid until she was quite sure he had given up looking for her.

Except that he didn't give up. It was one of the things that she learned about Callum. He never gave up.

When she came back to the crofthouse kitchen, he was still there, even though it was quite dark. She jumped when she saw him still there. But Callum smiled and held up his hand.

'All right, all right, Em. I promise I won't talk about it again.' Then he looked steadily at her, and added quietly: 'Not until you tell me you're ready.'

Then Emerald remembered it all. It was like a window which had opened and then banged shut. But she still pretended it wasn't there. Wasn't there at all.

Suddenly the boy picked her up again and hugged her, really hard, so she could feel his ribs crushing her and his strong arms around her. Emerald's cheeks turned scarlet with pleasure. When he eventually put her down, she was amazed to see there were tears in his eyes.

Emerald stared at the boy.

Of course she remembered the storm. She remembered the black monster who had come to eat her up. She remembered the soft green cave where she had played with the baby mermaids in the warm sand. But she remembered the story of the little mermaids, too. She could never tell Callum where she'd been – if she did, she'd belong to the mermaids for ever.

And she would certainly never see Callum again.

'See you tomorrow, little sister,' he said gently.

Later, when she was back in the favourite place she had found, a little plateau in the heather above the cottage where she now lived with the round person who smelled so nice, she considered long and carefully what the boy had said.

He would come back tomorrow. He had said he would. And then she would have to scold him, just a little, for not being there to save her from the black monster. She had been very scared when she was swallowed up by the monster, and she did not like to think about it. Not too much. Or the black monster would come and get you in your dreams.

Just the same, if you were going to be rescued, and Callum wasn't around to do it, the person who rescued Emerald was quite the right person to do so. Emerald hoped this someone was the person who was going to look after her till her real mummy came back to find her.

The next day when he came back and she scolded him, he quite refused to believe it was a monster who had swallowed him up.

Emerald knew better. She knew just why the monster had spat him

111

out. Of course. Boys were made of slugs and snails and puppydogs' tails, and all of those things tasted quite horrible.

But Callum said it was a great big wave which had carried him to the shore and washed him up in a cave. Callum had been found by the school-mistress. Emerald did not much like the sound of the schoolmistress. She was glad she had not been found by the schoolmistress.

She thought about it all that evening while she ate her bowl of porridge and cream and honey. She thought some more about it while she ate the snowy white scone and dipped little pieces in the boiled egg she had fetched herself all warm from underneath one of the marmalade hens.

You could tell when the hens had laid a brown egg because they clucked very loudly to explain how clever they were. Living in the croft was much more exciting than living anywhere else.

For the moment she didn't want to think at all. She simply wanted to remember the warm-hay smell of the boy's tousled yellow hair, his smiling face with the bright tawny eyes, and the strength of his arms around her.

She had a feeling about Callum, a warm happy feeling that stubbornly refused to go away.

He came to see her every day after that first time. When the sun had dipped to below a special clump of hazel every evening, she would know it was time to run to meet him after he had finished school.

She had to jump across the stepping-stones, and sometimes when the tide was high she got her feet wet.

Next year, when she was five, she would go to school, too.

But meanwhile, every Saturday, her nan – that was what she called her new mummy – took her to the school playground with the other children who were going to school next year, so it wouldn't all be too unfamiliar.

That was how she knew the schoolmistress had round spectacles and a thin cross face.

The main reason she didn't really want to live with Cal was that she'd have to live in the cold grey bungalow by the schoolhouse. Even with Callum there, it would still be terrible.

Then she would never see her nan again, or gather the sloes and bram-bles down the brae. She'd never be allowed to play all day on the beach and paddle out to find the feathery fronds of carragheen seaweed to set a milk jelly. Or carry back a bucketful of little sandy grey shrimps for her tea.

In the playground, there was a boy who paid her particular attention. The boy was another reason why she didn't want to live with the schoolmistress.

The boy was the schoolmistress's nephew and he was very old, much older than Emerald, even older than Callum. His name was Jack. Emerald giggled when he told her his name. 'Jack Sprat could eat no fat, his wife could eat no lean,' she sang. But she couldn't remember till later the bit about licking the platter clean.

Poor Jack. He didn't get much of a chance to lick any platter clean. Emerald knew, because he had told her so, that mostly he had only porridge without cream or honey for his supper.

Emerald always had much more than she needed in her Saturday lunch-box, and she would share her scones and jam with Jack because he always looked hungrily at them. Her nan made the nicest girdle scones on the island. Everyone said how lucky she was to have her nan to pack her lunch-box.

Jack was a bit of an outsider. He lived with his grandfather, but he didn't seem to spend much time there. Mostly he hung around with boys even older than himself.

Emerald would have invited him back to the crofthouse, but she knew her nan was not at all pleased with Jack.

And the schoolmistress, who was Jack's aunty but who looked after Callum, was cross with Jack, too. It all seemed to have something to do with Emerald – so she felt as if it was her fault. Which was another good reason to share.

Just the same, Emerald much preferred to be with Callum. She felt happy when she played with Callum. She didn't feel nearly as happy with Jack.

Jack watched her all the time with his little blue eyes under the sandy brows, a bit greedily, as if he was the black monster just waiting to swallow her up.

To Emerald, Jack was a person to be a bit sorry for, but a bit scared of, too.

To Jack, Emerald was quite simply the most wonderful creature he had ever known – and Callum was the boy who had deprived him of everything he had ever wanted.

Jealousy had followed so hard on the heels of love. Jealousy of the interloper who had so easily usurped his place. Jealousy of the little girl whose love he longed to earn.

Jealousy was a rat gnawing, the pain invisible – but just as sharp as the hunger of an empty belly.

Jack was used to the one, but the other he had yet to learn.

Emerald was happy, happier than she remembered being in her entire life. This wasn't saying much, because Emerald still couldn't remember

113

quite a few things about what had happened before she lived with her nan in the croft.

She remembered the things she wanted to remember. Callum was one of those things. Today had been the first day of school and she had spent all day with Callum.

Tomorrow she would again catch a lift with Archie Mackenzie Stuart the postman. Archie was Margaret Mackenzie's only neighbour on that corner of the island. You read the islanders' lineage in their names. Everyone was someone's second cousin or great-niece or brother-in-law. On an island it was always like that. Until the infamous Clearances, that part of Eas Forse had been full of folk. Archie was the last of his line, just like Callum was the last of his. Callum, with the Stuart blood in his veins, was a third cousin once removed of Archie the postman.

Emerald knew nothing of these things. She just knew she had been a bit scared when she had gone rattling round the island in the postman's trap for the first time, to be delivered to the little stone schoolhouse.

Emerald had to be brave.

Then she saw Callum coming out to collect her and take her into the schoolroom, and knew it was going to be all right.

Everyone, she soon discovered, did their lessons together, with the schoolmistress setting the bigger children more difficult tasks, and sometimes making them help the younger children. That first day Callum came over and sat beside her, looking at her smiling and occasionally squeezing her hand.

After school, Callum came with her up the hill to where the postman was waiting to take her home. He picked her up and swung her onto the cart, and then he climbed up beside her, and they went rattling round to the crofthouse together to give her nan a hand.

Emerald loved helping with the crofting tasks. Her nan said she didn't know how she had ever managed without her. There was the nanny-goat to be milked every day, the cow to be kept supplied with hay when she was in the byre through the winter, the sheep to be cared for through the spring lambing. In summer there was the line to be set for mackerel down by the point, and the seals to be shooed away before they dived down to help themselves to the catch. There were lobster-pots to be emptied, the geese and hens to be fed, and the hoodies to be chased from the henhouse. Every day was as busy as it could be.

There was not much housework as the house had only two rooms with an attic above where everything was stored. Downstairs the kitchen doubled up as the dwelling-room. On the other side of the little hall was the front parlour, which was never used except for funerals and weddings and the rare moments when someone important came to visit.

Behind the house was the but 'n' ben of a larder where food was kept and milk was churned for butter. Her nan had taught Emerald the proper songs for turning the handle to make the butter come quickly. And, almost too high for Emerald to see into, there was a big stone sink for which the water had to be fetched in a bucket from the well-spring.

Sometimes Emerald helped her nan collect the herbs she dried and used to cure anything from a baby's wind to worms under the sheep's tails. Every week Margaret went into Salen to see to the small problems the islanders brought to her before they had recourse to the doctor from the mainland. Raspberry leaves for an infusion to help mothers in labour, a tincture of thyme to cure the cough to which the islanders were prone, wormwood to stimulate a sluggish appetite.

Everyone helped the crofting families with the spring plantings and the autumn harvestings. When Callum was busy with his schoolwork, even Jack would come and lend a hand at the Mackenzie croft, now that Margaret had forgiven him his snooping.

Although the schoolmistress seemed to have forgotten her anger with him, Jack felt her change of mood had more to do with her pleasure in Callum than with anything to do with him. Callum even helped in the caravan with the filing of the island's news – which everyone knew was Jack's special responsibility.

So Jack had begun to keep his own record, scribbling his accounts of the island's happenings in a big line-ruled exercise-book.

Some day he knew his aunt would be proud of him.

But, above all, Emerald would be proud of him. She would look at him with bright shining eyes, just like she looked at Callum, and tell Jack how clever he was.

Emerald's admiration would be worth earning. Emerald's admiration would be the best. At that moment, Emerald's admiration was all Jack wanted.

17

The Bahamas: May 1945

'Darling Billy, we had such a divine gossip!'

The loud cackle of Wallis Windsor's laughter cut through the peace of the well-watered lawns which aproned Nassau's Government House, alerting the ex-king to his wife's imminent arrival.

'See you this evening.' The Duchess's voice floated over on the light breeze from the sea.

Wallis breakfasted early in the privacy of her own room, after which she usually joined her husband. The Duke took his stewed fruit and tea at the table set out in the shade of the overhanging jacaranda-tree.

Hearing her voice, the Duke bounced up to set a chair for his wife.

Wallis must be in a good humour this morning. He frowned at the thought of the probable cause: Sir William Beaumont. Edward Windsor did not approve of the raffish English baronet. He waited in some irritation for the roar of the departing motor-vehicle to be replaced by the familiar tap of his wife's high-heeled mules approaching across the wooden boards of the veranda.

Wallis knew her husband didn't like the Englishman, although he was happy to put up with her American friends. His reaction, she guessed, was probably to do with the way he felt that he – and, above all, she – had been treated by his own countrymen.

When the war was over, the Duke was convinced, everything would change. What he was really after was the post of roving ambassador to the United States. Wallis would enjoy that, and he could keep an eye on his investments in the New World. They were proving surprisingly profitable, and in his position, with the question of taxation unresolved and a wife to indulge, money was a major concern.

Meanwhile Wallis herself, restricted to the limited company Nassau offered, had plenty of time for the dapper little Englishman. She found in Billy Beaumont an amusing and well-informed companion, a delightful ally in the parochial island's life – always acknowledging, of course, that he was one of the more unreliable elements in the colony, and that his presence at Government House invariably led to some item in a gossip column.

Yet Wallis could do no wrong in the former king's eyes, even in her choice of friends. As soon as his wife came into view through the dappled shade, the Duke's face lit up with pleasure. He bounded forward to greet her.

'Darling!'

Wallis accepted the kiss on her cheek with a graceful inclination of her long neck. She took the chair her husband pulled out for her.

'You look wonderful this morning.'

Wallis gave her husband a small smile, secure in the knowledge that she did indeed, as always, look superb.

'It'll be even more wonderful to get back to Fifth Avenue. I feel so *dowdy*.' She paused and looked down at the soft sweep of her morning gown. 'Such a frump!'

'Nonsense, sweetheart.'

The Duke smiled reassuringly. But he knew how tough it had been right from the start. He would never forget that sweltering August day – was it two summers ago now? – when they arrived in the merchant ship from Bermuda to find that the whole of Nassau – black, white and chocolate – had hung out flags and flowers and turned out to greet their royal Governor and catch a glimpse of the American divorcee for whom he had surrendered his throne.

Wallis, of course, had managed to look cool and *soignée* – but, then, she always did.

She breakfasted on a single glass of freshly squeezed orange juice and a cup of sugarless coffee in her large light suite of rooms on the sea-side of the mansion. Even first thing in the morning, she was already perfectly coiffed, her make-up impeccable. She was not yet, however, in her street clothes. She was wearing one of her long loose morning robes: a plain round-necked column of gossamer-fine raspberry wool trimmed at the neck and wrists with cerise silk braid. She had a wardrobe of such gowns, a weapon in the armoury of sensual luxury which made her the undisputed queen, if not of England, at least of its ex-king.

The Duke briefly reflected that his wife had not been quite so attentive in that department of late – her explanations ranging from the heat to the exhaustion of her war-work in the services canteen.

The Duchess looked across the lawn towards the ocean, her face dreamy.

'Whatever comes next, darling, I can't wait to get out of this drab place.'

She stood up, the long folds of the bias-cut gown outlining the high small breasts.

'*So* much to do today.'

Back in her boudoir Wallis thought she would almost be sorry to leave this room. Two years had seen it transformed from an ugly uncomfortable hotel bedroom into an appropriate setting for the most famous seductress of her time.

The two maids bobbed to their feet as their employer appeared in the doorway.

'Thank you, girls. That'll be all.'

The Duchess walked over to the windows and drew the fine muslin curtains to admit as much as possible of the slanting rays of sunlight.

As always at this important weekly task, the Duchess dismissed her helpers in order to settle down alone with two of her Cairn terriers, Pookie and Prissie, to check the inventory of her jewellery in its soft rolls of dark-blue suede secured with fine leather straps and gold buckles.

Apart from the personal treasures which never left her vanity case, the rapidly accumulating Windsor trinkets accompanied the Duchess everywhere in a leather-covered jewel-case, itself the size of a small trunk. Some were royal heirlooms brought by the Duke into exile, others were grand pieces commissioned from fashionable jewellers.

The hand-tooled leather case was fitted with tailor-made drawers and boxes. As neat as a set of Russian dolls, the drawers accommodated the necklaces and earrings, brooches, bracelets, jewelled bags and boxes, and those assorted bibelots – jewelled combs and gold-mesh purses, diamond-monogrammed powder-compacts and cigarette-cases – that the jewellers of Paris call *les nécéssaires du soir*. There was a drawer, too, full of the love-trinkets – crosses for sorrow and hearts for joy – engraved with the messages which marked the stations of the grand romance which had ended in the loss of an empire.

Methodically she checked the inventory, satisfying herself that everything was there. The list included one small, highly personal piece: a locket which should, Wallis decided, be hidden from curious eyes.

Carefully she began to work her way tray-by-tray down the coffer until she found what she was looking for. The Fabergé boxes, packed two deep, filled the bottom layer. They were never disturbed. One of them would just accommodate the locket. She pulled up the portcullis, tucked the locket inside, shut the lid and laid the box back among its fellows.

Wallis paused for a moment, lost in thought, one hand absent-mindedly ruffling the ears of the small dog on her lap.

So brief a life, so tragically lost, commemorated in the red-brown curl which had fallen out of the envelope from Iona Fergusson which brought the news of the child's despatch. What if it had been different? What if the child had survived? What if . . . ?

Wallis shook her head firmly.

There was no room in her life for such imponderables. Wallis dealt in reality, not in the shadows of what might have been. Her task was to re-create a kingdom for the man who had counted a kingdom well lost for her love. Ghosts had no place in such a scheme.

She settled down to finish her work.

A cache of cloudy green gems in a velvet pouch reminded her that the Palace had managed to hold on to the rest of Queen Alexandra's dowry, the emeralds which had been bequeathed by his grandmother to the handsome young Prince of Wales – an inducement to choose a wife.

For a moment the Duchess's brow furrowed in anger. The Palace had treated David shamefully. Everyone said so. It was the breakdown of his relationship with his mother which had hurt him more than anything. Wallis had even written to Queen Mary herself, and received a civil enough reply, but there was still no indication that she might ever be prepared to agree to her eldest son's dearest wish and receive his bride.

Perhaps it would be better when the war was over. God knows what her mother-in-law would have done if she had got news of the child. For that reason alone, the trinket must never see the light of day.

The whole episode was closed. Dead. Buried. She could scarcely be held responsible for the little girl's tragic end, but she shuddered to think what might be thought of her if the news got out.

How the waspish little Billy would enjoy a story like that! Wallis was in no doubt that he gossiped *about* her as liberally as he gossiped *to* her.

The two Cairn terriers yapped. They had burrowed their way into the pillows on the bed.

The sun was streaming through the windows. It was time for the dogs to be taken for their morning walk.

The Duchess pinned on a wide-brimmed sun-hat, powdered her nose and filled in the contours of her mouth with a dark plum-red lipstick. For a moment she studied the effect. Yes, Elizabeth Arden's new colours suited her magnolia-pale skin. It had taken every string she could pull to get the new collection shipped in from Miami, but it had been worth it. Really, wartime was such a bore.

'Come along, Pookie. You, too, Prissie.'

She opened the french windows and paused for a moment as the waves of midday heat rolled towards her.

'Walkies, babies.'

The dogs trotted obediently behind their mistress into the mani-cured greenery of the Bahamas garden. Wallis watched their antics with pleasure and a sense of relief as her mind wandered back to an earlier moment of less well-controlled dalliance. A moment which had so nearly landed her with a serious and permanent little problem, the problem recorded in the inscription on the ring.

It was all very sad; but perhaps, in the end, all was for the best.

'Mummy loves you,' the Duchess told her four-footed companions. Dogs were so much more convenient than children.

18

London: July 1945

Two months after the Duke and his Duchess were packing up ready to leave their wartime exile in the Bahamas, Major Anthony Anstruther returned to London from Istanbul.

Anstruther's exile had been spent in rather less pampered comfort than his royal ex-employer's. The bespectacled former courtier had had what was described as 'a good war', with his DSO hard-earned as SOE's executive officer in the Balkans.

The day Lieutenant Anstruther, as he then was, arranged for Iona Fergusson's two children to leave Britain in the SS *Politician,* he received his own orders to go abroad on active service. The German panzer divisions had gone through the Balkans in early 1940 like a knife through butter, leaving SOE with virtually no-one on the ground and no control nearer than Cairo. All available Allied officers, many of them, like the short-sighted Anstruther, who'd originally been given office jobs because of some physical disability, were immediately assigned field postings.

Anstruther's briefing officer was an elderly diplomat who had just returned from a double tour of duty in Istanbul, where the Turkish government had declined the invitation to join the Axis.

His posting was Bulgaria. The former ambassador to the court of King Boris was driven up in an official car on the last day of Anstruther's perfunctory training.

'Wish I was going myself, young man. Subversive lot, the Bulgars. Had to be, really. Five hundred years under the Turks have left them with a taste for murder and mayhem. The king's a shit, of course. Dyed-in-the-wool Blackshirt. Thinks the sun shines out of Hitler's arse.'

By the time Anstruther found himself on his way through the Dardanelles, Hitler's forces were pushing on into Russia.

The Bulgarians were well used to occupation. There was little a young English officer who had never seen active service could teach them about subversion; all they lacked was back-up. Anstruther returned to Istanbul and set up shop in the Grand Souk as an arms dealer.

The word quickly went out that the new dealer who occupied the small room above the spice merchant's stall was prepared to pay good money for ammunition, guns, muskets, explosives, bombs – anything and everything which might fall off the back of a lorry, whether Axis or Allied.

As part and parcel of his arms business, Anstruther also found himself dealing in caviare, Istanbul's traditional trade with Russia having been obstructed by Hitler's advance. Much of the caviare was routed through British ports, where some of it found its way to London.

When in the early summer of 1945 he returned from his active posting to his desk at the War Office, Anstruther wryly reflected that the DSO he'd been awarded might owe more to his contribution to the well-being of the politicians and senior officers who dined at Claridge's than to his skill as an undercover agent.

With the Third Reich on the brink of surrender and Hitler dead by his own hand in a bleak Berlin bunker, all wartime personnel were ordered to return to civilian life as soon as possible. The only exceptions were the officers of the secret service.

Anstruther still had various ends to tidy up before he could consider his own future. One of these was his association with the ex-monarch.

His absence from Britain throughout the war meant that, although he was still on record as unofficial liaison between the undercover services and the Governor of the Bahamas, he knew nothing of the fate of Iona Fergusson or of the disaster which had befallen the SS *Politician*.

The Foreign Office team which had gone into Berlin after the Allies took over the city was already methodically working its way through the German foreign-policy documents in the Nazi archives, assessing what it found, and assigning them to those best able to deal with them.

The documents relating to the Duke of Windsor were marked for the attention of Major Anstruther.

The first document, B15/B002635-38, together with later addenda relating to the Windsors' sojourn in the Bahamas, arrived on Anstruther's desk within a week of his return to London. The document itself made startling enough reading, revealing as it did the extent to which Ribbentrop thought the Duke of Windsor's German sympathies made him a willing quisling, ready to take over as nominal head of a government of Britain after the capitulation which Hitler believed both inevitable and at the time imminent. In diplomatic language, it was a little embarrassing.

There was worse to come. Addendum 38M recorded Iona Fergusson's interrogation by the Gestapo in Lyons in the three days following her capture on 5 February 1941. The words were as chilling in translation as they must have been in the German of the senior Gestapo officer who had dictated them to his clerk under 'Utmost Importance Secrecy' – the classification created by Hitler himself.

The designation covered the most sensitive of all information about the President of the United States, Winston Churchill as Prime Minister of Great Britain, and 'close and intimate members of the British royal family' – members whose support for the Third Reich might help make the declared thousand-year domination of the world a reality.

After the loss of so many of his contemporaries, Anstruther thought nothing more could touch him.

Iona Stuart Fergusson was dead. She had died, brutally and unnecessarily, as a direct result of the irresponsibility of the spoilt royal couple who had passed the war years in the luxury of an island paradise.

Anstruther suddenly and bitterly regretted the whole business.

He read through the entire transcript word by word, as if, by sparing himself none of the horrific details of the young woman's agony, he might somehow be able to make it all worth while.

When he came to the end, he shuffled the documents neatly together and locked them in the safe. Then he walked across the park to his club in St James's. There, uncharacteristically and for the first time since his university days, Anstruther got very drunk indeed.

The following day, battling a roaring hangover, he called in at Admiralty House and asked for the papers relating to the SS *Politician*. Wartime left so many loose ends. On a bleak February day in 1941 two of those loose ends had taken passage in a ship in Liverpool bound for a little island in the Further Isles.

It seemed a thousand lifetimes ago.

The wartime regulations still in force in the summer of 1945 prohibited the release of details of shipping lost at sea.

It needed a call to the Home Office to verify Anstruther's special credentials before the Admiralty clerk could hand him the file recording the wreck of the SS *Politician* off the island of Eriskay. As he opened the file, Anstruther winced. The ship had sunk on the very day Iona Fergusson had been parachuted into southern France.

Stapled to the report was a note saying that the Governor of the Bahamas had been notified of the loss of the cargo on its way to him at Government House in Nassau.

Apart from that, the tattered pages recorded little more than that the ship had been lost with all hands. There was no specific reference to the fate of the passengers Anstruther was interested in. That wasn't surprising. Their embarkation had deliberately been kept on a need-to-know basis, and their names didn't even appear on the passenger-list.

Anstruther was a thorough and methodical man. He had to make sure neither of the two children had survived the wreck. That there was no trace in the records was not absolutely conclusive. Anything could happen in wartime. The Home Office was having a devil of a time coping with lost and abandoned orphans, evacuees who had somehow vanished in transit, unmarried mothers trying to trace fathers – it would take years to unravel the mess.

With hostilities over, he intended to slip quietly back into the practice of law. A well-respected chambers, keen to recruit a young man with his brain and his connections, had offered him an excellent opening. Anstruther had accepted. It was time to let others breathe the stultifying air of the Court.

So he had thought, until this.

The trouble was that Anstruther was a prisoner of his past.

Family tradition dictated that the Anstruther men put country before self, king before family. The family motto, *Ad astra semper fidelis*, 'Faithful always to the stars', underlined family tradition: to serve the luminaries of the royal house of Windsor.

The house of Windsor and one other – the bewitching, entrancing star of Iona Stuart Fergusson. The woman the feckless Prince of Wales, in Anstruther's opinion, should have made his bride.

She was also the woman Anstruther had sent to her death. Her last resting-place, in some Gestapo-dug trench outside Lyons, would remain unknown. But there would be no peace or forgiveness for him, he knew, until he'd made sure where her 'bairns', as Iona called them, were laid to rest.

Anstruther had made a promise. A promise he was duty-bound to honour.

'Excuse me, sir.'

Lost in his thoughts, Anstruther had not even heard the clerk approach.

'I thought' – the clerk hesitated – 'that this might be relevant, sir.'

Anstruther glanced up. 'What is it?'

'An enquiry. We received it after the ship had gone down. It should have been followed up. But you know how it is in wartime, sir. Things get pushed to one side. They get there in the end – but it takes a while.'

Anstruther stared down at the oblong of card the clerk handed him. The date was a week after the wreck of the SS *Politician*. The enquiry had been routed from the Glasgow record office and marked 'Nothing known – please hold'. The letters 'LP' indicated that the problem was reckoned low priority. There were plenty of lost orphans about, and plenty of such problems to be solved. Time enough when the war was over.

The enquiry had originally been raised by an unidentified inhabitant of the island of Eas Forse. The subject of the enquiry was the identity of two young survivors from the wreck of the *Politician*. The enquiry had not been pursued and the matter had been shelved.

A week later, just long enough to give himself time to clear his desk of the most urgent business, Anstruther booked a sleeper on the overnight *Flying Scotsman,* bound for Crianlarich on the way to the Western Isles.

The following evening he found himself sharing a cabin in the SS *Lord of the Isles,* the small battered ferry, successor to the coal-powered puffers, which made the two-day round of the little islands in the outer ring of the Hebrides.

Eas Forse was the last stop down the line.

19

Eas Forse: July 1945

The air was sweet and pure at midsummer in the Further Isles, and twilight reached round until morning.

'We'll be late for tea, Cal!'

Emerald's voice echoed down the ravine.

'OK, rascal!' Callum's laughter bounced back.

In spite of being four years older, Callum was slower than her at rock-climbing. Callum said it was because Emerald knew all the short cuts from going out on gatherings with her nan.

The island was enjoying its summertime. The war was over at last. All was well with the world. The soldiers were back in civilian clothes, and there were once again young men to harvest the land.

The wartime evacuees had nearly all been returned to the cities of the south. The process was taking a little time, since more than a few of the home addresses no longer existed.

There were those who had nowhere to go home to. Among these were Callum and Emerald – and neither of the two foster-mothers had any intention of triggering official enquiries.

Callum knew that his parents were missing. He had been bewildered at first, bewildered and miserable. Missing in action, in the performance of duties to King and country, had been all that the schoolmistress had been able to discover – and that was only because the notification had come to the island since the old laird had been his mother's next of kin.

After the war, the schoolmistress had told him, it would be easier to find out what had happened. But Callum must not set his hopes too high. No-one did in wartime.

After she had told him that, all Callum had left was Emerald.

Now, in the sunshine with the buzzards wheeling overhead, he began the long scramble up the rocky chimney to join the little figure high above.

Emerald, eight years old, wiry and brown as a hazelnut, lay flat on her back, stretched out in the heather, feeling the warmth of the sun on her face. The sky had been a clear azure a moment ago. As was the way in the isles, a flock of little white clouds had danced out of the west like spring lambs, casting small dark shadows on the green turf. She could shut her eyes and feel their passage overhead.

After a moment, Emerald wriggled over to the mossy pool and balanced on her haunches under the raggedy pine.

She dipped her cupped hand into the well-spring with its eddies of peat-brown water. She drank. The water tasted clean and fresh and icy-cold. It had taken her a long time to be able to look into the pool of water, a long time to forget the monster which had pulled her down into the water cave beneath the waves.

Today all was sunshine. Sunshine and peace.

Emerald could hear Callum scrambling up the brae. She wriggled to the edge of the steep ravine for a glimpse of the straw-mop bobbing in the distance below.

'Cowardy custard!' she called.

Emerald rolled over and gazed down into the clear water of the burn. She loved to watch the little speckled trout flickering among the stones. She loved to watch the blue kingfisher dive for minnows, arrowing down like a shooting star into the dark water, to reappear in a flash of silver droplets with a wriggling body in its gunmetal-blue beak.

Today the trout were all dozing in the shade, and the kingfisher must have gone home for his tea.

'It's not fair!' Callum grumbled as he arrived panting at her side. 'You should be more ladylike, Emmy. Doesn't your nan tell you that?'

'I'm not ladylike yet. But I soon will be. Girls always grow up faster than boys. I know. My nan told me so,' Emerald replied confidently.

Then she relented. 'Never mind. Nan says I'll slow down when I get to puberty.'

'What do you know about puberty, Em? You're much too little.' Callum raised his eyebrows crossly at Emerald.

Emerald liked it when he raised his eyebrows. Beneath them Callum's eyes were as bright as a wild cat's.

'Puberty,' she repeated, just to make Callum raise his eyebrows again. Then she giggled and said, 'Well, I know girls get it, and boys get it, too. Nan told me. It happens at around your age, Cal, so I expect you'll know about it soon. It has something to do with the tupping in the autumn. You know, when the rams go with the ewes and the lambs being born in the spring.'

Her voice trailed away. Her nan always told her things in a roundabout way. Callum liked things just so.

Callum sniffed and got to his feet. Puberty was not at all suitable for little girls, particularly not for Emerald. He walked on to show he was annoyed.

Emerald watched him. Whatever Callum thought was right, she *did* know about puberty – and a lot more than she was telling him.

Jack Sweeney had puberty. Jack's puberty was horrible. Emerald discovered about Jack's puberty on a day last autumn, when the rams had been put to the ewes and the berries were ripe. It had happened when Miss Sweeney took her whole class out on the hill to gather moorland fruit – strawberries and blaeberries and cranberries – to make jellies for the school's bring-and-buy.

Callum had not gone with them that day – perhaps he had been busy doing something for the schoolmistress in her archives.

Up on the moor, where the peat moss outlined the limit of the bog, Jack found a patch of yellow berries. Anyway, Jack was still being nice to Emerald then, and he took her away from the rest of the children to show her what he had found.

The berries were quite different from the others they'd been collecting. They looked like big fat yellow raspberries, but they grew one by one on little short stalks quite low to the ground.

Emerald examined the juicy little offering.

'What are they, Jack?'

'They're cloudberries. Here. Try it.'

'Are you sure it's not dhu?' Emerald shook her head doubtfully, using the Gaelic word for bad.

'Of course I'm sure, stupid.' Almost violently he pushed the cloudberry between her lips. 'Go on. Eat it.'

Surprised and a little frightened by the sudden violence of the gesture, Emerald spat the berry out.

'Don't like it!'

She turned and ran off, meaning to join the others. She could just hear their voices over the lip of the hill.

But Jack leaped after her. He caught her, pulled her down on to the sphagnum moss, and pinned her tight on her back. His body was all hard and bony against her. It was like when the rams chased the ewes and jumped on them.

She turned her head away and shut her eyes because she could just see his face above her. His chin was bristling with the beginnings of a beard, and for some reason his skin had flushed a strange hot scarlet. Suddenly he bore down and kissed her on the mouth, forcing his tongue roughly between her teeth as if it was the berry he had tried to make her swallow.

Emerald knew about kissing. She kissed Callum when he was nice to her. She kissed her nan goodnight every night. Nan's cheek was dry and soft and her lips fresh, but Jack's kiss felt scratchy and wet. It was slobbery and full of spit. Emerald hated it.

She fought Jack off, screaming and clawing with her fingernails. Afterwards she scrambled to her feet and ran all the way across the heather and didn't stop until she was safely back with the rest of the children.

Jack didn't come back to join them.

The next day he came to school with a face like thunder and a long raw scratch down his cheek.

Although she never told anyone what had happened, Jack was certain she had told on him, and the trouble – the taunting and name-calling – had started then.

But today Jack was far away, and Emerald was perfectly happy.

She bounded up again.

'Race you, Cal!'

The two children plunged away across the heather, not stopping until they reached the cliff-top and saw Margaret Mackenzie's little croft on the island-promontory below.

The scent of baking curled up to meet them.

However much Catriona Sweeney might disapprove of Margaret Mackenzie's stories, even the schoolmistress didn't dispute what everyone else on Eas Forse knew was true – that Emerald's nan set the best tea on the island.

The water sparkled in the sunshine. The tide was coming in.

Still a full night's journey away, bumping over the waves in the little ferry towards the string of silvery islands, Anthony Anstruther was brooding on what lay in store for him at the end of his journey.

There was nothing on the island which could harm Emerald.

Nothing except the arrival of Anthony Anstruther. If it hadn't been for him, Emerald might almost have been an ordinary child. Almost – but not quite.

There was something about Emerald which made her not at all ordinary – something at which Margaret Mackenzie could only guess. Meanwhile she had had the usual forewarnings and began to make her preparations, as she knew she must.

All Margaret meant to do was to keep her changeling safe, whatever the cost. And she knew that the cost would be high.

20

Eas Forse: August 1945

The word that the ferry was about to dock spread as fast as the seed from the buttercups which glowed in the summer meadows. On the harbour wall, those who had business with the mainland mixed with the small group of idlers who had gathered on the quay to lend a hand to the ferrymen.

Anthony Anstruther watched the gathering through half-closed lids.

He was well aware of the interest the islanders were likely to take in a visitor who appeared to have an official brief. And well aware that a closed community had an interest in keeping its business to itself – particularly when valuable salvage, such as the whisky, was concerned.

The previous evening, while watching the sun dip down to the horizon, he had shared a bottle of Islay Mist with his companion in the cabin, a travelling telephone engineer come to install a new exchange in the little post office. The engineer was a man whose business took him at one time or another into every home on the island.

The morning's hangover had been worth the investment. By the time he was ready to disembark, his briefcase and overnight bag over his shoulder, Anstruther had learned more about the lives of the islanders, including the goings-on at the Beltane fires, than the history books had to say about the massacre at Glencoe.

'A dram?' Anstruther proffered the bottle again.

'I wouldna turn ye down.'

The engineer held out his tumbler for his third refill, and settled back against the slatted wooden bench.

He took another sip of the whisky and considered the matter again.

'If', said Anstruther carefully, 'you were looking to trace a friend – someone who had gone missing in the war maybe, but who might perhaps have lost his memory – what would be the best way to go about it?'

'Well, now.' The engineer gratefully held out his glass again. 'If that was what I was about, I would pay a cordial visit to Miss Catriona Sweeney, the schoolmistress. Making sure, that is, that my visit coincided with some favour I might be able to do her. I know, for instance, that she has been wanting an extension line to the schoolroom, to save her legs when the telephone rings in the front room. Now, that is a favour I could be offering if it were me looking for a friend.'

He smiled.

'Now, if ye could see your way, say, with a telephone call to the Department of Education in Edinburgh, to obtain the authorization for a line, mebbe Miss Sweeney would be glad enough to open her boxes for ye.'

And that was how Anthony Anstruther came to spend half an hour the next morning, with a splitting headache – the second he had acquired in the discharge of his self-imposed obligations – on the ship's radio making contact with a distant office on the mainland. The office in its turn made contact with a not-quite-so-distant office in Edinburgh. By that afternoon, just at the moment when Anstruther followed the engineer down the gangplank and up the single metalled road, the postmaster received the authorization for the new line. There were instructions the authorization was to be handed to one Mr Anthony Anstruther – Anstruther had immediately abandoned his wartime rank – who would shortly be arriving on the ferry and booking into the Salen Arms, the island's only hostelry.

The landlady of the Salen Arms, her curiosity aroused by a stranger heralded by a telegraph, showed her guest up to the best bedroom herself, even carrying his shoulder-bag up the stairs and opening the windows to air the room.

Later, in the visitors' lounge, in answer to the visitor's query, she nodded.

'Ye'll find Miss Sweeney at the end of the street up the cliff. The bungalow's opposite the schoolhouse – ye canna miss it. But ye may catch her at work in the yellow caravan down the brae on the other side. School's all on holiday, as ye'll be well aware, no doubt. She takes a wee bit of rest of an afternoon. None of us are as young as we were.'

Then, unable to resist her own curiosity, she added: 'Is it the parish records ye'll be after? Or mebbe the school inspection?'

Anthony Anstruther shook his head and smiled back.

'Nothing so grand, I'm afraid. Just a personal matter – some family papers I'm anxious to trace.'

'Family papers?' The landlady raised her eyebrows. 'Then it'll be certainly Miss Sweeney ye're needing. She has more bits of paper in that caravan than a magpie's mate.'

'And with that', the landlady told her husband, Lachie, later that evening when they had their feet up on the fender in the landlord's parlour at the back of the pub, 'he was off up the street like a fox with a nostril full of rabbit.'

Meanwhile one of the junior pupils anxious for good marks from one of the main powers on the island had already alerted the schoolmistress.

Catriona's heart missed a beat when the youngster told her of the stranger's intention.

Her first reaction was to protect her own. 'Callum! Will ye come here right away?'

Callum, compensating for his day on the hill with Emerald, was finishing up his history homework at the kitchen table. He came through as soon as he heard the schoolmistress's voice. Next year was the first year of school certificate, and he aimed to do as well as he could. Catriona had promised him a camera if he did well. Above all things, Callum wanted that camera.

'Here I am, Nan.'

Catriona studied the boy's face. It had become as familiar to her as her own. My, but he was growing into a handsome young man. A bit skinny still, mind you, not filled out like the islanders would be at his age, but with the limbs well formed and growing in strength daily. But, above all, it was the straight intelligent gaze and tawny eyes which marked him out for who he was, the young gentleman Catriona knew him to be. Peasant or lordling, you couldn't beat the breeding.

All Catriona's archiving had taught her that inheritance mattered. Not the inheritance of material goods, but the kind of inheritance which made one line good and the other bad. Like the Sweeneys and the Mackenzies. Breeding was the most important thing you could have. And Callum Fergusson had the breeding. The blood of the Stuart kings ran in his veins.

In the past four years, since Callum had been washed up in the cave, she had told the boy only as much as she felt was constructive and useful to him. Of his past, Callum knew what he remembered of his life in his mother's house with his foster-sister. And he knew, too, that

133

he was the grandson of the old laird. And that the war had orphaned him.

To Catriona, the stranger's enquiries could only mean trouble for her – and for the boy she loved, in her own way, as dearly as if he had been her own. Callum must be kept out of harm's way until she could establish the nature of that trouble.

'I have an errand for ye to run, young man. Ye'll put aside your schoolbooks for the day. There's an important document to be taken to my brother's wife over by the Giant's Footsteps. Ye ken the Mackay farm? Good.'

As she spoke, Catriona had been putting papers in a brown envelope. She tied the packet with string and sealed the knot with a blob of scarlet wax, as she always did with private papers which were for no eyes but those of sender and receiver. Catriona Sweeney was always scrupulous in such matters.

'There you are. And tell my sister-in-law I've said to be kind enough to let you stay overnight. It's a long walk and ye'd no be away again before sundown. She has her niece, young Alison Mackay from Perth, staying down the road in the cottage. She's a well-spoken young woman. The two of you can get acquainted.' Catriona glanced across at Callum sharply. 'Someone of your *own* age to keep you occupied.'

'Right.'

Callum grinned at her. He knew the schoolmistress was referring to the amount of time he spent with Emerald. It was not a subject either of them discussed, but it was there right enough and – Callum sensed – a barrier between them. Catriona had her reasons, and Callum knew them well enough by now to know that she had to bite her tongue every time he went round the island to be with Emerald.

'Take a clean singlet for your back and a piece for the road and be off with ye now.'

Callum readily obeyed. It would be good to spend a night away on the far side of the island. And on his way back tomorrow morning he would pass by and collect Emerald.

They might even manage a bit of fishing from the shore. There had been a shoal of mackerel spotted round that side of the island, and once you found one of those there would be mackerel for tea for the whole population of Eas Forse.

He swung quickly down the village street. The ferry was just discharging its passengers. He did not join the throng, as he would usually have done. Today he had an errand.

*   *   *

134

By the time she heard the gravel crunch under the polished leather shoes of her visitor, Catriona Sweeney was as ready to receive him as she would ever be.

She came to the door to answer the knock, and listened attentively to what the man had to say in greeting.

'Indeed, Mr Anstruther? And what would be your interest in the archives of Eas Forse?'

The schoolmistress peered sharply at him through her bifocals.

'If it is to be official business, I shall need confirmation. If it is pleasure you are on, come back on Saturday, when my school work is done and I can give you my full attention.'

Anstruther smiled and held out the envelope.

'I thought this might be of use, Miss Sweeney. I happen to have a friend in the education department in Edinburgh, and the post office engineer was my companion on the ferry. He says he'll be along later to put up the line.'

Catriona accepted the paper and glanced at it quickly.

Anstruther watched the schoolmistress anxiously. He was relieved to see her face had relaxed into a thin-lipped smile.

'Well, Mr Anstruther' – she stood back from the caravan's door – 'as the bearer of such good news it would be churlish not to extend a welcome. Please come in. I only hope I can render service.'

'Thank you, Miss Sweeney.'

'Sit down, Mr Anstruther. What is it exactly you're after?'

'An enquiry. Something which may have come within your jurisdiction.'

Rapidly and cautiously Anstruther explained his business, leaving out anything which might lead anyone to suppose that the younger of the two children he sought was other than an unidentified orphan.

'So you see, Miss Sweeney, since I happened to be passing' – Anstruther knew it sounded a little limp – no-one just happened to be passing by Eas Forse – 'I had to make sure. Pay my respects, you understand.'

The schoolmistress had been watching Anstruther shrewdly. She was enough of a student of human nature to know that her visitor was not telling the whole truth. The man's voice was pitched unnaturally high, the fingers twisted a little too nervously.

'I think you know more than you say, Mr Anstruther. I think you have more than a casual interest in these children.'

'I do assure you, Miss Sweeney' – Anstruther's voice was less sure – 'this is no trivial enquiry. I *must* know the truth.'

'Which of the children would interest you most, Mr Anstruther?'

Anstruther's mind whirled.

'I will be honest with you, Miss Sweeney. The girl.'

'Not the boy?'

Anstruther hesitated. He had to keep faith, fulfil his duty, whatever the difficulties.

He said slowly: 'I would need to know the boy was well cared for. Safe. But it is the little girl I'm searching for.'

Catriona was beginning to feel more confident now. If she played her cards with care, the man might even prove an ally. She knew the boy's parents were dead and gone. After the death of the old laird there were no family ties. Nothing closer than a second cousin in Canada. She should know that well enough. The laird's lineage was at her fingertips, every twig on the family tree recorded in her own archives. It was just possible that, if she delivered the girl, the boy might remain in her care.

'And if I told you where you might find the girl?'

'Then, Miss Sweeney, I would be content.'

Catriona hesitated for a moment longer. Then she made up her mind.

'Mr Anstruther, ye can set your mind at rest. I think we can do business.'

Catriona drove a hard bargain. Anthony Anstruther, used to resisting the blandishments of the rug merchants of Istanbul, was astonished to find himself agreeing to every single one of her terms.

Some would cause him rather more work than others. A stipend to cover the boy's necessities, to be paid out of the inheritance, with Anstruther, if necessary, to pursue Callum's rights through the courts. The registration of Callum's right to his grandfather's estate as well as that of his parents. Everything to be held in trust, with Anstruther the trustee, until he came into his majority at twenty-one.

'And I'll be hoping that you yourself will be keeping an eye on the boy when it comes to him going to the big city, Mr Anstruther.'

'Indeed, Miss Sweeney.'

Anstruther's voice was calm, but his mind was in turmoil. What had he let himself in for with the boy? Above all, how in the name of all that was holy was he to cope with the little royal bastard?

One thing he knew, and knew for certain, and that was that there was little or no chance that the Windsors would care to take on a responsibility they believed themselves well rid of.

He remembered the brief conversation he had with His Royal Highness on the transatlantic telephone to New York. He had needed to know what the Duke would feel if the child had somehow, unlikely as it was, managed to survive the wreck. The answer was not encouraging.

'What d'you say? Survived? Well, what do you expect me to do, Anthony? I'm *unemployed*, man. Waiting on my brother's pleasure, don't you know? Sort it out. Good. Let me know how it goes, eh? Discreetly. Don't let the Duchess know. Delicate and all that. D'you hear?'

Anstruther heard.

He wrenched his mind back to the present.

Catriona Sweeney had risen to her feet and was holding the door open.

'Then, that's settled, Mr Anstruther. I'll have Archie the postman call for you in the morning, ten o'clock sharp at the publican's. The Mackenzie crofthouse is a wee bit round the island. A city gentleman like you will not want to be making the journey on foot.'

Anstruther held out his hand. Catriona noticed that, though the handshake was firm, the palm was damp.

'Thank you, Miss Sweeney. I will be in touch as soon as possible.'

'Indeed. Oh, Mr Anstruther . . . ?' The schoolmistress's voice was suddenly lighter. 'One other thing.' She hesitated for a moment, then made up her mind. 'Callum is an ambitious lad. I don't entirely approve, but he has the intention of becoming a photographer. Do you think you might – say, in a year or so – provide him with a secondhand camera? To come out of the stipend, of course.'

Anstruther smiled. 'I think that's one thing I *can* manage.'

His brow furrowed in thought, he walked back down the hill. The gulls screamed overhead, but in his mind he was far away on a chill spring morning in London before Hitler's war had begun. He was staring down at the tiny face framed in starched organdy and lace, who had received her baptismal blessing among strangers. How long ago was it now? All of eight years.

Emerald Mary Fitzwallace would now be eight years old. No longer a scrap of history lost on some stony shore, but flesh, blood and bones.

God help her, the bastard daughter of Edward VIII and Mrs Simpson was once more a flesh-and-blood reality.

21

Eas Forse: August 1945

'Hello, mister.'

At the sound of the child's voice, Anstruther felt the hairs rise on the back of his neck. For an instant he was paralysed. He had been prepared for everything but flesh and blood.

'Did I scare ye?' The child's voice was anxious. Surprisingly, it had a soft Hebridean burr.

After visiting Catriona Sweeney he'd gone back to the hotel and passed a troubled night. The wind had risen, howling off the ocean and bringing him nightmares.

As dawn came he slept briefly. Then, rattling and bumping round the coastal road in the mail-cart, he felt almost light-headed in the sunlight of the summer morning. His driver was a dour, taciturn man and Anstruther had been glad of the silence. It gave him a chance to gather his thoughts.

Callum would be better off on the island. There was no doubt that Iona had loved the land of her birth, and the schoolmistress had proposed a satisfactory solution.

No, it was the little girl who was the problem. She was a walking time-bomb – even now. With the Empire restless and the country struggling out of the anguish of war, there was a new republicanism on the rise. The world had changed, and the usefulness of monarchy was once again being called into question. The country was preparing to elect a Labour government, and there were those just waiting to find an excuse to dismantle a thousand years of privilege. A fresh scandal involving the King's own brother must be avoided at all costs.

The child could not remain on Eas Forse. It was too dangerous. The greatest threat was the link which might be made with Callum himself – and, through him, to the truth of her parenthood. Emerald must be spirited away immediately. The child had to grow up somewhere so remote there was no chance of any story about her existence or hint of her true identity coming out.

The most distant and isolated sanctuary Anstruther could think of was his mother's house in the forests of Mexico.

His mother Molly had been an Edwardian beauty – clever and bookish but, in the way of the time, completely uneducated. Anstruther senior was twenty years older than Molly, chilly and reserved by nature, and, worst of all, a royal courtier. His young wife had thought that marriage would give her freedom and independence and the chance to follow her own inclinations. Instead she found married life a dull and cumbersome thing, quickly tiring of chilly grace-and-favour accommodation and the philistine life of the Court. Soon after the birth of her son, she fled to the steamy jungles of Mexico with a poet who had offered love in a warm climate.

Molly had shed the trappings of her old life much as, when undressing after an evening's dancing, she dropped her clothes on the floor for her maid to retrieve. There was nothing unkind about it.

Her son Anthony had been her parting gift to her husband, a consolation prize. Inevitably young Anthony's childhood had been a solitary loveless business, lacking in both spiritual and physical warmth. Holidays had been spent following his father around the various draughty royal palaces, playing second fiddle to whatever young and bossy royals happened to be resident at the time.

When the poet had departed, Molly had taken against romance – in or out of wedlock. She had remained in Mexico ever since, returning briefly each Christmas, matronly and middle-aged, to spend a couple of weeks with her husband and son. After the death of his father, his mother's visits had ceased. From her infrequent communications, Anthony gathered that she was bored and lonely. She had even expressed regret that she had not been more responsible with her son.

He had never asked his mother for anything. Now he was about to. He was going to ask her to house an orphaned child and her nurse. He knew that his mother, provided she did not have to nanny the child, would find the idea intriguing. She'd almost certainly believe the child was his. And, if it served the child's cause, he wouldn't disabuse her.

None of this careful planning had prepared him for a face-to-face confrontation with the child herself.

Emerald had been helping her nan with her herbal potions, and had seen the stranger's arrival from the window. So she ran down to greet him, as she always did the rare strangers who made their way to Margaret Mackenzie's croft.

'I'm Emerald.' The voice was firm and confident. 'Who might ye be?' Now she looked at the visitor, her head on one side. It seemed like the cat had got his tongue, but Emerald was much too polite to say so.

Instead she said: 'I'm sorry. Did I frighten ye?'

Anstruther braced himself, and turned.

Not a ghost. Not a remote anonymous babe-in-arms who'd drowned at sea, but a living, breathing reality. A small heart-shaped face, nut-brown and freckled from the sun.

But the eyes were what held his attention most vividly. No longer the midnight dark they'd been when she was an infant, they were now a clear violet. The violet of amethysts, of the tiny wild pansy called heart's ease. Utterly unmistakably, they were her mother's eyes – the eyes which had captivated a king.

When at last he found his voice it sounded forced and unnatural.

'You rather gave me a surprise.'

Emerald nodded. 'Ye must have been thinking so hard about tying your shoelaces that ye didna see me coming.'

Anstruther stared at her, his brain churning.

She smiled – a glorious flash of sunshine. 'Come along. The kettle's on the hob.'

The child picked up the stranger's hand, turned and tugged him gently behind her. The visitor still looked a bit scared. She thought she should make him feel at home.

'You can call me Emmie if you like. Everyone does.'

'Emmie,' Anstruther repeated obediently, and followed the brown legs trotting up the slope which led to the crofthouse.

'We'd better be quick. Nan's brewing up.'

'Brewing up?'

'Making potions and things. It's fun. My nan's a white witch, but 'tis better not to tell anyone.' The child screwed up her face in thought. 'Miss Sweeney the schoolmistress says it's all stuff and nonsense. Except it isn't of course.'

'Of course,' Anstruther echoed, obediently.

140

The little patch of garden round the crofthouse was bordered by a thick hedge of blazing crimson and purple fuchsias. There was a yard at the back which seemed to be full of feathered and furry creatures, including a pair of fearsome-looking geese. The geese advanced, curious, hissing.

'Hush, then!'

The birds fell silent as a cheerful voice rang out. Margaret Mackenzie had come to the door in her apron. The woman's cheeks were pink with steam, and Anstruther could smell the scents of thyme and rosemary billowing out from the kitchen.

He held out his hand. 'Miss Mackenzie?'

'Ay. That's me.'

'My name's Anstruther, Anthony Anstruther.'

Margaret Mackenzie wiped her hands on her apron and took the pale hand with its manicured nails in her broad working-woman's fist. She could sense the fear in the stranger. She stood aside and gestured to the door.

'Come in. Take the weight off your feet.'

Anstruther took a deep breath. He followed her into the cosy kitchen lit by the soft glow of the peat-fuelled open range. The scent of herbs was almost overwhelming now.

As Margaret Mackenzie filled a kettle from a bucket in the corner, a pair of hens scuttled from under the kitchen table and out into the yard.

'Set ye down, Mr Anstruther.'

As Anstruther's eyes grew accustomed to the darkness inside, he saw there was another figure, a tousle-haired boy, sitting at the table, his face glowing in the warmth of the stove.

Emerald darted round and clambered up beside the boy. She placed her arm round his neck, and leaned her gleaming cap of dark russet curls against his shoulder. Absent-mindedly the boy ruffled the child's hair.

'Callum!' Margaret scolded. 'Where are your manners, lad? Stand up and say good morning to the gentleman.'

The boy blushed, stood up, and held out his hand awkwardly.

Anstruther felt the sweat break out on his forehead. Christ Almighty. He'd tried to prepare himself to meet the ex-king's daughter, but not Iona Fergusson's son at almost the same instant. Momentarily the shock left him speechless.

'Callum Fergusson. Pleased to meet you, sir.'

Anstruther managed to recover himself. He blinked and took Callum's hand. The boy's handshake was firm and strong, and his gaze level and direct. Iona Fergusson's child – twelve years old as he must be now –

had grown up straight-backed, strong-limbed and tawny-eyed. He was a fine-looking lad – the image of his father.

As Anstruther mumbled something – afterwards he simply hoped it had been appropriate – Margaret offered him a mug of tea. He accepted it gratefully and sat down.

Emerald had perched herself on the other side of the table. Anstruther stared at the little girl again. There could be no doubt. No shadow of doubt. Her mother's eyes, her father's charm – but her beauty was all her own.

Margaret Mackenzie set the kettle on the hook over the fire. She smiled at the two children.

'The gentleman, I think, has business with me. So be off and away. Ye can come back later for your tea.'

'Cal and me are going fishing.'

Emerald bounced up, pulling the boy with her.

'Pleased to meet ye, sir,' Callum said. He held out his hand again.

Anstruther shook it.

'Me now!'

Anstruther looked up with a start as Emerald spoke. He began to stretch out his hand, but Emerald ignored it. Instead, to his astonishment, she put up her face, puckering her lips to be kissed.

Anstruther had never kissed anyone in his adult life, not even a child. There was no escape. He bent down and touched her cheek with unpractised lips. As he did he knew he was lost. The one simple gesture trapped and held him as surely as if he had been tangled in a silken spider's web.

Dizzily he straightened up. The child, the changeling bairn as the croft woman called her, was magical. Whatever her birthright, she was a true princess. From now on, whatever lay in front of Emerald, Anstruther's own fate would always be linked to hers. *Ad astra fidelis*. Faithful to the stars – a single star.

Then in an instant the child was gone, tumbling down the hillside in the wake of the boy, leaving a trail of laughter in the air.

Margaret Mackenzie half-closed the door. 'Now, Mr Anstruther, make yourself comfortable. Then mebbe ye can tell me what's on your mind.'

Anstruther removed his spectacles and polished them with his hand-kerchief. The responsibility was his alone.

Margaret waited. She knew nothing of Latin mottoes, of grand codes of honour or oaths of loyalty. Her own gods were smaller and far older. But she'd seen the contact between them, the bairn and the stranger, and she knew Emerald had cast her spell. Anstruther might not be a

142

warm man, but he was a man who could be touched, however briefly, by love. It was enough. He would do her child no harm.

'Well, Miss Mackenzie—'

'If it's all the same to ye, I'm happier with Margaret.'

Anstruther coughed. 'Of course.'

He hesitated. He knew that almost on impulse he was taking irreversible, even dangerous, decisions which might store up trouble for the rest of his life. What he didn't know was whether it was fear or happiness which had so numbed his brain that the consequences no longer seemed to matter.

All he could see in his mind's eye was the warm cheek so confidently tilted towards him. And he knew, as surely as he knew anything, that the child must be protected against her own past.

As he talked, the plan crystallized in his own mind.

Emerald, he explained, was the daughter of very powerful people: people who could not admit their parenthood for fear of the child being made a scapegoat, of having to pay the price of what might be described as – Anstruther hesitated – a major indiscretion.

He was careful with his words. Economical. No-one, not even Margaret Mackenzie, could know the whole truth.

But he made the danger to the child clear. Emerald must never find out whose child she really was. Life would be hell for her if she did. She would never be able to make a move without attracting publicity – without the whole sorry business being dug up again. Worse, there would be official authorities taking decisions which would have nothing to do with the child's happiness and welfare.

When he finished Margaret Mackenzie sat for a long time in silence. Anstruther didn't hurry her for an answer. What he'd asked her to do was going to cause an upheaval in her life such as she could never have known. Her devotion to the child, he hoped against all the odds, would make her agree, but she needed time to take it all in.

'I'll do what ye ask of me, Mr Anstruther. For the sake of the bairn.' When she spoke at last, Margaret Mackenzie's voice was soft, but her eyes were bright and clear. 'For her sake I'll leave my island, the island where I was born.'

She did not add what else she knew. Nor did she explain that the stranger's request had come as no surprise to her. But, still, it was hard to speak the words – knowing, as the second sight had told her, that she would never return.

Meanwhile, down by the shore, Emerald, too, knew something was wrong. Something exciting and terrible was about to happen.

She and Callum had gone to the rocks where the seals basked in the sunshine. From there the ocean stretched all the way to the horizon. Callum set about baiting his mackerel lines.

'No fishing today, Cal,' said Emerald.

'What's the matter, Em?'

'That man. The man who's talking to my nan.'

'What?'

'He's come to take me away.'

'Don't be silly, Emmy.'

For a long while Emerald looked out over the water.

'Cal' – Emerald's voice was urgent – 'promise me something.'

'What?'

'You must promise in blood. I'll find a thorn.'

Emerald jumped up and set off up the slope. After a few moments she returned holding a sharp little hook pulled off a blackthorn bush.

'You do it,' she said.

Callum pricked first his own finger and then hers. Emerald's face was solemn and intent as she watched the little scarlet drops appear.

The two children rubbed their fingers together. The blood mingled. Emerald's face lit up with relief.

'Blood-brothers, Callum. You and me. Now we're blood brothers, whatever happens. Nothing and no-one can ever keep us apart.'

She was wrong. The man from London, waiting for them now in the crofthouse kitchen, had indeed come to do just that.

That evening, when Margaret Mackenzie was fussing with their bags, choosing the things they would take on their journey, Emerald was given the task of searching the chest which held her nan's small treasures – and, in doing so, found her own.

On the island, the affair was no more than a two-day wonder.

After a brief flurry of gossip and speculation, to which Catriona Sweeney contributed a well-crafted tale of parents abroad who had sent for Emerald, and Margaret Mackenzie's willingness to see her storm-orphan settled in her new abode, life for most of the islanders of Eas Forse returned to normal.

The exception was Callum. Callum knew his heart had broken clean in two. One piece stayed with him, the other had gone far away across the sea, locked fiercely in the small fist of the foster-sister he had loved and lost.

He had one consolation. The man from London had given him his word. He had promised that he would send him news of her. And

144

that some day, when the danger had passed, they would be together again.

What Callum did not know was that Anstruther had no intention of doing anything so dangerous. To Anstruther, lying for King and country came as easily as breathing. This time he knew that lying was the only way for him to keep faith with that bright-eyed young woman he had sent to her death.

He told himself he had lied for everyone's good, but above all for Emerald herself – now no longer a dim memory of the past, but a living child, bright-eyed and clear-sighted, who through that single kiss had had the power to move him.

You might even call it love.

The power of love can change everything – everything but the habit of a lifetime. And there Anstruther could not help himself.

Lies were so much easier to hide than the truth.

22

London: October 1946

It was a full year after Anstruther despatched Emerald and Margaret Mackenzie to Mexico before he found an opportunity to make provision for Emerald's longer-term future.

Naturally he had informed the Duke of the child's survival and of the arrangements he had made for her care. As he expected, the ex-king had been evasive, clearly unwilling to take responsibility for a problem he thought had been tidied away long ago. In fact Anstruther doubted if he'd even told the Duchess their daughter might have survived the wreck.

Well, Emerald had certainly survived. If the child was to have any sort of secure future, she'd need money, and the money would have to come from her father. To prise it out of him, Anstruther knew he'd have to wait for the right opportunity.

It came on 17 October 1946, when the Duke brought the Duchess to Britain for the first time since the abdication.

The Windsors' arrival produced a spate of headlines and press speculation. Perhaps the ex-monarch had come to seek a reconciliation with his mother. Perhaps he was after some formal recognition of his Duchess. Or, then, again, he might have arrived to negotiate with the King, his younger brother, for some role in public life.

In fact the Duke was after something much more practical. He wanted exemption from tax. An official diplomatic post, perhaps at the Paris embassy, would solve the problem.

The Palace was alternately anxious to accommodate him and worried by the effect any such appointment might have.

Tommy Lascelles, the one official at the Palace who had spanned both reigns, confided his worries to Anstruther over lunch at the St James's Club.

'A diplomatic posting's the obvious answer. But where and what? Washington's out of bounds. The Paris embassy's nervous of his pro-German history. The man's dynamite. Can't open his mouth without stampeding the horses. Anyway, he's still chasing the "Royal Highness" for his wife. I can't imagine why; it's flogging a dead donkey. Anyway, it would complicate the position over any heirs.'

Anstruther looked up sharply.

The expression on Lascelles's face was bland, innocent. Lascelles had been the Prince of Wales's private secretary – and as such was probably the one member of the Palace staff who knew about the child. But even he did not know Emerald had survived.

After lunch Anstruther walked thoughtfully back to the Inner Temple, where his career as a barrister was flourishing.

Back in his chambers he picked up the telephone.

The Windsors, Anstruther knew, were staying with Lord and Lady Dudley at Sunningdale just outside London.

'Anthony? Good to hear from you again, old man. How's tricks?'

If anything, the American accent and mannerisms were more pronounced than ever, but there was no hint of nervousness in the Duke's voice. He sounded cheerful and unconcerned, as if he'd entirely forgotten about the little 'difficulty' which had been the subject of his last conversation with Anstruther more than a year ago.

'Want to see me, do you? How about a turn round the links, Thursday afternoon? Wallis has some shopping to do in town, so we should have time to talk in private. Bring your clubs, and we'll get in nine holes before cocktails.'

The following Thursday a car picked Anstruther up from his apartment at Albany in Piccadilly. He had his golf clubs with him and he arrived at Sunningdale in good time, but the proposed nine holes of golf weren't played.

Wallis had changed her mind about the shopping trip.

That morning she had taken delivery of a new piece of jewellery from Cartier's, a marvellous bird of paradise with a huge sapphire forming the breast. The brooch was so superb, such a truly royal gift, she decided to show her appreciation to her husband by arranging a special treat.

He must see the jewel in its proper setting.

The Dudleys were both out for the day, and the Duke was taking the Bentley and the chauffeur for an early appointment with the Labour Prime Minister. As soon as the car pulled away from the front door, she set about preparing her surprise.

Edward Windsor expected to return to a solitary lunch. Instead, when the butler admitted him, he was handed a note in his wife's round clear handwriting. 'Follow the maid, David Thumb.' The use of the intimate nickname was a coded signal. In a moment he found himself being led upstairs by what he initially thought was a demure little housemaid, too shy to look him in the eye.

As they climbed he noticed the housemaid's shoes were remarkably expensive for a servant's. They had high, polished black heels, quite impractical for housework, which made her hips sway. His eye travelled up the impeccably straight seams of the black silk stockings. The skirt had a jaunty flirt, almost a French cut. The scent lingering behind her – vanilla and cinnamon with a sensual undertone of tuberose – might almost have been of Wallis's concoction. He smiled to himself. He hoped his wife was enjoying her shopping trip.

The maid paused for a moment on the landing, her hand lightly stroking the banister.

The Duke swallowed. The housemaid was very . . . *flirtatious*.

She walked on ahead of him, the hips still swaying over the high heels. He followed her down the deserted corridor, until she stopped at his wife's bedroom door.

Her head down, the little white lace cap bobbing demurely on the dark hair, the maid opened the door and stood aside.

The Duke caught another breath of the perfume as he walked past her.

Even though it was broad daylight outside, the curtains were drawn and the room was lit by candles and dancing firelight. The fragrance was overwhelming now.

A small table set in an alcove beside a chaise-longue had been laid for one. On the table a tin of Imperial caviare, nestling in a china bowl of ice, was open to reveal the little golden globules. A silver bucket flanked by a slender glass flute held a bottle of Dom Pérignon.

'Your Royal Highness?'

The door closed, and Edward Windsor turned.

With a shiver of anticipation, he realized the identity of his seductress.

'Were you about to commit adultery, David Thumb?'

Wallis's voice was throaty with triumph. She loved these games. 'You can, sir. You can ask me anything.'

She bobbed her head in mock submission, raising her hand to play with the buttons of her prim maid's uniform.

She whispered, 'Is there anything I can do for His Royal Highness?'

She came closer. Her eyes were deep dark violet, the colour they always went when she made love.

'Would sir like a little refreshment?'

She poured the champagne.

'Perhaps this?'

As she held the glass to his lips, she caressed his cheek, running her painted fingernail across the pulse-point at his temple.

'Or this?' Wallis raised her hands to the buttons again. This time the black silk slithered to the floor.

Naked now but for the jewelled bird blazing on a velvet ribbon at her throat, the Duchess dipped a long silver spoon in the caviare.

She had definite plans for the caviare.

The rest of the household, summoned by the housekeeper's bell for afternoon tea in the basement kitchen, didn't see the royal love-making in quite the same light as the participants.

The Duchess confided in her lady's maid, Yvonne; and Yvonne had just breathlessly described what was going on.

'Well, I never. You'd think they'd have better things to do with their time at this hour of the day.'

The housekeeper, a thin and irritable woman, sniffed and poured herself another cup of tea.

The maid was French of course. What could you expect?

'Sex-mad,' the housekeeper muttered under her breath. 'Like mistress, like servant.'

'Don't be a spoilsport, Lizzie Williams.'

Mrs Lane, the round-faced pink-cheeked cook, ranked equally with the housekeeper in the below-stairs hierarchy, but unlike the housekeeper she enjoyed a good belly-laugh.

'It's the best story I've heard in a long time. Come on, Yvonne, what else is Her Grace up to?'

'Well, there's the caviare . . .'

The maid giggled. Everyone leaned forward intently to listen to precisely what it was the Duchess did with the caviare. They were all so absorbed by the story, so intent on catching every word, that

149

no-one heard the furtive tread of the intruder's footsteps on the landing upstairs.

It was the Duchess herself who raised the alarm. Leaving her husband dozing after their love-making, she carried her clothes down the passage to her dressing-room. She took off the glittering new brooch and laid it in her travelling jewel-case.

She always found the exercise of power stimulating, and her power over what his previous mistress, Thelma Furness, had called the Little Man was absolute. Even the urchins in the streets of London had known it.

'Hark the herald angels sing,' they had chanted on that bleak December day when she was driven into exile, 'Mrs Simpson's pinched our king.'

So she had. For ever.

And perhaps now, after his visit to the Prime Minister that morning, David Thumb would at last get the official position he craved, and his wife might be accorded her proper royal title.

Wallis had decided to run herself a scented bath as a reward for her elegant little piece of theatre. She headed for the bathroom further down the corridor.

She was so preoccupied with her thoughts that she failed to notice that the dressing-room's sash window had been slipped open, and a rope was hanging down outside. Later the police decided that the thief must have thrown the rope up while the Duchess was 'speaking privately' with the Duke, and then climbed it while she was in her bath.

The thief worked quickly, so quickly he had almost emptied the Duchess's jewel-case by the time he was disturbed by her return from the bathroom. Certain aspects of the robbery – the precise timing, the rope, the open window, the convenience of the household summoned to tea – led the police to suspect that it might even have been an inside job.

The robber knew what he was doing. As he made his escape he discarded the lesser baubles in a trail through the flowerbeds and across the golf course, and kept only the most expensive pieces.

What grieved the Duchess most was that morning's gift from her husband. Like a child, the only toy that mattered to her was the latest one.

'Oh my God, David. It's gone!'

'Gone? What's gone?' The Duke's voice was drowsy, drugged with the afternoon's delights.

'The brooch – my beautiful bird – it's gone!'

Her husband sat up and rubbed his eyes.

'Good Lord!'

Alerted by the Duchess's cries, the household tumbled out into the hall.

By the time Anthony Anstruther's hired car turned into the drive, there were three police cars blocking the entrance and a dozen uniformed officers swarming all over the house.

Lord Dudley himself opened the door to Anstruther. He explained the disaster in a few words.

'Damn woman didn't lock up her baubles in the safe. Kept them under the bed like some common peasant. Fellow shinned up a drainpipe and pinched them. Plenty more where they came from, but there's one hell of a song and dance. Just hope the fellow didn't get away with my fishing rods,' he finished gloomily. 'In all the hoo-ha I haven't even had time to look.'

It was two hours before the ex-king managed to comfort his wife enough to feel he could leave her and see Anstruther. Even then Edward Windsor, dishevelled and with his cardigan buttoned up the wrong way, seemed incapable of concentrating on anything except the theft.

'I *told* the Duchess not to bring it all with her. Hopelessly under-insured of course. Twenty thousand pounds. It'll take double that to make up the difference.'

He took a deep breath.

'And now *this* – this news of yours. Anthony, it's absolutely the last straw.'

'I'm sorry, sir, but I didn't think it could wait any longer.'

Anstruther paused.

'Don't think I'm not *grateful*.' The Duke's voice became calmer, and the famous Windsor charm surfaced. 'Of course I am, couldn't be more so. You've done a quite splendid job in dealing with the child. But, as for money for her, I'm afraid it's blood from a stone. It'll be as much as I can manage to replace what the Duchess has lost.'

'What exactly was taken, sir?'

The Duke grunted. 'Fellow knew his stuff – took everything of any value.'

'Personal mementoes?'

Edward Windsor wrinkled his forehead. 'Not sure what was there.'

Anstruther hesitated. He remembered the many occasions when he'd been despatched to various jewellers to pick up the love-tokens with which the Prince of Wales, as he then was, had courted his mistress.

'I hope it's not indiscreet, sir, but did you give the Duchess a memento of the child's birth?'

Edward Windsor glanced up sharply. 'Certainly. Naturally. Keepsake

151

locket, damn pretty thing. Moon and stars – Georgian, if I remember. I think Iona sent over a curl of the child's hair. Seem to remember the Duchess put it in the locket with the others after the news came. Of the shipwreck, you know.'

'Would it be possible to see if the locket's gone?'

For an instant the Duke looked startled, almost fearful.

'The Duchess is deuced upset. Don't know if I dare ask – salt in the wound and all that.' He frowned in anguish. Then, realizing the gravity of what lay behind Anstruther's question, he nodded. 'I'll see what I can do.'

The Duke vanished upstairs. His wife's voice, dulled by closed doors, rose to a crescendo.

Anstruther paced the floor. Ten minutes later the Duke reappeared.

'All present and correct, thank God!' He was chuckling with relief. He held out the jewelled locket for Anstruther's inspection. 'Pretty little thing, isn't it?'

Anstruther caught a brief glimpse of a triple curl before the Duke slipped the crystal-faced trinket back in his pocket.

'It was in one of the Fabergé boxes. The swine must have turned his nose up at them – left them scattered all over the floor. Had to search through the whole damn lot to find it.'

Edward Windsor began to relax. 'Narrow squeak, eh?'

He went on chuckling.

Anstruther gazed at him. There had never really been any doubt in Anstruther's mind. Had there been, it would have been dispelled then. The former King of England and his consort would never acknowledge their child. They were both too vain, too selfish, too careless.

'Yes, sir,' Anstruther replied quietly.

'Imagine if the press got hold of it' – the Duke shuddered – *'that* would put the kibosh on any kind of official appointment. Saw the PM, that Attlee fellow, this morning. Think I can talk him into offering me Paris.'

'Excellent, sir. Perhaps if it happens—'

The Duke shook his head. 'I know what you're going to say, Anthony. The answer still is *no can do.* Even if my damned brother manages to talk sense into the Bolsheviks at the Foreign Office, it'll be as much as we can do to keep a roof over *own* heads. No. It's out of the question.'

'But, sir—'

'Hang on!'

The Duke suddenly interrupted him. His face had lightened and was glowing with the boyish enthusiasm that had once so endeared him to his subjects. 'I've had an idea. My grandmother Alexandra's emeralds are still in the vaults at Windsor. She left them to *me*. Everyone knows she wanted my future wife to have them.'

'Emeralds, sir?'

'Her dowry. She was the Princess of Denmark, as you know – family poor as church mice, of course, but at least they came up with the goods when she married Grandpa. They're supposed to be worth a fortune. Get that turncoat Tommy Lascelles to take the stuff down to the pawnshop. Just the ticket. If the matter comes up, everyone will think the stuff disappeared in the robbery.' His voice grew thoughtful, almost tender. 'She was a good woman, my grandmother. I know she'd want her legacy to go to the right place at the right time.'

Anstruther was silent for a moment. Then he said: 'I would need your authorization, sir.'

'For God's sake, Anthony,' the Duke snapped, 'Lascelles knows the story – took the king's shilling from both my brother and myself. Make it clear what the consequences would be. Tommy may have the loyalty of a polecat, but he knows the ropes. The Palace has been tight-fisted as hell as far as I'm concerned, but Tommy'll see it's in their interests as much as ours. Stir it up. So far, they've had it all their own way.'

'Perhaps just a note in your own hand—'

'Stuff and nonsense.' Edward Windsor's voice was petulant. 'Quite unnecessary. A word in the right ear. Far more effective.'

In the distance Wallis Windsor was having a word in a great many ears. Her voice could be heard haranguing the assembled servants, the high-pitched shrieks punctuated by the more reasonable tones of her hostess, Laura Dudley.

The Duke leaped to his feet, his face creased with anxiety.

'Think that's it, Anthony. Got to go and console the Duchess.'

Anstruther stared at his ex-employer. The former monarch seemed not merely in awe of his wife – he was almost frightened of her.

'Thank you for your time, sir.'

'My thanks to *you*, my dear fellow. Just see to it, Anthony, would you?'

Edward Windsor went over to the door. The audience was over. As far as the Duke was concerned, the matter of his inconvenient offspring was concluded.

Anstruther polished his glasses deliberately, the only gesture of dissent his training allowed him. As he took his leave, he noticed once again what a dandy the man was. Small but perfect, like a porcelain miniature, even hurriedly dressed as he was now.

'Goodbye, sir. Hope the job comes through.'

'Yes . . . well . . . sure there'll be something. *Has* to be something really.'

The Duke held out his hand, his bulbous blue eyes already shifting nervously to the hall.

'One other thing. Make sure none of this reaches my wife. Far too delicate under the circumstances. More than enough on her plate as it is. Get Grandmother's emeralds down to the pawnbroker's, and make an end of the whole damn thing. There'll be no problem, I assure you.'

'Yes, sir.'

As Anstruther left the house, the Duchess's tirade echoed across the neatly tended driveway. 'For God's sake, David, *do* something!'

As the car pulled away, Anstruther found himself heartily wishing the Duke would do just that – *do* something, take his own decisions, and not leave others to clear up the messes he made.

Remembering the glowing innocence of the little girl in the crofthouse kitchen, for the first time he was glad the child's fate had not been left in the hands of her true parents. Margaret Mackenzie had served Emerald well. Anstruther was glad the child had found a kinder hand to rock her cradle.

He had been pleased that his mother had readily agreed to his request to grant the fugitives safe haven. Briefly, as he ran over the events of the day in his mind, he wondered how the little girl was coping with her new home. It been a year since he had put the elderly islander and her charge on the steamship bound for the port of Vera Cruz in southern Mexico. Since then, he had had a couple of letters from his mother in which she had mentioned little except that the child was well and settling in.

'Endearing little creature,' his mother had written. 'She's a little wild, but perhaps that's usual at her age. As you know, I am not the best authority on such things. Rest assured, between us we shall manage.'

There was a postscript. 'By the way, dear boy,' his mother had written in her elegant copperplate, 'I am quite certain this child could not possibly be yours.'

A little irritated in spite of himself, Anstruther wondered how his mother could possibly have come to such a conclusion.

23

London: October 1946

'Private Office at Buckingham Palace, please. The back entrance.'

Anthony Anstruther leaned back in the cab. He had a 4.30 appointment.

The Palace was magnificent in the afternoon sunshine. The bomb-damage to the façade and forecourt had been repaired, and the sovereign's standard with its lions rampant rippled over the pediment. The pale stone looked bright and clean against its coronet of russet and gold autumn leaves. The red-coated Guardsmen in their towering black bearskins stared unseeingly past the knots of tourists who crowded the railings, hoping for a glimpse of some shadow behind the tall blank windows.

The war was over and all was well with the world.

At the back entrance in Buckingham Palace Road, Anstruther showed his pass to the policeman on duty. The cab was admitted to the courtyard which led to the rabbit warren of bureaucracy which kept royalty in business.

His ex-colleagues greeted him jovially. The Private Office was buzzing with gossip about the robbery in Sunningdale, and Anstruther spent the half-hour he had to wait describing the scene at Ednam Lodge. Listening to the laughter that greeted his account of the Duchess's tantrum, he felt a ripple of nostalgia. It was as if he'd never been away.

Suddenly a quiet voice cut into the merriment.

'Seems you're today's cabaret, Anthony. I don't want to interrupt the performance, but what can I do for you?'

Too clever by half was how his enemies described him – and Tommy Lascelles had made more than a few of them in his time. Among them, increasingly and with reason, was his former boss, Edward Windsor.

'A little local difficulty, Tommy,' Anstruther replied. 'Perhaps we could—'

'A walk? Of course.' Lascelles's thin pale face was expressionless. 'About time for my constitutional. We'll take some crusts for the ducks.'

Lascelles vanished down the corridor to the Palace kitchens. He reappeared after a few moments with a bulging brown paper bag.

'Always stuffy in here now the central heating's installed. Let's get some air.'

Anstruther followed him out. The two men walked side-by-side down to the lake in St James's Park. To a casual observer they might have been father and son – Anstruther in the dapper navy-blue pinstripe of a successful young barrister, lengthening his stride to match the taller and stooping older man who wore the long frock coat and sponge-bag trousers of an Edwardian courtier.

They threaded their way through the prams and nursemaids whose charges were playing tag among the drifts of yellowing autumn leaves. Then they stopped at a secluded spot on the lake's edge.

'Right, Anthony. What's it about?'

Anstruther outlined the sequence of events, briefly and colourlessly. Tommy Lascelles was not a man for drama.

'As you can see, Tommy, something needs to be done,' Anstruther finished. 'Discreetly of course, but it has to be done.'

'What do you want of us?' Lascelles's voice was noncommittal.

Anstruther took a deep breath.

'When HRH suggested the emeralds, I'm afraid I rather jumped at it. I did tell him it was bound to be awkward. But he seemed to think his brother would be willing.'

Tommy Lascelles nodded. He stood in silence for a while, his face thoughtful.

'A lot of things went missing in the bombing, of course,' he said eventually. 'Half the family's personal stuff has never been catalogued anyway.'

'The emeralds, for instance,' Anstruther suggested. 'Well, for the sake of argument, let's say they might have been sent to the bank for safekeeping?'

Lascelles nodded again. 'It's possible.'

'Possible?'

'We'd have to have some kind of receipt. Double-edged sword, of course. Could be taken to mean an admission of the child's claim.'

The two men walked on in silence, both of them lost in thought.

'It's damned awkward, Anthony, to be honest.'

'The whole thing's awkward.'

'Yes.'

Tommy Lascelles halted and leaned over the wooden bridge to stare at the waterbirds below. A pair of magnificent pelicans, pouched beaks stretched over snowy backs, were preening themselves under the arch of the bridge.

'Fine birds, pelicans.' Lascelles glanced at the younger man. 'Winston Churchill's, you know. Gift of some grateful African government. Never been known to breed. Just as well. Eat half a ton of fish a week each, I'm told. One thing leads to another and, before you know what's what, there's all hell to pay. Kings or pelicans, they're all the same.'

'The point is, Tommy,' Anstruther answered quietly, 'your boss's co-operation would take care of the problem for good and all. The child would be endowed.'

Lascelles stopped and looked hard at his ex-colleague.

'Well, if anything can be done, I'll – we'll – hold you responsible, Anthony, to make sure it's fireproof.'

Anstruther gazed steadily back.

'It'll work out, Tommy. When the time comes, the child will make a respectable marriage – on the other side of the Atlantic, if a suitable candidate can be found. That's the intention. She's still very young, of course. There's a limit to what one can plan.'

'Pity the shipwreck didn't solve it.' Lascelles's voice was flat.

'You really see it like that?'

'And you don't?'

'She's entitled to her life. A child's a child.'

'Except when it's a royal bastard. God knows, they've brought down empires before now.'

The two men walked on, matching each other's pace like soldiers, their polished shoes burnished to the colour of autumn leaves. Good shoes. Shoes which would last a lifetime.

Together, perfectly in step, they crossed the bridge which led back to the Palace.

On the bridge Anstruther paused for a moment to watch the ducks dabbling in the leaf-dark water. Their spring-born fledgelings had long since taken wing and dispersed. Compared to them, Anstruther reflected, the breeding habits of humanity were extraordinarily untidy. Only humans disregarded the laws of nature concerning season, food-source, timing.

The consequences could be immensely inconvenient.

Anstruther himself had never felt the slightest urge to reproduce. Having seen the mess it seemed to create for everyone else, he knew it was unlikely he ever would. And yet. And yet.

In his mind's eye he saw the little heart-shaped face and bewitching violet eyes of the shipwrecked child. He smiled to himself. Emerald was a daughter any mother would love, any father be glad to cherish. Any mother or father except those which nature had so carelessly given her.

Anstruther quickened his step to catch up with Lascelles. Neither said another word until they reached the entrance to the Palace offices. Then Lascelles stopped and held out his hand to his one-time colleague.

'Glad you came to me, Anthony.'

'I'll wait to hear.'

'Might take a week or two.'

Anstruther nodded. 'Here. Thought I'd forgotten something.' Lascelles held out the bag of bread-crusts. 'Forgot to feed the damn birds.'

Anstruther took the bag. 'Thanks. Feeding things – my role, it seems.'

Lascelles gave a thin-lipped smile. 'Absolute discretion, of course. I mean, *absolute*. We'll deny the whole thing. Dump you in the shit.'

Anstruther raised his eyebrows in mock surprise. 'You astonish me, Tommy.'

On his way back to his comfortably shabby flat in Albany, Anstruther fed Winston Churchill's conveniently infertile pelicans with the contents of the bag from the Palace kitchens.

Ten days later a parcel was discreetly hand-delivered to Anstruther at his chambers in the Inner Temple.

Usually the Palace courier left the packets which Anstruther handled in the normal course of his business with one of the junior clerks in the office downstairs. Today the courier insisted on being shown into Anstruther's own office.

'I'm sorry, sir,' the courier said, 'but they told me this one needs your own signature twice. One for you and one for me to take back.'

Anstruther studied the two sheets of the familiar Buckingham Palace writing-paper, with the royal crest deeply embossed on the thick cream surface.

The message read simply: 'Received – one packet of goods delivered to the Hon. Anthony Anstruther on behalf of His Royal Highness, the Duke of Windsor. Contents as agreed. Benefit to be applied at discretion.'

It was all very elliptical and discreet.

It was also, Anstruther thought with his lawyer's mind, evidence – circumstantial evidence, of course, but evidence all the same. If anything happened to the child, if anything threatened her, his signature on the receipt indicated that the Palace accepted responsibility for her.

'I think we should get my signature witnessed,' he said to the courier.

'Yes, sir.'

He went downstairs and signed in front of his clerk. He was surprised that his request had been granted so swiftly. He'd expected delay, denials, endless attempts to wriggle off the hook.

Instead it appeared that the Palace, notoriously close-fisted with anything like the Danish jewels whose ownership might be disputed, was as anxious to get rid of Emerald as her natural parents.

Later, after locking the door carefully, Anstruther opened the parcel and lifted the lid of the heavy little box. Inside was a bag made of thick dark-green suede, closed at the neck with a twist of plaited silk. The leather was stamped in gold leaf with the arms of the Danish royal family.

Anstruther loosened the mouth of the bag and peered inside.

The bag had little pouches sewn round the sides. Each pouch held a single uncut stone, slipped into its own small envelope of yellowing silk. It was indeed the legendary treasure whose whereabouts and ownership had been the subject of so much speculation over the years.

Gossip had always surrounded the gems. It was not even known if they truly existed. If they did, the general view was that Edward VIII had presented them to the woman he intended to make his queen. Or that he had taken them with him into exile as a reward for discretion. Or that the Palace had kept them as a surety for the ex-monarch's good behaviour.

The emeralds were held to be unlucky in love. Certainly they had not brought happiness to the gentle and dignified Danish princess in her marriage to an unfaithful lecher of a royal husband. Perhaps it was that which warned her love-besotted grandson that they weren't a suitable present for his mistress-wife, however much she loved jewels.

The emeralds had never brought anyone good fortune.

Until now. Now, finally, the Danish princess's bride-price would buy her great-granddaughter happiness. The emeralds would act as collateral for the child's needs until they were sold to provide her with a dowry.

Anstruther smiled to himself as his fingers played among the glowing nuggets. It was right that Emerald's endowment was to be her namesake. Grass-green treasure for a changeling child.

Perhaps, as Margaret Mackenzie believed, there had indeed been a fairy-godmother at the bastard princess's christening.

Anstruther left his office. He walked briskly down the Strand with its gap-tooth bomb-sites, across Trafalgar Square, and made his way past Eros, the bronze statue which acted as a rendezvous for lovers in Piccadilly Circus, threaded through the boisterous evening crowds milling round the lighted windows of Swan & Edgar; and turned thankfully into the tranquillity of Albany.

The courtyard was roomy enough for a carriage-and-four to turn in comfort, away from *hoi poloi* on the busy streets outside. In a way, Anstruther reflected, it mirrored the life he was destined to lead – comfortable and secure, a life of service which would, in due course, be rewarded by a knighthood bestowed by a grateful monarch. Some things in England never changed.

And yet, perhaps, it might have been different.

He might, like his mother, have escaped to the wild beauty of the Mexican forests, and grown up there in freedom and love. Except that for him, he knew, it could never have happened. He was his father's son, a bondsman by inclination as much as by inheritance.

Emerald could be different. She could grow to womanhood liberated from the shackles of her royal parentage – the same shackles which still bound Anstruther fast.

His mother had been right, but she was also wrong. Emerald was the child Anstruther knew he would never have. She could make a reality of what for him could only be a dream. Emerald could wander the forests in his place. She could grow strong and beautiful and free. She could fall in love, and live happily ever after.

'It's a little *irregular*, Anthony. We're not pawnbrokers, you know.'

Peter Trevelyan smiled and ran a hand over his Trumper's haircut, releasing a faint scent of lime hair-oil.

'We leave that kind of thing to the boys down Petticoat Lane.'

The tall, languid senior partner's voice was as smooth as cream. His family had been running Trevelyan's Bank for rather more generations than the reigning house had occupied the throne.

'Hogwash,' said Anstruther.

Trevelyan looked up in surprise.

'With the greatest respect, Peter – sanctimonious balderdash,'

160

Anstruther continued. 'Your founder – when was it, 1639? – started up in business making precisely such loans to Charles I against, if I remember, a bunch of baubles similarly prised loose from the crown of England.'

He paused, his glasses glinting.

'Your emblem is three gold balls. Three gold balls, Peter. One more than the usual. I presume you put your money where your emblem is.'

Peter Trevelyan raised his eyebrows. Then his face relaxed into a faint smile.

'Vulgar, but *touché*. What have you got for me, Anthony?'

Anstruther leaned down and picked up his briefcase.

Trevelyan's Bank handled the Windsor business – and Anstruther's. They already handled the administration of Iona Fergusson's estate, paying Callum's allowance regularly into his foster-mother's account.

Discretion brought the right kind of business. Anstruther laid the briefcase on the banker's desk, opened the lid and removed a dark green leather bag, running an index finger tenderly over the embossed initials. Delicately Anstruther loosened the silk cord which held the mouth of the bag closed and pushed it across.

'Magnificent, eh, Peter?'

Peter Trevelyan gazed down at the blazing cache of emeralds co-cooned in the soft folds of suede.

'Well . . .' Trevelyan's voice remained slightly uneasy. 'The circum-stances are a little unusual, but the partners have indicated that they can see their way to accommodate the arrangement.'

'You mean that *you* as the senior partner can see your way. I never imagined anything else.'

The banker smiled and sniffed the carnation in his buttonhole.

'Presumably there's a valuation. Proof that all parties are agreeable? Within the bounds of discretion of course.' He raised his eyebrows. 'Good. In which case your word will be sufficient, Anthony. Leave the relevant papers in there. We'll put the box in the safe together, and organize investments to produce the necessary income for a lump sum on matrimony.'

Trevelyan turned from the table.

'How's HRH? Never did understand why the blighter did a runner. The woman's obviously got him by the appendages you referred to earlier. Shame really. Could have made a decent monarch. Politically sound, if you know what I mean.'

Anstruther knew exactly what the banker meant. Conservative with a small 'c' was the least of it.

Trevelyan opened a white-gold Cartier cigarette case and offered it to his old friend.

'Balkan Sobranie? No? I forgot. More of an occasional cigar man, aren't you, Anthony? Moderation in all things.' He frowned. 'We're the last bastion of the old establishment.'

He lit the honey-gold oval cigarette and walked over to the high Georgian window which gave on to Threadneedle Street.

'See those young men out there, Anthony? They're after my job – the barrowboys and totters' whelps. They've never heard of a gentleman's word, let alone his bond. They'll be running the country soon. Along with the women. The rot's setting in . . .'

Trevelyan swung back. 'Some of my married female customers are actually running *separate* bank accounts. I'm told – and you should know well enough – there are even female barristers these days. We'll be getting a woman prime minister next.'

A wry smile crossed Anstruther's face. 'I don't think it'll quite come to that, Peter.'

'Mark my words, Anthony. This is the last of *us* – the gentlemen bankers of the City of London. The future belongs to *them* – the alleycats out there.'

Later that evening, walking to the Indian restaurant round the corner from Albany for supper with a retired colleague from his Palace days, Anstruther mused that Peter Trevelyan was right. The old order had already changed. The battlefield had seen to that. In fifty years, two world wars had achieved social upheavals which should have taken centuries.

The changes had been too abrupt. As a barrister he had to deal with the consequences every day. Nothing now was binding unless it could be held up in court. There were gentlemen's agreements which were no longer made between gentlemen.

Politically it was the same. An unwritten constitution was a delicate plant, a living organism: pinch off a bud, tear off a few petals, strip off some leaves, and the whole thing could wither away. It was a difficult time. A time for consolidation.

It was enough that the two children were safe and well and his obligation to Iona's orphans did not threaten what Anstruther knew was his duty to King and country – a responsibility which included keeping a watching brief on the King's brother's affairs.

Except . . . Except it was not so simple.

There is always that unpredictable factor in human relationships. Even the best-laid plans can go awry.

24

Mexico: 1947

The frog did not know it was being watched.

Nor did its dinner, a fruit-fly sipping nectar from the lip of a scarlet hibiscus.

'Got it!'

Emerald's shout of triumph echoed round the deep ravine, the barranca which formed the southern boundary of Molly Anstruther's rambling garden.

'Let's see!'

Nacho pulled himself into the pepper-tree beside his best friend. At just turned ten, the young Mexican boy was a few months younger than Emerald. He looked older – the Indios, the brown-skinned natives of the barranca – grew up much faster than the gringos.

Emerald leaned down from the fork and uncupped her fist so Nacho could see the inky velvet of the frog's back. The tiny creature's scarlet throat pumped with fright.

Emerald stroked it gently with one long, sun-browned finger.

Every living thing, even the reptiles who needed the sun to warm their cold blood, took refuge from the heat of the day. Now, in the early evening, the creatures of the barranca were beginning to emerge.

'You're not to do anything beastly to the frog, Nacho.'

Nacho, Emerald knew, considered life just as expendable as his ancestors the Aztecs had done. From them the boy had inherited a smooth honey-dark skin and slanting lizard's eyes. Given half a chance, Nacho would lay out the little frog on a makeshift altar and make a sacrifice to the old gods, just as he had done when they had found the old carved stone tablet down the ravine. Then it had only been a rat Nacho had caught in the dustbin, but Emerald wasn't taking any chances.

'I expect it's an orphan like me,' Emerald added. 'Or maybe a handsome prince just waiting for a princess to kiss it.'

Nacho grinned. 'Give it a kiss, then, Princess.'

He had heard Emerald's fairy-stories before.

Emerald looked at him doubtfully. 'You won't tell on me? Swear?'

Nacho turned his face until it caught the sun's rays slanting through the feathery leaves of the pepper-tree.

'By the snake-bones of Cuatlicue my blood mother, may our father the sun tear out my heart.' He turned back to Emerald. 'Go on, do it!'

Emerald puckered her lips and aimed a quick peck at the crown of the frog's head.

The frog, feeling the sun as Emerald opened her hand, leaped for freedom, a streak of black and scarlet.

Emerald lunged after it. The branch whiplashed down, and she had to scramble back, laughing, to the fork of the tree. The frog landed on the soft suction-pads which cushioned its delicate feet, and hung trembling three branches below.

Nacho snorted. 'You'd have done better to tear out its heart for the moon goddess. That nearly always works. It worked for my sister Conchita when she was crazy for my cousin Ito. Your ideas never work.'

'Esmeralda! Come here at once!' Lupe's voice floated down the steep ravine.

Emerald lifted her head. She liked the Spanish translation of her name. Esmeralda sounded so romantic, and the customary prefix – la Esmeralda – gave it distinction. It almost sounded like a film star.

Only her nan called her Emerald now. The old lady – she seemed very old to Emerald even though Margaret Mackenzie said Aunt Molly was only a little older than the Scotswoman herself – called her 'darling' and 'my dear'. Sometimes Emerald thought Lady Molly couldn't remember her name.

Lupe had no trouble with it. Lupe was the cook. More important, she was Nacho's mother. She could make Nacho obey her, and through Nacho she wielded power over Emerald.

Emerald was so wild, Margaret Mackenzie sometimes despaired of her.

Now the child had the Spanish and a smattering of the Indio dialect, it was becoming worse. Only Nacho could keep up with her.

'Nacho!' The voice rose again. 'Nacho, you send la Esmeralda back this very minute! *La nana* is waiting. She'll be very angry if la nenita is not at table immediately, you hear!'

Emerald sighed. She slid her long brown legs, scarred at the knees from many similar scramblings, down the tree-trunk and dropped to the earth, dislodging an avalanche of old tin cans with her leather sandals. Nacho, who always went barefoot, never made any noise.

'You come here right *now*, Esmeralda! If you don't, la nana says you're to be given a big tortazo!'

Emerald giggled. A tortazo was a spank. No-one had never spanked her in her life, not even when she had been out all night in the churchyard eating sugar-skulls and playing ghosts with Nacho on the Day of the Dead.

Nacho, on the other hand, was beaten almost every day. Particularly when, like today, he had cut short by twenty-five minutes the six hours for which he was paid to exercise his Uncle Felipe's fighting cocks.

They were beautiful birds, the jungle fowl, small and wiry and tough and fierce, just like Nacho's uncles who still lived in the mountains of the Chiapas. They arched their beautiful curved tail-plumes, turquoise and scarlet, topaz and obsidian – brilliant as the sacred quetzal bird – and their heads were crowned with rosy soft-fleshed combs which flared red when the battle-urge was on them.

Nacho's job was to walk them up and down the baked earth of the trellis-shaded yard until their thighs were so taut with muscle there was no flesh left on the drumstick.

Nacho loved his birds. But not as much as he loved la Esmeralda.

Which was just as well, he thought, as Emerald didn't have a mother or a father to love her. She only had Nana, her old nurse, and Doña Molly, the old English milady who owned the Yellow House where Nacho's mother, Guadalupe – Lupe for short – was the cook.

Nacho watched Emerald scramble back over the wall onto the road, wisps of red-brown curls plastered against her damp neck. She wore a pair of boy's shorts and a loose cotton shirt. As yet there was no sign of the soft curve of the growing breasts which Nacho's sisters had proudly displayed at her age. Emerald was long and skinny, not like a Mexican girl at all; but, then, she'd always been different.

Nacho had been her companion from the moment she arrived at Lady Molly's mansion. Doña Molly was pale and vague, and drifted round the house like a faded rose-petal. No-one knew how or why Emerald had entered the old lady's life or the life of the Mexican township. Two years ago, she and her nursemaid had simply appeared from nowhere.

Since then the household had come to revolve round the child and the sturdy Scotswoman.

Doña Molly continued to read her books and receive her few neighbours, while Emerald had the run of the rest of the house, with its airy white-painted rooms filled with dark carved furniture and endless library shelves. In the absence of a proper school, Doña Molly had decided, the books would have to provide Emerald's education.

'Take anything you please, dear.' Molly had taken the wide-eyed child round the shelves soon after Emerald arrived. 'If you don't understand the meaning of a word, look it up. Commit it to memory and carry on. You'll find all the literature and history any educated person needs. Biographies are more reliable than memoirs. Novels are the most likely to be true. Read Trollope for character and Dickens for plot. I have monthly book-parcels from London. Please ask me if there is anything you'd like, although I shall expect you to justify your choice.'

She opened the door and glanced back over her shoulder.

'In addition, my dear, we will have half an hour of French conversation every evening at six after my rest. On Saturdays I shall teach you double-entry book-keeping so you can keep household accounts. My mother was an excellent mathematician. It was the only skill she taught me which has ever been of the slightest use. For the rest – science, politics, biology and so on – no doubt you'll pick it up from the servants.'

Doña Molly waved her hand absent-mindedly and disappeared.

Emerald had the books – and she had Nacho. To some extent the boy replaced her foster-brother. The little girl's immediate assumption that, like Callum, he would be at her beck and call surprised and pleased him. No-one had ever needed Nacho before.

Nacho's playground was the barranca, the steep-sided dry river-bed which bordered the garden. The tamarisk-trees which fringed its pale cliffs accommodated wild cats and stray dogs, iguanas and lizards. Down by the railway siding, along the edges of the barranca lived the shifting population of mountain-bred Indios who'd come to the city to make their fortune in the silver mines, or in the orchid trade, or by selling fake fertility figurines and silk *rebozos* to the American tourists – or by anything, from pimping to supplying marijuana to the tourists from the north.

The barranca-dwellers were Nacho's people, and from them he'd learned everything anyone needed to know.

He knew how to string the hibiscus flowers with resin-soaked threads to trap the jewel-bright hummingbirds. How to rob the wild bees of their black honey. How to set traps for slow-worms. How to skin snakes and roast them in the embers of a fire.

But there were other things which Emerald could do and Nacho could not. Emerald was not afraid, as Nacho was, of plunging into the deep cool waters of the pool. Emerald could swim like one of the eels Nacho occasionally managed to catch in the debris-thickened depths of the barranca's winter spate.

Emerald could twist her tongue round strange alien sounds, chattering to her nan and Doña Molly in languages which to Nacho sounded like the piping of the forest parrots. After the first few months, Emerald could switch freely between her native speech, the servants' kitchen Spanish, and the Indian hill-dialect Nacho had taught her.

So Nacho decided he, too, must learn. There was only one place where the Indio children could go to learn their letters, and that was in a makeshift classroom behind the church in the square, where the nuns taught the shifting population of urchins a rudimentary curriculum. The nuns would tick off the roster and decide what the lesson was to be.

Emerald clamoured for permission to join the classes when Nacho went, and her Aunt Molly did not see any reason why she should not do so. Provided her nan fetched her and brought her home.

Sometimes, when it was very hot or the rains had been particularly heavy, Margaret Mackenzie would let Emerald come home alone. Those were the best times. Those were the times Nacho would take her down to visit the curandera, the witch who lived in a hut on the edge of the town, almost on the way home.

The curandera had a formidable reputation as a healer and weaver of spells – with more than a smattering of knowledge of the ways of the old gods. Doña Molly didn't approve of the curandera and had absolutely forbidden Emerald to go anywhere near her. But Emerald was fascinated, even a little frightened, by the curandera. She was a white witch like her nana; only she was a bit of a black witch too. Everyone down the barranca knew for sure that the curandera, for all that her back was bent with the weight of her own bones, could fly through the air like a bird, dive deep in the earth like a snake, swim oceans like a dolphin. Everyone down the barranca came to the curandera to have their problems solved and their illnesses attended. The curandera made potions with strange little fungi and subterranean plants which had to be dug out of the earth on a special day by moonlight.

The curandera tolerated Emerald for the sake of her strange eyes – the same pale eyes of the Spanish conquistadores which had deceived

Montezuma into hailing their leader as Quetzalcoatl, the long-heralded blue-eyed god from the skies.

Nacho found Emerald's eyes extraordinary, too. You didn't see the colour of Emerald's eyes at first as she kept them hooded under their soft-veined lids. That was because she was always reading books. Proper books. Not just the wordless photo-romances which Nacho's four sisters devoured. But books without pictures – fat books, sometimes with leather covers and gold tooling, which she was allowed to take down from the library shelves. Nacho knew that must be where she got her ideas about princesses and frogs.

When he asked her what was in them, she'd look up and her eyes would shine with such an intense violet brilliance he'd have to blink and glance away. She did it now. Nacho shook his head and turned his attention back to the frog and the fruit-fly.

The fly had finished its nectar, and the frog was crawling carefully down the tree-trunk towards it. Nacho jumped out of the tree, and landed softly beside the cactus hedge below.

Its pulse throbbing, the frog waited for the danger to pass.

Threading his fingers through the spines, Nacho picked out the trembling creature. There was no sign of it turning into a prince. Nacho was glad. He had no wish for la Esmeralda to find herself a consort.

He placed the frog back on the branch for luck. He was going to need all the luck in the world tonight.

Swiftly he made his way back through the rubbish which had silted up in the dry stream-bed of the ravine. He had an hour to make his charges ready for the evening's cockfight. There were the leather leg-straps to be greased and softened, and half a dozen of the ferocious steel spurs to be sharpened and polished.

Later he would go up to his mother's kitchen in the yard behind the Yellow House and see if Emerald could be persuaded to risk the grown-ups' anger and sneak out. Tonight his own special bird, Xuma, was to fight for the first time. He wanted la Esmeralda to share what he was certain would be his triumph.

If Nacho's hopes were the saving of the little black tree-frog, the fruit-fly was not so fortunate. Down in the barranca, the frog seized the fly, swallowed it, and tucked itself into a damp patch of scrub to wait out the cold hours of darkness.

25

Mexico: 1947

'I kissed a frog today, Nana.'

'And what happened, my pet?'

'Nothing at all.'

Emerald's voice was doleful.

'Never mind. He may have turned into a prince when he went home for his tea.'

Emerald put down her spoon.

'I don't believe you, Nana. And I don't like soup.'

Margaret Mackenzie looked up. Instead of her usual gentle reply, she said: 'More fool ye, then. Supperless to bed it shall be.'

The Scotswoman picked up the plate and looked severely at Emerald.

It was a dangerous time in a child's growing, when childhood ended and adulthood began. Like a butterfly born into the sunlight, its wings still wet and crumpled from the cocoon, she could neither crawl nor fly.

'Up to your room, young missy,' said Margaret firmly. 'No doubt your schoolwork needs a little attention.'

'See if I care,' Emerald said scornfully as the door of her bedroom shut behind her nan.

Margaret sighed and went downstairs.

Emerald hugged herself happily. Her plan had worked. Her nana would not be up to see her again tonight.

Emerald waited until the click of her nana's door told her the coast was clear. Then she crept down the polished stone staircase, crossed the veranda on tiptoe, avoiding the loose plank, and made her escape into the thick shrubbery.

Beyond the shadowed tranquillity of the Yellow House and its walled garden, the sprawling town was wide awake. Emerald headed into the middle of the town where Nacho would be waiting for her.

However much Aunt Molly and her nan disapproved, Emerald loved the great tumbling antheap of the rumbustious baked-earth streets. They held no danger for her. She knew the labyrinth of alleyways like the back of her hand.

Above all, she loved the scents and colours of the wares offered by the kerbside foodstalls. Each street-corner had its own speciality, and Emerald knew most of the vendors by name.

'¿Que hay, Maria-Jesus?' she called out. 'Aren't you coming to the fight?'

'Get along with you, child.' The old woman who supplied the Yellow House with its daily bread of maize-flour tortillas shook her head and laughed. 'I have a living to earn. Toma, neita, take this – you need flesh on those bones.'

Maria-Jesus held out a crisp round of refried tortilla.

'You'd have me as fat as Lupe,' Emerald laughed, 'and then how would I find myself a husband?'

'Aiee, nenita, You gringos are so stupid. Fat is good. No real man wants skin and bones. You'll find out!'

Emerald laughed. Sometimes she helped Maria-Jesus sell the tacos she made. Emerald was an excellent salesgirl. She would give a big smile which crinkled the corners of her violet eyes. All the boys would crowd round, until Nacho would spot her and threaten to tell her nan.

Today she had no time. She was on her way to the cockfight.

In the market-place Cristóbal was setting up his stall for the holiday. He was fanning a charcoal brazier under a steaming vat of tamales: maize dumplings stuffed with spiced meat neatly parcelled in maize husk. On the next corner old Pedro the pork-butcher was putting out a cauldron of boiling blue-hazed fat ready to fry strips of crackling for those who were hungry after drinking at the cactus-beer stall.

Emerald didn't like the vinegary beer, but she loved the crisp little salty chicharros which burned her tongue if she didn't blow on them first.

'¿Que tal, nenita?'

'¡Bien!'

170

She hurried on past the piled vegetable-stalls. Familiar smells filled her nostrils. There were herbs everywhere: great bundles of coriander with its strange beetle scent, bunches of green onions and garlic, posies of epasote - the rank feathery weed which went into a green mole stew.

Emerald paused by a rickety table.

'Hey, Ricardo, two centavos' worth.'

The boy behind the stall, no older than Emerald herself, was piling an earthenware dish with great slabs of wild honeycomb – black bee-grubs gleaming through pale wax cells. He broke off a piece and wrapped it in a twist of maize-husk, the broad thick leaves which were the universal wrapping-paper of the market.

Emerald exchanged the two-centavo coin for the little packet. Nacho loved honeycomb.

She hurried on towards the beaten-earth market square at the far end of the town. Beyond was the sprawl of tin huts which housed the Teatro Chino, the mysteriously named 'Chinese Theatre', where the town's live entertainments were staged. Last year there had been a freak-show with a two-headed pig with four eyes and only three ears, and a lady so fat even Maria-Jesus was amazed. Tonight it was the cockfight which had drawn the crowds. It was a special event in honour of St Sebastian, patron saint of the town, whose fiesta it was. Sebastian, the most popular saint in all Mexico. The Indios liked all the arrows the saint was stuck with. Those were the kind of gods the Indios understood.

The prize-money was good, and competition was sure to be fierce.

Emerald slipped through a gap in the boards at the rear of the wooden shed which housed the cockpit, and climbed to the hayloft above. Nacho was already in position.

Nacho heard her. He poked his head over the rafters and put his finger to his lips. Emerald nodded. Neither of them was meant to be there. If the clamour of the betting on the next contest hadn't been echoing up from below, she might well have got both of them caught.

'Here,' Emerald whispered as she crawled up beside him.

Nacho accepted the piece of honeycomb. Then he returned to his scrutiny of the brightly lit arena below.

Rubber balls filled with betting slips and banknotes flew from side to side across the small wooden-walled ring. The circle of sawdust glowed white and hot in the light of dozens of tall candles thrust into sconces set in the ring-posts. If it hadn't been for the noise and the tobacco smoke, Emerald thought, the darkened shed would have looked and smelled like the cathedral of Our Lady of Guadalupe on a day of High Mass.

171

The noise quietened as the far door opened. The third bout of the evening was about to begin. This was the star turn.

Everyone knew that Nacho's uncle believed his new bird, Xuma, was a champion, and that Nacho had been employed to exercise the creature for six hours a day to make sure it became the strongest fighting animal in Mexico. Now it only remained to be seen whether Xuma had the heart and liver for the ring.

Nacho's slant eyes narrowed. 'Look, Esmeralda,' he whispered. 'My Xuma! Isn't he fine?'

Below them Xuma had made his appearance, pinioned under Nacho's Uncle Felipe's arm, with his head bobbing and weaving like a prize-fighter's. Emerald's breath quickened. She crept closer to Nacho and peered over the edge of the hayloft.

Smoke wreathed up in the candlelight. The bookmakers were milking the crowd for bets as the two birds darted out their long reptilian necks, their beaks gaping soundlessly, bristling feathers smoothed by quick flicks of the handler's palm.

Emerald studied Xuma's opponent. He was big and lean with a heavy breastbone and a torn coxcomb. On his naked legs were the thin white scars of earlier battles. The experience might give him an advantage, but the money was being wagered evenly.

'Did you bet?' Emerald whispered.

Nacho nodded, his eyes gleaming. 'Every penny I earned for the walking. How can he *not* win?'

The bell clanged.

'¡Toma su querencia! Each to his corner!' the referee called, and climbed into the ring.

The two owners with their birds faced each other across the sandy circle. The wooden walls were draped with white cotton sheets to protect the spectators from spurting blood. Emerald could see they were already well spattered from the previous bouts. The spectators at the ringside had tucked the cloth into their collars like a long dining-table napkin.

Momentarily the bouncing of the betting-balls ceased. Both birds crowed, a great soaring scream which echoed round the rafters.

'¡Vámonos! Let's go!'

Tío Felipe and his opponent, a large man with a cactus-beer belly that bulged over bell-fringed leather chaps, launched their birds at the same instant into the circle of trampled sand.

Xuma spread his wings and shot out his neck feathers.

The pointed plumes on his mantle stood out stiff and straight like a Spaniard's ruff. His opponent stretched on to his toes, wattles quivering, the steel spurs harnessed to his legs curving outwards like twin scimitars.

For sixty long seconds the two birds darted and stabbed, their feet thrust forward like an eagle's stoop and their beaks gaping furiously below glittering diamond eyes. The two owners circled them, clucking and hissing.

Suddenly Xuma's opponent slashed sideways, catching Xuma a glancing blow on one naked plucked leg. Blood spurted, spattering the rows of eager dark faces, and the rubber betting balls began to arc over the ring again.

Beside her, Emerald could feel Nacho's thigh jerk with Xuma's pain.

Xuma crouched back for an instant. Then he launched himself. One slash. Two slashes, and the blood soared again. Voices rose in excitement above the bouncing balls and circling men: 'I'll take twenty! Give you fifteen! Done!'

The noise died away. The birds were ready for the kill.

Suddenly their screams rose above the fading shouts. Steel spurs daggered out. Blood fountained up so high Emerald felt a warm wet drop on her cheek in the loft. She licked it, tasting the metallic flavour. Below her the two cocks tumbled over and over in a frenzy of slashing fury.

There was no winner or loser. Everything was lost in rage and blood. The last frantic pelota-ball bets showered across the bright arena. Then there was silence.

Emerald buried her head in the straw.

When she lifted her face the crowd was roaring. The white sheets were drenched with scarlet, and the two owners were hunched with the umpire over the birds in the middle of the ring.

Nacho had gone.

Suddenly she glimpsed him below, his elbows flailing as he pushed his way through the crowd towards the brightly lit circle of sand. As the men pulled back Emerald could see the two birds, their shining feathers dark and sticky now, half-buried in the sand.

'Xuma!'

Nacho vaulted the wooden barrier and scooped up one of the bundles in his arms.

The boy hurled himself through the open door and out into the dusk. His uncle glanced up briefly. He had been arguing with the umpire. It was a matter of points and strikes, and Felipe had won the argument. His bird, the younger, was the winner by four strikes to five. The rubber balls flew again.

Emerald slid quietly down the ladder.

She knew where Nacho would have taken Xuma. After the disaster in the ring she was certain Nacho would have taken Xuma to the curandera.

Emerald was wrong.

The old woman sleepily drew back the tattered curtain that covered the doorway. She saw Emerald and shook her head. No, Nacho had not been there.

Emerald walked away into the darkness. Dawn was breaking above the mountains when she eventually found Nacho. The fighting cock was clasped in the boy's brown arms, and they were curled up together under the pepper-tree where that morning she and Nacho had watched the black-velvet tree-frog.

Xuma lay in the sleeping Nacho's lap, a bedraggled bundle of feathers, his bronze plumes dull against the yellow lizard-skin of his stiff legs, his once-bright eye misty blue in the pale light.

Emerald sat down beside them. Clumps of dry grass prickled the soft skin at the backs of her knees. She put out her hand and stroked Nacho's cheek. Nacho's eyelids fluttered open.

Emerald said: 'We won.'

Nacho shrugged. Emerald was silent. The sun's rays slanted down the barranca, casting the shadows of the pepper-tree's leaves across Nacho's blood-spattered shirt. Nacho's eyes were wide open now – wide open and midnight-dark.

Emerald hesitated.

Very gently she leaned over and kissed him, her violet eyes half-lidded, her russet hair, lightened now by the sun, soft against the skin of his chest. Her lips touched his. She felt the warmth of his body and her own tears on his smooth cheek.

Suddenly she leaped up and ran away, scrambling back up the barranca to the shade of the jacaranda tree and the silky waters of the pool.

Nacho watched her go. His heart pounded with longing.

La Esmeralda. Her eyes were as deep and soft as the evening sky. She was as skinny as a boy, as his mother Lupe the cook, just like Maria-Jesus the taco-seller, was fond of complaining as she piled Emerald's plate with yellow corn-muffins and dollar-pancakes with maple syrup. Skinny, skinny, skinny, Lupe moaned, and nothing I can do, madre mia, to fill the child out. Where will she find a man who wants a sack of bones?

But Nacho knew that Emerald was perfect. Even if she *did* kiss frogs. He leaned over to watch the tiny black-velvet tree-frog creep out from under the prickly pear to warm its cold reptilian blood in the early-morning sun. It was readying itself for the day's fruit-fly hunting.

174

Soft and vulnerable though the frog looked, it, too, was a predator. It was a lesson Emerald would have to learn. There were bad people in the world. Even in Emerald's world. He would tell her, he would explain it once again as he showed her how to use a skinning-knife, how to fight for herself, how never to show fear, that only the strong survive. The rest have no importance.

La Esmeralda was deeply important – to Nacho, of course, the most important person in the world.

Nacho touched his lips. Emerald had just kissed him.

Emerald was, quite simply, magic. But it was no good thinking a kiss would turn a frog into a prince. Not even Nacho.

You had to be more practical than that.

Nacho thought for a while.

He would take the cockerel to the kitchen and give it to his mother so that Emerald could have it for her supper. That would be a proper burial for a hero, a kind of completion of the sacrifice it had made – although he doubted she would understand that.

Nacho considered again. He might be wrong. Emerald liked chicken spiced with green chillies and coriander and baked in banana leaves, just the way his mother made it. She learned quickly.

Perhaps, after all, she *would* know what he meant.

175

26

Glasgow: 1950

The streets of Glasgow were paved with gold.

Or so, three years ago, Jack Sweeney had been led to believe when he left the island of Eas Forse at the suggestion of his old hero, Peter Mackay, a newly apprenticed docker in Glasgow's port.

The quays, Pete said, were a goldmine for those who knew how to look after themselves. There were three of them now, the lads from Eas Forse, and they had taken lodgings above a chandler's. Jack was welcome to join them.

Jack leaped at the chance – even though he had plans which would take him far beyond the Clydeside docks. And at sixteen he did not have to ask permission from anyone.

He intended to come back to the island, if he ever came back, with more money in his hand than the islanders had ever dreamed of – and fame, too. He would be rich and famous, and then his aunt would be sorry for all she had not done for him. Sorry for the years of neglect when she had abandoned her own nephew to care for young Callum Stuart Fergusson.

If she noticed her nephew at all, it was only to make unfavourable comparisons with the boy who had stolen his place. Or to rap Jack over the knuckles with her steel ruler when she caught him skiving over his books and writing up his endless stories instead.

'First, you must have the foundations of knowledge,' she said. 'Then you can use what you know.'

Sometimes, in his dreams, it was he, Jack Sweeney, who was the rightful laird of the Further Isles. In his dreams he walked out onto the battlements of Forsa House to survey all that he owned. By his side, gazing at him adoringly, was a glorious woman. The woman had the heart-shaped face, the violet eyes, the wild russet hair of the child who once lived in the crofthouse below the castle.

Jack, at nearly sixteen years old, was already full-grown, with powerful shoulders and ready fists. He had lately assumed leadership of Salen's ratpack – depleted as its older stars, Willy McCrone and Andy Cameron and Peter Mackay, reached eighteen in turn and got their call-up papers. The war was over too soon for Jack to join them.

The leadership of the pack was no consolation, considering that, in Jack's view, all the good 'uns, or bad 'uns, if you took that attitude, had no intention of demobbing back to the island.

'I'm away south, our Marie,' he had said to the publican's daughter, now a forward young woman of seventeen, as bored as he by the lack of entertainment and opportunities on the island.

After the others had gone, he had inherited certain rights, as much by default as because he was chief of the new crop of ne'er-do-wells who hung round the harbour pub of an evening.

Marie was one of those rights. 'Ye'll take me with ye, Jack?' she asked on his last night on the island, after she had allowed him to feel her breasts and put his hand between her legs. Jack liked the feel of her, and the way the nipples rose under his hand when he pinched them. Marie had squealed when he did that. So he did it again. He liked the sound of her squeal. But he did not like the price of her favours. On an island like Eas Forse, such intimacy was as good as a promise of marriage. And Jack Sweeney had no intention of falling into a trap which would keep him imprisoned on the island.

Jack squinted at Marie and shook his head. 'No,' he said carefully. 'I don't think ye'll be coming with me, Marie.'

Marie drew back, pulled down her skirt and buttoned her blouse, her face suddenly clouded with anger. Then she slapped him hard. Twice. After that she ran back into the protection of her father's den at the back of the pub.

Jack shrugged. She would not be telling her father, or the publican would take a strap to her for being the trollop she was. It was no loss. There were girls in Glasgow who did things that Marie would never even dream of.

*   *   *

The first lesson Jack learned down the Clydeside had nothing to do with girls.

Jack hadn't wanted to meet his old mates with his pockets empty. He wanted at least to have the price of a round.

It had been a long time, and Jack knew he would have to prove his worth. The others had been the lucky ones. They'd experienced life. Been to war, seen men killed – maybe even killed a man themselves.

You didn't let hard men like that buy a drink for you; you bought a round for them.

Jack had picked his target carefully out of the rough tattooed crowd of dockers and sailors in the Cottar's Revenge, one of the many pubs – half drinking-den, half pick-up parlour – which punctuated the gap-toothed line of boarding-houses fronting the Glasgow docks.

Jack had a knife.

He hadn't thought the man might have a weapon of his own, let alone a wickedly curved skinning blade of the kind fishermen used on the slippery silver herrings – slitting their bellies and tossing the scarlet guts to the screaming gulls, just like Jack knew the man would do to him now if he moved a muscle.

Jack Sweeney had misjudged; he'd misjudged badly.

'Ya wee scarrit bugger!' the man hissed.

Jack could smell the stench of fish mingled with whisky on the man's breath, half-choking as he was in the grip of an iron fist. The man's other hand held the knife to Jack's throat.

Jack had jumped the sailor from behind after he came out of the pub door, belching and rolling from the liquor. The man had been drinking pints of bitter with whisky chasers, round after round, paying with five-pound notes peeled off a thick wad.

Just as Jack knew he would, the man turned down the dark alleyway which served the pub's customers as a makeshift urinal. He waited until the man had unbuttoned himself. Then he jumped him.

Jack never knew what happened next.

How, one moment, armed with the short rubber-handled flick-knife he used to terrorize the young boys on Eas Forse, he was launching himself on an apparently defenceless victim. And, the next, how the knife was sent spinning from his hand, and the man had whirled him round and was holding him in a brutal half-nelson with his own knife levelled at Jack's throat.

Jack could feel the point of the blade against his skin, as sharp as a hornet's sting.

178

Christ, the man was going to kill him.

The smell of urine and fish mingled with another richer stench. 'Ya daft loon!' The man's voice was disgusted. 'Ye shat yerself.'

The man hurled him away with a brutal street-wrestler's throw. Jack cannoned off the soot-dark wall, dislodging a dustbin lid with a deafening crash.

The noise funnelled down the alley. A cat howled – a high-pitched scream like a child in pain.

In the corner by the open dustbin, Jack coughed and moaned. He could smell the rank rich stink from his bowels, and he wondered dizzily how many of his bones had been broken.

Silence fell. No-one came to help him. Why should they? The incident was nothing out of the ordinary, just another spark of the savage violence which flared every moment of the day or night in Glasgow's thin dark streets.

Jack lay where he'd been thrown.

He watched the man, his victim-turned-aggressor, calmly finish urinating. The man zipped up his fly and tossed the knife in his hand. He wiped the blade on the seam of his trousers and slipped it into a well-worn leather sheath at his belt. Then he spat on his hands and smoothed back the wiry grey hair which had become ruffled in the fight.

Almost as an afterthought, he walked over to the wall where Jack was lying. Casually, without any apparent malice, he kicked Jack hard in the small of the back. Jack felt tears welling in his eyes as the pain coursed through him.

'Let it be a lesson to ye. Dinna jump yer elders and betters,' the man said.

He spat in the gutter inches from Jack's cheek, a great globule of nicotine-coloured phlegm, and kicked him again. Then he walked away.

Jack lay on the ground, listening to the man's retreating footsteps and watching the trail of spittle spreading slowly across the stones.

Somewhere a woman screamed. Silence fell again.

Footsteps approached. Jack hunched himself round his aching body. Perhaps the sailor had come back to finish the business. The footsteps slowed, and then halted close beside him.

After a few moments, Jack ventured to look up.

The sailor had not returned. Instead a middle-aged man in a threadbare tweed jacket, a chewed cheroot sticking out of one side of his mouth, was leaning against the wall looking down at him.

'Ye learned yer lesson the hard way, then, laddie?' The man's voice was hard, laconic. 'Just arrived in the big city, eh? Saw you in the pub. Knew ye had a lesson coming to ye. No bones broken?'

Jack scowled up at the man. Then he shook his head.

The man went on cheerfully. 'Come on then. On yer feet. We'll get ye down to the Sally for a wash and brush up.'

Jack pulled what was left of his clothes and his dignity round himself and stood up.

'The Sally?' Jack had never heard of the Salvation Army. On Eas Forse, there was always a bothy for anyone who needed shelter, and every housewife on the island would part with a cup of tea and a piece for a stranger.

'That's better, my young turkey-cock,' the man said. 'I like to see a man back on his feet. D'ye no ken the hostel? Ye have pleasures in store. The bedbugs are no respecters of prayer, but it'll be a bed and a wash for the love of God and the price of Hallelujah. I'll take ye down there. And on the way we can mebbe have a chat.'

'Chat?' Jack's voice was suspicious. He'd heard stories about such chats.

'It's no yer wee body I'm after, if that's what yer thinking.' The man pulled the cheroot out and examined it. 'I wouldna fancy ye even ye if didn't smell like a shite-house on a Saturday night.' Then he grinned. 'The name's McGlashan. But my acquaintance call me Scottie. I'll no shake hands; we'll save that pleasure for when ye've cleaned yerself up.'

Jack fell in behind the man as he turned and began to walk down the alley towards the lighted quay.

Jack said, 'I'm no parting with anything, ye understand. I have friends.'

Scottie's face split into a grin. 'I can see we'll get along fine, laddie. In the line of business I'm in, I'm thinking ye can mebbe help me. Give me a wee bit of an insight into where ye come from and how ye come here. What's yer name, to begin?'

'Sweeney. Jacob Sweeney.' Jack narrowed his eyes and peered at the man. 'I'm no saying onything more.'

'Ye will, my lad. Ye will.' The man gestured at the rubbish-strewn alley. 'I've a story to write, and you, ma braw wee laddie, are just the ticket. I'm a journalist – ye ken what the word means?'

'A journalist? Ye're a proper journalist?'

Scottie laughed. 'Ye could call me that if ye've a mind to it. Improper, more like.'

Jack gazed at the man in awe. To Jack Sweeney, a journalist was the most glamorous thing anyone could possibly be. He'd seen the green-shaded heroes of the printing-room in the movies on the flickering screen in the Salen ceilidh-tein when the man with the projector came over from the mainland.

He never had the price of a ticket, of course, but there was a crack in the sheiling wall. But what he had seen was all fast cars and faster women. Nothing like this seedy middle-aged man in a threadbare jacket. The only thing right about the man was the cheroot.

The man grinned. 'I know what yer thinking, my lad. Yer thinking: What has a wee green scarrit bugger like meself to interest this very important person?'

'Ay,' said Jack carefully. 'Sommat like.'

Scottie sucked his cheroot and looked hard at Jack.

'Since ye ask, I'll tell ye. I'm covering a slot for the paper on gadgies such as yerself – come to Glesga messin' among the keelies, keepin' bad company. Human interest. The editor's awfu' strong on the human interest. "Scottie," he says, "sod the politicians. Get oot on the street and find me some real people." '

Scottie gave a short bark of laughter. 'Don't grow on trees, real people. Real people, people like me and you, Jack, grow in the gutter.'

'What's in it for me?' Jack narrowed his pale blue eyes and stared up at the man with what he hoped was a mere flicker of cautious interest.

Scottie grinned again. There was something about the scrawny sandy-haired youngster, like a puppy who has been kicked too hard and too long, which reminded him of his own beginnings.

'Fame, laddie, fame.' Then he added swiftly, 'And a tenner, just to keep yer head above water.'

He spread his hands to show the headline. ''Jack Sweeney – His Story.' What d'ye say, gadgie? We'll have a man out for the photies. It'll make ye the talk o' the toon.'

Jack laughed aloud.

The gutter. Real people grow in the gutter.

That's what the man had said.

To Scottie McGlashan, Jack Sweeney was a real person. A person with a future. Even a person with a past. Jack could see it now. It all made sense.

At that moment, for the first time in his life, Jack knew he had come home.

'And if yer a good wee scarrit bugger, and promise not to shite yerself again with a' the excitement, there might even be a wee bit o' scurrying around ye can do at the paper. Mebbe get ye out of the gutter for good an a'.'

That was how Jack had got his start.

*　　*　　*

Two and half years later, as he sat on his luggage in the third-class carriage listening to the train wheels rattling over the sleepers, he could hear the drumbeat of success. He was on his way to the big time.

Jack had come a long way since that seminal moment in the gutter. The job on the Glasgow *Clarion* had been an apprenticeship, a reward for his contribution to what the paper had seen as a major coup: the exposure of a gang of thieves whose activities had been terrorizing every honest, and dishonest, citizen who made his way down the Clydeside. For a few months the waterfront had been the fiefdom of what the police described as a gang of old-fashioned footpads. No more nor less than highwaymen.

That first break, his involvement in the paper's coup, had been a baptism of fire, a salutary lesson in elementary sleuthing which had stood him in good stead in his career.

After he'd cleaned himself up at the Salvation Army hostel, Jack had, on Scottie McGlashan's instruction, returned to the streets. It had been a piece of blessed good fortune for Jack, although rather less so for Willy McCrone, that the leader of the footpads happened to be his old friend, the very man Jack had been on his way to join when he had been waylaid in the alleyway.

Jack hung out with the old gang, picking up where he had left off, until he knew the business inside out. And then he had turned King's evidence. The judge congratulated him on his courage. The *Clarion* offered him an apprenticeship, and Jack was on his way.

His former mates, all first-offenders, were given three years in Barlinnie gaol. With remission for good behaviour, this was reduced to two.

Just before Willy McCrone was due for release, Jack thought it prudent to move south before anyone came looking for him on a dark night.

One good turn deserves another, and Scottie managed to secure Jack a job with an old acquaintance in Fleet Street as a junior reporter on the *Daily News*. There were plenty who hailed from north of the Border in Fleet Street. The joke was that there were more Glesga patter-merchants holding up the bar in El Vino's than rats ever came out of the Clyde Tunnel.

Jack grinned to himself as he rattled south on the overnight Pullman. 'Hold the front page. Jack Sweeney's on his way.'

27

————◆◎●◎◆————

Mexico: 1951

In the jungles of Mexico, the tigre was the fiercest hunter of all. Nacho had been stalking the spotted cat for a week. He had fetched Emerald for the expedition that morning, shinning up to her balcony at dawn to wake her before the household was up and about. Anyway, Doña Molly was away on her annual trip to the city, and Emerald's nana had other matters to occupy her time these days. The women of the neighbourhood had discovered she had skills with the herbs which grew in the old monastery gardens – now long abandoned, but still thicketed with the monks' imported pharmacopoeia.

With the school on holiday, Emerald was left more or less to her own devices.

It was the first time Nacho had taken her to hunt the tigre. He had already shown her how to set traps for the fat scarlet-mouthed iguanas which fetched nearly as much money as chicken in the market. And how to tell which of the succulent mushrooms that grew on the fallen tree-trunks tasted as good as meat.

Nacho called the animal a 'tiger'. But her Aunt Molly had shown Emerald a picture of it in the encyclopedia, and Emerald knew by the rosette markings and pale pelt it was the jaguar, the smallest and most savage of the great cats, and the only one of its kind native to the Americas.

When it was a matter of books, Emerald knew everything. In matters of the hunt, Nacho had the last word. A tiger was what they were hunting.

The two young people hitched a lift on the roof of the rickety old bus which made its way slowly through the shanty-sprawls which edged the town. They paid half-price on the bus because they travelled on the top, with the bundles of clothes and the chickens in wire coops.

'It's half a day's journey on foot, and we must be back before sun-down,' Nacho explained. 'La Mama said so. And it's always me who gets beaten.'

Emerald had wrinkled her nose, but she had obeyed. She knew Nacho was right. She could not walk as fast as Nacho. Even though they were the same age – just fifteen – and her legs were longer and she could always sprint ahead of him over a short distance, long distances were Nacho's strength. He could keep up his peculiar half-walking, half-running gait all day without tiring.

Just the same, it was a matter of pride to protest at not making all the journey on foot. It was like the hare and the tortoise, Emerald told Nacho, and explained the story she had read in a book of French fables.

When they reached the banks of the river, Nacho, stripped to the waist, his feet bare, blue-black hair long against his neck and coppery skin rippling over the bunched muscles of his back, slipped down behind the tangle of ferns which marked the edge of the water.

'Tigre!'

Nacho's voice was an urgent whisper.

'Where?'

Emerald peered through the undergrowth, her heart thumping. She was scared. Even with Nacho there.

'In the cave – see, up there—'

Nacho moved to her side. Emerald's skin prickled with excitement.

'On the other side of the water. Beyond the big tree—'

Emerald squinted through the branches, moving her head to follow Nacho's line of sight.

'Too slow, nena. But she's there. I know and *she* knows. It will be a long wait.'

Emerald watched Nacho slip back down the bank, and rolled over to look at the sky.

She loved the way the sun shone through the green canopy of leaves to make patterns on the bare earth, the soft rustle of the jungle creatures, the feel of the damp loam beneath her naked feet, the woody scents of the undergrowth.

Emerald liked Nacho's scent, too. It was a sort of warm spicy smell, like pepper sprinkled on the skins of limes which have been warming in the sun. She liked his blue-black hair, straight and soft like a cat's pelt, and the way the muscles moved under the conker-brown skin. She liked the way he was good at things. Physical things.

'Nacho,' she whispered. '*Mi amigo*, Nacho.'

She lay back, listening to soft murmurings of the the river. The sun was warm on her own golden skin. She had freckles. Nacho thought her freckles were funny, like sunshine through leaves, he said.

She felt safe with Nacho in the forest. Safe and loved. Often these days she felt neither. Doña Molly, delicate and beautiful and careless, had never made anyone feel safe. And she had lately felt Margaret Mackenzie drawing back, letting her spread her wings.

Emerald was growing up. The changeling child was no longer a child. It was hard sometimes. Emerald thought sometimes that no-one loved her. No-one but Nacho, of course. And Nacho, her Aunt Molly had as good as told her, didn't count. He was only the cook's son, she said. Just as it didn't matter if the servants, the Indios, heard what you said, saw you in your underwear, even naked, you could assume they saw and felt nothing.

Emerald knew her guardian was wrong. Emerald knew Aunt Molly was wrong, too, about Nacho's feelings. She knew Nacho felt many things. And particularly one thing.

Emerald knew Nacho loved her, just as she knew the sun would rise over the flat ochre plain in the morning and set over the high blue mountains at night. She had read his feelings in the way he watched her when he thought she wasn't looking. In the way he had always jumped to her protection when, playing with the other children in the street, he thought the games were too rough. She had read it in the way he wanted her to be with him at important moments, like at Xuma's fight.

Emerald trusted Nacho completely. She told him whatever came into her head. Just as she had talked to Callum about everything in that time – the long-ago time – on Eas Forse. Callum, blood-brother Callum.

But it was the curandera who had explained to her about women's bodies. She had explained about the monthly bleeding, when Emerald had gone to her in a panic. Told her how it meant that her body was getting ready to make babies. And then she knew she had puberty – just like Jack Sweeney had had it.

She went to look for Nacho.

'Nacho, *how* do people make babies?'

It was a question she did not dare ask anyone else. Nana would have told some fairy-story. Doña Molly would have been disapproving.

185

'Nenita, didn't anyone teach you anything?' Nacho laughed, as he usually did when Emerald asked him about things which everyone else, it seemed, already knew since they were small. 'Come with me. I'll show you how it happens.'

Nacho had taken her down the barranca and made her put her eye to a gap in the cardboard wall of the shanty-hut, so she could see Nacho's cousin Conchita with Ito, making babies. It was very dark, and Emerald had not been able to see much. But whatever it was, it was quite noisy and not at all neat and quick, like the cockerels who mounted the hens in the yard. Sometimes Emerald felt all her book-reading taught her nothing important at all.

A few months later, the curandera had fetched her to watch Conchita's baby being born. Emerald had stayed until it was nearly over, and then she had been shooed out, along with the sow with her little piglets who lived in the box by the bed, and Ito's little sister who was only five and just like Emerald had never seen a baby being born.

After that, Emerald was not sure she ever wanted to make a baby. It all seemed very complicated at the beginning and terribly painful at the end. Perhaps it had been *that* which made her real mother give her away. Perhaps for the gringos like her it was even more complicated and the pain was really bad.

Doña Molly said it had all been a terrible *bore*. But Emerald wondered if her Aunt Molly had really done all those kind of things. All the underpinnings and laces and whalebone must have got terribly in the way.

Both Aunt Molly and her nana were quite firm on one matter. You had to wait for the right man to come along before it could happen. Until then you were a virgin.

Emerald was a virgin.

Lady Molly had told her it was an important thing to be. Even Nacho seemed a bit hazy as to what exactly being a virgin meant.

She knew it was important to be in love when you made babies.

Lady Molly said so.

'What's "in love", Aunt Molly?' Emerald asked.

She had wanted to ask if 'in love' was what Ito and Conchita had been doing. But something told her Doña Molly would not approve. Certainly *not*.

'All in good time, child,' her Aunt Molly had said, and her eyes had taken on that faraway look. 'When you fall in love, you will know.'

All her nan said was, 'Wait till Mr Right comes along.' And then she told her a long rambling tale of snowstorms and a handsome young man.

186

Emerald listened patiently, trying to understand. She could remember snow when she was very little on Eas Forse, but she knew nothing about war, except that they had to keep the curtains shut so Mr Hitler couldn't find them.

So Emerald looked in the library. There had to be books to tell you about things you needed to know. She devoured all the romantic novels she could find. None of them told her what she needed to know.

Once again she had to ask Nacho.

'What's "in love" Nacho?'

Nacho just looked at her oddly through his slanting eyes. Then he shrugged.

' "In love" is for gringos, Esmeralda.'

'What about Conchita and Ito?'

Nacho shrugged again, but this time he grinned. 'They make babies, nena.'

Emerald nodded. That made sense. She had been worried for a moment that 'making babies' and 'in love' were the same thing.

She rubbed her cheek thoughtfully. Then she said slowly, 'Ito made the baby, but Conchita had to grow it. And it hurt terribly when she pushed it out. I don't think I want to make babies.'

Nacho laughed then.

'You want to be a boy, nena?' he said.

And then he laughed again. But he wasn't really laughing at all.

After that, Emerald stopped asking anyone about love. She wore boy's clothing and cut her hair short.

Today Emerald felt absolutely perfectly happy.

She threw herself down on one of the large slabs of moss-covered stone which lay half-buried where the forest reached down to the water.

Nacho turned to look at his treasure, his Emerald. She was becoming more beautiful every day. She was willowy and strong-limbed, even though with her hair cut short as it was, and wearing a boy's rough cotton shorts and loose faded blue top, she could still almost be mistaken for a boy, there was no way to hide the new curves the last year had bestowed on her.

Nacho moved snake-like up the bank until he lay beside her.

'We will have good hunting, Esmeralda. The gods are with us.'

'How d'you know, Nacho?'

Emerald was curious. Nacho's gods were quite different from Doña Molly's stern saints, or even Margaret Mackenzie's fairies.

187

Nacho's gods were strange animal-people, with snake-heads and bird-bodies and claws instead of fingers. They were the sort of gods you might expect to come across suddenly, when you least expected it, perched up a tree or hiding under a rock.

Nacho grinned, a flash of ivory teeth in the dark skin.

'I'll show you.' With his skinning knife he began to scratch a patch of thick green moss off one of the stones.

Emerald looked over his shoulder.

Soon the sign-writing underneath began to emerge, confident gougings in the hard lichen-spattered granite. Nacho had shown her how to read the vigorous hieroglyphs, the stories of hunting and conquest and sacrifice which were his heritage.

'See here the warrior, here the hunter,' Nacho whispered.

Emerald nodded. With her finger she traced the outlines of the warrior figures. Otomi and Olmec, Toltec and Maya – the conquerors adopted the gods of the conquered: with so many earthly enemies, there was no sense in incurring the wrath of heaven as well. So there were many of the old stellae buried in the deep vegetation of the jungle, a random scattering of ancient battalions, a resurrection waiting for the trumpets. Nacho seemed to be able to find them as easily as a water-diviner can find the well-spring.

Emerald turned to look at Nacho. He was studying the lines with a fierce intensity.

Then he looked up at Emerald. 'I am a warrior,' he said. 'One day I shall reclaim the land of my ancestors.'

Emerald smiled. She liked it when Nacho talked like that.

Anxious for confirmation from a reliable source, she said. 'Did the curandera read it in the bones?'

Nacho nodded. 'On the Day of the Dead, she told me.'

Emerald nodded thoughtfully. Then she said, 'The curandera says *I* shall be a great warrior in my own land.'

'But you're a girl—' Nacho sounded cross.

Emerald said firmly, 'The curandera says that doesn't matter. I shall be a different kind of warrior. Anyway, I can use a knife just as well as you. You told me so yourself.'

Nacho scowled. A shadow had fallen over the brightness of the day, the shadow of loss.

In my own land.

Some day, some day soon perhaps, Emerald would be gone. To lose her would be as terrible a fate as that suffered by the human sacrifices his ancestors had made to propitiate their fierce god.

Nacho crouched back on his haunches. He said: 'You will see. I shall be a greater warrior than anyone has ever been. They will draw my picture on stones, bigger pictures than have ever been drawn before.'

His fist closed over his precious catapult, his weapon of war – a beautifully polished forked root of tamarisk, sinuous as a muscled wrist.

The catapult was no child's toy. In the hands of the smooth-skinned Indio, the weapon was as deadly as a gun. With it Emerald had seen him kill a six-foot snake at forty paces – and she had no doubt that it could, as he boasted, kill a man.

Nacho sighed. His muscles loosened.

Then he slipped back down the bank and settled down to wait, his gaze fixed on some movement still invisible to Emerald. After a few moments he reached into the little embroidered pouch which hung from the same silver-studded belt, and pulled out one of the smooth obsidian pebbles he used as ammunition.

On the far bank the forest reached right down to the sluggish river, the trees dense and thick and hung with vines. Through the upper branches swagged with grey loops of Spanish moss could be glimpsed the green landscape of the upper canopy, pierced with the occasional shaft of sunlight.

A flock of white parrots flashed albino wings in the cathedral-high darkness, slicing the air with their harsh cries.

Nacho whispered: 'Fine eating, nenita. The tigre eats parrot, too. Be patient.'

'I'm always patient, Nacho.'

'Here, nenita,' Nacho whispered.

He stretched out his hand towards her. Along the palm lay the slender-bladed skinning knife he always wore on his silver-studded belt, his most precious possession.

Nacho had taught Emerald how to use the knife like a street fighter, making her strop it on the dampened leather strap until the edge was razor-sharp, showing her how to hold it low in a short grip and use a quick upward thrust to the belly, a sharp downward thrust behind the neck, teaching her not to hesitate or flinch as it entered the target – a straw-stuffed bolster he fixed to an overhanging branch.

'Patience,' he whispered again.

Emerald took the knife and slipped it into the soft dry moss by her hand. Then she lay back in the long grass and stared up into the forest canopy.

The flock of white parrots, clattering and preening, were moving cautiously, branch by laden branch, down towards the water for their evening bath.

Meanwhile the jungle, accepting the incursion of the human intruders, settled back to attend to the essential business of filling its belly. A covey of small brown birds squabbled as they cropped the berries and leaf-shoots high in the tree canopy. A silvery sloth moved hand over hand along a vertical branch, like an ancient acrobat unable to resist a final turn of the ring. A water snake slipped down the river bank and into the shallows, scattering a school of tiny fish.

Nacho relaxed, every muscle dormant. Time passed.

A blue-green lizard darted down the bank to lie motionless a yard beyond Emerald's bare toes. The polished surface of the rock on which the reptile basked shimmered with reflections from the river, the creature almost invisible in the pattern.

Emerald propped herself on her hand. She loved to watch Nacho when he was hunting. He became almost a feline predator himself, lying in wait, coiled immobile and tranquil, until the moment came. She had learned to recognize the moment itself by the tensing of the muscles, the sudden sharpening of focus when the pupils of the eyes contracted to pin-pricks. Like hunter, liked hunted.

The flock of parrots moved slowly further down towards the water.

Not yet.

Emerald dozed, the knife by her hand. In her day-dream the lapping water of the river became the slap of the wavelets on the beach of Eas Forse. Another young man, his hair blond from the wind and the weather and his eyes like a tiger's eyes, kept her company on another river bank.

'¡Allí! There.' Nacho's whisper cut through her day-dream.

Emerald opened her eyes. Nacho was pointing urgently into the tangle of creepers round the great grey trunks on the opposite bank of the broad slow stream.

Emerald narrowed her eyes to focus. She could see no movement at all. Not even the flicker of a bird's wing.

'Allí – ¡tigre!' Nacho's voice was a sibilant hiss. 'See? Look for the tips of the ears.'

Then she had it. A twitch of the dark ear-tufts suddenly brought the whole body into focus. Stretched full-length along a splinter of bleached tree-trunk overhanging the river lay a graceful, slender, feline form, creamy fur camouflaged to near-invisibility by delicate rose-markings random as sunshine and shadow. The tail, ringed with a ripple of dark bars, braced the animal for its inevitable strike.

190

Emerald drew in her breath. The jaguar was the most magnificent creature she had ever seen.

A twig snapped, a pistol-shot in the silence.

The dark pupils in the slitted topaz eyes expanded suddenly and the ear-tufts went up again.

Emerald froze. This was the moment when all might be lost.

But the tigre was hunting. Mistress of the jungle, she knew there was no rival who could harm her. Once and once only she had fought over prey, competing with a cocodrilo – one of the fierce little alligators – for a plump water-rat which had been a fraction slow in returning to its burrow in the river bank. The tigre still bore the scars of that encounter. She had learned to leave the waters to those better equipped to hunt them.

The flock of white parrots had come down to drink. The tigre, crouching low on her haunches, head lowered between powerful shoulders, was hungry.

Emerald held her breath.

One of the birds, bolder than the rest, had hopped onto the very tip of the branch along which the great cat lay. The bird, oblivious to danger, preened itself with the silver droplets. The other birds, emboldened, came down to join their fellow.

The jaguar was ready. Only the emergence of the wickedly curved talons betrayed her decision. With a flick of the dark tip of tail, the great cat launched herself into the white flurry of screaming birds.

At that moment Nacho stood up and unleashed a pebble from his catapult. Emerald heard the sharp crack as the deadly little missile hit its mark, full between the eyes on the satin-patterned skull.

The jaguar, its body wire-tense as its talons reached for the prey, spun round in mid-air, teeth bared in a snarl of surprise, and tumbled forwards into the shallows of the river.

Nacho hurled himself down the bank and across the slow-moving stream towards the flailing body. But the jaguar was merely stunned, her senses half-restored by the shock of the water. The great cat jack-knifed round and clawed her way upwards, frantically trying to escape the fearful water.

Emerald was on her feet now, the knife in her hand.

A quick flurry of movement at the edge of the river had told her that Nacho was not the only predator with an interest in the birds.

The cocodrilo was fully five foot long from nose to tail. He made scarcely a splash as he slid down the bank and into the water.

In the few seconds after she had seen the creature, Emerald had been literally paralysed with fear.

The parrots screamed, scattering like a flock of white-flounced debutantes.

At last Emerald found her voice. 'Nacho – behind you!'

And then she leaped down the bank, the knife held low in her hand. She plunged into the water, cutting through the sluggish stream with her powerful crawl, her eyes fixed on the flat dark head with the protruding eyes.

The alligator moved steadily and swiftly against the current towards the double prey.

Nacho had swung back again to face the wounded cat, the catapult braced on his arm. Swiftly, calmly, he loaded it and let fly. Once again the great cat jack-knifed in mid-air.

At the same moment Emerald's feet found a submerged rock. She braced herself and stood up. The alligator was still moving upstream, all five senses fixed firmly on the carrion which must result from the battle between the boy and the dappled cat. Swiftly and surely, Emerald brought the knife down behind the creature's wicked flat head, severing the spinal column with one swift thrust of the blade.

Beyond her Nacho had swung away from the now-sprawled body of the big cat, and started towards her.

The anguish on his face, sheet-white under the dark skin, told Emerald what she already knew. Nacho would gladly have died for her. Instead she had risked death for him.

Emerald held up the knife and laughed in triumph.

'See, mi niño,' she called. 'Show me the boy who could do as well!'

Nacho grunted and grinned, the relief visible in the white flash of teeth.

The alligator's body, the tail thrashing against the current, had drifted level with him. He stooped down, pulled out the knife, and heaved the creature up onto the bank.

Then he tugged the limp body of the spotted cat up the steep escarpment to the soft grass where Emerald had lain day-dreaming only minutes before.

Emerald followed, barefooted, picking her way carefully over the rocks.

The thickets were silent as the creatures of the river bank watched and waited for the danger to pass.

Nacho said gruffly: 'You did well, nena. Give me the knife.'

He settled down on his haunches, Indian-style, and set to work, quickly and deftly, to skin first the alligator, then the dappled cat, taking care to slit the pelt so skilfully the soft fur was not marked. His long slender

192

fingers worked delicately and surely, cutting skin from the lithe sinew and muscle.

Emerald lay back lazily and watched the canopy overhead. Finally Nacho stood up.

He said, 'Good hunting, nena. The cocodrilo skin is yours. The tigre is mine. She has not yet shed her winter coat. It will be worth at least five, maybe even six pesos.'

'What will you do with the money, Nacho?'

'You'll see.'

Nacho grinned.

Then he set off back through the shining arcades of the shadowy forest at his usual silent barefooted lope. Behind him trotted Emerald. Under her arm was the rolled alligator skin neatly tied with a length of strong creeper.

The sun was casting long shadows across the wide plain when they at last began the descent towards the road to hitch a lift on the returning bus.

Darkness had fallen by the time Nacho left Emerald at the entrance to the Yellow House.

With Doña Molly away on her annual visit to the capital, there was no-one to mark Emerald's comings and goings. Only her nan and Lupe to cluck and fuss.

But this evening Lupe was not in the kitchen, and not even her nan came out to scold her.

28

Mexico: 1951

The Yellow House was deserted when Emerald returned with the cocodrilo skin. This was just as well, as Emerald knew full well that neither her nana nor Lupe the cook would have approved.

It was a holiday tomorrow, the feast of the Virgin of Guadalupe, so perhaps Lupe was out visiting her sister.

With everyone out of the way, Emerald thought she might pay a visit to Lily.

Miss Lily Lovage was Doña Molly's only near neighbour in the valley, and she was Emerald's friend. Perhaps because she had no children of her own, the old lady and the child saw each other as equals, and enjoyed each other's company.

Lily had been a famous beauty, a mannequin, much sought after in Paris society, she told Emerald – a very long time ago it must have been, because Lily was very old now. About a hundred, Emerald thought. Much older than Margaret Mackenzie, much older even than her Aunt Molly.

Sometimes her Aunt Molly would take Emerald with her when Lily had company. Lily's company was plump and pink and smelled of gin – not nearly as interesting as the company Emerald chose for herself, such as Nacho or the curandera down the barranca.

Lily called these occasions her salon.

But Emerald liked it best when, like this evening, she visited Lily on her own.

If it was raining, as it did in summertime in great torrents of water, she would be allowed to play in the walk-in cupboards which lined Lily's dressing-room.

It was like a fairy cavern in those cupboards, with Lily's spangled and embroidered dresses, all covered with silk overpinnies, hanging in long lines and smelling faintly of mothballs. Emerald had never imagined anyone could possibly have so many clothes.

Beneath them were the shoe racks, rows and rows. And on the shelf above, there were round boxes for hats and square boxes for handbags and long thin boxes for gloves. The old woman kept a special box of make-up for her, too. Her nan and Lady Molly would never have allowed Emerald to experiment with lipsticks and false eyelashes, like all the town girls did.

Now she was neary fifteen, Emerald would visit Lily, on her own, without telling anyone – not even her nan. Not even Nacho, who knew everything she did. Then she would spend all afternoon with Lily, messing about in the cupboards.

'I'd never tell a soul but you, child, but I was born all of eighty years ago – 1871 it was. Imagine that, my dear? There were six of us girls, two to a bed in the tied-cottage on the estate where Father was the gamekeeper. We had rabbit pie for dinner every day.'

'Tell me about the Quality, Miss Lily.'

Emerald loved to hear Lily's stories of the 'Quality'. These days she liked them better than Margaret Mackenzie's tales of the Little Folk.

'Come and sit by me, child,' Lily would say, and then she would begin. 'Well. I was only a scrap of a girl, just about as old as you, when I went into service at the Hall—'

Emerald settled down with a sigh of pleasure.

Lily had been lucky – if, as she said, you took the long view – in that her neat fingers and pretty face had earned her admission to the privileges of the life below stairs in a Victorian household.

There she had learned to mend the linen, darn the hose, and embroider and trim the beautiful dresses. All was well for a couple of years, until her figure as well as her face had caught the eye of one of the young gentlemen who came courting the daughter of the house. His advances being declined by the young mistress, he had turned his thoughts to the servant-girl who had darned his shirt-sleeve when he tore it on a rose-thorn.

More fool the young mistress, Lily had thought. *He* was a handsome fellow all right, in his fine silks and linens and polished boots. The lure of him had been irresistible. The dalliance had led to the inevitable.

'What's "the inevitable", Miss Lily?' Emerald had enquired.

'Lord,' Lily had replied, 'a baby.'

'Ah,' said Emerald.

'I had no complaints, mind you. The young man saw me right.'

Seeing Lily right meant he had paid for her lodgings in the town, and arranged that the Irish nuns who had seen to her accouchement sent the baby to a good home.

'Boy or girl, Miss Lily?'

'The nuns don't tell you that, my dear.'

Lily's voice was a little sad.

'Oh,' said Emerald. The story gave her a funny feeling. Sometimes she imagined Lily's little baby might have been her.

'And then?'

Lily smiled. After what she called 'the inevitable', Lily had gone to London to seek employment as a milliner.

The fashion business had been very different in those days, said Lily, when she had first gone down to London to earn her living.

'It was all fine things. All frills and furbelows. No lady of quality would leave her house – even to put out the cat – without a *hat*.'

Lily's neat fingers soon earned her promotion to a fashionable dress-maker's workroom, cutting out the plain muslin *toiles* to the patterns of the itinerant designers who took their drawings door-to-door.

'Then, my dear, the designs were not important at all. It was not the shape of the clothes, but the fine trimmings, the braids and lace, the buttons and bows, which made the height of fashion. There were no *couturiers* then. But everyone wanted their dresses to come from Paris just the same.'

So, by the time she was twenty, she had worked her way across the Channel and was established in the capital of dressmaking, where her pretty face earned her a new career, this time as a mannequin in the house of the great Doucet, featuring in her first season in a hobble skirt and Byzantine breastplate in the fashion magazine *La Gazette du Bon Ton*.

From then on Lily was the toast of Paris, until, on her fortieth birthday (give or take a year or two), she retired to open her own millinery shop on a corner of the Tuileries. Everyone wanted a Paris hat, and Lily was the name to conjure with. Her fortune was made.

In 1940, warned by one of her famous admirers of Hitler's impending advance on Paris, she packed up her wardrobe in hampers and took passage in the first available merchant ship out of Le Havre. The *Aztec Star* was bound for the banana-port of Vera Cruz on the east coast of

196

Mexico. From there she made her way to the interior, to Oaxaca – where the climate was agreeable and the living cheap.

'And that, my dear, is the end of the story,' Lily finished. 'Here I am, and here I stay.'

Lily's great hampers lined with oilskin, in which were packed the marvellous clothes which came from Lily's days as the toast of Paris, were a treasure-store. There was outerwear and underwear – 'unmentionables', Lily called them – all embroidered and inset with lace. And there were wonderful bodices stiffened with whalebone so they stood up on their own like soldiers standing to attention. They had special hooks and ribbons down the back to lace them up tight.

Each of the hampers had a date on it. Lily would sit up in her bed and make Emerald unpack the one she had chosen.

'Nineteen twelve,' she would say. And Emerald would open the hamper, and take the garments out one by one and lay them on the silk cover of the bed. Lily would stroke the clothes with little soft murmurs as if they were small birds, or even babies, and tell Emerald where and when and in whose company she had worn them all.

And then she would show Emerald how to put the garments on, wasp-waist whaleboned stays, layer on layer of frills, bugle-beaded bibs and stiffened satin skirts. And then Lily would lie back, her head on one side, and clap her hands with pleasure, and tell Emerald wonderful stories of Paris and London and the grand balls she had attended and the fine gentlemen she had known.

She taught Emerald how to pirouette and parade to show off the garments to the best effect.

'Act the clothes, child. You are a great *actress*. Put your heart into it. That's better. You must *believe*.'

She taught her to model a toile, how to move her body so that the sleeves might be cut, a shoulder draped. How to work her fingers into the long kid gloves, how to drape a feather boa, how to whisk a train just so.

For Lily, the child was the mirror to her own lost childhood, perhaps even the child she had lost.

For Emerald it was even more simple. With Lily she was a girl. Every day, with Nacho and everyone else, Emerald was as like a boy as she could possibly manage. Being a boy was safe. Boys could do things which girls couldn't. There were many things Emerald was not allowed to do because she was a girl, including going to watch Nacho's fighting cocks.

But, with Lily, it was all right to be a girl.

Girls, Lily said, were really *girls* in her day. And it was true that the whaleboned bodices and stiff petticoats and heavy beaded overskirts were not like anything Emerald had ever seen. Nothing like Lady Molly's elegant body-skimming tea-gowns. Nothing like her nan's neat white blouses and firmly tailored woollen skirts. Not even like Nacho's girl-cousins' bright flounces.

The hampers were a secret Emerald shared with Lily.

To Emerald's relief there were no guests in residence that day. Emerald found Lily's guests something of a trial since she had grown a few curves.

The old men would remark, 'My, my, we *have* grown.'

Then they would look meaningfully at her chest.

And the young men would look down their noses at her and boast about the parties they had been to in New York and Paris and London. 'Such a party, my dear. Never seen anything like it.'

But that evening, with no visitors to disturb them, Lily and Emerald had been able to play their special game. Lily had closed her eyes and said: 'Nineteen twenty-seven.' The hamper was full of feathered capes and beaded shifts and bathing dresses with little skirts. Lily had put on a jazz record and explained to Emerald how to flip up her heels and dance the way they did in those days.

'Nineteen twenty-two, my darling. We were all flappers and we danced the Charleston till we dropped.'

Emerald wondered if Nacho would like to learn the Charleston. Maybe not. She thought Nacho liked her best as a boy.

It was late when Emerald finally returned to the Yellow House. Lupe came out to scold for her supper being cold. While Emerald ate up her beans with fried eggs and chillies, Lupe explained the nana had retired early. She had not been feeling herself all day. She thought it must the weather. It was so heavy and hot her limbs felt like lead.

There was a marsh-fever which wafted up in the hot damp days of summer from the swamps below the town.

The fever struck at random, entering the bloodstream of its victims from the water, or from the food, or from whatever path it chose. The fever cleared away the old and weak, and the sickly infants, just as the leaves fell from the trees in the autumn.

It was part of the rhythm of the turning seasons. The young and healthy shook it off. Those who were not able to resist, succumbed.

Lupe was worried the old white woman might have caught the fever.

29

Mexico: 1951

'No! No! No!' Emerald screamed.

The noise bounced round the whitewashed colonnades of the Yellow House, catapulting the rooftop-roosting doves skywards in a cloud of snowy feathers. A few plumes drifted down through the heavy air.

She waited for the tears.

Emerald never cried. She had not cried since the storm pulled her out of her safe world and sucked her into the night-black tunnel of the monster's maw. It was a disability, like being a person who was hard of hearing or short-sighted; or a dog who couldn't bark, or a cat who couldn't purr. But now the sobs racked her body.

Over in the kitchen quarters, Lupe the cook put down the knife with which she was chopping chillies for the evening stew. She wiped her hands on her apron and opened the door to the main part of the house. She knew what the scream meant. Those who had not the habit of death, who did not know how to welcome it as every Indio child was taught from birth, could not seem to accept it comfortably.

The poor orphan gringa would not find it easy, even though she, Lupe the cook, had taken her own son Nacho and the little gringa together, as if the blue-eyed child was her own daughter, to play in the churchyard with sugar skulls all night long each year on the Day of the Dead.

She crossed the courtyard which divided the kitchen and servants' quarters from the main house. There were duties to be discharged. Arrangements to be made.

Lupe had done all she could – made daily visits to the curandera for soporific infusions and soothing ointments brewed up in the hut in the barranca.

In accordance with what she knew would be the absent Doña Molly's wishes, Lupe sent for the local doctor, a plump round-faced young man who had had his training in the big city hospital. He had administered such medicines as he had, and advised bed-rest and drinks of salted water. What would be, would be. The fever would pass, or it would not pass. The young doctor had more than enough to do without wasting his time on what would either cure itself or not be cured at all. He made his brief daily visits on the way home from his surgery. There, in a bare-boarded little room with a tin medicine cabinet on one wall and a kitchen table covered with a blanket against the other, he stitched up the knife wounds inflicted in the bar-brawls and struggled to repair the damage inflicted by back-street abortions.

Violent death was his business. Natural death was a matter over which he had no jurisdiction. In the house of the rich foreigner, he would stay for five minutes, shrug and leave again. In Mexico, even the young and healthy died, every day, all the time. They died on the streets, under a pile of old tin cans in the corner of the market-place, in the doorway of the church of Our Lady of the Seven Sorrows. If they were very fortunate, they came to die in the fullness of time, in their own bed, in a cool room shaded by wooden-slatted blinds, between clean fresh linen sheets.

Lupe agreed with the young doctor. Margaret Mackenzie was old. Just the same, it was a pity she was so far from her own, with no-one but the poor child to mourn her.

The old should be allowed to die in peace, without interference, in their own land. And then their families could visit them each year in the graveyard on the great festival of All Souls, and everyone could make merry at the banquet laid out on the cold stone, living and dead together, with the clear conscience of duty discharged.

At the same hour every morning and evening Lupe had gone in to smooth the sheets, plump up the pillows and go through the ritual of coaxing the old woman to eat, feeding her little sips of broth with a spoon.

Then there was the washing and the bedpans. You have to love someone very much, or not at all, to do such things.

Just the same, thought Lupe, the curandera's remedies did at least bring comfort, memories of ancestral paradise to assist the dying on their journey.

Esmeralda would take it hard.

Lupe quickened her pace.

Afterwards Emerald remembered very little of the dark days of her nan's fever. When she had returned from her visit to Miss Lily, Lupe had been anxious to keep Emerald away from the sickbed.

'No, nenita. Doña Molly would be angry if you go to her.'

Emerald shook off Lupe's restraining hand and took the stairs two at a time.

'She's my *nan*!' Emerald shouted in anguish as she raced upwards.

Margaret Mackenzie was propped on a heap of pillows in her bed by the window. The old woman turned her head towards the door. Her eyes were unnaturally bright and her cheeks were flushed.

'Is it ye, my bairn?' The voice was weak and hoarse.

Emerald ran forward and kneeled by the bedside.

'Nan. My darling nan.'

Margaret Mackenzie struggled to sit upright. Then her head fell back on the pillow.

'Away wi' ye, child. A sickbed's no place for a bairn.'

Emerald picked up the hand which lay on the sheet, feeling the pulse in the wrist, the skin all hot with fever.

She shook her head. 'I'm not leaving you, Nana. Never again.'

Margaret Mackenzie sighed. 'Open the window, my bairn. I've a sore longing for the scent o' the heather.'

The old woman turned her head towards the light. She could see quite clearly now, not the shadowy attic-room under an unfamiliar sky, but the purple hills, the shimmer of sand and the lapping of the waves on the shore of Eas Forse.

' 'Tis uncommon dark. There'll be a storm coming over the headland.'

It was time and past time. Her strength was fading. She could feel the fever surging through her bones, lapping her flesh, blinding her eyes.

Soon. It would be soon. Gifted as she was with the second sight, she had always known when she had taken ship that never again in life would she return to gather harebells on the hill. And now she was going home at last. Home to the heather and hill of the rain-washed Western Isles, the loveliest islands in the world. She saw through the darkness of her fever the blazing summer slip green and gentle into autumn. She felt the touch of the first snowflakes of winter, heard the curlews cry on the headland, watched the sun rise over the silver sea.

The sickness ebbed and flowed for a week. In all that time, Emerald never left the sickbed, except so that Lupe might do the things she could to make the old woman comfortable. Or when the young doctor made his brief and hurried visits.

At times when the fever was fierce, Margaret Mackenzie would cry out. Then the storm would abate, and the old woman seemed to recover for a few hours, only for the raging heat to return again.

Once, unable to resist her own despair, Emerald cried out: 'Nan, my nan, forgive me!'

'My bairn . . .' The voice was barely audible, but the blue-webbed lids had fluttered open. 'There's nothing to forgive.'

Weakly the old woman reached out, gathered her changeling in her arms and held her close as if she held once again the half-drowned storm-orphan she had found on the shore.

'Hush, my darling. There's nae man nor monster can harm ye, nor ever could.'

Night fell suddenly, like a dropped curtain.

The sky was brilliant with stars. Through the arches of the bell-tower Emerald could see the pale circle of the moon, hear the shrill squeaking of the little blunt-nosed bats which hunted the evening's hatch of moths.

Moths lived for a day, and then they died.

'Nan,' she whispered. 'Don't leave me, Nan.'

Emerald stretched out her arms and gathered the old woman close. As long as they held each other, her nan would not leave her.

Child of my heart, my changeling babe.

In the long black moment just before dawn, Emerald heard the silence creep into the room.

And then, as Lupe had told her she would, she heard the retching bone-clicking rattle of death.

It was then that Emerald opened her throat and screamed, the long anguished wail of the child she had been and was never to be again.

High in the hills, Nacho stopped and listened. It wasn't the physical sound he heard. He was too distant for that. But when Emerald was in trouble he had always been able to hear her call as clearly as if he had been in the room.

Emerald couldn't understand how he could do it.

'*Claro*. Of course,' he would say, and smile, showing his strong white teeth.

Hearing the anguished cry, Nacho quickened his easy lope to a run.

In the sickroom, Lupe drew the heavy curtains shut. She drew the sheet over the old woman's body, the paper-white face, the skin drawn taught over the cheekbones.

'Aiee . . . !' called Lupe respectfully as she pulled the eyelids down over the sightless pupils. They had strange pale eyes, the gringos.

She would have to send down the barranca for the curandera to help her lay out the old white woman in the proper fashion so that she would not go empty-handed into the great cavern of Tezcatlipoca. There must be a burial in the proper style. After all, the old white woman had been a curandera, too, and well respected for her skills with the white man's simples. Death was an expensive business. The twin deities of death, Mictlantecuhtli and Mictlancihuatl, permanent residents of the nether world, did not come cheap. Heaven only knew how it would be paid for, with Doña Molly away.

Lupe had sent for her, as soon as the old woman had fallen ill. But the roads were bad, and travelling took time. In the fever-days, death waited for no-one, and the burial must be swift.

She would have to find Nacho. The boy was never around when anyone needed him.

Gently she led Emerald from the deathbed. She must come to the kitchen for a bowl of maize porridge.

Emerald took it out into the cool of the garden and sat down under the jacaranda–tree. She was not hungry, but still she ate. Lupe said she had to eat.

The church bell tolled the angelus. A flock of blue-grey doves rose briefly from the crenellations in the tower. The warm breeze touched Emerald's cheeks, a feverish breath. She shivered. She willed time to pass. If the end of the world was come, time would still pass. She felt anger and fear. Fear and a dull unreasoning ache. Time passed. She felt hurt and betrayal. And loneliness. Above all, loneliness.

The sky and the doves were mirrored in the dark water of the pool. The tiles edging the black depths echoed the viridian of the roofs. A flotilla of jacaranda blossoms, their violet petals browning at the edges, had fallen in the water, and the blooms sailed on like tiny boats in the sky's reflection, making little ripples on the drifting clouds.

Emerald trailed her hand in the water. She closed her eyes, reclaiming once again the darkness of her nightmares, seeing the white foam of the churning waves of Eas Forse, feeling the icy current which pulled her down, down the long tunnel into the maw of the monster.

30

Mexico: 1951

With naked feet impervious to cactus thorns, and runnels of sweat coursing into his eyes, Nacho slowed his pace only when he reached the shrubbery of the Yellow House.

He stopped to catch his breath in the shadows.

He had been in the mountains, doing his first deal with the tigre pelts.

Nacho was a sin-camisa, a shirtless one. There was only one way for a sin-camisa to haul himself out of the barranca. There were men who had once been as poor as he who walked around in alligator shoes. The men in the alligator shoes made their money in the only way anyone could make their fortune who came out of the barranca.

Such men changed their shirts every day – the guayabera with its starched pleats and neat pockets to carry wallets stuffed with banknotes. The men were dealers. They dealt in marijuana – mary-jane – the weed. Whatever you called it, the gringos paid good prices for the soporific leaf.

The people of the barranca worshipped the dealers for the hope they gave, for the possibility that others, too, might become like them. Such men were better than gods, since their acolytes could share, however modestly, in their good fortune: by starching the guayaberas, polishing the alligator shoes and performing all the small services which such men could afford.

Nacho meant to join the ranks of the dealers. Only then could he make the revolution which would earn his people freedom. It was a terrible injustice that the children of the barranca died of hunger while those who owned the land grew crops for the gringos' pleasure.

Like all the best plans it was simple. He needed an introduction – something the gringos wanted which he alone could supply. The gringos who bought the crop had an appetite for luxuries such as the beautiful rose-patterned pelts, very rare, to throw round the plump white shoulders of a wife or a mistress when they returned home.

The tigre Nacho had just hunted was the last pelt he needed for his first trading bundle, the precious skins which would serve as his calling-card.

His first deal had been conducted high in the hills, at the disused monastery which served as the clearing-house for the marijuana crop. He had been on his way down the mountain when he had heard Emerald's cry. Now, across the courtyard, through the mosquito screens which veiled the high windows, he could see his mother moving around the old woman's room.

When Lupe's hand drew the heavy curtains, Nacho knew for certain. His mother did not need to tell him what to do. Everyone knew what to do when the hollow-eyed horseman came for his own. Everyone except the gringos.

Nacho looked around for Emerald.

Under the shadow of one of the arches Nacho's eye caught the edge of movement. He crossed the space silently. He put his arms round Emerald, just as she had embraced him on the day that Xuma had died.

Emerald looked up at him, her eyes huge and round like fragments of the summer sky.

'Oh, Nacho,' she said, 'why weren't you here?'

He said, 'Ven, nina. Come.'

Emerald shook her head.

'She's dead. My nan is dead.'

There were tears in her voice, and bright droplets brimmed her eyes.

Nacho nodded. He stroked her bent head. His heart went out to her. *Emerald, my Emerald. There is birth and there is death – why is it so hard for you to accept?* Emerald had so many lessons to learn.

'Come,' he said gently. 'The dead have to start on the long journey. The living must help them depart. There are things to be done.'

Hearing his voice, strength flowed back into her limbs. She lifted her face to the light. She had not even known the sun had risen.

'Did you see her, Nacho?'

Nacho shook his head gently. 'That is women's business. We must fetch the curandera. Come.'

Emerald obeyed. In all practical matters, Nacho knew so much more than she.

After the rains, the sides of the barranca were steep and overgrown with wiry grasses and a dense thicket of cactus. The witch's lean-to was buried in a mass of yellow flowering shrubbery, carpeted with herbs. Crushed underfoot, their scent was rank and powerful.

The old woman came to the door. A single glance at Emerald told her all she needed to know.

'It is finished, child?' The curandera's voice was kindly.

Emerald nodded. She felt braver already.

'What money do you have?'

Nacho hesitated only for an instant. Then he pulled out the dollar bills from the sale of the skins.

The wise woman fingered the notes and nodded again.

'It will be a fine funeral.'

Then she turned to look at Emerald. The gringos took these things too hard. There was birth and there was death; life was merely the journey between.

She said briskly, 'You, nena, will fetch honeycomb and cacao from the market. Nacho, you will collect the herbs for preparing the body. I shall need sage of the oracle and leaves of God for washing, and morning glory and mint of the divinity for the ointment. Your mother and I will prepare the dish of the dead. We will leave for the cemetery as the sun goes down.'

The curandera watched the two young people disappear down the barranca again, and then she made her way up to the big house where the body of the gringa lay.

Lupe came to the door to greet her. The two women went in from the blazing heat of the morning, through the cool hallway to the attic room where the corpse lay cold and silent. The skin was stretched so taut over the bones it looked like the silk canopies the spiders wove over dry grass to catch the summer grasshoppers.

'Aiee. The long journey must begin.'

'Aiee,' the curandera agreed.

Lupe had already fetched the priest from his tequila-sodden stupor and brought him up to the house for what both considered to be the necessary incantations. It was an unspoken arrangement, and no-one stepped outside the boundaries. Propriety must be observed, but in its proper place.

The priest returned to his church, the women set about their business. There was the body to be prepared and robed, the food of the dead to be cooked.

For Emerald, returning with the necessary articles from the market-place, there was a soothing rhythm to the careful preparations the two women made. The ritual had a purpose to it: death was a familiar visitor, his ceremonies as well known and understood, as casually accepted, as the rituals of birth.

The funeral cortège assembled throughout the day, the low murmur of the women's voices occasionally broken by the soaring cry of the high-pitched mourning keen. There were many who had availed themselves of the old woman's skills and wished to accompany her to the Monte de los Muertos, the Hill of the Dead.

By the time the sun had lost its warmth, all was ready. The body had been washed, anointed with sacred herbs and wrapped in a blue shroud, tightly bound with the sacred scarlet thread which gave protection against evil spirits. The face and hands were left uncovered for the mourners to kiss. Great banks of marigolds, the flowers sacred to the dead, cushioned the corpse.

In her time among them, the white woman had earned the respect of the townspeople, and her status was reflected in the long queue which stretched up the street to the table set up under the arches. Lupe as the only 'family' the old woman had – Emerald not yet having attained adulthood – accepted the condolences and offered those who had viewed the corpse the house's hospitality in return: tiny cups of hot sweet chocolate.

At last the body, on its couch of orange petals, was loaded onto the wagon decked with blue and white paper flowers.

'That is good. All is order.' The curandera nodded approval as she inspected the bier. She set the dish of honeycomb beside the right hand; on the left went the blue pottery jar which contained the food of the dead: unleavened bread made with white maize flour, soaked with fermented cactus juice. Without such provisions, no voyager to the underworld could hope to cross the nine rivers. 'Aiee, it is well done.'

A funeral was an event, a family affair. The people liked to have a chance to pay a visit to their own ancestors, although it was hard to tell, once the branches had rolled or rotted away, which debris belonged to whom. The men went up to the Hill of the Dead alone to lay the body in the earth. That was men's business. The women's task was pay their respects to the bereaved, and to prepare the dead for the ceremony.

A hedge of sinicuichi shrubs, the sacred leaf which induced golden

207

visions, divided the boundary of the cemetery from the fields which spread outwards from the town. Apart from the three skeleton trees which crowned it and the wild greenery covering the slopes, there was nothing to indicate that the place was a burial-ground at all.

The young men of the barranca, Nacho among them, formed a group apart on the hill, strong and high-cheekboned, brown limbs under tattered cotton clothes, silver-studded belts heavy with weapons – knives and catapults, with here and there the dull gleam of gun-barrel. The warriors were the guardians of the living. The dead were the business of those past fighting.

The torchlit procession wound up the steep slope to lay the corpse of the old white woman at the foot of the three tall crosses which crowned the Monte de los Muertos. The crosses formed a visible link between life and death – living bones, their branches stripped of leaves, on which had been nailed rough-hewn cross-bars. The trees were Christian symbols, but with ancient meanings: the bear-god Tezcatlipoca, lord of life, and the snake-plumed Quetzalcoatl, master of death, gave precedence to the fearful Chachalmeca, king of the underworld.

Emerald watched with the other women from the shelter of the yellow-flowered sinicuichi hedge. At the end, when the body had been set to rest, the women moved up the hill to keep the mourning vigil. All through the night, they sang the songs of life and death, the songs of gods and men, which soothed the departed souls and sent them safely on their way.

In the dark time before dawn, the time when the spirits are released from their earthly prison, Emerald heard for the last time the beloved voice, the voice she knew so well, thread through the keening of the women.

She heard it as clearly as if her own nan's arms had been around her, that same lullaby which so long ago, on that cold grey morning when the sea-monster had been cheated of its prey, had served to call back the changeling child from the cavern under the waves.

Emerald heard the song, and lay down on the cool grass beside her nan, and slept at last.

31

Eas Forse: 1952

The island's ladies clicked their knitting-needles and gossiped, in the way of all island ladies everywhere. With the Beltane fires so close, they were matchmaking.

Alison Mackay, overhearing the gossip, smiled to herself.

'They'd make a fine couple, wouldn't you say?' Minnie MacBean remarked to her husband Lachie, landlord of the Salen Arms, when Callum Fergusson came in the evening before, cutting as fine a figure as anyone might imagine with young Alison Mackay on his arm. The young man had changed out of his working breeks into a plain brown kilt and newly knitted white woollen stockings. Before the old Queen Empress had popularized the coloured plaid, such kilts were the usual dress of the highlanders, doing double duty as blankets out on the hill or on the march. Many of the island families, including the Stuart himself, had worn them at the battle of Culloden.

This morning, as the steamer picked its way into the little harbour, Lachie, who had an in-comer's interest in all the comings and goings on the island, went over to the window and glanced up the street.

'You'll not be seeing the schoolmistress again today.' Lachie nodded towards the small figure of Catriona Sweeney vanishing into her caravan down the hill.

'How so?' said Minnie absently, her mind on the shoulder of lamb she was roasting for the lunchtime special. It had been a well-grown yearling hogget, near-enough mutton, and she hoped it would be done on time for the ferry passengers.

'No, indeed,' Lachie continued. 'Miss Sweeney will not be walking out on the day of the Beltane fires.'

'The Beltane fires would never have been allowed in Devon,' said Minnie, inspecting the bloodied skewer with satisfaction. 'After-chapel tea it is, where the young folks meet, and folks know how to keep themselves to themselves.'

'Very true, dear. There's no doubt there's many a wickedness at the Beltane fires,' Lachie agreed, a note of regret in his voice which made his wife glance up sharply.

He went over to the bar and started to polish the beer-glasses.

Catriona Sweeney, as Lachie MacBean had observed, had retired to the end of her fuchsia-hedged patch of garden to spend the afternoon cataloguing in the old caravan.

Catriona's greatest frustration was that she hadn't been able to give birth to Callum. Deeply as she loved the young man, he would never be more than her foster-son. What she was able to do, thanks to her passionate diligence as an archivist, was give her storm-orphan his birth-right – his past and beginnings of which, in the spinster schoolmistress's austere view, his wayward natural mother had deprived him.

Catriona shut her door against the fires of Beltane, and settled down patiently to put the finishing touches to the dossier she had spent ten years compiling. It was to be her gift, the gift of the past: the handwritten family-tree, the faded photographs, the documents which confirmed the conjunction of bloodlines which had culminated in her own Callum Fergusson, last of the Stuart line of Eas Forse.

Perhaps, if you could give credence to the legend (though Catriona gave no credence to legends), back to that bonnie prince, the Stuart himself, last of the line of Celtic kings, who had crossed the water and lost a kingdom.

But that was idle speculation. Catriona dealt in realities.

Realities were proof of ancestry, certificates of birth, marriage, death. Of baptism and legacy. Anthony Anstruther would finish the task she had begun. That had been the agreement. She had kept her side of the bargain. Now, since the boy was eighteen – it was his birthday the following day – it was time for him to take over responsibility for his own life.

She laid out the papers and set to work.

Tomorrow, after the Beltane fires had come and gone, she would show Callum his past and, through the past, his future.

210

*   *   *

Alison Mackay also had Callum and the Beltane fires in mind. But she was concerned with the immediate future, not with the past.

From her vantage point at the table outside the island's only shop cum post office, Alison watched the young man guide his small boat through the harbour mouth.

Alison expected admiration. At nineteen her large brown eyes, rosebud mouth and silvery-blond hair had already made her much in demand in London as a house model for Susan Small, one of the major fashion houses. Her success had brought her the public recognition she knew was her due, a smooth continuation of the adulation of doting parents – a father who delighted in spoiling her, and a mother with nothing else to do but dress her daughter in hand-embroidered smocks and parade her round the front parlours of snobbish Perth.

The lesson she had learned from her childhood was that her looks would get her anything she wanted. Today she wanted Callum.

Alison leaned back and raised her face to the spring sunshine, composing the image for Callum's lens. She knew of the young man's ambitions to be a world-famous photographer.

The boat bumped gently against the sea-wall of the jetty. Callum stood up to make the bows fast against the topmost of a line of weather-beaten iron rings on which half a dozen other small boats were already moored.

A fraction under six foot, the young man was tall for his eighteen years, already taller than most of the islanders, which allowed him to reach that particular ring even at low tide. With a sailor's care he clipped the rowlocks to their neat hooks in the prow. Then he carefully transferred his oilcloth-wrapped Rolleiflex and two rolls of film to his fishing-bag, dismantled the short split-bamboo rod and buried its triple-barbed hooks securely in a lump of cork buoy. Finally he reached into the sawn-off petrol-can which served as both fish-bucket and baler, to check on the dozen or so fat mackerel still twitching in the bottom.

Feeling in the pocket of his jacket, he pulled out a curved steel knife. With a quick movement of sinewy wrists, he slit open the pale bellies. Then he tossed each hank of scarlet innards to the screaming pack of herring-gulls which had trailed him back to harbour.

Alison Mackay saw none of these things. She saw only the breeze-tousled mop of chestnut-gold hair as Callum leaned over the gunwale to rinse the fish in the water. As a young boy his hair had been white-gold when bleached by the sun, fair as the Vikings who had liberally seeded the women of the Western Isles. Later it had darkened to the golden brown of an otter's back.

211

She saw, too, the movement of the muscles beneath the sun-freckled skin of his broad shoulders as he reached up to hook the rope over the ring, the knotted ropes of tendon in his arms as he heaved himself over the sea-wall. Lazily, like a cat extending its claws, she stretched her fingertips as if to stroke the thick strong column of his neck.

Callum did not look at all like the slender, dandyish young men who squired Alison around the nightspots of London. Callum had the slender hips and heavy muscular thighs of a hill-shepherd. He could walk for miles across the tops when the sheep were to be gathered for the lambing or the dipping. And in the summer, when the tourists were looking for a bit of fishing, he could row a boatful of passengers single-handed across the sea-loch even when the wind off the Atlantic churned the water into a white frenzy.

Feeling the warmth of the spring sunshine on her bare shoulders, Alison stroked the down on her own white arm, city-pale still at the start of the annual holiday. Then she shut her eyes with pleasure at the thought of a triumph still only a few hours old.

And there was more and better, with the Beltane fires to come. After that . . . well, that was anyone's guess. Alison knew herself well enough to understand her own attention-span only lasted as long as the wanting. Callum would do well enough as a holiday diversion. There would be other fish to fry than a young man's catch of mackerel, which would surely be all the dowry Callum might offer her, whatever his ambitions.

Callum at that moment was not aware of Alison's presence at all. Although, of course, he had certainly been more than aware of her down on the shore yesterday evening. After, that was, she had managed to divert his attention away from the viewfinder and the play of light and shadow on the tide-washed rocks and on to her own ripe beauty.

Yesterday had been the first day of real spring. As it had shaded into dusk the air had still been soft with the warmth of the approaching summer. Down on the shore, the brilliant cobalt sky was reflected in an indigo sea. Callum, torn between the black and white images in his lens and the reality beckoning him on the shore, turned his camera towards his companion.

Alison laughed and took it gently out of his hand. She said, 'I want to see your eyes.'

Callum's eyes were honey-coloured with sandy green flecks in the them. Brown-eyed Alison loved his tawny eyes.

'Tiger's eyes,' she said, shadowing her own against the dipping sun.

She bent down to snatch a limpet, big as a penny, from its rock, deftly so the muscular foot had no time to clamp down on the hard black

212

granite. Straightening up again, she turned the shell over to expose the soft underparts of the mollusc.

Using her thumb-nail as a spoon, she scooped out the morsel of limpet flesh and slid it into Callum's mouth.

She glanced up at him under lowered lashes as she sipped the salted juices from the shell-cup.

Callum rolled the limpet flesh around his mouth. It tasted of sea-spray and sand.

Alison laughed again. Then she caught Callum round the waist and pulled him down beside her onto the damp sand. Before he knew it, Callum had kissed her full on the lips. It was a little rough and nervous, but for the first time in his eighteen years he had kissed a girl. He felt the response stirring his body. Scarlet with embarrassment he rolled over and sat up, his face burning.

He knew Alison would immediately push him away: there was no doubt that what he was feeling now was, as Preacher McInnes had dinned into all of them as he thundered from his pulpit Sunday after Sunday, a sin. A mortal sin.

'Alison,' he stammered, 'I . . . '

His voice trailed away.

Unbelievably Alison did not slap him and run away giggling as the young girls he shared a schoolroom with always did. All the *nice* girls, that is. In island life there was no room for dalliance. You were courting or you were *not* courting. To discourage those who were more adventurously inclined, there was always Jack's mother to be held up as an example. Courting was one thing. Playing the field was quite another.

But Alison Mackay was different. Outsider-different. Instead of re-buffing Callum, or even playing come-and-get-me flirting games, Alison stretched out her body confidently on the damp sand on the edge of the ocean where the oystercatchers picked with their scarlet bills among the discarded limpet shells.

Alison raised herself on one elbow to look at Callum with her big brown eyes. Slowly and deliberately she caressed the outline of her breasts beneath the thin cotton of her shirt, her hand travelling down to smooth the curve of her hips where they met the rounded slope of her thighs.

'Shut up,' she said, and pulled Callum's head down towards her own.

She brushed his cheek softly with her own, unbuttoned her white cotton shirt and guided his hand so that his clumsy fingers could explore the rounded warmth beneath. Alison had known well enough that the shepherd boy would have no knowledge of the hooks and straps and buttressing girls customarily wore as their underpinnings. So she had done without.

The buttons of her nipples hardened under his fingers.

Then she kissed him. Nobody had ever kissed him like that before. Her small strong fingers stroked the short hairs on the back of his neck as she held him to her, her salty tongue flickering in and out of his mouth, seaweed-sweet and flavoured with limpet juices.

Callum felt the blood race round his body until he thought the earth would split open and swallow him into its hot centre. When Alison finally took her mouth away, Callum blinked. He looked, Alison thought, rather adorable and very young.

'There, baby,' she said, and patted his cheek. 'That's a French kiss. Just a little taste.'

Then the tide had swamped them, and they had scrambled up laughing, clothes sodden with salt water. Alison's blouse was so wet that her rosy nipples showed through the white fabric.

So Callum kissed her again, more confident this time, feeling the sweetness of her mouth as her tongue caressed his – until finally she pushed him away and ran up the slope, leaving Callum to follow her back to her family's farm just up the bay with the bucket of mussels for their tea.

Alison Mackay had been holidaying with her family on the island each year for as long as Callum could remember. Certainly ever since that summer, six years ago, when his beloved Emerald had been taken away from him.

Of course, Alison's mother had been a Mackenzie. Alison would tease Callum that everyone on the island, except Callum, was a kissing cousin, since everyone on the island, except Callum himself, was related to either a Mackenzie or a Sweeney. It was a Mackenzie aunt who had left Alison's mother the little cottage out on the headland, on condition that the family visited it once a year.

Alison knew all about Emerald. No-one who knew Callum could fail to know about Emerald. At the beginning, the first year she had been on the island, Alison had tried to get rid of what she saw as her absent rival.

'So what's so special about Emerald No-name?' Alison asked when the two youngsters were fishing with bent pins from the boulders at the end of the pier. 'I'll tell you what's special. My Aunty Jessie told me your Emerald No-name's *dead*. All dead and maggoty – like the hoodie on your nan's back fence.'

Callum lost his temper. 'You're lying!' he shouted. Then he snatched up her bucket and threw the catch of silvery fish back into the water.

Alison ran home howling with rage and told on Callum to her mum,

214

and her mum told her Aunt Jessie. Jessie went and complained to the schoolmistress, the boy's guardian. Catriona Sweeney confiscated Callum's fishing rod for the rest of the summer, and gave him a sharp switch across the knuckles with it for being a bully.

After that Callum had had maggot nightmares for a month.

As the years passed, the two young people came back together warily. Lately they were thrown together more and more, because Callum had taken summer holiday work on Alison's aunt's farm, as he had done for the last two years, as soon as he was old enough to earn the basic wage.

Last year Alison had been to the Beltane fires along with the rest of Eas Forse's diminishing population of young people.

After the Beltane there had been stories about Alison and Isaac Finlay, who was, after all, four years older and had been on the mainland to Glasgow. Alison had made sure Callum knew all about the rumours.

This year both Alison and Callum would be going to the fires, and Alison had decided to douse the torch Callum carried for his lost playmate for good and all.

In the process she would have a little fun. She slipped her hand between her thighs, and waited for the young man to come up the street to join her.

The preparations for the Beltane fires had been going on all day.

The ceremony was an ancient one, a direct throwback to the pre-Christian fire festivals. Early that morning as the sun rose the young men who had attended the ceremony for the first time the previous year had gone up to the Rock to make the Beltane altar – four deep trenches cut into the peat-turf dug down to the bare rock so as to leave a raised rectangular table in the middle. On this the young men piled tinder-dry heather, birch twigs and rowan branches.

The island's first-year initiates – Callum himself, red-headed Duncan Cameron and Bobby Lamont, the son of the radio-operator in the lighthouse at Burg – were charged with bringing up the *tein-eigen*, the needfire in the ceilidh-tein from which the bonfire was lit.

As a symbol of its importance to those whose livelihood and very survival depended on the annual return of the sun, on this one night of the year all the fires on the island had to be extinguished, so that the powers of the needfire might be concentrated in the single sacred flame. The hearth-flames were rekindled from the returning needfire as the sun rose again – newly fortified, as the old belief had it, by the ceremony – to begin its daily climb towards the summer solstice.

The ceremonies were about to begin.

The three young men, dressed in the rough woollen overshirts and plain brown blanket-plaids which did duty on the island for the tartan kilts and tweed jackets sported on the mainland, assembled outside the ceilidh-tein. Each carried a russet-brown wedge of tinder-fungus, gathered in the birch woods beneath the Beltane Rock that morning.

'Good people, douse your hearths!'

The cry echoed from house to house as the torchbearers carried the needfire up the main street of the little town and out on to the cliff-road.

Tonight was the night when tales were told round the dying embers of the hearth-fire, the night when young children huddled close to their parents while the grandparents told stories of long ago, keeping company with the spirits who lived in the green hill and who might otherwise have been tempted to mischief.

'Douse your hearths!' the people sang as they passed the crofts on the island road. 'We wait on the tein-eigen!' came the reply as the people crouched round their cold hearths.

The procession took four hours to reach the table dug beneath the Beltane Rock. By that time, thrashing from side to side like a many-footed dragon, it had sucked into itself all the islanders of an eligible age and unmarried status – including a few who were neither but had awarded themselves honorary bachelorhood for the night, giving husbands or wives the slip in the dark. At least a hundred eager faces danced in the flickering light of the kindling torches.

Afterwards none of the participants could remember much of what happened that night. The truth of the matter was that not one of the three young men, the novitiates, who brought the *tein-eigen* which set the Beltane fire ablaze in a shower of firework sparks and dancing flames was meant to remember, even had he wanted to.

Each remembered being handed a bowl of carved birchwood frothing with some bitter-sweet liquid which had to be drained to the dregs. After that, the dancing began, and no-one who was at the Beltane fires could hold anyone else responsible for what happened.

That was the rule, as it was always the rule when the lord of misrule held the sceptre.

Callum held Alison, sweet Alison, in his arms, twisting and tumbling as he plunged into her body. She encircled him as a cave pulls in the tide, the scent of herbs and crushed heather rising as her thighs arched towards him against the rough cloth of his plaid. The dancing firelight flared from her half-naked body. Her hands raked his back, salt from the night wind stinging the fine tracks of her nails.

216

'How do you like it, sweet Callum?' she whispered in his ear, her breath warm and soft as the summer hay.

Then she turned him over and climbed aloft, riding him, one hand behind her gently stroking him, her breasts tilted towards the moonlight, her hair wild around her face as pale as moonbeams.

'Sweet Callum, like this?'

Afterwards, spent, Callum lay dizzy as he gazed up at the wheeling stars.

Alison had held Callum in her arms – sweet Callum, young Callum. And then she danced away. That night she held many men in her arms. But no-one, as was the way at the Beltane fires, knew or cared who danced and lay with whom, whose juices mingled, whose bodies locked together, pounding sea to sand like the surf on the shore below the Beltane Rock.

That was the law of Beltane.

Next day Alison walked, her body swinging free and loose, up the gangplank, to return to the mainland on the ferry which, on this one night of the year, had put into the island overnight so the visitors could share the ancient Beltane rituals.

At that moment, Alison Mackay had no thought but of the city – and none at all for Callum's tawny eyes.

32

Mexico: 1952

'Sit down, child, over there where I can see you.'

'Yes, Aunt Molly.'

Obediently Emerald went over to the window seat, sat down and waited.

As soon as Molly received the letter from her son Anthony outlining the answers to her questions concerning Emerald's future, she sent for the girl.

The year had turned full circle since the death of the old nursemaid, and Doña Molly was once more due to leave for the capital on her annual summer visit.

Molly knew she should have tackled the problem sooner. And there was certainly a problem. Yesterday she herself had been vividly reminded of it. She had just settled down on the veranda to begin the new Evelyn Waugh – *Men at Arms,* it had been, a subject so divorced from the scented tranquillity of her garden that her mind had wandered – when Emerald came down for her morning swim.

The girl had not even glanced round before she stripped off her shirt in one long graceful movement, and plunged, clad only in her shorts, into the dark waters of the pool. In spite of the wiry strength of the limbs, the breasts were filling out and the waist was curving in.

The wide-set eyes sparkled mischievously under the thick lashes. The lips had a sensuous fullness which reminded Molly of her own wild young womanhood, in the twenties, after that other war, the Great War, had liberated her own generation from the tight-laced prison which had been Queen Victoria's legacy.

Emerald surfaced among the flotilla of jacaranda blossoms, hauled herself up the edge of the pool, the slender golden body gleaming, the nipples of the young breasts tipped upwards from the cold, and shook out the shining cap of hair which clung close to the heart-shaped face. Then she laughed and called to someone out of her line of sight. No doubt that young ruffian, the cook's son, was somewhere about.

It had been easy enough when Emerald was still a child and Margaret Mackenzie had been there to run around behind her – in so far as she had done any running at all in the last years, after she had, as the old hands might say, gone native. And since the death of her old nursemaid the child had been allowed to run completely wild.

Now, not a moment too soon, the proper decisions had to be taken. It was the first step in the grand plan, in so far as anything so deliberate as a grand plan might be said to apply to the arrangements made for Emerald's future.

Although Emerald herself seemed unconscious of her own attractions, Molly had no doubt of the effect she would soon have on the opposite sex. The delicate face, like a neat little violet, gave her an air of vulnerability. Vulnerability – real or imagined – was so attractive to men.

Even the boy Nacho, with every young strumpet down the barranca after him – if his mother Lupe's tales were to be believed – was completely besotted by her. The result was that the girl was as wild and wilful as the tuft-eared forest lynxes which patrolled the barranca.

Only the other day, Lily Lovage had offered to take her in hand, saying that she thought the girl had promise, that she might be able to earn her living as a mannequin. Not that that was an occupation for a girl with prospects.

And Emerald certainly had prospects. Anthony's letter had outlined her expectations. She was the beneficiary of a discretionary trust – modest enough when you considered the American heiresses on the marriage market, but perfectly adequate to provide a respectable dowry when the time came.

Molly herself had neither the time nor the inclination to give the girl the gloss which would make her marriageable – and marriageable she must be. To be acceptable in society, the girl must be tutored in the social arts.

The only obstacle was likely to be Emerald herself. The child was practically a savage. Lupe said she kept a rolled-up alligator skin under her bed, and even boasted that she had killed the animal herself.

It wouldn't do. Wouldn't do at all.

Today, as always, she was dressed in ragged shorts. And her boyish Aertex shirt, open at the throat, accentuated rather than hid the new curves the body had acquired.

Doña Molly sighed and went over to her rose-garlanded Hepplewhite desk. She picked up the letter again and studied it.

She glanced up. 'My dear, you're growing up. I'm sure you realize it's time to put childish things behind you.'

Emerald looked warily at her guardian. 'Childish things, Aunt Molly?'

Doña Molly smiled, her faded-rose smile.

Emerald's stomach turned over. She knew the smile well. It conveyed disapproval. Mind your manners. It was the smile which was applied to her expeditions to visit Miss Lily. Or when she had been off in the hills with Nacho.

'Among other things,' Doña Molly repeated thoughtfully. 'For instance, running wild with that young ruffian.'

Emerald waited, seething with anger. Nacho might be a young ruffian, but he was a worth a thousand times more than the limp young men she met at Miss Lily's.

Molly's temples throbbed. The whole business had given her a headache. It had opened emotional doors which were better left shut – brought back memories.

She picked up her son's letter and studied it again.

A husband mature enough to take care of the girl was the obvious answer, and fifteen was not too early to begin to look at the prospects. Edwardian girls had considered themselves on the shelf if they had not found a husband by the time they were eighteen.

No. There was no time to lose in making Emerald marriageable.

What her son had in mind, Molly surmised, was a discreet alliance with some rich expatriate family of English stock. One of the ranching millionaires in the south of the American continent.

They were by all accounts respectable and well off. Certain standards had to be maintained. Those very standards she had once rejected at least offered some kind of order in an increasingly disorderly world.

Marriage was a certain standard.

Everywhere the old social barriers were breaking down – and not just in the world of politics, which impinged little on Doña Molly's tranquil retreat. Although Molly had chosen to throw off the straitjacket of her husband's stultifying milieu, she had not found anything with which to replace it. As she grew older and her beauty faded, she had retreated into a cocoon from which she only emerged with reluctance.

Interviews such as this were quite exhausting.

She looked across at her ward. The girl's face was shuttered, almost defiant.

There was no doubt Emerald had courage – whatever else might be said. She would need it. Life never worked out as one would wish.

Poor child, she thought.

Molly continued, more gently this time: 'It's time to think of the future, my dear. *Your* future. One has to acquire the social graces. Deportment, flower-arranging, proper modes of address, all those kinds of thing. All the kinds of thing your dear Miss Mackenzie, God rest her soul, could not possibly have provided. I blame myself. But what can one do? There's been no-one to take you in hand. We have to think of your future. And when you have acquired the social graces I'm sure between us we can find you a suitor.'

'A suitor?' Emerald was taken by surprise. 'I'm only just fifteen, Aunt Molly. Why should I need a suitor?'

'Of course. In two years you must be thinking about marriage seriously. In six – when you are twenty-one – you will already be a woman. By then you will need to have found a husband. You have the potential to be a pretty girl, if we let your hair grow and see that you wear the proper underpinnings. Certainly you shall have suitors. Perhaps not of the best family, under the circumstances, but someone who can take care of you, provide what you need . . .' Molly's voice trailed away.

Emerald held on to the back of the chair. Her knuckles were white. A suitor. Like the young men with their manicured hands and flabby bodies she met at Lily's. Or worse – one of the old men, those same old men who tried to put their hands on her knee and feel the soft skin of her thighs.

Emerald shuddered. She said: 'I don't need someone to take care of me, Aunt Molly.'

Doña Molly smiled. 'You do, my dear. Believe me. Marriage will give you independence. Freedom.'

'Did marriage give *you* freedom, Aunt Molly?'

Emerald's face was innocent, her brows raised questioningly. But she knew very well the story of Doña Molly's escape from her own marriage. She had learned it from Miss Lily.

'That, as you very well know, Emerald, is impertinent. Your remarks merely prove my point. You must learn to conduct yourself with propriety. You will have to acquire better manners.' Doña Molly's voice was sharp with irritation. 'Manners, my dear, make a lady.'

221

Emerald stared at her guardian. In her Aunt Molly's estimation, lack of manners was the worst thing which could be said about anyone.

Suddenly Emerald didn't care about manners. Still less did she care about being a lady.

The only person she liked being a lady with was Lily Lovage. And Aunt Molly didn't think Lily was a lady at all.

Emerald said quietly, 'I don't think I want to be a lady.'

'Behaving like a child won't change anything, Emerald.'

Molly looked at the lowered lids and relented a little. It could not be easy for the child. When she spoke again, her voice was more kindly.

'You'll get used to it, my dear. We can make quite a respectable marriage for you, I'm sure.'

'*We?*' Emerald's head jerked up.

Molly hesitated before she replied. 'Others concerned for your welfare—'

A cold wave washed over Emerald. 'It's from my real parents, isn't it?'

Molly shook her head emphatically. 'No, Emerald. Absolutely not. I can promise you that.'

'I don't believe you.'

Molly heard the fear in the girl's voice.

Fear of the future, certainly. Fear of the past, perhaps. Molly was not an insensitive woman; she just couldn't understand the young. How could she? She had no experience of such matters.

Molly shook her head, her voice more kindly this time.

'No, child. That letter was not from your *real* parents, whoever they may be. You are – were – a foundling. Miss Mackenzie *found* you. I am your guardian until we find you a husband. Then he will take over the responsibility for your welfare. As for the rest of it, I can only tell you, child, some things are better left unasked.'

Emerald stared at the letter in her guardian's hand. A thought had struck her. 'Would it be impertinent, Aunt Molly, to ask who wrote that letter?'

'Since you ask, child, it's the man to whom you owe your presence here. My son Anthony. And I can assure you, he and I have only your welfare at heart.'

Emerald felt the blood rise to her cheeks. 'And what is his interest in me, Aunt Molly?'

'That, child, is not any of your business. Anthony has a finely developed sense of responsibility.' Molly sighed. 'He has that from his father, as I know only too well.'

222

'I think it's very much my business,' Emerald said quietly. 'Mr Anstruther is the one who had me and my nan sent here from Eas Forse.'

'Emerald, in life one must learn discretion.'

She looked at her ward. Even for those who had everything, there were prices to be paid, as she herself had found out.

Molly put out her hand in a gesture of sympathy, and said quietly, 'My dear, it's not the end of the world. It's for your own good.'

Emerald shook her head fiercely. Emerald knew all about her own good. It had been for her own good when she and her nan had left Eas Forse. When Callum had been taken from her. And now it was for her own good she should be found a husband. *For your own good* meant absolutely the opposite. From now on Emerald knew she must be the judge of her own good.

She stood up.

'Can I go now, Aunt Molly?'

Her guardian nodded. But her mind was already on the journey ahead. So fatiguing, travelling. And so much to be done.

'Yes, my dear. It'll all work out for the best. You must pack your things and be ready.'

But Emerald was no longer listening. She already knew exactly how to foil her Aunt Molly's plans. She would do it immediately. Before it was too late.

33

Eas Forse: 1952

After the ferry had pulled away, Callum waited patiently for his turn at the post-office counter. The postmistress peered at him over her half-moon spectacles.

'Young Callum Fergusson. Here ye are: the letter from the south, I see.'

The postmistress knew everyone's business on the island. The postmistress was sister to the island's telephonist. And the sister was married to the lighthouse operator who manned the shortwave radio. So between them there was nothing they did not know about the islanders' affairs.

'Ye'll be on tenterhooks, I'm thinking.'

She pushed the pile across the counter. 'I set Catriona Sweeney's bundle with it.'

'Much obliged to ye, missus.'

Callum picked up the bundle and stared at the envelope with the London postmark. He turned the envelope over in his hand, hesitated for an instant. What if it was not the reply he had been longing for, the reply which would take him down to the city and into his new life?

It was not the kind of letter you opened with all the island's eyes upon you. He tucked the letter into his pocket, picked up his foster-mother's thick wad of newspapers and carried them out into the sunlight.

It was the schoolmistress who'd made him write the letter applying for the job in London in the first place.

Catriona Sweeney had retired that year, after the island's school was relegated to infants only, the seniors amalgamated with one on the mainland which Eas Forse's children now attended as weekly boarders. The new school might be larger and much better equipped, but in Catriona's view it didn't begin to offer the education she'd provided for her pupils for years. None of them, she was fond of repeating, had ever lacked for the three r's, or had been excused the duty of getting by heart passages of Shakespeare and Milton – under threat of her fiercely wielded ruler.

Catriona loved the classics, but she also had a passion for modern literature. Over the years she had badgered and bullied the librarian on the mainland into sending her parcels of all the latest novels for her charges. Once a month, as a special favour, the librarian would also send her a bundle of the library's old newpapers. Callum had been entrusted with the task of searching for and cutting out any story that might have to do with island affairs.

Quite early on, as the boy combed through the newspapers under her direction, Catriona became aware of his passion for the grainy photographs that studded the pages. After he had his camera – the smart new Zeiss Contax, the best professional camera on the market, sent up from the south with the compliments of Anthony Anstruther, together with a big box of film and the equipment to blow up the images – she helped Callum convert the lean-to shed at the back of the cottage into a darkroom.

The schoolmistress watched with pride as he produced his first smudged images, sifting the prints through shallow tin trays of foul-smelling chemicals.

Callum had accepted the camera eagerly – but that was before he had realized he was never going to receive the promised news of Emerald. Not, at any rate, from that particular source.

Emerald and her whereabouts was not a matter he could discuss with his foster-mother. The old antagonism between Margaret Mackenzie and the schoolmistress had not mellowed, in spite of the temporary truce. Any mention of Emerald brought a thunderous brow and two days of silence.

All the more reason for him to go south. There he might be able to have news of his foster-sister.

As he grew more skilful, photography had taken over Callum's life. Soon he was recording everything on the island from the winter storms that raged over the tops, to the shepherds' outdoor feasts in the lee of the stone fanks that marked the end of a successful gathering-in of the flocks.

When he was sixteen, without his knowledge Catriona entered a group of Callum's pictures in a competition sponsored by the *Oban Times* for scenes of highland and island life. The photographs won not only the main prize, but also the subsidiary prizes for almost every other category that was advertised.

'It will do well enough, laddie,' Catriona said as she read the results. 'Shall we call it eight out of ten? Ye missed out on studies of home baking and floral arrangements.'

Callum stared at her. He flushed scarlet with happiness. From the schoolmistress, never mind that she was also his foster-mother, eight out of ten was unheard of. None of her pupils had ever been awarded marks like that.

'I'll do the home baking and the florals for next year,' he said.

'Next year ye may have other business on your mind,' Catriona said severely. 'Ye can leave next year to me. I shall be considering.'

It took her six months. Six months when, unknown to the young man, Catriona Sweeney scrutinized the employment advertisements in magazines and newspapers that had rarely, if ever, reached Eas Forse before but which now poured on to the island in a weekly stream. The cost bit deeply into her savings and made the Salen postmistress, Morag, work overtime to bundle them all up with rubber bands and direct them to the cottage.

Finally Catriona found what she was looking for.

A London photographer wished to extend his practice of 'portraiture and elegant fashion modelling in natural settings, as the mode of today requires'. He wanted an assistant. Catriona Sweeney had exactly the assistant for him.

'I'll draft the letter of application for ye,' she said to Callum. 'Then ye can transcribe it in your own hand. It's the job ye've been looking for, and it's what you're going to get.' She beckoned at the kitchen table. 'Sit down, laddie. We'll do it right here and now.'

That was two weeks ago. The letter had been written and sent off in the puffer. Now the reply was in his hand.

Callum walked up the main street until he reached the bench which overlooked the bay. There he slit open the letter.

'Dear Mr Fergusson,' he read. 'I am pleased to be able to offer you' – his eye skipped down the paragraphs – 'modest starting salary of five pounds a week' – he scarcely needed to read further. He scarcely *could* read any further, his heart was beating so fiercely.

Catriona must be the first to know.

His foster-mother came to the door at his knock, and saw by Callum's face and the letter in his hand the news he brought. Her face lit up with pleasure.

'I scarce need ask if the news is good. And at the right moment, if I'm not much mistaken. If ye'll hand me the bundle of papers, I'll no be long in the completion.'

Callum raised his eyebrows questioningly.

'Your papers, lad. I'm not the island's archivist for nothing. It's all here,' she said proudly. 'Every man, woman and child of yer ancestry. And this packet ye've brought me has the last piece of the puzzle, if I'm not mistaken. Now, put the kettle on, and give me space to spread it out.'

Catriona had done her work diligently. It was not till the far end of the day, when Catriona had made her gift, had set out all she knew of Callum's past (holding back all she knew of that other victim of the storm, now long gone from the island) that she triumphantly dropped into his hand the final entry, the official announcement of the declaration of probate.

So eagerly did she anticipate the future that she forgot to care for the past – had forgotten that the past itself might be a burden too great to bear.

For Callum, the bald declaration was the news he had been dreading ever since that night when the storm had tossed him on to the shores of Eas Forse. He, and everyone else on the island, had known always that he was Callum Stuart Fergusson, the grandson of the old laird who had been drowned on the night of the storm on his way to fetch his only grandson off the doomed *Politician*. It was also known to all and sundry that the old laird had died penniless, all but for the ruin of a castle on the headland, which would scarce keep the rain off the rats which were all the living creatures that inhabited it.

As far as Callum knew, all his foster-mother had succeeded in eliciting from the Ministry was an admission that Iona Fergusson had been on a secret mission into enemy territory and that she was listed, as all such casualties were, as missing in action. And then, almost as an afterthought, came the sting. 'Presumed dead' had a double purpose in wartime: it softened the blow to the bereaved and it minimized the official casualty lists. It was a magician's trick, a sleight of hand.

Except that Callum had believed it. It had somehow brought reassurance that all might have a happy ending, that now-you-see-it-now-you-don't trick of the light.

The wording held out the possibility, however faint, that there might have been a mistake. That somewhere, God alone knew where, there might be that very same beloved mother who still, in his dreams, brushed his cheek with her lips.

It was not that he had lacked for care. Catriona saw he wanted for nothing – as much as anyone wanted for things in wartime. And later, as he grew older, she had been as good as any mother might ever be with her son.

It was not Iona's absence but her presence that he felt. He missed her in the summer breeze which carried the faint trace of her rose perfume. He missed her in the wind from the sea which brought him, in that moment just before waking or sleeping, the echo of her voice. He missed her, above all, in the companionship of the little girl with the violet eyes – once lost, regained, and lost again, it seemed, for ever.

When Emerald had first gone, he had run down to meet the ships which called at the island, searching the faces eagerly. Later, as the memories of his childhood faded, he had no longer greeted each passing ship with a surge of hope. Yet, as he grew to manhood, Callum did not forget. Even had he wanted to, the island did not let him forget. He would climb the castle walls, and set himself down to gaze out to sea, wondering about the grandfather who had set out to reach him on that black night of the storm. Try to conjure up the father he had scarcely known. Save until last the image of her own dear face, etched into his memory as indelibly as if it had been gouged into every stone of the crumbling citadel.

Somehow his heart had not credited what his head told him must be so: that his mother was dead. Now he stared down at the black-ringed entry in the newspaper. 'Died bravely. Probate granted.' That was all. That was the end of it. Raw, naked and unequivocal.

For a moment Callum looked steady and unseeing at Catriona, dry-eyed, blindly aware of her anxious face; dimly aware, too, of the pain he must be causing her, his foster-mother, who had given him everything.

Then, silent and grieving, he went out into the night.

Catriona let him go. What else could she do?

Callum walked all night long on the hill, offering to the first woman he had ever loved that one single night for all time, from moonrise to the moment the sun rose blood-red over the sea.

All night long he tasted the bitter pain of loss, walked with the ghosts on the headland, kept company at long last with the dead. All that long night he remembered his childhood, remembered his boyhood, laid all his memories at the feet of his own sweet mother-love, rocking her in his arms, soothing her brow as once she had soothed his own.

Until, finally, gazing out at dawn over the rolling waves which had carried him, tossed on the storm which had changed his world for ever, he had offered her, his sweet mother-love, one long night of his remembering.

And then, for Callum at least, it was done.

His childhood behind him, the pain of his loss locked in his heart, accepted and buried along with the mother whose ghost he had finally bid farewell, he went back to Catriona to take charge of the legacy she had assembled, to plan his future and bury his past for ever.

The following week, his arrangements complete, he packed his belongings, including his precious photographic equipment, took leave of the schoolmistress, embarked on the ferry and took the train south for London.

In his wallet, tucked in beside the precious contract of employment, was a letter of introduction to Anthony Anstruther.

Although he had not liked to mention it to Catriona, when she gave him the letter and told him of the role the barrister had offered to play in his life, his only thought was that he might at last have news of his childhood companion.

What Catriona failed to mention was that she had kept back the letters which, soon after the little girl's departure, had arrived for Callum regularly, clearly addressed in a familiar round childish hand, bearing a foreign stamp. It had been fortunate that Catriona had anticipated trouble, and had a confidential word with the postmistress.

It was better that way. She only had Callum's welfare at heart. Even if it had gone against her principles to suppress the written word, she was sure it had been the right decision. Sure enough, over the years the letters had slowed to a trickle, and finally stopped.

Least said, soonest mended.

34

Mexico: 1952

All Emerald had to do was find Nacho and tell him what she had decided. She was quite certain he would help her. The trouble was, Nacho seemed to have disappeared. She searched for him everywhere. Emerald went down to the kitchen. Lupe would know where Nacho might be found.

Lupe was bustling about unloading the morning's marketing.

'Dreaming with the little angels, nenita?'

The phrase was her usual greeting when Emerald had risen late.

'Si, Lupe.' Emerald gave Lupe a speculative look. Lupe would certainly not approve of her plan.

'Well, then, mi nena. You need food. Eat your breakfast. The tortillas are fresh.'

Lupe cleared a space among the groceries and set out a knife and fork. Then she went over to the stove and ladled out a cup of thick hot chocolate.

Emerald sniffed hungrily.

She picked up one of the black-blistered maize-pancakes and rolled it round to make a cornet for some of Lupe's guava jelly. It was lovely with the chocolate.

Lupe smiled as she watched Emerald chewing. As long as she ate, all would be well. News travelled fast, and Lupe approved of Doña

Molly's plans. When the time came, the child would make a beautiful bride. Skinny, but what would you?

Meanwhile there was work to be done. Food to be prepared. Thank the gods for meat and the strength to enjoy it. She 'had picked out a fine young turkey in the market and carried it home by the legs. It was filling its belly in the yard right now. Not for long. Lupe rolled up her sleeves. There was the sauce to be made.

Emerald finished the tortilla and made herself another.

Lupe picked up the heavy stone mortar, set it in the middle of the floor and began to throw in handfuls of spices for a *mole negro*, a rich black stew which took a whole day to make properly. After that the turkey would no longer be gobbling about in the yard. Lupe made the best turkey stew in the town.

Emerald watched Lupe as she worked the pestle, pounding up the crimson chillies with green tomatoes and cinnamon and sesame and garlic and nuggets of grainy unsweetened chocolate. Lupe was strong. If anything, she was even stronger than Nacho.

Emerald filled her nostrils with the sharp peppery scents. They reminded her of Nacho.

When she had finished the second tortilla, she licked her fingers and said, quite casually, as if it wasn't the most important thing in the world: 'Where's Nacho, Lupe?'

Lupe set the pestle down and shook her head. 'La señora says you are to be a good girl and stay at home today.'

'Just a hint? He'll be back for the stew?'

Lupe smiled. She had a round brown face with slanting black eyes and high cheekbones, just like Nacho's.

Emerald gave Lupe a hug. 'Please, Lupe – it's really important.'

Emerald could always get round Lupe.

Lupe said, 'That boy is going from wild to crazy. Some business in the hills he had with Ito and all the rest of them. Crazy boys, stirring up trouble for themselves and everyone else.'

Lupe's position as Doña Molly's cook-housekeeper gave her status – and Nacho a full belly and a bit of education. At least the boy could read and write. Not like his cousin Ito, who had never been to school at all. It was a cut above life down in the barranca, and Lupe did not approve of the company her son kept.

'But no doubt he'll be back for his supper.'

'Thanks, Lupe.'

Emerald thought for a moment. Then she grinned and went out into the sunshine of the yard.

Lupe shouted after her. 'Don't you go looking for him, Esmeralda. La señora would never forgive me.'

But Emerald was already climbing down the barranca. There was no time to lose. At this very moment Doña Molly was planning her future, contacting suitable husbands, telling them she had 'expectations'.

Emerald had expectations. But her expectations had nothing to do with Doña Molly.

Emerald had decided to wait for Nacho at the piragua pool.

The pool acted as a natural reservoir for the ancient aqueduct that brought water to the town below. It was small but very deep. Because of its cup-like shape, the pool was called for the piraguas, the little wooden shell-boats which the Indios used to ford rivers and cross marshes. Nacho told Emerald the water reached right down into the middle of the world.

Nacho would know where to find her. The piragua was where Emerald always came when she wanted to think.

The piragua pool had been the first place Nacho had shown Emerald after he had decided to take her under his protection. That first day had been Emerald's tenth birthday. Her nan had said they could all go out on a picnic – the three of them, Nacho and Emerald and her nan. Nacho had led the way, striding out on his strong legs, with Emerald trotting as close to his heels as she could, and her nan with the basket behind.

Overhanging it, bending over the clear still depths, was an ancient avocado-tree, its silvery branches weighed down with thick green leaves and heavy emerald fruit.

'This is Xochipili, the ancestor of all avocado-trees,' the brown-limbed boy had told her proudly. 'No tree can bear fruit which has not had a fruiting branch grown on it from another of its kind.'

'And in the beginning?' Emerald asked.

'There was Xochipili. He was both mother and father.'

Emerald was surprised. Even *she* knew that everyone needed a mother *and* a father. Unless, of course, they were changelings like Emerald.

She stared up at the tree. Xochipili must be very special.

Nacho smiled. Emerald loved his smile – the strong white teeth and the way his eyes crinkled at the corners.

'Here.' In a moment, Nacho had picked up Emerald and swung her up on to the top arch of the aqueduct, so that she could reach into Xochipili's branches.

Emerald had climbed up into the greenery, pulling herself from arch to arch on the aqueduct, until she could reach the hard green fruits. She pulled one off and bit into it. It was as hard as wood.

'It tastes horrible!' she called down.

'¡Claro!' he called back. 'Those are Xochipili's unborn children.'

Emerald jumped back down beside him.

'What do you mean, Nacho?'

Nacho laughed. Emerald, for all her books, had so much to learn.

'They are like you, Esmeralda. Young and green and still on the branch. Like all of us, Xochipili's fruit must fall before it can ripen.'

Nacho bent down and picked up one of the fruits which lay on the ground. He pulled off a piece of the skin. It peeled off easily.

Emerald poked her finger into the soft flesh. Inside it was creamy and yellow. She licked her finger.

'You like it, nenita?'

But Emerald's mouth was full, and she could only nod. It was delicious.

Then they raced each other down the aqueduct, straight into the waiting arms of her nan, toiling up the path behind them.

When Doña Molly had heard where Emerald and Nacho and her nan had been, she had scolded everyone. She made Emerald promise not to go there again.

Emerald had promised, but she had crossed her fingers behind her back. Everyone knew that Emerald kept her word. No-one would go looking for her when she visited Xochipili.

From then on Xochipili was the place she went when she was sad – when she was missing Callum, or missing her nan after the marsh fever had carried her off. And Xochipili put out his arms and comforted her.

Emerald also visited Xochipili when she was really happy, so that he could share that with her as well. It wouldn't have been fair otherwise.

Today, when she needed him, Emerald knew that Xochipili would help her.

She climbed steadily, listening to the trickle of the stream imprisoned in the channel carved into the stone. The water went all the way down to the town. It tinkled gently, like goat-bells.

When she reached the piragua pool, she climbed the aqueduct until she reached Xochipili's lower branches, and worked her way along until she was hidden among the leaves just like when she was as young and green as the fruit he carried.

All she had to do was wait for Nacho. Xochipili would do the rest.

The bees were busy among the tiny white flowers on the tree, and the water bubbled softly in the conduit on its way to the town.

If there had been a breeze to shake the branches, Emerald often gathered the ripened fruits from the ground and brought them down for Lupe to make her a bowl of guacamole for her supper.

Lupe never told on her, even though she surely knew where the fruit had come from. She would peel off the knobbly rind and chop the rich yellow curds with green tomatoes, coriander and a specially fiery green chilli.

Emerald would sit on the steps outside the kitchen door with the bowl of squished avocado and scoop up the scented pulp, like green porridge, with a bit of tortilla – just as she had once sat outside the crofthouse door with an oatcake to scoop up her dish of crowdie curds.

Today there would be no time for such childish things.

Emerald closed her eyes, drifting back in her memory to another time when she had come up to take comfort from Xochipili.

She had been – then as now – day-dreaming among Xochipili's branches. She had fallen into a doze from which she woke with a start to the sound of soft laughter below.

Propping herself on her elbow, she looked down through the leaves. On the bank beside the piragua pool, beside a pair of discarded cotton wraps, lay two wedding-garlands of trumpet-shaped hibiscus flowers. The scent of tuberoses mingled with the thick rich smell of the fruit in the grass beneath Xochipili.

There were two people, a boy and a girl standing very close facing each other under the tree, hands lightly pressed together. Both were naked, clothed only in the dappled evening sunlight which made their bodies freckled as the spotted cat she had hunted with Nacho.

The boy moved towards the girl. Emerald caught her breath. The boy's sex was enormous. Emerald had never seen anything like it, not even when Conchita was making Ito's baby in the hut down the barranca.

The boy smiled as he moved closer to the girl's body, pressed back against the trunk of the tree, out of Emerald's line of sight. The boy's smile was as bright as sunlight.

The girl moved away from the tree trunk. The boy pulled the girl's thighs towards him. He began to move in and out of her body, making little murmurs, stroking the girl's hair.

Emerald could feel the boy's touch, felt it in her own body, all up and down her legs and in her secret places.

Then the girl wrapped her legs across the boy's back, making the linked bodies look like one of the beasts drawn on the stone slates in the forest. The double-backed creature rolled over and over until the glade was full of the sweet smell of damp earth and ripe fruit.

At last they lay still, the creature separated itself, and once again became what it had been at the beginning, two children playing in

234

the glade. Xochipili had already shown Emerald what she must do. Meanwhile, she had only to be patient, and Nacho would come to her.

Day turned to evening. The moon rose clean and new.

Emerald waited for Nacho in the twilight, cradled in Xochipili's arms.

Nacho had been up in the mountains all day, working in the stony fields alongside his ragged barranca army, harvesting the crop which would bring them brotherhood and liberty.

When he reached the outskirts of the town, he changed course and, instead of returning to his mother's kitchen, climbed the path which led to the piragua pool. Until that moment when he knew she needed him, he had not thought of Emerald for an hour at least.

Where the spring rose, bubbling out of the earth into the pool, the great tree splayed long fingers into the earth and sky, the water's surface a perfect burnished mirror for its heavy tresses.

He looked round the glade, and then up into the branches. He knew, felt it in the nerves of his fingertips, that she must be close. He settled down to wait.

Emerald, high in the branches, waited for Xochipili to cast his spell.

The air was sweet and warm, and the moonlight almost as bright as day. The water looked cool and inviting.

'Nacho?' There was soft laughter behind the familiar voice.

Nevertheless, the whisper caught him by surprise.

Nacho searched the glade again. And then stared up into the branches.

'Esmeralda?'

'Who else?'

Nacho felt his skin prickle with the nearness of her.

The rustling of Xochipili's leaves punctuated the young woman's descent from the branches above his head.

'Close your eyes, I have a surprise.'

All at once Emerald was by his side.

'Look now.'

Nacho obeyed.

Her apricot-skinned, moon-bright body glimmered against the dark bulk of the tree's reflection in the shining waters. She was naked. Nacho's body was nut-brown and smooth beside her.

Above them, Xochipili trailed long green fingers towards the double image reflected in the pool.

At once her slender form arched into the water, the ripples closing behind the dark cap of hair as she vanished into the night-black depths.

Emerald surfaced, shaking her head so that bright droplets shone like stars gathered back into the dark pool. Nacho's hands were on her now, light in the water as a fish's fins. She felt the sinewy warmth of his body against her own, slipping like silk against her naked skin.

No-one had ever touched her like that before – the fluttering of the fingertips covered her like a cloak, as if she was caressed by a thousand little fishes.

'Alma de mi corazon, soul of my heart, come.'

Nacho's voice was low and urgent. Gently he drew her to the edge of the pool.

Droplets of water glistened on their bodies as they came out into the warm night air.

Nacho picked his princess up in his arms and carried her to the grass under the tree. He laid her down among the warm ripe fruit beneath Xochipili and lay down with her, his brown limbs strong and warm. She felt an unbearable excitement, as if something extraordinary was about to happen. Just as it had happened when she had watched the boy and the girl twined together among that same ripe fruit.

The same perfume rose to her nostrils, mingled now with Nacho's scent, the familiar scent she knew and loved.

Every nerve in Emerald's body tingled with astonishment. Nacho's lips moved against her shoulders, to her breasts. At his touch, it was as if there were fine threads tugging at her, her limbs helpless as one of the clay puppets the market-children played with.

Nacho's voice was close to her ear: 'Are you sure, my soul? Sure this is what you want?'

Now he was kneeling beside her. She could feel his breath on her skin. He crushed the buttery green flesh of the pears in his strong brown hands. He rubbed the leaf-scented pulp all over her body, lingering and slow. She closed her eyes, the better to understand what his hands were telling her. There was no need of words as he showed her the secret places – here and here and here were the pulse points, the nerves of fingertips and toes, the delicate mysteries in the soft small folds between her thighs – which unlocked her body's joy.

Soon it would happen. Soon.

Wordless, Emerald pulled him to her, feeling the hot length of him against her, parting her thighs to draw him within. The flesh of the fruit made her body receptive, liquid as velvet.

He was gentle. So gentle it was almost unbearable.

Emerald felt the resistance in her body opening to him, the tender membrane parting, closing round him. And then he was inside her and she knew it was done. Almost as if there was nothing there. No veil to keep them apart.

Was this all it was? This small thing, this spider's web which separated, as Aunt Molly said, the good girls from the bad?

Nacho made love to her then, as he had never made love to anyone ever before. He made love to her not just with his body, not the baby-making that he made with the girls down the barranca, but with all his heart and soul.

The night sky sang to her. The stars danced for her. The moon smiled to see them there together, on the grass, by the piragua pool, cradled by the tree which was as old as all the world.

From that moment she knew she had changed, knew she had discovered something in herself which was all her own. Something which had nothing to do with anyone or anything, which had nothing to do with who she might be or how others saw her. Something which set her apart, now and for ever. The gift of Xochipili.

At the end, when the final explosion had come and gone, she held him close, drawing him into her, as if he was no longer Nacho but Xochipili himself, the dancing god whose branches shadowed the moon.

It was as if all the sun in the world had come to shine on her. As if all the oceans of the world were lapping over her. How could it be bad, this marvellous feeling?

Afterwards, when Emerald thought about that moment, it slipped away from her, elusive, leaving behind no print of its passing, but a slick of honeyed juices between her thighs.

Emerald smiled up at Nacho. His slant-eyes were dark as the piragua pool. She had not even had to ask. She had not had to find the words, the words she had not even formed in her mind.

So she said: 'Nacho, sweet Nacho.'

Nacho leaned on his elbow and looked down at Emerald, tracing the lines of her body, the secret folds, with a gentle hand.

She said: 'I knew you would.'

'Would what?' he said. 'This? And this?'

Emerald's laughter was joyful.

'Again,' she said. And then she pulled him to her once more.

Nacho's smooth brown body arched above hers, and their bodies came together a second time, hot on the cool rock pillowed by a bed of fallen leaves, limbs lapped by the ripples of the pool.

Afterwards they lay together, the night breeze drying their bodies, and Emerald knew that nothing would ever again be the same. The old Emerald, whose goodness or badness had a price, was gone for ever.

She was no longer the foundling who belonged to whatever and whoever might choose to claim her. Emerald no longer belonged to anyone.

And Nacho, his face tender in the aftermath of love, looked down at the girl in his arms, and knew without being told that she had taken what she wanted of him.

Emerald was nobody's. Not even Nacho's.

35

Mexico: 1952

Emerald's rope-soled espadrilles made no noise as she padded across the shadowy garden towards the Yellow House.

The beating of her heart sounded like a drumbeat in the still night air. Even the crickets down the barranca seemed to be holding their breath.

The light in Doña Molly's boudoir gleamed through the heavy linen curtains, but the rest of the colonnaded building was in darkness.

She moved silently up the steps, unlatched the door and began to tiptoe through the wide marble hall.

The door of her guardian's room stood slightly ajar, allowing a beam of light to trace a slender triangle on the pale ochre floor.

On the other side of the line the shadowy stairwell rose towards the safety of her room. She was absolutely certain that what she had just done must be clearly written on her face, on every line of her body. She had to see herself, look at herself, compose her words. She had not even clearly worked out what she was to do, where to go.

Too late. The shining thread of light widened and then vanished. Doña Molly's bulk filled the doorway.

Emerald froze. 'Emerald? Is that you? Where have you been, child? I was worried.'

Emerald shrank back into the shadows.

'Nowhere special, Aunt Molly. Up the hill.'

'Up the hill?' Her guardian's voice was irritated. 'Really Emerald, I thought we had been through all that. We agreed it was time to put childish things behind you. And I had important news for you.'

In her hand she held a thick yellow manila envelope. Emerald knew what it contained.

She suddenly drew herself up. If she was no longer a child, it was time to stop behaving like one. It was time to be an adult.

'I have important news, too. I lost my virginity, Aunt Molly.'

Emerald's voice was as confident as she could possibly make it. 'I'm nearly sixteen, and Conchita lost hers when she was twelve.'

'What are you *saying*, child?' Molly's voice rose in anguished disbelief.

Emerald smiled calmly, even though she didn't feel at all calm. Emerald knew that you had to be a virgin when you married. All the books said *virgo intacta* was what you had to be. You had to save yourself for Mr Right. Or even, as Lily had done, for Mr Wrong. And if you threw yourself away on a nobody – well, that was that. Doña Molly thought Nacho was nobody at all.

'And so you see, Aunt Molly,' she finished, 'I can't possibly marry anyone. So there's no need to finish me at all.'

'Who?' Molly's voice was low. The kind of low which meant she was really angry. 'I want to know *who*.'

Emerald shook her head. 'No-one really, Aunt Molly.' Emerald knew that, in Doña Molly's view, that would be no more than the truth.

'You *will* tell me, child. You will come to me in the morning, and you will tell me.' Molly looked hard at her ward. 'Was it one of those young men at Lily's?'

Emerald thought of the soft-fleshed boys who lounged round Lily's pool in their shirts covered with palm-trees, pale eyes shielded by sunglasses, thin hairy legs all pink from the sun. They talked of stock markets and gambling and girls. In her mind's eye she shook them out of their linen trousers with the creases down the front. She very nearly giggled aloud. Not a bit like Nacho. Not at all like Nacho. Not ever.

'No, Aunt Molly. Not one of them.'

'Child, I cannot possibly leave you here after this. You will have to come with me to the capital—'

'That really won't be necessary,' Emerald said firmly.

Molly stared at her ward. She was at her wits' end. She would have to write to her son immediately and tell him what had happened. He would have to bring the plans forward. It was all much too much for her to cope with on her own. *How* it had happened was beyond her. If Emerald hadn't

240

explained the event in such graphic detail, she would not have believed her. The only information Emerald had *not* given was her partner in what Molly could only describe as a gross error of judgement.

It could not possibly be Lupe's young ruffian. Except that she could not imagine who else it could possibly be.

She hoped to heaven the child would not be in worse trouble as a result of her pig-headedness. Girls did not simply throw away their chances as Emerald had done. Molly felt quite faint with the anxiety of it.

But Emerald did not wait for her guardian to put any further plans into action. The next morning, before even Lupe was about, she packed a bag with her few belongings, searched her nan's room till she found the blue book she knew was the passport she needed for her travels, tucked the rolled-up alligator skin under her arm, and slipped out of the garden door.

'Given name?'

'Esmeralda.'

The moustachioed official, pen poised, looked up expectantly.

'Father? Mother?'

'Noname,' she said, and wrote the word out carefully in her best capital letters on the top of the form. Then she slid across the blue book with the gold stamp on its cover, placed the rolled-up alligator skin on the desk and gazed steadily back at her questioner. It was a risk, but it was all she had.

The man set down his pen and looked closely at the young woman, noting not only the ragged clothes but also the violet eyes and paleness of her. In part gringa, if he wasn't mistaken, in spite of the dialect of the barranca and the barranca-dweller clothes. The booklet was not much good as a travel document. It had clearly belonged to an old woman travelling with a child. The child who was now a grown woman herself.

Then he looked back at the delicately patterned leather the girl had brought, and prodded it thoughtfully. There was a price for everything – either in metalico or in kind. Alligator shoes were a status symbol for anyone who was anyone in the town.

Esmeralda. At least she was well named. This one was certainly a jewel – and the official had an eye for such things. More than a few paid for his official services in kind. This one was not that sort. He could always tell.

However, if all the pretty one wanted was a travel document, who was he to argue? She would soon be across the border, soon find a rich gringo to take care of her. Perhaps even had one already. And that was more than could be said for most of his compatriots, obliged to swim the shallow red waters of the Rio Grande to reach the promised land, the cities of the gringos, where the very sewers ran with golden dollars. For them, papers were an unnecessary extravagance, and the trade in official passes was not the business it had once been.

The official looked up at the young woman again, and back down at her offering. He flexed his feet in his worn shoes. The skin was worth ten pesos in the market, a reasonable price for what she required.

He nodded. What was a piece of paper when set against a pair of alligator shoes?

He bent back to his task: the fabrication of a human identity. This was a service for which the State, swamped by the paperwork required to keep track of a mushrooming and illiterate population, paid him a token wage – expecting their employees to make up the remainder through private enterprise.

Date of birth? At least she could inform him of that. Half the population had no record of an event which one of the two material witnesses was too young to recall. Place of birth? Among the shifting populations of the barranca dwellings, razed to the ground every few months, such questions were greeted with a smile and a shrug. He wrote her down as eighteen, just to be on the safe side.

Name? No name. The official was not a stupid man. He prided himself on his education, or he would not have reached a position of such responsibility. Well, if the pretty young woman did not care to admit or even could not acknowledge her parentage, that was not so unusual either. It was not his business to enquire into public morality, merely to see that the formalities were properly observed.

There was a shorthand, a code to overcome such problems of birth, domicile and parenthood. Slowly, deliberately he worked his way down the forms. He enjoyed his work. It had a creative side to it.

He signed the document with a flourish, sealed it with the official stamp, gummed down the blurred black-and-white photograph, and glanced up at the original herself, watching him anxiously from the other side of the desk.

'Buena fortuna, Esmeralda Sin-nombre,' he said, just so that she knew he knew exactly what she was up to, and that the exchange was a fair trade. He pushed the document towards her and laid his hand on the leathery skin.

The young woman smiled and picked up the precious paper. Such a lovely smile. Good fortune was hers already. With a face like that she would have no need of fortune.

Buena fortuna was for those such as he, and that girl there, who knew how to take it for themselves. He propped his feet on the desk and draped the worn shoes with the new skin. He would cut a fine figure on the evening paseo.

Meanwhile, Emerald, her precious papers in her pocket, threaded her way swiftly and determinedly through the busy morning streets. Her heart sang. She had claimed a name which was hers alone. She was Emerald Noname. It was excellent.

At last she reached the arched gateway which gave admittance to the grounds of Lily Lovage's sprawling white mansion on the outskirts of the town. She knew that Lily would give her temporary sanctuary – might even manage to persuade Aunt Molly that this was an interim solution. It would give her time to make proper plans. Lily might even be able to help.

But Lily already had every intention of playing fairy godmother to Emerald. Better still, she knew just where to find the magic wand.

36

New York: 1952

The magic wand Lily had in mind for Emerald was Sir William Beaumont, New York's premier social fixer.

Billy had stumbled on his vocation almost by accident. After spending the war years in the Bahamas playing jester at the court of Queen Wallis, the dapper baronet had found himself on his uppers in Manhattan. In the land of opportunity, New York had the most money, the tallest skyscrapers, the richest bankers, the most lavish shops. In short, it had everything except class – that sheen which, like the patina on old furniture, comes from years of patient polish. Class was all Sir William Beaumont had. Class – and the address-book to go with it.

But class did not earn the daily bread – unless that was what you called free dinners.

It did not take him long to identify the gap in the market.

To earn his share of the goods on offer, Billy set up a highly specialized finishing school. You could really call it *the* finishing school. Social acceptability could be bought. At the end of three months, Billy's well-dowered young ladies, lighter by a thousand dollars or so, but with their rough edges smoothed to a veneer of European sophistication, could with confidence be despatched in search of titled Englishmen hungry for fortunes which might put the roofs put back on their crumbling ancestral piles, and whose table manners would at least not frighten the horses.

'Where there's demand, I supply,' was Billy's motto.

It was also a nice little earner.

Once a year he accompanied a chaperoned party of his young ladies – only those who met his strict standards of fortune and polish – to experience a little Old World culture at first hand.

For every ancestral pile in need of reroofing there was an heiress in need of a handle. The young mistresses of commerce fortunate enough to show Billy the hand of fortune would find no stone unturned, even if all that crawled out from underneath was a feckless fop of a younger son.

And for such favours a discreet finder's fee was, of course, in order. In addition, if any of his young ladies happened to catch a title worth having – one of the big ones, ancient or modern – well, Billy shared in the joy and, in a modest way, the worldly goods exchanged with the contract.

Billy taught the young ladies everything he felt a young lady should know. In fact Billy's enterprise was not so different from what Molly Anstruther had had in mind for Emerald. Billy kept a few places for what he considered to be investments for the future – what he liked to think of as 'scholarship girls'. This was what Lily had in mind for Emerald.

There were lessons in what Billy considered the usual social arts: the selection of menus, the proper shaking of a cocktail, the construction of canapés, the rituals of teatime, the stocking of the guest bathroom, the arrangement of flowers, how to lose gracefully at bridge and cheat at patience. Billy did the best he could to turn his young ladies into women of the world. At the very least, he told himself, he was performing a vital social function.

In spite of the fees he charged, each year Billy's annual expenditure exceeded his annual income. Savile Row suits and a taste for caviare saw to that. So he had added a new string to his bow. What was sauce for the goose suited the gander as well. In the course of dealing with the daughters' fond papas, he came across more than one homespun millionaire who had outgrown his small-town wife and was looking for a bit of Old World class to hang on his arm. On one or two occasions, quite by chance, Sir William had been able to oblige with a blind date – the sisters or daughters of the owners of the crumbling piles. Discretion was of the essence, but even young ladies of quality were not always averse to a little present or two in return for an evening keeping company not of their own choosing. Surprisingly often the relationship turned into a more permanent arrangement – even marriage.

The exchange could equally well work the other way. A bit of fresh blood from the New World revitalized an Old World fortune.

There was even a rumour – which Beaumont did nothing to discourage – that it was the one-time poor little girl from Baltimore who had given him, in gratitude for a certain confidential but empire-shaking introduction, the sapphire dress studs he wore in his fashionable white picqué dress waistcoat. Billy neither confirmed nor denied that particular rumour. However, he did acknowledge that he had engineered the introduction which provided Wallis Windsor with the man the newspapers called her *cavaliere servente*, the Woolworth heir, Jimmy Donahue. As a millionaire in his own right, young Jimmy was supremely well qualified for the task of escorting Manhattan's most famous socialite. Particularly now her royal husband, deprived of the purpose for which he had been born, seemed increasingly reluctant to play the social game.

'Darling heart, over here!'

Jimmy Donahue's high-pitched shriek rose above the din of New York's fashionable 21, – 'Jack and Charlie's' as it was known to its regulars since the days when it was a speakeasy offering bootleg liquor in the obligatory teacups.

'There he is!' Wallis Windsor said to her husband – somewhat unnecessarily, the Duke thought, since the plump young millionaire was by far the most visible guest in the place.

The Duke and his wife made their way across the crowded restaurant towards their host.

Wallis Windsor graciously proffered her cheek before taking her seat. She crossed her thin legs with a rustle of taffeta underskirt.

Jimmy put his head to one side and examined the Duchess with a mock-critical eye.

'Perfection!' he shrieked.

The Duke frowned. 'For God's sake, Donahue, keep your voice down.'

'Hush, darling. Poor Jimmy only wants to help.'

'What with?' The Duke turned his popping blue eyes on his wife's admirer.

Wallis clicked her tongue disapprovingly. 'Honestly David. With the ball, of course.'

'What ball?'

'Don't be so tiresome, darling. The Duchess of Windsor Ball. We've already discussed your wardrobe. Now it's time for little me.'

'Oh,' said the Duke. 'That ball. How could I have forgotten?'

Wallis made a face. 'And to think it was to please you that it's to be in aid of wounded ex-servicemen. Such a sensible cause, and so unpartisan. You said so yourself.'

The Duke stared at his wife. 'Bit of a performance.'

'Nonsense.' The Woolworth heir put in his pennyworth. 'It'll be wonderful. Everyone needs a party.'

'Genius,' said the Duchess, patting Jimmy's hand.

The Duke scowled.

At first the man had been amusing – and Wallis loved, above all, to be amused. But these days his wife seemed to prefer the company of young Donahue to his own. Dashed odd, as the Woolworth heir was not even her type. He was on the plump side and as bald as a coot.

It was no longer a joke. He watched his wife and the Woolworth heir put their heads together to whisper.

The newspapers were always gossiping. It was annoying – even though no-one of any importance read the gossips. But he had begun to get irritated when she was photographed sitting up late with the man in nightclubs. Finally she had absolutely refused to accompany her husband on his last trip to Europe.

All of a sudden Edward Windsor had had enough. Abruptly he rose to his feet.

'I'm off. Suddenly remembered. Got an appointment.'

His wife looked up. 'Busy day at the office, David?' Wallis's tone was mocking.

Her husband winced. 'Things to do.'

As Wallis well knew, he had nothing at all to occupy his time. Unless you could call hacking out his memoirs an occupation.

'Be a good boy.'

' 'Bye, darling.' His voice softened.

The Duke was quite certain the man was a pansy. Quite sure the only use the portly American millionaire had was to pick up the bill. And in these hard times, with the Privy Purse at sixes and sevens after the death of poor old Bertie, that was no mean advantage.

He rested his hand briefly on his wife's shoulder, and then bent his shining blond head to brush her cheek with his lips. 'Enjoy your lunch.'

The Duchess raised her hand to smooth the perfect chignon.

She said: 'Don't forget the dogs go walkies at three.'

The Duke inclined his head briefly towards his wife's companion. His gaze flicked to his wife. A shadow fell over his face. Wallis had eyes only for her *cavaliere servente*. He reflected that they had come a long way since that wild night at Fort Belvedere. But all he said was: 'Look after Her Royal Highness, Jimmy.'

247

'Yes, indeed, sir.' Donahue half stood to attention, his voice was eager, deferential.

The Duke turned and retraced his steps towards the door, and was gone. Wallis stared after her husband.

When she spoke again, her face was suddenly sombre.

'I've always been scared of that.'

'What, dearest?'

'People leaving. When I was little I was terrified my mother would leave me. My father already had – he died when I was five months old.'

'Poor darling.'

'Not at all. It was probably the best thing that ever happened to me. I made up my mind, as soon as I had the chance, I'd do the leaving. And at eighteen I did it. I left home for good, and I've never looked back. Not once. Not ever.'

'I'll never leave you, *belle dame.*'

'Silly boy. Never at lunchtime, anyway.' Wallis Windsor gave her short bark of laughter. 'I always say I married the Duke for better or worse – but not for lunch.'

'So witty!' shrieked Jimmy, rolling about with exaggerated joy.

Jimmy's mirth was interrupted by the arrival of the main course – a roast pheasant *en demi-deuille,* slivers of black truffle slipped under the skin of the buttery bird.

Jimmy stopped giggling immediately and tucked his napkin into his collar.

'Fabulous,' he said, gobbling greedily.

Wallis lifted a morsel to her lips, nibbled, and put the fork down.

'Be serious, Jimmy.'

Her companion glanced up, and wiped the gravy from his chin, instantly contrite.

'There's only one thing more serious than lunch. And that's the most important event of the year.'

'Good.' The Duchess took another peck at the roast meat. 'Elsa Maxwell's offered to do it all.'

'Elsa's perfect. She's an old cow, but she knows the business. Just like your sister-in-law,' Jimmy said with another hoot of laughter.

'Don't be flippant, Jimmy.'

Wallis's mood had changed. He watched her anxiously. June was scheduled for the coronation of the young Princess Elizabeth. It would be a milestone for Wallis. In her heart of hearts, Jimmy knew, the Duchess had still not accepted that she would never be Queen.

She pushed at a slice of truffle, and then laid down her fork again.

'Anyway, it's absurd. The girl's far too young. They should have sent for the Duke as soon as his brother died – made him regent or something.' Then she brightened. 'Of course the ball'll send Cookie *mad* with rage.'

'Cookie?'

'Bertie's widow. My sister-in-law. The dumpy little *hausfrau*.' Wallis smiled. 'But *our* ball will be the event of the year. Buckingham Palace couldn't manage anything like it.' She stretched out her hand to admire the blazing diamond on her finger. 'Their jewellery will all have to come out of mothballs. So dowdy. None of it's been reset for centuries.'

'No-one, but *no*-one, has your taste, my star!'

'Silly boy.'

Jimmy reached out and patted the Duchess's bony hand.

He loved touching her hands. They were so deliciously thin.

One of the things Jimmy liked about Wallis was how extraordinarily slender she was. Flat as a boy.

He watched admiringly as she blotted her lips on the napkin, leaving a great slash of scarlet lipstick on the white linen. She took out her powder compact, and dabbed a little pressed powder on her nose and chin, and prepared to remake her lips with a Van Cleef basketwork lipstick.

'*So* sexy, making up in public!'

Wallis raised her carefully arched eyebrows and smiled. The compact had been a present from Jimmy, one of many – a gold heart set with a huge cabochon aquamarine, a piece from the Duke of Verdura, Chanel's aristocratic Sicilian designer.

Jimmy sighed appreciatively. Wallis's collection of jewelled *nécéssaires* was famous. She knew how much he enjoyed watching her play with them. She slipped the trinkets back in her new crocodile Hermès bucket-bag and settled back on the velvet banquette.

'It's so marvellously exciting, a party. Elsa says the Waldorf's *perfect*. And Billy Beaumont's agreed to vet the guest-list. In January, too, just when everyone's in the mood after Christmas.'

Wallis made a little moue with her scarlet lips. 'I never had a coming-out ball – I think I deserve one now.'

'So tragic.'

'Elsa's booked young Beaton for the décor. Simply delicious drawings.' The Duchess creased her forehead: 'Not the flowers of course. I trust no-one but myself. White lilac, jasmine, lemon blossom – divinely romantic. All white – like eastern mourning clothes.'

'Deliciously pure! And the frock?'

'*Frocks*. Absolutely secret. But I think Balenciaga for one. Ivory *faille* with a stream of bows all down the back. I raised the neckline just a tiny bit – much more flattering. And a change before the dancing. So boring otherwise. Maybe Mainbocher – full-skirted taffeta. Dusty pink. Pale anyway. White's so virginal.'

She paused reflectively. 'My first long frock was white satin. My mother's nigra seamstress made it. Stitchin' and stitchin' away, por ol' Ellen . . .'

Wallis sighed. 'We were poor as church mice – all Scarlett O'Hara and make-over. I think we even chopped up the curtains. I remember what I wore on my wrist, too: a blue velvet ribbon pinned with a white rose. It was a sensation.'

Wallis's voice soared into a parody of a Deep South drawl: 'My, my – and ain't Wallis just so *original.*' She shook her head. 'How little they knew. Mother had sold off all her jewellery. What else could one do?'

'Poor diddums.'

'Diddums nothing. This time I shall be positively *dripping* with jewels.'

'And I shall pay the bill!'

Wallis Windsor playfully tapped her companion's hand with her gold-rimmed lorgnette. 'You're such a vulgarian, Jimmy.'

Donahue beamed. '*Divina*! We have so much in *common.*'

The Duchess looked at him sharply. Sometimes he went too far. Then she laughed. She could never be cross with Jimmy for long. He really was the most amusing companion. Like that party he had given in his flat, where all the servants were completely naked. Not even a figleaf. Perfectly shocking. And he knew all the best places, and would happily stay up partying all night. While poor David, fussing over his book, was quite content to slip home early – or, better still, as he missed all the gossip, stay at home in Paris.

Jimmy giggled again; he was off and running. '*Divina*, I have it. A fashion show. You shall lead the defile. The couture-houses will *queue* to lend us the grandest ballgowns. Everyone will be quite bewitched.'

'I shall have Alexandre come over from Paris to do my hair.'

'Remember the time he did Elsa? My dear, chopped it right off! Miss Maxwell was mortified. La Vreeland said she looked like a toad in a wig.'

'She's dying to have him do it again.'

'That's not all she's dying to have done again, *bellissima.*'

'Naughty boy. Put on your thinking-cap. We need a theme. I thought, maybe, "Bridge across the Atlantic".'

'Genius!' the Woolworth heir shrieked.

'Then there's the menu.' The Duchess's voice was suddenly alive. Jimmy had noticed she much preferred talking about food to consuming it. It was another of the accomplishments he found wholly admirable.

'It must be absolute perfection – not too extravagant, but completely surprising. First, the merest hint of caviare in an exquisite soufflé of Maine lobster. And, to finish, a perfectly English savoury. Marrow bones served in the whitest of starched napkins. You have to scoop out the marrow with those long silver spoons.'

'So sexy! The main course?'

'I have it!' The Duchess's pale cheeks flushed quite pink with excitement. 'It shall be grouse. *À la royale* – roasted with bacon, with bread sauce and rowanberry jelly just as they do it at Balmoral. Fruity can arrange to get the birds shipped over. Think of the delicious surprise.'

Jimmy clapped his fat little hands with pleasure.

'And I wonder . . . I wonder', the Duchess continued thoughtfully, 'if I could persuade David to pipe in the birds. He takes a set of bagpipes everywhere. It would be such wonderful theatre. He could wear his kilt.'

'His kilt and his pipes and his sporran!'

Then, to the fascination of 21's surrounding guests, who included a stringer for New York's *Daily Mirror,* the two collapsed into helpless laughter, Wallis's harsh sqawks counterpointing the rippling shrieks of her companion.

The following day the story of the lunch and the premature announcement of the Duchess of Windsor's Ball appeared in Walter Winchell's acid-penned society column. As soon as the news broke, the applications for the fifty-dollar-a-plate tickets flooded in. Fortunately, as Wallis said to Jimmy, neither of them had to bother with such things. Billy Beaumont was just the man to sift the wheat from the chaff.

The press interest in the unlikely duo was fuelled by the excitement generated by the party. No matter, as they told each other over a shared pre-dawn breakfast in a secluded red-velvet-upholstered booth at El Morocco – who cares about the press?

37

London: 1952

That gossip sold newspapers was a universal truth not lost on Jack Sweeney.

Gossip columnists had expense accounts and fast cars. They had access to beautiful girls. They enjoyed the kind of lifestyle ordinary people could only dream of. There were few more ordinary than Jack.

With this in mind Jack had offered to do unpaid legwork for his newspaper's all-important society column – he had come a long way since he had first smelled printer's ink as a general dogsbody in the newsroom of the Glasgow *Clarion*.

With his weekly wage-packet from the *Daily News*, Jack found himself a place of his own. He took a short-lease tenancy of a cold-water flat above a strip-joint in Soho. From this vantage-point he plunged head-first into the dungheap, gravitating naturally to the paper's sex-and-sleaze desk. Soho was full of sleaze and sex – and the great and the good who were not so great and good when their trousers were round their ankles.

Jack had done it longer than most. Now it was time to move on. He got himself a new wardrobe, a fashionable haircut, and offered, for the price of the invitation, to fill in for 'Dandy Dan's Diary'.

The incumbent Dandy – a public schoolboy with all the right connections but whose appetite for the bottle was only matched by his skill at recycling stories – was only too glad to pass on the out-of-town events to his enthusiastic apprentice.

'Just keep your eyes peeled and your ears flapping, my young cockerel,' the public schoolboy advised him. 'And get the name spelled right. It's all most of 'em care about.'

Soon Jack was handling the second-best parties and less-fashionable race-meetings, and – never one to forget a lesson well learned – embarked on the task of transforming himself from a seedy hack into the very picture of a young-man-about-town.

If you want to beat 'em, join 'em.

He went down to the market off the Mile End Road on a Sunday morning and equipped himself with a secondhand dinner-jacket and piqué-fronted shirt with collar and bow-tie attached. For the race-meetings and point-to-pointing, he acquired a pork-pie hat, a jacket with double vents, a pair of dark glasses, a check shirt, and a tie which proclaimed membership of a minor public school.

Jack was after the gossip editor's chair. He could see it opened many doors – doors he had learned to peer through when he was helping his aunt the schoolmistress with her archiving. He dreamed one day he would belong to the world he had so far only glimpsed.

In particular one image haunted him. One day, he knew, he would walk up to the most beautiful young woman in the room. He would gaze into her heart-shaped face and see the admiration, the longing in her violet eyes. And then he would turn on his heel and spurn her, just as she had once spurned him. Or perhaps not. But it would be his choice.

Jack set about remodelling himself. He slicked back his fiery ginger mop with scented creams and had his fingernails manicured. He even took evening lessons from a middle-aged lady recently retired from a career on the stage, to have the edges knocked off his accent.

Then he sat back and waited for the plum job to drop in his lap. Even its most devoted readers had to admit the column had lately been slipping.

There had already been eight incumbent Dans since the Diary had first seen the light of day – or, more accurately, the glow of candlelight. Generations of readers – from the idlers of the nineteenth century's coffee houses to the mid-twentieth's busy housewives – knew what they liked. And what they liked was true confessions – sex-and-tell, preferably wearing a tiara, but certainly washed down with champagne.

'Between you and me, the job's yours – if we can get the bugger out of the door without him tripping over his own feet,' said the editor to Jack. 'Think you can handle it?'

Jack grinned and nodded. Previous experience of rooting around in dustbins was the perfect qualification for a gossip columnist. Soon it would be Jack Sweeney, man-about-town, recipient of a post-bag stuffed with engraved invitations. There would be dinner at Quaglino's, dancing at the 400, gambling in Monte and yachting at Cowes. It would be anyone for Wimbledon, and croquet on a thousand lawns. It would be Jack in clover, a meal-ticket for life.

However, the incumbent Dandy had proved rather more tenacious than Jack had anticipated.

'Trouble is,' said the editor gloomily, 'our Dan's had the good sense to date the proprietor's daughter. Blood, my lad, is thicker than Beaujolais.'

After six months as a stringer, Jack got tired of waiting. He decided to take matters into his own hands – discreetly. He waited until the Dandy had had a particularly heavy night on the vintage port, and – under cover of the imminent deadline – slipped in a titbit under the Dandy's personal by-line which revealed that the proprietor's mistress had been two-timing him with the owner of a rival paper. The editor sent for Jack, and the job was his – discreetly at first; then, if it worked out, with his own by-line.

What Jack needed was a nice juicy little story, something to open his editorship of the Diary with a bang. Jack was certain he'd found it. As part of this preparation, he had taken to reading the personal announcements in *The Times*. The paragraph which had caught Jack's eye was brief and unsentimental, as such announcements always were. It had been buried in the small print of the front page, at the end of the column which recorded the nation's more noteworthy births, marriages and deaths. It was one of those poignant little paragraphs which those who have a professional interest recognize as placed by official sources. The announcements record some event, previously covered by the Official Secrets Act, which has just come into the public domain.

'Fergusson, Iona née Stuart. Widow of the late Major Frederick Fergusson, Scots Guards. Died bravely for her country Feb. 2, 1941, at Lyons. George Cross awarded posthumously. Survived by one son, Callum. Probate granted.'

On the face of it, it was not going to set the Thames alight – let alone devotees of Dandy Dan. But to Jack it spoke volumes. He had already done all his homework on Callum Fergusson.

He had only to check the facts with the private office at the Palace – that the *Politician* had been on her way with a cargo for delivery to His Royal Highness the Governor of the Bahamas. The Palace could neither confirm nor deny – and they immediately contacted the man who kept a watching brief for the Windsors.

For Anthony Anstruther the news was the second time that day he had been vigorously reminded of his self-imposed responsibilities. The first had been in the course of a transatlantic telephone call from his mother, in itself an usual event since Molly Anstruther had a deep distrust of the newfangled instrument.

For a moment the barrister was left speechless.

Then he said: 'Good heavens!'

'For the Lord's sake, Anthony, you can do better than that.'

'But how on earth did it happen?'

'Even you know *how*. The question is what do we do now?'

The barrister shook his head. The news came as a real shock. Only that very day he had been congratulating himself on the completion of his plans for Emerald's future. The disaster outlined by his mother was like a bucket of cold water on all his plans.

'But what was the motive?' Anstruther asked, and then instantly regretted the question which unleashed a torrent of justification.

Molly blamed herself, she blamed her son, she blamed the child, she blamed the world. It was precisely in order to avoid such responsibilities that she had left his father all those years ago. His mother wanted to wash her hands of the whole business. The wilful creature had put herself beyond the pale.

'I'm sure we can sort something out, Mama.' Her son's voice was as soothing as he could make it. 'Where is she now?'

'Over at Lily Lovage's. Absolutely unsuitable, of course. I thought the culprit might have been one of Lily's young men – heaven knows, Lily's not one to discourage such things – but she says there's no question.'

'Then, perhaps she might stay with Lily, even if it is "unsuitable"?' Anstruther smiled wryly at his mother's choice of epithet.

Respectability has a way of creeping up on old age. Just the same, you had to hand it to the girl. For imagination and determination, one could almost say, her mother's daughter. He would have to complete his arrangements rather earlier than anticipated.

'Just until I can get something organized,' he added.

'It's really too vexing. I simply can't understand what she thought she was up to. Lily seems to be the only one who can do anything with her at all.'

'Let the dust settle, then. I'm sure she'll see reason. Leave it to me. I'll be in touch through the embassy as soon as I have it all finalized.'

Anstruther shook his head as he replaced the telephone.

It was very bad timing. With George VI not yet cold in his grave and a slip of a girl about to ascend the throne, it was a delicate moment.

It seemed that Wallis Windsor was not the only one who thought her husband should be permitted to reclaim at least some kind of official position. There were those who still considered Edward VIII the proper incumbent of the throne, and many who believed he should be offered some kind of regency – at least until the young princess had proved her mettle.

It was no time for a new scandal involving royalty – particularly one which would open old scars.

Trouble always comes in threes. First the diary item, then his mother's news. Now the third was on his way up the narrow stairs of Anstruther's chambers.

'Visitor for you, sir. Says he has no appointment but he hopes you might see him just the same. I checked the PR graveyard.'

Polite rejection – 'the graveyard' – was what happened to those seeking redress from the law, but whose custom was not encouraged by the chambers to whom they applied. Those without the right recommendation from a 'friendly' solicitor, those whom the grapevine had branded reluctant payers or labelled potential vexatious litigants, all fell into the PR category.

Anstruther knew that anyone who had got through his clerk of chambers must either be a very pretty woman or a most persuasive talker.

'Should I see him, Mr Baring?'

'I think maybe you should, sir.'

Anstruther sighed. 'If you say so.'

A few minutes later there was a knock on the door.

'Come in.'

The door opened to admit a tall, well-built young man with tawny hair and hazel eyes which were somehow familiar. The rough tweed suit proclaimed him a countryman.

The young man stood uncertainly in the doorway, twisting his cap in his hand. 'Fergusson, sir. Callum Fergusson.'

Anstruther stiffened. 'Of course. Come in. Take a seat.'

Anthony Anstruther stood up and held out his hand. The young man shook it. Anstruther winced at the strength of the fist.

''Tis good of ye to see me, sir.'

Anstruther noted that Callum's voice had the soft inflexion of the islanders – a reminder of the barrister's last meeting with that other little problem which stubbornly refused to vanish.

'Not at all. Naturally – always welcome.'

Anstruther looked at the young man uneasily. He would have been far happier if Iona's son had stayed well out of the way on his mist-shrouded island – particularly at a delicate time like this.

'Aunt Catriona sends her compliments sir.'

'Good, good. Got the notification, I expect? Probate, and all that?'

'Ay. Miss Sweeney said you had agreed to be good enough to give me some guidance with the paperwork.'

Callum set his tweed flat cap carefully on his knee. He reached down into a battered leather case he had placed on the floor beside him, pulled out a small bundle of papers and set them down on the desk in front of the barrister.

'My foster-mother is a very methodical person. She has always kept records as best she could.'

Anstruther leaned forward and pulled the pile across the desk. A few of the documents bore the stamp of officialdom. The rest were press cuttings, neatly clipped, mounted and dated. They were all there, the weddings and christenings, family gatherings, society occasions – everything which went to make up the complete and perfect record of a past. The beautiful clear-eyed Iona stared up from almost every page.

Anstruther peered at Callum again. How his mother would have loved to see her boy now, been so proud to see how tall and handsome he had grown. A wave of nausea suddenly swept over him. It had somehow knocked the stuffing out of him – out of all his generation – the loss of the brightest and the best.

But what choice had there been? What choice for any of them?

The young would never understand the price of war. If they did, they would never again undertake that terminal adventure. Anstruther had been fortunate; had been allowed the luxury, in middle age, of regret.

Anstruther studied the young man closely.

A little rough at the edges and somewhat lacking in the social graces, but what would you expect with the boy's upbringing? The stock was good; there was no doubt of that. And there was no doubt of the parentage, either: the boy was the spitting image of his father.

'All in order, then. No doubt you are who you say you are. I'm afraid the Public Trustee and His Majesty's courts grind slow and small. There are a great many cases like yours left over from the war.' Anstruther tapped the papers. 'Leave these with me. If you give Mr Baring your address and telephone number, we'll be in touch as soon as the position is clarified.'

'I've taken digs in Ebury Street, sir.'

'Very suitable – until you have your own place available. As I expect you'll have gathered, there's the house. At least you'll have a roof over your head and something in the way of stocks and shares to fall back on.' Anstruther shuffled the papers together absent-mindedly. 'What's the work?'

'Photographic – studio work, society portraiture. I'm only a trainee, of course, and there's nae much money yet. But, as Miss Sweeney told me ye ken already, it's what I've always wanted.'

Anstruther nodded. He remembered the boy's foster-mother's original request for the camera.

'Pleased to hear it. I look forward to seeing your work – *Country Life*, *Tatler* – that kind of thing? But if you want a wider market, as it happens I read a couple of the newspapers for libel. If you need a friendly word in someone's ear, I may be able to put it in . . .'

Anstruther paused. He turned to look out of the window. Then he said abruptly. 'Yes. The press. If anyone should get in touch with you, refer them directly to me. There's been a little interest – the probate announcement brought a rat or two out of the woodwork. It's always better to say nothing until one's sure, you know, and things are cleared up.'

'Cleared up?' Callum asked in surprise. 'I thought 'twas a formality.'

'There's no problem,' – Anstruther's voice was reassuring – 'but these things simply can't be hurried.'

'How long will it take, sir?'

'Couple of months to have the deeds transferred and so forth.'

'Thank ye, sir. I'm most grateful for the time and trouble.'

Callum hesitated. 'There's one other thing, sir. A promise ye made me a long time ago. My foster-sister. You told me I should have news of her.'

Anstruther stiffened. 'Yes. Of course. She's fine – all that kind of thing.'

Callum's eyes blazed with a sudden anger. 'Ye made me a promise. Ye failed to keep it. Why?'

'Circumstances made it . . . inadvisable.'

Anstruther spread out his hands. Callum looked at the pink manicured nails, the long white fingers and the heavy gold signet ring. The bile rose in his throat. He leaned over the desk. 'The hell it was! Emerald's my responsibility – far more than yours. She's old enough to make her own choices. I must know her wishes – if not from ye, then from my own efforts.'

'I wouldn't recommend that, Callum. There might be problems. Unavoidable delays in the inheritance.' The barrister's face was shuttered, blank. The sooner the interview was over, the better.

'I'll thank ye to let me be the judge of that.'

Anstruther leaned back, putting physical distance between himself and his questioner. For a second he wondered if he should ring for Mr Baring – if Callum's upbringing had led him to a ready use of his fists.

No. The young man did not look the sort. He said: 'It was a matter between . . . your mother and myself. I made her a promise—'

'I mind ye didna keep your promises to me.'

Anstruther hesitated. 'I know what's best for her. Trust me.'

'I'll trust ye right enough when ye tell me where I may find her.'

'I can't do that, Callum. Not yet.'

'When?'

'When the time is right. Now it would only make trouble – for her.'

'Not "her". She has a name. Emerald. Flesh and blood.'

Anstruther held the young man's furious gaze. The young were so arrogant. As if he didn't know very well that Emerald was flesh and blood – and the consequences of that.

'It's not,' – Anstruther hesitated, choosing his words with care – '*politic* at the moment. Maybe later. Have patience.'

'I've had seven long years of patience.'

'I can only assure you—'

'With respect sir, I no longer give credence to your assurances.'

Anstruther stood up and went over to the door. The interview had to be brought to a close as swiftly as possible.

'That is your choice, young man. Meanwhile I shall continue to pursue your interests. You will hear from my clerk as soon as the inheritance is settled.'

'Ay. For that, at least, I am beholden.'

Callum turned on his heel. At the door he swung back.

'For the other matter, I shall expect ye to change your mind.'

The steel-studded hill-walker's boots clattered on the stone steps.

Anstruther stood for a moment looking down into the courtyard to watch the young man out of sight. Then he walked back to his desk.

Sometimes he thought the responsibility would never end.

The press interest he had mentioned in passing to Callum had been from a society diarist on the *Daily News*. The piece had been a little near the knuckle. Some over-eager gutter-hack had come up with a story about the Fergusson inheritance – triggered no doubt by the announcement in *The Times* – and suggesting that there was some mystery to the business of the wreck of the *Politician*.

There had been quite a minor flurry over it. Anstruther considered himself fortunate to have caught the story in time to defuse it – stop it going any further. Nothing official, of course – the newspaper's proprietor had picked up on the passing reference to the impending Coronation Honours List. Such considerations carried considerable weight. In fact, the regular lists of those the sovereign wished to honour personally were the one reliable form of pressure the Palace could put on the press.

Anstruther was always surprised that it had an effect even on the most left-wing of proprietors. One would have thought that the war had put an end to such intangible rewards. Strange, the power of snobbery.

38

Mexico: 1952

Snobbery was what kept Billy Beaumont in business.

'My dear, she's absolutely delicious. What *shall* we do with her?'

Billy Beaumont stared down at the slender figure twirling on the makeshift catwalk in the courtyard of Lily Lovage's house.

The question required no answer. He already knew what must be done with Emerald.

Sir William, fixer to the *haut monde* of New York and confidant of the Duchess of Windsor herself, knew just how to organize life for a beautiful young girl – with the greatest propriety, of course.

He had taken a little holiday from sifting the favoured applicants for the Windsor Ball. There's no pressure like social pressure; and with the ball only a month away he had decided he absolutely had to get away for a few days.

It had been quite fortuitous that Lily's invitation to visit had come at exactly the right moment. Lily was such a delight, the place so absolutely out of the way, with nobody to see and nothing to do but gossip.

Lily adored hearing everything about what was going on in the big world. And she always had some delightful little surprise up her sleeve, some new singer, or a dancer she had found, or even, one year – he remembered with a shiver of pleasure – that charming young masseur with the sensitive fingers.

261

This time Lily had excelled herself. The young girl was quite exquisite.

Lily had had the girl put on a little show for him. Now she was modelling a glittering twenties cocktail gown, a gossamer confection of pearls and chiffon which caressed her lithe young body as she moved to Gershwin's 'Rhapsody in Blue' – the music underlining the period of the clothes.

'Pirouette and turn. Pirouette and smile.' Lily kept the rhythm and orchestrated the movements with a tap of her maribou-trimmed fan. 'Toss the head. Look up. Turn. Now. Again.'

Billy leaned back into the shadows. 'Impeccable, my dear. It's the sort of thing one *lives* for. It's just so gloriously unexpected. Whose is she anyway?'

Lily smiled. 'Such an indiscreet question, Billy dear.' She leaned over the balcony and called down: 'Thank you, darling.'

Emerald came to a halt, dipped into a brief mock curtsy and smiled up at her audience.

Emerald knew Lily had a plan. Lily's friend was important to that plan. Emerald trusted Lily. She was sure there must be a good reason for the morning's small piece of theatre.

When Emerald had disappeared, Billy turned to Lily. 'She's a natural. La Vionnet herself couldn't fault her. Tell me who.'

Lily laughed. As she had hoped and expected, Billy was hooked. 'Not a *name*, as you would have it, Billy dear.'

'Let me be the judge of that.'

Lily beamed. 'A mystery. She doesn't know anything about herself – or, if she does, she won't talk about it. Not even to me. She has a formidable guardian. Old Molly Anstruther.'

'Molly Anstruther?' Billy's forehead creased. 'Husband something at court. A scandal? Yes – ran off with a long-haired scribbler—'

'You know it all, my sweet.'

'How else can one survive?'

Lily patted his hand. 'Such a fixer.'

'Mystery. Orphan. Better and better. More.'

'Well . . .' Briefly, and with a quick glance to make sure that Emerald was still out of earshot, Lily told Billy Emerald's tale of her lost virginity.

'And there you have it,' she finished, her eyes bright with laughter. 'What could I do? She was so gorgeously innocent about it all. Thought she had come up with the perfect answer. Molly was *outraged*.'

Billy roared with laughter. 'And then?'

'Molly went off up to the city to lick her wounds and make new arrangements. And the child – I think, if I hadn't been here, she'd have swum the Rio Grande. Oh, my dear, such a delight. Did I tell you about the alligator skin?'

'Tell.'

Lily recounted the story of the passport, with embellishments.

'Magnificent. And poor old Molly?'

'Back home with a new plot. Sent for Emerald this morning.'

Billy frowned. 'I heard Molly has become terribly respectable in her old age.'

'Yes. But I think the dear girl is more than a match. Such spirit. A child after my own heart. She's getting quite a good little sempstress, too. So important if you want to understand clothes.'

But Billy was no longer listening. He was too busy watching the girl's return. He held his breath as she came out into the sunlight.

Emerald had changed into what he assumed were her ordinary clothes: a boy's shorts and singlet. In her hand she carried a sewing-basket and the sparkling dress she had been wearing. She paused for a moment, glanced upwards, waved, then walked across the grass and settled down just out of earshot.

Billy sighed with happiness. The girl was really quite remarkable. She had the same quality in repose as she did in movement – an ability to sit absolutely motionless, creating a pool of tranquillity around herself. She would be perfect as a photographic model – and that was certainly the future.

'So fresh, so new, so now, as La Vreeland says,' he breathed. 'I know just the thing. Can I take her with me?'

'For heaven's sake, Billy, she's not a parcel. There's still Molly to be convinced.'

'She's a natural. You said so yourself.'

'I know. I was the same at her age. But how? I've tried my best with Molly, but she thinks being a mannequin is not "respectable". And Emerald's still very much a minor.'

Billy laughed. 'I thought the child had already established her lack of respectability – and more than proved her majority. Anyway, I can assure Molly the profession is much more respectable these days. Boringly so.'

He put his hand over Lily's.

'Dearest Lily, you and I – we were both so unrespectable. That was our greatest charm.'

'*Was*. Thank you, old friend.' Lily said drily. 'As we get older we can see ourselves more clearly in the beauty of others. Emerald holds a mirror to my youth. I enjoy her. I'm not ready to lose her.'

'Of course you are. You'll enjoy her success.'

Billy stared down at the young woman stitching under the palm tree. A mirror to the youthful beauty which had once been Lily's? No. Lily was wrong. Emerald was no mirror to the man-made fantasy Lily had been – no dimple-limbed boudoir Venus. Lily – of the hour-glass figure, milk-and-roses complexion, the curls and curves – had been a deliberate artefact, a triumph over nature. Her perfection had been achieved with whalebone and corset, powder and paint and curling-papers.

Emerald was as unlike Lily as nature could make her. Emerald's beauty needed no adornment. The skin was tanned and smooth as silk. The breasts small and high. The long slender legs were taut and muscular. The shoulders broad and strong. Lily had trained her well; she moved with confidence and authority, as if she was wearing the garments as much for her own pleasure as for her audience's admiration.

But now, dressed in what Lily could see only as ragged clothes, with the shadows dappling her golden skin, she had come into her own.

Emerald. The name suited her to perfection.

Where Lily had been a hothouse flower, Emerald was made of fire and earth. Like some wild jungle creature, the body muscular and untamed – as untamed, if Lily's stories were true, as her mind.

But the girl's mind was not what interested Sir William Beaumont, master-fixer to the *haut monde*.

'So that's settled, Lily my dear. I'll take her. It'll be a challenge. The kind of challenge I adore.'

'The kind of challenge which earns your living.' Lily looked at him steadily. 'Remember, if you harm her, old as I am, I'll come after you myself.'

'She'll come to no harm. Rest assured.'

'I can't vouch for her good behaviour, Billy. She's not at all predictable.'

'It's a risk worth taking.'

'Something tells me Emerald will make up her own mind what she wants.' She leaned forward over the balcony and called out: 'Tidy up, darling. Molly wants to see you.'

'Aunt Molly's back?' Emerald dropped the dress and jumped up. 'What does she want?'

'The usual. "Send over the prodigal nightmare," I think was what she said. I believe she has plans.' Lily glanced at Sir William. 'Rival plans.'

Emerald's eyes widened. 'It can't be. *Won't* be.'

'What can't be, Emerald?' Lily's elderly friend cut in.

'Aunt Molly doesn't understand. I can't be what she wants.'

'What's to fear? The future? Or the past?'

Emerald stared up at the speaker. 'I *have* no past.'

Her voice was fierce with conviction. There was nothing to hold her now. Not her beloved nan. Not even Nacho, prowling in the hills like the fierce little cats he hunted.

'Then, my dear, you have nothing to lose.' Billy smiled. 'Let me tell you what I have in mind.'

A jewel like Emerald was never meant to glitter unseen. The limelight was where Emerald belonged. The limelight was what Billy resolved she should have.

Molly returned reinvigorated from the capital. She had followed her son's advice, left Emerald with Lily, and let the dust settle while she made her annual trip. The rains were too fatiguing in the lowlands.

Looking at Emerald now after the intervening weeks of her absence, Molly felt much more optimistic.

Lily had effected a remarkable transformation in the child. Today, in a pretty dress, with her hair neatly brushed, she was looking quite charming. Girlish even.

Molly's son Anthony had bestirred himself. He seemed to have come up with the perfect answer: a finishing school in fashionable Buenos Aires, where Emerald would be welcome as companion to the daughter of an elderly beef-baron and his wife, who had been an Anstruther on her mother's side.

Anthony had the package which ensured Emerald's future – documents, introductions, all the necessary paraphernalia of a lifetime – delivered in the diplomatic bag to the embassy in Mexico City, and from there by special messenger to his mother's hand.

This was the package Molly now handed to Emerald.

She began to explain the contents. The family was one of those Anglo-Argentinians who had made enormous fortunes out of the cattle ranches. The beef-barons lived in prewar splendour, with town houses and country estates and all the luxury money could buy. Better still, they had an old-fashioned sense of duty and loyalty. The couple (fed a suitable tale of truth and half-truth) had offered to treat the foundling as one of their own.

'It's a golden opportunity, my dear.'

There would be polo and tennis and canasta-parties – and plenty of well-brought-up young people. It was an old-fashioned community, a little strait-laced perhaps, but they looked after their own.

'And later, they plan a discreet emergence into society. I'm told they give the most splendid parties. Quite the thing.' Molly paused. 'Well, my dear?'

'Do I have a choice, Aunt Molly?'

Molly tapped the yellow envelope sharply. 'You are still a minor, Emerald. You must accept that others must choose . . .' The violet eyes met hers. 'I hope you won't make difficulties, my dear. It's just what's needed – after your reprehensible little adventure. And that, I trust, we will never mention again.'

'And if I refuse?'

Molly turned away. 'Then I can do no more. Young as you are, you must make up your own mind. I'm sure you know we have only your own interests at heart.'

Left alone, Emerald stared down at the envelope, turning it over and over in her hands. Without even opening it she knew the for-your-own-good that it contained. Mr Anstruther's own good.

There had been a time – no longer – when Emerald had wondered what it would have been like to have a mother. A real mother. Not someone else's mother. Not a nan. Not even a guardian like her Aunt Molly. But a real mother. Someone of whom people could say: 'Oh, doesn't she look like you?' Someone who belonged to you. Someone to hold you and love you and wipe away your tears when you cried. Emerald never cried when she was little. It had been her own answer and it was simple. That way there was no risk there would be no-one there to dry the tears.

Now the tears formed. She held the past in her hands, the monster which had come to claim her. A letter. A fat letter which confirmed what she already knew but refused to accept. That she had a mother who had never even wanted to wipe away her tears. That she had a father who had never longed to carry her in his arms.

Emerald stared into the black water of the pool in the garden, rippling it with her hand and watching the small eddies swirl. The same black water which had reflected her sorrow when her nan died. It seemed so very long ago, so long she had been alone.

Then, very gently, she floated the letter unopened on the little waves, watching the bundle whirl in the flotilla of papery blossoms until, sucking the water into itself, it vanished into the dark depths.

Now Emerald had no past, except of her own choosing. No future, except of her own making. Only the present – and that Lily had shown her she could claim for herself.

She thought again about Doña Molly's parting words.

Emerald had had enough of people who had her interests at heart.

266

39

New York: 1952

New York's high society had no-one's interests at heart but its own.

The Windsor Ball promised a chance to celebrate the new aristocracy of money; and, with a brash confidence which ignored the labyrinthine rules which still governed social life in Europe, the price of the ticket was the price of admittance.

There had never been, nor would ever be, such a party as this one. The King has abdicated. Long live Queen Wallis.

Each day brought fresh news of who was joining whose party, which society beauties would be chosen as catwalk models, which designers were dressing which *mannequins du monde*, those fashionable ladies who received their clothes at very special prices; the soaring unobtainability of black-market tickets, and, the most glorious accolade, the most ferocious speculation of all, which of the season's crop of débutantes had been picked for presentation to Him and Her. There had been talk of nothing else ever since the announcement in Walter Winchell's column.

On his return to the discharge of his social obligations after the little interlude in Mexico, Wallis Windsor had entrusted Billy Beaumont with the selection of the society mannequins for the fashion show.

Emerald was certainly not what Lily called 'a name'. But with a little spit-and-polish she would do very nicely indeed as one of his scholarship girls. The ball was the ideal launch for his young protégée. After that, he would stand back and let nature take its course.

For the required spit-and-polish, Billy had the perfect teacher in Dido Delal. The daughter of one of his old gambling partners, Dido was learning the ropes before taking on the European end of Sir William's profitable little business.

The reason she was so valuable to Billy was that she already had a fully paid up entrance-ticket to Europe's social whirlpool. The price had been high in Dido's case – a lifetime.

From the moment she was born, Dido's life had been public property. Her mother had been the daughter of a Swedish match-millionaire. She had eloped with the first charming young ne'er-do-well who had lit her fire – and incidentally got her in the family way. The young woman had not survived the birth of the child whose conception had precipitated the lovers' flight. The distraught match-millionaire, the blood of the Vikings pounding in his veins, caught up with his son-in-law outside the Casino in Cannes, but in the ensuing scuffle the luck of the longshipmen deserted him.

The French newspapers whipped up public sympathy for the tiny victim of the double tragedy, compounded by the imprisonment of the newborn's only surviving relative. The story had even made the centre pages of *Life*. On appeal, Dido's father had been acquitted of murder on grounds of *crime passionnel*. He had inherited responsibility for the fortune along with the child, now a considerable heiress. From that moment her father's sole concession to parental responsibility was to put enough aside to pay Dido's fees at the Swiss boarding school she attended as soon as she was old enough.

In addition, every holiday, he would send her a ticket to whatever gambling palace he had selected for his attentions.

It took eighteen years for her father to unload Dido's inheritance on to the wheel of fortune and leave his daughter penniless.

On Dido's eighteenth birthday, the day she reached the majority specified in her grandfather's will, he confessed all and announced his intention to start a new life in the ample bosom of a diamond-mining widow with more money than sense. Her weakness for charming rogues did not extend to their daughters. Particularly one with a slender figure, slanting green eyes, flaming red hair – and her grandfather's temper.

Her father's departure for the fleshpots of Cape Town left Dido with her living to earn. Billy provided the perfect niche.

Billy and Dido agreed that Emerald needed the gloss – the glamour, the finishing sheen which only the catwalk could give.

Whatever Molly Anstruther's objections might have been, a career as a mannequin by no means precluded a good marriage. As American *Vogue* put it so comfortingly in the announcement for their annual competition to discover new modelling talent: 'You can reassure yourself, your husband or your son, on one point: modelling is terribly respectable. Whatever you do, you will always be exemplarily clothed and excessively chaperoned – by photographer, photographer's assistant, fashion editor – my dear, *stickler* for form – studio girl . . . '

The timing was perfect. Emerald could simply take her place in the line-up of favoured débutantes who were to show the clothes for the fashion show which was to be the highlight of the Windsor Ball. And after that, Billy was certain, her career would be made.

'Call it an investment,' Billy explained to Dido. 'Like your own dear father, I can't resist a little flutter.'

'Paris?'

'Paris.'

That was for later. For now, New York was excitement enough.

The ball was scheduled for the eve of Epiphany – the last feast of Christmas, the night the Three Kings brought their gifts to the newborn Christ. For the New York gossip columnists the Windsor Ball *was* Christmas, or at least the best excuse since *Woman's Home Journal* serialized the memoirs of Crawfie, the former royal nanny, for making imperial mountains out of common-or-garden molehills.

Everyone loved a royal, even if only in the form of a secondhand retread, as the insiders unkindly put it (speaking in whispers because they didn't wish to jeopardize their chances of a place at the high table).

Even Hollywood, usually so preoccupied with its own scandals that it paid no attention anywhere else, was enjoying the gossip about little Jimmy Donahue, the Woolworth heir. Everyone said the Windsor Ball would be the party of the year, rivalling – and with any luck outdoing in splendour – the forthcoming coronation of the new young queen in Britain.

The British newspapers, for once inspired to report beyond their own shores, had bestirred themselves to send journalists to cover the event.

The *Daily News* was first among those to clamour for a press invitation.

'It's the chance of a lifetime, lad. So don't waste it,' the editor had said when he assigned Jack Sweeney to the team.

Jack had earned his spurs as a royal gadfly. The fact that some bastard from the Private Office had managed to screw the lid back on his story of the missing children and the royal cargo ship, had been neither here nor there. The Palace's reaction had been enough proof to give the story credibility.

'No matter, son,' the editor said. 'It'll come again – and next time we'll nail 'em.'

Whatever the left-wingers said, the readership loved a royal. Royals sold newspapers.

'On your way, Jack. Unlike you, my lad, I've got work to do.'

So Jack took the triple-hop flight across the polar route in a Bristol Britannia, the engines rattling like a coffee-grinder, the shadow of the great winged bird moving in miniature across the snowy wastelands below. He sipped cocoa in an airport hangar in sub-zero temperatures while the aircraft refuelled at Gander and Halifax.

Finally, after more than twenty hours in the air, notebook at the ready, Jack Sweeney touched down at New York's Idlewild airport.

As the cab delivered him to the second-class hotel in Brooklyn – currency regulations were still in force, even if his newspaper had not kept a tight rein on expenses – Jack felt a thrill of excitement at the glimpse of the tall canyons of glass and concrete.

The public was hungry for gossip. Dandy Dan was there to satisfy that hunger – and in the process earn a meal-ticket for life. The Windsor Ball would surely provide more than a cocktail canapé; it promised the full five-course banquet.

40

New York: Christmas 1952

Emerald was in love. Not with one of the smart young men in button-down shirts who, brothers or cousins of the Academy's young ladies, came and went in the brownstone house. Not with one of the middle-aged Wall Street brokers who lunched with their daughters among the Jackson Pollocks at the Four Seasons restaurant and kindly invited her to join the party. Not even with one of the elegant elderly gentlemen who took her, along with their granddaughters, for hamburgers at P. J. Clarke's.

She had been in New York for a fortnight, and she was in love with a city.

In all honesty, Emerald would probably have been in love with any city in which she happened to find herself that Christmas of her sixteenth year. But it was a stroke of particular good fortune that the city was New York, muscular as a young prizefighter under its thick blanket of Christmas snow.

She was head over heels in love with the fairy-tale which had been laid at her feet, which towered over her head and rattled beneath the pavements. In love with cavernous squares and thronging streets, with subways and shopfronts; with black limousines and yellow cabs; with forests of marble and caverns of crystal. She was in love with the hurrying fur-muffled crowds, the bright faces of children under the falling flakes of

271

white. In love with the icicles on the eaves of the pale tall buildings and the frost on the leaves in Central Park.

The towering city overwhelmed her with its beauty. With multi-layered department stores and the lifelike mannequins in the windows of Bergdorf Goodman. With the waterfall of merchandise piled high in boxes, stacked on shelves, pyramided on the counters of the vast emporia of plenty. With the faces of film stars forty feet high on the hoardings. With the scrawls of neon which lit up the night. With the mouth-watering scents of roasting chestnuts, frying onions and steaming hotdogs which rose from the tiny portable kitchens on every street-corner.

In the city streets, Emerald knew with all the fierce conviction of youth that she had come home. But, in the brownstone which housed the Academy for Young Ladies of Quality, Emerald might as well have come from the moon.

The young women seemed so utterly knowledgeable, so vastly superior, so infinitely more sophisticated than Emerald could ever hope to be that she was almost in despair. Furthermore, Emerald's clothes, chosen for her with infinite care by Lily out of the mothballed trunks, were all completely wrong.

Had it not been for Dido Delal, Emerald might well have run all the way back to Lily, or even thrown herself back on the mercies of her Aunt Molly.

But as soon as Emerald had settled herself into her little attic room at the top of the brownstone Billy had delegated Dido to show his new protégée the ropes.

If Emerald was in love with a person, it was probably Dido, the most sophisticated and glamorous young woman in the Academy. She was also delightful and funny and knowledgeable and, best of all, didn't mind at all that Emerald's wardrobe was a bit old-fashioned.

'Darling child, secondhand clothes are all the rage in Paris,' Dido said.

Dido had lived in Paris – as, it seemed to Emerald, she had lived in every other city in the world.

The first thing, Dido decided, was to take Emerald's wardrobe in hand.

'It's all very beautiful, but not quite practical enough. You need two pairs of slacks, at least three comfortable tops, and a good haircut.'

She went to find Sir William himself.

'Billy,' she said firmly, 'Emerald has absolutely nothing to wear.'

'How much?'

'Bring your wallet and no grumbling.'

So Billy, grumbling, came too.

'It's one of my skills – separating a gambler from his small change,' Dido said cheerfully as the two young women walked down Fifth Avenue with Billy trotting behind. 'It's a matter of timing.'

She did indeed seem to have an uncanny knack of getting dollar-bills out of her employer.

Dido said that denims were all the rage on the left bank in Paris, particularly if you chose, as Emerald did, the boy's ones with the zip-up flies.

'Perfect,' said Billy contentedly as he paid in cash.

Dido said that big sloppy sweaters were a must for every young girl of fashion in Manhattan.

'Of course,' said Billy. 'Take two.'

Dido said that Emerald must have her hair hacked right off short – not that it was not like a boy's already, but it had to be properly done, in a proper salon. Rat-nibbled, *Vogue* called the new look.

Billy smiled and paid the bill.

That Christmas was the happiest Emerald had ever spent. Billy arranged a small party on Christmas Eve for those of his protégées who remained in the city for the holiday. And on Christmas Day itself there was a little tree and a turkey dinner – and Emerald and Dido spent all evening walking the streets and marvelling at the Christmas lights.

Many of the shop windows were decorated with flakes of imitation snow and glass icicles.

'It reminds me of Christmases when I was little, Dido. There was no snow in Mexico, so it's ages since I've thought of Eas Forse where I used to live. My nan's crofthouse always looked so pretty in the snow. I had a brother then. Well, a sort of brother. A foster-brother. He was called Callum. He had bright eyes and tousled hair, and I loved him more than anyone in the world.'

'What happened? Where is he now?'

Emerald shook her head. 'I don't know. My guardian said I shouldn't talk about him. I should just forget all about him. I had a new life now. And when I asked her my nan just made up one of her stories which never tell you what you really want to know.'

'Didn't you write to him?'

'At first – lots. I had to send them care of his foster-mother the schoolmistress. But Callum never wrote back. So I supposed he must have forgotten all about me.'

'Maybe he didn't get the letters?'

Emerald considered the possibility for a moment. It was inconceivable that Miss Sweeney would not have passed on the letters. She always said that you must treat the written word as sacred.

'I'm sure he did.'

Emerald felt a sudden wave of loneliness.

Callum had certainly forgotten all about her by now. He would have a new life, a new family, maybe even a new sister.

The following week, with only a hectic few days to go before the Windsor Ball, Billy took the two girls – his professionals as he called them – to the Waldorf Astoria, where the preparations for the ball were in full swing. He had to present them to Madame Agnès Bertrand, just in from Paris on the transatlantic liner.

Agnès Bertrand was the Duchess's favourite *vendeuse*, the orchestrator of the Ball's fashion show. Madame Bertrand was part of Billy's grand plan for Emerald.

It was then that Emerald found her feet at last – if anyone could call sitting cross-legged on a table finding your feet. They found the *vendeuse* barricaded behind ten trunks of couture gowns, in despair over the alterations. The strong-limbed broad-shouldered young women who were to be her models were not at all the same build as the salon mannequins on whom the dresses had been fashioned.

On the first day of the fittings, the *vendeuse* was almost in tears.

'Is there no-one here who can so much as turn a hem?'

'Me,' said Emerald. 'I can sew.'

'Que le bon Dieu soit bénit, ma fille.'

It was then that Emerald discovered that she had a skill which none of the other young mannequins possessed. Whatever else Lily had taught her – and Madame Bertrand had allowed herself a small nod of approval when Emerald had shown her paces on the catwalk that first day – Emerald could stitch a seam and set a sleeve with the best.

So Emerald, just as she had done at Lily's, settled herself cross-legged on the table and sewed her fingers raw, while Agnès Bertrand pulled and tucked as best she could at the material she had been given – both animate and inanimate.

In that week before the ball, Emerald learned more about the couture business, the stitching of a toile, the fitting of darts, the drop of a taffeta lining, than any professional mannequin.

There was no mannequin more valuable than one who understood the dressmaker's art. Such a mannequin was worth her weight in gold. She could be a Muse, said Agnès. Every salon had one, the girl who served

274

as the embodiment of the collection, the inspiration for the couturier, a living dummy on which the first toiles would be cut and draped.

'There will be a word in the right ear when the time comes, *ma petite.*'

Emerald was of far more use in the workroom than practising out on the catwalk with the others.

'I intend no flattery, but you are cut from a different cloth.'

There were to be seven tableaux vivants – a revival of the twenties fashion for such little extravagances. The scenes were designed to reflect the Duchess's career – carefully edited, naturally.

The Duchess herself was to take the central role, with appropriate supporters and props. No acting ability was required, only an audience – and on this occasion that was certainly guaranteed.

Jimmy Donahue had come up with the idea for the parade. 'The seven ages of woman – and that means *you, divina.*' Jimmy squealed and clapped his fat little hands.

Madame Bertrand decided that Emerald was to appear as the bride.

She was to be seen once only, alone – probably in white, although the choice was a little tricky, considering Wallis Warfield's three bites at the matrimonial cherry.

That last afternoon, Madame Agnès was putting the finishing touches to the Duchess's wardrobe.

'Do you know what this is, *ma chérie?*'

Agnes held up an exquisite column of sapphire-blue crêpe. The heart-shaped neckline was draped into a full bust gathered into the most slender of waists.

Emerald glanced across at the *vendeuse* and smiled. 'Tell me, Madame Agnès.'

'This – this was the Duchess's wedding gown when she married the Duke. The very same. Such a magnificent passion. Every paper carried the picture. I was at Mainbocher, learning my trade – how long ago? So many years – as long ago as you were born, *ma chère p'tite. Son altesse* had it altered a little here, and a little here. And the buttons re-covered just so.'

Agnès stroked the gown lovingly. 'Such memories in such clothes. Each one an affair of the heart.' She glanced up at the young woman stitching away on the table. 'Come here, child.'

Emerald set down her work and came over. Agnès Bertrand held up the garment against the young girl's body.

'Perfect. So chic. The colouring just right. You're a little taller of course, and a little fuller in the bust perhaps. One might almost say—'

'What, Madame Bertrand?'

The *vendeuse* shook her head thoughtfully, and held her peace. But she wondered just the same.

Agnès Bertrand was not the only one to notice the curious likeness between the middle-aged duchess and the young unknown. It was not immediately obvious, but it was there.

41

New York: 5 January 1953

'Cinderella *shall* go to the ball.'

In the tiny hotel room which smelled of old cigarette smoke and boiled cabbage, Jack Sweeney stared at the photograph which had triggered his headline. He chewed his pencil reflectively, turning the phrase over in his mind.

This was to be his big chance. Everyone who was anyone was to be at the Windsor Ball, including every gossip writer in the business. He had to find the right angle, find it fast – and get it on the wire before the early editions.

He rolled a clean sheet of paper into the typewriter and began to punch vigorously.

'Deadline New York, 5 January, 1953. Windsor Ball hot line. Dandy Dan reporting.'

He hesitated for a moment, then crouched back over the keys.

'So what's new on the eve of the Big One? Shake out those frocks, girls. The spotlight shines for *you*.

'Gloria Vanderbilt? A little bird at Mainbocher tells me the Marchioness of Milford Haven plans identical scarlet taffeta. Girls will be girls.

'Claire Booth Luce? Last year's Givenchy. She's tipped as ambassadress to Rome. No wonder the poor thing's economizing.

277

'Marquesa Casati could show Claire a thing or two. She's chosen floor-length sables – and that's only for her Nubian footman.

'Fleur Cowles? Vernier's tiger-striped silk, and watch for the diamond solitaire. Escort Harry Winston is expected to toss her a few carats in the near future.'

Jack finished his roll-call of society beauties, paused and took his hands off the keys.

He needed someone the readers could identify with. The common touch. He'd found her right there that very afternoon: the young woman in the new street-uniform of jeans and Sloppy Joe sweater, her hair hacked close to her finely shaped head, stitching at the beautiful clothes in the mannequins' changing room.

It was she who had inspired his headline.

He had called over one of the staff photographers and framed the shot he wanted. No-one knew who the mysterious young beauty might be. All he'd been able to discover in the chaos before the ball was that she was to appear in the fashion parade. Just the same, there was something oddly familiar about her. Something about the eyes perhaps – they were such an unusual colour. And then the face, the little heart-shaped face.

He shook his head. It would come to him. Sooner or later, it always did. Finding things out was his business.

Meanwhile he had his copy to file.

New York took its pleasures seriously and on time.

The fashion parade was scheduled for eight o'clock. Those who were to host their own tables were due to meet in the anteroom at seven-thirty to be received by the royal couple.

By seven o'clock, the early arrivals were already descending from their shiny Cadillacs into the icy gale, mobbed at the red-carpeted entrance by the celebrity-hungry crowd and the popping flash-guns of the photographers.

Behind the scenes, Madame Bertrand at last expressed herself satisfied that the gowns approximately matched the shapes of the wearers – as much as she would ever be satisfied.

Emerald was briefly released from her last-minute stitching for a glimpse of the preparations in the ballroom. Trapped behind the scenes, Emerald had begun to feel that the ball might be nothing but a dream. Now she couldn't bear to wait another moment.

'Come *on*, Dido.'

Dido had already changed into the green cut-velvet gown she was to

278

wear for the first parade, and now she was impatiently teasing her unruly red hair into a neat French pleat.

'Hang on, you'll spoil the effect,' Dido protested as Emerald, still in her working clothes, propelled her friend through the door.

'We'll have to be quick. I've found a way up to the gallery.'

From the banistered minstrel gallery – strictly forbidden as it led directly to the Windsors' private apartments – the two girls had a perfect bird's eye view of the scene below.

The transformation of the cavernous ballroom was complete. The scent of spring filled the air. Blossoming cherry branches billowed like pink candy-floss. Delicate loops of greenery twined round draperies of coral silk. High overhead, the ceiling was tented with indigo velvet scattered with tiny star-shaped lanterns.

Everywhere, on every table and in every alcove, there were silver candelabra twined with lily of the valley. From a forest of lemon-trees, planted in terracotta pots set among tables, rose the perfume of flowers and fruit, mingling with the scent of beeswax and honey from a thousand flickering tapers.

Emerald closed her eyes and let the glorious scents billow round her.

'Oh, Dido,' she breathed, 'pinch me. This can't possibly be real.'

Dido laughed. 'It isn't. But it's marvellous fun to pretend.'

At that moment the doors to the anteroom were thrown open and the guests streamed in, eddying round the tables and swirling through the pillars. The women were like brilliant peacocks in their sculptured brocades, jewel-encrusted bodices and glimmering French silks trailing shimmering trains.

The men, too, were resplendent in their tuxedos and starched white shirts – a sea of black and white to set off the Florida sun-tans which were the hallmark of New York's high society.

The crowd shifted and stirred as the serving staff handed round trays of champagne. From the gallery above, the girls could hear snatches of conversation. Who was with who? What would the Duchess be wearing? And the Duke?

All at once the hubbub ceased. Down below in the well, every face turned up towards the gallery.

Just in time, the two girls pulled back into the dusty darkness of the drapes as the royal party passed within inches of their noses.

Even if she hadn't been keeping as quiet as a mouse for fear of discovery, Emerald would have held her breath. In all her life she had never seen anyone as perfect as the star of the ball. The grooming was impeccable. The gleaming cap of dark hair was parted in the centre, and held in place by tiny jewelled bows was a crescent halo of flashing fire. On each earlobe gleamed a single gigantic sapphire, the colour of the gems exactly matching the brilliant blue eyes. The dress was a deceptively simple sliver of gunmetal-grey slipper-satin, its stiffened skirt curving the body, the high neckline framing a thick plait of diamonds and rubies.

But what set the Duchess apart from every other woman in the room was the sheer indisputable romance of her escort. The Duke was a perfect foil, a matched miniature with gleaming cap of blond hair and impeccable midnight-blue tail coat, as polished and neat as the bridegroom on the top of a wedding cake.

Below, the applause swelled from a few hand-claps to the full twenty-one-gun salute.

Whatever her styling, Wallis Windsor was every inch a Royal Highness. She raised a gloved hand in that peculiarly regal gesture which is neither greeting nor blessing, but an acknowledgement of homage due.

Then, to the strains of Elsa Maxwell's tinkling piano, the Duchess glided down the wide flight of red-carpeted stairs to take her place at the head of the official receiving line.

Back in the mannequins' changing room, Madame Agnès was quite pink with excitement.

'Emerald, where have you been? Mary-Lou needs a tuck in the waist. Dido, what have you done? What is this cox-comb of a hairdo?'

The *vendeuse* circled her charges, pulling and clucking like a mother hen grooming her chicks.

The advantage of Emerald's single appearance at the end of the parade was that she could help with the dressing of the *mannequins du monde* – the amateurs, as the *vendeuse* called them with an eloquent shrug of the shoulders.

Considering the unpromising material, Agnès Bertrand thought to herself, it was a miracle that everything was as ready as it was. It was as much thanks to Emerald as it was to herself. There would be a bright future for the child, if she had anything to do with it.

'Ten minutes, my little sirens,' called the *vendeuse*. 'Keep your eyes on *son altesse*.'

The society mannequins twittered and gossiped as they waited for the Duchess's signal. But Dido and Emerald found a narrow slit in the looped-back curtain where they could catch a glimpse of the crowded ballroom, see the sparkle of the jewels in the candlelight, watch as the spotlights played through the darkness, illuminating each table in turn.

Dido seemed to recognize everyone, and Emerald listened enthralled to her roll-call. Here were Rothschilds and Rockefellers and names seen only in lights. There a gaggle of Guinnesses and matching Greeks. And over there in the corner Cecil and Noël held court in a wreath of scented smoke. Emerald knew all their faces from Lily's magazines – their doings reported, their dresses catalogued, their fortunes enumerated. One face was new to her – perhaps because the fashion editor of *Harper's Bazaar* did not herself seek the public eye.

'Diana Vreeland,' Dido hissed in her ear. 'The most powerful woman in the room. Isn't she amazing?'

A hook-nosed woman in clown-white make-up, raven-black hair scraped back, bone-thin shoulders in a froth of scarlet and gold, moved through the silvery river of guests till she reached her ringside seat.

If the Court of St James could appoint a Mistress of the Robes, then the Court of Queen Wallis had Diana Vreeland. With DV in position, the parade could begin.

The band struck up with a waltz as the lights came up on the catwalk. The Duchess herself had taken the stage in a new outfit, this time a blazing yellow. Her jewels flashed fire. Over her elbow-length white kid gloves, she had fastened a huge sapphire bracelet; round the neck, left bare to the shoulders, was a barbaric gooeen collar, wide as a baby's bib, encrusted with emeralds and rubies.

Like a bright flock of cygnets, the first rank of mannequins tripped out onto the gold-carpeted catwalk to meet her. The parade unfolded in a mirage of shimmering gowns. The mannequins advanced and re-treated, whirled and bobbed; all of them had brothers and fathers, mothers and aunts to cheer them on, to greet them by name, to chant encouragement.

With only one tableau to go, Agnès turned to Emerald. 'Your turn now, *ma belle.*'

Swiftly Emerald stripped down to bare skin while the *vendeuse* laid out the many layers of the wedding gown.

'Here. First this, and this and this.'

Clucking and tutting, Agnès began to hook Emerald into the silk underskirt of the beautiful dress.

'Now this. Bend down, arms out.'

She topped the layered silk with a sliver of snowy chiffon, and stood back.

'There. So. From now on you don't sit down.'

She turned Emerald so that she could see herself in the tripled-winged mirror, see the slender naked torso rising from the graceful drapery, watch herself reflected a dozen times from every angle.

'You must learn how to admire yourself, *ma fille*. This body is a gift of *le bon Dieu*. See, these small breasts, so perfect. The firm shoulders, such a gleam to the skin. The curve of the spine and the length of the neck.'

Emerald, suddenly aware of her nakedness, crossed her hands over her breasts. The *vendeuse* gently took her hands away.

'Non, non. You do not hide such things. Beauty is in the mind. Every Frenchwoman knows that. Some of it in the body, a little of it in the face, but most of all in the mind. And then, when you are comfortable in your skin, so you may cover it up. It is very simple. Now. We have admired. We are prepared.'

Agnès clipped the bodice round Emerald's waist and secured the tight petersham.

'Allez. Breathe in.'

The bodice had stiff whalebone stays and half-moons of soft padding to push up the breasts and hold them in place. The stiff shell clasped her ribs, folded into her waist, flared round her hips.

'Lean forward, child. There. So the bosoms fall into the cups.' Agnès stepped back and examined her handiwork.

The bridal gown was the pinnacle of the fashion show, the last to be shown – the embodiment of romance.

'Is it not good?'

Emerald turned to the mirror again. For a moment she didn't recognize the fragile beauty reflected there, so perfect was the transformation. With Lily, the dressing-up had always been a game – two children playing at grown-ups – but now the beauty in the looking-glass was real, as real as any of the glittering women in the ballroom, as real as the star of the ball herself.

Emerald, her heart beating so loud she thought the whole audience must hear, took her place in the wings, waiting for the signal to claim her place in the limelight.

And then, at last, her moment had come. The band switched rhythm to the Wedding March.

As soon as Emerald stepped out into the lights, the applause lapped around her, lapped and ebbed, and fell away to silence.

There was an audible intake of breath and a low murmur of astonishment. It was not even the exquisite dress, so pure and pale after the rich jewel colours of the ballgowns, but the shimmering incandescence of the young woman herself, the sheer innocence of her own bright beauty, which caught and held the audience spellbound.

At that moment Emerald was truly a bride, all snowy and new, a young girl on the threshold of womanhood, leaving her past to embrace her future.

In that single instant Emerald felt as if this was what she had been born to do: to spin round in this swirl of satin, feel the caress of the silk-cased whaleboned bodice, the roughness of the underskirts, the warmth of the lights, hear the music played just for her, drink the admiration in the upturned faces.

The audience, sensing the young girl's pleasure, responded. It could not have lasted for more than half a minute, that swift pirouette of joy alone in the middle of that fairy-tale stage.

Half a minute was too much for Wallis Windsor.

The Duchess, the uncrowned queen of the ball, turned sharply to locate the focus of attention. The jewels flashed as she raised one elegant kid-gloved arm in a gesture of dismissal.

The audience sighed, hesitated, then broke into wild applause. This time the salute was not for the Duchess, but for the unknown young beauty who had stolen the show.

The audience loved a queen, but best of all they loved a Cinderella.

In the wings, Dido was waiting with outstretched arms as Emerald came out of the darkness. 'You were sensational!'

Emerald laughed with joy, her cheeks were flushed and her eyes were huge and bright.

'Did you really think so? The lights – it was all so fast—'

'Absolutely!' Dido's voice was exultant. 'Get back in there fast. The Duchess looked daggers – and you'll be the toast of the ball!'

Back in the ballroom, the lights had dimmed, the catwalk had been rolled back and the spotlight swivelled to illuminate the royal couple.

'Imagine what it must be like to be married to a real prince,' Emerald whispered. 'When I was little, I used to kiss frogs, just in case.'

'It works in reverse,' Dido said with a giggle. 'Look.'

The Duke, no longer crisp and dapper, was sprawled in a chair with a bottle of J & B by his elbow. The bulbous eyes were staring fixedly into the middle distance. He looked supremely bored – like a frog on a lily leaf, Dido whispered to Emerald. Now it was Emerald's turn to giggle.

Beside him his duchess was oblivious to her prince as she leaned her sleek head close to her dinner companion.

'Jimmy Donahue,' Dido whispered. 'They say he's her lover.'

Emerald was startled. 'Surely not?'

'Surely yes.'

Emerald shook her head. She could not imagine how the Duchess could find the man interesting. He looked just like the young men at Lily's. Emerald could no more think of taking him as a lover than of flying to the moon.

Soon, as they circled the room, Dido was pointing out half a dozen other couples she swore were other people's wives and husbands.

'Is absolutely everyone having an affair with everyone else?'

'Of course. It's the social whirl. If they stopped for a moment, they'd be bored to death.'

At that moment a roll of drums banished the waiters to the sides of the ballroom. On that evening of imperial splendour, there was one more ritual to be completed.

'Your Royal Highnesses, my lords, ladies and gentlemen. Pray take your places for the presentation.'

The Duchess disengaged herself from her whispered conversation and moved forward to a small carpeted dais.

A line of débutantes, white-frocked and pink-cheeked beside their matronly escorts, formed a queue to have their names called out, drop a curtsy and be rewarded with a few gracious words of acknowledgement. The heads topped out with egret plumes, the flurries of tulle and silk bobbed and shuffled.

The sapphire bracelet glittered on the Duchess's wrist and her fingers sparkled with rings. Even the lorgnette used to examine the list of those due to be presented was worked as a golden tiger with enamelled stripes.

Emerald wondered what it would feel like to be one of those privileged young women, to be the apple of a father's eye, the focus of a mother's dreams.

As if in answer to her thoughts, Emerald felt her arm seized. The hawk-nosed woman was by her side. In a moment, in spite of her protests, she found herself thrust towards the dais.

'I can't—'

'You *must*, my dear. I absolutely demand it. Name?'

'Emerald.'

The woman looked at her speculatively. Then she said, 'Perfect.'

Emerald's heart beat faster. The hawk-nosed woman pressed her forward. There was no escape.

All at once she was face to face with the Duchess.

'Your Grace, may I present Emerald? Our newest star.'

The delicately plucked eyebrows arched.

The encounter lasted only an instant. But in that single second, as she

284

raised her head from her curtsy, Emerald saw a look of surprise, perhaps even of fear, in the Duchess's icy blue eyes.

At that very moment – or the whole audience might have wondered at the strange intimacy of the encounter – the spotlight swung back to the royal table, where the Duke, an expression of petulant irritation on his face, was fitting together a set of bagpipes.

He stood up and began to push his way through the glittering river of diners, nodding and greeting as he went. The spotlight followed him through the haze of smoke until he reached the stairs and disappeared momentarily from view.

A few moments later the drums rolled again, the lights dimmed and the plaintive strains of the Highlander's Lament soared out from the gallery above.

The Duke, obeying his wife's request for a tune on the pipes, had chosen to play his ancestor's requiem for the loss of the land over which he had once been undisputed sovereign.

To Emerald, listening on the sidelines, the wail of the pipes was unbearably nostalgic. Eas Forse seemed a lifetime away. She wished her nan could see her now. She would have been so proud of her. And Callum – she would have loved to have him by her side.

As the strains of the lament died away and the buzz of the table-talk resumed, she felt a hand on her shoulder.

'My dear, you must forgive me.'

'Mrs Vreeland – I don't think the Duchess was pleased.'

'Of course not. Such snobbish nonsense, and so ungracious. I told her so myself. You were so delicious up there in that famous wedding gown. You may not have noticed, but every man in the room – and half the women – fell in love with you instantly. A triumph. A true début. Come and sit with us. Whatever the Duchess thinks, you are the sensation of the ball.'

Obediently Emerald followed the woman through the crowd.

When she had settled her by her side, Mrs Vreeland fumbled in her little gold evening bag and perched a pair of half-specs on her nose. She looked even more like a bird of prey as she darted out a bony hand to tip up Emerald's chin.

'Now let me see you properly.'

The appraisal was almost a physical assault – as if a grappling-iron had been tossed over the side of a ship.

Emerald held the gaze, her violet eyes unflinching.

'Good girl!' The woman's harsh voice was triumphant. Then she added, almost to herself: 'And the body – like a little dancer. No need

285

for all that whalebone. Marvellous eyes. Excellent bones. With a bit of powder and paint . . . ' She considered for another moment, then flicked one long elegant finger. 'Tomorrow, then. Come and see me at the office. Tell Billy I said so.'

On that night of the ball, Mrs Vreeland was only the first of many to assure Emerald, obliquely or directly, that she had a career ready and waiting. Most of those who did the assuring were gentlemen.

Emerald scarcely managed to swallow a mouthful of the delicious dinner, the creamy lobster soufflé, the delectably tender little birds – scarcely even had a moment for a sip of champagne, she was in such demand.

From that moment on, Emerald danced. She danced with old men and young men, with fat men and thin men. She danced with husbands and sons, cousins and brothers. It seemed as if there was not one man in that room who did not want to hold her in his arms and whirl her round the floor.

That she was the belle of the ball there was no shadow of doubt; the eyes and the whispers followed wherever she went. It was exhilarating, the feel of rough male cloth against her bare arms, the closeness of muscle and flesh, the intimacy of moving to music clasped in the arms of a stranger.

The crooner sang of love and hearts surrendered, of a waltz to make a dream come true. Emerald knew he sang just for her.

As she danced, her heart was beating not from the champagne, not even from the compliments whispered in her ear, but from the knowledge that she was beautiful, desirable – that she had a power which could, if not change the world, at least change the way the world saw her.

At the end of it all, when the last waltz had been played, as she slipped out of her beautiful frock and fell into her small bed in the attic room in the brownstone house, she was dizzy with happiness.

After that evening she was no longer a problem for someone else to solve. She had found what Madame Agnès called her vocation. Nothing and no-one could stop her now.

42

London: 6 January 1953

The next day, the story of the ball was in all the papers. Most of them gave wide coverage to the young beauty who had made her début on the catwalk. Everyone predicted a glittering future for the unknown young girl who had snatched the limelight from the Duchess of Windsor.

The Duchess was furious. She did not relish having her triumph stolen by anyone, let alone by a chit of a girl whom everyone said looked just like the Wallis Warfield of thirty years ago. The past was not something Wallis Windsor liked to have aired in public. Some of the papers even dusted down an old proof photograph of Mr and Mrs Ernest Simpson on the day they were married, with the bride in the gown the girl had worn at the ball. It was extremely vexatious since the former Mrs Simpson had thought she had had all the prints destroyed. The pity was that she had not instructed Agnès Bertrand to burn the damn dress as well.

No-one seemed to know who the young woman might be or where she sprang from. No-one at all could put their finger on anything about her – no-one, that is, except those few in whose various interests it was to keep their knowledge to themselves.

The Duchess knew – and feared the consequences when the Duke confirmed her fears that the child had indeed survived.

Mrs Vreeland guessed, but knew where angels feared to tread.

Even Agnès Bertrand had noticed the likeness – but was far too discreet to question.

Jack Sweeney knew he had seen the young beauty before, but had not yet guessed the truth.

Anthony Anstruther recognized disaster in its most familiar form – when it stared up at him from the newspaper.

But, that particular morning, he had not had a chance to scan the papers before he kept his appointment with Callum. At exactly the moment Emerald was confronting her future in Diana Vreeland's office, Anstruther handed Callum the keys to his past.

He had telephoned the young man at his digs on the first day of the New Year to make the appointment.

'Callum? The papers have come through. Congratulations. It's mainly the house – not in the best area but up-and-coming I'm told. There's a bank account in escrow and a small portfolio of stocks and shares. All in all, quite a nice little set-up for a young man. Welcome to the club.'

Callum met the barrister at his chambers. They had taken a taxi together.

Anthony Anstruther had seemed to Callum almost nervous, certainly taciturn, but there was no doubt he had the air of a man not entirely at home in his skin.

The taxi drove down Pall Mall and past St James's Palace, up Piccadilly where the gap-toothed façades bore witness, even after ten years, to the destruction of the Blitz.

They drove along the newly replaced railings of Kensington Gardens alongside the procession of nursemaids trundling babies in perfectly sprung lacquered prams home for tea.

The taxi turned up an avenue of white-stuccoed houses with crumbling pillars, and drew up at last opposite a closed and shuttered mansion set back from the road behind a stone balustrade.

As they stood on the pavement opposite the house in Notting Hill, Anstruther shivered. He'd be glad when the whole business was over. Too many memories. Too much water under the bridge.

Anstruther walked slowly up the steps to the dusty front door. The brass door knocker was a dull green, the once-golden shine crusted with verdigris. The unswept porch had little heaps of dried autumn leaves in each corner.

When he spoke, his voice was crisp, emotionless.

'Well, here we are. Would you like to . . . ?' Anstruther held out a delicately carved brass-inlaid key.

To Callum, even the key was a memory. He fumbled with the lock.

He pushed open the door on to a darkened hallway and stepped inside. The place smelled of disuse and cobwebs. He paused for a moment, accustoming his eyes to the gloom.

Anstruther's voice cut through the blanket of silence.

' 'Fraid it's a bit neglected. But sound, structurally sound. I've kept an eye on the place. Knew your mother, you know. Worked with her in the war.'

After a pause he added: 'She was a fine young woman. Headstrong, but heart in the right place. Generous. A kind woman.'

'Kind? To Emerald?'

'Emerald? Yes . . . well, we won't go into that now.'

Anstruther's eyes closed, his face shuttered. 'I'll leave you to it, young man. There'll be a few more details. The bank accounts and so forth. We can deal with them at another time.'

The door shut behind him. It was a heavy door with solid panels of lacquered oak – a door with brass knockers and expensive tumble-locks designed to keep out unwelcome visitors. The kind of door which protects the property of those who have from those who have not.

Callum sat down abruptly on the stairs.

His mind was still numb. He thought of small things. Domestic things. He remembered that on Eas Forse no-one shut their door unless they had gone visiting. Then they left the door shut but never locked. No-one had locks on Eas Forse unless they had secrets, like Catriona Sweeney in her caravan. And even then the key was on the mantelshelf or under the rug. Certainly not held hostage for more than a decade until the recipient reached his or her majority.

There were many things about life in the big city which Callum's upbringing had made him distrust. One of them was the goodwill of officialdom. In any event, he had the Celt's hereditary lack of respect for rules and regulations. Twelve years was a long time to wait for the key of a door which was his of right.

'What can one do?' Anstruther had shrugged. 'The law is the law.'

Now Callum breathed in the stale air of his mothballed childhood.

By the door stood a curved, carved satinwood chair, its polished surface inlaid with a delicate miniature pastoral scene. He remembered coats and scarves piled, a gentle hand buttoning a child into an overcoat.

He looked up the stairs. Long beams of sunshine filtered jewel-bright through stained glass.

Under the window, on the mahogany half-moon table, lay a scattering of papers. There were cardboard invitations speckled with age. 'At Home – air-raids permitting.'

The silence pressed down on the stirrings of memory.

He heard again the screaming sirens and the whine of bombs; smelled the cold breath of earth as he was hustled down the steps and into the dark cellar.

Callum opened door after door, knowing, from the deep recesses of memory, what he would find.

Ghostly rooms crowded with furniture shrouded in dust-sheets. Guttered candles in tarnished brass candlesticks hurriedly brought out during a wartime power-cut. Under all the windows, piles of neatly folded blackout curtains, ready for the next air-raid.

In the middle of the hall a crystal chandelier like a half-submerged iceberg, swathed in eiderdown and pillows, the glittering crimson and blue crystal exposed where mice had eaten their way through the cambric cover, powdering the polished tiles beneath with tiny feathers.

In the bedrooms above, empty beds bulked high with folded blankets, mothball-scented. Red gingham, faded in patches where the light had fallen. Most poignant of all, cupboards full of clothes. Tweed jackets with leather patches for the stalking, a tail-coat awaiting a wedding. His mother's wardrobe with the delicate teagowns, taffeta-skirted ballgowns with lace-frilled bodices, satins and velvets, soft wool and faded cottons.

Then there were shoes. Children remember shoes. His mother's shoes: sturdy wartime brogues nestling among maribou-trimmed slippers faintly mildewed with age. His father's: black with laces for the city, brown with little patterns of punched holes for the country.

Now, in this silent shuttered house, memory woke.

At the top of the stairs, a wooden gate led to the nurseries. The latch was stiff under his fingers.

Cracked linoleum on the bathroom floor. A half-empty bottle of shampoo, a plastic duck. Small slippers set ready for powdered toes.

Emerald's nursery. The frieze of hurrying rabbits so much smaller than he remembered, the walls of the room shrunk, Alice-in-Wonderland.

Emerald's memories. He felt almost like a thief in that small room. The little box which held her past, the memories she had denied with such passionate conviction when he had found her again on Eas Forse.

And, in the corner, Emerald's desk. His fingers felt beneath the carved lip and applied the gentle pressure which released the catch of the secret drawer. He lifted out the little handful of treasures squirrelled away by the child who had once inhabited the room.

It was not much, that childish treasure. An ivory shoehorn, a pink coral teething-rattle with a tarnished silver handle, three buttons made of deerhorn, a tortoiseshell comb. A blue linen envelope, funnelled, tipped out a glittering little stream into his cupped hand.

He went to the attic-window to study his find. It was a very fine chain bracelet set with tiny diamonds, one link bearing a small emerald-studded cross.

He remembered the tiny wrist the chain had once encircled – made for an adult, it had taken four loops of the wrist to secure it.

He remembered as if it were yesterday the crying bundle in his mother's arms, the little fingers which clutched his own. In the half-world of his memory, the violet eyes stared solemnly up at him from the cradle.

Emerald. How could he so carelessly have accepted the legacy of his past, when his past was also hers? What was missing in the tall house full of memories, her presence lingering in every corner, was Emerald. Emerald had to be found.

He knew, with all the vigour and strength of his being, that the glittering trophy was an omen, fortune's hostage to Emerald's return.

43

Eas Forse: 1953

Jack Sweeney had not been back to Eas Forse since the day he left, and he would not be back now if he had not been looking for Cinderella. Now Jack stood at the top of the ferry's gangplank and breathed in the salty air of the island of his birth.

On his return from covering the Windsor Ball, he had asked for a week's leave to follow up the story of the young woman whose photograph had been printed on the front page. His editor had expressed satisfaction – his highest form of praise – with the way the young reporter had handled his first major story as Dandy Dan. Jack's proposal for a follow-up story sounded promising. He was granted three days' leave of absence, provided he took it over the weekend. With *reasonable* expenses.

Jack was exultant. Reputations were made on one good story. And this promised to be one hell of a runner.

Jack had taken a risk in returning to Eas Forse. He had no desire to be recognized on his arrival by any of his erstwhile mates who might bear a grudge.

He counted on his city slickness to maintain his anonymity. Jack flattered himself that he was altogether a bird of a different feather, a positive peacock – the very picture of a young-man-about-town. Just the same, the dark glasses were a sensible precaution.

Now Jack surveyed the small knot of travellers waiting to disembark on the island.

On the overnight passage, the ferry had been unusually crowded for the time of year. In February the spring storms kept the islands in semi-hibernation. But spring was the time for weddings. There was to be a wedding on the island, and there were guests arriving from the mainland.

Among them was his companion of the previous evening, a young woman with blond hair and the sort of figure which looks terrific as the wrapping round the fish-and-chips. Alison had agreed to meet him down at the bothy – the hut where the errant husbands overnighted when they had taken too much of the usquebaugh to return to their wives. She had not at first understood why he was not attending the wedding like the rest of the ferry's passengers.

Even though Jack and Alison were second cousins, they had not had much contact in the times when Alison was on the island for the summer holidays. Alison's mother had not encouraged her to play with the rough island boys.

It was while taking a dram in the ferry's little bar that they discovered their kinship. At first Jack had been nervous of discovery – until he had sworn her to secrecy and told her why he had to come back to the island without a welcoming committee.

To celebrate auld acquaintance, Jack had offered to buy her a drink. As many drinks as she wanted.

As the evening wore on, he found himself increasingly drawn to her. He enjoyed young Alison's stories of the Beltane, his appetite for her sharpened by her description of her conquests. Alison liked boasting of her successes. It was one way of getting back at her scheming mother and the proper ladies of Perth. Alison was wonderfully indiscreet, a gossip columnist's dream – particularly her characterization of his old rival, Callum.

By the end of the evening, with the whisky fiery in their veins, they were getting on just fine. And later, down in the bothy, after Alison had finished at the wedding and Jack had concluded his business with his aunt, they would get on even better.

Now, from the top of the gangplank, Jack watched Alison vanish among the crowd of islanders. It was a pity he had to return without a fanfare. If there hadn't been the little business in Glasgow, if there hadn't been the certainty of more than a bit of bad blood pumping around the island as a result of it, his homecoming would have been a different matter. He would have swaggered into the Salen Arms and ordered up the best whisky in the house.

He wondered about the welcome the schoolmistress would give him. She should be proud of his success. She would admire what he had achieved. He closed his eyes briefly, a child again, to savour the thought of his great-aunt's admiration.

After all, they were family. She and he were the last of the line, ever since his grandfather had been taken with the pneumonia last winter, if you didn't count the baby girl and the young wife.

The one and only communication from the island since he had left had been the notification of the old man's death. It had been forwarded care of the *Daily News*, pinned to a formal little letter from his great-aunt as executor to the deceased, along with a cheque for fifty pounds on condition he did not contest the claims of his grandfather's young widow. He had cashed the cheque and blown the money in one night with the girls at the Kit-Kat Revue.

Even though he had not been the best of correspondents, blood was thicker than water. She would not refuse him.

Catriona Sweeney came to her door to answer Jack's knock.

'Ay? And what can I do for ye?'

Jack removed his hat, adjusted the knot of his smart new tie, slicked his hair back with the flat of his hand, and waited for the cry of joy which was his due. He waited in vain.

'Don't you recognize me, Aunt Kate?'

The schoolmistress was wearing her reading spectacles and her eyesight was not what it was. She peered at the young man's face.

After a moment she said: 'That I do, Jacob.'

Jack shifted uneasily from foot to foot. This was not the warm welcome he had hoped for.

'Ye can surely do better than that, Aunt Kate.'

'Ay. If I've a mind to it.' Catriona stood aside. 'Will ye come into the parlour? Ye ken your way.'

His aunt settled her glasses more firmly on her nose. She returned to her desk and patted the pile of newspapers she had been clipping.

'Set yourself down, young Jacob. I'll be with ye right away.'

The schoolmistress bent over her work, as if Jack had been no more than one of her young pupils wanting help with his sums.

A wave of bitterness washed over him. He had thought it would be different. He had earned respect – for all that he had made a few enemies on the way.

Nevertheless he hung his smart new hat on the hook by the door, and threw himself down on the settle to wait while his aunt completed her task.

294

When she had finished the last paper and set it neatly on top of its fellows, she took off her spectacles and leaned back in her chair.

'You're looking well, Jacob.'

'So's yourself, Aunt Kate.'

'As well as may be expected. I for one am pleased to see ye in such good health – although there's others on the island, I'm told, who might feel differently. Ye should watch your step. But that's your own business, no doubt. Tell me about yourself.'

Jack leaned forward eagerly – almost as if he was once again the child in her classroom.

'Ye can be proud of me, Aunt Kate.' Jack's voice had slipped back again into the soft inflexion of the Gaelic-speaking islanders.

Jack pulled the newspaper out of his pocket. He had brought the edition with the photograph of Emerald.

'I want ye to take a look at this.'

Catriona stared down at the photograph in silence.

'Ay. 'Tis her right enough. But ye did not need to come all this way to hear something ye already knew well enough.'

'Always the sharp one, Aunt Kate. In a manner of speaking, I'm here on business.'

Catriona looked up at him, frowning.

'Business, is it? I know all about your writings and the paper ye work for, Jack Sweeney, as ye will no doubt be aware from the fifty pounds sent on from my brother's bequest.'

'Thank you kindly, Aunt.' Jack smiled his thin smile.

'Kettle's on. Tea'll be up in a minute.'

She went over to the range and swung the kettle over the pot.

'Still keep busy, Aunt Kate? Time on your hands?'

His voice was sly. He knew what his great-aunt thought about time on people's hands. Retirement would not be suiting her.

'I keep busy enough.'

She poured the tea and handed him a cup.

'So what brings ye back in all your finery?'

Jack grinned. 'Something right up your street, Aunty.'

'Ay?'

'In a manner of speaking. Information.' He hesitated and added hurriedly. 'Paid work. Research.'

'And what would that be?'

'To begin at the beginning . . .' Jack's voice was careful, lazy, almost uninterested – the technique he had perfected when interviewing those who did not welcome his attentions. 'I had news of young Callum Fergusson from Alison Mackay on the ferry – she's over for the wedding, as she told me.'

His aunt's eyes narrowed. 'Alison Mackay indeed? A Mackenzie on her mother's side.'

Jack nodded. Good. Still the same old obsession. He said, 'It's information about the Mackenzies – by association, you might say – that I'm after.'

Catriona studied her great-nephew shrewdly. He hadn't changed, for all his fancy clothes. Magpie pick-poking was what he was about – but that, she had sometimes thought as she filed his press-cuttings, he had had from her.

'And what would it be precisely that ye're after, Jacob?'

'This. The story behind *this*.'

Jack put his hand on the newspaper. Then he began to explain. His aunt listened, and as she listened her mind tumbled back, back to that moment on the shore when Callum had been delivered to her from the ocean.

Back to the violet-eyed child who had fallen into the care of her arch-rival Margaret Mackenzie. Her heart hardened with anger as she listened. Anger at the memory of that long ago night of the Beltane, when the snows fell on the high tops.

And as she listened she was assessing the consequences of her nephew's request. What effect would it have on her beloved Callum, on the future she had planned for her foster-son?

'So ye'll see it's the papers – the evidence of kinship, association, that I'm after, Aunt Kate.' Jack finished up: 'That and the wee disc I gave to you, the one which must have come from the girl's wrist. Ye'll remember ye said ye'd keep it safe.'

Catriona nodded. She had kept everything. Of course she had.

Yet at the end, when she had let her nephew have his say, she had made up her mind.

What he wanted, even if she had been able to give it him, could do Callum nothing but harm. Might even mean that the girl, the girl he swore was his foster-sister, might claim a share of his inheritance.

No. What Jack Sweeney wanted would surely jeopardise Callum's future. The girl was not her affair. The lawyer would have done all that was required for Margaret Mackenzie's foundling. He would have known what was right and proper.

She shook her head decisively. 'I'm sorry, Jacob. It canna be done.'

'What do you mean, Aunt Kate?' Jack stared at Catriona in disbelief. 'What harm can it do? The girl's almost a Mackenzie – by adoption and upbringing if not by birth. And there was I believing blood was thicker than water – that the Mackenzies were the very devil as far as the Sweeneys were concerned—'

'I said no, Jacob Sweeney. And no is what I meant.'

Jacob stared at her again. Then he tried another tack.

'The paper will pay a good fee, Aunt Kate. A bit in the bank now you're retired – maybe even two hundred pound, as much as a year's full board and wage for your own flesh and blood—'

'Though ye be my own flesh and blood, I will not do it.'

Jack clenched his fists, suddenly reduced by the schoolmistress's tone to a frustrated child: 'Aunt Catriona, I need it – for all that I've never asked ye a favour. For all that ye've ever done for me—'

Catriona raised her hand. 'That will do, Jacob. I've given my answer.'

Jack stared at the old woman. A red wave of anger flooded over him.

He said, 'I'll be back, Aunt Kate. Back to hear ye change your mind when ye hear what your precious Callum was up to with Alison Mackay at the Beltane . . . '

Catriona drew in her breath: 'Tattle and tales out of school, Jacob, and ye a grown man. No doubt ye know the way out.'

'Ay. And I'll have what I want and know the truth – with or without your help.'

Jack, his face black with rage and frustration, pushed his way past the old woman and walked out of the door. The last ties of blood had been severed.

The key to Emerald was Catriona's dossier on Callum. Of that Sweeney had no doubt. He had a right to the information he sought. Of that, too, he had no doubt. With or without his aunt's permission, he would take what he needed.

But first he needed a diversion, some way of ensuring that the schoolmistress didn't catch him as he raided the caravan. She would certainly not be going to the wedding – with the bride a Mackenzie, there was no question of that providing the solution.

He knew who would help him – if he played his cards right and made it worth her while, in one way or another. Jack shivered in his fine clothes, and his shoes slipped on the wet rocks of the burn as he climbed down to the bothy to keep his tryst with Alison Mackay. The meeting on the ferry had certainly been a stroke of luck – the kind of luck with which Jack earned his living.

It was to be the first step in a profitable collaboration, even if it did turn out to be rather more profitable for Jack than for Alison.

*   *   *

As soon as he had seen Alison disappear into the schoolmistress's bungalow, Jack slipped down the hill to the caravan.

He felt under the edge of the door-jamb where he knew his aunt hid the key. His fingers closed on the sliver of metal.

Swiftly he unlocked the door and slipped inside.

The place smelled musty, as it always had. Old newpapers were piled in every corner, as they had always been.

Until Callum had usurped his place, the caravan had been Jack's playground. He knew it like the back of his hand. It was in this small room that he had served his apprenticeship, learned his skills. Now, once again, taking his time, Jack worked his way through the neatly labelled stacks.

It was all there: the letters, the press cuttings, the complete record of the events which had happened on the island as long as the schoolmistress had been keeping her archives.

The strongbox where he was sure the identity disc had been hidden was padlocked. It was no trouble to Jack, experienced in such matters from childhood, to tumble the rusty metal spokes. Once again he stared down at the roughly etched inscription on the verdigris-encrusted disc. He slipped it into his pocket.

Then he turned his attention to the files, working patiently through until he found the bundle of letters to Callum from Emerald. Eagerly he slit the unopened envelopes – clearly the schoolmistress had hidden them from her foster-son, but had not betrayed her principles as far as actually reading them. The letters were almost like diary-entries, as the little girl told her foster-brother what life was like for her now, reminding him of shared memories. Clearly she missed him terribly.

There was no doubt the young man had indeed once shared his nursery with the violet-eyed child. But why and how had she come to be there? Why had there been no mention of another child in Iona Fergusson's obituary notice? What was the secret of Emerald's parenthood that it had to be kept hidden? There had to be a reason for the child's presence in that nursery. If there was a blood-kinship with Callum – and on Eas Forse such things were commonplace – he might even have stumbled on a conspiracy to defraud the young woman of her inheritance.

That would be a scandal well worth breaking – and one which would pay Callum Fergusson in kind for his theft of what Jack saw as his own birthright.

Back in London, Jack dropped Alison off to collect her things from the basement flat in South Kensington she shared with two respectable young ladies from Perth, and took the taxi straight on to Fleet Street.

There was plenty, in his new position, which Jack could do for Alison. And plenty that Alison, with her society contacts, could do for Jack.

Jack was well satisfied with the trip. The following day he took Alison out for a slap-up meal at Wheelers in Old Compton Street, fed her on *sole Véronique*, topped her up with Black Velvet – half champagne and half good strong stout – and explained exactly what he wanted her to do for him.

Alison was well placed to gather little items of gossip, moving as she did on the fringes of café society. She was as keen as mustard to get her name in the society columns, an ambition which Jack could certainly facilitate. As a pretty young woman, she could also gain access to those places and people which might be barred to the young reporter.

It was the perfect partnership, both in bed and out of it. Alison set up home with Jack in his cold-water flat in Soho. Her family left the safe respectability of their Scottish town and journeyed to London to express their shock at her decision to live in sin. Her mother was shrill, her father gruff with anger. As far as they were concerned, nice girls didn't. If the news got round Perth, they would never be able to hold their heads up again. And that, her father said, was that. As far he was concerned, he had no daughter. Her mother's imagery favoured the domestic: her daughter had made her bed and now she would have to lie on it. Alison was only too happy to oblige.

The afternoon of his return from Eas Forse, Jack typed up his story. Just a preliminary salvo, linking the beauty at the Windsor Ball to the shipwrecked wartime cargo-ship which had been on its way to fill the cellar of the Governor of the Bahamas.

It was no more than a little taste-tickler for the readers of his column, a whiff of scandal, just a hint of what was to come.

It was a story which would run and run – he was sure of that. A sexy story. A story with staying power. A Jack Sweeney story.

What he could not have known when he turned in his copy was that Catriona Sweeney had already betrayed him to Anthony Anstruther.

What he had not yet grasped was the power of the Establishment to protect its own.

44

London: 1953

'Kill it, Manny. Just kill it.'

Anstruther's knuckles whitened on the telephone. Thank God Catriona Sweeney had alerted him in time.

The night editor at the *Daily News* was astonished by the request, even though it came from so unimpeachable a source.

'Why the hell should I kill it? It's just a two-bit gossip story.'

'Because it has a bloody D-notice on it.'

'A D-notice? On a gossip column?'

'Messenger's on the way.'

'Look, Mr Anstruther, give me a break. The editor'll kill me if I have to stop the presses—'

'The Palace'll have your proprietor's balls if you don't.'

'Jesus wept!'

'Just do as I say. Spike the damn thing.'

Anstruther slammed the telephone back on its hook. For God's sake!

He rubbed his face wearily. It had been a risk, but he had had to take it. Fortunately Manny Braithwaite was used to such directives from the Private Office. Although D-notices were the heaviest hammer of all, the night editor had not thought to question Anstruther's authority.

In reality the Palace had issued no such instruction – with or without the imprimatur of the Ministry of Defence. Far too busy with the preparations for the Coronation to pay attention to a paragraph in a gossip column.

Anstruther knew better. It was the tip of the iceberg. He should have known some sort of disaster would be lurking round the corner as soon as the girl had surfaced at the Windsor Ball.

Manny Braithwaite replaced the receiver. He had never heard the Private Office so steamed up. And on a mere whiff of gossip. Young Jack had certainly stirred up a hornet's nest – and if there was one thing Manny disliked it was anything which threatened his pension.

A few minutes later the instruction was confirmed by the arrival of the official notice.

Manny rang the bell for his newly appointed Dandy Dan.

'You spiked it? What the devil *for?*' Jack stared at the night editor in disbelief.

Manny shrugged. 'Editor's decision is final.'

'I don't believe it!' Jack thumped his notebook down on the desk. 'All the evidence is right there!'

The night editor looked up wearily. He was due for retirement next year – back to the Yorkshire village where he had been born – and teaching young men like Sweeney the ropes was exhausting.

'Just do what I say, lad. Don't bite off more than you can chew.'

'The hell I will! I'm going to find the fucking proprietor. I know exactly where the bastard is – we're supposed to be covering his wife's charity evening.'

As Sweeney swung on his heel, Manny said quietly, 'OK, OK. It was a D-notice.'

Jack stopped and turned. 'What the hell's a D-notice?'

'A defence notice. An instruction issued by the Government that revealing certain information isn't in the country's interests. The piece has to be spiked. Voluntary, of course, but compliance is assumed – or else. The proprietor doesn't get his favours or his K or whatever it is his wife's after.'

'But *why?*'

'How do I know, lad? I'm only the editor.'

Manny sighed. Then he laid down the blue pencil with which he had been cropping the photographs for the early edition, and stared hard at Jack.

'Take an old man's advice, Jack. You're doing just fine, but you've a lot to learn. The first lesson is to accept your limitations. Understand who and what you are. The goddam sensitive reporters – the crap-merchants who get a by-line bigger than the headline, claim they're *writers*, observers and recorders of the human condition.'

Manny leaned back. 'Bollocks. Hacks like me and you get paid by the column inch, just like a gigolo. The bigger the prick, the better the tip. Except that you don't get the action. You're a voyeur. Your business is to keep your flies buttoned and your eye to the keyhole. After that, it's easy. Just get the copy in on time, to length, with all the names spelled right. Christ, you should know. If the fucking story gets killed, that's it. So tomorrow's fish and chips won't have your name on it. Tough shit.'

Manny paused for breath. 'And one other thing. The bottom line's my fucking pension – and yours. Some people will pay you to keep their names *out*, and some people will pay to get their names *in*. It's up to you to tell one from the other. This time you got it bloody *wrong*.'

Manny pushed the D-notice into Sweeney's hand and nodded towards the door. 'Now, get the hell down to the printroom and kill the fucking thing.'

Bewildered, Sweeney stared down at the official document. When he saw the signature, he almost laughed aloud.

Anthony Anstruther.

The man who had signed the D-notice was the barrister who had come to fetch Emerald on Eas Forse – the man who, he knew from Catriona's archives, had taken such a personal interest in Callum's future.

After he had done as Manny asked, Jack made his way down to the paper's cuttings library. There were several references to Anthony Anstruther, most of them relating to wartime activities. But it was the entry in *Who's Who* which was the most interesting.

There was a royal connection all right. As a young man Anstruther had been an equerry to Edward VIII; his service extended briefly after the Abdication. He had been one of that privileged band of courtiers who had the run of the Private Office – an association which had presumably continued when he joined the legal chambers which dealt with royal affairs.

One judicious phone call confirmed that none of this gave Anstruther the right to authorize a D-notice.

It was clear the man had taken a serious risk to keep the young woman's past out of the papers.

Jack had learned a valuable lesson that day. A window of opportunity had opened. From now on he would bear in mind that there was more money to be made from *not* filing certain stories than there ever was in printing them.

*   *   *

Anstruther had just put down the telephone when the clerk of his chambers announced Callum. In the morning's anxiety, he had quite forgotten to check his diary.

The young man had requested an appointment a week earlier – and the timing should have warned Anstruther that there was more trouble brewing. Sure enough, in Callum's hand was a newspaper – one of those which had carried the story of the unknown girl at the Windsor Ball.

'Mr Anstruther, why the hell didn't you tell me?'

Callum's eyes were blazing with anger.

'My dear boy, I had no idea she was going to do such a thing.'

'That's not the point. She's my sister. She must share the inheritance.'

There could be absolutely no doubt it was Emerald. And he had absolutely no doubt that as his sister – foster-sister or no – she should share everything he had.

'She's not your sister, Callum. You know that perfectly well.'

'So who the hell is she?'

Anstruther stared down at the front-page photograph. He spread his hands. 'You'll just have to accept she has no claim on your parents' estate.'

'The moral obligation's perfectly clear. I want her to have one half.'

'Impossible.'

'Why the de'il not?'

Anstruther walked over to the window to give himself time to think. When he turned back, his voice was quiet, reasonable.

'Many reasons. One of them is that the Public Trustee will not allow it. As a minor, you are still under the protection of the Crown. That protection can be extended on request – if a responsible person such as myself makes a proper case.'

'Is that a threat, Mr Anstruther?'

Anstruther returned the young man's gaze steadily. 'Take it as you will.'

Then he said more kindly: 'Far more important is that what you propose could only do Emerald harm. That is why I cannot allow it.'

Callum leaned across the desk. The barrister flinched, wondering for an instant if the rough upbringing would lead Callum to land a punch.

'Ye cannot *allow* it? What the hell does that mean – considering it's yourself and whoever gives ye the orders has been pulling the strings? God knows why, but we were helpless wee bairns. You juggled with our lives as if we were of no more account than a pair of half-dead rats.'

'Believe me, Callum, I had no choice.'

'The de'il ye had no choice! It seems to me ye've been the only one to hae any choice. What choice did Emerald have when ye shipped her out without so much as a by-your-leave? What choice did I have when I lost my sister – and she was that in all but blood, whatever ye may say? What choice when I remained in ignorance of her whereabouts?'

'You know her whereabouts now.' Anstruther's voice was dry.

'Ay. And I mean to act on the knowledge.'

'It's none of your business, Callum. The child already has provision.'

' 'Tis nae what my mother told me. Provision? That story of the Austrian cousins? Mother told me she had nothing in the world.'

Anstruther stared at the young man. My God, but he looked like his father. It was a pity he did not have the same tolerant temperament. And clearly he had not inherited Freddie's willingness to take orders for King and country – whatever the personal cost.

'Your mother didn't know the whole story.'

'I'm no sae much in the dark as ye think, Mr Anstruther. And Emerald shall have what is owed.'

Anstruther shook his head wearily. 'For pity's sake – for your mother's sake – will you sit down and *listen*? I'll try to explain as best I can.'

Callum subsided, his eyes narrowed. 'This time I'll trust it's the truth.'

'The truth. If there is ever any such thing.'

Then, taking his time, as night fell in the quiet cloister beyond his window, Anstruther began to tell Callum a web of lies. As a barrister, it was his vocation to make the truth seem what it was not.

It was not that what he told Callum was so far from the truth. Emerald was a bastard certainly. She was the illegitimate daughter of very important people. That was no lie. After the war, they had settled a certain sum of money on her – Anstruther could assure Callum it was a considerable fortune. But her right to inherit was dependent on her origins being kept absolutely secret. And that meant wiping out all trace of the arrangement which had been made with the kindly Iona, and which might lead back to the true identity of her parents.

'She was a very special person, your mother,' Anstruther finished carefully. 'I have no doubt at all that this would have been what she would have wanted.'

As Callum listened he remembered the letter his mother had given him to read to Emerald. The letter which was to explain what was to happen.

Hesitantly he said: 'When our mother put us on the ship, there was a letter. We were to read it the morning after the storm. Emerald wanted to keep it, so I let her.'

Anstruther looked up sharply. 'A letter?'

Callum nodded. 'Then there was the storm – and of course the letter was gone. I mean, we lost everything. I always wondered what it said.'

'Well, there you have it.' Anstruther's voice sounded deeply relieved. 'I'm sorry, Callum. I suppose the situation was simply allowed to drift. No doubt we were all to blame. At first it was circumstances. Politics. I cannot be specific, but you must believe me, it was so. Your mother offered a solution. To be fair, it was never intended as anything more that, just an interim measure. But then there was the war. Chaos. Nothing seemed to matter any more. And, of course, the shipwreck seemed to solve everything.'

'The de'il it did!'

Anstruther shrugged. 'You were children. Children vanished all the time. For God's sake, man! You have no idea what it was like in wartime. No-one had any means of knowing you had both survived. And then – well, by the time the pair of you turned up again it seemed better to leave you where you were. Always loathed public school myself – wouldn't do it to a dog. No. It seemed to me you were far better off with old Catriona – and believe me, Callum, there was no-one but her and me to worry about you. You were the last of your line, and you were at least in safe hands. You were fed, clothed and educated. As far as I can see, it's done you no harm in the long run. And I kept an eye on what was coming to you, as you know.'

Callum stared at the barrister. Perhaps the man was human after all.

'Ay, I know that – and I'm grateful. But what of Emerald?'

'Ah. Emerald. Well, I had to take a decision as fast as possible. These things have a way of getting around. So I shipped her out to my mother in Mexico – discreet and comfortable. I intended finishing school and a suitable match when the time came. Buenos Aires actually. Very civilized. Anyway, she kicked over the traces. Showed us all a clean pair of heels. Took over. The result is plain for all to see.'

He put his hand over the photograph, as if by the gesture he could wipe out the evidence.

'It's a nightmare, if you want the truth of it. And I can't do anything for her until the dust settles. But perhaps it was inevitable, considering. The trouble is, the money won't be available until she marries. Then it'll be released – but only if the alliance is suitable. That means *discreet*. With no chance of the story of her origins coming out later. God knows, there's nothing to be gained by blowing the whistle now. Even you must see that.'

Callum's mouth had set in a firm line. 'It doesn't give Emerald herself an option—'

'As I have told you, young man, it's out of the question that you should come storming out of the blue offering to share all your worldly goods with your foster-sister. The press would get wind of it in no time. And that would mean everyone would deny everything – officially. There's no proof naturally. The system sees to that. It's good housekeeping – and *that*, at least, we do supremely well. The result would be no dowry, no acknowledgement – and a notoriety which would make Emerald's life public property. In other words, absolute hell.'

After a moment he added: 'No-one knows the whole story except myself – and now you.'

Anstruther paused and studied the sturdy, strong-limbed young man, judging the effect of his words. Then he said quietly: 'Whatever Emerald may choose to think, and however she may behave, she's still very young. She has to be allowed time. Till she's able to cope, make her own decisions. You must see the logic in that.' Anstruther shook his head. 'Don't rock the boat, Callum. The scandal would be . . . *expensive*. For both of you. But more simply because Emerald won't tolerate it. She's run away once. She'll do it again.'

'How can you be sure?'

'I can't. I can only deal in probability. Think about it. Quite apart from the realities of the situation, and my own sense of duty – which I fully appreciate you may not share – consider the effect on a young woman of the news that she has parents who chose, and still choose, to ignore her existence. Who took a conscious decision to abandon her. What good do you think that would do?'

'It would hae the merit of allowing her to make up her own mind.'

'About what? It's all water under the bridge. All it can do is cause pain. Later perhaps, when she's a full-grown woman.'

He sighed. 'Believe me, it's for her own good. It's always been a holding operation. Until she has a life of her own, that's all it can be.'

'A life? You mean a husband. What kind of man would that be? Bought with whatever de'il's pact ye've constructed?'

'Your characterization's a little dramatic – not to say unkind. There are a thousand reasons why people do such things. The best matches have always been arranged.'

Anstruther shook his head. Callum was wrong. He did care about Emerald – after his own fashion. Wilful and difficult as she might be, she had been given into his charge, and he meant to discharge his obligations as honourably as possible.

The young were so romantic. Couldn't understand the notion of duty and honour.

Honour dictated Emerald be found a husband, provided with a future which had absolutely no connection with her past, a family of her own to replace the parents she had never had.

A new identity. Spies in wartime could expect no less. In a sense, Emerald came under similar rules.

Whatever his own uncertainties, Anthony Anstruther was still an honourable man. But he could not expect this angry young man to accept that.

'Knowing the price,' he said quietly, 'would you be the one to tell her that her parents chose to disown her – will still disown her? Would you?'

He had played his cards. There was nothing to lose now but the game itself.

Callum picked up the cutting again and stared at the photograph. Whatever the considerations Anstruther might feel took priority, Emerald's happiness was all that mattered to him.

Callum raised his head again to meet Anstruther's gaze. Behind the glasses, the barrister's face was drawn and weary. Suddenly the dapper middle-aged ex-courtier looked tired, almost worn out.

After a long moment of silence, Callum spoke again. His voice was firm and steady. He had made up his mind.

'Very well, sir. For Emerald's sake – for her sake alone. I'm a man o' my word – and you have it. I'll keep my distance.'

For the first time in the entire interview, Anstruther's face relaxed. He polished his glasses and put them back into his pocket, made his customary steeple with his fingers, and began to enquire after Callum's career.

Callum answered politely, mechanically. His future, once so bright and clear, was now once again shadowed with loss. The loss of the little sister, now growing to womanhood without him.

Yet what Callum forgot to include in his calculations – what everyone had always forgotten – was Emerald herself.

Even as a tiny child held in Iona Fergusson's arms, unnamed and unacknowledged at the baptismal font, Emerald was fiercely her own self. Not Anstruther's. Not Callum's. Not even Jack Sweeney's, stalking her from the shadows.

45

Paris: 1954

In Paris it was the first day of spring.

The wind marked the changing year by whipping the bare twigs off the lime-trees which cast spidery shadows on the wide boulevard, swirling dead leaves in little eddies down the gutters, snatching playfully at the fashionable pleated skirts of the office girls hurrying to work.

Emerald swung easily along the Avenue Georges V in her flat ballerina slippers. Her long legs were unconstricted in slender black pencil-pants, a billowing blue workman's shirt worn over black high-necked pullover masking the willowy model's figure. No-one, seeing the girl in those clothes – a uniform worn by every student in Paris – would have recognized her as the mannequin-muse of the famous couturier Christian Paradis.

Or perhaps they might have done, since the freshness which Emerald brought to her work was the reason Monsieur Paradis had chosen her to be his muse, the inspiration for his house style. Emerald's trademark on the catwalk was the long barefoot-hunter's stride, the fluid grace which came to her naturally after her childhood in the forests of Mexico.

'Le dernier cri, c'est Paradis!' was the theme of the spring collection.

Paradise was hard work. For those who earned their living in the couture business, the hours were long and there was little time for romance.

When the collections were being prepared, as now, the sempstresses and mannequins were on twenty-four-hour call.

Emerald had been working through the weekend. On Monday morning, with the first fitting in the neon-lit workrooms at eight o'clock, she was a few minutes late. Reluctant to miss the first day of spring, she had loitered by the river Seine, filling her lungs with the sweet breath of the new season.

'Emerald – where have you been, child?'

Madame Verdun, the chief *vendeuse*, came out from her cubicle, her brow furrowed. It was unusual that Madame Verdun was in early enough to scold late arrivals. However, the whole House of Paradis was in turmoil on this particular morning.

'I have no objection to what you girls do with your private lives, as long as it does not interfere with the profession.'

Secretly she rather hoped *la belle Emerald* had indeed been up to something in her private life. To the girls' employers, a single mention in the society columns – with a suitably glamorous photograph – was worth an acre of paid advertisements in *Vogue*.

Employment with any of the big couturiers – let alone being the star of the House of Paradis – gave entrée to Paris's raffish postwar society, and the girls were encouraged to borrow the clothes they modelled and show themselves in the evening as walking advertisements for the fashion houses.

The Paradis models reflected their employer's status. They were the *mannequins-vedettes*, the star turns of the season, receiving invitations to the grandest parties, and seen at all the fashionable restaurants and night-clubs. Acceptance of such engagements was almost a condition of work.

Madame Verdun frowned. As usual Emerald had not arrived with her maquillage in place.

That Emerald's nonconformity was also reflected in a reluctance to play the social game had not escaped Madame Verdun's notice. Her friend Agnès Bertrand, who had recommended Emerald's employment at the Paris salon, had warned her that the young woman would not be likely to toe the salon line.

Emerald hated the pancake make-up required of the professional mannequins, and just as she would change the structured clothes for slacks when she was not working, so she preferred her own clean-scrubbed skin to the rouge and false eyelashes which were part of the salon uniform.

In fact, in the little flat she shared with Dido Delal, Emerald made her own face creams and cure-alls to the recipes she had learned from Margaret Mackenzie and the curandera of the barranca.

But it was this natural look, her scrubbed, unpainted beauty, which led Christian Paradis to launch his new fragrance, a blend of spring flowers with mossy undernotes. The perfume, he felt, perfectly reflected the new liberated woman who earned her own wage-packet and had the freedom to spend it.

The campaign was all-important. After the war, every couture house had been obliged to cut its coat according to its cloth – to develop subsidiary, cheaper products from shoes to costume jewellery to make-up and perfumes. A successful fragrance could make the difference to a couturier's financial viability.

It could also make Emerald a star. A mannequin-muse was a star, to be sure, but in a very tiny sky. Soon Emerald's face would be famous far beyond the confines of the mansion in the Avenue Georges V.

That was for the future. Meanwhile there was work to be done. Victoire Verdun bustled Emerald up the wide stairway towards the mannequins' changing rooms.

'Allez, ma fille. Monsieur Paradis himself has been asking for you. We have a *very* important client this morning.'

A slight smile softened her features as she hurried up the stairs behind Emerald.

The girl really had a *feel* for the clothes. Not only was she a natural mannequin, but she also understood exactly the processes which turned a simple length of cloth into a couture creation. And, of course, the gossamer silks and shimmering organdies looked wonderful against her clear pale skin. Monsieur Paradis himself would often ask for her when he wanted inspiration for the cut and drape of a new fabric, whether the grandest of gold-threaded brocade or a simple length of cashmere jersey.

What Emerald really disliked was the corsets. She hated the tight bands of elastic and whalebone, the waist-nipping merry-widows and long-line brassières, cantilevered and foam-padded, which served the mannequins, along with every other fashionable woman, as a substitute for the good strong muscles and well-exercised limbs Emerald considered her birthright. All the more so since her physical strength had been hard-earned – first on the heather and the hill of Eas Forse, and later in the jungles with Nacho.

'What do we do with this *enfant terrible*?' Victoire Verdun would say every time she caught Emerald in what she called her *déshabillé*.

Emerald won the battle. She became the first mannequin on the Paris catwalk whose curves were all her own. In spite of that minor victory, there were other standards which had to be maintained.

Professional mannequins were expected to arrive with their make-up already perfect.

Almost without glancing at Emerald, Madame Verdun said, 'Do your maquillage right away, you bad girl. And do not think I will not *know* if you come in with black rings round your eyes.'

The Duchess of Windsor was due in at midday, the second of her fashion appointments that morning. Agnès knew from her friend Paulette, the chief *vendeuse* at a rival house, that *son altesse* had been due at Givenchy's at ten. The *vendeuses* made it their business to know such things.

Important private clients such as the Duchess who, merely by wearing one of the house creations, could trigger orders for five hundred copies, would come to the shows and take notes of the numbers of their favourite outfits. Later the client would return for a private showing in one of the small salons, where Monsieur Paradis would be on hand, the house models would wear the clothes she had liked, and the *vendeuse* and one of the workroom girls would tuck and pin and adjust to order.

The Duchess of Windsor's patronage was always a coup, a guarantee of success, even for the House of Paradis. It was a good sign that she would be taking her lunch – chicken sandwiches packed in a miniature picnic-hamper – in the company of her favourite *vendeuse*, Victoire Verdun.

The couturiers paid attention to the tastes of their important customers, and the collections always included outfits designed with a specific client in mind. It had become a kind of game between the designers and their star clothes-horses to guess which these were – and it was a running joke that the Duchess could always identify those dresses for which she was the inspiration.

Today Wallis Windsor was to pick the three items she would order from the spring collections.

'*Son altesse* knows herself by heart. Purity and simplicity of line are her trademark. We are here to confirm her choice,' Victoire Verdun lectured Emerald as she arranged the beautiful garments on the numbered hangers on a portable rail in the mannequins' dressing-room.

'The Duchess has asked for three short evening dresses. Emerald, you will wear first number thirty-nine, the yellow with the pearl bugle beads. You have the same colouring as the Duchess, even if your curves are a little more lavish. No more millefeuilles, *ma petite*! Next will be the navy with the jet fringe, number thirty-three, and afterwards fifty-one, the rose-pink with the cream embroidery.' She paused and glanced up from the hem, her mouth full of pins. 'Daytime, *son altesse* prefers pastels in the summer. For those you will wear first the raspberry linen, then the blue-grey silk crêpe.'

The Duchess had her own dressmaker's dummy made to her measurements, as did all the couturier's regular clients, so that the tape-measure did not need to come out every time. After she had made her choice, there would be a first fitting with the toile, a stiff cotton pattern from which the final garment would be cut. After that would follow two or three further fittings, the final one to adjust the set of the sleeve, the placing of buttons, the length of the hem. The Duchess's dummies were always made of a special blue linen with a small monogram in one corner.

'As long as I have known her, we have never had to change the measurements of the dummy. Now, Lady Diana Cooper, she has put on two kilos since her last visit. We will have to unpick the dummy again.'

Emerald stood patiently as the sempstress, a new recruit, put a few marker threads into the shoulder of the jacket.

'How does it feel?'

Madame Laurent, the head tailor, put her head round the door to check the fit of a jacket which went with a black silk dress lined with taffeta. The two silks rustled softly together as Emerald lifted her arms to demonstrate the set of the sleeve.

The tailor considered the effect for a moment, then hitched up the shoulder. 'Monsieur P designed this as the season's robe-écran. The Duchess chooses one every year as a backdrop for her jewels.'

She removed a pin and stuck it on her wrist-pincushion. 'The sleeve set high. *Son altesse* likes the cut of her jackets as narrow as possible, and your shoulders are a little more square.'

Emerald laughed. 'Do you have a corset for that, too, madame?'

Madame Laurent – the courtesy title of madame was accorded to all professional women, married or not, who had reached a certain seniority – pursed her lips, and brushed a few threads off her severe black dress. Then she put her eye to the gap in the curtain.

'You keep watch, *ma belle*. When Madame Verdun signals, come through into the salon.'

Reached by a grand sweep of staircase, the salon, the theatrical showcase for the clothes, was decorated in soft shades of grey, with a deep-piled battleship-grey carpet. During the biannual official showings of the collections, a raised parquet catwalk bisected the great room. For the rest of the year the room was divided into tented passages and curtained cubicles, with the viewing-area restricted to a space at the far end, and the rows of little gilt chairs replaced by two upright Louis XV sofas upholstered in pale pink velvet.

A flurry of activity at the far end of the room marked the arrival of the important client.

Emerald smoothed down the thick satin of the pale yellow evening dress she was to show first. She checked her appearance in the triple mirror and went through to the small curtained-off anteroom in which the mannequins waited for the signal to present themselves.

'Christian, you can read me like a book.' The voice floated through the heavy curtain.

Emerald lifted the velvet drape gently to one side so she could see the *vendeuses* fluttering around their star customer.

Wallis Windsor, a tiny figure in a cream bouclé wool suit, her neat head wrapped in an ocelot turban which defined her square jaw, stood at the top of the stairs, feet slightly turned in, talking animatedly to the bald-headed designer.

'Of *course* I knew the lilac was meant for me.'

A squawk of laughter scythed the perfumed air.

This time, unlike those wild moments in the New York ballroom, Emerald had the chance to examine the salon's most valued client.

The Duchess walked over to the sofa and settled herself, feet precisely crossed at the ankles, her stick-thin wrists and large square kid-gloved hands folded over the crocodile clutch-bag which bore the Windsor monogram – two entwined Ws topped with a crown. The Duchess had brought two pugs with her. The snub-nosed wrinkle-browed little dogs stared pop-eyed from their vantage point by the Duchess's crocodile-shod feet.

'Victoire, you know perfectly well I *never* tire of shopping! When a woman tires of shopping, she's going to the wrong shops.'

The Duchess's voice was surprisingly loud. The eyes were hard and bright – a clear blue accentuated by the careful make-up and severely parted hair, exposed as she unpinned the hat and laid it down beside her on the velvet upholstery.

She began to unpack a small hamper, describing the contents to Madame Verdun as she did so.

The *vendeuse* smiled and nodded, and then flicked her index finger towards the gap in the curtain.

'Allez, ma fille,' whispered Madame Laurent.

Emerald took a deep breath and walked forward into the glare of the salon lights.

The Duchess glanced up, the eyes bright as searchlights, the voice continuing smoothly, uninterrupted.

' . . . those little grey shrimps – the kind children catch with shrimping nets.'

Number thirty-nine, walk, turn, smile, turn, walk, smile, exit.

'Melt a lump of butter and mix in black pepper, a dash of wine vinegar and a mint leaf, stir in the shrimps, mix and chill. So easy. No, Victoire, I don't think so.'

The click of approval or the nod of dismissal.

'Delicious for tea – such an English meal. Of course I'd *buy* that, but I'd never *wear* it.'

Number forty-four. Again. Turn, walk, smile. The Duchess nibbled the tiny sandwiches.

'Victoire, *do* have some. All my French friends are mad about them. *Wafer*-thin cucumber sandwiches – the cucumber cut lengthwise, with all the pips taken out.' Her voice suddenly changed. 'Wait, child.'

Emerald stopped in mid-twirl.

The Duchess dabbed at her scarlet lips with a scrap of embroidered linen.

'Trooper, Imp, do we approve?' A scrap of chicken was posted into a pug's jaws.

Emerald waited, smiling.

'I think, yes. Perhaps.'

The pop-eyed pugs, licking their drooping chops and following the direction of their mistress's eyes, looked like indulged pink-tongued caricatures of their adoring owner.

'*Son altesse* knows exactly what suits her.'

'Ye-es.' The lengthened vowel trailed in the air as the Duchess turned her gaze for the first time on the young woman modelling the clothes. Her eyes narrowed.

'So this is the new mannequin. Come closer, dear.'

As the Duchess lifted her hand to beckon her over, Emerald noticed that Wallis Windsor was wearing a child's charm bracelet round her wrist, a narrow chain decorated with small jewelled crosses and tiny hearts. It looked oddly incongruous among the diamond-studded slave-bangles which were the royal trademark.

'Your Highness.' Emerald bobbed a graceful curtsy.

The Duchess examined the young woman coolly. 'What's your name?'

For an instant Emerald hesitated, remembering the inexplicable flash of anger on the Duchess's face when Diana Vreeland had insisted on presenting her.

Quietly she said: 'Emerald, Your Royal Highness.'

'Really.' The Duchess's face was a mask. 'A pretty name. We had a pug puppy once called Emerald.'

The Duchess gave her quick dry bark of laughter. 'I had to give her away when we left France. The trials of war.'

Wallis Windsor leaned forward, patted the nearest pug's wrinkled skull.

'We – His Royal Highness and I – always say the dogs are our children.'

She smiled, a thin-lipped slash of ruby lipstick.

For a long moment Emerald held the icy blue gaze. It was almost as if a fine thread linked them. Then, abruptly, the Duchess looked away. The thread snapped.

The star customer of the Maison Paradis waved her hand in the familiar gesture of curt dismissal, the wrist sparkling again with its bright jewelled circlet.

It was not until she was back in the mannequins' changing-room, hanging up the magnificent jewel-encrusted dresses, that Emerald remembered.

All at once the parade of rich silks and taffetas, moulded and flowing to take the shape of the woman for whom they were designed, seemed as bloodless and stiff as the tailor's dummies on which they were cut and stitched.

The memory reached far back down the vortex of dark water into which she was sucked and pulled in her dreams. As it did so, Emerald shook her head frantically. No power on earth was going to drag her back down that tunnel of remembrance. She tried to make her mind a blank, but stubbornly an image floated to its surface.

A narrow band of golden chain with a single tiny glittering cross, the exact replica of those on the charm bracelet the Duchess was wearing, was wound twice around the tiny wrist of a child.

Later, after her fittings, the Duchess returned to the magnificent mansion in the Bois de Boulogne which the municipality of Paris had generously put at the Windsors' disposal on a twenty-five-year peppercorn lease. There she explained to her devoted husband (the little business over Jimmy Donahue now forgiven and forgotten) that what she had suspected at the Windsor Ball was all too true.

'I have absolutely no doubt it was her. Something must be done about it, David.'

With that, the Duchess removed herself to the Mill, the Windsors' recently acquired country establishment, conveniently only half an hour from the centre of Paris.

There she awaited results.

315

46

Paris: 1954

'Anthony. Need to see you immediately. Matter of the utmost urgency.'

'Yes, sir. Paris or the country?'

'I think the Moulin.' Edward Windsor's voice crackled down the line. 'More discreet. You'll stay for the night, of course. Teatime on Saturday, then.'

Anstruther replaced the telephone on the cradle and rubbed his cheek thoughtfully. Although he had general overall charge of the Duke's financial and legal affairs, there was no meeting scheduled in the near future.

This time he could scent trouble. And trouble could only mean one thing. Trouble meant Emerald.

It was not the Windsors' way to ask questions – of each other, still less of outsiders – to which they might not wish to hear the answers. And Anthony Anstruther was too much the courtier to bring up a subject which was never discussed.

Anstruther resigned himself to whatever the fates might have in store, packed up a few papers for signature in his briefcase, and warned his clerk of his impending absence.

The Windsors' country house was a handsome rambling old mill, the Moulin de la Tuilerie, in the Vallée de Chevreuse, twenty-five miles outside Paris – a mere half-hour from the Windsors' much grander town house in the Bois.

In their country retreat, the Duchess had re-created as best she could the surroundings the Duke had enjoyed at Fort Belvedere, redecorating the interior in an Americanized version of an English country house. The Duke himself spent most of his time digging and planting up an English herbaceous border. His latest project was the establishment of an alpine garden among the boulders which fringed the mill's stream.

As usual Anstruther enjoyed the chance to get away from the office for a day or two. He took the opportunity to try out the dark-blue Jaguar saloon which was his modest reward to himself for a successful year. He liked the comfort and the leather seats and the walnut facings, the sheer *reliability* of the vehicle.

Long avenues of poplars, silvery trunks and flickering leaves rimmed the road. Wheezing tractors and lumbering horse-drawn carts slowed to let him pass. Rural France had healed her wartime sores, the rhythms of harvest re-establishing their hold on the lives of the small farmers whose homesteads dotted the landscape.

The countryside of France was looking clean and fresh and green. Anstruther spun the wheel, turned off the main road and drove through the pretty little village of Gif-sur-Yvette.

Privilege hid its face behind high walls. The Windsors' privacy was protected from sightseers by ivy-covered stones and solid wooden doors. The old gatekeeper peered out through a small wooden *portière*, nodded as he recognized the numberplates on the car, and waved Anstruther through.

'Passez, monsieur.'

A short drive led to the little seventeenth-century house on the millrace, set in an untidy jumble of barns and steadings.

Anstruther parked the Jaguar to one side of the little cobbled courtyard, noting a silver Mercedes and a Humber with British numberplates as well as the Duke's Bentley, and walked up the steps to the porch. In August the soft red brick of the façade was garlanded with clusters of pale apricot roses.

The front door swung open before he could press the bell. Anstruther always marvelled at the efficiency with which the Duchess organized her household. There must have been a footman with his eye glued to the spy-hole.

The open door gave immediately on to a large airy hall, where a handful of other guests had already assembled.

Even though the evening was fine and warm, a fire blazed in the grate. The stick-thin Duchess always felt the cold, although the Duke, accustomed to the draughty royal houses, had removed his tweed jacket and was in his shirt-sleeves.

The Duke came forward immediately to greet his visitor.

'Come in, my dear fellow. Delighted to see you. Whisky? Champagne if you prefer?'

'Thank you, sir. Champagne would be just the ticket.'

'Good. Excellent.' The Duke waved a half-smoked cigar. 'Take it with you while you change for dinner. Cocktails in an hour. Dinner at nine. We'll be able to slip away later. Settle the business.'

Anstruther had been given one of the chintz-curtained bachelor-rooms at the back. He took a quick shower and unpacked his dinner-jacket – obligatory even in the country. The Windsors always changed for dinner, even if they were alone.

An hour later he was back on parade.

'Over here, Anthony. This'll interest you.'

The Duke's hand was on his elbow. Anstruther joined the group which included a tall stooping Englishman and his plump wife.

The Duke waved his hand. 'You know Berkeley Ormerod and Bea? Old friends, of course. Lent us her place in Nassau while the Duchess was making Government House habitable. Good. Well, Bill is a financial wizard – just published a book on the Dow Jones. Pump him for a few tips.'

The Duke was in his favourite Royal Stuart tartan kilt worn with a white kid sporran, cream silk shirt and loosely tied plum velvet bow-tie, dark-blue velvet jacket with crested silver buttons. Knee-length Argyll socks and buckled shoes completed the romantic but slightly incongruous outfit.

The Duchess was as sleek as a heron in sunflower-yellow Balenciaga, the gleaming satin complementing her jewellery – a wide bib of tooled white gold patterned with yellow diamonds.

There were to be eight for the meal, including the Windsors themselves.

The dining-room was perfect as always. The table, covered with a pale primrose starched linen cloth and set with gold-rimmed plates and silver-gilt cutlery, was heaped with tiny gold-ribboned bouquets of yellow pansies – the bright little flower-faces exactly matching Wallis Windsor's outfit.

'I do so enjoy pansies,' the Duchess's harsh voice rose about the chatter, 'both in my garden and at my table.'

The guests laughed nervously – and Anstruther was not the only

318

one to notice the sudden look of pain which crossed the Duke's face. There had been plenty of truth in the rumours about young Jimmy Donahue.

Two white-gloved footmen in the dark-green monkey jackets designed by the Duchess as the indoor servants' country uniform, served the dinner.

Filets of sole in cream were accompanied by a Rhine Riesling, its flowery bouquet chilled to complement the rich sauce.

'So clever of David – he's wonderful with wine.'

As if in confirmation, a 1948 Lynch-Bages was poured with the roast partridges. The Duke waved away a dandelion salad.

'David! You know perfectly well . . . '

The Duke took a helping of the re-proffered greens. Anstruther watched with some amusement as he pushed the leaves around the plate.

He cheered up when the plates where changed, examining with pleasure the cork of the Château Yquem which was to accompany the iced *bombe aux fraises de bois.*

'David!' The Duchess made a disapproving little *moue* at her husband. Then she turned back to her guests. 'The strawberries are ours. David has such wonderfully green fingers.'

Wallis took a tiny helping of the berries, but waved away the wine. She left the rich dessert untouched on her plate. If her dressmakers dictated her diary, her figure dictated her diet.

Anstruther, his mind drifting in the sea of chatter, was content to think his own thoughts. From Callum's photographs, Emerald certainly favoured her mother. Physically the likeness was startling. But there, it seemed, the resemblance ended. In the way they chose to live, mother and daughter could not have been less alike.

But, for the rest of it, there was no doubt that Emerald had inherited her feckless father's charm. Combined with her mother's driving ambition, the quality would surely prove – had already proved – a potent mix.

'The drive was pleasant, Anthony?'

The Duchess's voice interrupted his thoughts. His hostess adhered rigorously to the royal protocol of changing conversation partners with each change of course.

The arrival of the savouries announced that the meal was drawing to a close. Whole fried mushrooms on toast, each fragrant black cap topped with a spoonful of hollandaise, were handed round with the port. This was the sign for the ladies to withdraw, following the English custom of leaving the men to themselves after dinner.

319

Wallis Windsor liked to underline the Englishness of her exiled royal household. She stood, smoothed down her skirt, and gracefully moved towards the door. The ex-monarch's eyes – pale Hanoverian blue – anxiously tracked his wife's movements.

'We'll join you in a moment, darling.'

There was no doubt the man was still besotted, Anstruther reflected. Someone had once said – perhaps it was the waspish Cecil Beaton – that the two had been irretrievably welded by the tragedy of their mutual sex-urge.

Left to themselves in the dining-room, the men's talk was all of stockmarkets and property values. The Duke was always interested in money. Without the safety net of the vast family fortune, it had become an increasing preoccupation.

Meanwhile the Duchess led the ladies up to her rooms for coffee. The upstairs drawing-room was a converted loft filled with chintz-covered sofas and low tables – the room high and airy and roofed with dark beams. The sloping levels of the mill gave access to the garden through french windows, half-open in midsummer so the guests could enjoy the long twilight.

The ladies discussed the costumes for a forthcoming fancy-dress ball. The Duchess was bored. She did not like fancy dress and did not intend to wear it.

When the men joined the women, the talk turned to politics. The resurgence of the new Germany. France's problems in Indo-China. The mounting losses in Vietnam. The riots in Algeria. The troubles the United States was likely to have with the emergent young nations in Latin America.

After a polite interval, Anstruther wandered out into the scented garden.

'See you in the barn, Anthony.' It was the Duke's voice. 'Take a whisky. I'll be over in a moment.'

The barn was the Duke's private domain. Everything that had ever marked him out for what he had once been – the anointed heir to the greatest and richest empire the world had ever known – was stored and displayed in the high airy room.

A huge map covered the fireplace wall. There were mementoes of his official visits to India and Canada on every surface. Cap-badges, buttons, silver cups and engraved salvers, ribbons and decorations from the Duke's service in the First World War, all neatly labelled as reminders of the exalted status of the ex-monarch.

Most poignant of all, the ceremonial brass drum of the Welsh Guards served out its retirement as an ornamental coffee-table. Not unlike its owner, Anstruther reflected wryly as he settled down to run through the Duke's portfolio.

Anstruther placed his leather attaché case on the table, opened it, and carefully laid out the few papers which needed attention.

As he did so, Anstruther felt a sudden wave of anger at the sheer feckless irresponsibility of the ex-king and his duchess – so wrapped up in the trivia of their own lives that they were completely oblivious to the fate, let alone the happiness, of others. The signs had been there for years. There had been the great betrayal of the Abdication itself which had disappointed millions of his subjects. Then there had been the minor betrayals – like poor faithful Fruity Metcalf, left to hitch his way alone to Cherbourg when the Duke and Duchess, fearing the fall of Paris in 1940, abandoned their household and ran for cover in the neutrality of Franco's Spain.

It had not always been so. There had been a time when, as the sword-and-buckler Prince of Wales, the heir to the victor of Agincourt had won his own spurs – and the Military Cross for valour – on the battlefields of the Great War.

Not any more. Love – and there was no doubt he loved the woman – had unmanned the people's hero. Unable to make her a princess, the ex-prince was now a slave to his infatuation.

'Make yourself comfortable, Anthony.'

The Duke was standing in the doorway, his jacket over his arm, his bow-tie loosened.

'Thank you, sir.'

The Duke threw himself down in one of the leather armchairs.

'I expect you're wondering why I brought your visit forward?'

'I did rather, sir. There's not a great deal to report on the investment side of things. Just a few transfers for signature. Nothing significant.'

'It's the child.'

'The child?'

'The Duchess says . . . Well, how shall I put it? Her Royal Highness and I . . .' He hesitated.

'Yes, sir?'

'It's the young woman's career . . .'

'What about her career?'

'I don't know quite how to put it. But it's rather in the way.'

'In the way?'

'Well, you see, she's quite in the limelight over here. Paths cross. Paris is not exactly Timbuktu. It's becoming quite noticeable. Uncomfortable.

The Duchess is not at all happy . . .' The Duke's voice trailed away helplessly.

Anstruther's face was stony.

'Meaning, sir?'

The Duke began again, his words tumbling over themselves.

'Since you insist. Lay it on the table. Wallis is absolutely adamant she won't come back to Paris until the girl's out of the way.'

He paused and looked pleadingly at the barrister. 'There it is. Now you know. Had sleepless nights. At my wits' end. Anthony, you have to help me. I depend on you. Frightful mess, all of it. Too late to do anything now, except make more of a mess.'

'Sir, the Duchess is going to have to live with it. With the best will in the world, I don't see what the hell I can do.'

'She must have some kind of passport. Work permit. Official stuff. That kind of thing.' He took a deep breath. 'You know your way around. Talk to the Quai d'Orsay. They'll help. They do that sort of thing all the time. Undesirable alien. Make it up to her. Use the collateral.'

'Undesirable alien?' Astruther's voice was quiet.

'Buy it.'

'Buy it?'

The Duke nodded. 'Any way you can.'

Anstruther, courtier though he was by birth as well as by inclination, was angry. Helplessly, blindly angry.

He stood up abruptly. 'Mind if I go out for a moment, sir?'

The Duke flushed. Then he waved his hand. 'Of course. Think about it. Only natural. Know you felt bad about Iona and all that business. Terrible. Still. Spilt milk. Happened all the time in the war.'

Anstruther walked through the door into the silence of the garden. The blood pounded in his temples. Christ. The price was too high. But, then, the price of loyalty was always too high.

'And so I said to Christian, if that woman wears the Chanel I shall positively die of laughter . . .'

The Duchess's harsh voice floated down through the damp night air.

Anstruther clenched his fists, feeling the sharp edge of nails against his palm. Suddenly it was as if a great weight had been lifted from his shoulders. He had made up his mind. For once, Anthony Anstruther, ex-courtier, ex-lapdog to an ex-king, was going to take the side of the angels.

One angel. His ex-employer had been right in that he felt he had betrayed Iona. He would not now betray the child she had entrusted to his care.

The Duke glanced up anxiously as Anstruther came back into the room. 'Well?'

'Can't be done, sir.'

The Duke stared at his ex-equerry. The boiled-sweet eyes hardened to blue pin-pricks. 'What the devil's that supposed to mean?'

'Simply that it's not possible.'

The Duke swallowed. The Adam's apple popped up and down in his throat. Then, astonishingly, he stamped his foot. The kilt danced.

'The devil it isn't. What am I supposed to tell Her Royal Highness?'

'I'm sure you'll think of something, sir.' Anstruther allowed himself a fleeting smile. 'Try giving her a trinket. Suitably engraved.'

'You tendering your resignation, Anthony?'

'Yes, sir.'

'Bloody stupid.'

'Yes, sir. And now, if you'll excuse me . . .'

Anstruther went straight up to his room. Early next morning he packed up his briefcase and left before breakfast.

His heart lifted as he swung for the last time out of the shadowy driveway and emerged into the bright air of the clean spring morning.

For the first time he felt that he had laid the ghost of Iona to rest. He had taken a decision he was not likely to regret.

Meanwhile it would be as well to make sure that Emerald suffered no repercussions in the future. On the way home, he passed through Paris and called on an old comrade-in-arms, now a very senior official at the French Foreign Office on the Quai d'Orsay.

It happened there had been certain favours rendered, dating back to wartime troubles, which opened doors. Anstruther used the Palace's receipt for the Alexandra emeralds to reinforce his confidential briefing on the wishes of the Duke's brother. The French understood that these things needed delicate handling.

Forewarned was forearmed. And if the Duchess continued to sulk in the country, then the Duke would have to appease his wife as best he could.

The scene was set. Emerald could enjoy the limelight in peace. The better she made her own mark, the less anyone would search out her past.

There was just one last obligation to fulfil. The career Emerald had chosen had its own built-in obsolescence. For all the young mannequins it was a road which led to the altar.

For Emerald it was not simple. The marriage settlement was still in place; not even the Duke would dare to vary that agreement. Everything depended on finding the right – discreet – match.

For that Anstruther needed a broker. However wide the range of his skills, arranging marriages was not one of them.

The modern world believed in true love.

Anstruther's world had more sense than to count on anything so fickle. Arranged marriages were always the most successful.

47

Astley Keep: 1954

An arranged marriage was exactly what his mother and her old acquaintance Billy Beaumont had in mind for Thomas, 17th Baron Sherwood.

Tom Sherwood had just turned thirty. The 'wake' he had thrown to mark this tragic event had received extensive coverage in the popular press – a chance to rail against the decadence of the young bloods of the aristocracy. The invitations had been edged with black, and the guests were instructed to wear mourning. The all-night party had been held in a disused village cemetery in the hills overlooking the principality of Monte Carlo, Tom's chosen place of residence.

It was the bill for this extravaganza which had triggered his mother's uncharacteristic flurry of activity on her son's behalf. Tom's preferences did not indicate marriage was something he was likely to choose for himself. Nevertheless, given Tom's particular circumstances, married he must be, and to an heiress at that.

His contemporaries had been quick to spot Tom's proclivities when, just into his teens, he had transferred from a brutal preparatory school to the equally brutal public school the males of his family automatically attended.

The term 'public school' was a ludicrous misnomer, since admission to that most privileged of prisons was anything *but* available to the public.

The new boys were called squeakers.

'Do you know why you're called squeakers?' the fag-master, a sixth former of supreme power and towering elegance in a scarlet brocade waistcoat, asked his trembling audience.

'No, sir,' came the piping reply from short-trousered thirteen-year-olds lined up on one side of the ancient monastic quadrangle.

'I shall tell you, then, my dears,' the older boy continued. 'Squeakers are baby pigeons. Like you they come from nice warm nests, and like you they are ripe for the plucking. Also like you, they open their beaks and squeak for their mummies.'

The fag-master glared at the line of initiates.

'Those of you who came to Open Day will have no doubt been treated to a tour of the magnificent grounds of our venerable Alma Mater. You will have admired the fine dovecot which, true to the tradition of the Cistercian monks who founded our centre of learning, we keep well stocked. It will be your pleasant duty to perform, in strict rotation, a service which has been part of our weekly chores for five hundred years. The doves have to be fed twice a day, morning and evening.'

'Please, sir?' One of the boys put up his hand.

'Yes, squeaker?'

'We have a pigeon-loft at home, sir.'

'I've no doubt we *all* have a pigeon-loft at home, squeaker.' A syco-phantic twitter of laughter punctuated the reply.

'Follow me.'

The fag-master set off across the quadrangle, through the double-arched clocktower with its sundial, across the square of lawn until he reached the stone-built miniature castle which housed the doves.

As he ushered his charges inside, a sharp ammoniac stench billowed up to greet them from the damp straw which covered the stone floor. The gloom, pierced with arrow-slits of light, was criss-crossed with perches on which the birds shifted restlessly, filling the air with their rustle and soft cooing. The noise echoed eerily in the hollow structure, punctuated by the beat of whiplash flight-feathers as the adult birds moved in and out of the nesting boxes.

The older boy reached up to the nearest nest and felt inside. He pulled out a pair of ungainly pink-fleshed young, their huge beaks out of proportion to the helpless soft bodies spiked with embryonic quills. He turned over the fledglings and beckoned his audience forward. The plump young birds' legs had been tied together as for a three-legged race.

'See that, my dears?'

The fag-master held up the grotesquely twinned birds, twisting them in the shaft of light from the open door. They looked like little pink balloons.

'As soon as the squeakers show signs of fledging, it is the responsibility of the duty-squeaker – which ever of you it is – to tie their little legs together in pairs so they can't leave the nest. The consequence is obvious: the parent-birds continue to feed their young, the squeakers continue to fatten until they are ready to have their necks wrung. It's simple. The parallels to your own lives are obvious. We have squeaker pie every second Saturday of the month.'

The boys filed out into the sunshine again.

'Right, squeakers. You can go to your dorms and settle down on your little perches. All but the one with the pigeon-loft.'

'Yes, sir.' The boys scattered, leaving one behind.

The older boy stared at the younger, his eyes narrowed. Then he said. 'Name, squeaker?'

The new boy was small for his age, his big round brown eyes, rosebud mouth and curly gold hair contributing to his air of cherubic innocence. Tom's mother, her mind on the breeding cycle of the hawk-moth, had not provided him with the regulation uniform short trousers. So Tom Sherwood, in a countryman's tweed jacket, knee-breeches, thick woollen stockings and heavy brogues, stood out like a gamekeeper in a pack of merchant bankers.

'Thomas Sherwood,' said the new boy.

'Thomas Sherwood, *sir.*' The fag-master's voice was cold.

'Sir, sir.'

'Better, squeaker. So you're the little lordling? My, we *are* a pretty boy.'

Tom blushed scarlet. He glanced up through long chestnut-brown lashes, noticing with admiration the dark fuzz on the older boy's upper lip. He liked the way it expanded like a little concertina as the fag-master smiled.

'Say thank you, Baggot, sir.'

'Thank you, Baggot, sir.' Tom's voice, just on the verge of breaking, soared in and out of its baby register.

'Cheaky squeaker. Come to my room at teatime. I just might have a job for you.'

The job, it turned out, was not the shoe-polishing and button-sewing duties which Tom Sherwood had expected. He was not even required, as Harmsworth Minor had warned, to warm the lavatory seat for his mentor. Instead the chore involved young Tom Sherwood's initiation into a practice which, in more than one such venerable institution,

327

was considered an intrinsic part of a public-school education.

The older boy took the younger down to the dovecot, where he arranged him tenderly against one of the lower beams which provided the birds with their perches. As Sebastian Baggot expertly Vaselined the younger boy's bottom, before taking a brief but satisfactory pleasure with him, Tom Sherwood discovered for the first time that sex was neither a solitary occupation which risked the growth of hair on the palms, nor something girls – effectively absent from his upbringing – might or might not let you do to them. Instead of the dangers of heterosexual dalliance, homosexuality provided a way to peer-acceptance and special privileges in a fiercely competitive world.

Anyway Tom Sherwood liked his relationships with men, particularly if he could arrange a little tenderness in a pigeon-loft. It was a habit he had no desire to kick, whatever his biologist mother told him was the accepted breeding pattern. He never regretted his choice for a moment, not even much later when he was discharged from his late father's regiment for being so indiscreet as to get himself caught with his trousers down in public. He had been enjoying the company of a young Guardsman in the shrubbery in Kensington Gardens, in full view of the pigeons resting their weary wings on the bronze statue of J M Barrie's Peter Pan.

None of this would have mattered particularly had it not been that, after the death of his father in a hunting accident, Tom had inherited a title which could be traced back to William the Conqueror, plus the house and land which went with it. The estate had belonged to his family even before the title itself had been created.

Astley Keep, as the house was named for the Saxon moat which once surrounded it, was listed in the Domesday Book – making it at least a thousand years old.

Over the generations the Keep had spread outwards and upwards, piling up layer upon layer without paying the slightest heed to architectural principles. Tom's great-grandfather, influenced by the sights and trophies he had acquired on the Grand Tour, had had the main house rebuilt from scratch. He dismantled most of the ancient Keep, filled in the moat, and replaced the original sprawl with a reproduction of the turreted Transylvanian castle of Vlad the Impaler, the inspiration for Count Dracula, whom his wife, a beautiful Romanian countess also acquired on his travels, claimed as a direct ancestor.

This reduced at one stroke the ancient Saxon hall to a flight of theatrical fantasy, a maze of Victorian plumbing with enough servants' quarters to house an entire cavalry regiment, horses and all. The expense finished off the last remnants of the family fortune, reducing the estate to near-penury.

By the time Tom's father came into his inheritance, the house was in a sad state of disrepair. Fortunately for everyone the young heir had the good sense to fall in love with an heiress. That she happened to be Jewish and very very clever was something the family was happy to overlook, provided she put the lead back on the roof.

Bertha Goldberg, Tom's mother, was by any standards a remarkable woman. She was a scientist, a passionately serious scholar. She was eccentric. She was also, to those accustomed to admire small tiptilted noses and round blue eyes, extremely plain. And, as a member of an ancient family of diaspora Jews, she was, in the eyes of the County, profoundly foreign.

Tom's father married Bertha Goldberg not for her banking-family fortune, but because he loved her. He himself was not at all clever; in fact he was sent down from Cambridge after failing his preliminary exams because, in the acid view of his tutor, of the 'inordinate amount of time Lord Sherwood spends with companions he clearly, and perhaps rightly, believes to be his only intellectual equals at the university. I refer of course to his horses.'

He was never quite sure why he loved Bertha. In part, it was unquestionably because she was everything he was not – even physically he was as blond and handsome as she was dark and plain. In part, too, it was because he had the gypsy blood of the Romanian countess his grandmother in his veins – and the eccentric Bertha, with her raw-boned strength and wild dark hair, seemed exotic enough to provide him with an escape from the programmed rigidity of his own upbringing.

But the mainstay of their conjugal happiness was Bertha's attitude to sex. She loved everything about the mating process – in and out of the laboratory.

'When you spend as much time as I do peering at the sexual organs of plants,' she would explain cheerfully, slipping an exotic scarlet bloom under her microscope, 'it gives you an appetite.'

Bertha tackled the business of lovemaking with a gusto and imaginative breadth which would certainly have shocked the County had they known – and completely captivated her husband.

The day she told him she was carrying the child who turned out to be Tom, was the last day of the fox-hunting year. The season's last meet was always held at Astley Keep. The hunt and the hounds, with the whippers-in in their scarlet coats, were about to move off from the forecourt, when Bertha appeared.

She had not been feeling well that morning. But now she came out on to the cobbles still in her nightclothes, white-faced and wearing a white silk dressing-gown. To her husband she was the most exciting and beautiful woman he had ever known or could ever imagine. Only Bertha, still very young and the master's wife, could have come out in her dressing-gown and got away with it in the eyes of the County. For Bertha, rules didn't exist. In a very short space of time the County had been forced to accept that.

'I hope the Countess's genes are as strong as mine, my dear,' she said to her husband as he sat straight and tall, magnificent in his scarlet coat and top hat, on the roan stallion. 'Because in a few months' time you're going to see a whole new cocktail of them.'

She smiled up at him.

Bewildered, her husband leaned down and kissed her. He laughed. He didn't know what she meant. He was simply delighted she had come out to see him off.

The hounds bayed, and the hunt servants blew their horns. He swung his horse round and set off behind the pack already streaming away through the park. An hour later they picked up the scent of an old dog fox, and the first of the day's runs started. Man and horse were leaping the third fence in the wake of the now-racing hounds, when Tom's father realized what his wife had told him.

He gave a shout of delight, took off his topper and tossed it exuberantly into the air, and urged his horse into a gallop. The horse miscalculated the approach to a tall hawthorn hedge. Both hoofs caught the top of the hedge. Horse and rider fell on the far side. The rider was thrown clear, but his unprotected head smashed against the stump of a felled oak. He died instantly.

Six months later, Tom was born.

Bertha's substantial marriage portion had been put into a trust fund on her wedding. The Goldbergs did not trust the English aristocracy. They had made too many loans to profligate younger sons for that. The capital was entailed, and therefore not available for distribution, except to fund Bertha's researches – the family had a healthy respect for science – and to keep the roof on the building.

So the year Tom turned thirty Bertha Sherwood, although she had never before concerned herself with her son's choice of bedfellow, decided it was high time she found her only child a wife to provide a successor to the paternal line. She owed it to the boy's father.

Once she had made up her mind, Bertha normally achieved her aims.

The medium she chose to put her plans in motion was her husband's old schoolfriend Sir William Beaumont, who had just, at Bertha's invitation, spent the weekend at Astley.

Bertha had never particularly liked the dapper little baronet on the rare occasions their paths crossed. She found him plausible, greedy – and more devious than a Baghdad rug merchant. But Billy had a reputation as a marriage broker – a good old-fashioned matchmaker. The services of a matchmaker were one of the few areas in which Jewish tradition and that of the aristocratic Gentiles coincided.

Billy would know instantly what she was looking for: a young lady of the very best but with a touch of mongrel breeding in her ancestry. As a biologist Bertha knew the value of the mongrel in the mix. Hybrid vigour strengthened the line.

Billy said he understood perfectly. As a matter of fact, given a little time and patience, he had the very thing – just coming to ripe young womanhood on the catwalks of Paris. And, if he was not mistaken, he knew she had a nice little marriage portion, payable on her marriage to the fortunate husband. All very discreet. It was an unusual story. But, whatever she lacked in acknowledgeable pedigree, hybrid vigour she had in plenty.

Billy had stumbled on Emerald's expectations almost by accident. Except that the connections that Billy made were never truly by accident.

The writ of the *Almanach de Gotha*, continental Europe's bible of genealogy, does not run in Britain. Just as her laws depend on precedent and her constitution remains unwritten, so her social system does not depend on lists and lineage. Dynastic marriages are arranged through intermediaries, over lunch in a club, tea at the Dorchester. The arrangement has one overwhelming advantage. In the self-limiting social circles of an island, it allows a more flexible view of genealogy than that laid down by the strict rules of lineage. In other words, who actually fathered whom is not information recorded on the family tree. A well-informed dependable broker will know exactly who is half-brother or half-sister to whom, and make sure there are no unfortunate misalliances. Some element of choice is permitted the young people. New money is welcomed. Even the odd barmaid is permissible. But inbreeding and bad blood are best avoided.

It was Billy Beaumont's business to make suitable connections. He already had a good notion of the girl's pedigree, and he had listened carefully enough to Lily to realize that if anyone knew why and how Emerald had ended up in Molly Anstruther's care, it was likely to be her son.

Billy made it his business to run into Anthony at his club.

To Anstruther, Billy came as a chance to regain control of a situation which threatened to spiral out of hand.

The cautious barrister had not given him the whole story, of course. Billy understood the need for discretion. But, over a whisky at White's, Anstruther had told Billy just enough to make it clear that the girl – effectively an orphan, for reasons which were not so uncommon in postwar Britain – would before long be in need of a husband.

Both agreed that Emerald was the perfect solution to Tom's problems. And Tom was the perfect solution to Emerald's.

48

Paris: 1956

Emerald hurried up the escalator of the Paris Métro, taking the steps two at a time. Heads turned as she passed, but after three years in the city she no longer noticed the effect she had on casual passers-by. In Paris every red-blooded male automatically turned his head to follow any beautiful young woman's progress.

With the autumn air cold on her face, she paused for a moment in the square in front of the great cathedral of Notre-Dame for a glimpse of the soot-streaked gargoyles which grimaced from the cathedral roof. Although for nearly three years now she had followed exactly the same route, she never tired of the intricate carvings; there was always something new to admire. Paris was full of such surprises; shadowy and subtle as New York had been bright and brash, the ancient city never failed to enchant her.

The sun was already setting in a pool of liquid scarlet over the asymmetrical twin towers. The great shrine, no longer a place of religious pilgrimage but a tourist Mecca obedient to the demands of commerce, closed its doors at sunset.

Now, in the dim half-light, the great courtyard was empty of tourists, the honey-coloured flagstones dotted with scavenging pigeons. On the far side of the square, a girl and a boy, no older than eight or nine, their bright hair gleaming in the late sunshine, drew out a game of hopscotch.

Emerald paused for a moment to watch the two shining faces, so intent on their game. For a moment her mind wandered back to her own childhood – to the tousle-haired boy whose nurseries she had once shared, who had been her companion on the hills of Eas Forse.

She shivered. A shadow had fallen – the shadow of loss. Surely Callum would have forgotten all about her by now; he would have plenty of other girls to claim his attention. He might even have fallen in love.

She frowned. Absurdly she felt a sharp stab of jealousy.

Callum in love? She remembered the strong arms which had once held her safe, and surely now held another. The tawny eyes which had once lit up only for her would be smiling for a new love.

She shook her head. That was the past; and, dearly though she had loved him, Callum was part of that past. Emerald feared the power of the past. It had never done her anything but harm. She had made her own life, which owed nothing to anyone. She earned her own living, made her own friends, chose her own destiny.

Then she walked on swiftly across the bridge which led to the Île St-Louis and the apartment she shared with Dido Delal. The tide was high, and a light breeze ruffled the calm surface of the Seine. She pulled off her beret and shook out her cropped mop of dark hair, the russet glints picking up the reflections of the water.

Soon she reached the busy little street which led to her apartment building. Her spirits lifted, as they always did, as the scents of home-cooked cassoulet wafted through the open door of the traiteur. She joined the queue of returning office workers, selecting a couple of slices of wind-dried ham, a wedge of ripe Camembert, a scoop of celeriac in mustard mayonnaise, a crisp-crusted baguette.

After a moment's thought she added a bottle of flower-perfumed Chambéry, Dido's favourite apéritif. Not that Dido was likely to spend an evening at home – unless the previous evening had left her with more than the usual hangover.

The greengrocer next door to the traiteur was her last stop. The proprietor was a cheerful round-faced grandfather whose thick rolling consonants spoke of the fertile valleys of the south. Now, at the end of the day, the old man was carrying in the boxes of vegetables displayed on the pavement before he put the shutters up for the night.

Emerald was his favourite customer, and he would put aside little treats for her, presented with courtly elegance after she had made her purchases.

'Bonsoir, mademoiselle,' he called as soon as he caught sight of her. 'You're home late.'

Emerald waved and crossed the road to greet the old man.

'We had a busy day, Monsieur Revel. You'll be seeing my face all over the hoardings soon – the new perfume's due out in a month.'

'But of course – what else?' The old man smiled, the weatherbeaten face creased with pleasure. He was proud of the pretty young woman, as proud of her as he might have been of his own daughter. She was an ornament to the *quartier*.

'Tenez.' He held out a plump strawberry, turning it so that Emerald could admire it, rosy-cheeked as a painted mannequin. 'Les derniers. The last of the season. Just arrived from the Gorges du Tarn. From Florac, where they have all the market gardens. Take it. It will remind you of summer.'

Emerald accepted the berry and rolled it round her tongue. Its perfumed sweetness reminded her of the magenta-dark berries of the Mexican markets.

She sighed. 'It tastes of sunshine. How much for the box?'

'Too expensive for you, *ma belle*.' The old man smiled. He pulled out a sheet of yesterday's *Figaro*, and began to wrap up the box. 'Much too expensive, A gift.'

'You spoil me, Monsieur Revel. I shall have to buy flowers.'

Emerald selected an armful of heavy-scented tuberoses and held out the coins to pay for them.

The old man counted the money carefully. 'Merci. And the other *belle demoiselle*? I've not seen her for a while.'

Emerald laughed. 'You'll have to move to the Faubourg Saint-Honoré if you want *la belle demoiselle*'s custom, Monsieur Revel.'

The old man shook his head. 'Young girls . . .'

'Not like in your day?' Emerald teased. But it was true enough that Dido's shopping trips were more likely to be to the smart boutiques of the fashionable Faubourg than to the greengrocer round the corner. A childhood spent between strict boarding schools and luxurious hotels had not left Dido with a taste for cooking or cleaning. Fortunately for both girls, Emerald, well accustomed to life below stairs, enjoyed taking charge of the housekeeping.

In fact, she reflected as she swung down the street with the shopping bag, it was easier to share living space when their interests did not coincide.

It was even easier that the two young women chose the opposite ends of the social spectrum for companionship. While Dido was wined and dined at the glamorous Tour d'Argent, spending her weekends in the gamblers' palaces of Deauville or Monte Carlo, Emerald had never shared her tastes.

Every evening, after she had left the pampered world of fashion behind her, she vanished among the Left Bank's student population, queuing for gallery seats at the Comédie Française, browsing up and down the wooden-fronted book-kiosks which lined the bridges, hunting for bargains in the Marché aux Puces.

She turned into the rue des Mendiants. Nearly home. The rich perfume of the armful of lilies filled her nostrils, and was joined by another, even more delicious: a billowing breath of caramel and toasted almonds.

She hesitated for an instant outside the pâtisserie. Then she shook her head and walked on, smiling to herself as she remembered the strictures of Madame Verdun against putting another inch on her curves. The strawberries would have to do.

As she turned through the archway into the courtyard of the apartment-block, she looked up at the elongated double window of the flat. Tonight the curtains were drawn. A thin crack of light showed between the heavy prewar damask. Emerald breathed a sigh of relief. Dido must be home; she hadn't been home all night.

Such overnight absences were becoming the rule. From the first, Dido's life had been as disorganized as Emerald's was orderly. Emerald could never work out how Dido earned her living – only that sometimes she had fistfuls of notes, and at others she didn't even have the price of the cab. Dido's main source of income seemed to be the commissions Billy Beaumont paid her for introductions. Then there were chaperon duties for his visiting young ladies. For the rest of it, Dido's affairs were conducted at night at the wild parties for which Paris society had an insatiable appetite – a public display of affluence which fuelled the students' anger.

Emerald was content with her own far simpler existence. She loved the apartment. It was the first home she had ever known where she didn't feel an interloper. The comings and goings which were the inevitable result of Dido's busy social life were kept firmly out of Emerald's room. Her bedroom was her haven.

There was only thing lacking. Paris was a city for lovers. It was impossible to avoid them. Young lovers were everywhere, gazing into each other's eyes under every street-lamp, kissing on every park bench, strolling hand-in-hand round every corner.

In spite of Dido's best efforts to introduce her to eligible young men, in spite of the glamorous world in which she earned her living, Emerald refused all suitors.

She was hungry, not for love, but for life itself. Paris was life. Like a baby suckling at its mother's breast, she loved the taste, the smells, the sounds of the city. The city itself nourished her.

Lovers were part of the scenery. Someone else's scenery.

At the far end of the courtyard, Madame Rappaport the concierge, plump and waddling in her widow's weeds, twitched the corner of her yellowing lace curtain and tapped on the window to attract Emerald's attention.

There was nothing which Madame Rappaport did not know about the comings and goings in her building. As she described the day's visitors to her best friend, the concierge in the neighbouring apartment block, she explained that she herself was the soul of discretion when it came to which gentlemen – or lady-friends – of the inhabitants she allowed into the building.

Some time – Madame Rappaport hoped it would be soon – she would retire on the fruits of her discretion.

Take Mademoiselle Dido, for instance. Her numerous visitors dictated liberal helpings of discretion. But tonight it was the other young lady, the quiet beauty, who had the visitor. An old acquaintance, he said he was. A childhood friend. Almost a cousin really. Madame Rappaport had been doubtful at first. But he was very well dressed, polite – and persuasive.

'Tenez, madame. My card.'

Madame Rappaport stared at the proffered oblong of thick ivory card. It was engraved – you could feel that without even looking down by the bumpy surface. Above the name was a little coronet. Folded neatly beneath the card was a banknote of a surprisingly large denomination.

'D'accord, monsieur. Perhaps you might like to wait inside?'

A real gentleman, Madame Rappaport told herself as she showed the gentleman up. Impeccably presented, perfect manners – and spoke such beautiful French, with only the smallest hint of the English accent which sounded so *soigné* when the speaker was as tall and fair as the wheatfields in summer.

A *cavalier de bon ton*, romantic and handsome – just the sort of visitor she, Françoise Rappaport, would wish for the beautiful *demoiselle*.

49

Paris: 1956

Emerald was sure it must be a mistake. She expected no visitor. Any gentleman – particularly one of whom Madame Rappaport approved – could only be looking for Dido.

She rearranged her armful of shopping, took a deep breath, and began to climb the six flights of stairs. The lift was almost always out of order. It had served the inhabitants for fifty years, and the landlord saw no particular reason to pay good money to change its rusting clockwork for an expensive modern shaft of steel and plastic.

Emerald and Dido lived on the fourth floor. Most of the inhabitants were young and fit, so the stairs were no great hardship. There was only one elderly resident, a one-time chorus-girl who lived in the attic. She let a basket down into the well sharp at eight each morning for the concierge to send up her breakfast croissants. Emerald could always tell it was time to get up by the bump of the basket against her bedroom window-pane. The old lady would sometimes ask Emerald up for coffee and regale her with stories of life at the Café de Paris.

Next to her, in the warren of tiny rooms at the top of the building, lived Étienne, a young philosophy student who had made it his business to improve Emerald's education. They had quite literally bumped into each other on the stairs one evening soon after she had arrived in Paris. Emerald had been on her way up to her own apartment with a big bag of groceries. The young man, his arms piled so high with heavy volumes he could not see where to set his feet, had been on his way down. Both had dropped their burdens, which went cascading, intermingled, down the stairs.

'Allez! Your shopping!'

'Oh Lord! Your books!'

Emerald watched in horror as a large bag of ripe tomatoes cascaded downwards, spilling a scarlet snail-trail over the shiny white paperbacks.

'Such beautiful tomatoes!' The young man sat down on the stairs, elbows out of the black jacket, threadbare as a beggarboy, his face such a mask of tragedy that Emerald burst out laughing.

The young man looked up at her, his eyes serious. 'Body and soul must suffer equally. You have lost your supper. And I have lost' – he sighed, and began to wipe off the covers – 'a thousand years of argument.'

He held out his hand. 'Companions in misfortune. Étienne. Et toi?'

'Emerald.' Emerald took the hand and smiled.

'Marvellous. Tu viens avec?'

Emerald, startled, accepted the invitation. So Étienne took her down to the café on the Left Bank. Here, under the sponsorship of the young philosopher, she found herself a spiritual home among the crowd of students who thronged the smoke-filled rooms after the lectures at the Sorbonne.

Étienne treated her like a delinquent younger sister – insisting, even after she had had a long day at the salon, that she accompany him on his evening forays. In return Emerald would sometimes cook him a meal, most of which he pushed uneaten to one side as he expounded on the day's lectures.

Emerald enjoyed her vicarious tutorials, arguing fiercely over the latest theories which had caught Étienne's imagination.

'You feed nothing but the mind,' Emerald would say finally in exasperation as she dished up a foaming omelette. 'How about the body?'

Étienne would smile and shrug. 'A vehicle, no more. Inconvenient.'

'Inconvenient maybe. Vehicles need fuel. Eat.' Étienne would laugh, and obey.

Dido disapproved of Emerald's relationship with Étienne.

'I can't think why you bother. He's broke. He leaves half his food on the plate. And he doesn't even make love to you.'

Emerald laughed. But it was true. Étienne's relationships with girls rarely lasted more than a few days. His dark eyes lit with passion only for his beloved philosophers – whether dead or alive, it mattered nothing.

But he had given Emerald an existence of her own, an existence which she took care to keep separate from her life at the salon.

The apartment which Emerald and Dido shared was not large, but it had high airy ceilings built for the more generous domestic spaces of the previous century. The cornices had delicate rococo mouldings, the edges softened by ancient tides of paint.

There were three rooms: a bedroom each for Emerald and Dido, and a living-room. The minute kitchen backed on to a tiny noisy bathroom into which was crammed a huge chipped enamel bathtub with claw feet, a handsome porcelain washbasin, a bidet with brass taps and a throne-like mahogany lavatory. Emerald loved the grandeur of the bathroom.

The living-room furniture was heavy prewar mahogany and Emerald had brightened up the room as best she could. She had thrown a couple of threadbare Turkish rugs from the Marché aux Puces over the tattered sofa and armchair, and sewn a pair of bright Indian bedspreads over the faded moquette curtains.

On the doorstep, Emerald set down her shopping and fumbled in her pocket for her keys. The scent of a Balkan Sobranie cigarette curled under the door.

Then she remembered.

Dido had been nagging her for months to join one of her weekend forays.

'Poor old Billy will be so disappointed if you cut out,' Dido begged. 'Just this once. Someone special. You'll really like him. At least he'll pick up the bill.'

'You always say that, Dido,' Emerald had answered, pulling on her student's weeds and scrubbing her face clean of make-up.

'Think of the future. It's good for you to meet eligible young men.'

Finally Emerald had agreed to make up the numbers on a trip to Monte Carlo.

A week earlier, Dido had held Emerald to her promise.

Emerald ran over the conversation in her mind as she paused for a moment in the hall.

'Come on, Emerald. It'll be great fun. No strings attached, promise.'

'Oh God, Dido. I was going to take in the new show at the Louvre.'

'You promised. My date's already fixed, and I can't handle two of them. Billy's really sold on this one for you. Says it's made in heaven.'

'Worse and worse. I'll do it, but only to stop you complaining. No dressing up, mind. I'm on holiday.'

Dido inspected her friend. As so often when she was away from the Maison Paradis, Emerald looked more like an athletic tomboy than a

340

high-fashion model. Dido herself was never without her full man-hunting outfit – today a little tailored suit with nipped-in waist worn fashionably with no blouse beneath. Just a peep of exquisite lace-trimmed petticoat under the tailored revers.

'You have to dress up, silly. Monte Carlo. The Salle Privée's very grand. Black tie *de rigueur*.'

Emerald sighed. 'What's his name?'

Dido giggled. 'Little Lord Fauntleroy. Otherwise known as Tom Sherwood, seventeenth Baron. Billy assures me he comes complete with crumbling ancestral heap and ancient retainers. Although there won't be much of that left if he goes on hitting the wrong side of the red-and-black. Tom's a gambler. I've seen him drop more in one evening than Dad lost in a month. A bit of a black sheep, but very charming and fantastically handsome. In fact', Dido dropped her voice conspiratorially, 'he's a dead ringer for the Archangel Gabriel.'

'Just up your street, Dido.'

Dido shook her head. 'Who needs it? Mine's no oil painting, but he does have matching Renoirs. Friday evening, then? Good.'

Until that moment on the doorstep, the whole arrangement had gone out of Emerald's head.

The door of the sitting-room was ajar. Emerald popped her head round the door. She could only see the back of her visitor's head outlined against the window. A blond halo of golden curls dimly seen against the light.

'Be with you in a moment!'

Then she added, laughter in her voice: 'Make yourself at home!'

She dropped her flowers and the boxes of goodies on the kitchen table, glanced in the rococo-framed mirror by the window, and ran her hand through the short crop Alexandre had given her. She pulled a face at herself. She owed it to Dido to look her best.

She went through into her room, struggled out of her student black, and pulled on a pair of pencil-thin shocking-pink Pucci pants and a roll-necked silk sweater which matched the colour of her eyes.

She paused in the doorway. The sharp scent of Trumper's lime aftershave wafted across the room.

'Sorry to keep you waiting. You must be . . . ?'

'Tom Sherwood, at your service, Miss Emerald.'

The public-school drawl was unmistakable.

As the young man came towards the light to greet her, Emerald could not help a sharp intake of breath.

Tom Sherwood was not just handsome. Tom Sherwood was without a doubt the most beautiful young man she had ever seen.

*   *   *

Tom had made first-class reservations on the overnight Blue Train to Nice. Emerald and Tom shared an excellent supper in the train's luxurious dining-car.

Emerald was tired and more than a little irritable about having her weekend monopolized by the favour she had promised Dido, however handsome.

That first shared meal was not a success. Afterwards Tom wished Emerald a courteous goodnight and retired to his own sleeping-compartment.

Emerald fell into a deep dreamless sleep as soon as her head hit the pillow. She did not stir until the train pulled into the station the following morning.

Tom had left his Bentley parked in the station carpark. It was a convertible, and Tom wound down the heavy canvas roof so Emerald could feel the sun on her face and enjoy the scents of the citrus groves, wild rosemary and thyme from the surrounding hillsides.

The drive along the sea was spectacularly beautiful, winding past little white fishing harbours, round rocky headlands alongside white beaches dotted with sun-worshippers.

At midday Tom swung the wheel towards a little harbour nestling at the foot of a steep ravine. There, in a quayside bar, he was greeted by the proprietor as an old friend.

Tom enquired after the day's catch, and then ordered lunch. The scent of hot oil and roasted garlic rose from the lean-to kitchen at the back. The proprietor poured wine, dark and dusty. A huge oval dish piled high with crisply frittered rockfish appeared, sea-flavoured and subtle. Then there was a salad of thickly sliced tomatoes dressed with slivers of garlic, torn leaves of basil and thick green olive oil.

It was simple and delicious, and Emerald ate with relish. During the course of the meal, she found herself enjoying Tom's company more and more. He seemed very sure of himself – very confident and worldly-wise after the students who were her usual companions.

As they ate, Tom talked. And as he talked Emerald wondered what story Billy had spun about her to make Tom think she would even begin to appeal to him.

Tom was everything Emerald was not. While she had no past, he could trace his lineage back for a thousand years. While she had to earn her own living, he clearly had no need for such mundane exertions. While her own interests were in painting and music and books, he had no time for what he described as 'serious talk', preferring to amuse her with stories of the world he and Dido shared.

342

There were physical differences, too. While she was happiest in her student's black, he was clearly a dandy. And, to her surprise, she found herself admiring Tom's manicured beauty: the thick mop of wiry blond curls, the tanned skin, the fine-boned arrogant profile, the tall rangy body casually dressed in a heavy cream silk shirt tucked into impeccably creased linen trousers thrust into Spanish riding boots polished to a deep mahogany sheen.

The rest of the journey passed swiftly, and Emerald was already beginning to feel as if she had known Tom all her life. The afternoon sun glimmered off the blue sea by the time the Bentley drew to a gentle halt under the palm-trees which fronted the second-largest of the stucco-pillared buildings in the main square of Monte Carlo, the world's most fashionable playground.

Tom switched off the engine, swung his long legs out of the car and came round to open the door for his passenger.

'Welcome to my world, Miss Emerald.'

He waited, smiling.

'Well? Is it what you expected?'

'You – or the place?'

'Both. Either.'

Emerald examined her escort with mock-seriousness. Tom was indeed all and more than she had expected – physically at least.

She widened her eyes mischievously.

'Dido described you' – she paused – 'beautifully.'

'I accept the compliment, my dear. And Monte Carlo?'

'Not what I expected at all.'

'How so?'

Emerald grinned. The wine at lunch had made her feel happy. 'I thought it would be more like a bank, not a pink-and-white wedding cake in a shiny blue plate. I didn't expect Toytown.'

Tom's bright head of curls dipped as he followed her gaze. 'Don't be deceived. It may look like Toytown, but the games are real. Dangerous. There's a sharp edge to it. A pretty jewelled scabbard but, within, a sharpened sword, just waiting to draw blood. That's why I love it.'

Tom took a deep breath. 'Such a whiff of nostalgia. Nothing like it. Snobbery and money. Happiness. Built by Rainier's bankrupt father as a last turn of the wheel. So appropriate. Rien ne va plus. And lo and behold – Lady Luck flicked her finger, and the little ball fell in the right hole.'

His face grew thoughtful. 'Never used to be the place to go. My maternal grandfather was not a gambling man, but he liked to watch others gamble. A sort of vingt-et-un voyeur. He always took me to

Deauville. Everyone was there. The Dolly Sisters and Gordon Selfridge. The Aga Khan and the Russian grand dukes. Marvellous stuff. The rich always crowd together – safety in numbers.'

He waved at the flight of marble steps which led up to the most ornate façade of all.

'Your billet, mademoiselle. We're booked into the Hôtel de Paris. It's the best, of course. Belongs to the casino. Serves as my accommodation address. They like an English milord. Adds a bit of class. I get a special price, and the credit's good.' He smiled. 'They keep the attics for us pretty people. We dilute the rest of them – the skinny old widows and the fat old men.'

Tom ran up the wide marble stairway which led to the foyer of the huge hotel.

Emerald followed more slowly, taking in the lavish surroundings. The hotel was as ornate as an Indian pavilion. Massed ranks of pink-and-white balconies were shaded by candy-striped awnings.

Inside, she stood for a moment, holding her breath. An avenue of columns topped with white stucco cornices picked out in gilt arched above cream marble. The red-and-gold carpet, deep as a mown lawn, matched the heavy crimson curtains which draped the tall windows. Crystal chandeliers cascaded from dim frescoed ceilings.

In spite of the sunshine outside, the hall was as shadowy as a night-club. Fitted into the curve of the arches were brightly lit gilt-framed alcoves which displayed a millionaire's shopping-list: trinkets and baubles with which those on a good run at the tables could pamper them-selves and appease their women. Cigar-wallets and solid gold lighters. Crocodile handbags with gold clasps and shoes with Gucci horse-bits. Loewe's lizard-skin belts with tiger-head buckles. Hand-stitched ostrich-skin luggage by Louis Vuitton. Monogrammed silver water-bowls for pampered dogs. Sulka dressing-gowns in navy-blue polkadot foulard. Charvet shirts. Van Cleef's twists of diamonds. A thicket of miniature trees hung with Cartier watches.

The opulence was overwhelming.

'Window shopping, my dear?'

Startled, Emerald swung round.

An elderly man with a bald head and pebble-glasses, his Savile Row suit speckled with cigar ash, thrust his face very close to hers.

'Such a pretty child.'

He pressed something into her hand and murmured: 'My card. Should you decide on shopping.'

Emerald giggled. 'Merci, monsieur. But I'm with a friend.'

She looked round for Tom, and spotted him leaning over the polished mahogany reception desk. He had been watching her, an expression of amusement on his face.

The concierge, distinguished from his clerks by a morning coat and striped trousers, glanced up to follow his customer's gaze.

'Excuse me, milord.' The concierge's eyebrows rose in a twin arch. 'You are meeting someone, mademoiselle?'

The concierge's eyebrows were famous for their ability to convey polite disapproval. Single young ladies in hotel foyers were part of his training. There were other hotels where young ladies arrived without the customary six cabin trunks and a lady's maid. When they did it was by invitation – and only after making due arrangement with the manager, the senior concierge, the doorman, the bellboys.

'The young lady's my guest, Gaston.'

Tom's finger moved down the day-ledger, hesitated, and then stopped.

'Of course, milord.' The eyebrows descended smoothly. 'Mademoiselle has her luggage in the motor-car?'

Emerald held up her carpet bag. 'That's it.'

'Of course, mademoiselle.' The concierge's eyebrows indicated that it was perfectly normal for young ladies to arrive with practically no luggage.

'I trust mademoiselle enjoys her stay.'

'See you later, my beauty.'

'Much later . . . '

As Emerald passed the display cabinets again, she noticed her elderly bald would-be suitor deep in conversation with a pretty young blonde in a low-cut red velvet cocktail dress. He had clearly found more promising pastures.

In the principality, it seemed, most things were for sale. Including an evening's company.

Tom – the enigmatic, beautiful Tom – had bought her company. Somehow she knew that was all that he wanted.

What was it Dido had said?

'I always wondered about angels. In those Italian Annunciations, Gabriel always looks so sexy. But I suppose the whole point of an angel is absolutely no surprises under the nightie.'

345

50

Monte Carlo: 1956

Much later, as she had promised Tom, when the sun was already dipping over the blue headland beyond the crowded harbour, Emerald rose from her scented bath in the pink marble bathroom and wrapped herself in one of the hotel's enormous white bathrobes.

She curled up in the chair on her balcony, watching until the lights of the port and the yachts bobbing at anchor had sown the little waves with bright sequins.

The square in front of the Winter Casino was crowded with tables. It was time for the evening apéritif, a revolving carnival of brightly dressed gamblers readying themselves for the evening's entertainment.

Emerald dressed carefully. She had borrowed one of her employer's simple narrow linen sheaths in a deep indigo-violet which complemented her eyes. She slipped contentedly into the borrowed finery. Then she dialled Tom Sherwood's room number.

'Tom? Are you ready?'

'La belle Emerald' – Tom's voice was cheerful – 'I've just been having a conversation about you.'

'Who with?'

'Mutual friend. Good things. Tell you in a moment. Come on up to the housemaids' floor.'

Emerald frowned. It could only be Billy again. Whatever it was, there would be money involved. There was not likely to be anything sentimental about Billy Beaumont's manoeuvrings.

Emerald took the lift to the attic floors. Tom's room was a tiny bedroom with a sloping roof, tucked under the eaves. He had changed into a beautifully cut dinner-jacket worn over a plain silk-twill evening shirt in a pale oyster pink.

Two glasses and a bottle of champagne in an ice-bucket stood on a small table.

'Come on in. Thought we'd have something before we go over to inspect the tables.'

He poured out two glasses and handed one to Emerald.

'Sit down, my little Emerald. I want to talk to you. Seriously.'

The handsome face was shuttered, the lids lowered.

Emerald accepted the glass and sat down obediently.

'I would like you to consider a proposition,' the voice continued lazily. 'Maybe not a proposition. More in the nature of a proposal.'

'A proposal?'

Tom looked up at her, noting the startled violet eyes. Clearly Dido had been discreet – the girl had no idea of Billy's suggested arrangement.

'I can see I've caught you on the hop.'

Emerald took a sip from her glass. 'Must be the champagne.'

'Not that kind of hop.'

'Tell.'

'This is perfectly serious. So no interrupting.'

'I shall say nothing until given permission.'

Tom grinned. 'Somehow I don't think that is your way, *ma belle*.'

His eyes were glittering, and his shoulders were hunched. A hunting cat, thought Emerald. She waited.

After a moment he said. 'I have a problem which you can help to solve.'

'Me?'

'You and you alone.'

Tom hesitated. Then he made up his mind. 'I see no reason to beat about the bush, *ma belle*. I need to be married.'

'Anyone special in mind?'

'Yes. There's a problem, of course. I'm afraid I have two drawbacks as a marriage prospect. The first is that I have no money.'

Emerald smiled. 'That'll raise the concierge's eyebrows.'

'You're not taking me seriously. It's not a matter of credit.'

'Good. Nice not to have to volunteer for the washing-up. The second?'

'Far less serious. I prefer boys.'

Emerald studied him quizzically. 'Something else we have in common.'

'Are you shocked?'

'Don't be silly. But I still don't understand what any of this has to do with me.'

It was true that she wasn't shocked. In Oaxaca, the boys who earned their living from selling their favours were known as *pajaritos*, little birds – a reference to the tiny bright-plumaged hummingbirds which darted down the barranca, sipping nectar from the trumpets of hibiscus flowers. It was a way of earning a dollar or two, and by no means precluded marriage and children. And of course many of Paris's most famous designers were partnered by young men; in fact it was unusual to find a couturier who *did* prefer women. They were known as kind and considerate employers, and Emerald enjoyed their company.

However, the news did explain why, wonderfully handsome as Tom was, there'd been a total absence of any physical electricity. The archangel problem made flesh.

'Dear Tom, your choice of bedfellow is none of my business.'

'You haven't heard me out.' The lazy lids flicked. 'My dear girl, I have just made a proposal of marriage.'

Emerald's champagne went down the wrong way.

'Tom, you're completely crazy.'

'Not at all. The very reverse. Give or take a little accommodation, we're perfectly matched.'

Tom leaned back in his chair to examine Emerald. The broker was right. Whatever else, the young woman had *style*. Poor old Billy and his *style*. As if it mattered a tuppenny damn. But she really was quite delicious – for a girl.

Tom was not used to romancing women. Billy had advised him how to play it. He had warned Tom that Emerald had no idea she was an heiress – or, to be more accurate, that there was a bride-price on her pretty head.

'That's all? Just that?'

Tom leaned back. 'Of course. What do you say?'

'What do you expect?'

'You could try "yes".'

'Seriously?'

'Seriously.'

'Seriously. No.'

Tom nodded. Emerald was clearly neither fool nor gold-digger.

Then he frowned. He would have to come up with a convincing reason for his offer. A little storytelling might be in order. Tom was good at storytelling. After all, it was only a little bending of the truth.

Meanwhile Emerald had risen to her feet and gone over to the window. It seemed that Tom meant what he said. She'd have to let him down a little more gently. When she swung round again, her face was calm.

'Look, Tom, I don't want to upset you, but I had something more . . . *involved* in mind for a husband. Let's forget this ever happened, not let it spoil a lovely weekend.'

'Emerald, sit down again. Please.'

Responding to the urgency in his voice, Emerald obeyed. It was all Dido's fault, she thought crossly. She and Billy had landed her in this. God alone knew why.

'Don't get me wrong,' Tom said softly. 'There's money coming my way – and it's a great deal, if I play my cards right.'

That was true enough – if Emerald accepted his offer.

'I'm not interested in money, Tom.'

'Naïve, my sweet. It makes life so much more enjoyable.' Like all gamblers, Tom thought fast on his feet. Like all gamblers, lies came easily to his lips. 'I should explain. The money's held in trust until I marry. Which is where you, my dear, come in.'

'That's all?'

Tom Sherwood threw back his curly blond head and laughed. 'My dear child, what do you expect? Declarations of undying love? Down on one knee in the conservatory?'

'I've read about it in books.'

'Lies, all lies.'

'Why me?'

Tom shrugged. 'Why not? You come well recommended. You seem a steady, independent young woman. Essential – as we would live separate lives. You would have a life-tenure of the family acres, social acceptability, and so on and so forth. All the things you lack.'

He glanced up at her slyly, and took a sip from his glass. 'You see, my dear, I've done my homework.'

'So I can hear.'

'Good. We will understand each other perfectly. Naturally I should wish to continue with the life I've chosen. I have an agreement with my trustees for them to pay all the bills which come from abroad. It's a device to keep me as far away as possible, and I delight in it. So you wouldn't be too much burdened with my expenses or my presence at home – Astley Keep, it happens to be called.'

'Look, Tom, I may be naïve but I know perfectly well you don't even want to sleep with me.'

349

'True. And so refreshingly different. We all have our little foibles. They make us what we are. Look at Toulouse-Lautrec. He'd never have painted those wonderful *filles de joie* if he hadn't been permanently at knee-level – the ideal position, as you would have it, for a proposal. Also the best position for looking up a lady's skirt. You can rest assured it wouldn't do anything for me. But, then, happily I don't have short legs.'

Emerald stared at Tom for a moment, and then burst out laughing. Molly would have disapproved thoroughly. But Lily would have adored him.

'That's better.'

Tom uncurled his rangy body and came over with the champagne.

'I can at least declare you're quite beautiful when you laugh.'

The bubbles sparkled as he poured out the golden wine.

He waited until she had taken a sip. Then he sat down beside her and picked up her hand. He raised it to his lips, turning it palm upwards. Emerald watched the golden head bend over, felt the lips, full and soft as a girl's, brush the sensitive skin of her palm.

He looked up into her eyes.

'Well, then, beautiful girl, what's your answer?'

Emerald hesitated, the laughter still on her lips. She reclaimed her hand gently.

'I'm flattered, sir.'

'*Flattered?* My dear girl, this is not a new hat for Ascot. Nor is it romantic dalliance. You will hear no lies about undying love. No. This is much more permanent. A deal. A dynastic alliance. Matching fortunes.'

'Now you really sound crazy. I have neither fortune nor dynasty.'

'Quite so. Together we would have both. What young lover could offer more?'

Tom raised Emerald's hand to his lips again, his eyes unfathomable. Emerald shivered at his touch.

He said: 'All I lack is you.'

Emerald felt dizzy, almost seduced by the beauty of the man and the effects of the champagne. It was crazy. She shook her head, as much to clear the mist as to deny what he was saying.

'Why not? It's perfectly usual. The British aristocracy survives because it can accommodate aberrations like me. We're experts at the business. Marriage to me will give you not just respectability, but freedom.'

'I'm free already.'

'Nonsense. Every day you do at least three things you don't want to do because someone more powerful than you makes you do it. No sense in denying it.'

350

Tom stretched, cat-like, again.

'Anyway, you'd like my mother. She's so eccentric she's beyond respectability. Doesn't give a damn what the neighbours think. That's real freedom. Just what you need. I know she'd fall in love with you instantly.'

'It's not your mother making the proposal.'

'That's where you're wrong, my beauty. I've little doubt she cooked the whole thing up. She's fed up with keeping me in the style I have chosen. And she's longing for a grandchild. Feels she owes it to my late lamented father.'

'A child?'

'Why the surprise? Of course, a child. Astley has to have an heir – and I certainly have no stomach for the task. I thought you might enjoy choosing someone to father the next Baron Sherwood.'

Emerald stared at him in amazement. Tom was completely outrageous. Once again she was nearly seduced by her own laughter.

'I assure you, my dear Emerald, you'll never get a better offer.'

Emerald stopped laughing.

She said gently: 'Thanks, Tom. But no, thanks.'

Tom stared at her for a moment, a curious expression on his face. He shrugged. 'I think you'll change your mind, my dear. As a gambling man, I'd stake my shirt on it. I leave my cards on the table. Think about it. Astley Keep always knows where to find me.'

He pulled a heavy white silk snuff handkerchief from his pocket and held it behind his back.

'I'm glad we've had our little chat. Don't look so serious, my beauty. Here's something to cheer you up.'

He flourished the handkerchief, and the room was suddenly filled with an overpowering scent. Emerald sniffed. The smell was rich, heady, overripe.

'Guess.'

Emerald shook her head. 'Seaweed? Steak?' Then she said, 'Sex?'

Tom let out a whoop of happiness. 'Oh, you know it, my beauty, you know it. I could tell that as soon as I saw you. Think back. Out of decay comes forth the most exquisite of aromas.'

He spread out the handkerchief.

'I show you this side. I show you that. Nothing. I reveal all. The handkerchief, sprinkled with a little almond oil, had been wrapped up all night in this.'

He pulled out a small tin from behind the dressing table and carefully unlocked the lid. The room filled with a much stronger distillation of the extraordinary scent. He held out the tin for Emerald's inspection. Inside was a small black nugget, its earthy surface as gnarled and rough as cracked mud.

'See that? My talisman. All gamblers have one.'

Emerald breathed in again. The smell was almost overpowering now, rich and heady and disturbing.

'*Tuber melanosporum*,' Tom explained, chuckling. 'The black truffle. The scent you recognize is pure sex. It has an electric effect in a crowded room. Quite imperceptible at first. But then there is a kind of ripple of excitement which I hope puts everyone off their game. I save it for very special occasions.'

Tom paused.

'I know an old man up in the hills.' He waved his hand towards the mountains behind. 'He has his own patch of truffle oaks. Every year I go out with him and his old black mongrel bitch. We pick a warm damp day, when the earth is not too hard to dig, and we try to interrupt the course of nature. When the truffle is perfectly ripe, at the precise moment it begins to decay, it attracts the attention of a particular red fly, no bigger than a flea.'

Tom tucked the handkerchief into his pocket.

'To the fly the smell means food for its larvae. It lays a million eggs. If the dog does not find the truffle first, the little worms will hatch. They will eat their way through the truffle until they're big enough to grow wings. The flies are eaten by birds. The birds excrete the spores. And so on round and round. Life in all its predatory simplicity.'

Tom put out his hand, lightly touched her cheek, fingertips soft as a cat's paw.

'All we can do is try to beat the system. Such an elegant deception, sex. Such a snare for the unwary. Enough to put anyone off their game. That's the way it goes, my dear Emerald. For us all.'

He stood up, tall and blond and handsome.

'I can see I shall not persuade you at once.' He sighed. 'Anyway, there's no hurry. Faites vos jeux, mesdames messieurs. Let's go find young Dido and her friend. We have far more serious business than matrimony to attend to.'

51

Monte Carlo: 1956

The casino was reached through an underground passage which connected the Hôtel de Paris with the only diversion in which its guests were truly interested: the green baize tables in the Salle Privée.

Unlike other casinos, the bank at Monte Carlo had no highest permitted wager. 'Jeu sans limites' meant exactly that. Whatever you wished to gamble, the bank could match. There were legends about gamblers who had broken the bank at Monte Carlo; but the stories, like all gamblers' legends, had more of myth than of truth.

'How about it, *ma belle*?' Tom's face was bright with excitement. 'Terrific?'

Emerald gazed around.

The place was crowded even though the evening was only just beginning. The roulette-wheels and gaming-tables in what Tom told her was called the Kitchen – the servants' quarters – accommodated those players whose bets were not likely to rise much above a bank manager's monthly salary. The round plastic chips clattered down, bright as confetti, to be raked back and forth by the dinner-jacketed croupiers. At the far end, a bar served as a meeting-place for the restless gamblers.

Tom leaned towards her, his breath coming quick in her ear. 'Can you smell her? Lady Luck has a special scent. Cheap perfume, damp armpits, expensive cigars, liquor, and that peculiar stench of fear. Marvellous. Your people should bottle it. It'd sell a million.'

Emerald laughed. 'You'd have trouble persuading Monsieur Paradis.'

'More fool him. Nothing like it.'

Tom began to move through the tables, tugging Emerald in his wake, filling his lungs with the smoke-laden air, greeting the tellers and the cloakroom girl by name, pausing to exchange greetings with the slim-hipped fast-dealing croupiers.

After a few minutes, Tom halted and turned.

'This is just the playpen. We're heading for the grown-ups' toy-cupboard.'

He gestured towards a pair of double doors at the far end of the room. 'We go through there. The Salle Privée.'

Emerald followed.

As they approached the doorway, a distinguished-looking elderly man in a discreet grey uniform stepped out of the shadows and laid his white-gloved hand on the handle.

'George is the keeper of the keys,' Tom whispered. 'Nothing and no-one gets past him. He knows all the gentlemen-gamblers – and the ladies or not-such-ladies who accompany them. Not to say there's not the odd merry widow or two – they're the most formidable of all. Anyway, no *hoi poloi* get through, unless invited. Once George has seen you, it's all on file – together with the *nom de plume*, alias, whatever you please. It's all there, isn't it, George?'

The uniformed doorman nodded and swung open the door. 'Milord.'

The private rooms were nowhere near as crowded as the Kitchen had been. Quality replaced quantity under the shaded lights which swung low over the green-baize tables. Emerald sniffed. The air was still thick with cigar smoke, but laced with expensive scent. Pretty young women in spruce maids' uniforms circled the tables with trays of champagne, canapés and cigarettes, all courtesy of the management. The tables were more widely spaced, the gamblers were in black tie, while the women were in mid-calf cocktail-dresses – their throats and arms weighed down with jewellery.

The gamblers could take their choice. It was blackjack or vingt-et-un, baccarat or chemin de fer, the inevitable roulette. No poker or bridge, or backgammon or any of the other games in which the bank did not take a cut. Large oblong chips, the plastic embedded with flecks of gold, indicated the size of the bets. The largest of all were big ovals of pale ivory.

Dido and her millionaire (from Pittsburgh, Dido had explained proudly) were already settled into the evening's gambling. Dido came over immediately and pushed her arm through Emerald's.

'How's it going?' she whispered.

Emerald laughed, her violet eyes sparkling. 'Let's say it makes a change from the Deux Magots.'

'Glad you came?'

'Of course.'

Dido smiled. 'I simply love it. Brings my childhood flooding back.'

'I can see. You look like a kid in an ice-cream parlour.'

' 'Course. My date's scattering his chips around like the proverbial bread on the water – with about the same hope of return. How's it with yours?'

Emerald hesitated. 'What did you expect?'

Dido shrugged. 'Billy has something going with Tom. He expects results.'

'Results?'

'You know Billy's "results". D'you like Tom?' Her voice was suddenly anxious.

Emerald stared at her friend. 'He's made me a proposal, if that's what you mean.'

Dido's face relaxed. 'Good. And?'

Emerald laughed. 'Thought you had something to do with it. Crazy.'

'But you're at least interested?'

'For heaven's sake, Dido, what's all this? I'm not a chip on the roulette table.'

Dido looked at her speculatively.

'Don't you believe it, sweetheart,' she said, her voice suddenly deadly serious.

'Now, let's see if you can give a tweak to my millionaire's luck. He's promised me the most divine little clip from Cartier if he wins.'

Emerald giggled. 'Honestly, Dido.'

'Honestly. And that's only the beginning. The place is filling up – the Greeks must be in town.' She nodded to a group of swarthy-complexioned middle-aged men who were settling in at a blackjack table in the far corner.

All but two of the tables were in play. Beside one of them, the blond girl in scarlet velvet Emerald had seen before at the hotel had turned to watch the two young women.

'Who's that?' Emerald whispered.

Dido glanced across. 'Don't know for sure, but I'd say a stringer for one of the London papers. Saw her the other day at one of the private clubs in London with a sandy-haired little fellow from the *Daily News*.

The casino's pretty cagey about that kind of thing – none of the customers likes publicity. She must have come in with a punter. Seems to specialize in the high-rollers.'

'It's that easy?'

'Sure. The newspapers all use the same trick – a pretty girl. Sometimes, even when they suspect, the casino finds it easier to turn a blind eye. Don't like to upset the escort. That's how most of the stories get out. Until the backroom boys don't like the cut of someone's jib – and then doorman George will do the rest.'

'He of the piercing stare?'

'Dear gentleman George. Never forgets a face. No-one can bounce with more finesse than George. I love him. He used to lend me the cab-fare home when my father was on a losing streak. And, God knows, that was most of the time.'

Across the room Tom Sherwood, a glass of champagne by his elbow and a pile of the ivory oval chips in front of him, had taken over the blackjack shoe.

Tom beckoned Emerald over.

'Pull up a chair, lucky penny. Now, don't move. Just watch the cards.'

Then Tom hit a winning streak. Hand after hand, luck was on his side. Not a card fell wrong. It was as if Emerald formed part of a chain which drew the right cards towards him by magic.

Each time Emerald shifted in her chair he put a restraining hand on her arm, throwing her a fierce glance almost tangible in its intensity.

'No. Stay where you are.'

All night long, Tom rode the winning streak.

At last – long after dawn had broken – he rose from the table.

'Thank you, gentlemen.' As she rose to follow him, Emerald's head was spinning and her body was drained of all energy, but she had watched Tom's small pile of chips mount to a pyramid.

As she followed Tom to the caisse, the girl in red glanced up and rose swiftly to her feet. Almost, thought Emerald with surprise, as if the young woman was shadowing them.

Meanwhile Tom had cashed in his chips for what seemed like more money than she had ever seen in her life.

'You see?' Tom's hands were full of banknotes. 'I absolutely knew it! You *are* my lucky penny.'

Whatever his faults, when Tom won he was wildly generous. Everyone from the croupier to the cigarette girls had a fistful of the flimsy notes.

Even the imperturbable George was moved by the size of the tip the

English milord slipped into the velvet-trimmed pocket of his tailored uniform.

'Now, *ma belle*,' Tom said as they walked back to the Hôtel de Paris arm-in-arm through the underground tunnel, 'it's your turn. A bauble to mark our first collaboration.'

He turned his head to study her for a moment, his head on one side. 'I think I know just what's required.'

Emerald shook her head, laughing. 'I couldn't possibly accept anything, Tom.'

Tom stopped abruptly and turned to face her. His expression was no longer light-hearted, but deadly serious – almost angry.

'You don't understand. Gambler's luck has to be paid for. A tithe of the winnings. You have to take what is yours – or the cards will never forgive me.'

Emerald stared at Tom. His handsome face was creased with tiredness, but the mouth had set in a stubborn line. The eyes were bloodshot, and Emerald sensed it was not only from sheer exhaustion. Whatever fuelled Tom's passions, gambling was more than a flirtation. For Tom, gambling was not a single battle, it was a lifetime of war.

'All right, Tom,' she said gently. 'Whatever you want.'

'Good.' His face lightened instantly with a smile. Once again, she thought, he looked a dead ringer for the Archangel Gabriel. So unlikely. Emerald giggled.

'Penny for them?'

Emerald told him. He laughed.

'Appropriate in a way. Androgynous bunch, the angels. Very wise of the Almighty to pick 'em. Saves so much anxiety.'

His moods, Emerald realized, were as changeable as a gambler's luck.

'Breakfast. Boucheron won't be open for an hour. Stoke up for the most important decision of the day.'

Tom, his energy levels restored by the bright sunshine of the morning, bounded up the steps of the hotel, turned into the pink-napped restaurant, and began to explain to the *maître d'hôtel* exactly what was required.

When it came, breakfast was absolutely sumptuous – a meal, Emerald thought to herself, far more suited to a honeymoon couple than to a gambler and his moll. It began with ripe black figs wrapped in slivers of pink prosciutto, moved on to slabs of rich pink foie gras spread on buttery wedges of toasted brioche washed down with fresh orange juice laced with Veuve Clicqot, and finished with tiny cups of thick strong coffee.

An hour later, Tom steered Emerald, dizzy from wine and tiredness, into one of the little Aladdin's cave treasure houses which lined the hallway. There a deferential tail-coated assistant pulled out tray after tray of glittering jewels.

Tray after tray was greeted with an abrupt wave of the hand.

'Ah. Got it,' Tom said at last, holding up a pair of matching earrings, sprays of tiny flowers set with diamonds and centred with clear blue-violet gems. 'Perfect.'

Tom pulled her over to a mirror and stood behind her, beaming over her shoulder as he held the beautiful little jewels against her ears.

Emerald caught her breath. She had never owned any real jewellery. Let alone something as beautiful as that.

'See. Twin sapphires to match your eyes. You should never wear anything else.'

'But, Tom,' Emerald protested, laughing. 'They must cost a fortune.'

She stopped instantly, seeing the change in Tom's face.

'Yes, Tom,' she said quietly. 'Thank you.'

'Don't mention it, my dear.' Tom stared at her. The fierce expression had returned to his handsome face. 'Ever.'

A shiver went down her spine. To Tom, she sensed, people were merely adjuncts, handmaidens to serve a cause. His true partners were the cigar-chewing opponents at the table. But even they were merely companions-in-arms, soldiers fighting in the same battleground.

There was something about Tom which reminded her of Nacho. Suddenly she realized what it was. Both were hunters; the only difference was that one stalked the steaming forests of Mexico, the other the gilded halls of Europe's pleasure-palaces. Both were predators, obeying nothing but the law of the jungle: kill or be killed. Both were dangerous, even to those they loved.

Whatever his preferences in bed, boy or girl, only one thing fuelled his energy: beating the odds – the crazy, all-consuming love-affair of the obsessive gambler.

The bright jewels Emerald laid in their tiny velvet-lined box on her dressing-table as she dropped exhausted into her bed were an offering not to Emerald, not to a woman of flesh and blood, but to the reigning queen of the wheel, the presiding genius of the cards, Lady Luck herself.

Meanwhile, back in the hotel lobby, Alison Mackay, her blond hair gleaming against the crimson velvet of her dress, was on the telephone to Jack Sweeney at the *Daily News*.

52

London: 1956

Jack Sweeney leaned over his typewriter and punched in his headline. 'THE GAMBLER WANTS A WIFE.'

He straightened up, and then bent back to his task.

The Dandy predicts wedding bells a-tinkle for gambling peer Tom Sherwood.

Domestic bliss would certainly be a new departure for His Lordship. More at home among the gaming tables of Monaco than in the muddy fields of his Dorset estate, Tom has never been noted for his romantic links with the fairer sex.

Nevertheless my spies at Monte Carlo's exclusive gaming-tables whisper that the russet-haired beauty Lord Sherwood escorted to the Salle Privée this weekend was none other than Emerald – favourite tailor's dummy of the great Christian Paradis.

Faithful readers of this column will remember a royal connection when the young beauty shot to stardom as the belle of New York's Duchess of Windsor Ball.

Has Cinderella found her prince at last? Let's hope it's not too much of a disappointment.

A little bird tells me the couple shared a champagne breakfast in the exclusive Hôtel de Paris, and later were spotted choosing a love-token in a certain well-known jeweller's.

Postscript. Close friends who share Tom's artistic tastes hope he will not turn his back on fellow-members of the Cherwell Cherubs, the exuberant bachelor bathing club he founded during his university days.

Jack Sweeney straightened up, replaced the final punctuation with an exclamation mark, and reached into a brown manila envelope and pulled out a photograph of Tom Sherwood taken at a swimming party during his brief sojourn at Oxford University.

The photograph showed a fenced-off bend of the Cherwell river traditionally reserved for male nude bathing. A group of bare-bottomed young men were shown indulging in a little horseplay in the shallows. Tom Sherwood was clearly identifiable as one of the more enthusiastic members of the group.

The subtext was all too obvious. The law of the land declared homosexuality an offence punishable by a prison sentence – a Victorian statute under which Oscar Wilde had been incarcerated. It was not much used these days, but the law still stood. Discretion was held the better part of valour.

Discretion was not young Tom Sherwood's way. On one famous occasion he had attended a ball at Blenheim Palace partnered by a young Moroccan boy dressed in full-length débutante white – from elbow-length kid gloves to matching white satin pumps. All would have been well had not one of the visiting earls been smitten enough to invite the boy to take champagne in the conservatory after he had partnered him in the Gay Gordons. After the furore had subsided, Tom had been frogmarched out through the gates.

There were plenty of other stories about Tom Sherwood. The miracle was his activities had not yet been chronicled in the popular press.

Jack had no intention of being the first to do so. He had other uses for his literary endeavours.

Satisfied with his work, Jack yanked out the sheet of paper and took it down to the typesetters' floor.

'In proof please, Iris.'

The typesetter glanced up at the young reporter, and then set to work.

Iris was used to Jack Sweeney's methods. She knew exactly what he was up to. She condoned it partly because he was nice to her at the office Christmas party, but mainly because he slipped her the occasional fiver. The article was not for publication, it was a trade

360

item. It was not Iris's business to do anything but run off one copy and file the original. Jack said a trade item always looked so much more convincing when it was typeset.

Jack waited while the woman's quick fingers flew over the little steel blocks. She crossed the room to the hand-operated proof-press, pulled a single sheet, and handed it to the red-haired reporter.

'Thanks.'

Jack took the proof back to his desk and pinned the photograph to the piece.

After he had spoken to Alison Mackay, he had decided the time was right for a little discreet milking of his favourite story. The story of Emerald No-name, the girl from nowhere.

This time there would be no confusion as to whose best interests might be served by *not* printing the item. Since the young peer's preferences were a matter of common gossip, it was unlikely that romance alone had influenced his choice of companion. Jack knew enough about the ways of the Establishment to understand how these things worked. His Lordship – or more probably His Lordship's formidable mother – would be looking for an heir.

Emerald, Jack reckoned, would have no idea what she was in for.

Jack put two and two together and came up with Anthony Anstruther.

'Shit.'

Alison Mackay stared round the grimy little cold-water flat she shared with Jack Sweeney.

At the very moment Jack had set out to keep his appointment at Anstruther's chambers, Alison had arrived home from Victoria Station after her weekend trip to Monte Carlo. Although she was on a small retainer as Jack's assistant, it was scarcely enough to cover expenses. It had been a hellish journey on the boat-train across the Channel – the *Daily News* was too tight-fisted to stump up the air fare for a humble stringer.

Jack had left the place a tip – as he always did when she was away. Overflowing ashtrays and empty glasses littered the table. She was dog tired and the place smelled like a badger's set.

She opened the cupboard for something to make her feel better.

Shit again. Jack had even finished the last of the vodka.

She had given up her salon work as soon as she moved in with Jack, replacing a regular income with casual work for a modelling agency. It was well paid enough when it came her way, and allowed her to take time off to see to Jack's business.

She worked hard for Jack. Sometimes it puzzled her that many of the juiciest little stories she followed up for him never got into print. But Jack said that was always the way with journalism. And she had to admit she enjoyed her little jaunts around and about the social scene. Increasingly, too, she enjoyed the free booze.

She gazed round the little room. A rubbish-tip. The bedclothes were tangled up all over the floor.

Anger rose in her throat. There was another reason for her exhaustion. She had missed her period. In fact it was the second period she had missed. And that on anyone's calculation made at least six weeks gone.

Tonight she would have to tell Jack.

She wondered what he would say.

It was not what her parents had had in mind for her. If her father had not pulled up the drawbridge long since, he'd have been after Jack with a shotgun.

For a second she considered what marriage to Jack might be like.

Her mouth set in a hard line. She knew exactly what it would be like to spend the rest of her life in a one-room dump with a screaming infant and a husband who was most likely to be spending the housekeeping down in some sleazy dive with a tart for company. Jack made no secret of his intentions to continue his bachelor pleasures, whether or not Alison was sharing his bed.

She shook her head. Shit and shit and shit again.

She tugged angrily at the bedclothes. A scrap of dark cloth caught her eye. She pulled it out.

A pair of panties. A pair of cheap black silk knickers with lace inserts.

The bastard. And in her own bed, too. The matrimonial bed in all but name. The bed where he had got her pregnant. Insult piled on injury, like the greasy plates in the sink. While she had been flogging back third class on the overnight cattle-truck, doing all the hard work and getting no credit for it, he had been up to his old tricks paying some whore to keep her bed warm.

This time she'd show him. Teach him a lesson he would never forget. Methodically, her anger now replaced by a cold calculation, she began to smash up every item of use or value in the flat.

Finally she pushed her hand under the mattress and found what she was after: a small, flat metal cashbox, its catch held in place by a steel padlock. It took a heavy screwdriver to force open the lock. Jack, magpie Jack, had never lost the islander habit of keeping his money and his small treasures in the urban equivalent of a tea-caddy on the mantelpiece.

She reached inside the box and pulled out a bundle of white fivers. Jack's whore-money. She stowed the crumpled notes in her handbag, then tipped the rest of the contents of the box out on the floor.

Boyhood treasures, pathetic in their worthlessness. A polished shell, a trinket off some girl's charm bracelet, a single cufflink – and the metal disc she had helped him to steal from the schoolmistress's caravan on Eas Forse.

It was hers by right. She slipped the little disc into her pocket. Something told her the loss of that little piece of metal would mean more to Jack than anything.

The whoring lying bastard.

She stared into the mirror. Time to climb out of the gutter. She repaired her make-up carefully. Then she put on a sexy little black dress which set off her blond hair; it was lucky the pregnancy did not yet show on her curvaceous figure.

Time to stop flogging a dead horse. Time to look for a new billet.

The trip to France had put her in mind of an old acquaintance: Emerald's foster-brother. She had crossed paths with her ex-playmate on several occasions since the young man had come to the city to make his way in the world of which she was a long-time inhabitant. She had even managed to put a little work his way. It'd be fair exchange.

She retrieved the telephone directory from the debris, and looked up Fergusson. There were quite a few of them. At last she found it. Notting Hill. She underscored the address, searched in her bag for a stub of pencil and a scrap of paper, and wrote it down.

Then she packed her suitcase, locked the apartment behind her, threw the key down a drainage grille, and spent the afternoon at the cinema watching Brigitte Bardot's new movie.

Alison identified with the blond sex-kitten. For too long skinny little dark girls like Audrey Hepburn – even Emerald, the Paris model Jack seemed to be obsessed with and whose activities she had been sent to report on – had had it all their own way.

She felt better.

And then . . . who knows? She would grow her hair longer like Brigitte, wear it all wild round her face, and buy some new clothes.

She checked her watch. Callum would be home by now.

She hailed a cab.

Half an hour later she pressed the doorbell of the tall house she was confident would be her new home.

363

Callum would be no match for Alison Mackay. She had no doubt of her ability to rekindle an old flame, blow new life into those embers which had first smouldered that night of the Beltane fires.

Jack Sweeney stood on the pavement outside the offices of the *Daily News* and stared ruin in the face. He was bewildered. Bewildered and angry.

The interview with Anthony Anstruther had not gone as he had expected.

He thought he had perfected the technique. It was not the first time he had augmented his income in the way old Manny Braithwaite had suggested. Until now his judgement had been faultless and his victims had been grateful for the opportunity to avoid embarrassment in Dandy Dan.

His mind churned, running over the conversation with Anthony Anstruther again, as he had done many times that afternoon.

Jack had been confident. The barrister's attitude had been so promising. Jack usually had sensitive antennae for that kind of thing – for that kind of betrayal.

'Yes, Mr Sweeney, what can I do for you?'

The barrister's chambers were certainly imposing; but Jack was too old a hand by now to be intimidated by snooty lackeys, leather arm-chairs and polished mahogany.

Jack sat down and leaned casually back in his chair. 'Well, sir, it's not so much what *you* can do for *me*. It's perhaps something *I* can do for *you*.'

Jack's voice was pitched just right. Neither threatening nor wheedling.

'Oh?' The barrister was watching him. Jack felt the eyes were gimlet-hard behind the round bifocals.

'I thought you might like to see this, sir.'

He pushed the proof copy of his article, the photograph pinned neatly to it, across the desk.

There was silence while Anstruther studied Jack's prize offering, his face expressionless. After a moment, he glanced up.

'A fascinating story. What makes you think it might be of interest to me?'

Jack shrugged and grinned. 'A little bird.'

'I see.'

Anstruther paused. Then he leaned forward and appeared to rearrange the papers on his desk. Jack had thought it a sign of nervousness. He had been wrong. That was the moment which should have warned him that all might not be going as planned.

'So, Mr Sweeney, what do you intend to do with this?'

'Publish it. You may have read my column in the *Daily News*. Our readers lap up this sort of thing.'

'So I've noticed.' Anstruther's voice was dry. 'In this case, that would not be wise.'

'I thought you might feel like that.' Jack could scarcely control the triumph in his voice. 'Of course, under certain circumstances—'

'An arrangement?' Anstruther's voice was smooth.

Jack smiled. It was going beautifully. 'If you felt the young woman's happiness—'

'Was in jeopardy?'

'Something like that.'

'Of course, there are the laws of libel.'

Jack shrugged. 'I've had our lawyer check it out—'

'Ah. Libel. Always a matter of opinion.'

Jack felt the first stirrings of unease.

Anstruther took off his glasses and polished them. Then he made a little steeple with his fingers.

'You had a figure in mind?'

Jack hesitated. 'A pony.'

'Horsetrading, eh? Never was a betting man myself. Five hundred sounds rather a lot.'

Jack stared at the barrister. 'I can simply go ahead and publish.'

'I wouldn't advise it, Mr Sweeney. You may find you've bitten off more than you can chew.'

'Meaning?' Jack raised his sandy eyebrows and narrowed the small blue eyes, preparing to bluster.

'I'm sure you're a busy man, Mr Sweeney. Far better things to do with your time than sit around tittle-tattling with me.' Anstruther's voice was clipped, expressionless. 'Such as looking for a new job.'

'What?'

Manny's warning came back to Jack too late. 'Pick on something your own size.'

'I think it may be . . . *politic*, Mr Sweeney.'

Anstruther leaned forward and pressed the intercom which connected him with his clerk. 'Mr Baring? Mr Sweeney is ready to leave now. And, Mr Baring . . .' He paused and looked up at Jack. 'You can switch that damn recording machine off now.'

Jack stared at the barrister in dismay.

For the first time in the interview, Anstruther smiled.

'Modern technology, Mr Sweeney. Marvellous. I'm sure in your work you must find it extremely convenient. One does like to make sure one hasn't overlooked the finer points of a discussion. I can never work out how to handle the things myself. Fortunately my clerk sees to all that. Of course, he takes it all down, too. Just to make doubly sure I don't overlook anything.'

He stood up and went over to the door, standing by it expectantly as he watched Jack Sweeney struggle to his feet.

'For God's sake—'

'Not even for His sake. Or I think you may find yourself explaining your behaviour to your proprietor.'

Anstruther glanced down the stairwell. 'Mr Sweeney, you have exactly' – he glanced at his watch – 'three hours in which to hand in your resignation to your newspaper. I happen to be dining with your proprietor at seven-thirty at the Garrick. I shall expect a copy of your letter to be awaiting me at the porter's office. If so, you will hear no further of the matter. If not— Ah, here's Mr Baring now.'

Later that afternoon, as he strode up Fleet Street on his way to deliver the required copy of his letter, Jack seethed with rage and hatred. Anstruther had managed to turn the tables so neatly he had nowhere to go, no option but to obey.

He'd show him. He'd show them all.

All he had to do was produce his trump card: the identity-disc. Jack didn't know exactly what its significance was, but he understood enough to reckon that, to those in the know, the battered little coin told a dangerous story.

It was a story the barrister had been at very considerable pains to conceal. The story which had lost Jack his job. In short, it was a very valuable bit of flotsam indeed.

And to whom might it be more valuable than to Emerald herself? She'd come a long way since he had first seen her, that day after the storm, in Margaret Mackenzie's crofthouse on Eas Forse. A long way, but not far enough.

This time Jack would pick on something his own size.

53

London: 1956

'Shit,' said Alison.

'Surprise,' said Jack, and grinned.

Alison had been comfortably installed in the tall house in Notting Hill for a week. Jack was the last person she wanted to see.

'Fuck off,' said Alison.

'Language. That's no way to talk to a friend.'

'Some fucking friend.'

'Rude, but accurate.'

'How the hell did you find me?'

'Call it luck. Call it genius.'

Alison said: 'I'll call the police.'

'What for? So you can tell them why you pinched the petty cash?' Jack's eyes glittered. 'Come on, Ali. Just a chat.'

'Chat nothing.'

Alison swung her body against the door to block his path, but Jack was too quick for her. There was no-one faster than Jack at getting a foot in the door.

She stared at him. 'How did you guess?'

'Easy. You don't want to be traced, you don't underline your new address in the book.'

'I don't *need* this, Jack. I don't owe you anything.'

'It's not the money I'm after. Honest.'

Alison hesitated. The last thing she needed was an ugly little scene on the doorstep. Already the old gardener who cleared up the leaves in the square was resting on his broom and watching with lively interest.

'Please, Ali. I need your help.'

'You've had plenty already.'

The gardener moved closer. Alison scowled. At least in Soho no-one poked their nose into anyone else's business – unless invited to do so. And Jack had done the inviting just once too often.

Gossip. The place was as bad as Perth for doorstep gossip.

Reluctantly she released her pressure on the door.

'That's my girl.'

Jack stepped inside, swinging the door shut behind him with his heel.

Alison folded her arms. 'Make it snappy. I'm busy.'

Jack propped himself against the doorpost. 'Come along, Ali. Give it over.'

'Give what over?'

Alison stared at Jack. He looked terrible. Red tufts of hair sticking up and little pink eyes. For a moment she wondered why on earth she had ever got involved with him in the first place, let alone got herself knocked up.

'You know exactly what. The identity-disc.'

'For a moment I thought you meant me.'

'For God's sake, Ali. I've lost my job because of that little witch. I need it; it's all I've got.'

'Finders keepers.'

Alison smiled triumphantly. She had thought the loss of the disc would upset him more than the money. She had been perfectly right. And doubly more so now that she knew what she knew.

'Look, Ali' – Jack tried to keep the desperation out of his voice – 'there's money in it, for both of us. You and me, Ali . . .'

'No. Paddle your own canoe.'

'Partners?'

Alison laughed. 'Not with you, Jack.'

'Found yourself something better?'

'Maybe.'

'Loverboy?' He jerked his thumb towards the staircase.

'Think I'd tell you? So you can add to your list of titbits which might be worth a bob or two?'

'I told you. I handed in my resignation.'

'Tough. What now?'

'I'm good. I'll find something. I've got a plan.'

'So have I.'

Alison had a plan, but Jack was not part of that plan.

Christ knows, she deserved a break, and she had taken it. Had she not been in the family way, it would have been perfect.

Just as she had expected, Callum had swallowed her story hook, line and sinker. That it happened to be mostly the truth made it all the more convincing. The bit of the truth she kept to herself was the pregnancy. This was part of the plan.

At first, Callum had been as gallant as she had hoped. He gave her the run of the house for as long as she needed it. Even offered to contact her parents to effect a reconciliation. Alison had quickly dissuaded him. Her parents were the last people on earth she wanted to see.

'As you say, Ali. Of course, you're most welcome. I rattle around in this house. Be nice to have a—' He hesitated. 'A woman's touch around the place. You could have the guest bedroom.'

Callum led Alison up to the second floor and opened a door. The room was large, high-ceilinged, shrouded in dustsheets. Callum walked over to the window and pushed the casement open.

'Bit musty, I'm afraid. Still, it'll do till you find a place of your own.'

'It's lovely, Callum.' She bounced on the bed. 'Comfy.'

'Good. I'll bring up your things.'

Alison glanced round the room. She smiled. She had no intention of finding a place of her own. She had every intention of moving – but not nearly as far as Callum supposed. She meant to move only just down the corridor. In fact she meant to move into Callum's bed, and from that vantage point persuade him the child was his.

Callum reappeared with her single suitcase. He set it down gingerly and turned to face her. His face was serious.

'I want you to know, Alison, I wouldn't dream of . . . taking advantage of the situation.'

Alison could have laughed aloud, his anxiety was so evident. Callum Fergusson. Such a gentleman. So unlike Jack – so simple and direct. An honourable man. He'd make a wonderful husband and father.

The object of this speculation shifted uneasily from one foot to another.

'Look, Alison. I wouldn't want you to think . . . I mean I'd consider myself, as Aunt Catriona would say, "*in loco parentis*".'

'And vice versa,' Alison said sweetly. 'It might not be the first time we'd taken advantage of each other, Cal.'

'I know.' Callum's eyes were level. 'But I can assure you it won't happen again.'

'You mean my virtue is quite safe in your hands? Not very gallant.'

Alison's voice was teasing, but she was watching him shrewdly.

Perhaps he was warning her off. Maybe he had a girl. There was no sign of female habitation, but still . . . She'd have to tread softly at first. But, if there *was* someone, whoever it was clearly hadn't yet staked a permanent claim in the bachelor house. Foolish.

Whatever the obstacles, she was sure Callum was no match for her. All she needed was a little time. As she had reminded him, the Beltane fires had been ample proof Callum was susceptible to her charms.

She let the dust settle for a few days, and then took action. She had been shopping; at least Jack's little nest-egg had come in useful for that. She had bought herself a sexy little number with broderie anglaise round the Brigitte Bardot décolleté. It showed off her milky bosom to perfection.

She spent the afternoon at the hairdresser having her hair restyled with the new Bardot highlights. The hairdresser had even managed to persuade her to invest in a very expensive hairpiece to give that *rumpled* look.

Alison valued her own powers of seduction highly enough to expect that sooner or later Callum would succumb to them. She intended it to be sooner. She prepared a little dinner for two. Nothing overtly seductive – Alison was too subtle for that.

The meal, served at the kitchen table – no candlelit intimacy to set alarm bells ringing – was designed to remind him of their days in Eas Forse. A single oyster apiece, sea-juiced in its pearly shell, to put him in mind of the moment he had first kissed her. And then lamb with barley, just the way they made it on the islands, with the soup served first and the meat and tatties after.

It was all very cosy and intimate. She thought she was getting on just fine, chatting about old times – nothing contentious such as the Beltane fires, but all very cosy.

Later she thought perhaps the reminders of island life might have been a mistake. Immediately after dinner, Callum suddenly rose to his feet.

'That was delicious, Alison. Leave the washing-up – I'll do it later.'

'Where're you going?'

'Nowhere. Up to my study.'

'Where's your study?'

He hesitated. 'In the attic – where the old nurseries are. Not really my study. It's just that it's quiet up there and it . . . has associations.'

'Can I see?'

Callum shook his head. His face was unhappy. 'Look, Alison, it's something of my own. Nothing to do with anyone.'

He looked embarrassed. Almost as if he had a girl up there. Suddenly Alison guessed. Knew in that one instant who her rival might be.

'The attics were your nurseries, weren't they? You and Emerald, when you were children together. Before Eas Forse.'

Callum shook his head again – whether in denial or in unhappiness, she could not yet fathom.

She persisted. 'You still carry a torch, don't you?'

'Don't want to talk about it. Sorry, Alison.'

Alison, blond Alison with her newly highlighted Bardot hair, was suddenly annoyed. She tossed the rumpled curls and pouted. 'Miss Emerald No-name? First Jack. Now you. What the hell's the attraction?'

Callum took a deep breath. 'That was a very nice supper. Thank you, Alison. See you in the morning.'

'Callum, wait.' The urgency in her voice stopped him in his tracks. 'What if I told you I'd seen her?'

Callum swung round. His eyes were blazing. 'Then, I might well – as politely as possible – tell you to mind your own bloody business.'

Surprised at the sudden anger, Alison recoiled. 'I was only . . . I just thought you might like to know. About her. She's famous now – all the rage. The new Paradis girl. But I expect you know that – you must have seen her photographs.' She paused, her eyes cunning. 'Jack sent me down to Monte to get a story. She's got some beau or other . . .' Alison's voice trailed away.

Callum seemed to be paying attention, but his eyes were blank. It was almost as if Alison wasn't there, didn't even exist.

Abruptly he swung on his heel. The door closed behind him. She could hear the footsteps mounting the stairs. The attic door banged shut.

After a few moments, Alison tiptoed up behind him, and put her ear to the door. Silence. Then a faint creaking, as if a casement was swinging open. Or maybe a rocking-chair. She tried the door. It was locked.

'If you feel like that, why the hell don't you just go and get her?' Alison shouted.

Silence.

'It's not difficult. Maison Paradis. Better make it snappy. Jack says she's getting hitched.'

The door swung open. Callum stared at his tormentor.

'To set your imagination to rest, I haven't seen Emerald since she left the island. Now, will you please get the hell to bed?'

That was how Alison worked out who her rival really was. A ghost, a figment of the imagination. And Callum, like Jack, was obsessed. It was crazy. Unhealthy.

The next morning Alison could hear him banging round the kitchen early. She slipped into her dressing-gown and went down to find him.

He was already making himself coffee. His eyes were red-rimmed. He looked as if he had been up all night.

' 'Morning, Callum,' Alison said brightly.

Callum glanced up. 'Look, Alison. About last night. I'm sorry. It's just that . . .' He paused unhappily. 'Go where you like. Make yourself at home. But leave the attics to me.'

Alison, mindful of her plan, agreed immediately. ' 'Course, Cal. I wouldn't dream of it.'

Naturally she had meant not a word of her assurances. When Callum left for work, she searched the house until she found where he kept the keys.

The attic nurseries were silent, the surfaces thick with dust. In the day nursery, the only sign of recent occupation was a rocking-chair by the window, slewed towards the light, its cushions still indented from what must have been an all-night vigil.

Pinned to a cork board on one wall were cuttings from glossy magazines. Some of them were clearly Callum's society belles – a sea of airbrushed smiles. But there were fashion shots as well – and they were all of the same young woman.

The captions beneath the photographs confirmed the model's identity. Spring, summer, autumn collections of the Maison Paradis. The latest creations of Christian Paradis, shown on his favourite mannequin. Three years of changing fashion: full skirts with petticoats, slender pleats, narrow-hipped jackets, the new fashion christened 'the sack'. Three years of Emerald.

Emerald No-name. Alison clenched her fists. What had the girl done to deserve her luck? That's all it was. Certainly Alison had the beauty and the brains. Luck – and maybe an accident of birth. Whatever that might be.

She began to explore, pushing open the doors one by one.

Up in the eaves, time had stood still.

From a corner of an empty playpen, a battered golliwog cast a single beady eye at the interloper. Alison pulled out drawers, peered in cupboards. Rows of small coats and jackets. Little garments neatly folded and scented with lavender. Wooden building bricks stacked in a wooden chest. A bookcase carelessly stacked by childish hands.

Everything had been left exactly as it was, as if the children who had once filled it with life and laughter might at any moment return.

She discovered the secret drawer quite by accident.

She was rummaging without any particular purpose through a little desk when she found the bundle of yellowing photographs. Two children stared up. There could be no doubt of the little boy's identity. Solemn-faced and tousle-haired, Callum was unmistakable. But as for the companion tugging at his hand, a bright-eyed toddler wearing what could only be her brother's cut-down shorts, it would have taken the eyes of a mother – or a lover – to realize that this scrawny child and the favourite clothes-horse of Christian Paradis were one and the same.

Alison picked up the bundle. Beneath it, set flush, was a small brass button. Spring-triggered, the secret drawer slid out at a touch.

At first she thought it was empty. Then, right at the back, she caught the glint of gold. She pushed her fingers into the cramped depths, feeling the sharp edge of the metal.

Alison examined her find in the light: a little jewelled cross, set with tiny emeralds, dangling from a bracelet. Delicately worked. An expensive trinket from a fashionable jeweller. On the reverse of the cross an inscription, clearly etched.

It was in some kind of private code, designed to be understood only by the giver and the receiver: EANUM WE R 3 and a date. She turned it round to see if it made more sense the other way. If it hadn't been for the date, she might not have given it more than momentary attention.

As it was, she made the connection immediately.

That very morning, she had again examined the small trophy she had stolen from Jack. She went down to fetch it, just to make sure. She was right. The dates exactly matched. 5 March 1937.

She did not know what it meant, except that it had to be more than coincidence. It was evidence – of something. She didn't yet know what.

She had been around Jack long enough to realize she had stumbled on something which might be valuable – to the right person, extremely valuable. For a moment she was half-tempted to telephone Jack and tell him about it.

The bastard didn't deserve it.

He didn't deserve her, either.

While Alison was considering her next move, the doorbell rang.

Timing had always been Jack's strong point. Timing – and knowing other people's little weaknesses.

373

Now he had gained access to the house it was time to exploit Alison's little weakness. Jack pushed his hand in his pocket. He had picked up a half-flask of vodka on the way over, just in case.

'I brought a little something to celebrate our reunion.'

Alison hesitated. Callum did not seem to keep any drink in the house. She remembered that his foster-mother had been strictly teetotal. Probably Callum had never even thought about it. Alison was not quite secure enough yet to bring in her own.

She was feeling pretty rough this morning, what with one thing and another.

'How about a Bloody Mary? For old times' sake.'

Alison shrugged. But her eyes were fixed on the liquor.

'There's no tomato juice.'

'Un-Bloody Mary, then. Where's the glasses?'

'In the cupboard.'

Alison's voice was still sulky. She watched while Jack poured the vodka into two glasses – one full to the brim, the other only a splash.

'Friends?' He handed Alison the full glass.

Jack looked her up and down. 'You're looking good, Ali. New hairdo suits you. All rumpled like that. Nice.'

Alison looked at Jack over the edge of the glass.

'Jack the rat.'

'That's me.'

Jack raised his glass. His lips barely touched the rim. He could not afford to let her get to him. Not even the use of that ugly little nickname from Eas Forse.

Alison took a sip, and then another.

'Bastard.'

Alison took another sip. Jack smiled. The less of her wits Alison had about her, the better.

'That's my girl.'

'Not your girl.'

'Cheers anyway.'

After a moment he said, quite casually: 'We can still work together, Ali. I've been thinking. This thing – the disc. We could do something with it. I know it. Bet your landlord knows something.'

Alison took another sip of vodka. She frowned. Jack didn't know what she knew. Callum didn't know, either. They only knew one thing each. She was the only one who knew both things about Miss Emerald No-name. Bet your life she did. Connections. That was what you made. If you were clever.

She felt better. The vodka made her feel much better. A bit dizzy, though, on an empty stomach. Not so empty, the stomach.

She looked at Jack again. The bastard. A child. Even if she could persuade Callum that it was his – and after last night it looked as if she'd have her work cut out – what the hell could she possibly do with a child? She must have been crazy even to think of having it.

The vodka made you see things much more clearly.

She stared at Jack.

He said: 'What's the matter, Ali? It's me. Jack. Your old friend Jack.'

'Never a truer word.'

She made up her mind.

'I'm pregnant.'

'Jesus.'

'Great. You want to do something about it?'

'Be reasonable, sweetheart. I'm not husband material. You know that.'

'I don't want it. He. She. It. Do you?'

'We can handle it. I know a doctor—'

'Bastard.'

Alison stared at him. Callum or Jack. Jack or Callum. All men were bastards.

She narrowed her eyes. 'Who'll pay?'

'For heaven's sake, Ali. You took the money – and I don't begrudge it. Should be enough to get yourself fixed.'

'Fixed! That the advice you usually hand out? Your other lady-friends do things more professionally?'

'I'm sorry, Ali, it's not my fault. I took precautions—'

'Like hell.'

Stupidly, he said: 'You sure it's mine?'

'Fuck you, Jack Sweeney. You think I could get myself knocked up in a week?'

Alison swung her arm back. The contents of the glass caught Jack full in the face.

Jack reached out and took the glass from her hand.

'OK. Calm down.' He wiped his face with his other hand. 'No need to waste good liquor. ' 'Course I'll see you right. Be reasonable.'

'Why the hell should I be reasonable? Would you be reasonable, if you had this thing growing inside you?'

Her eyes filled with tears. Jack handed her the flask. She held it up to the light. 'Not much left.' She lifted it to her lips. Then she said: 'I had a plan. A good plan. Now it's all gone wrong.'

'What was the plan?'

'None of your sodding business, Jack Sweeney.'

After a moment she said: 'Anyway, I've spent the money. So who'll pay if I get it . . . *fixed*?'

Jack spread his hands. 'You've got all I had. Give me the disc and I'll get some more. Plenty more.'

Alison could see it all perfectly clearly now. She knew very well who deserved to pay.

She looked at Jack slyly. 'And if I . . . give you the disc. And show you something even more interesting?'

'Partners.' Jack's voice was eager.

'Equal partners?' Alison thought her voice sounded a little slurred. She said 'partners' again, making sure the last syllable came out neatly.

'Sure. Whatever you say, Ali.'

She smiled. Poor old Jack. Maybe he wasn't so bad after all. Alison noticed that Jack's nose was quivering. He really did look foxy. Like a red dog-fox who'd scented a rabbit. She giggled. The liquor always made her feel giggly. Giggly and friendly. Unleash the fox to catch the rabbit.

'Come along, then.'

She dragged Jack upstairs behind her, her breath coming in short eager gasps. She fished in her pocket and laid the identity-disc on the desktop. Then she pressed the brass button. The bracelet was still in the secret drawer.

'See?'

Triumphantly she held the little trinket to the light; showed Jack, foxy Jack, the inscription on the reverse of the cross. And then she showed him how the dates exactly matched.

Jack was jubilant. 'Now, this is what I want you to do.'

Swiftly he explained his plan. Then he took the precaution of pouring enough black coffee into Alison to iron out the slur in the voice before she did what he wanted.

Directory enquiries yielded the telephone number of the Maison Paradis.

He dialled, and handed Alison the phone.

'Now, sweetheart. Your best.'

Alison nodded. She was used to doing such things for Jack. Women were so much more convincing.

Even so, it had been surprisingly easy to persuade the flustered young receptionist at the Maison Paradis that Alison was ringing on behalf of American *Harper's*. Mrs Vreeland herself was to be over in Paris for a few days the following week. Yes, Mrs Vreeland knew the perfume launch was today. She was anxious to interview their star mannequin. Talk to her about how she had come to be chosen as . . . the Spirit of Paradise, wasn't it?

'But of course. I'm sure Mademoiselle Emerald would be delighted. At the salon? When would be convenient?'

Then Alison proved her worth. Her voice was smooth, soothing. 'Mrs Vreeland suggested it would be so much more *natural* if they could chat in Emerald's home environment. Our readers are so much younger these days; the informal touch is so important.'

The young woman hesitated. She took advice. They must put the proposal to their star. Could she ring back, or would the caller hold?

Alison would be happy to hold the line.

The reply came back almost immediately. Mademoiselle Emerald had agreed with pleasure – naturally, since it was Mrs Vreeland who had made the request.

'Marvellous. We'll confirm next week. Wonderful. And the address?'

She had it. Easy as candy from a baby.

All's fair in love and war. And this, at last, was war.

54

---•◆●◆•---

Paris: 1956

'Cousin, indeed!'

Madame Rappaport sniffed loudly to show the young man what she thought of his claim.

Did these English have no imagination? If she had a thousand-franc note for every young man who was *la belle demoiselle*'s cousin she would be as rich as the queen of England. She would certainly have no need to sit out in a cold little box on a wet winter's evening.

She sniffed again to show that she did not like the look of this particular young man at all. She supposed the fellow had managed to wheedle the address out of mademoiselle's employer. So indiscreet. No wonder there was so much crime and violation of young women in the city.

Madame Rappaport refused the proffered banknote and sent the fellow packing. She had standards to maintain.

But the self-styled relative had not been seen off so easily.

Not Jack Sweeney. He was far too old a hand for that. He felt a wave of nostalgia. It was just like old times, when he had his nose in the dustbins of the rich and famous. He liked the smell of dustbins.

He had what he wanted. The concierge had glanced up to the fourth-floor window, checking that the lights had not yet come on in the young mademoiselle's apartment. That had been quite enough to tell Jack Sweeney what he needed to know.

'Merci, madame,' he said. And meant it.

He strolled casually round the block until he found the alleyway which he knew would give access to the fire-escape at the back. The old apartment-blocks all had sturdy wrought-iron staircases which also doubled as rubbish-chutes. The structures were a godsend to thieves and – important in so flirtatious a city – to lovers escaping jealous husbands.

Jack was neither thief nor lover. Yet. But in his chosen profession he was well used to gaining access through such discreet entrances. It was a matter of moments to reach the back door of the fourth floor. It was a matter of a few seconds to slip the lock.

He slipped inside, pausing for an instant on the threshold, straining his ears for signs of occupation.

Satisfied, he set about familiarizing himself with the layout. Swiftly he worked his way round the rooms, selecting the right setting for the little drama he had in mind. He did not want his quarry screaming for help as soon as she got through the door.

He felt in his pocket and laid the little trinket on the table. The gold of the chain and the emeralds in the cross twinkled prettily.

He wondered what memory was worth. He wondered what she knew. What she could remember of the past. What the little bracelet might tell her.

They would strike a deal. An agreement – for mutual benefit. Her story for his story. Tell the story – that was what he knew how to do. That was his part of the deal really. A bloody good story.

Emerald would be grateful; surely she would welcome his help.

He needed a good price, of course. For Alison. To sort out the little problem. The bracelet was worth good money, a great deal more than the market value – to the right person. Emerald was certainly the right person. Even if he took the trinket down to the pawnbroker's, it would be worth the price of getting Alison fixed up.

He anticipated many more such visits. Many more times when Emerald, the beautiful unobtainable Emerald, would welcome the knowledge he brought.

He felt in his pocket for the reassuring presence of the disc. That was not a bargaining counter for today. It was for the future. Call it insurance.

He checked his watch. She should not be long now. Six o'clock and the office workers were already piling back into the busy *quartier*.

He had brought his binoculars – a most important piece of equipment in Jack's profession. Cautiously he moved to the outer edge of the window, glanced down to make sure he could not be observed from the courtyard below, and raised the glasses to his eyes.

He had a good view right down the street. Suddenly he tensed.

It had to be her. Even after all these years, there was something about her.

It was certainly not the clothes the young woman was wearing. They were cheap chain-store stuff – not at all the kind of thing one might expect to see on a famous mannequin. No. It was something about the way she moved – something about the lightness of the step, an easy swing to the hips, the carriage of the head – which set her apart from the bustle of other young women returning home from the day's work.

His quarry hesitated for a moment and then vanished into the corner delicatessen. There must have been a queue, and it was fully ten minutes before she came out again, a carrier-bag swinging from her hand.

Jack was hungry. He wondered what she might have purchased. Something delicious no doubt – something to share with an evening visitor.

Next time it might even be for him that she prepared an intimate little meal, set flowers, lit candles.

In his mind he rehearsed the little scene. He wondered if she would recognize him as easily as he did her.

She was coming through the gateway now, giving him a chance to study the face magnified by the powerful spy-glasses. The violet eyes sparkled and there was a half-smile on the curved lips. The familiar smile. For a moment his heart stopped.

He kept the glasses trained on her, following the curve of the hips, the tilt of the breasts as she turned in through the gateway which gave access to the courtyard below. The clothes were drab, shapeless. Didn't show her off to the best advantage. He might have a word with her about that – when they were friends, as they surely would be.

Now it would be different. Now he had something of value to trade.

He could see the concierge's curtain twitching. Voices echoed in the courtyard. The old bag was explaining about the visitor.

A few moments later he heard light steps outside the door. The key turned in the lock. Jack waited for her in the shadows of the darkened room.

Jack was not the only one who had decided to act on his knowledge of the young woman's whereabouts.

Callum was also on his way to see Emerald.

The morning after the confrontation with Alison, he had arrived early at the studio. He had spent the night thinking about his foster-sister: trying to come to terms with what Alison had told him, battling with the reality of the undertaking he had given Anstruther.

After the shadows which haunted him through the night watch, it was a relief to walk into the familiar chaos of the workplace. There was a rush job on that morning. When he had agreed to do it, he had not even known where and what it was. Just that it was an assignment, and it would take his mind off his troubled thoughts.

Had he realized, he would never have taken the risk. His resolution that he could not – must not – interfere in Emerald's life had been shaken enough as it was. When he heard that the assignment was in Paris he did his level best to get out of it. Paris was Emerald. Paris was too close to sleepless nights.

'How about sending Mike?' His voice was casual. Mike was the studio junior – a position until recently occupied by Callum himself. 'He handled the Hartnell shoot pretty well.'

'Mike my arse,' his boss interrupted roughly. The thick cockney accent and lack of social graces were his trademark. 'Pardon my French, but what's the matter with you, ol' cock? Gay Paree. Beautiful birds. Spread in *Queen*.'

He peered at his employee. 'Christ. You look 'orrible. You should give it an 'oliday or it'll drop off. On yer bike, loverboy. Train leaves in an hour.'

There was no help for it. Callum packed up his photographic equipment and prepared to do as he was told.

'Good lad. Got enough film?' The boss glanced up from his scrutiny of a stack of contact prints.

' 'Ere you are.' He pushed the yellow briefing sheet across the desk. 'While yer there, take the weekend. Buy yerself a toothbrush, hole up on the Left Bank and see the sights. Brush up on the parlay-voo. On expenses – the bastards can afford it. Mike can handle anything that comes up over here. Make a change from handlin' 'is weddin' tackle.'

Callum laughed. Then the laughter died in his throat as he glanced down at the paper in his hand.

It had been easy at first – while the shoot was in full swing.

There must have been fifty photographers crammed into the winter-darkened salon when the spotlight came up to reveal the beautiful young woman whom Christian Paradis, the most famous couturier in the world, had selected to personify the Spirit of Paradise.

In the London studio, as soon as Callum had learned the identity of the young woman he had been summoned to photograph, he had nearly turned tail and run. Nearly made his escape. Nearly risked the sack. Nearly telephoned the studio from the station and told them all the trains had been cancelled.

Then he had told himself that he must face up to it. Told himself he was strong enough, committed enough to his profession, to treat this particular day's work as just another job.

All he had to do was make sure Emerald herself didn't spot him. So he had been careful to take up a position at the back of the salon, so that he was just another blurred face obscured by another camera.

Silence fell.

Then the curtains swung back, revealing a beautiful young girl, face alight with laughter, rocking gently on a flower-twined swing. There was an audible intake of breath – even from the posse of hardened professionals.

The painted slant-eyed beauty, the body skimmed by a smooth bell of flower-strewn silk, the spotlight brilliant on the smooth cap of gleaming russet hair, seemed a creature of fantasy. She was indeed, as Christian Paradis had proclaimed, the Spirit of Paradise.

The air was suddenly filled with the scent of rose petals, violets, a faint trace of heather and fern, the powdery perfume of primrose. The girl began to move, her body dipping and swaying with the movement of the ropes.

At first his delight in the shadow blinded Callum to the substance. All passion was funnelled down the small square frame, no bigger than the palm of his hand, which dictated his vision. Even now, when he had the girl he loved almost at the tips of his fingers, happiness was measured by the success of the black and white images he captured.

His work was his obsession, and Emerald was the most magnificent subject he had ever had. It was not her beauty alone. She had an extraordinary vivacity, a quality of youth and energy, which transferred itself undiluted to the celluloid.

It was only when the little square shutter ceased to register, when the spotlight had faded and the uproar had died down, that he truly realized what he had seen.

That the *mannequin-vedette* of the House of Paradis was one of the most beautiful women in the world had not come as any surprise. He knew that well enough from her photographs. The trouble was that nothing had prepared him for the turmoil he felt at the reality of her. Still less for what he would feel when he waited, hanging back in the shadows like any lovestruck stage-door Johnny, for her to finish her day's work.

Suddenly she was there, bright as a sunbeam among the group of chattering sempstresses, so close he might almost have reached out and touched her. Her face scrubbed, the full dark skirt tightly belted into the narrow sweater, this was the Emerald he recognized.

Unable to let her out of his sight, he followed the hurrying figure through the cold grey streets, seeing not the smooth beauty she had become but the bright-eyed child who had shared his attic nurseries – the infant whose first steps he had encouraged, whose first words he had framed, who had once been all his joy.

Undimmed by time, memory flooded back, filling the deep pool of longing he had always known was there. The damage was done. Emerald was no longer a painted icon whose image he and others might capture, but a living, breathing reality.

So real that he knew he could no longer keep his word to Anstruther. So real that, whatever the consequences, he could no longer deny the truth.

For the first few moments, Callum had been tempted to declare himself immediately. Caution prevailed. If his own mind had been in such turmoil, if he had felt such anguish over the reunion, might Emerald not feel the same? Better to wait. Once he knew where she lived, he would make the meeting casual. Perhaps she had a favourite café. It would be much better to pick the right moment.

His heart beating wildly, Callum settled himself in the doorway opposite the entrance to the apartment block into which Emerald had vanished.

The lights came on in the front room of a fourth floor apartment.

For an instant, until an unseen hand yanked the curtain closed, there were two figures outlined against the light.

One of them, Emerald. The other . . . Callum's blood ran cold. How could he have dismissed Alison's story so easily? How could he have imagined that Emerald would not have a suitor? How could he have thought for a moment that there would be no rival, that her heart and life would be as empty of love as his own?

Callum loved Emerald. He had always always loved her. There had never been a moment when he had not loved her.

He knew it now. Knew he was lost, as he had always been lost. In the cold light of that winter morning, he told himself that, even if it was only once, he must touch her again. Feel the softness of her skin, smooth the sheen of her hair, look into depths of those sparkling violet eyes. He must take her into his arms once more, whatever the price to her or to him.

Even if he never held her again.

383

55

Paris: 1956

Emerald paused on the threshold of the apartment, her hand on the doorknob.

Her skin prickled. Something was amiss. If Dido hadn't been away for the week in hot pursuit of the Pittsburgh millionaire, Emerald would have sworn there was someone inside. Perhaps her flatmate had come back early. She set down the shopping.

'Dido? Is that you?'

Silence. A faint stirring of the air.

'Anyone there?'

Silence. Maybe Étienne, her young student friend from upstairs, had gone to sleep on the sofa. He had a volatile new girlfriend who sometimes locked him out. Emerald had given him the extra key to her own backdoor so he could take refuge.

'Étienne? Is that you?'

She pushed open the door of the living-room. In the evening gloom with the light from the hall behind her, the room appeared to be empty. Then she saw him, a shadowy figure by the window, half-hidden by the undrawn curtain.

'Étienne?'

The answering voice was a whisper. 'Emerald?'

She put out her hand, searching for the light-switch.

Behind her she heard a sharp intake of breath. The curtains yanked shut.

Light flooded the room.

She turned, a smile on her lips. 'Really, Étienne—'

The smile faltered and died.

'Who—'

Jack stepped forward. 'Emerald. It's me. Jack. Jack Sweeney.'

She stared at him, startled. Her breath was coming in quick short gasps.

'Jack!' She took a deep breath. 'Lord, you gave me a fright.'

Jack leaned forward eagerly. He said: 'Sorry. Didn't mean to startle you. Just passing.'

He hesitated, and then decided to come clean. 'The old bag at the gate wouldn't let me in. I had to sneaked up the back. I thought . . . old friends and all that. Nice to talk over old times.'

Emerald breathed again. At least it wasn't a thief – or worse. This was the 'cousin' Madame Rappaport had warned her about.

'How did you find me?'

'Easy.' He grinned. 'You're famous.'

Emerald looked at him. His face was innocent, the sandy brows lifted, the small eyes watchful but giving no hint he meant her any harm.

'I've seen your by-line, too, Jack. That Windsor Ball piece – I wondered if you'd recognized me.'

'Took a moment or two.' His eyes narrowed. 'In fact, it's more or less about that that I'm here.'

'Is that so, Jack?' Emerald's voice was wary.

Jack's reputation had even reached her in Paris. The Maison Paradis didn't like the wrong kind of publicity. Dandy Dan was certainly the wrong kind of publicity.

'I live a very quiet life.'

' 'Course you do. Monte Carlo. High life. Aristocratic company. Tom Sherwood.' Jack laughed, a little bark without mirth. 'And now we have Étienne – whoever he might be.'

Emerald stared at Jack. She didn't like his tone. 'Étienne lives upstairs. He's a student. A friend. And as for Tom – none of your damn business, Jack.'

'Just plenty of good friends?' Jack tapped his nose and winked. 'Everyone's damn business is my business. But especially yours. I take a very personal interest in your welfare, Emmie my beauty. Always like to keep an eye. Quite a little handful, Tom Sherwood. I hope Étienne's more forthcoming.'

Jack didn't like the way Emerald looked at him then. It looked as though young Emerald was not the easy innocent he had supposed.

'Anyway, that's not why I'm here,' he added hurriedly. 'I brought you something – sort of a memento.'

He bent down and picked up his talisman from the table. He dropped the sparkling chain into her hand, turning the cross over so that she could read the inscription on the reverse.

'Thought you might like it.'

Emerald stared down at the trinket. It smelled faintly of talcum powder – very old and stale, but talcum powder none the less.

An icy hand reached out for her. 'Recognize it?' Jack's voice was eager.

'Where did you get it?'

Jack disregarded the question. 'Recognize the date?'

She stared at Jack. 'Of course.'

Memory opened its black maw. Her skin was cold, but the cross felt burning hot. She closed her fist on it, feeling the heat in her palm.

Jack said, 'It'll cost you. I had to pay good money.'

Emerald's violet eyes were wide and dark. 'Who to, Jack? Who sold you this?'

Her voice was calm now. She no longer felt the burning metal or the cold of her skin. She simply felt numb.

He shrugged. 'A friend.'

'What friend?'

Jack hesitated. Any minute now, she'd want to know if it came from Callum. The last thing he wanted was to bring Callum back into Emerald's life. Two was company, three was none.

'Who did you get it from, Jack?' Her voice was gentle, persuasive. She sounded like Catriona Sweeney. Like the schoolmistress when she caught him red-handed. Magpie Jack. Jack the rat.

Jack stared at her. Any minute now she was going to accuse him of thieving it.

After a moment he said: 'A girl. A friend. She found it . . .'

Emerald waited.

Jack stumbled on. 'This girl – she got herself into trouble. You know how it is.' His voice rose. 'Pregnant. That's all. I promised her the money to get it fixed.'

'Is that the truth, Jack?'

Jack looked into the steady violet eyes. He felt like a delinquent small boy.

He nodded. 'It's the truth.'

'Then, of course I'll help.' Emerald's voice was calm. 'How much do you need? I'm afraid I don't keep much in the house. I'll see what I have.'

Emerald turned and left the room. A faint trace of rose petals hung in the air. Rich and rare, the scent of rose petals and spring flowers. Clean and sweet to leave in the air in her wake.

Jack stared after her.

A favour. She was going to do him a gracious favour. What did he expect? A girl like that would be bound to do him a favour.

So what the hell did she know of such things? Girls like that didn't get knocked up. Even Alison, with all her talk of being a good girl, she was just another one. Just another girl who was no better than she should be, whatever airs and graces she might give herself.

Girls like Emerald were different. Girls like Emerald could pick and choose. Girls like Emerald never chose Jack.

The red wave swept over Jack – the red wave of anger.

He remembered the moment in the heather on Eas Forse, when he felt her struggle, when the butterfly wings fluttered, when his body stirred.

Lust followed hard on the heels of anger.

Anger hardened into rage as he remembered the risks he had taken for her sake. As he remembered the young boy's loneliness on that island hillside. Remembered humiliation. Remembered blood and tears in a Glasgow gutter. Remembered Catriona's refusal to give him what was his by right. Remembered the long reach of Anstruther's protective arm which had cost him his livelihood.

A girl like that – a girl like that who could summon up such forces with a click of her fingers. How could he ever have been so crazy as to imagine for an instant that she might look at him with tenderness?

She would have many admirers – and not all of them, no doubt, as indifferent to her charms as Tom Sherwood. Or as content to admire from afar as Callum. Callum who didn't even have the gut-courage to confront a woman of flesh and blood. It was men like that who could afford a jewel like Emerald.

A blackmailer. That's how she would see him. Yet it was his birthright she had stolen. She, not he, was the thief.

The red wave of anger washed over him as he waited for the favour which was his due. As he waited for the favour which he would take.

Emerald, returning with a handful of banknotes in her hand, had no chance to defend herself. Jack launched himself at her, cannoning the breath from her body. The blow caught her below the ribcage, stifling her scream in her throat. Oblivion, merciful oblivion drowned her as black night descended.

Jack plunged down. Rage fuelled lust. His body crushed her. Angry hands ripped the cloth. Plunging into her again and again, the monster of her nightmares bore down.

When it was nearly over, spiralling upwards through the darkness, she found her voice and screamed. Nails gouged soft flesh. She struggled free. The knife. Where was the knife? She carried the knife slipped into the belt at her waist. Nacho had taught her to use it.

Gone. Her belt. She had it. She turned, teeth bared, knife arcing. He pulled back, rage spent in the violence of his lust, suddenly fearful. Blood on his cheek.

She ran. The door banged. Fear focused her feet. Drummed downwards on the twisting iron, eyes blinded by anger, breath short and quick.

Her voice echoed, her own voice in her ears.

O Lord, let him not come after me. O Lord, let him not follow.

56

Paris: 1956

It was as black as pitch in the alleyway. The light from the street-lamps did not reach into the backyards of the tenements. The few thin beams of light which escaped from under the doors, stacked one over the other up the brick well of the courtyard, speckled the darkness.

Emerald, motionless at the foot of the iron staircase, was no longer afraid. She was angry. She was angry at her own trusting stupidity. She was angry at whatever it was which had turned her gesture of friendship into an outrageous act of violence. She shivered in the cold.

She looked down at her dishevelled clothes, smoothed the full skirt, pulled down the sweater. Her body was no longer part of her, she no longer felt the bruises, the ache between her thighs, the cold of the air on naked skin.

Her fist tightened on the skinning-knife which had been Nacho's present to her after the battle with the alligator. It had been a long time since she'd had reason to remember Nacho's training. What had Nacho taught her? Never be cornered. Choose your territory. Strike the first blow.

Straining her ears for the footsteps which she knew must follow her, she glanced round, looking for an open space.

Ten paces along the alleyway was the street which led to the back of the greengrocer's shop, shuttered now and with the stacked empty vegetable-boxes awaiting collection on the pavement.

Emerald moved swiftly, covering the distance to the mouth of the narrow street. There she stopped, her body pressed back into the pile of empty crates, the stench of rotting cabbage in her nostrils.

She waited.

Sure enough, footsteps echoed down the dark tunnel of the alleyway. Odd. She had expected to hear the rattle of the iron fire-escape. He must have come round from the front of the building.

A figure was silhouetted against the dim street-light at the entrance to the alleyway.

'Emerald?'

Bewilderingly Jack's voice had changed. There was anxiety – almost panic – there.

The man moved forward slowly – whether cautious or uncertain, she could not tell. She only knew he moved softly on the balls of the feet – the movement of a hunter or a thief. She held her breath. The footsteps slowed, deliberate.

Emerald shrank back into the shadows, the blood pounding in her temples.

'Are you there? Emerald?'

The face moon-pale, shadowed from the light, was turning from side to side, searching.

Adrenalin pumped through her limbs. He could surely hear the drumming of her heart.

Still she waited.

The man's footsteps slowed. The face was turned towards her, the eyes black mirrored holes.

Her muscles bunched.

She sprang. Like the tigre in the jungle she sprang, four-footed, knife extended.

The man whirled, recoiled, turned. She heard the tearing of cloth, felt the spring in the slender blade. Again she struck.

The man's hand came up palm outwards to take the force of the knife. There was blood on the extended palm, shielding the face.

The man's face was close to her, his blood warm on her hand.

She screamed, the noise bouncing, echoing down the narrow alleyway.

Then she began to run, her shoes slipping among the oranges and overripe pears underfoot.

The smell of rotting fruit filled her nostrils. 'Emerald!'

The man was closing on her now. She spun round, body held low.

Again: 'Emerald! For God's sake, Emerald!'

He was close to her now, caught and held her – the strong arms

390

holding her prisoned, helpless as a wild bird in a trap. Blind-eyed with rage, her breath choked in her throat.

Until he heard the scream, Callum had waited in the shadow of the door-way opposite the apartment block into which Emerald had vanished.

Across the street, the windows remained shrouded, silent.

The street-lights came on. The hurrying faces of the passers-by were suddenly livid in the bright cold light.

Callum stared up at the darkened window, his mind in turmoil. What if it was too late? What if Emerald was already lost to him for ever?

One after another, the shutters of the shops clanged down. Windows opened and closed. Voices echoed across the courtyards, snatches of greeting, laughter, a voice raised, the barking of dogs, the cries of children, rattle of rubbish chutes. Scents of cooking began to drift under doorways, garlic and hot oil, billowing fragrance of a hundred stewpots.

The sounds and scents which reached Callum's blunted senses were nothing out of the ordinary, neither more nor less than those of any winter's evening in the city. The *quartier* settled down to break its fast. The office workers, the housewives, even the pair of young tarts who had inspected him with interest when he first took up his vigil, disappeared indoors. In Paris even the ladies of the night took the dinner-hour seriously.

All at once, over the murmur of domestic activity, rose a new sound – urgent, fearful, abruptly muffled. A momentary silence, then again the noise arced upwards, bouncing off the walls of the enclosed courtyard. A scream – and another and another, intermingled. The bang of a door and the rattle of an iron staircase.

It was this which restored Callum to his senses, which brought him running in search of her.

Now he felt the pain of the knife-wound, the warmth of the blood.

'Emerald! Do you hear me? It's me, Callum!'

'Callum?' The noise in her ears. Sweat running, salt on her tongue.

She shook herself, pinioned. She felt the rough cloth against her face. Rough cloth and a familiar scent, reminding her of hill and heather.

'Emerald, what is it? What frightened you?'

Fiercely Emerald pushed the man away. She knew it was Callum, not Jack. Anger rose in her throat. He was a man. *Rape*, she screamed silently. Do you not understand? Men do this thing to women. You are a man. You, too, betray.

'Emerald, tell me.'

His arms were still round her, offering his strength, comforting her.

391

His heart ached, the throb of the wound in his hand a welcome earnest of the pain he longed to share.

She pushed him away, spinning round in search of that other man who must still surely follow.

The alleyway was empty.

Callum's voice was gentle, anxious. 'What can I do if you won't tell me?'

Can you not see it on my face? Smell it on my body? How can you not know? She was angry with him. Angry that by his absence, by all those years when he was not there, he had allowed her to be betrayed.

'Why now, after all this time? Why do you come to find me now?'

Her words tore at his heart. How could he explain the pact he had made which had kept him from her, how explain why he had not been there to protect her always?

His arms were around her again. 'Hush, sweetheart. It's over. You were scared, that's all. It's over now.'

She heard the anguish in his voice.

She remembered him so gentle, so kind. Callum had been all her own. Tears rose suddenly, as if she were a child again, when as father, brother he had been all things to her – when he was all she had.

'I was . . .' She hesitated, not wanting to give the word, the silent scream, reality. 'I was attacked. A man attacked me.'

Stupidly he said: 'Where? Who?'

His hand outstretched, there was blood on the palm. She remembered the knife entering flesh. She took his hand in hers, turned it over, saw the open wound.

She said: 'I hurt you.'

Unreasoning, she was glad. She was glad that he, too, could feel the pain she would not, could not share with him.

'It's nothing. See? It's almost stopped bleeding.'

She stared down. She remembered Jack Sweeney's blood. Rage gripped her once more. *But we three were only children then, when we knew each other. What could have made Jack do this to me?*

Emerald's body was as cold as ice, as cold as the black water of the night of the shipwreck.

Her strength returned as Callum's arms circled her again. She beat his chest with her fists, trying to break the gentleness, the calm. Fiercely she pushed him from her. Her safe haven no longer safe.

Her mind was suddenly clear. She said: 'I'm going back. If I find him, if he's still there, I'll kill him.'

'No. This time, it's my business.'

Now Callum, too, was full of rage. Rage at his own failure to protect her. At the long years he had not been able to watch over her.

He pushed past her and began to climb the stairs towards the arrow of bright light.

They paused together, one behind the other as close as children, breathing softly together, listening.

Callum made a gesture to Emerald to stay, his hand held up in warning. Then he moved forward, silent as if he was stalking a deer on the hills of Eas Forse.

Inside, the sounds of movement. The door to the sitting-room was ajar. The creak of a floorboard told him the intruder was still there.

The man's back was turned. Whoever he was, he was absorbed by the confusion of upturned furniture, proof of a struggle, oblivious to all but the scene before him.

Callum was glad.

The man was lightly built, there was a studious stoop to the shoulders – more like a skinny black-clad scarecrow than the thug Callum had expected.

All this Callum took in at a glance before he tackled him, cannoning into the back of the man's knees. The man went down like a willow-tree in the path of a raging torrent.

Behind him Callum heard Emerald laugh, an edge of hysteria in the voice. 'Callum! Stop!'

Abruptly Callum's triumph turned to comical bewilderment.

'Stop?'

'Let him go, Cal – please! It's only Étienne.'

Callum inspected his cowering catch. 'Étienne who?'

As the two outraged faces turned towards her, Emerald's laughter lost its hard edge of fear – the two white knights in shining armour riding to her rescue seemed so absurd.

'Please let him go, Cal. He's my neighbour.'

Callum tightened his grip.

'Then, why did he attack you?' he asked reasonably.

'He didn't. Étienne lives upstairs; he's my friend. For heaven's sake stop growling at him, Cal.'

Meanwhile Étienne had taken advantage of the lull to wrench himself free, scuttling away behind Dido's rubber-plant like a frightened rabbit.

After a moment he poked his head out. 'Emerald – as you know, I do not believe in physical violence. You will please explain who is this man?'

Emerald hunched her shoulders and spread her hands in the French gesture of exasperation.

'Étienne, this is Callum, my foster-brother. Callum, meet my official philosophy tutor, Étienne.'

The two men glowered at each other.

Emerald looked from one to the other.

Suddenly she had had enough. She had to be alone. Alone to clean up the debris, to mend what had been broken.

'Gentlemen, grateful as I am, you are now leaving. Push off.'

'What is this "push off"?' Étienne's frustration was so comical that even Callum began to laugh.

'Go. Fous le camp. Finis.'

Étienne's face lit up with relief. 'Now, that at least I understand. That Emerald has explained to me many times.'

This time all three joined in the laughter.

'Étienne. Callum.'

She put her hands gently to each face in turn.

'Now, go. Both of you.'

'I am a sensitive man,' Étienne said seriously. 'I can see I am de trop.'

Callum looked at Emerald. 'Are you sure?'

'Sure.'

Callum followed Étienne over to the door. He hesitated, and then turned back.

'Why, Emerald? Now that I have found you again?'

'Because I need to work this out. It's not so easy. I've had to learn to live without you – without anyone.'

Seeing the anguish in Callum's face, she paused. After a moment she said gently. 'Sweet Callum, because I'm different. I was always different. You above all should know that.' She stretched her hand again to his cheek, touched him lightly. 'Remember our agreement? When we pricked our fingers with the blackthorn spike?'

'But we were only children. We didn't know the price. We should never have let them part us.'

'I knew. Even then, I knew the price. And now I don't know how to make you understand.'

'Try.'

'Because – ' She hesitated. 'Because it's . . . *dangerous*. There are sleeping monsters – I feel them.'

'The past? Is that what scares you?'

She nodded. 'Always.' She took a deep breath. 'The man – it was Jack Sweeney.'

'Jack? Jack Sweeney was here?'

She nodded. 'Him. Magpie Jack. He brought me this.' She held up her wrist. Turned it so that he could see the bracelet with its little cross. 'Recognize it, Cal?'

'How on earth did he get hold of it? How did he know it was yours?'

'I thought you might tell me.'

'Mama kept it in the bureau in the nursery. In the secret drawer—' His voice trailed away. Alison. It must have been Alison. But why? What did she know? What did she have to gain? What did Jack have to gain?

'I can't think how—'

He could feel her eyes on him. She said: 'Jack had some story about a girl you both knew. A girl who'd got into trouble. He felt it might be worth . . . *money.*' She hesitated. 'He felt I owed him something.' She turned her back, so that he did not see the tears well up. 'Except it turned out not to be what I had to offer . . . freely.'

Callum reached out for her, caught her shoulders, turning her to face him. 'What happened? Emerald, you must tell me!'

Emerald held up her hand. The little jewel sparkled.

'Why? So that you can undo what was done?' She shook her head. 'No. Only I can do that. That's all I'm going to tell you. All I'm going to tell anyone. Ever.'

'Oh, my darling.' Callum tried to take her in his arms. 'I'm so sorry.'

'No.' She shook her head, pushing him away. 'It's over. Done. Finished. It wasn't your fault. No sympathy. Blood brothers? We agreed?'

'If you say so.'

'Don't sound so miserable. I thought . . .' She pushed him gently towards the door, holding back her still-churning anger. 'It'll be all right. I need time – to pick up the pieces. That's all. Then come for me. A few days. We'll start again. It's not so long. I won't run away. Promise.'

And with that promise, for the moment, he knew he would have to be content. Emerald never lied. He could only hope. Wait and hope.

57

Paris: 1956

After Callum had gone, Emerald stood silent in the room where Jack Sweeney had been.

Methodically she began to set the room to rights. She fetched dustpan and broom to clear away the debris, cloths and polish to wipe away the evidence of what had happened. She worked fiercely, fuelled by her rage, as if by the very gestures she might undo what had been done.

Finally she threw the casement wide, letting in the night breezes.

Already she was beginning to impose her will on memory. The laughter had begun the healing. When she was ready, Callum would complete the forgetting.

She scrubbed her body clean – not, as she usually did, luxuriating in the scented water, but angrily, scouring her limbs now until not a trace of what had taken place remained.

Nevertheless it was three long days before Emerald could put Jack Sweeney out of her mind. Three days before what he had done did not haunt her every waking hour. Until, like an oyster with a speck of grit, she knew she had laid the first thin veil of pearl which made the memory bearable.

Meanwhile Callum roamed the city alone. The wound in his hand, though healing fast, had made the use of his camera difficult. So, for the first time since he could remember, he was obliged to see the world no longer as an image within the confines of his lens, no longer as a peepshow, a world bordered and contained and available for capture, but as reality.

He telephoned the studio, lying to cover up his protracted absence. The salon had promised him an exclusive. He had to delay his return.

'Exclusive my arse. Fuckin' free 'oliday, more like,' his boss grumbled.

For those three days, Callum – as Emerald herself had done – wandered the city, seduced by its beauty, by the scents, the sounds, the glory of the ancient stones. For those three days, Emerald was never out of his thoughts.

For those three days, Callum courted Emerald. It was a gentle courtship. Each morning, just before she left for work, he would deliver some little delicacy for her via Madame Rappaport. A chocolate éclair, done up in a little box with a red ribbon. A jar of rose-petal jelly. A vanilla-scented honey-cake.

At night, just before the time he knew she returned from her day's work, he would leave flowers. A bunch of violets, a sheaf of lilies of the valley bundled in their own dark leaves, a posy of pink rosebuds with their petals just beginning to unfurl.

'Allez, mademoiselle,' Madame Rappaport said approvingly as she handed over the small gifts each day. 'This young man is surely in love. When will you receive him?'

Emerald accepted the offerings, but she shook her head and smiled. She was not yet ready.

Callum, hearing that she had not refused his gifts, was content to wait. Emerald had always done things in her own time and in her own way.

On the third day, Emerald took early leave from the salon.

'I have family visiting, Madame Verdun,' she explained. And it was true. Callum was all the family she had.

That evening Emerald was waiting for him by the *portière*.

Callum saw her instantly, as soon as he turned into the street. She was wearing some kind of cloak which swirled as she moved. It was made of soft dark wool, witch-like, lined with scarlet.

They were both hesitant, feeling the awkwardness in each other, fearing the unknown, like two teenagers out on their first date. She stopped suddenly just before she reached him, shy as a young girl.

'Hello, Cal.' Her face was bright, her eyes clear. Nervously, not knowing what to say, she said: 'Am I late?'

Tawny eyes, so dearly remembered, searched hers.

'Three hours. Three days. Twelve years.'

She laughed joyously, the anxiety gone. Gently she picked up his hand.

'Poor Cal. How's the wound?'

'Healing.'

'I'm sorry. Sorry I hurt you. Sorry I threw you out.'

'It doesn't matter. I understand.'

'Do you, Cal?'

'Tell me.'

She shook her head. 'No.'

'You look . . . *fine.*'

'You, too.'

They stood close, feeling the nearness of each other.

He said, 'We'd nearly given up hope – me and Rappaport.'

'Rappaport's on tenterhooks. She thinks I deserve a much more exciting love-life. I think she enjoys being disappointed in me. I should hate to spoil it for her. Yet.'

She tucked her arm through his. 'I thought we might walk. Walk and talk.'

Emerald matched her steps to Callum's long hillwalker's stride along the banks of the Seine. Below, their reflections danced in the river's quiet waters.

On the Pont St-Louis they stopped.

'Where are we going?' Callum asked.

'Are you hungry?'

He smiled. 'Now you mention it, yes.'

'Good. I have plans – wonderful plans.'

'Such as?'

'I'm so happy you're here with me, Cal.' She looked at him seriously. 'What took you so long to find me? I thought I'd lost you for ever.'

'I would have come before.' Callum hesitated. 'Heaven knows, you're not hard to find – your photograph's everywhere. Except— Anthony Anstruther. He made me promise not to contact you. Told me our mother would have wanted it so. I believed him. He said you would run away. That you wanted nothing of the past – not even me.'

'Oh, Cal, how could you have thought such a thing?'

'There was something else. He threatened to block the inheritance. Made me give my word. I had nothing to offer you. The house was mothballed until I was old enough to take it on. And then – when the papers came through, I wanted to share it with you.'

'Oh, Cal,' Emerald said softly, 'that's Catriona's talk. Agreements. Inheritance. Worldly goods. None of it matters.'

'What matters, then? I want to be able to look after you. Give you the world.'

'None of it is of any importance. Now is what matters. Us. You and me.'

'Where do we begin? We have so much to catch up.'

'We're still the same. Whatever they may have done, it makes no difference.'

Callum stared down into the water.

Emerald laughed. 'Serious Cal. So serious. It's easy. We tell each other what we want to know. Anything. Ask about anything at all. We answer yes or no – and no-one's allowed to fib.'

Callum grinned. Then he said, 'You start.'

'First and most important – are you a virgin?'

'Honestly, Emerald—'

'Yes or no? Truth.'

Callum hesitated, his face scarlet. 'All right. No.'

'Terrific. Ask me.'

'Ask what?'

'If I'm a virgin, silly.' She giggled. 'You could try "Do you like avocado pears?" '

'What's that supposed to mean?'

'Darling Cal. Always so good. No, I'm not a virgin. You wouldn't want me to be – would you?'

Callum blushed even more deeply. 'No. I mean, yes. Oh, Em, what am I supposed to say?'

'You're supposed to say: "Very nice, Emerald. I'm so pleased for you." As if I had passed an exam or something. "Go to the top of the class." ' Emerald giggled. 'Anyway, did you enjoy your first?'

'Yes. I mean, no. For heaven's sake, Emerald,' he finished up lamely.

'Next. Do you have a lover?'

He hesitated. 'No.'

'Just as well. I might be jealous. Would you be jealous, Cal? If I did?'

'Certainly.' He looked at her very seriously. 'Who taught you to use that knife?'

She smiled. 'Are you sure you want to know?'

'No.' Callum's voice was rueful. He looked at his healing wound. 'Whoever it was, he was good.'

'Of course. He was good at other things, too. Would you like to know what else?'

'Now I *am* jealous.'

'Better and better. I wrote to you all about him.'

399

'You wrote to me?'

'Of course. Lots. After all, I knew where *you* were, but you didn't know where I was.'

'Oh, Emerald, I never got your letters.' Callum stared at her. 'How terrible.'

'It *was* pretty terrible. It was probably old Sweeney who snaffled them. They all said I wasn't allowed to write to you. But I got Nacho to send the letters in secret. And then you didn't write back, so after a time I gave up.'

Callum's face was miserable. 'I'm sorry.'

'It's OK. It wasn't your fault. I've forgiven you anyway.' Emerald giggled. 'Nacho kissed it better.'

'Emerald!'

'What did you expect?'

Emerald giggled again, and tucked her arm through his. Then she drew him with her until they were under the shelter of the arch of the bridge, where the lovers go.

'Kiss me, please, Cal.'

She held her face up towards him, offering him her lips.

Surprised, he touched his mouth to hers.

He was clumsy, inexpert, nervous at the unexpected request.

'I always wanted to do that. Kiss under the arches.' Gently she stroked his cheek. 'Do you mind?'

'Of course not.' He was confused. He had the feeling he was in the vortex of a whirlpool, that he had no control whatsoever over what was happening to him.

Studiedly, he said: 'What took you so long?'

'To kiss under the arches?'

'Yes.'

'I had to wait for you.'

Callum's face split into a reluctant grin. 'And now?'

'Oh, Cal, so much to catch up with. Kiss me again. Properly this time.'

This time Callum responded, all the longing of the waiting concentrated in that long deep kiss, his body tingling with awakened hope, his mind dizzy, his senses drugged with the scent of her.

She thought of warm bread and honey, rough and sweet on the tongue.

He felt her stir in his arms, pull back to look at him.

She traced the outlines of his remembered face. Boy to man. Man back to boy.

'You haven't changed at all,' she said.

In his mind's eye, at the tips of his fingers, he saw the woman-curves, felt the softness of her.

'You have,' he said.

The words that lovers use are never what they mean. The meaning trickles through fingers like water, and is gone.

A passer-by, casting a furtive glance, seeking to relive young love in those tender looks, in the glowing faces of those lovers under that particular bridge on that particular winter night, would have known what they meant.

She could feel it in his eyes on her, felt the print of his fingers on her skin, felt it at the rosy centre of her body, knew all at once what it would be like when he made love to her. The waiting was so sweet, the anticipation so sharp, that their coming together must surely set the world aflame.

What she said was: 'Tiger eyes. I always loved your tiger eyes.'

'Always?'

'Always.' After a moment: 'We might walk some more.'

What she meant was: Stop me, take me in your arms, love me.

'As you say,' he replied.

But what he meant was: To the ends of the earth, till the world spins on its axis and the heavens fall.

She took him to her favourite places – to the student cafés where Étienne and the others argued.

Among her friends, Emerald was bright, brilliant, beautiful. She wore Callum like a rose in her buttonhole.

'Mon frère-copain,' she called him proudly. And, laughing, she explained: 'We shared our childhood.'

Her friends smiled acceptance, drew him into their conversations.

She realized what it was that she had felt, the meaning of her dreams, her memories. Even making love to Nacho, he had been there.

They drank coffee laced with anis, hot and strong. They talked and laughed. She ordered little glasses of sweet white wine, perfumed with herbs. She would not let him be alone with her. Not yet. She could not bear it to begin, knowing that it would end.

They danced, slow-dancing, cheek-to-cheek to the ballads on the jukebox. Callum held her close, his heart pounding.

What can you expect? What can anyone expect? It's natural in Paris to be young and in love.

'Ce n'est pas rationale, mais c'est l'amour,' said Étienne with a shrug, and returned to making his philosophical point in a long-running argument on the nature of existence.

401

'J'espère bien que c'est l'amour,' muttered Madame Rappaport, summoned at last to give admittance to the young lovers.

Emerald stood close to Callum as they waited for the door to swing wide, holding on to his arm, the wine making both of them light-headed.

'A soft spot for you, Cal,' she whispered.

She enveloped him in her cloak, bright face mischievous, hands busy. She was so close he could feel the warmth of her breath light on his cheek, his senses filled with her.

Aloud she said: 'Madame Rappaport, may I present my cousin? Enfin mon vrai cousin.'

The concierge nodded and smiled. 'We have met before, monsieur and I.'

Callum, his skin alive to Emerald's caress, his face scarlet at the response his body made, nodded solemnly and shook hands with the old woman.

'Enchanté, madame.'

Emerald, seeing Callum's embarrassment, let her fingers stray a little further, keeping him there a moment longer, teasing him, postponing one last time the sweet moment when they might be alone. And all the while she held him close, under the witch's cloak.

58

Paris: 1956

Midnight. Cinderella's hour.

Emerald had made her preparations carefully. All had been left in order.

There were beeswax candles ready to be lit in the old iron candelabra. There was a bottle of champagne set on ice in a cracked Sèvres porcelain vase. Two fluted glasses waited on the table.

The apartment was filled with flowers – Callum's posies and her own. On her way home that evening, she had bought from Monsieur Revel a sheaf of creamy-blossomed tuberoses and a branch of lemon blossom with its fruit. The greengrocer, hoping *la belle demoiselle* was entertaining a lover at last, had thrown in a single spray of white orchids.

Now, alone at last, she led Callum into the darkened room. She lit the candles, filling the room with fragrance, shedding soft light on the blooms.

He held his arms towards her. She kissed her fingertips and put them to his lips.

'Not yet. Soon. Open the champagne. Sit over there, with your back to the door. I want to surprise you.'

She vanished, smiling.

Emerald wanted everything to be perfect.

'Make 'em wait,' Lily's parting advice had been. 'Men love surprises

403

– all those buttons and bows to unpick. However beautiful the gift, the pleasure of the present is in the packaging.'

So, before the old woman had packed off her young protégée to Billy in New York, Lily had laid out a froth of what she called her frills-and-furbelows, making Emerald try on the bodices and soft silks stiffened with rods of hand-split bone. There was a merry-widow – a whaleboned rib-corset in pale dove grey, embroidered with tiny violets, all laced up with crimson velvet ribbons, pulled so tight she could scarcely breath.

'We all had handspan waists then – the men loved that,' said Lily. And then she brought out real silk stockings with garters of Brussels lace; an embroidered slip in palest blue crêpe de Chine, so fine it scarcely veiled her curves.

'I know you won't wear them now, little savage that you are. Call it a present for your trousseau. Some day, when you find your prince, you'll thank me.'

Now Emerald took her time. Knowing that Callum was longing for her, that the moment was approaching, she made herself ready for him.

Finally, her body perfumed and smooth under her fingers, she slipped on the silk and lace next to her skin, laced up the ribbons, slipped on the silk stockings and the feathery slip, chose a shawl, embroidered with green leaves and blossom, thick and rich, to throw round her shoulders.

She came to him softly, where he was, sipping his wine in the armchair by the window. She thought: *How beautiful you are, my love.*

She hesitated then. She was suddenly uncertain, wondering what she could offer that would bind him to her. Whether he wanted her as much as she did him.

She set her hands over his eyes, pressed her breasts against the tender curve of his neck, reached forward, feeling the hardness of him under her hands.

Callum caught and held her. He pulled her down to him, his mouth greedy for her lips. He took the soft stuff which covered her, crumbling it in his hands, feeling her body beneath.

With nimble fingers, he unlaced the ribbons, releasing the beautiful breasts, tracing the curve of the hips and the narrowness of the waist.

Emerald looked down at herself, seeing her body in the mirror of his pleasure.

He lowered his head towards her, his mouth searching for hers, stopping her laughter with his lips.

It was his turn to hold back, to make her wait. He put his hands on her, caressing her, the tips of the nipples, the soft breasts so perfect in his hand, watching her glittering eyes, smoothing the hair until it was a fiery halo round her shining face.

He explored her body, all rosy now with the blood racing under the skin, tracing the central path, the soft valley between her breasts, the belly-button, the line of soft curls between her thighs, the blue-violet pulse under his fingers, slipped his hand between, feeling the nether lips open, melting, ready for him.

She reached for him, fumbling, laughing, buttons tangled in her fingers.

Callum guided her. Then he, too, was naked. Her hands reached out for him.

Her arms were round him, feeling the strength of him in the width of the shoulders, in the long ropes of muscle down his back. Her fingers strayed to the soft skin of his thighs, and there, in the heat and hardness of him, the tangible proof that he found her as beautiful as she found him.

She kissed the soft hair at the edge of his cheekbones, drew her finger down his spine. She licked her finger, tasted the salt sweat, finding it silvery sweet.

His mouth was on her breasts, warm and soft as an apricot.

The sofa creaked, sloped, cascading them laughing to the floor. Naked they clung together, bodies shaking with the joy of it. She pulled the cushions to the floor, spread out the shawl, lay waiting for him. He came towards her, his manhood proud.

'You're beautiful,' she said.

Callum looked down at her, kneeled beside her.

She put out her hand, delicate and light-fingered, felt the velvet tip, the fine rope which ran beneath, the pulse at the base. He shivered, every nerve-end quivering at her touch.

She felt the hard muscles of the stomach, ran her hands down the strong thighs, the curve of his hillwalker's body.

He pulled her close, his chest pressed against her breasts. His tongue touched the tender oyster of her shoulder. His hands caressed her. All her body welcomed him. She was like a blossom opening to the sun.

'Hold me, Callum. Feel me.'

And Callum was lost, drowned in his love for her. On his lips the taste of her – seaweed and surf, milk and honey.

'Sweet love.' His hands on her – his rough hands were gentle. Tracing lips, above, below, he asked unspoken questions – here and here?

She replied, a little shy at first, but certain of what she felt. His body fitted itself to hers, fiery and urgent. Her body's response was melting, cool as the summer snows. Flame and ice together fused as one.

Then, for the first time, Emerald felt in the velvet depths of her

405

that closing and caressing, that clenching and unclenching, the rippling waterfall which left her gasping, spent. Only to begin again, slowly gathering and then spilling down anew, fresh and strong, riding the waves of their passion.

Her limbs twined round him, her body vibrant, triumphant.

He felt her nails dig into his flesh, the arch of her back as she pulled him deep inside her. She felt her inner core melting around him, no longer snow-cool but molten lava erupting in the fiery heavens.

Then at last the whirlpool claimed them. Spinning and surging, the world was lost. The last trump could have sounded, the angels fallen from the sky, and they would have been oblivious.

At that moment, the very last moment, when he could hold back no more, he cried her name. She felt the explosion of his loins, welcomed his seed into her body, knew in that moment that she had claimed her own. She was every woman who had ever been. Since the beginning of the world, it had been the same – paradise lost and found in that single instant of creation.

And then it was over. The tide pulled back, little waves of pleasure lapping.

Emerald had always known there was something more – something which could not be stolen, which was in her gift alone. It was something Jack Sweeney had not been able to wrench from her. Something which, even when she gave her unwanted virginity to Nacho, she had not understood was there.

This was the true flower of love. More than the pleasure she had taken in the careful preparations she had made. More than the luxury she found so sensual. More than anything and everything in all the world. And it was Callum, Callum who had shown her what it was.

For a long while they lay entwined, content.

For Emerald, it was as if Callum belonged there, soft and dormant within her, as if she had always been incomplete, as if by the act of love she was made whole.

To Callum it was as if this was the reason he had been born, as if all his life had been a preparation for this moment, as if all the past and future melted into this coming together. For both of them, it seemed, nothing again would ever be the same.

It seemed to her then, in the aftermath of love, that their bodies were transparent, fragile as glass, so bright and clear she could see the blood pounding in the veins, feel the ropes of sinew binding soft flesh.

'So beautiful,' she whispered.

'Sweet love,' he answered, sleepy.

'Did you always know?'

'That it would be like this? Never.'

She pressed her lips to his. He felt the curve of her smile against his cheek.

'Again?' There was laughter in her voice.

He smiled up at her. 'So greedy.'

'Of course. More. Isn't that what it's meant to be? Like chocolate, or vanilla ice-cream with strawberries?'

She hesitated, suddenly unsure again. Her eyes wide and dark, she cupped his face. 'Callum, do you think I'm a bad girl?'

'Come here, and we'll find out.'

She held back. 'Cal, are we in love?'

'Yes.'

'So it's all right, then – to be greedy?'

For answer, he pulled her to him.

This time it was Callum's turn to dictate the terms of the love-making. He was hungry for her pleasure, knowing what he had given her, knowing it could be more perfect still.

Gently he cupped her soft breasts, feeling the nipples rise to his touch; slowly he traced the curves of her strong firm body, feeling for the response he now knew he could arouse. Drawing out the sweet agony, until he himself could bear it no more and buried himself in the cool ravine of her thighs.

Again and again she cried his name. Again and again her body dissolved, liquid as molten gold around him.

At last it was over.

'Breakfast,' she said.

'At this hour? Where?'

Laughing, she gathered up his clothes, dumped them down beside him.

Together they rose, dressed. Emerald pulled the curtains, letting in the early light of day.

'Lazy-bones. I'm ravenous.'

Callum followed her down the winding stairwell, caught up with her as she reached the street, swung her round, kissed her.

'Now tell me where.'

'A secret! I've saved it just for you.'

Her face lifted to his was bright, mischievous.

'Race you, Cal!'

Then, just as they had when they were children so long ago on Eas Forse, they raced each other through the silent canyons of the city. This

time there were no rocky outcrops to clamber, no rowan trees to skirt –
only the narrow streets and arched bridges of the shuttered city of lovers,
deserted now in the early dawn.

Their companions in the empty streets were those who for one reason
or another burned the midnight oil: sleepless poets; *filles de joie*; those
who had come to the city to make their fortune and those who had lost
the little they had; lovers such as they – all made rendezvous in the cafés
which ringed the ancient market of Les Halles.

The scent from a hundred cooking-pots curled out to greet them.

Here night turned into day – and the day's business was nearly done.
Long before dawn the porters and loaders, merchants and dealers had
unloaded their goods onto the worn cobbles. By dawn it was time to break
their fast.

Onion soup was the restorative: thick and rich, fragrant with wine
and oil, and served with crisp-crusted bread baked in one of the many
boulangeries which set their dough to rise at midnight and were ready to
bake long before dawn.

The young lovers picked their way through the noise and debris, drawn
towards the rich aroma of cooking which curled out from a little corner
shop, its window bricked up with cans of olive oil, stacks of bottled peas,
asparagus, artichokes, scarlet peppers gleaming in glass jars.

Inside the narrow counter was lined waist-high with barrels of salted
anchovies, pickled olives in big metal drums, glistening herrings arranged
in golden cartwheels in wooden barrels.

The air was dusty with the scents of the east, each one distinct. Here
the warmth of cardamom and cumin, ginger and turmeric, pungent cloves
and dusty cinnamon – perfumes as old as time.

There was noise and people. At the back of the shop, a small dining-
space accommodated one long table flanked by benches.

At the table there were workmen in *bleu de travail*, their jaws already
working busily on the steaming plates.

'Vas-y, les mecs,' the barrel-bellied patron greeted the new arrivals
as he came through from the tiny kitchen carrying two more plates and
spoons. 'Bon appétit.'

He dumped a fresh tureen of soup on the scrubbed wooden board and
pushed across the basket of thick-cut corn-coloured bread and a slab of
hard salty cheese with its grater. Next, a carafe of thick dark wine, two
tumblers balanced on the neck, with a bunch of rosy radishes and rough
salt.

They both ate ravenously, tasting with tongues sensitive as a blind
man's fingertips, savouring the sweetness of onion and broth, slick of

oil, slippery caramel threads dripping on to their chins, a soft sponge of soaked bread, sharp salt flavours mingling.

They laughed together, eyes drinking as well as mouths, as the workmen taught them to *faire chabrot*.

'Voilà – ça se fait comme ça.'

A glass of red wine, oak-scented, slopped in the dregs, tipped straight down open throats, the strong wine-rich broth fragrant and heady on empty stomachs.

'Comme ça?' they asked, and drank.

Afterwards, warm and content, they returned towards her quiet room, knowing they would make love again. They threaded through morning streets tangled with busy city-dwellers, with the scents of hot bread, of buttered croissants, the sharp clean perfumes of winter fruit: oranges and clementines, sweet wizened grapes, fresh yellow dates and dried brown figs, fragrant winter melons and pears with their stalks sealed with scarlet wax.

But they were hungry for each other in the bright new light of day.

Back in the room, her cosy rumpled room, she turned to him and held out her arms.

'Sweet love,' she said. 'Again?'

He met her passion with his own. Limbs twined, gentler this time, as if all their empty nights might be filled with the joy of that one night.

Later she said: 'This can never end.'

But it was a question. Lovers never say the words they mean.

He said: 'Never, sweet love. For now and for ever.'

Sweet Callum with his tawny eyes.

O my lord, my love. Hold me and never let me go.

Hearing the silence, Callum held her close, finding in the sweetness of her lips the oblivion he needed, losing in the brightness of her eyes the shadow of his broken promise, knowing that there was a price to be paid for this night of love.

Callum and Emerald. Emerald and Callum. There was ever-and-ever talk. Talk of now and what was yet to come.

As for the past, the monster held his peace, slumbering in his cave.

Midnight had come and gone, and Cinderella danced on, happy in the arms of her prince. It seemed as if nothing now could bring her any harm.

59

London: 1956

The trail of blood started as a line of small glistening blotches which blended almost invisibly into the Turkish rug on the hall floor.

Callum saw it as soon as he walked through the door of the Notting Hill house.

For the month after he had returned to London, Callum rang Emerald each evening. Emerald was working overtime at the Paris salon, and Callum was covering the London collections. Both of them were working too hard to have anything more than brief conversations to catch up with each other's news.

This was not because Callum did not think about her every waking moment. The very reverse: Emerald was so strong a presence in his life that it seemed as if they had never been apart. He was so deeply in love that to him Emerald was life itself.

He had waited for Emerald for twelve years. Those years could not be ignored. He knew that she had made her own life, and he knew that it would take time for her to accept what he longed to offer. He knew of the fears which governed her memories of the past. He had determined that he would wait for her as long as necessary. He just hoped it would not be too long. And when she came to him he would present Anstruther with their decision, and nothing and no-one would keep them apart.

For this reason, he was content to wait in patience, knowing that she would come to trust him as she had when they were children.

One person at least was well aware of the position she occupied in Callum's affections.

Today, as usual, Alison Mackay was the last person on Callum's mind.

If it hadn't been for the interest taken by the neighbour's neutered tabby cat who followed Callum into the house, he might not have noticed the blood until the morning. By then it might have been too late.

The tabby moved delicately down the broadening tick-tack trail, licking the glistening drops, until she came to an expectant halt on the second floor.

Callum threw open the door.

The blood-trail led all the way to the bed, where Alison lay curled in a pile of blankets. Until he saw her there, Callum hadn't realized how stick-thin she had become. For the past few weeks he had left the house before Alison was up and about, and had only been dimly aware of her return in the small hours of each morning.

Today Alison had not left her bed at all. Her eyelids flicked open as he came into the room. From where he stood, he could see that the bedcover and her lower clothing were spattered with a viscous trail of scarlet.

'God, Alison, what happened?'

Alison's voice was a croak. 'Get me the box of pills in the bathroom cupboard. I couldn't make it that far. They're supposed to stop the haemorrhage.'

Callum raced into the bathroom. He found the small white box and fetched a glass of water, watching anxiously while Alison tipped the contents into her hand, poking among the multicoloured sugar-coated pills. She picked out four small blue ones and swallowed them, her throat working painfully with the effort.

Then she lay back again.

'Christ. That's better. It'll take a moment for them to work.'

Callum waited. After a few moments, some colour began to return to the sheet-white skin.

Gently he said: 'Tell me what happened, Alison.'

Alison stared at him. 'What the fuck do you think? I've had a scoop-out. An abortion. No big deal. It happens all the time.'

'Jesus. Who did it?'

'Some backstreet abortionist my boyfriend recommended. Bloody Jack Sweeney. No doubt he got a commission. All men are bastards. Including you, sweetheart.'

'But why were you let out like this?'

Alison shrugged. 'Bad luck. It's all right while the local anaesthetic's still working, but later you can go into birth contractions, and all this stuff starts pouring out. The bastard must have done it with a meat hook. Get the towels and a basin of cold water from the bathroom, will you, Cal? Looks worse than it is. It'll be all right now I've got the pills.'

It took Callum half an hour to clear up the mess.

He dumped the bloodstained sheets and clothes in the bath to soak, shooed the tabby back out of the house, and finally managed to get Alison, the flow stanched and the contractions subsiding, tucked up in clean sheets.

'Thanks, kid.'

Alison sat up, pulling the sheets up to her chin.

'Now all I need's a drink. There's some in the cupboard over there.'

Callum looked at her anxiously. 'You think you should?'

Alison said: 'Bet your life I should.'

Callum hesitated.

Then unhappily he went over to the cupboard. The bottle of vodka was half-hidden in a pile of underwear. It was half empty. He pulled it out, fetched a glass and poured a short measure. He brought it over to the bed.

Alison pulled herself upright and drank greedily. She held out the glass for a refill.

'Thanks. Only medicinal.' She drank again.

Callum watched the colour come back into her cheeks, her eyes brighten.

'Much better. Help yourself. Join the party.'

'No thanks.'

'Don't look so disapproving, Cal. Vodka's good for you. It's a *cheap* idea. It solves all the people-problems. Throws up a barrier. Just like you and your precious camera. No different. What do you expect out of life? A rainbow with a pot of gold? Life's a bitch, that's all. This is *normal.*'

Callum sat down on the bed.

'Why did you do it, Ali?'

'Easy. All you need is money. Or maybe you mean getting pregnant? Easy, too. Maybe the rubber had a hole in it. Maybe I forgot my diaphragm. Maybe I was drunk. As I expect you noticed, it's not the first time – and it won't be the last.'

'For God's sake, Ali—'

'Not God. Jack Sweeney.'

412

Callum stared at her, remembering Jack's visit to Emerald. Jack Sweeney seemed to be the one constant factor in every disaster.

'Look, I'd have helped. Told your parents. Talked to Jack.'

'Fuck off, the lot.' Alison shook her head. 'And that includes you, my sweet innocent. I didn't notice anyone taking precautions at the Beltane fires.'

'But, Ali—'

'Shut up Cal. Think about it. Could have been yours.'

Callum took her hand anxiously. 'Look, Ali, I know how you feel.'

Alison scowled and pulled her hand away.

'That's rich, Cal. Got an attack of conscience? Want to make an honest woman of me?'

She laughed. The liquor had brought a flush to her cheeks.

'Some hope, sweetheart. Anyway, it makes no difference. Life and death – who cares? There's black *nothing* out there. I know. Away it went, flushed down the drain. Whoosh. Nothing to it. This lot's just a little bad luck.'

'You'll feel better in the morning. I'll get Jack over.'

'The hell you will. I never want to see that bastard again in my life. *Ever.*'

'Ali, I'm so sorry—'

'Sorry? What the fuck's sorry?' Alison's voice was shrill with rage. 'You're not going to wreck your life for me, are you, Cal? Well, Jack isn't, either. And I'm not about to wreck mine for some bastard's little bastard. What d'you *expect* me to do? Run back to Mummy? Hello, Daddy, I'm home? Where I come from, good girls don't get knocked up; they get knocked down. To the highest bidder.'

Callum picked up the bottle. Alison watched him, her eyes glittering.

'Leave it there, sonny boy. I'm going to need some more.' She held out her glass again. 'Right now.'

In spite of the vodka and the pills she still felt lousy. Callum. Fucking Callum who had been so good to her. She had had such hopes. Callum who had done everything. Who had taken her in. Everything but fuck her. Unfucking Callum.

'So how was it over there, loverboy? Anyway, what do you care, so long as you get your fucking pictures? Christ, do I know about *that*.'

She had tried. God knew she had tried. Callum. The bastard with his romantic attachment and his look-don't-touch. His precious obsession with a nameless, motherless, fatherless young trollop. Emerald No-name. The bit of fucking *flotsam*.

He had been to Paris. Just like Jack. And when he came back he looked

413

as if he had been screwing the daylights out of her. Maybe they'd both been screwing the daylights out of her.

Alison was beginning to feel better. She pushed her hair out of her eyes.

'Want to take my picture, Cal? Click? Bit of a mind-fuck?'

'Shut up, Alison.'

'No. I mean it. What is it that you feel – really feel – when you've got someone in your sights? When you press the trigger?'

'We've done that scene.' Callum's voice was weary.

'No. Shall I tell you what happens? You think it's so easy. Shall I tell you what price *real* people have to pay?'

Callum's body went cold, willing the voice to stop.

'I'd better get a doctor—'

'No!' Alison's voice rose. 'You know where the money came from? Your precious sweetie-pie. She's the one who paid for this little trick. You can blame her for the mess you so generously cleaned up. Except that it's not her fault – any more than it's mine. It's yours – and Jack Sweeney's – and all the rest of you bastards. Fuck the lot of you.'

'Oh Jesus.'

'I'm a bad girl – what do you expect?' Her face was cunning. 'You want to know why she paid up? Seems Jack got hold of a story about some fellow she's dating.' She giggled suddenly. 'Seems the prospective bridegroom's bent as a corkscrew. But there again, he's got a title – and God knows what all beside. Seems she didn't want the story to get out. Funny that. Swings and roundabouts. Jack took it to that lawyer of yours first, but it backfired, and Jack got the sack.' She giggled. The vodka made everything seem funny. 'Poor Jack, got the sack.'

Callum stared at her. 'What lawyer?'

'You know. Whatever he's called. Anthony Anstruther.'

'How the hell did Jack know about him?'

'Don't ask *me*.' Alison shrugged. 'You know Jack. Magpie Jack. He's got a whole file on your photogenic girlfriend.'

'But why? Why is Jack so interested in Emerald?'

'Has his reasons.' Alison narrowed her eyes slyly. 'Jack's a ferrety little bastard.' She tapped her nose. 'Smelled a rat a long time ago – way back on Eas Forse. Jack's good at saving up little bits of useful information. It pays – even if it isn't always in the currency the bastard expects. Anyway, he got some money out of your girlfriend – just like he promised me he would.'

'What?'

Alison lay back on the pillows, her eyes glittering slits of anger.

'For God's sake, Callum. Join the real world. Fuck me. Fuck her. Fuck anything. And if you can't – fuck off.'

'Oh Christ.' Callum put his head in his hands. Emerald. What if . . . what if she, too? He looked at his watch. Midnight. Too late to ring her now. Surely she would have said something?

Tomorrow. Tomorrow he would confront Anstruther. Tell him that he meant to marry Emerald. Whatever the cost. By the evening, he would have it all arranged.

Tomorrow all would be well.

60

Paris: 1956

The next morning in Paris all was not well at all.

For the past few days, when she got up in the morning, Emerald had been feeling unaccountably queasy. She hadn't told anyone about it. There was no-one to tell. Étienne was studying for his finals and scarcely even came down to the café any more. Dido was still away on Billy's affairs.

Had he not been her lover, she might have told Callum.

Emerald knew with absolute certainty that she loved Callum. She thought of him when she rose in the morning, reached for him in memory as she drifted into sleep at night. She missed him every moment of the day. Yet being in love with him somehow set him apart from the world she made for herself. For the first time since the death of Margaret Mackenzie, her happiness was in another's keeping.

She knew that Callum loved her, too. She knew that at the first hint that she was ready to accept the life he offered her he would run to her side, give her the world. But it would be his world, the world they had once shared, the world of the past as well as of the future. Somehow she knew she was not yet strong enough to claim it.

Soon, she promised him. They would be together soon. And it was true. Every time she heard his beloved voice the dark shadow of the past lifted, her fears faded.

416

And then came this peculiar illness. Emerald was never ill; but for the past week she had scarcely been able to drag herself out of bed in the morning.

So it was Madame Verdun who first noticed that the star mannequin of the Maison Paradis was not herself.

'Are you all right, *ma belle?*'

Her concerned enquiry had produced a sudden inexplicable torrent of tears.

'I'm sorry, madame. I don't know what's happened to me. Every morning I feel so terribly ill.'

Victoire Verdun looked at her shrewdly. 'Have you missed your time of the month?'

'I'm a bit late . . .'

'In that case, I have an idea what's the matter, *ma petite.*'

The two woman looked at each other.

Emerald hesitated. 'It can't be . . .' Then she flushed scarlet. 'Do you think that might be the reason?'

'There's nothing for you to worry about *en ce cas,*' Victoire Verdun nodded briskly. 'It's all perfectly natural. You are just – for the time being – a little emotional.'

'What am I to do?'

'For the moment, nothing.' The Frenchwoman's voice was matter-of-fact. The violet-eyed beauty was by no means the first – and she would certainly not be the last – of the House's young ladies to get herself in such a situation. There was a simple solution. She said: 'When you are six weeks, then we can do something. Attend to the matter.'

Emerald shook her head fiercely. 'If I am . . . what you think I might be . . . there's no question—'

'Ma petite—'

'No!' Emerald shook her head again.

Victoire Verdun sighed. That was what they all said – until the reality of the situation caught up with them. Then good sense prevailed. It was all very well if you were a country girl and you had a mother who could shoulder the burden. But in Paris young ladies were more sophisticated. And Emerald – she had a career. It was a financial matter. There had been an enormous investment by the fashion house in the new campaign to promote Emerald as the Spirit of Paradise.

The Spirit of Paradise could not possibly be pregnant.

'Voyons, ma jolie. Think of the complications. Your duty to your work – responsibility to your friends, to the House of Paradis. You must see that it would be a disaster.'

417

Emerald's eyes widened. 'A disaster?'

'Of course. I have seen it happen. Not many times, because our *demoiselles* are sensible. Modern. Perhaps less innocent than you, *ma belle*. But if you carried it through, naturally it would be a disaster. Ça va sans dire. You could not continue to work. You would lose everything you have worked so hard to build. Your independence. A wonderful career. And for what?'

Emerald said fiercely: 'For a child.'

Victoire Verdun said gently: 'A child needs a father. What of the father?'

The question crashed on her head like an icy wave. What of the father? What if the father was not Callum, but Jack? What if the child which would soon be stirring in her womb was not the product of love but of hate?

What of Callum himself? He knew about Jack. He, like her, would hear that unanswered question. How would he respond to what she had to tell him?

All she knew was that she and Callum loved each other. Of that she was absolutely certain. And yet how could either of them be sure that the child was an expression of that love?

What of the father?

What of the child?

She made up her mind. Only Callum could answer.

Victoire's voice was still ringing in her ears when Emerald took the overnight ferry. It was still echoing as she climbed down onto the platform from the boat-train. It was still foremost in her mind when she caught a cab to the house in Notting Hill.

She would be with Callum before he left for work. Somehow it was not something she could explain on the telephone. It was something they must face together. Emerald and Callum. Callum and Emerald were in love – and fairy-stories always have a happy ending.

'He's not here. Gone to work.'

Emerald stared at the dishevelled young woman who had opened the door of the familiar tall narrow house in the square in Notting Hill.

Callum had said nothing about a lodger.

Emerald said: 'Callum didn't tell me—'

Alison rubbed her eyes. 'I bet he didn't.' She stared at the intruder. 'I'm Alison. Who're you?'

Emerald hesitated. For the first time it occurred to her that perhaps Callum had not told her the truth. Perhaps he did have a girlfriend. This

418

one was certainly pretty enough, even if she did look as if she had just got out of bed.

Emerald hesitated. 'A friend.'

Alison giggled. 'Join the club.'

Emerald smelled the liquor on the young woman's breath.

Alison shook her head. She didn't feel good at all. She had treated herself to a drink as soon as she woke. Several drinks. And a handful of the little blue painkillers, just to make sure.

Emerald said: 'Are you OK?'

'Sure. Why shouldn't I be? None of your damn business.'

She pushed the door to close it.

But Emerald, suddenly angry, thrust the young woman aside. The door swung open again.

Alison shrugged and stepped back. 'Be my guest.'

In the hallway of the house which held her childhood memories, Emerald gazed round. Memory surged. Somehow it looked smaller, the ceilings lower, the stairwell less forbidding than she remembered. Nevertheless it was her home. The home she had once shared with Callum – in which, God willing, she might once again claim shelter.

Emerald said quietly: 'I used to live here.'

Meanwhile Alison had slumped down on a convenient chair. She narrowed her eyes. Suddenly she realized who the young woman was.

'Did you, then? Well, I live here now. He probably didn't tell you about me. Me and Cal – we're like that.' She held up two fingers side by side, rubbing them together. She giggled again. 'See what I mean?'

Emerald stared at her, her heart pounding. 'No. I don't.'

'He wouldn't tell you, would he? Men are such shits.'

Alison giggled again. It was too good an opportunity to miss.

'It's Emerald, isn't it? He's told me all about you.'

Alison jumped up and disappeared into the depths of the house. Emerald could hear the tinkle of the dial and a muffled conversation.

After a few minutes she reappeared.

Alison could see her visitor more clearly now. She swung her arm in an exaggerated gesture of welcome.

'He says make yourself at home. He's on his way. Then we can discuss this like adults. Except I'd much rather discuss it like two-year-olds.'

Alison had had a very good idea. Her limbs suddenly filled with a manic energy, she ran up the stairs.

'Up here. Up here. Come *along*.' Alison's voice floated down the stairwell – urgent, more than a little crazy. 'The nursery's up here.'

419

Bewildered, Emerald followed. Drawn upwards, her senses alert to every familiar shape, the curve of the staircase, the glitter of sunbeams through stained glass, the scent of old lavender and pot-pourri which even now hung from the heavy folds of the curtains, the satin-smooth feel of the banister under fingertips. There was the memory of small fingers reaching up to steady first stumbling steps. Baby memories of the boy who had been Callum, laughing, running up these same stairs to find her on his return from school.

The attic gateway creaked on its hinge. Her heart beating, she moved forward until she stood in the open doorway of her night nursery under the eaves.

Memory flooded back. Unable to help herself, Emerald pressed her own hands to her belly, reassuring the child within.

In a flash, seeing the gesture, Alison understood why her visitor had come. She was surprised at her own cleverness. As always when the vodka got her, she could see things much more clearly. Callum – Jack – they had all betrayed her. And now she had her chance to take revenge. And she knew exactly how to do it.

She reached in her pocket and pulled out a little bottle. She had decanted some of the vodka into a medicine bottle. It made it look so much better. She took a quick nip, just to fortify herself.

'Sorry I couldn't give you more of a welcome. Not myself today,' she said in a conversational voice, taking care not to slur her words. Then she repeated, 'Not myself at all. I've just had an abortion. Takes it out of you.'

Emerald stared at the young woman.

'Oh God, I'm sorry.'

'Sorry? Why should you be sorry? Nothing to it.' She picked up the abandoned golliwog. 'Is there, Golly?'

She glanced slyly at Emerald out of the corner of her eye.

'Have I offended you, sweetie? You ever had it done? No? Thought not. Gather round, children, and pay attention to Aunty Ali. Just in case either of you get yourself in the family way.' She smiled reassuringly at the toy.

'The snotty nurses is the worst of it, isn't it, Golly? As if they had never spread their legs for a man – and, if they didn't, as if they didn't wish they had.' She squeezed the toy, her knuckles white. 'Did I tell how they do it, Golly? They put your legs up in these stirrups – like a mare on heat or whatever they do to animals. Then they leave you there. Just like that. Waiting for the man in the white coat to come in and shove things up you. Then, when he's got a good grip, he wrenches everything inside-out.

Plop. Into a bowl. And then goes home and screws his wife.' She smiled at Emerald, her eyes glittering. 'Interested? I can give you an address. You'd be surprised how easy it is. All in the day's work.'

Alison began to laugh. She sat down suddenly on the floor. She had started to bleed again. A pool of viscous dark liquid began to spread out on the worn brown lino.

Alison looked down. 'Fuck.'

Emerald stared at the spreading stain in dismay. 'Look, can I get a doctor?'

'You already did.'

'What do you mean?'

'The money you gave Jack. That paid for it. That bastard Callum wanted me to have it. But you and me, we outwitted them, didn't we?'

Emerald stared at Alison, a cold wave of fear sweeping over her.

'Surprised? Don't be. What cock-and-bull story'd he spin you, sweetie? What does it matter? You did me a good turn.'

Alison's mood had changed. She no longer felt despair. She felt powerful.

With an expression of deep concentration, Alison dipped her finger in the pool, making a little pattern with the dark red liquid. She did a heart, and then two entwined initials. An A and a C. Then she added another: an E. She felt generous. Why not? The vodka and the pills were beginning to catch up with her properly now.

Emerald stared down at the mess, trying to understand what Alison was telling her.

'What can I do?' Emerald's voice was agonized.

Alison narrowed her eyes shrewdly. 'Nothing. It's done. Don't worry about it. I'll be fine. You'll be fine. We'll all be fine.'

Alison looked up at her rival, pleased at the effect, at the pain in the girl's eyes. Then her attention suddenly switched. She'd seen something she knew was hers.

'What's that on your wrist?'

Emerald glanced down. 'A bracelet—'

'Mine!'

Now she was angry. Alison reached out and yanked at the fragile chain round Emerald's wrist.

Alison held up the trinket and screamed, a high wail of rage and triumph. 'Bitch! Get out!'

Emerald turned and ran back down the stairs, clattering downwards on bare boards. Even in that safe house of her childhood, the monster had come to claim her.

She wrenched open the front door. The winter air rushed in. Her feet pounded on the pavement, escaping what was now the house of her nightmares.

All she knew now was that nothing on earth was going to make her part with what was hers, with the child which was hers alone. Not Alison. Not Victoire Verdun. Not even Callum. Not all the angels in heaven or the devils in hell.

61

London: 1956

Crazy Alison, alone in possession of her kingdom, savoured her triumph. Sweet – oh, so sweet – the triumph of possession.

She had defeated the enemy. She felt absolutely calm, completely in control.

Now she had seen the girl, she hated her.

With urgent fingers Alison tugged the bracelet on to her own wrist. It fitted perfectly, Cinderella's glass slipper. She knew it by the smell of it, the feel of it, the blind touch of it. Crazy how she knew it. Bright jewels whirred like Catherine wheels in her head. She read the inscription on the little cross, laughed aloud.

It was hers, all hers. All of it by right of conquest. Routed. The enemy routed. Who cared for Alison? Not Callum. Not even Jack. She wept. Spinning in the sea of paper, she wept.

High in the nursery grate, she piled the nursery furniture, the desk, the rocking-chair. She would burn the forest, the emblems of her lost hopes. Burn it all.

With clumsy fingers she found matches, struck flame.

She lit the fire. She fed it, thrusting the splintered wood into its greedy maw. The flames uncurled and licked. Ashflakes fluttered like snow, dancing down the stairwell, lying lightly on the Turkish carpet in the hall. The carpet with its tick-tack trail of rust-dark blood.

Downstairs, summoned by Alison's telephone call, Callum stood in the darkened hallway of his house. The door had been ajar, left loosely on the latch.

He had returned in answer to Alison's telephone call.

'Your bloody girlfriend. She's turned up.' By the sound of her voice, Alison had been on the vodka. She had been near-hysterical. All he had been able to gather was that Emerald had arrived on the doorstep, and Alison had taken her in. In her present state, he was fearful of what Alison might say or do.

'I'm on my way.'

'Do that.' Her voice had been low with venom. 'Don't expect to find me here. I'm getting the hell out.'

That very morning, Callum had made an appointment with Anthony Anstruther for the evening, intending to pave the way for the future he meant to share with Emerald. Instead, when Alison had telephoned, he had cancelled his meeting and hurried home.

Now Callum listened quietly, motionless in the hallway. The house seemed deserted. There was a faint smell of smoke and a crackle as of flames consuming dry leaves. He glanced through the open door into the square. There was a fire somewhere – perhaps a bonfire.

Upstairs in the attics, Alison watched the flames flicker upwards. She fed them greedily, her only friends. She was talking to the friendly fire, tending to the needs of the hungry fire.

In her mind she was far away. Alison was happy. She was seventeen again, careless and wild, dancing round the Beltane blaze. Faces floated before her eyes, all haloed in the sparks.

The flames roared up the chimney.

Inside the chimney, cocooned in the smouldering soot, the cylinder of metal, dormant for so many years, expanded gently. Fifteen years it had lain there, the legacy of war – ever since that night of the bombing, the famous night of the Blitz when half of London seemed to be in flames, when St Paul's itself was only saved by a whisker from destruction, that self-same night on which Iona Fergusson had been delivered to her death.

Now, at last, triggered by the rising heat, the allotted time had come.

The bomb, the sleeping beast in the chimney, detonated without warning.

The force of the explosion as the ancient mechanism of the incendiary device was finally cranked into life by the first fire to be lit in the grate since it slid into its soft bed caught Callum full in the back. The blast propelled him, like some cannon-blasted circus clown, through the half-open door and into the small overgrown patch of garden which separated the house from the pavement.

The house, dust-dry and skeletal, went up like a tinderbox, showering debris high over the greenery, blazing splinters spitting and hissing as they landed in the pooled water of the pavement.

The flames, sucked up through the wide stairwell, paused for a moment to lick the melting lead of the stained-glass odalisques, illuminating them briefly and brilliantly from within, and at last made their escape through the windows of the attic nurseries, sprinkling sparks, firefly-bright, towards the sky.

Onlookers craned necks, silent in fear, held spellbound by the unfolding disaster, waiting for the tragedy to claim its victim.

They had not long to wait.

It was the voices which woke him. Sibilant and insidious, the voices tugged and pulled, drawing Callum up through the thick mist of oblivion induced by the painkillers administered in the ambulance.

Callum's mind began to work, slowly groping its way through the darkness. Gradually his senses returned.

Pain was the first sensation. Dimly he was aware that his body hurt. His nostrils filled with an unfamiliar scent, a hospital scent: disinfectant and clean bleached sheets. He opened his eyes, and then shut them again immediately. The light blinded his eyes.

The voices hissed again, ebbing and flowing. He strained to disentangle the disjointed groups of words.

Lucky to be alive, said the voices. *An inferno. Had to tie him to the stretcher to stop him going back into the place.*

Someone groaned nearby. It took Callum a moment to realize the voice was his own.

Footsteps echoed on hard polished floor. The voices were closer now.

'I think he's coming round.'

A single voice pulled at him: a man's voice, the precisely rounded vowels and clipped consonants familiar.

'Callum? Are you awake?'

Anstruther. It was Anthony Anstruther.

Callum kept his lids tight-closed. He struggled to remember.

'Callum?' Again the voice.

Callum fought the light. He turned his head. Even through his tight-shut lids, the light was blinding.

425

Now he remembered something else. Emerald? Where was Emerald?
'Come on, young man. Time to wake up.'
The voice was a woman's. Emerald? No. Not her.
'All right, Mr Fergusson,' the voice continued briskly. 'The hands are bandaged. You were very foolish. But there are no bones broken. A little concussion. We'll soon have as you right as rain.'
Callum remembered now. He remembered a sheet of lightning – blinding, screaming white light and the roar of flames. Then came the thunder. A drum roll of noise beating and crashing against his body, propelling him through the open door, tossing him into the air as if he was no more than a rag doll in a child's fist.
He remembered fighting for breath. Voices ebbing all around him. Just as they did now. Black night had descended. After that he remembered nothing except that something had to be done – someone had to be found.
It came back to him now, and with it the urgency. He sat up abruptly, dizzy with fear.
He gazed wildly around at the faces bending towards him.
'For God's sake!' His head felt as if it would split open like a watermelon. 'Got to find her. She may still be in there! Got to find her!'
'Don't upset yourself, Mr Fergusson.' There was a note almost of panic in the nurse's voice. 'Mr Anstruther?'
'Calm yourself, Callum.' Anstruther's clipped voice again. Quiet, sympathetic.
'I'm afraid there's bad news. Very bad news. We didn't know who it was at first. But then the firemen found this.'
Callum turned his head. Desperately he searched Anstruther's face for the negation of what he already knew could only be.
'Oh God, no.' Callum's voice was hoarse, low, filled with a blind misery of despair.
Anstruther bowed his head. He held out his hand towards the young man. Slowly he spread his fingers.
In Anstruther's opening palm lay the glittering jewel, the bracelet with the emerald cross, the token which had so lately sealed love, and now all too horribly confirmed its death. Gently, almost lovingly, he slipped it into Callum's hand.
Callum stared down, closing his fist on the talisman, as if by so doing he might keep its owner safe.
Then, his body refusing what his mind could not accept, he spiralled back down into oblivion. And all Anstruther's coaxing could not unloose his grip.

*   *   *

Every cloud has a silver lining.

In his rooms in Albany, Anthony Anstruther heaved a sigh of relief.

Emerald was at last safely embarked on the course he had arranged she should follow. With fair weather and a following wind, he felt he might be able to enjoy a well-deserved retirement from the discharge of his responsibilities.

His troubled conscience was his own affair. It was not the first time he had to live with betrayal.

For a moment he felt regret for what might have been. For Anstruther, regret, even pity, was a new feeling. He reflected briefly he must be getting old and sentimental.

Anstruther thought of the arrangements concluded over the last forty-eight hours. Emerald, as always, had been no puppet. In fact he sometimes thought the young woman was rather more in control of her own destiny than those attempting to pull her strings.

As he left the hospital bedside, the one-time courtier, the man who still earned his living telling lies for others, told himself that the lie was justified.

If Callum had been an unsuitable match before – with his proximity to Emerald's past and the danger of people like Jack Sweeney chancing on the connection – he was doubly so now that he had lost the little security he had.

Callum had been left penniless. No insurance company would pay out against an act of war. Unfortunately the sleeping monster in the chimney had been exactly that.

There would be some government compensation, of course, but nothing which might constitute a lifetime's security. It was hardly a substitute for what Tom Sherwood had to offer. Unfortunate about Callum. An alliance which would at best have been extremely risky was now completely out of the question.

He told himself Callum was young. The boy would recover. He intended to throw himself into his career – switch to newspaper reporting.

Anstruther had been able to help there.

'I understand absolutely. Leave it to me.'

Callum, in his innocence, had been grateful for what Anstruther had managed to arrange: an assignment to cover the aftermath of the Hungarian uprising.

'And, Callum, I'll see to the paperwork over the house. Sort out what I can.'

Anstruther felt it was the least he could do.

'Thank you, sir. I mean to take the first plane out.'

Later, when it was all over, Anstruther might be able to convince himself that the means justified the end.

Anstruther would never count himself a gambler. Nor was he – unless you counted the gambles he took with other people's lives. Nevertheless he knew the rules – and the first one was that there is no such thing as a wager without a reckoning.

The first of these was presented that very afternoon. In person. By Jack Sweeney.

It had fallen to Anstruther to identify the body of the young woman who perished in the tragedy. Until Jack turned up on his doorstep for the second time, Anstruther didn't know exactly whose charred and unrecognizable remains had been found in the burned-out wreckage of the Notting Hill house.

Nor, in the nature of things, had he any real interest in discovering who the young woman might be – although, had he known of her relationship with Jack, he might have trodden more warily.

All he knew was that, in spite of what he had led Callum to believe, the body wasn't Emerald's. Emerald was safe and well and on her way to her wedding day. He knew that because he had just concluded the financial arrangements.

Meanwhile nothing must be allowed to interfere with the wedding plans.

Anstruther had learned of the disaster almost immediately. Catriona Sweeney, contacted by the authorities as Callum's next of kin, had been the first to get the news that her foster-son was in hospital – and she had telephoned Anstruther.

The police were anxious to know whose body it was in the attic. Before he visited Callum, Anstruther had volunteered to identify the remains of the unfortunate young woman.

There was no question of foul play; the young man who owned the house had been seen entering only seconds before the tragedy.

Except that it was hardly a body Anstruther was asked to identify. It was an object, the only article of apparel which had not been burned to a cinder: a delicate little piece of jewellery he had last seen on the wrist of a small baby in a lace christening-robe.

Anstruther identified the bracelet as belonging to Emerald, explained to an understanding chief inspector the need for discretion in the light of the delicate nature of the identity of the wearer. He also undertook to clear the matter through official channels.

Had Anstruther not known exactly where Emerald was at that very moment, he would have been forced to conclude, as Callum had, that it had been she who had perished in the flames.

Anstruther had not even been sure that Callum would know that the little trinket was in Emerald's possession at the time of the accident; so, in a way, Anstruther felt that he had been absolved from deliberate deception.

That investigations and dental records later revealed a case of mistaken identity, with the investigators contacting the unfortunate young woman's parents and setting the record straight, was no business of his. It was only a matter of a week or so.

Meanwhile Anstruther had bought the time he needed to ensure Emerald was safely on her way, using his own funds to pay the price Jack Sweeney asked for his co-operation.

'I suppose I have no option but to agree to your price, Mr Sweeney.'

Anstruther exchanged the little metal identity disc for what the foxy-browed ex-reporter described as 'severance pay'. In return he secured Jack Sweeney's agreement to delay registering the disappearance of the young woman who had lately been his lady-friend.

Jack did not seem unduly concerned about the tragedy.

'Only one more thing, sir.'

Jack was smooth, polished, scrupulously polite. Anstruther noticed it was part of his stock-in-trade.

'I mean to make a new start. Abroad.' Even the trace of the Scots accent had been ironed out. 'I've set my heart on America, sir. I had a taste of New York when I was over there to cover the Windsor Ball. You might remember?'

Anstruther remembered.

'I thought perhaps, sir, you might give me some assistance – with my career. I shall need a guarantor. Under the circumstances, do you think you might oblige?'

Anstruther would indeed. And the further away the recipient of the guarantee the better. Meanwhile he paid up in cash, hoping the man might crawl back under the stone from which he had emerged, hoping to God it was the last he had seen of Jack Sweeney.

62

London: 1956

Emerald made up her mind instantly and without hesitation, as soon as she left the house which held her past.

If she hadn't done so, she knew she might not be able to resist the temptation to confront Callum, hoping that somehow, somewhere, the evidence of betrayal might not be what it seemed.

She knew only one thing. The horror in the attic had told her that she wanted the child more than anything in the world. All that mattered was that the baby was allowed to be born – not flushed away into black oblivion. Not even, as she had been, abandoned to the care of strangers.

Her unborn child needed a father. She knew now it could never be Callum. She left herself with no choice. She booked herself into a hotel in Paddington. She made a telephone call. She had to do it immediately, before she changed her mind. Fortunately Tom – unusually for him – was at home.

'Of course, my dear,' Tom's lazy drawl curled round her. 'It suits just as well as ever. But – if it's not indiscreet – what made you change your mind?'

'I'm pregnant, Tom.'

'My sweet, how simply marvellous. Saves so much embarrassment. I'll come and collect you instantly. Just say when and where.'

Tom rang his mother's marriage broker immediately.

'Absolutely no reason to complicate matters by involving the young woman herself,' he agreed with Billy Beaumont. 'Young girls are so emotional over money. Might take it the wrong way.'

It was, after all, a bride-price. It was not as if Emerald was being deprived of anything which was hers of right.

Tom heaved a sigh of relief. The money would come in the nick of time. He had virtually exhausted his credit-lines, which was why he had been obliged to return to Astley Keep. By burying himself in the bosom of the ancestral nightmare at least he gave his bank account a rest. Even his tailor was beginning to make murmurings. Wretchedly inconvenient, tradespersons.

To compound his financial embarrassment, his new fancy had expensive tastes – making up, no doubt, for the deprivations of the public school from which he had only just made his escape.

Tom's pleasure in Emerald's final acceptance of his proposal was exceeded only by his relief that she was to present him with an heir. Otherwise his mother would have been nagging him to do his duty by the young woman.

'Stuff and nonsense, Tom,' his mother had said over his initial objections to the whole idea of producing an heir. 'Look at the Ancient Greeks. Boys for pleasure. Women for procreation. Get on with it. Houses need children.'

'I think you're wonderful,' Tom said as soon as he was admitted to the seedy hotel room where Emerald was busy repacking her small suitcase. 'So wonderful I'm not even going to ask who had the good fortune. Just tell me he's tall, handsome and doesn't gamble.'

Emerald thought of Callum, of his broad shoulders and long-striding legs, of his keen strong-jawed face, his tousled straw-bright hair and his tawny eyes. She thought of his betrayal. Her face darkened.

'Yes,' she said coldly. 'All those things.'

Tom glanced sharply at her face. The violet eyes were hooded, the cheeks flamed with something which was surely anger. For a moment he wondered what had gone wrong. Why she had chosen him over the father.

Whatever the reason, it was not likely to be for material goods or status, or for any of the reasons young women thought him a good catch. Or even, as was not uncommon, the conviction that they and they alone might save him from himself. Tom had long been plagued with the attentions of such females. That in part was why he had agreed to accept Emerald. He only hoped the girl was not looking for more than he could deliver.

Emerald held his gaze steadily. After a moment she said: 'One thing.'

'Ask. For you, anything.' His voice was light.

'That we never discuss the father. Ever.'

'Agreed. Written in stone.'

He looked at her. Her eyes were bright, too bright.

Tom feared weeping women. He had had his share. He had chosen Emerald, made his offer, because she was different. He had been sure she was made of sterner stuff.

His mother would know what to do. It was not Tom's affair. Tom had other affairs.

'Time for the road.'

He picked up her luggage, two cases, one in either hand. Two small suitcases for a lifetime.

'This all?'

'All I have in the world.'

Tom smiled. 'Perfect. Wait till you see the attics at Astley. A thousand years of *stuff*. You can rummage for years. Used to love it in when I was a child.'

Tom hesitated and glanced slyly at Emerald.

'Come and meet young Tobias. I left him in the car. He can't wait to meet you. So I brought him with me.' He laughed – a quick snort. 'Toby's to be my best man.'

Emerald was startled. She had not expected Tom to make things so plain so soon. She followed him down to the hotel's reception. He paid her bill, signing the cheque with a flourish of the single surname.

Tom grinned at her. 'Soon be yours. No doubt you'll take better care of it than I.'

He threw Emerald's luggage into the boot of a gleaming navy-blue Bentley. Several Vuitton bags and a heavy old leather case with the Sherwood crest on it already occupied most of the space.

Waiting for them in the passenger seat was a young man in tight blue jeans and a blue cashmere sweater.

'Emerald, meet Tobias Jones.' Tom glanced sideways at her. 'Toby dabbles in interior decoration.'

Tom settled Emerald into the rear seat. 'You'll have more room. It's a bit of a drive.' Then he swung his lean body behind the wheel and patted his companion's knee. 'All right, Toby?'

Emerald understood exactly what Tom was about. The young man's presence was a clear warning. Tom had begun as he meant to go on.

Now he turned the key in the ignition and the car began to move forward, the engine steady and powerful. Everything Tom did was at the far edge of acceptability. Now he drove fast and dangerously, leaving a trail of white-faced drivers in his wake.

Whatever the consequences for her, Tom was making it abundantly clear that marriage was not going to change his lifestyle.

Tom had never said otherwise. But, like the shell-shocked soldier who does not quite understand that the regiment has retreated, Emerald knew that she had not altogether believed him.

Now, at that moment, and for the first time, she was obliged to contemplate the physical reality of her decision. The two heads in front, one dark, the other fair, were leaning together. Toby was giggling and whispering something in Tom's ear.

'Each to his own, Emerald my dear,' he had said. 'Rest assured I shall not press my attentions on you. Which will no doubt be a relief to you in your present interesting state. It makes everything so much more convenient, a ready-made heir. And after that you, of course, are free to arrange your own affairs. Just be discreet – which of course I'm totally incapable of.'

He had laughed and turned his brilliant blue eyes on her, crinkled the corners of the lazy lids. And Emerald had suddenly wondered, in spite of his words, what he might be like as a lover.

What would Lily have said, had she known that Emerald had such foolish thoughts? That she imagined that she herself, given time, might be the one to change Tom Sherwood?

Lily's warning echoed in her mind. 'Listen, darling, in my dancing days I had more than my share of public schoolboys. It takes all sorts. But if it's a certain sort you can forget it.'

Emerald listened and nodded wisely. But still she didn't really believe Lily – didn't really believe what the old woman said could really be true.

If she couldn't do anything about his preferences, she could certainly do something about his driving.

She leaned forward. 'Tom, go slower. In what you call my interesting state, I think I may be sick.'

'Ladies are never sick; they are indisposed.'

He laughed, but he lightened his foot on the accelerator.

Soon they turned off the main road and began to wind through narrow lanes, their progress delayed by haycarts and herds of cows. The huge car slid past hedgerows starred with wild roses and bramble blossoms, five-bar gates leading on to green pastures gilded with buttercups, fields of ripening corn starred with scarlet poppies.

'Such beautiful country.'

'I hate it. There's nothing so boring as the countryside. Particularly beautiful countryside. It's like innocence – just another word for stupidity.'

Pulling into a lay-by to let a tractor go through, he glanced over his shoulder at Emerald.

'Don't look so worried, sweetie. I'm quite nervous enough for both of us. The old trout says we have to have the estate workers up for champagne and cake – not that there are very many of them – and at least *some* of the neighbours. It'll be fearsome. I loathed gatherings like that when I was young. The County wearing little pursed lips and truly horrible hats.'

He chuckled. 'By the way, you'll be billeted at the big house with the old trout. Toby and I share a gardener's cottage I've had made over. Keeps us out of harm's way, doesn't it, Tobias?'

I'll bet, thought Emerald.

The drive from London to Astley Keep in west Dorset took three and a half hours, much of it through winding lanes.

Emerald, exhausted by the events of the previous forty-eight hours, closed her eyes.

This time she would be safe. However odd the arrangement Tom had offered her, it offered an escape – a name for her unborn child, shelter. It might even be, as he had pointed out, a kind of freedom.

'Face-to-face with your destiny!'

She woke with a start when the heavy car swung between a pair of turreted gatehouses. Tom swung the wheel, attempting to miss the craters in the drive. Almost immediately the pale turrets of the house came into sight, rising above the dark wreath of the surrounding cedar trees.

'Your empire, my dear. A little threadbare, but all yours. My mother is absolutely delighted. She considers herself a temporary custodian of the family acres – can't wait to transfer responsibility. I'm afraid I've been a sad disappointment.'

Emerald gazed up, enthralled. She had never seen anything so tranquil and beautiful in her life.

Tom glanced over at her. 'Rural, peaceful, the symbol of Old England. In other words, a hell-hole. Presided over by a skeleton staff of ancient retainers headed by Mrs Piggot. Salt of the earth – but her cooking has to be tasted to be believed. I don't know how my mother can stand it.'

Tom shuddered. 'Every day, tomato soup, then meat hacked from

434

some unidentifiable quadruped in a thick brown gravy of which only old Piglet knows the secret. Poor old thing's convinced I actually like the stuff.' He screwed up his face in comical distaste. 'A minor consolation – my grandfather laid down an excellent cellar, and my father didn't live long enough to drink it. We'll have a 1905 Montrachet with dinner. And I think I might look out the last bottle of 1882 Tokay. Dessert wines are my weakness.'

The car slid through a pair of tall wrought-iron gates which marked the beginning of the garden – a once-formal arrangement of box-hedges and statuary. The car came to a halt.

Disturbed by the arrival, a young cock pheasant rose from a neglected rosebed, whirring away with a harsh rattle of alarm.

'Beastly things,' said Tom. 'Remind me of my childhood. My grandfather used to raise a thousand brace. I remember the corpses lined up on the terrace, and all the County taking a march past. The men in hairy knickerbockers and the women in those headscarves printed with stirrups and whips. Barbaric. Of course we had to eat the damn things. But not until they were positively rotting. You could smell the game-larder from one end of the stableyard to the other.'

'I used to hunt in the forests in Mexico,' said Emerald. Then she laughed. 'Maybe it was bit different, though. We had knives and catapults. And we hunted wild cats – jaguars – which you could get good money for in the market. And alligator-skins to sell to the Americans. For eating, parrots are the best – the pure white ones. They taste a bit like pheasant, only stringier.'

'I can see you'll educate the neighbours, my sweet. In Dorset, Polly is pretty, but rarely served up roast for luncheon.' Tom swung his legs out of the car. 'Quite in the family tradition. The Sherwoods have a reputation for eccentricity to maintain. You can restock the park. Wild cats and parrots. Suitably exotic.'

He opened Emerald's door with a flourish. 'Welcome to the family nightmare. No doubt my mother will give you the rundown. At least she can see it as entertainment. Comes of being, in a manner of speaking, only a relation by marriage.'

Emerald no longer heard his words, her heart was beating so fiercely.

So this was to be her home. Her home and the home of her unborn child.

It was like a fairy castle, all towers and crenellations.

She gazed up. 'It's amazing. Like a movie set. Wonderful.'

'Good. Glad you think so. 'Fraid you won't find anyone to agree with you. It's the most famous eyesore in the county.'

Tom stood back to consider his family home in the light of Emerald's admiration.

'Architecturally it's very unfashionable. The prettiest part is the stables – they're the only remaining bits of the Elizabethan mansion. The dovecot on the lake – my favourite hideaway – is Georgian. The bit of moat's a Norman improvement, and I remember my grandfather telling me that some of the beams which roof the dairy came from the Saxon hall listed in the Domesday Book. Quintessentially English down to the inadequate heating and rattling plumbing.'

'I'm not going to be discouraged.'

Tom grinned. 'I can see you're hooked already.' He glanced back at the young man. 'Tobias, make yourself scarce. Business before pleasure.'

Tom ran up the wide shallow staircase and ducked under the stone canopy which sheltered the heavy oak front door.

He tugged a polished brass handle by the door, triggering a shrill clatter somewhere in the depths of the house.

Footsteps clicked on polished stone. Mrs Piggot, the cook-housekeeper, plump and comfortable in her black uniform and starched white apron, swung open the heavy oak front door, its glass panels etched with delicate Victorian tracery.

'Your mother's expecting you, Master Tom.'

Mrs Piggot used the half-formal, half-familiar form of address of those who have known their employer since he was still in nappies.

'And this would be your young lady?'

'Of course. What Piglet means, Emerald, is "about time too". She's been longing for me to bring home a wife – nagging me ever since she took me to be measured for my first pair of long trousers. Haven't you, Piglet darling?'

'Now, then, young man. You'll embarrass the young lady.'

Emerald smiled and held out her hand. 'How d'you do, Mrs Piggot?'

The hand which took hers was firm and dry. There was genuine warmth in the smile.

'Delighted to welcome you to Astley, miss. I do hope you'll be happy here.'

Mrs Piggot held open the door. The hall was shadowy and dimly lit. Dark-pigmented ancestral portraits lined the walls, interspersed with sets of antlers and stuffed trophy heads.

'Bloodthirsty lot, my ancestors.' Tom waved a hand at a stuffed brown bear, its outstretched paws draped with an assortment of battered hats, shooting-sticks and leather-patched tweed jackets.

'Your mother's in the writing-room, Master Tom. She said I was to bring you both right in.'

Mrs Piggot walked ahead of them down a wide passage. As Emerald's eyes accustomed themselves to the gloom, she saw the walls were banked with glass cases crammed with more dead creatures. A faint scent of mothballs hung in the air. There were jewel-bright stuffed hummingbirds and pinned butterflies, prowling foxes and stiff-necked herons. A menagerie of glassy-eyed trophies – tiger and wildebeest, mouflon and elk – stared down from the rim of the high ceiling. It was clear the Sherwoods had enjoyed their sport.

Mrs Piggot came to a halt at a door at the far end and knocked firmly.

'Come in, come in.'

The voice was impatient and surprisingly deep.

63

Astley Keep: 1956

Emerald paused for a moment on the threshold.

The room was beautiful. More beautiful even than Molly Anstruther's room in the Yellow House.

But, where Doña Molly had loved to create pools of shadow, this room was filled with light. Shimmering white walls gathered every ray of sunshine. Linen curtains of a delicate bird's-egg blue caught the sunbeams which flooded through tall-paned windows. Underfoot was a creamy carpet scrolled with pink roses and green garlands, its worn threads pale with use.

The illusion of airy impermanence was underlined by the shrouds of heavy white linen which covered each piece of furniture – sofas, chairs and tables, everything but the desk at which Bertha Sherwood continued to shuffle her papers.

It was as if someone had pitched temporary camp in an alien landscape. As if it would take only a flick of a feather duster to return the whole place to its ornate Victorian gloom.

The occupant, a large elderly woman, was almost hidden behind a pile of dusty tomes which loaded a magnificent Louis XV escritoire. Incongruously, the desk was encrusted with ormolu cherubs and painted porcelain plaques and had clearly never been meant to play host to more than the private correspondence of a lady of leisure. Under Bertha

Sherwood's hand, mountains of manuscript rose to right and left, held in place on one side by an ancient microscope, on the other by a pile of specimen-boxes. The whole surface groaned under heavy leather-bound volumes, the inlaid drawers overflowing with more papers.

' 'Morning, Mother.' Tom leaned over the desk to plant a kiss on his mother's cheek.

'Tom.' Bertha Sherwood glanced up over her bifocals, and spotted Emerald at the door.

'Come along in, child. You'll soon get used to the chaos. Emerald, isn't it? Such a pretty name.' She patted her son's hand. 'Off you go, Tom. Go and find Ben – he'll just be finishing the milking, if you can remember where the cowshed is. He was complaining the other day he can't remember when he last saw you down there. I promised him you'd pop in.'

'As you say, Mother. Emerald – leave you in the lion's den. Her bite's worse than her bark.' The door shut behind him.

'Silly boy. Pay no attention. Sit down, my dear. I'm so glad you're here. There's tea and a biscuit, so help yourself. I won't be long. Just have to finish the labels.'

Bertha Sherwood replaced her bifocals on the end of her nose and went back to rummaging in the piles of paper.

Emerald quietly poured herself a cup of tea and took it over to a leather-buttoned window-seat which gave a view of the balustraded terrace and the lake beyond. Surreptitiously, she took the chance to examine her future mother-in-law.

Bertha Sherwood could not have been more different from her son. A strong craggy face devoid of make-up, grey hair twisted into a loose bun at the nape of the neck, a man's shirt, loose and baggy, worn under a shapeless tweed suit, everything indicated that Lady Sherwood, unlike her impeccably groomed son, did not bother overmuch with appearances.

Emerald looked back across to the lake, wondering what the future might hold, whether she had made the right decision.

Bertha's deep voice cut across her thoughts. 'Bit neglected now, I'm afraid, the gardens. The war, of course. No servants, indoor or out.' Her voice trailed off. 'Now, where did I put it?'

Bertha began to poke again in the pile of reference books on the table. Their titles confirmed her chosen field of interest: *The Reproductive Cycle of the Hummingbird Hawk-moth, A Histology of Papillonidae.*

'I lose things all the time. It's cumulative – a hazard of old age. Your memory goes. Cells drop out of commission.'

439

She smiled, strong white teeth stretching the papery skin. The face was benevolent, kindly. Emerald began to relax. She felt peaceful in that white room.

'Well. What do you think of your first glimpse of Astley, my dear?'

Emerald hesitated. 'It's very beautiful. I hadn't expected anything so . . . *flamboyant.*'

Bertha laughed, showing a line of strong teeth. 'Family's always been as mad as hatters. Well, you know my son. Breeding will out. My husband was the only sane one, and he had to go and get himself killed. Nice fellow. Good-looking but a bit dim. What can one expect – with those genes? Just the same, rather endearing. He was Tom's father, of course – the first one's always the husband's. The system's rigged – all that virginity before marriage.'

Emerald was startled, wondering how much Bertha Sherwood knew about her. Bertha pushed a box towards her.

'Turkish Delight? I'm afraid I live on the stuff. My little indulgence. Have one, dear – help yourself. Where was I? Ah, yes, genealogy. You'll gather I'm Jewish, of course. *My* family name was Goldberg, so you can imagine the fuss – *my* side, not his. The English are anti-Semitic naturally, but they've never been averse to marrying a little Jewish money. My family was *furious*. Nearly cut me off without the proverbial shilling. Came round in the end, of course. Snobbery really. The house and all.'

Emerald smiled. She was beginning to like the forthright old woman.

'It's a marvellous place.'

'It's peaceful, at least. Cold, of course. No central heating until I came. But the aristocracy has never believed in comfort. Poor old Vlad – my late husband – loved the place. Knew every nook and corner.'

She glanced round at the white-shrouded room. 'As you can see, I seem to have pitched tent – like my ancestors, no doubt. I'm sorry Tom never seems to have taken to the place. More of a nomad – takes after his mother's side of the family. I hope you'll like the place better than he does. It needs some love and care.'

Bertha paused and looked at Emerald thoughtfully. 'Just to get it clear, I couldn't be more delighted with your news. Tom told me all about it.'

'All about it?' Emerald was startled. Until she had arrived at Astley, she had had very little idea of what to expect from Tom's mother. The enormity of the decision she had taken was only just beginning to dawn on her. Somehow Bertha Sherwood had managed to make it all seem very simple.

'*All* about it.' Bertha's voice was firm.

Emerald hesitated, then she swiftly crossed the room and gave the old woman a hug. The papery skin felt dry and warm against her own, and she could feel the cheek crinkle into a smile. The answering pressure made her eyes fill with tears.

After a moment the old woman gently disengaged herself and put her hand up to Emerald's cheek.

'There now. That's settled. So glad you're here, my dear. The timing's perfect. Mrs Piggot will show you how the place works. I shall shortly be delivering a paper in Stockholm. Mating habits of the cabbage white butterfly. Fascinating stuff, and there's big money it. Commercial agricultural interest and all that. Grants from everywhere.'

She patted her pile of papers. 'I shall be here for the birth, of course. Couldn't possibly miss that – particularly as you won't be able to count on my son. Men are perfectly useless around childbirth. I'll be able to get him as far as signing the register, and then – well, I don't have to explain to you, my dear. We've made up the bed in the Green Room, but you must choose your own when you've settled in. Don't worry, we'll get on famously.'

As she followed the housekeeper up the stairs, Emerald reflected that Tom had told her no more than the truth. The moving spirit behind the marriage was certainly Bertha.

As she gazed round at the faded chintzes and the delicate watercolours painted by long-ago Sherwood ladies, she felt the gentle old house had made her welcome. Almost as if she had come home.

After supper – which was exactly as Tom had described it – Bertha Sherwood returned to her study, leaving the three young people on their own.

Tom stood up. 'Port in the gun-room, my dears. At least there'll be a fire laid. This horrible place never warms up, even in a heatwave.'

The gun-room was a cosy little oak-panelled room, but there were no guns or guncases in evidence. As Mrs Piggot gave her a preliminary tour, Emerald had learned that most of the rooms at Astley were called for functions long since defunct.

The breakfast-room was used as the dining-room, afternoon tea was served in the morning room. And when Mrs Piggot had shown Emerald up to a pink bedroom draped in faded carnation-printed chintz she explained with a smile that it was known as the Green Room in honour of a famous actress who had a brief fling with one of the Sherwood ancestors.

Tom stretched out long bony legs – he had changed into well-washed rusty-brown corduroys and heavy cream-silk shirt under a Fair Isle pullover – and propped his feet, shod in well-polished but battered brogues, up on the leather-upholstered fireguard.

Then he looked across at Emerald.

As women went, he reflected, she would do well enough. She looked at her best without make-up, when she was tired, with the red lights in her hair picked out by the firelight, the transparent lids drooping down over the big violet eyes.

He felt protective towards her.

He said: 'So that's settled, then, my dear. The mother is agreeable; she seems absolutely to have taken to you. Last hope and all that. Can't wait for you to take over. Longing to be a granny.'

All in all, he thought, a satisfactory outcome – two birds as it were, with one stone. The bank had been most co-operative.

'A week from today – eleven o'clock in Wimborne registry. Reception afterwards. Nothing grand, of course. Beer and pork pies for the estate workers. Pimms and sausages on sticks for such of the County as the old trout cares to round up. No sense in champagne and cake, or the word'll get out and we'll have the hounds of the press howling at the gates.'

Emerald watched him quietly. After a moment she nodded.

Tom sighed. 'Good. Anyone you want to invite? Might get Dido to catch the bouquet?'

Emerald shook her head. 'Heaven knows where she is.'

'Anyone else?'

'Absolutely not.'

Tom looked at her startled, the emphasis had been so strong. Whatever and whoever she had left behind, the past was certainly something she did not care to be reminded of.

Emerald shivered. Who else could there be she could possibly want to ask? Her life had been a series of escapes. Even her marriage was an escape. There was no-one and nothing she wanted to bring into her new life. No-one and nothing except the child in her womb.

'That's all right, then.' Tom looked across at Toby, perched gloomily on an upright chair on the far side of the room.

'Cheer up, Toby. Party time.'

'You know I hate that sort of thing.'

'Don't look so irritable; it'll give you lines.'

Tom considered the sulky young man, his head on one side.

'I'll tell you what. We'll give a parallel party. We'll invite all my most delightful, most *unsuitable* friends from London. It'll give the neighbours something to talk about for years.'

'Here?'

'No, silly. The piggery.'

'The piggery?' Emerald asked in surprise.

'Absolutely. Astley's piggery is one of its architectural treasures. Built by the tenth baron – he much preferred pigs to people. You can see exactly why when you look at the portrait of his lady – East Anglian sheep fortune, I think – on the staircase. You can tell who she is from the heavy black moustache and the currant-bun eyes.'

Tom grinned happily, the corners of his eyes crinkling.

'Anyway, the piggery was her husband's contribution to immortality. Three linked hexagonal halls for his fifty breeding sows with a domed hall where they could be brought out for his inspection. Late eighteenth century, of course, when frivolous domestic architecture was fashionable. And my family was always fashionable. My mother thinks my sexual preferences fall into the same category. Toby, what do you think of the plan, dear boy?'

'In the piggery?' Toby's voice was doubtful. 'It's a bit of a ruin.'

'You can do it up. Everyone knows you're marvellous at that sort of thing. Might get you a few commissions.' Tom stood up and ruffled the young man's hair. 'Seven days. Enough for all Creation. I've absolutely no doubt we'll be holding our party in a palace.'

The evening before the wedding, Emerald, left to her own devices after supper and too nervous for sleep, wandered upstairs, drawn into the labyrinth of the old house.

Each evening the two young men joined Bertha and Emerald for supper at the main house. Then the two men retired soon after to their quarters, the gardener's cottage at the end of the walled fruit garden where Tom and his occasional guests stayed whenever he came to Astley.

Bertha rose at dawn, worked in her room all morning, and rested all afternoon. Mrs Piggot, excited at the thought of a new mistress in the house, busied herself with preparations for the wedding breakfast.

During the day Emerald kept out of the way, wandering the woodlands and fields which surrounded the house, poking around in the complex of farm-structures and follies which were the legacy of a thousand years of activity by what Bertha referred to as the building-barons.

Physically the whole place was crumbling.

The stables had been gutted to provide garaging for a division of armoured vehicles which had taken part in the Normandy landings at the end of the war. A pile of rusting oil-cans and spare parts testified to their hurried departure. The roofs of most of the outhouses gaped wide to the sky. A lethal avalanche of the old slate tiles slid into the courtyard each time the wind blew from the north.

The conservatory which adjoined the house – arches of rusting iron, brick floors trenched to accommodate manure from the stables to supply the heating – had lost most of its glass.

Inside the house, in spite of the constant labours of Mrs Piggot and two cleaning women who came up from the village each day, the ceilings were dark with long years of smoking chimneys, the curtains tattered and hanging in shreds, the carpets worn threadbare.

By the end of that first week, Emerald already knew that Astley Keep was sorely in need of love, attention – and money.

As she began to know it better, drawing its old fabric round her like a well-worn cloak, she found tranquillity in the shadowy rooms.

The family bedrooms – including her own and Bertha's – were on the first floor. Although most of them were closed and musty from disuse, they still bore traces of previous occupants.

A threadbare teddy-bear on a window-seat told of someone's childhood – perhaps that of Tom himself. A cupboard full of heavy woollen black garments marked the widowhood of an earlier baroness. Suddenly, painfully she was reminded of the house in Notting Hill.

A wave of loneliness washed over her. She shivered and buried her head in her hands. If only it was Callum who was to be by her side in the morning.

Then her jaw set firm and she tilted her head up.

In all her twenty years, she told herself, she had never, finally, needed anything or anyone.

She had taken her decision. She had turned her back on the past – both the known and the unknown – to take on the mantle of Astley Keep.

But Astley was a house whose very fabric was the past. Where nothing and no-one had ever been discarded. From the portraits, to the book-plates, to the naming of the rooms, it seemed as if the house was swaddled in layers of ancestral debris – as if no occupant of Astley had ever thrown anything away.

The passing of the centuries was stacked in towering cupboards, piled under stairways. Tom was right. Emerald, in losing her own brief past, had inherited the baggage of a thousand years.

She could contribute no quarterings to the coat of arms proudly carved over the lintel. At the brief ceremony tomorrow, she would claim a new name – a reality truly of her own making.

Emerald gazed upwards into the darkness of the stairwell. Then she slipped off her shoes before tiptoeing upstairs. Until tomorrow, when she was mistress of Astley, she felt like a thief. At the top of the stairs was a green-baize door. She pushed it open and walked through, moving quietly through the gloom in stockinged feet.

On either side stretched heavy oak doors, brass-knobbed and hinged. Some of the doors still bore the names of prewar guests written in careful copperplate on crested cards slipped into little brass frames. Here, in faded script, was the roll-call of old England – the bright young things, who, in the sunny days before the gardens of the West had closed, enjoyed Astley's lavish hospitality.

Quietly Emerald pushed open the doors one by one. There were four-poster beds with embroidered hangings. There were polished grates still laid for lighting by early-morning between-stairs maids.

There must have been balls and shooting parties, hunt breakfasts, summer evenings on the lake to amuse Lord Anthony Willoughby-Hoare, Miss Fiona Baggot-Coutts, the Fermor-Hamilton-Curzons – their pedigrees delineated in the hyphens which linked dynasty to dynasty, bankers to landed gentry, merchant fortunes to peers' daughters.

Emerald knew she brought no such baggage, no dowry to be perpetuated in hyphenated splendour. Just as these rooms were now shuttered and dim, empty of life and laughter, Emerald brought no legacy to Astley but the child she carried – and that, it seemed, was dowry enough.

She sat down on a large brass-studded leather trunk which someone had left in the passage. After a moment she wondered what it might contain. The trunk was not locked. The lid swung back on creaking hinges.

Carefully Emerald folded back the oil-cloth lining which enclosed the contents, releasing a dusty breath of lavender and camphor. Inside, neatly folded between layers of rustling tissue, was a rainbow of dresses: yellow crêpe de Chine and purple satin, slithers of silk, a burgundy velvet cloak trimmed with swansdown, beaver collars on brocade jackets, fringed frocks for dancing, beaded capes and gowns trimmed with cobweb lace.

Emerald caught her breath. It was as if Pierrot and Columbine had just abandoned the carnival, leaving behind their bright disguises. She, too, had need of a disguise. Tomorrow she was to play the bride.

Gently she unfolded the beautiful gowns. She knew she had found what she wanted as soon as she lifted it out. It was long-skirted, bias-cut, slender with the broad shoulders and precise tailoring of prewar days. The colour was the exact shade of violet to match her eyes. Swiftly she stripped off her clothes. The dress fitted her to perfection. And with it, to hold back her cloud of dark hair with its russet lights, was a beautiful curved aigrette, a plume of amethyst-dyed feather held in place by a glittering cut-steel clip.

The grandfather clock in the hall below had chimed midnight before she finally curled up in her bed, her wedding dress laid out on the chaise-longue by the window, ready to catch the first rays of morning.

64

Astley Keep: 1956

The wedding party climbed into a single vehicle.

The bride, the curious onlookers noted, wore violet to match her eyes. The groom was impeccable in white. The best man wore daffodil yellow. The groom's mother wore black, absent-mindedly forgetting if she was to attend a wedding or a funeral.

The civil ceremony was brief and unromantic. In record time – witnessed by the new mother-in-law, the giggling Toby who nearly forgot the ring, a pleased Mrs Piggot, and taciturn old Ben Witherspoon – Tom and Emerald found themselves man and wife.

Mrs Piggot had polished up the drawing-room for the occasion, removing the dustsheets which covered the stiff-backed silk-uphostered furniture and spending a whole day on her knees giving a thorough beeswaxing to the floor. Trestle tables had been set out, and the beer-and-pie brigade congregated on one side, the Pimms-and-chipolatas on the other.

Happily Fleet Street had not got wind of the affair – Tom was far too shy of the press to tell his London friends that the party in the piggery was to celebrate his marriage. And Bertha, concerned to keep the wedding as discreet as possible, had not told the few invited neighbours ahead of time that they were to celebrate her son's nuptials.

Naturally the village knew what was up – the two cleaning ladies who

did for the Big House were too excited to keep *that* news to themselves
– but *they* were all sworn to secrecy. The village of Astley was a close
enough community to keep the matter private for the week.

So the party was a low-key affair, and Emerald, towed in her new
mother-in-law's stately wake, smiled and greeted her way round the
guests until her cheek muscles ached with the effort.

Bertha sailed from one group to the other, scattering her new daughter-
in-law like bread on the waters – and, she whispered to Emerald in a quiet
moment, with almost as little hope of return.

Everyone was curious about the mysterious new mistress of Astley.
Later, rumours would fly. But that afternoon the County had been
caught unprepared and unprimed, *far* too well bred to press the beautiful young bride. Even so, the *dress* – so unfashionable, not at all
the thing for the new lady of the manor. Still, there was no doubt it
became her pretty figure, complemented her colouring. And the husbands were all as keen as mustard. There was no doubt the new
neighbour should liven things up a bit.

When the last of the guests had left – scattering invitations to the
young bride to join them for coffee, bridge, anything she cared to name
– Emerald, her head dizzy with new faces and strong Pimms, helped to
clear up the debris.

Tom's party was not due to get under way until after sundown.
The last of the mud-spattered station-wagons and battered land-rovers
pulled out just as the racy little sports cars and smart saloons began
to crunch up the drive. Young men sprayed the sparse gravel onto
the threadbare lawns. A motley crew decanted itself onto the overgrown lawns, squealing greetings.

'Just as well they didn't all come earlier,' said Mrs Piggot disapprovingly
to Emerald as she watched the exquisite young men tumble out of their
vehicles. 'Milk and lemon don't mix.'

Emerald laughed, even though she did not feel much like laughter.

Much later that night she found out just what a curdled mess milk and
lemon made.

The church clock struck midnight. The wedding day was over, and
Emerald was alone with the consequences of her decision.

She had not gone looking for Tom. Instead she went down to the lake
to escape the sound of the music and revelry which floated out on the
breeze from Tom's private party.

The noise lapped and crashed against her window, beating at her temples
and pounding in her head. She knew what the shouts and laughter meant.

448

And what they meant was not for her.

She had only intended to watch the moonrise, keeping company with the wild pigeons which flighted in and out of the slender slits in the graceful dovecot on the island.

The punt bobbed gently on its rope in the boathouse. Emerald climbed in and pulled herself hand-over-hand, no more than twenty yards or so, across the still dark water. Little brown ripples, broken mirrors to the moon, marked the wake of the boat. Trailing her hand in the water as the boat slid into the landing-place, she felt the water silky and cool against her warm skin.

Holding her dress high, she clambered out onto the soft leafmould which carpeted the island. Then she tugged the rope which returned the punt to the shore – hand-over-hand, hand-over-hand, the hemp rough against her palms – until the boat slid back into the dark mouth of the boathouse. With the punt back in its shelter, no-one would know she was there.

At midnight Tom's festivities were just getting under way. Judging by the frescoes in the piggery, it was likely to be a wild night. The previous occupants of the domed extravagance would have been much surprised – even shocked – by the behaviour of their successors.

The place had been transformed into Toby's notion of a Greek bath-house. The wall-paintings were distinctly daring: heroic youths wearing no more than thonged sandals disported themselves in athletic positions against a backdrop of blue Greek sea and crumbling pilasters.

If the accommodation was reckless, the food was even more so. On the strength of Emerald's marriage portion, Tom had revived his moribund charge account at Fortnum & Mason. The food had been selected not for sustenance – absolutely no pork pie for the piggery – but for its aphrodisiac qualities. Pewter plates were piled high with oysters on their own pearly shells, glistening with milky juices. There was succulent pink foie gras studded with nuggets of Tom's favourite truffles. Pyramids of purple grapes and pink-cheeked peaches towered over pitchers of golden wine.

'Sweet wine, so much more *lascivious* than champagne,' Tom said, curling his tongue round a sticky rim.

Swaying, he pushed his way happily through the all-male throng dancing frenetically beneath the new frescoes. It was becoming hard to know where fantasy ended and reality began. But it was fortunate it was a warm spring night. Clothes had been discarded and togas issued as the guests arrived, and some of the celebrants had even disposed of the minimum cover.

449

'Eat, drink and be merry, for today we marry – marry I merry,' he shouted, his voice rising exultant over the din.

As his gaze ranged across the room, he spotted a young man he had had his eye on earlier in the evening. Unfortunately, just as he had established the young man's name and status – only loosely attached to a decorator friend of Toby's – Toby himself had popped up and thrown a tantrum. Tom loathed scenes, so he had simply shrugged and walked away.

Now, two hours later, Toby had conveniently disappeared into one of the converted sties – passion pens, Toby had christened them – with the young man's protector.

Setting his wine down, Tom crossed the floor swiftly towards the boy.

Pip, he said his name was. As Tom approached closer, he knew he had been absolutely right. First impressions are always the best.

The boy was quite delicious: short brown curls and eyes like a new-born calf's – all wet and anxious.

'Come along, little Pipkin,' he said with his mouth to the young man's ear. 'We're going to slip away for a little fun. No-one's going to miss us in this madhouse, and I've something rather delightful to show you.'

Tom put his hand through the youth's arm and drew him out into the darkness.

Pip was flattered by Tom's attentions. He admired older men. Not only did he admire them; he was accustomed to obey them. At eighteen years, older men made him feel secure – and he had plenty of insecurities to haunt him. Quite apart from being a belted baron – or an *unbelted* baron, the boy thought with a suppressed giggle – Tom, with his golden curls, sardonic blue eyes, and lanky muscular body, was the most attractive and confident older man he had ever met.

Pip knew he would do whatever Tom asked of him.

Tom punted his young admirer across the lake to the island with its graceful dovecot.

There was a pulley-rope which linked the punt to the swimming-pontoon. Tom made the punt fast to the rope and led the youth inside the dovecot. The place was warm and dark and smelled of bird-droppings.

Tom's eyes glittered. 'Pipkin. So pink and plump.'

Pip's mouth was dry with excitement.

'OK, squeaker, up you go.' Tom's voice was authoritative.

Pip glanced upwards. A ladder led into the cavernous gloom. The curved beehive roof must be pretty high, Pip guessed, but he obeyed Tom without question. As he climbed he felt giddy. All round him, the birds rustled their wings and shifted on their perches.

At last Tom, who was leading the way, stopped and swung his long legs over a beam.

'Here we are, squeaker. Watch out for the nests.'

Pip crawled along the beam beside Tom, his heart pumping with a mixture of exhilaration and fear. Tom's fingers brushed Pip's cheek.

'Take a swig, squeaker.'

Pip accepted the bottle.

The trouble was, he'd been emulating Tom. Pip was in no condition to remonstrate or even refuse, not that he wanted to. He gulped the sticky liquid down. It was cold and very strong.

'Good, squeaker?'

'Lovely!' The giggles spread uncontrollably all over Pip's body. 'Why d'you call me squeaker?'

Tom told him.

Pip found the explanation overwhelmingly, unbelievably funny. As he finally controlled his high-pitched laughter, he took another swig of the wine.

Tom Sherwood took off his toga.

'You, too, Pipkin. Or you'll get pigeon-shit all over you.'

The ammoniac smell of the birds burned Pip's nostrils. Stray feathers tickled his naked skin as he crouched to offer his buttocks to Tom.

'Too tight?' he said anxiously.

'Tighter.'

Locked and heaving together, Tom and Pip squatted in the rafters. When it was over, Tom said: 'Good squeaker.'

Pip giggled again.

'I'll tell you what,' Tom continued. 'Let's see what it's really like. To be squeakers, I mean. Tie your ankle to mine.'

Even to Tom his own voice sounded strange, hollow and strange and echoing, but he felt good. The liquor had taken hold. It was a fine idea. No-one had ever suggested that before.

Pip stared at Tom. 'Like in the three-legged egg-and-spoon race. Be lovely. Used to egg-and-spoon with my sports master.'

'Use this.' Pip felt a strip of cloth pushed into his hand.

The next idea struck Tom with blinding clarity. It was the most obvious idea in all the world, the greatest single idea since the world began. Squeakers flew. They could fly. When the mood was on him, he could do anything at all.

Why not?

He stood up, pulling Pip with him, and stretched out his arms, one

451

of them tucked across Pip's shoulders. Pip shivered with pleasure. The length of Tom's flanks was warm against his skin.

Tom said: 'Good squeaker. Now fly.'

'Fly?'

'You heard, squeaker.'

Pip gazed into the shining eyes.

He knew he would do anything, anything at all, for Tom.

Tom looked down. It was then, precisely at the moment when the two of them took flight, that he saw the shadowy figure in the corner, lit by a shaft of moonlight.

Bemused, Emerald was gazing upwards.

They looked ridiculous, the pair of them up there in the rafters.

But not as ridiculous as when they took off, three-legged Icarus, plummeted downwards and landed with a soft splat in the four-foot-deep layer of ancient feathers and pigeon droppings below.

The adult pigeons above, disturbed by the intrusion, the rush of air and the displacement of warmth, took wing in a flurry, whiplashing across the darkness on scimitar flight-feathers, the soft down of the disturbed nests drifting down to settle over the beams.

Tom stared up at Emerald.

Her eyes shone in the darkness; he couldn't tell if it was anger or hurt.

Tom hadn't meant to hurt her. He stood up, his lower body covered in a thick layer of sticky debris.

'Sorry about that, Emerald. Meant no harm.'

Pip started squealing hysterically. Tom swung round.

'Bugger off, Pipkin. Up the ladder and throw down the damn togas.'

Pip scrambled back up the ladder. A few moments later, the togas came floating through the air, disturbing the birds once again.

Emerald could think of nothing. Nothing at all. Except that the stench was horrible.

Tom said again: 'Look, Emerald. I'm sorry. What can I say? It wasn't as if I told you lies.'

Emerald shook her head. Her body was cold but her cheeks were flaming. Perhaps some day, tomorrow even, she would find it funny. As funny as Pip had found the story of the squeakers. But now, right deep down, she felt nothing but an icy miserable rage. Rage against Tom for being the way he was. Rage at herself for being so foolish as to think for an instant that she might be able to change him.

She said none of these things. There was no point. No point at all.

All she said was: 'Tom, you smell disgusting.'

452

'Easily solved, my sweet.'

He walked past Emerald and plunged head-first into the lake.

In a moment he had emerged again, shaking himself, drops of water flickering in the shafts of moonlight.

Then, casually, carelessly, he picked up the length of cloth the giggling Pip had retrieved, and knotted it round his waist.

Meanwhile Pip had followed Tom's lead into the lake and was splashing noisily in the shallows. Now he, too, had emerged and was busily rubbing himself with the toga. Then he stood looking from Emerald to Tom, his eyes wide, the pupils dark, a soft, foolish grin on his face.

Tom glanced up. 'Scram, squeaker.' His voice was curt.

Then he turned back to Emerald.

He still could not tell what she was feeling. She was so young, still wet behind the ears.

So he said gently: 'Look, I'll walk you back to the house.'

Emerald shrugged. Above all she felt rage – rage not at Tom, but at her own crass stupidity.

Emerald and Tom walked through the moonlit fields back to the house in silence, the noise of the party floating across the meadows on the night breeze.

Astley itself was dark and silent. Neither of them turned the lights on in the shadowy hall with its regiments of dead beasts lining the walls.

Emerald was numb. She heard the blood pounding in her temples, felt the night-breeze warm on her ice-cold skin. Nacho had said prey-beasts go limp, that they make some drug to kill the pain when the fangs of the predator grip their throat.

Tom followed her up the stairs.

Emerald opened the door of her little chintz-draped bedroom.

She turned to face her bridegroom. No bridegroom at all.

Tom stopped on the threshold. He leaned, long and careless, against the doorframe.

He said: 'Would it be all right if I stayed?'

Emerald looked back at him, her violet eyes huge in the dim light.

A tawny golden cat, a *tigre*, she thought. Careless and brutal. The scene in the dovecot had shown her that.

Or perhaps it was not so. Perhaps Tom Sherwood, no less than she, was a prisoner of his past. But he, unlike Emerald, could not escape.

'Why, Tom? What for?'

Tom stared back at her in silence for a moment. Then he spoke.

'Company. No-one should spend their wedding night alone.'

Emerald turned her back to him.

The moonlight streamed in through looped-back curtains.

She thought: *see the moon through glass.*

In one single movement she took off her beautiful dress, stripped it from her body – the violet crêpe dress she had found with such hope the night before. She wore no underthings but a long sliver of satin petticoat.

She showed her body to him, turning it slowly in the moonlight. *See what you're missing. Look at the beauty you have chosen to disdain.* She ran her hands down the soft round breasts, the slender thighs, the triangle between. Woman-like, sure of her power – astonished he did not respond.

He said: 'I know.'

'Then, why?'

Silence.

'What is there to say?'

She slipped between the sheets. She turned her body away, curled like a dormouse in a nest. She felt his bony muscular body against hers, his arms round her, body curved to fit her own, like that other body she had known and loved, but this time the limp soft sex told its own story.

Breathing slowed. Drunk on the honeyed wine, Tom slept.

For the rest of the night, the long cold night of her wedding, Emerald stared dry-eyed into the velvet darkness.

It was not as if anyone had lied.

Certainly Tom had made no secret of what he had to offer. It was she who had refused to face the truth, the consequences of the contract she had made.

Although the child in her womb betrayed itself by no more than a slight thickening of the narrow waist, an almost imperceptible swelling of the breasts, she was aware of the changes in her body. Aware that there was no going back.

After tonight the die had been cast.

As the dawn crept through the drawn curtains she heard Tom quietly rise and leave her bed. Suddenly, bitterly, she knew she had exchanged substance for shadow. From now on she had only her dreams. It would be Callum who was in her mind in the long nights while her belly grew. In spite of his betrayal, he would be there. It would be his imagined hand, not the reality, she felt on the swelling curve of the child, just as on the night of her wedding she had only had the ghost of a bridegroom. In spite of everything, whatever the truth of what he had done, of what Alison had told her, it would always be Callum's laughter, the feel of his strong arms around her, which would haunt her.

Emerald slipped her hand between her thighs for comfort, like a baby sucking its thumb, rubbing gently until her body responded to memory – until she had, if only in her dreams, held the father of her child once again in her arms.

65

———◆◆◆◆———

Astley Keep: 1956

The groom and best man left Astley the morning after the ceremony for the tables at Monte Carlo.

'Well, that's the end of him for the moment.' Bertha patted Emerald's hand sympathetically. She knew well enough the meaning of the black rings under her new daughter-in-law's eyes.

'It's just as well, my dear. Men are no good around babies. We're much better off without them. You're home now. Go wherever you please and get up to whatever you like. Don't pay any attention to me.'

Bertha, with her absent-minded kindness and her keen mind, knew instinctively that her daughter-in-law, like a wild animal, needed to turn in her leaves, make her own space.

So Emerald settled down. There was no help for it. Her mind tranquillized by pregnancy, she drew the fabric of the old house round her like a cloak, feeling the security in its ancient folds.

Above all now, with the changes her body was undergoing, Emerald needed to feel safe. Christmas came and went, and the days began to lengthen into spring.

The bedroom Emerald chose for herself was in a round turret up a circular stair, womb-like and comforting. She collected pieces of furniture from around the house. An old armchair upholstered in purple silk was rescued from a back bedroom. She brought down a little round table with carved legs from the attic, and found a mirror framed with seashells at the back of a cupboard. Most exciting of all, she came across a blanket-box in which lay folded a delicate blue-and-gold patchwork bedcover made of tiny hexagonals of flowered cambric which looked as if they had come from a Regency beauty's summer wardrobe.

Meanwhile Mrs Piggot spruced up a nursery for the baby, polishing up the family's steel-and-brass cradle, lining it with quilted cotton and a little down-and-feather mattress. Then she set to work knitting and stitching a tiny layette, dragooning the two daily cleaning women into crocheting shawls and bootees, sewing tiny vests and nighties in the finest lawn and softest wool.

Emerald spent most of her time in the garden, the burgeoning spring echoing her own swelling belly. The walled gardens were a tangle of weeds, blazing blossom and overgrown plants. And the whole place, filled with the hum of bees and the shimmering wings of dragonflies, smelled of fecundity, of damp earth and young shoots.

Only one part of the garden was still under cultivation. Bertha had kept the two huge greenhouses in production, filling them with the exotic plants she needed to provide food and nectar for the insects she bred for her research. Oleander and passionflower, valerian and sedum – the plants spilled out all over the house as well. Flowerpots overflowing with what looked to Emerald like unruly hanks of weeds lined every window-sill.

That was the extent of old Ben's capacities; he had plenty else to do around the land and farm. The once-productive vegetable gardens had reverted to an overgrown jungle of weeds, topiaried box hedges long since sprouted into full-sized trees. As the spring wore into summer, the beds became a wild tangle of rose-bay willowherb, drifts of forget-me-nots and towering stands of nettles. Apricot and peach, pear and apple trees threaded with tea-roses sprawled unpruned against the warm red brick of the boundary walls.

But it was the herb garden, its herringbone-patterned paths still starred with clumps of flowering thyme, which gave Emerald most pleasure – providing her with the raw materials for the herbal remedies whose preparation and application she had learned in her girlhood.

Armed with a copy of Culpeper's *Herbal* picked out from among the dusty leather-bound copies of Pepys and Thackeray in the library, Emerald found she could identify an astonishing pharmacology of medicinal herbs and aromatics.

'Ah, yes, the herb garden,' said her mother-in-law, briefly returned from one of her conferences. 'Good, isn't it? I used to keep it up while we still had gardeners. It was Cuthbert, the plant-collecting baron, who laid out the knot garden – seventeen fifties, I think it was. Remarkable collection. Glad you're taking an interest. I had a man down from Kew. There's a list somewhere.'

Emerald established herself in a tumbledown summerhouse in a corner of the walled garden, gathering and sorting aromatic plants and petals to make pot-pourri. Searching her memory, she selected leaves – lovage and dill, fat hen and mallow, burnet and sweet cicely – for Mrs Piggot to add to the salad-bowl.

'I'm sure I don't know what all that stuff is,' Mrs Piggot would complain to Annie Wilson, her friend in the village post office. Mrs Piggot was blessed with the true countrywoman's deep distrust of the unknown. 'Marigold petals we had the other day. Tasted most peculiar.'

Preoccupied by the changes in her body, Emerald gathered camomile, lavender and rosemary to scatter in her bath, made herself soothing teas of lemon balm and water-mint, harvested rosehips as they ripened from green to blazing scarlet to make syrup for the baby now stirring in her womb.

But mostly she sat, tranquil and content, in the summerhouse, feeling the sun on her face and the baby kicking in her belly.

Of Tom there was no sign, and Emerald had ceased to fret over him. Even Callum only haunted her in her dreams.

Somehow the eccentric old woman who was her mother-in-law and the kindly care of the housekeeper were enough.

Bertha, seeing her daughter-in-law's contentment, decided to wait until the child was born before she turned over Astley's affairs. That they were in a dreadful state there could be no doubt. She herself had let things drift too long.

Heaven knows, she thought, Emerald deserved some kind of honeymoon.

The first birth-pain came just before dawn.

In the bed in her turret room, Emerald lay curled up round her swollen belly.

Sleepless with anticipation, she felt the sudden involuntary tightening of the womb muscles, almost imperceptible at first, which told her that the baby was ready to be born.

The huge house was quiet, apart from the tiny creakings and flittings which Emerald knew were as much a part of its fabric as the extravagant turrets and hidden cubby-holes.

Tom's visits to the house had become fewer and shorter as the months wore on. Emerald had known from the start he'd never liked Astley. It seemed that whatever lingering responsibilities he'd felt towards the place had been discharged by his marriage.

Occasionally, particularly during the long dark winter evenings, Emerald felt a twinge of regret that he didn't come home more often. His presence would have given his mother pleasure, and Emerald herself would have enjoyed his flamboyant company, his laughter and his cynicism and his gossip. It didn't happen.

When she thought about it, Emerald knew it didn't matter.

Tom had long ago chosen his own path. Bertha had her moths, her microscopes, and her scientific papers to write.

Emerald would soon have her child.

The long months of pregnancy had passed as slowly as such times are bound to do. Emerald swelled like a ripe peach.

The local midwife – a cheerful round-cheeked Irishwoman – included Astley in her round of visits to the expectant mothers in her practice. Every month, as regular as clockwork, she would chug up the drive in her battered Morris van for the routine examination.

In the final month, the midwife's visits increased to weekly intervals. Only three days earlier, she had laid her hand on the bulge, expertly feeling the outline of the limbs, the positioning of the head, and delivered her verdict.

'There now, my duck. Not long now.'

Mrs Piggot had burst into frantic activity at the news, whisking her dusters into every corner of the old house, polishing and sweeping in preparation for the new arrival.

Emerald took long walks through the abandoned park, filling the house with the sweet scents of rose petals and jasmine, dried and piled in pitchers set out in all the rooms. She made clove-stuck pomanders, stuffed soft lawn pillowslips with hop-blossoms, camomile and catmint.

The house smelled of clean linen and hot starch.

The night the contractions started, Bertha Sherwood arrived back at Astley. She had returned without warning, commandeering the only two taxis to carry herself and her luggage from the station. For a moment, listening to the heavy cars grinding up the drive, Emerald had thought it might have been Tom.

She was infinitely happier to see Bertha.

'Am I too late?' Bertha said as she hurried into the hall.

Emerald, leaning her heavy belly over the stairwell, laughed.

'It's me that's late.'

'Good. Something in my bones, my dear. I had a feeling you might be needing me.'

The two women had taken to spending their evenings together whenever the old lady was around. They usually chose the little second-floor sitting-room which had become Emerald's refuge against the draughts of the cavernous halls.

That night Bertha sat up late with her daughter-in-law, listening to Emerald running over the events of the previous few days. She was pleased to note that already her daughter-in-law was beginning to take an interest in the estate.

Two of the cows were in calf. The ewes would be early with the lambing. Another pane of glass had gone in the greenhouses.

'Perhaps I'll just go on swelling up for ever.'

'Soon. Babies thrive in the spring.'

'Like lambs.'

'Birth should be seasonal. Only humans breed out of season. Curious that our species is the only one which fucks when the females aren't ovulating.'

Emerald laughed. She was used to her mother-in-law's objective views and forthright vocabulary. The rough words had a practical take-it-or-leave-it sanity.

'Breeding . . .' Bertha went on thoughtfully. 'I always wondered about Tom's choice of love-object. Probably my fault – if such a thing can be fault. There's plenty of homosexuality in animals. It's always supposed to be abnormal, but I'm not so sure. Perhaps it's a necessary bonding – young males in packs need to have a reason not to kill each other. We humans think about sex all the time. Pretend we don't, but of course it's there rumbling away. First priority is a full belly – and, after that, procreation. And if it's not convenient – well, whatever comes to hand.'

Bertha went across to the window and drew the heavy curtains.

'When the mind takes over – what we like to call romantic love – it's much less predictable than the body. And once that happens . . . The Sherwoods have always been wilful. Romantic. Which reminds me: a collaborator of mine in Australia has come up with a nice bit of research on the sex-hormones of the flea. Limited, but useful.'

Bertha pulled out a lined pad and began to make notes.

Emerald watched her mother-in-law at work. She used fine-nibbed pens and lined paper with a shiny surface so that the ink went on more smoothly. She maintained that the physical act of writing helped her to think.

Emerald loved to listen to the rhythmic scrape of pen on paper.

For an hour, Emerald sat watching Bertha work. Then she stood up and stretched.

'You make me feel ashamed of myself. I've never been so idle. Pregnancy seems to be a full-time non-activity.'

'You look wonderfully well, my dear.' Bertha set her work aside and examined her daughter-in-law over her half-moon spectacles.

Pregnancy did indeed suit Emerald. Her face was glowing with health, her eyes sparkled and her dark hair shone, the russet lights gleaming golden in the firelight.

Bertha smiled. She enjoyed beauty – wherever she found it. Emerald looked like one of the ancient Greek fertility goddesses with her full belly and madonna-like tranquillity. Even the clothes underlined her quiet contentment. She had worn loose flowing white garments throughout her pregnancy, searching through Astley's cupboards until she found a boxful of soft voluminous Victorian men's cotton shirts which would accommodate her swelling girth. These she wore over woolly leggings or long skirts, refusing to wear the ugly maternity garments which were all that were available in the shops.

Emerald sighed and stretched. 'I wish it was over.'

'It'll come soon. I couldn't do anything when I was carrying Tom. It was the sheer *inconvenience* of it. And afterwards such an interruption to one's day. I remember handing the poor boy over to Mrs Piggot and telling her to feed him – quite forgetting he was at the breast at the time.'

Emerald laughed. 'Sounds just like you.' There was real affection in her voice. 'What shall we call it – her – him?'

Bertha wrinkled her strong-boned face. 'There are the usual Sherwood names. James. Cuthbert perhaps. Thomas might cause confusion.'

'What if it's a girl?' Emerald stretched. 'Funny, but I hadn't thought that might matter. But of course it does. With Astley and all.'

'Doesn't matter a bit, dear child. In this family the firstborn is the heir. Unusual, of course; but the Sherwood title is one of the few which can pass to a woman. James I handed out the barony; he had a bastard by one of the Sherwood daughters – Charlotte, I think, was her name. Anyway, James was a Scot; north of the Border he was James VI. He at least had the good sense to apply Scottish rules to the fruits of his own dalliance. It's only the Anglo-Saxons who are obsessed with the male. Absurd. The Jews are so much more practical: we take our genetic inheritance from the mother. It saves so much unseemly argument. What do you think to James? Reliable. Something tells me it'll be a boy.'

Emerald looked down at her belly and smoothed the curve.

'Hello, young James. Whatever you are, you've been kicking all day.'

'I'm not surprised. They were a pretty irresponsible lot, the Stuarts. Careless with their seed. Ploughed the fields and scattered.'

Emerald laughed. 'Jamie. Ploughman Jamie. I like that.'

'Good. That's settled, then. Pity it's not a girl. Women are so much easier to live with.'

Bertha leaned back in the chair and coiled a stray wisp of hair back into the thick bun at her neck. She looked over at the young woman stretched out on the chaise-longue, her arm wedged behind her back to support the weight of her unborn child.

Bertha appreciated her daughter-in-law. Emerald was certainly much more of a woman than her wastrel offspring Tom deserved. Maybe a little wild, but that was all to the good. And who wouldn't be, with that upbringing? In any event, Bertha herself had given the County plenty to gossip over when she had first arrived as a young bride and filled the Victorian stillrooms with her test-tubes. The County had surely grown used to the eccentric Sherwoods by now.

When the new young mistress found her feet – and it would not take her long once the child was born – it would be in the way Emerald herself had chosen. And the County would just have to get used to her.

'You've done well, my dear.'

Emerald looked up, her eyes suddenly filled with tears. The absent-minded old woman, brilliant and eccentric as she was, had been kind to her, truly gentle and concerned.

'I'm afraid I'm not feeling very brave, Mother-in-law.'

'None of us is brave. We do what we have to.'

'Hybrid vigour?'

'The best.'

Emerald laughed, and then caught her breath. The child had turned in the womb – a short stab of pain under the rib.

'I think – I think – I'd better get to my room.'

66

Astley Keep: 1957

Bertha did not leave her daughter-in-law's side for an instant throughout the night.

'Wouldn't miss it for the world. It's so sexy, giving birth to a child. I really regretted I only did it once. It's not surprising, considering all the organs are in full production.'

Emerald could feel her body opening, and Bertha's hands were knowing and gentle as they kneaded and moulded the heaving bulge.

'That's right, my darling. No different for humans than for cows or cats. Our ancestors thought nothing of it; the wise woman was there if you needed her.'

'Like you, Mother-in-law?'

'Maybe. It all went wrong when the men took over. I'd have been burned as a witch long since.'

As the night wore on the contractions began to come fast and hard and at quickly decreasing intervals. To her surprise, Emerald found that Bertha was right: the body did indeed respond to the child.

'I think it's time for the midwife.'

As the sun came up, casting long beams of light on the bed, Emerald heard the familiar sound of the little van throwing up gravel in the drive. A few moments later the midwife's voice echoed up the stairs. 'On our way? Good girl.' Her voice was brisk and confident, her examination swift and expert. 'Just as well I cut short my beauty sleep. We're nearly there.'

'Breathe in, my darling, breathe in.' Bertha's voice, and her hands. 'Two fingers. Three, maybe.'

To Emerald, the voices were distant, triple-echoed, instructions half-heard through a mist.

'Push down, my darling. Here it comes. And another.'

Emerald, frantic now with the pain of it, bore down.

'Easy now. See the head?'

Emerald thought: Is this how it has to be? The sheer weight of the pressure on bone, split to cracking-point, the transparent elasticity of flesh and cartilage stretched to breaking. Down a dark tunnel, pressing down as if there were no limitations imposed by gravity, no centre to the earth.

'There we are, my sweetheart. Take it slow. Push again.'

On and on to eternity, again and again the irresistible unimaginable weight of muscle and limb forced into the narrow bowl of her hips, through yielding bone and taut-stretched flesh.

'Easy, my sweet.'

A thin wail split the air.

And then, all at once, it was over. Sucked down and spewed out down the vortex, there was a newborn creature.

'Will you credit it now? A beautiful boy!'

The midwife's voice was triumphant. She scooped black mucous from the mouth, quick and sure, slapped, held the baby up for admiration, swiftly tied and severed the umbilical rope, showed him to his mother for approval.

Emerald looked. First in terror, and then in wonder.

A promissory note of a person. All unfinished, with the soft pulse beating just under the skin. Like every newborn creature, the head too large, the limbs too limp, the bones too soft. Too vulnerable, too delicate, too impossibly fragile to have made that fierce journey.

Emerald held out her arms.

'There you are, now. Such a handsome fellow already.'

The baby's mole-blind eyes blinked unseeing. Starfish fingers snatched anxiously at invisible spider's webs. Tiny Chinese-doll-woman feet, curved like spoons, ending in miniature kitten-pad toes tipped with silvery fish-scale nails.

'Is he . . . ?' Ridiculously, Emerald asked the question all mothers ask.

The midwife laughed. 'Sure and he's perfect.'

Most miraculous of all – two eyes, two ears, ten fingers, ten toes. The child's sex evident. Nature does not equivocate on gender in a newborn child.

The midwife was busy, bustling.

'Come, now. He'll catch his death.'

She was swift and confident as she washed and patted and wrapped.

'Here you are, my duck. All clean and new.'

Emerald gazed down at her son. My love, my sweet. So inadequate for such overwhelming feelings, the words of love. We use the same language to our lovers as we use to our children.

Then Bertha took the child and cradled him in her arms. Talked softly, caressed, took him away to show to Mrs Piggot, called in old Ben for admiration.

Later, Emerald and Jamie, mother and son, suckled and slept.

Emerald woke again to watch the child, so perfect, cocooned in his cradle, lying like a crumpled flower among the old lace and embroidered lawn.

Child of my heart, my newborn butterfly.

For the week which followed the birth at Astley Keep in the bedroom which overlooked the lake, Emerald and Jamie woke and ate and slept again, unaware of anything except each other.

Two weeks later, Tom put in a brief appearance for the christening, bringing an exultant Dido to stand godmother. Dido was full of her own news: her elderly Pittsburgh millionaire had at last proposed to her.

'His fifth, darling. Isn't it thrilling? Billy's as pleased as Punch. He's to be best man.' Dido laughed as she tucked a coral rattle decorated with silver bells into the baby's cradle.

Tom unpacked an extravagant froth of tiny lace-trimmed garments from the White House in Bond Street to acknowledge the new arrival.

'I was certain it must be a girl,' he said, ruefully holding up a rosebud-embroidered petticoat. 'I don't know how I shall get on with a son.'

Emerald, absorbed in her newborn child, scarcely even noticed the arrival and departure of her husband and her best friend.

After that, Dido would make occasional transatlantic telephone calls retailing the high spots of life in Pittsburgh, and Tom's contact with her – and, indeed, with his mother – dwindled to the occasional communication from the grand hotels on the Riviera, and then only to issue instructions for the transference of funds from the estate's account to his own.

After the first three months, during which the four-hourly feeds necessary to satisfy the baby's voracious appetite had kept her permanently at the beck and call of her little son, Emerald had turned over some of the full-time chores of motherhood to Mrs Piggot. The housekeeper doted on the contented baby.

With time on her hands again, Emerald began to turn her attention to a new interest – preparing simple goods for sale in the village shop. Soon her pot-pourris and perfumed candles, herb bath-sachets and flower-perfumed soaps made to recipes in Astley's household books found an outlet in the local market town.

In the long summer evenings, after she had given her son his bath, she would sit on the window-seat in her sitting-room with the baby on her lap, feeling the growing strength in the young limbs, enjoying the delighted surprise with which he greeted each new experience.

The tall window had a view of the little artificial lake, its shores fringed with willow and elm, providing a stopping-off point for migrating skeins of geese and ducks.

Together they would watch the birds take off and land, wings flashing crimson and gold in the slow sunset, while Jamie waved pudgy fingers and tried out his new repertoire of nonsense noises.

To Emerald, Jamie was pure joy. The child grew like a weed. Every day, it seemed, he learned a new small skill. He was curious about everything. Every blossom, every scent, every moving creature which crossed his path received his rapt attention.

Each day Emerald saw the father in the son. The baby-hair – rubbed bald at the back of the egg-delicate skull when the baby turned in his cradle – soon turned a tawny gold. The shining eyes remained the deep violet of Emerald's own. But Jamie's firm little chin looked as if it must be his father's legacy, and his rapidly lengthening limbs promised his father's height.

Her worries that the child might be Jack Sweeney's swiftly evaporated. There was no longer any doubt in her mind that Callum was Jamie's father. There was nothing of Jack in the clear-eyed, vigorous little boy she held in her arms each day.

Emerald's life took on a new contentment – an invigorating happiness which Bertha noted with pleasure. Emerald's new-found energies must be turned to good account. It was time her daughter-in-law took over the reins of the estate.

Astley might have provided Emerald with sanctuary, but there was no doubt the need was mutual. And it would need all of Emerald's formidable willpower if the estate was not to crumble into the stones from which it sprang.

Bertha had served her time as mistress of the manor. She was quite confident that her new daughter-in-law would be the making of Astley Keep. And just as confident that Astley would be the making of Emerald.

*   *   *

The making of Jack Sweeney was New York. New York was Jack's town. Jack was a swell – top of the heap in the most exciting city in the world. Jack had power. He had respect. He was feared for the acid pen he wielded through his column in the city's most popular scandal-sheet.

' 'Morning, Luther. How's the family?'

Luther was the doorman of Jack's apartment block. Jack prided himself on retaining the common touch. Bouncers and doormen – particularly the tough back-street mafia who, like Luther himself, came from Harlem – were often the key to his work. He provided Jack with a great deal of inside knowledge on which celebrities were walking out – and in – with whom. And which ones were not averse to illegal substances to improve their performances, both in and out of the public eye.

'Well enough, sah. Thank you, sah.'

Luther's 'family' was the brotherhood of bodyguards and doorkeepers who supplied the raw material for Jack's column. The doorman pocketed the small roll of greenbacks which were the price of his co-operation, and swung open the heavy plate-glass door.

'Excellent. Good work, Luther.'

'Fine day, sah. Cab?'

'No, thanks. Think I'll walk.'

He swung down Fifth Avenue, his pork-pie hat at a jaunty angle, his wallet making a comfortable bulge in the breast pocket of his Brookes Brothers suit.

Jack had the good sense to write about what he knew. He specialized in the newly emergent Euro-groupies who were earning themselves a reputation as the wildest of the wild – and whose frequent misuse of defunct titles and mythical soon-to-be-inherited fortunes earned them the entrée to New York's glittering salons. The nightclubs were full of them.

It was Jack who first christened this glittering gypsy-mob. He made his name with an article titled 'Meet the Euro-trash', widely syndicated all over America, in which he listed and gave brief knife-sharp biographies of the high-swingers. Euro-trash was the 'in' word, and Jack was its begetter.

The attention earned him his own column, 'Jack's Trash', which was syndicated across the country. The readers of *The Whisper*, New York's popular weekly all-colour all-star all-truth magazine, trusted Jack to bring them all the dirt, hot from the heap. It was Jack who overheard what Mamie said to Queen Liz when they met in the White House rose garden. Jack who was the fly on the wall when Larry bawled out Marilyn on the set of *The Prince and the Showgirl.*

467

Meanwhile, not even Anstruther's long arm could reach right across the Atlantic, and he made sure his readers were regularly treated to little reminders of the doings of the beautiful Emerald and her wastrel playboy husband.

Once Jack had seen the announcement of the child's birth in *The Times*, he had drawn his own conclusions. He knew enough about Tom Sherwood to dismiss him as the father. Emerald's child, Jack believed, could only be the result of his own encounter with Emerald. Truth blurred into fiction. He had long since convinced himself it was love and not hate which had joined them.

His own son. Whatever the circumstances of the conception, it was a triumph – Jack's triumph. Looking back on it, the night in Paris had probably been the best thing that had ever happened to him. And as for Emerald – well, she had taken a sensible decision. For herself, and for his son.

Sometimes he thought of his knowledge as his insurance policy – the story which would win him immortality, maybe even the Pulitzer Prize.

It would be quite a scoop. And he was no longer an observer; he was an insider, right at the heart of it. He and he alone had the power to tear away the veil of deception and reveal the truth.

In his more rational moments, he thought of Emerald and her son – his son – as his little nest-egg. Whatever his aunt had done, Catriona had at least taught him the value of patience. Patience and an efficient filing system – the raw material of his profession.

He had not forgotten what he had learned in the caravan on the island. He may have surrendered the hard evidence – the little disc which named the child – to Anstruther; but that did not mean that he could not make connections. Connections lead to conclusions.

Jack had drawn his own conclusions.

What price the tale of the bastard daughter of the house of Windsor?

What price her bastard son?

In his wilder moments, he could see the headlines: the call for the return of Edward Windsor, the revocation of the instrument of abdication, and then, in due course and most fantastic of all, the accession of his, Jack Sweeney's, own blood to the throne.

That kind of knowledge was like money in the bank; it could only accumulate interest – until the moment was right to cash it in.

Some day he knew it would make him a very rich man.

67

Astley Keep: 1957

Jamie's first Christmas was sheer happiness. The energetic youngster was crawling everywhere, scampering sideways at lightning speed, his face wreathed with laughter, bubbling with the new noises he acquired daily.

As the festival approached, Emerald filled every vase in the house with sprays of winter berries – scarlet hips and deep crimson haws twined with ivy and evergreens. She garlanded every room with pine branches and holly. The stairwell was decorated with a big mistletoe bough Ben had lopped from an old apple-tree in the orchard.

She loved the scents of winter, and filled the pot-pourri bowls with handfuls of dried lavender and verbena leaves, spiced with bay and cloves and rolls of cinnamon bark. Each evening she threw handfuls of rosemary branches on the fire, and lit home-made scented candles in all the rooms.

On Christmas Eve, Tom appeared on the doorstep with armfuls of presents for everyone. Ben brought in a small fir-tree to set up in the hall among the stuffed animal heads. Mrs Piggot came down from the attic with several boxes of glass balls, a huge roll of crimson velvet ribbon hoarded since prewar days, and a handful of real beeswax candles.

While the two women decorated the little tree, Jamie hurtled round the floor, ecstatic with joy, thrusting a chubby fist out at every bright scrap of decoration which came within reach. Christmas Day passed with the excited baby the centre of the household's attention.

At midday on the day after the festival, when Tom had already vanished again, Bertha put her work aside and set to work to search through the archives until she had assembled the papers which related to the estate.

It was afternoon by the time she had everything ready.

Through the window she could see Emerald and Jamie returning from their daily ramble through the woods. She heaved herself to her feet and went into the hall to meet her daughter-in-law.

Bertha watched the young woman as she swung easily down the wide hall, the infant balanced on her hip. Emerald's figure was as perfect as it had ever been: the waist was as narrow, although perhaps the breasts were a little fuller, the hips a little more curved. And certainly there was a confidence in the carriage, a maturity in the violet eyes and the firm tilt of the chin which had not been there before.

It was time and past time.

'Come and see me, dear, after you put my grandson to bed.'

She returned to her study. When Emerald came down, Bertha's mind was already on other things. She waved her hand absently-mindedly at the table with its heap of bills and accounts.

'There you are. I'm afraid it's a mess. Sort it out, my dear. No-one else will. Should have turned it over months ago, if it hadn't been for young James.'

'Where do I begin?'

'At the top of the pile. I imagine you can read, write and add?'

Emerald smiled. 'Jane Austen, sixteenth-century poetry, thank-you letters and double-entry book-keeping.'

'Good. All you need. Business is not my strong point. Can't stand bankers and lawyers, myself. I always hoped Tom would take it over. Now there's you. And Jamie, of course. But we'll have to wait a while for him.'

Bertha hooked her half-moon spectacles over her nose.

'No Sherwood has ever been much good at making money. Good at spending it, of course. But, as for income, that's always come from the wives.' Bertha Sherwood picked up a pair of tweezers and began to pin an insect specimen carefully on to its cork display-board.

Emerald worked her way patiently through the pile of paper.

It was a sorry story. The overdraft, swollen daily by interest, was secured by a general charge on the estate. If she was going to have any hope of saving Astley before the loan was called in and the place sold,

470

Emerald knew she would have to start with its main asset: the land.

The home farm had to be brought back under the plough before the spring sowing, seed had to be bought and the estate turned round as soon as possible. There was machinery to be leased, labour to be engaged.

Meanwhile the only source of income was her own small business, still in its infancy but showing signs of profitability. Bertha's private income had been tied up so tightly by her father that she was able to do little more than pay the housekeeping expenses.

The week after Emerald took over, her agricultural suppliers informed her that the cheque she had issued to pay for the seedcorn she had ordered – enough to get a hundred acres of pasture into profitable cereal production – had bounced. The estate's bankers in Threadneedle Street, a firm with a long pedigree and a clientele which read like a copy of *Burke's Landed Gentry*, had a reputation for understanding the requirements of those whose main assets were the land – and for never bouncing cheques. It seemed the estate was mortgaged down to the last blade of unproductive fallow. Something had to be done, and done fast.

Emerald examined the bank records for the last ten years. For the previous decade, ever since Tom had reached his majority and acquired his own chequebook, there had been regular withdrawals and very few credits. With one exception. The most interesting item in the previous year's statements was a credit for a hundred thousand pounds received on the date of his marriage to Emerald. According to the entry immediately beneath it on the statement, three-quarters of the money had been withdrawn as soon as cleared. The remainder had paid off the previous decade's interest charges on the estate's overdraft.

That had now been exhausted.

Emerald went in search of her mother-in-law. She found Bertha busy pouring liquids in and out of test-tubes in the stillroom.

'Be with you in a moment, dear. I'm nearly through.'

Emerald waited until her mother-in-law straightened up and plunged her hand in the box of Turkish Delight.

Then she said: 'A question, Mother-in-law. Probably naïve, but I need to check. What's this?'

Bertha glanced across at the piece of paper Emerald held out.

'The bride-price, of course – marriage settlement – bribe. Whatever you like to call it.' She paused and looked at Emerald. 'Your dowry.'

Emerald stared her mother-in-law, her body cold with fear.

'What do you mean, *dowry*?'

'My dear, why do you think Tom married you?'

471

'He told me he needed a wife so that he could have the use of his fortune.'

'Did he indeed?' Bertha peered over her glasses. 'So no-one told you anything? About the arrangement?'

'What arrangement? All I knew was that there was money in trust which would be released when he was married. That he needed an heir.'

'My dear, what Tom needed wasn't an heir. He needed an heiress. You.'

The old woman's voice was exasperated. She had thought someone – the broker, even Anthony Anstruther – terrified though he was of direct involvement – would have told the young woman at least that much. These English – so spineless. And the old guard was the worst.

Bertha shook her head. Then she glanced back at her work. Using a pair of tweezers, she picked up a small caterpillar, its yellow-patterned flanks streaked with crimson fur. She held it up to the light. The little creature wriggled, its suction-padded feet searching for a toehold.

'Now, here's something *really* interesting. This little fellow will grow up into a hawk-moth. At this stage he—' She flicked up the wriggling tail. 'It *is* a he – has a digestive system capable of concentrating enough oleander toxins to kill anything it touches – including cancer cells. Any bird which catches *that* worm won't go back for a second helping. What I need now is the *chemistry*.'

Bertha placed the multi-coloured caterpillar back on a glass slide, picked up a surgeon's scalpel, and began to slice up the wriggling segments.

Emerald withdrew and shut the door quietly. It was no good asking Bertha for help. The old woman had one interest, and one interest alone – and that was certainly not Astley Keep's tangled accounts.

She spread the papers out and settled down again. The accounts must be made to balance if she was to begin to rebuild. And rebuild she must. For Jamie's sake.

It was nearly midnight when the door opened and Bertha poked her head in.

'Emerald? Go see the bankers. Tell them what you want.' Bertha gave her short bark of laughter, the fine skin stretched taut over the moulded cheekbones. 'All you need to mention, dear, is that you know about the emeralds.'

'The emeralds?'

'The emeralds. Your namesakes. At least someone had a sense of humour at the christening – or whatever it was they did to mark your appearance on the planet.'

'I was in no position to notice, Mother-in-law.'

'Quite. Anyway, if you have any trouble, tell young Trevelyan to give Anthony Anstruther a call.'

'Anstruther? What has he to do with it?'

'Trust me.' Bertha looked at her sharply. 'Just mention Anthony and the emeralds. You'll enjoy the effect. If I didn't need to finish this paper, I'd come with you just for the pleasure of watching Trevelyan wriggle. The Establishment's terrified of powerful women. Reminds them of the school matron. Stand your ground, and they'll eat out of your hand.'

'Then, come with me. I'll need moral support.'

'Quite unnecessary. Start as you mean to go on. Sole responsibility. You'll be more than a match for Peter. Don't take any nonsense, my dear. They enjoy bullying women. Don't give him a chance.'

'Why should he listen?'

Bertha snorted. 'He'll have to listen. You have power of attorney.'

69

London: 1958

The private bank which handled the Sherwood affairs had two branches. There was a head office off Threadneedle Street – handy for the Lloyd's 'names' with whom it did much of its business, those private investors who used their otherwise unproductive landholdings as collateral; and there was a branch office in Park Lane for the convenience of the ladies, the wives of the clients. The bankers also had expensive wives, and were well aware that ladies liked to shop in Mayfair.

Peter Trevelyan was the partner who handled the personal accounts; important clients were not expected to deal with anyone as lowly as a bank manager.

Emerald made an appointment with Trevelyan for the following week. She spent the next few days drawing up the plans for expanding her new business. Her small cottage industry had already brought her as many customers as she could comfortably supply. Drawing on her involvement with Maison Paradis cosmetics, she already had good contacts in the business. She would have to identify new markets and set up the organization to fulfil larger orders if she was to bring in the kind of income which would make Astley profitable.

Bertha took time off from her work to help her daughter-in-law with the closely written projections and overdraft requirements.

'Looks excellent, my dear. Very professional,' she said finally. And that from Bertha was the highest possible praise.

Emerald went up to London the day before her appointment and bought herself a new outfit in Bazaar, Mary Quant's newly opened boutique – a bright-pink linen shift. The shorter skirt and body-skimming lines suited her slender figure. Then she had her hair clipped into the new short curls in a King's Road salon frequented by the Chelsea Set, where her face was still familiar enough from her days on the catwalk to guarantee her special attention and the model's discount.

Afterwards, her confidence boosted by the becoming hairstyle, she had persuaded the hairdresser's buyer to try out some of her herbal hair products in the salon's little boutique. It was her first London opening.

By the time Emerald walked up the steps and into the ornately pillared hall of the Threadneedle Street bank, she felt she was as well prepared as she would ever be.

She gave her name to the uniformed receptionist at the entrance.

'Please take a seat, Lady Sherwood. I'll buzz Mr Trevelyan.'

After a few minutes Peter Trevelyan appeared. The tall, silver-haired banker – Bertha might think him young, but to Emerald he looked a well-preserved fifty – held out his hand, shooting out a blue silk cuff secured with crested gold cuff-links. His dark-grey flannel suit was curved into the waist, the double vent allowing a flash of scarlet lining to match the scarlet carnation in the buttonhole. Peter Trevelyan was clearly a dandy. And almost certainly a lady's man.

'Sorry to keep you waiting, Lady Sherwood. The fairer sex is not usually so punctual.' He smiled. A flash of expensive dentistry. 'The ladies always like to keep us poor men waiting.'

On the way up in the lift, Emerald fought back a wave of irritation. It sounded very much as if Bertha was right. Peter Trevelyan knew a woman's place. And that clearly wasn't in the banking hall.

If it had not been for the patronizing tone, she would have turned round and gone straight back to Astley Keep. As it was she was irritated enough to overcome her nervousness.

'Please sit down, Lady Sherwood.'

Emerald settled into the brass-studded leather armchair which faced the banker's gleaming mahogany desk. There was nothing on the mirror-bright surface which separated them but a leather blotting-pad with a pad of cream-laid writing-paper, an ornate ormolu pen-holder and a discreet black telephone.

'How's your admirable mother-in-law?'

'Still admirable.'

The banker leaned back. 'Now, perhaps you might tell me what you require of me?'

'What do your lady customers generally require, Mr Trevelyan?'

Peter Trevelyan stared at his visitor. She was a little sharp, the new Lady Sherwood. He decided to show her the ropes. Gently.

'The wives of our clients – our lady customers – like to have their own pin-money. An allowance. Their own chequebook. It gives them a little independence, bless them.'

'You have no female customers who run their own affairs?'

'We're a little old-fashioned, I'm afraid. Needing guarantees and so forth. Usually we find our ladies like it like that. It's for their own protection.' The banker had nearly added 'my dear', but caught himself just in time. Something in Emerald Sherwood's voice warned him against such paternal phrases. He finished lamely: 'Of course, your mother-in-law is the exception – a law unto herself.'

Emerald turned her violet eyes on the banker. 'You'll find me an exception too. When we do business.'

'Business, Lady Sherwood?'

The eyebrows rose.

For the first time the banker noticed his visitor was carrying a briefcase instead of a handbag.

'Business, Mr Trevelyan,' Emerald repeated calmly.

He pursed his lips. If Emerald Sherwood thought she was going to get anywhere with *him*, she was going to be disappointed. With that wastrel young man controlling her purse-strings, she hadn't a snowflake's chance in hell of raising anything.

No. Someone would just have to bite the bullet and sell off some of the assets.

'Your husband, Lady Sherwood—'

'My husband, as you know well enough, has no head for business, Mr Trevelyan.'

And no eye for a woman – *any* woman – either, Peter Trevelyan thought. Everyone knew about Tom Sherwood.

'However,' Emerald continued carefully, 'I have power of attorney.'

'Have you indeed?' The banker's voice was startled. 'It's still a complicated matter, Lady Sherwood.'

He smiled politely. As a banker he was trained not to let his emotions show, but inwardly he knew that the new mistress of Astley was going to give him trouble. Plenty of trouble.

'Mr Trevelyan, bouncing the cheque for the seedcorn will not bring the harvest in.'

'I'm sorry about that, Lady Sherwood. There's the matter of the overdraft.'

'I'm aware of the figures, Mr Trevelyan.'

With a rare touch of humour, Peter Trevelyan allowed himself the thought that he, too, was aware of the figures. But perhaps not the same ones as Lady Sherwood.

Emerald reached into her briefcase. She dropped the file on the desk in front of the banker.

'I have such confidence in your co-operation, Mr Trevelyan, that I've taken the liberty of bringing you my own projections for the future of Astley.'

Trevelyan's eyes narrowed. Sooner or later it had been bound to come to this. Women were unlucky. Every sailor knew that – and Peter Trevelyan had spent his war in the Navy. Women brought bad luck in a ship. And they brought bad luck in a boardroom. All right in the bedroom. But death in the boardroom.

'I shall need time to study your proposals, Lady Sherwood,' he said smoothly.

'And I need that cheque to our seedcorn suppliers cleared. Now. After that I shall need working capital to put the estate back on its feet.'

Trevelyan stared at her. Surely the young woman didn't expect him to take a decision on the spot?

By the way she leaned back in her chair, it was clear that she did.

'I'm more than happy to wait.'

Trevelyan said nervously, 'We're not merchant bankers, you know. They handle this kind of thing.'

'You surprise me, Mr Trevelyan.'

He stammered: 'I haven't the authority, Lady Sherwood. I have partners to consult.'

'We're on the same side, Mr Trevelyan. There's only one way to recover your money. And that is to invest in the future.'

'Future?'

'Of course. At least I have learned in my time at Astley that we cannot harvest if we cannot sow. Here is what I wish to sow. We have already tested our local markets. Now we are ready to expand.'

Emerald leaned over the desk and pushed the papers across the blotter.

Trevelyan studied her with a new interest. She had spirit – and she was a beauty, there was no doubt of that. That smooth white neck would look marvellous collared with the royal pearls. In a less censorious age, and if his ex-Majesty hadn't been such a besotted fool and abdicated; if he had done things in the right way, let things take their proper course – who knows but he might have got away with making his mistress his queen, and the young woman might have been wearing her great-grandmother's jewels as of right?

'Yes. I'm not sure of the correct procedure. There is a little matter I'll have to clear up first.'

Emerald smiled. 'With the greatest respect, Mr Trevelyan, I wouldn't be here if I believed that to be true. I think that Anthony Anstruther is the one you are obliged to consult.'

Her voice was cool. It was time to play her trump card. Bertha had told her so. And it was the first time she had knowingly used her past. But it was not for herself. It was for Astley, and for Bertha, and for Jamie. Above all, for Jamie.

Trevelyan stared at her. 'Anthony?'

'Certainly. I'm sure he's well aware that the Sherwood estate is mortgaged to its limit. And, of course, there's the matter of the emeralds.'

'The emeralds?'

'Of course. And no doubt you wish to explain their connection with the hundred thousand pounds made available to my husband on the date of my marriage.' It was a more than a guess – Bertha had as good as told her so. 'I presume you are aware of the provenance of the funds?'

Trevelyan's face went white. Anthony had assured him the young woman did not know, *must* not know, of the arrangements made to secure her future.

Trevelyan's voice rose an octave. 'Indeed. The settlement. We saw no reason to question the . . . *depositor.* The position as presented to us was that this was a marriage settlement.'

'*My* marriage settlement?'

'You could say so, yes, Lady Sherwood. It all seemed in order. The collateral was more than adequate.'

'That doesn't tally with your returning my cheque.'

Trevelyan stared at her. He noticed that the young woman's eyes were a most remarkable shade of blue – violet perhaps, or sapphire.

'Such matters are absolutely confidential, Lady Sherwood. The bank has a responsibility . . .'

His voice was calm, but his hands were icy. Who could have told her? How much did she know? What was he to tell Anthony Anstruther?

Emerald knew she had him – and she had no intention of letting him off the hook. 'The bank has a responsibility to whom, Mr Trevelyan? Or is that also confidential?'

Trevelyan hesitated, then reached forward and began to flick through the papers.

'Perhaps I'd better glance through these.'

Emerald noticed with interest that his hands were trembling slightly. At that moment, for the first time, she knew it was possible to win.

She smiled, uncrossed her legs and stretched them out so that the banker might have the full benefit of the short skirt. It certainly suited her. And that morning, before leaving for her appointment, Emerald had deliberated whether to wear high heels. She had worn flat shoes for so long while she was carrying Jamie that she had almost forgotten how uncomfortable high heels could be. But bankers, after all, were men. And, Emerald knew well enough, a man was more likely to do what you wanted if your heels were high and your lipstick scarlet.

Sure enough, Trevelyan glanced down. Then he noted two things: that the skirt was extremely short, and that the legs were exceptionally shapely. Trevelyan was a man who appreciated a leg. Particularly clad, as these indubitably were, in the sheerest of nylon stockings. His face softened. They would look good against the flanks of a horse, those thighs, rising and falling against the saddle, moving with the rhythm of the trotting horse. The sweat started on his temples. Yes, on the hunting field – that was the place for those thighs. Trevelyan never missed a hunt in the season. Some men went for the bosom. But Trevelyan had always been a buttock man.

'I'd be most grateful if you would consider my proposals seriously.'

There was amusement in the young woman's voice. For one wild moment Trevelyan permitted himself to wonder how grateful the beautiful Emerald Sherwood might be prepared to be.

'Perhaps you'd excuse me a moment.' Trevelyan's voice rose an octave.

'Of course.'

After ten minutes, the banker returned. This time his voice was cheerful, almost jaunty.

'Well, Lady Sherwood, I think we can see our way to accommodating you. Within reason, of course.'

By the time she packed up her briefcase and stood up to leave, the banker had agreed to everything Emerald wanted, including expansion capital for her new business.

Emerald's parting shot was delivered with a final dazzling smile. 'I'm so glad we have reached an understanding, Mr Trevelyan. And I trust that you will never bounce one of my cheques again.'

Trevelyan hesitated. Then he smiled back. A gentleman could concede defeat with grace. Whatever the Establishment might have done or not done for her, whatever Anthony Anstruther had engineered, Emerald was a survivor. Maybe even a winner. All bankers love a winner.

'Certainly not without full consultation – as we bankers put it.'

'Good. Then, I trust our association will be long and profitable.'

'It will be a pleasure, Lady Sherwood.' There was genuine warmth in his voice.

Peter Trevelyan saw her to the door and then sank back gratefully into his heavy leather armchair. The velvet glove had indeed concealed an iron fist.

His mind went back to when he had first had dealings with her, albeit *in absentia*. When Anstruther had first come to the bank during those sensitive times just after the war, the child's parentage had been one of the most explosive secrets the Establishment had ever had to hug to its chilly bosom.

At that moment, with a socialist government in office and republicanism in the air, the monarchy would have been hard-pressed to survive such a scandal. Now . . . well, things were more stable.

Even so, if anyone got their hands on the Palace's release of the Danish queen's emeralds, it could still be dynamite. The payment of what was effectively hush money was as good as an admission the young woman had a claim on the throne. Edward VIII had abdicated, but what of the child, subsequently legitimized by marriage? Did she have no rights? Under British law any claim would not be upheld; but under international law there was plenty of precedent which permitted legitimized children to inherit.

Anthony Anstruther had done well to keep the business under wraps. Damage containment.

But those *legs*.

For a few moments, he flicked through the projection figures again. Such attention was a formality.

A woman like that could do anything she wanted. A woman like that could change the world. And he would not be the only one who would feel the same.

Trevelyan did not usually permit himself such thoughts. But, then, Emerald was enough to set any man to thinking. Trevelyan knew his own wife would no more dream of doing what Emerald Sherwood had just done than fly to the moon.

Meanwhile Emerald had forgotten the discomfort of her high heels and was almost skipping down the street. She smiled at the office-bleached faces under the bowler hats. City men bobbed back at her, their minds fixed on the movement of the money markets, uncertain whether she was a madwoman or just a young woman in love.

Emerald was neither. Quite simply, she was exultant. Whether it was the lipstick or the lip-service which had done it, the trick appeared to have been turned. And there was just a chance, given what Callum might have called a calm sea and a following wind, that Jamie might one day have something to inherit.

The thought of Callum – the pain of what had happened dimmed by the joy of the child he had given her – drew her irresistibly back to the house which had formed her first memories.

She could not help herself. Callum was so deeply embedded in her life it seemed impossible she would never see him again. She had an almost tangible longing for him, to catch a glimpse of him even if only for a second, even if only through the windows of the tall house in Notting Hill.

Now, with the strong wine of success coursing through her veins, she hailed a cab and gave the familiar address. This time she would have the strength to face the past as well as the future.

69

London: 1958

'Oh my Lord, no!'

Emerald stood under the leafy canopy of the Notting Hill square and gazed up in shock at the gutted skeleton of the house.

The explosion had blown the attic roof wide to the heavens. Blackened spars of twisted ironwork reached spider-fingers into the sky. The water jets of the fire-engines had streaked the creamy façade with soot.

The front door, blown into the street by the blast, had been hammered back into place, held by rough planks of wood. The window-panes on the ground floor were miraculously still intact. Through the glass she could see that the elegant curved staircase had crumbled into a heap of rubble.

'Terrible business.'

Emerald swung round to find the source of the voice. She had been too intent on the house – or what remained of it – to notice the gardener sweeping up the leaves in the square.

She ran over to the railings.

'You were there?'

The old man put down his broom and came over.

'Here every morning and evening, regular as clockwork. Rain or shine. But I've not seen the like of that since the war. Mr Hitler's love-letters, posted neat as Santa Claus right down the chimney, it was. London's full of them, they say. Just waiting. Same thing as happened to that publican and his wife down in the East End – Mile End Road. Just the other day, it was in all the papers. Digging around in the cellar, he was, using a blow-torch, and up it went. Blown to smithereens, the pair of them.'

Emerald felt ice-cold. 'But here – was anyone . . . ?'

The gardener nodded. 'Started in the attic. Must have been a fire in the grate, they said, triggered the thing. Some young woman fancying around with matches and sticks. Never found much of *her*, I can tell you. Not after the explosion. Blew the gables clean off. Two years ago now, and I'm still picking the slates out of my flowerbeds. The flames came right down the staircase – like a bellows, it was. Threw the young man clean over the road. I thought to myself: Someone up there loves him. Few bruises and no bones broken. Went a bit crazy, though. Raving on about the girl and how he had to rescue her. Had to tie him to the stretcher to stop him. Flesh and blood wouldn't have lasted more than a minute.'

Emerald's heart turned over. Alison's fate might have been her own. Hers and her unborn child's. She shivered. Jamie might never have seen the light of day. And Callum? What terrible remorse had he suffered?

The gardener watched her shrewdly. 'Thought as much. Bit of a shock? Friend of the young man, are you, miss? Fine young gentleman, Mr Fergusson – like his father and mother before him. Used to know them all. I keep an eye out for my residents. Very polite and well spoken, the family. Gentlefolk. Not like that young woman – the one who copped it. Never speak ill of the dead, but if I'd been her dad I'd have taken a belt to her. Up at all hours in her nightie and arguing on the doorstep with the boyfriend.'

Emerald swung round. 'Boyfriend?'

The old man nodded. 'Her fancy man, if you ask me. Red-headed and a sharp dresser. Not a gentleman; more of the other sort. Used to get a lot of them after the war.'

Emerald's heart leaped. Jack Sweeney – it had to be him. What if Alison had been lying? The girl had been beside herself with drink and pills. What if it was Jack who had been telling the truth? She shook her head. If so, why had Callum not moved heaven and earth to find her? Surely that was proof enough of his guilt.

She had to know. Had to make sure.

'And the young man – Mr Fergusson – have you seen him?'

The old man shook his head. 'Not since the accident. Gone abroad, they say. The house is to be put on the market once the work's been done. There's a gentleman handling the business – very well spoken.'

The gardener lowered his voice. 'Gave me a tenner at Christmas for keeping an eye out for vandals. Very considerate. Gave me his visiting-card in case there was any trouble. Very smart address.'

The old man fumbled in the ticket-pocket of his waistcoat. 'See?'

Emerald stared down at the proffered oblong of dog-eared cardboard. The engraved letters leaped up at her: Anthony Anstruther, QC, 6d The Albany, Piccadilly, London Wl.

She shivered in the sunshine. Her mind tumbled back to that moment in the heather of Eas Forse, when, little knowing the part the balding bespectacled visitor was to play in her life, she led him up the brae towards Margaret Mackenzie's crofthouse.

The print of Anstruther's hand had been on everything which had happened since that moment. She shook her head angrily. All that was behind her now. Her marriage at least had been her choice alone – of that she could be certain.

'Are you all right, miss?'

The gardener was watching her anxiously.

Emerald, suddenly aware of the effect she must be having on the old gardener, fumbled in her purse and found a pound note.

'I'm fine. Thank you.'

The old man nodded. 'Much obliged. Remember me to young Mr Fergusson. Mr Anstruther will know where to find him.' He shook his head again. 'My, but he was the lucky one.'

The phrase rang in her head all the way back to Astley, echoed in her mind until she held Jamie once again in her arms.

'The lucky one.'

Callum evidently had suffered no lasting injury – and with that she must be content. She had made her choice – for herself but, above all, for Jamie. Whatever the truth, she must keep faith.

Yet secretly, in her heart, she told herself that the dead girl must have lied. That Callum's self-exile was no proof of guilt. That there had to be another reason for his disappearance. And now it was too late. The die was cast. Callum, no less than she, was the victim of Anstruther's manoeuvrings.

From today, all that was in the past. From today, she would have no need of anyone. Today she had laid the foundations of Jamie's inheritance. What she would build for Jamie would owe nothing to anyone or anything. She needed strength and patience – and she had both.

70

Astley Keep: 1959-63

Spring came early to Astley that first year of Emerald's grand plan. The corridors of the ramshackle old house rang with Jamie's laughter. The overgrown orchard, pruned back the previous autumn, blossomed as it had not done for years. The work Emerald had put into the herb garden began to show results. The long rows of tender young shoots, carefully tended and weeded, promised a bumper harvest. The fields were gradually being brought back under plough and new crops planted. There were two brawny young farm-hands to take direction from old Ben. Next year she would be able to afford new machinery.

Bertha stopped her travelling – ostensibly to return to her research, bustling round the greenhouses and conducting her experiments, but in reality to give her new daughter-in-law a much-needed hand in her self-appointed task of restoring the estate.

Jamie was growing faster than the weeds in the flowerbeds. The little boy kept company with Emerald in the mornings while she made her rounds of the farm and tended the young plants in her garden.

When she was at Astley, Bertha liked to work from first light until midday. Then she broke off for the day to take over the care of Jamie, leaving Mrs Piggot free for her work.

These few hours gave Emerald a chance to work on a new project: a range of natural cosmetics and, perhaps later, a perfume.

Using the knowledge she had acquired from Margaret Mackenzie, Emerald cropped the young leaves and plants for her pharmacopoeia, remembering the skills learned from the *curandera* as she brewed up delicately scented creams and lotions made to recipes she found in the household books in the library – rejecting some and taking others to Bertha for chemical analysis and advice.

The days lengthened into summer, and it was time to harvest the aromatics. Camomile and rosemary for herb-scented shampoos, pennyroyal for astringent lotions, borage and infusions of rose petals for skin tonics.

The household books assumed skills which Emerald could only acquire by trial and error. She pored over the recipes, trying to work out what an eighteenth-century housekeeper might judge to be a knifetip of gum arabic, how many hours were covered by the instruction to simmer from Matins to Evensong.

Bertha could always be relied on to provide the answer.

'Listen to this, Mother-in-law. "Essence of lavender. Very good. Take six handfuls of lavender flowers stripped from the stem. Pack into a pitcher and pour in as much clean spirit as will fill a pipkin." '

'Pitcher and pipkin? Second shelf, third cupboard, left of the pantry. Housekeepers being creatures of habit, I imagine they're still the same ones.'

Laughing, Emerald went off to fetch the containers.

She bent back over the book. 'It says here: "Set in water and boil for as long as takes to recite the Miserere." Bet you can't answer that.'

'At least Christianity had the good sense to appropriate King David's magnificent poetry. Try the fifty-first Psalm.' Bertha smiled as she peered over her half-moon spectacles.

Soon the kitchen was filled with wonderful perfumes and bubbling pots of unguents. There was always a pot of honey-scented beeswax dripping through clean linen by the side of the stove, always some new problem to be solved as Emerald struggled with the precise balance of the emulsions which were needed for her creams.

She set up a distillery in one of the back kitchens, adapting a pressure cooker to concentrate the precious oils. Bertha pitched camp at a bureau in one corner, keeping a comfortable eye on her daughter-in-law while she worked. Bertha's involvement in her enterprise gave Emerald the confidence to experiment.

Only one problem remained: the packaging.

Emerald's experience at Maison Paradis had taught her that this was all-important with a new product. She knew that Christian Paradis had spent more money on the development of his new perfume's elegant Lalique jar than he had on the contents.

'It's like *haute couture, ma belle,*' he explained to Emerald. 'It's the *look* that must be recognizable. A woman must feel that she can walk into a room, take out a lipstick or a flask of my perfume, and everyone will know *exactly* who she is.'

Emerald smiled at the memory of the couturier's lecture. Christian was right – for his own market. The Paradis perfumes and cosmetics cost a fortune and looked a million dollars. The Spirit of Paradise, youthful and flowery, was bought by well-heeled mothers for their daughters, and rich old men for their young mistresses.

This was not the market Emerald meant to capture; she had a far larger constituency in mind. The new generation of working women had had enough of fancy packaging and the advertisers' blandishments. They earned their own money and had the sense to spend it wisely.

She spent days poring over suppliers' catalogues. Nothing seemed quite right.

And then one evening, following the inquisitive little Jamie on one of his forays, she came across a huge stock of old preserving jars in one of the stable-lofts. In every size and shape, they had been stacked away during wartime, ready for the time when sugar would no longer be rationed.

Emerald knew immediately that they were perfect.

She washed the jars carefully and sterilized them overnight in Mrs Piggot's huge old kitchen range. Once each jar was filled, it was topped with a layer of paraffin wax, then sealed with oiled parchment tied on with string – the old countrywife's way of potting up jams.

In the evenings, after Jamie was securely tucked into his cot, Emerald settled down to write out neat brown labels in the clear copperplate she had learned in her days under Doña Molly's instruction. Then the jars were finished with a tiny posy of dried herbs. They were packed in old wine-crates, and delivered by Ben to her small but widening network of outlets.

By the end of the third year, most of the new King's Road boutiques who catered to the newly affluent young stocked the Astley Meadowsweet range, and they couldn't get enough of it.

Even Peter Trevelyan was impressed by the figures. So impressed that the young Lady Sherwood was invited to lunch in the partners' dining-room at the bank – an unprecedented accolade for a woman.

It was an occasion which reduced Bertha to tears of laughter when her daughter-in-law described the experience.

'Would you believe a special addendum to the company's articles of affiliation so I could be allowed to enter the gentlemen's washroom? There's no provision for anything but waitresses – "persons of the serving classes", I think the phrase was. Social trip-wires everywhere – worse than old Ben's rabbit-traps.'

Success brought more success. With the new season, Emerald was determined to increase her turnover to a level where next year she could take on paid help in the garden and in the cosmetic business. Ben's joints were stiffening up. Not all the herbs in her pharmacopoeia could do much for old age.

Tom reappeared two or three times a year, settling himself in his cottage in the walled garden with a new young man in tow, and spending a single token evening with his wife and his mother. He watched Jamie's progress with a wary fascination, and would bring him beautiful little wooden toys bought in foreign markets.

Emerald welcomed Tom's arrival and enjoyed his stories of the goings-on round the watering-holes of Europe, but soon learned to steer clear of any involvement in his imported social life.

Tom was as charming, entertaining and well mannered as ever. He was everything – except a husband and father. The experiment of the wedding night was not repeated.

Jamie was increasingly bold and adventurous. The boy loved everything about Astley, and as soon as he was able he joined in the activities of the farm, helped with the feeding of orphaned lambs in spring. In the summer he would slip out of his bed at dawn to help with the milking, staggering across the yard with the skimmed milk to slop into the piglets' trough. Ben said he was the best apprentice he had ever had.

Increasingly, as Jamie needed her less, Emerald's thoughts turned to Callum.

Sometimes, willing the father's features sketched in miniature on the child, her heart ached, her body reached out to his memory, the memory of that wild night of their first lovemaking, the lovemaking which had given her her son.

Nevertheless, for the first time in her life, Emerald felt secure. The pain of her memories gradually faded into the old stones. The house was carpeted with its own memories, they seeped from the walls and crept under the doors.

Happiness was Jamie – and Bertha's absent-minded care, and the success she was beginning to enjoy with what was turning into much more than a cottage industry.

After the success of the third year, she decided to add a small range of make-up, Jewels of the Meadow, which she persuaded a local firm with spare capacity to manufacture. The clean pale lip-colours and kohl-based eyeliners were an instant hit – the perfect complement to the vigorous crop-skirted fashions which were all the rage in the city.

By the fourth year, she was ready to dip a toe in the export market. She made a brief visit to New York, leaving Jamie with Bertha and Mrs Piggot, and took her products to Diana Vreeland.

'Wonderful, darling. Delicious – and so *now*. I was wondering what you'd been up to. Just the thing for the May issue. I'll give you a teeny hand.'

Mrs Vreeland did even better than that. She featured Emerald's products over four pages in *Harper's Bazaar*, and put Emerald herself on the cover. In New York, London style was all the rage, and the beautifully packaged natural products sold like hot muffins on a cold morning. The result had been rush orders for Bergdorf Goodman and Macey's.

With international success, Emerald's Jewels of the Meadow had come of age.

Trevelyan was talking about bringing the business to the stock market in a couple of years' time. Then Astley's future, underpinned by the farm and Emerald's increasing experience, would be secure.

At the end of the fourth year, Emerald began work in earnest on her perfume. Maison Paradis had taught her how valuable the market could be. She began to experiment, using vervain and lemon balm for the muscular underpinning, wild rose for a delicate top note.

Bertha added her own secret ingredient. 'I've been concentrating on the chemistry of sex-hormones. Nothing like a pheromone – drives the male swallowtale butterfly mad with lust. The little brute can pick up a female across a ten-acre field even in a gale. Imagine what it'll do to the human male.'

Emerald had exactly the right packaging, too. The essences were to be supplied to the outlets so that the customers could make up their own blend in refillable flasks, copied from nineteenth-century medicine bottles. The secret ingredient was added from an eye-dropper. The bottles were then corked and sealed with scarlet wax.

'Perfect,' Bertha laughed. 'Everything absolutely simple, but with just the right hint of mystery. We'll call it for you, my dear: "Emerald's Secret". Launch it at Astley next spring. Which, by the way, is when we should hold the heir ale for Jamie. It can be a double celebration. So cost-efficient.'

'Heir ale?'

'Didn't I tell you? One of those peculiar Sherwood traditions. Held to mark the birth of an heir to Astley. Instituted at the time of the Black Death. After five years, the child has at least a chance of survival.'

Bertha smiled and ruffled her grandson's hair affectionately. 'Jamie seems to pass muster.'

'Shouldn't Tom be here?'

Bertha shrugged. 'No doubt he'll find a reason to absent himself. He loathes that kind of thing. We'll go ahead with or without him. The County will have its say anyway. And it'll be good for Jamie, stand him in good stead later. It's a kind of official nod. The expense will be considerable, the trouble vast. But, believe me, you won't regret either.'

The County was consumed with curiosity when the invitations arrived from Astley for the heir ale.

Of course, the birth had been in all the local papers – with pictures. But, when all was said and done, the County told itself, that husband of hers was . . . well, not exactly breeding material.

Hopes had been high when the baron was a young man doing the rounds of the social season. There had been more than one daughter of the gentry disappointed who had had her eye on him at a hunt ball. Not a ladies' man, the word was. Never grown out of that public-school horseplay like the rest of the County's brothers and sons.

Not much of the father there, said the County.

The County enjoyed a scandal. The County told itself it was a scandalous business anyway – the registry wedding and then the birth seven months later.

But, then, there was many a skeleton in many a County cupboard. A little rattle of the bones livened up a sherry morning.

Hearing the stories retold by Mrs Piggot, Emerald shrugged and laughed. Communities loved a gossip. It was not so different from Eas Forse.

Bertha helped her daughter-in-law make out the guest-list.

It was important that the day should be a success. Yet more important than the County's approval was what the celebration meant to Emerald.

Five years. Five years of unremitting work which had seen the dead and almost bankrupt estate struggle back to life. It wasn't finished yet; there were still debts to be paid off, and sometimes Emerald wondered if the task she'd set herself would ever be finished. But the Keep was alive again and it was alive for a purpose. As a family home.

Just the same, Emerald could never look at Jamie's hazel-flecked eyes and the strong confident little face without her heart turning over.

490

Emerald had never had an inheritance, not even a name she could call her own. Her son was going to have both.

At least Tom had been true to his contract.

Whatever she felt, there was no doubt Tom saw Emerald's arrangements as none of his business – and considered his none of hers.

Emerald hadn't taken advantage of her liberty – although not because, in the past five years, she hadn't had more than her share of admirers. She could have taken her pick among the rich County neighbours. Most of the husbands were bored – commuting to the City during the week and entertaining their own kind at the weekends. It was an equable balance: most of their wives had time on their hands and were more than happy to look for a little extra-marital excitement with their best friend's husband.

It was all kept discreetly and cosily within the community family. The County expected newcomers to acknowledge the rules and pull their weight. It was a weight Emerald singularly failed to pull.

On more than one occasion she had to fend off the amorous attentions of a neighbour, avoiding snatched advances in darkened corridors, or politely declining discreet suggestions of lunchtime meetings on one of her trips to London. One lovestruck young man, her companion at a dinner party, had laid siege to her for a month, deluging her daily with flowers and poems.

'Well, he's certainly persistent. You could always give it a try,' Bertha suggested absent-mindedly, her brows knitted in concentration. She was using a fine paintbrush to fertilize a captive female swallowtail butterfly. 'Take this little beauty. Not ready for it. Unlike your suitor.'

'Sorry, Bertha. Freddie's just not my type.'

'No? Never mind. He's not *clever*, but then he's not proposing a meeting of the minds, is he? Still, you must please yourself. That kind of thing is all very time-consuming – if immensely entertaining.'

Emerald laughed.

It worried her not at all that the County thought her most peculiar that she chose not to join its circular games. But, then, there was a lot about the Sherwood set-up the County saw as peculiar.

Yet the truth was that Emerald had no need of amorous diversions. In spite of everything she was still in love – a love which was kept alive in her love for her son.

She had news of Callum – even if only at secondhand. His credits were appearing increasingly regularly in the newspapers, and she could trace his assignments in the headlines. But it was the extraordinary photographs he had taken in Hungary – it must have been just at the time Jamie was born – which had made his name. One photograph in particular had caught the public imagination. It had been reproduced worldwide in all the weekly news-magazines. The image was of a young soldier, his body spreadeagled against the skyline, taken at the precise moment that the bullet passed through his body.

Callum had chosen a dangerous profession. In moments of loneliness, when Bertha was away on one of her trips and Jamie was tucked up in his cot, she longed for his touch. Till one night, still sleepless at dawn, the longing had become unbearable.

She had written to him then – even slipped in a photograph of Jamie – thinking to send the letter care of Anstruther. Later, in the cold light of day, she had torn the letter up.

'What of the father?' Victoire Verdun had asked her. For answer, Emerald had made her own choice.

She had married Mr Wrong, and she was doing her best to live happily ever after.

The business – and its growing success – was her chance to take revenge. It was her answer to those shadowy presences, unseen but still felt, who cared nothing for her happiness, who had tried, through the barrister's manipulations, to consign her to a convenient oblivion.

The following week, she wrote to Callum again – a short note telling him briefly of her life, of the happiness Jamie had given her. And this time she did not destroy the letter, but sent it care of Anthony Anstruther at his address in Albany. After that, she wrote faithfully once a month, always briefly, always enclosing the latest photograph of Jamie. She did it not for Callum, not even for Jamie, but for herself – needing the acknowledgement, even if only in her own heart, that her child had what Bertha would call a biological father.

As for suitors to take on the marital duties of her absentee husband, Emerald could not help what the County thought. The heir ale would give them a chance to satisfy their curiosity – at least on appearances.

And, on a more practical level, the press always enjoyed a bit of theatre. The heir ale would indeed, as Bertha suggested, make a wonderful launch for Emerald's Secret.

Emerald had had her work cut out to break through the monopoly of the big cosmetics companies. She owed her success as much to her career as the Paradis perfume girl as to the intrinsic honesty of her products. In spite of the support she had wrenched from the banker in Threadneedle Street, it had been an uphill struggle.

All these thoughts raced through her head as she listened to Bertha's plans for the party.

'The timing's perfect. The gardens will be looking quite spectacular – roses roaring out of every orifice. Ben'll open up the greenhouses, and

Mrs Piggot can organize tea. She loves that sort of thing – no cupcake left unbaked. Jamie can hold court in the nursery; no doubt the neighbours'll bring their own little darlings, hand-smocked to the nines.'

Bertha gave a roar of laughter.

'Poor Jamie. We'll have to make sure he's not flattened in the rush. In twenty years or so, he'll be quite a catch.'

71

Astley Keep: 1963

The day of the heir ale dawned bright and clear.

'Nature's on our side, my dear,' said Bertha, bustling round with Mrs Piggot.

By midday all was in order. The County came to eat and drink, to toast the child's health, to inspect the young mistress of Astley and her eccentric mother-in-law.

The County poked its nose into every corner of the estate, and confessed itself impressed.

'Truly extraordinary,' said the ladies with a twinge of envy. The energy with which the new mistress had set about restoring the grounds was amazing. The lawns, so long neglected, were neatly mown, the box hedges well on their way to the elegance of Edwardian times.

'So fortunate in the weather,' said the owners of lesser horticultural displays.

Someone – the village ladies said it was the young mistress herself – had been hard at work on the Victorian flower borders, pruning back the tangled roses so they flowered thick and new, planting sweet peas and pansies, delphiniums and ox-eye daisies, edging the brick paths with tiny clumps of scented herbs.

'A Dutch oil-painting,' agreed the ladies.

But, in the view of their husbands, all these visible achievements paled beside the fact that the beautiful Lady Sherwood had managed to raise the capital for the business whose profits had transformed the once-derelict estate.

'Such acumen – for a woman,' said the gentlemen.

All could see that the source of the restored prosperity was the walled gardens. Although they had not been cultivated since the war, the three enclosures had once supplied two households – Astley itself and the family's London residence – with all the fruit and vegetables they needed, in season and out of season. The beds had been painstakingly cleared, manured and replanted, and the long-neglected acres carried a harvest of the scented blooms and herbs Emerald needed for her expanding business.

Whatever gossip there might be about Emerald and her curious marriage among the neighbours, there was no doubt of her popularity among the villagers of Astley. She had brought work and a new prosperity to the little neighbourhood, dependent as it was on the estate for its employment.

In one way or another there was plenty of work for the locals in the harvesting of the aromatics, the preparation and packaging of the creams and lotions, shampoos and soaps whose chief selling point was that they were pure and natural products, made to the traditional household recipes of Astley Keep itself.

There were even plans to restore the great conservatory for the cultivation of tropical plants and trees. Already the graceful Victorian glasshouses accommodated lemon- and orange-trees, tuberose and jasmine. Soon, rumour had it, the old stables were to be converted into stillrooms.

There was a fine tea for the estate workers and the business's employees – a thank-you from Emerald for all the hard work which they had shared – and a dram of whisky for those who had a fancy for something more fortifying.

The business was indeed expanding. You could see the evidence everywhere – not least in the press excitement engendered by the launch of the new perfume.

'Emerald's Secret? So appropriate,' murmured the ladies, their collective mind focusing on the unknown pedigree of the young lady of the manor.

The launch achieved all Emerald had hoped. The afternoon brought a trainload of reporters from London to join the crowds surging round the grounds. The press kits were considered quite a prize, with beautifully packaged sample-bottles of the new fragrance, each one finished with its tiny posy of dried flowers.

Naturally Emerald was in much demand among the photographers, posing with professional courtesy among the riotous profusion of the borders.

Young Jamie, unused to all the attention, raced around at the head of a pack of visiting children, and it was past ten that night when Emerald and Mrs Piggot between them managed to pack the wildly excited little boy off to bed.

At last Bertha and Emerald could relax and talk over the events of the day. It had been a great success; there was no doubt of that.

The only cloud on the horizon had been the absence of Tom.

Bertha shrugged and patted Emerald's hand. 'Never mind, my dear. It was perfectly predictable. You know Tom.'

Wearily, Emerald reflected that she didn't really know Tom at all.

It was not really Tom's fault that he failed to put in an appearance at the heir ale.

He had fully intended to arrive at Astley in good time for the celebration. He felt he owed it to his mother, to the little boy who was his acknowledged heir – and, above all, to Emerald.

Emerald had told him she intended to launch her new perfume at the heir ale; and he was, after his fashion, proud of his wife's success.

Tom felt something rather special in the way of a present was required. He had already spotted the very thing in the window of the jeweller's where he had selected the earrings which marked the beginning of his courtship of Emerald: a delicious little sapphire-and-diamond ring which would perfectly complete the set.

The morning before the heir ale, Tom nosed the bows of the Fairey Huntsman between the twin arms which enclosed Monte Carlo's harbour. He glanced up at the casino perched on the heights above, and down at his watch.

After an expensive weekend in Tangier, he planned to make the necessary pocket-money to complete the purchase of the pretty trinket. Emerald would be enchanted. He wanted to come home a winner. Today he felt like a winner. He would have plenty of time to catch the midnight flight out of Cannes.

With a quick flick of the wheel, Tom threaded the sleek clinker-built hull through the lines of tethered pleasure-boats until he reached his mooring.

Tom was a skilful sailor, and the *Dorian Gray* – as he'd gleefully renamed the boat in honour of Oscar Wilde's most famous hero – was a beauty. Nothing flashy – no girl looking for a good time would have given her a second glance – the Huntsman attracted attention only among those who really knew their speedboats.

With her narrow lines, her fine mahogany decks and her polished brasswork, she was infinitely more beautiful than the huge gin-palaces which dwarfed her on every side. Fast and sturdy, she was ideal for weathering the sudden squalls to which the Mediterranean was prone. Her speed and safety allowed Tom – without notifying any authorities or answering to any officials – to make the journey between the Côte d'Azur, where he gambled, and the coast of Morocco, where the rules of the game were also *sans limites*.

Tangier was full of compliant young men. His favourite hunting-ground was the Bordello Edward VII, named after the libidinous old monarch who had given his patronage to at least half the brothels of Europe. There Tom had an arrangement with the proprietor and access to an unending supply of pretty boys with kohl-rimmed eyes.

Tom smiled to himself at the memory. He always felt good after one of his forays to Tangier. Today Tom felt he could conquer the world.

Twelve hours later, in the casino overlooking the sleek boats moored in the yacht basin, Tom was not so sure. By then his obligations had faded into insignificance. He had forgotten everything but the way the cards were falling.

He picked up a glass of champagne from the tray proffered by a passing waitress, sipped it once and immediately replaced the glass on the tray. It was a bad sign when the best vintage champagne tasted acid on the tongue.

He rose from the *sans limite* table and walked out on to the balcony of the Salle Privée to watch the sunrise over the headland. The sky was stained a deep dark violet – a colour which matched his mood.

The disastrous run of the cards had been the worst experience he had ever had as a gambler. He had started the evening with a bit of luck and a modest win. A little later, but while it was still early, he had taken a small loss against the Greek who had bought the baccarat shoe. It was nothing serious, but just enough to unsettle him. To give his luck time to change back, he had joined friends for dinner on the balcony overlooking the harbour. After dinner Tom felt so confident he absolutely *knew* luck was riding with him again.

He was wrong.

Hand after hand the cards were against him. He refused to give up. With the same lazy smile on his face, but with his stomach growing colder and colder, he plunged on. When his cash and then his credit with the casino were exhausted, the Greek offered to play him privately head-to-head. By then Tom was in so deep he had, he thought, nothing to lose. The cards couldn't run that way for ever. All he needed was a little luck. A rabbit's foot, a dried mole hand, the black truffle – anything to change the run of the cards.

It was not to be.

At dawn the Greek called it a day. For Tom the cards hadn't changed. Remorselessly they'd continued to fall against him. When the table broke up, Tom owed the man over half a million francs.

'I'll need a little time to have the transfer telegraphed from London,' Tom said with his most winning smile.

'Don't worry!' The Greek grinned back at him expansively. 'I'll give you all the time you need. Say, forty-eight hours. We Greeks have a saying: "What cannot be done in a day cannot be achieved in a lifetime." We allow you two lifetimes. Meanwhile you sign this, no?'

The IOU Tom signed had a call-date of exactly forty-eight hours by the clock in the square from the moment they walked out of the casino.

Tom spent the morning on the telephone. His call to his London bankers merely resulted in a chill refusal to extend the credit raised on the security of Astley Keep and its lands.

There were times when he knew he'd sailed too close to the wind; but this hadn't, he thought, been one of them. He felt he had invested the marriage settlement wisely.

He had made a clean sweep and paid off his old debts – tailor, hatter, shoemaker, shirtmaker, turf account, wine merchant – in cash. He had even repaid, with handsome interest, the four-figure sum he owed to the doorman of his club – a man beloved among the younger members of the aristocracy for his ability to come up with the necessary bob or two, in cash, when unofficial creditors pressed.

The balance he'd used as his gambling float, taking only a proportion to buy the beautiful motor-yacht he could see bobbing at anchor by the quayside below.

It had never been the slightest use asking his mother for money. She was not her father's daughter for nothing. She had not even provided bail the time he had been taken in for possession of marijuana. 'Let the boy stay there,' she had said cheerfully. 'It'll teach him to be more careful.' He had spent a cold and uncomfortable night in the cells.

This was different. The Greek ship-owners were the highest rollers in the world. If they weren't paid, they could see that he was blackballed in every casino where they took their custom – and that was in every gambling-hall from Monte to Havana. He would be finished in his chosen world. To a gambler there was no worse fate.

This time the *Dorian Gray* would have to go. Except that the *Dorian Gray* was his lifeline. Without her he was lost. Finished. There had to be another way.

Emerald. She had bailed him out before – even though she hadn't known it. Now she was in a position to bail him out again.

He hoped to God it would be his wife and not his mother who picked up the telephone.

Emerald was his only hope.

It was one in the morning on the night of the heir ale when the telephone rang at Astley Keep.

Sleepily, Emerald reached for the instrument.

As usual, the timing and the crackling line heralded the identity of the caller. When Tom made his calls it was always from some casino bar at peculiar hours of the night.

'Emerald?'

'Tom?'

'Thank God it's you. Thought it might have been the old trout. You on your own?'

Emerald rubbed her eyes. 'Sure. I'd certainly have noticed if I wasn't.'

'Good. Look, old girl, I'm afraid I'm in a bit of a spot.' The voice was cautious. 'Circumstances beyond my control.'

Emerald wrenched her mind out of sleep. 'What happened, Tom? Why didn't you come to the heir ale?'

'Sorry, sweetheart. Didn't mean to let you down – or Jamie.' Tom sounded like a penitent small boy. 'How did it go?'

'Fine. Terrific.'

'Good. So glad. Makes it a little easier.'

'Makes *what* a little easier?'

'Not very sensible, I'm afraid. Money.'

'Oh God. How much?'

There was silence. Then Tom's voice again. 'Twenty thou. Sorry, old girl. Not very wise.'

'What on earth *for*, Tom?'

' 'Fraid I've done it this time. My luck ran out. In a manner of speaking, I did it for you. Wanted to bring you and Jamie back a present. Should have had you there as my lucky penny. Remember that first time?'

Emerald's voice was quiet. 'I remember.'

'Then, we understand each other. Look, Emerald, I'm desperate. I've tried everywhere. You're my last hope.'

'Tom, I haven't got that kind of money.'

There was another crackle of static and the sound of coins falling in the telephone-box.

'Emerald? Are you still there?'

'Yes.'

'You'll get it back in a few days. My luck'll turn – and there's always the *Dorian Gray*. You know I wouldn't ask unless . . . there was no alternative.'

Behind the lazy drawl Emerald recognized the hard edge of panic.

'Tom, are you in danger?'

'Just do it, my sweet. Cash – no banker's drafts. For me and for your – our – son.'

Emerald's blood ran cold. Tom had called in a debt. It was his to call.

'It'd have to come from the business. I'll need time.'

'Haven't got it, my darling. Pistols at dawn, figuratively speaking.'

Emerald was silent. Then she said: 'When and where?'

'Monte. Tomorrow at sunset. Six o'clock. No later. Down by the *Dorian Gray*. I'll be waiting.'

The line went dead.

The following morning, Emerald set out for London at first light. Somehow she would have to make Peter Trevelyan do what she asked.

72

Monte Carlo and London: 1963

When Tom put down the telephone after his conversation with Emerald, he did a very foolish thing.

It was partly because, hearing Emerald's voice, he suddenly felt guilty.

It was partly because, as long as he was not required to warm her bed, Emerald brought out the best in him. They did not see each other very often but, after his fashion, he loved her. It was a strange irony that, in making his marriage-bed, for the first time in his life he had been able to offer a woman what she needed. Although all he had asked from her was the bride-price, Emerald had given him far more than that.

By rebuilding Astley – however much he disliked the place – she had discharged his debt to his forebears. His ancestors would have understood their arrangement. The crusaders had gone off to the wars and left the women in charge. If necessary, they, too, had had to pawn the family lands to ransom their men.

The arrangement between Tom and Emerald had never been anything but an agreement between equals. Had things been different, he reflected, their life together might almost have been . . . a *marriage*. As it was, they both had to do the best they could.

And the best Tom could do was find another way to recoup his losses. He would ride into battle in the only way he knew how. He owed it to Emerald. To Jamie. To Astley.

Roulette is the gambler's last resort. Lady Luck reigns supreme over the spin of the wheel. There are those who believe that the lady can be beaten; that the fall of the little ball in the red or the black can be predicted by the laws of mathematics.

Tom knew better. In the hand-to-hand street-fighting of those games where one man pitted his wits against another, and the fall of the cards, there was at least an element of certainty – of skill.

Like all gamblers, Tom had developed his own rituals. When he knew that Lady Luck had truly abandoned him, he threw himself on her mercy, played the game which was hers alone. It was an act of homage to the lady – and it had never failed him yet.

All he had to do was follow certain rules. Red or black. Double or quits. All he needed was a stake.

There was one avenue still open to him. It was dangerous, foolhardy, but it was there. Now, certain that Emerald would deliver, he felt brave enough to take it.

He went down to the harbour front and started up the speedboat's engines and headed along the coast. The *Dorian Gray* was the only instantly negotiable asset he had. There was only one way he could raise the money and not have to part with her – unless, of course, he defaulted on the debt – and Tom had a gambler's certainty that the last throw of the dice would scoop the pool.

Dawn was just breaking as the boat bumped against the quay of Vieux Port in Marseilles. The time of day was immaterial. The pawnbroker Tom intended to visit kept unusual hours. He had to. He ran an usual business.

In a back room of a certain chandler's on the Canebière, a sober-suited agent of the milieu, the local branch of the Mafia, acted as an unofficial banker to those whose cargoes were of interest to Interpol. Drug-dealers and gun-runners had rather more need of credit than most – and their activities were most comfortably conducted in the dead of night, or the small hours of the morning, or whenever the local *flics* were safely tucked up out of harm's way.

The dealers pledged their boats against the price of the cargo. Since delivery depended on the debtor retaining the use of his pledge, the agreement was strictly credit – belief between gentlemen, honour among thieves. There was little danger of the customers reneging on their debts. One way or another, the milieu could always collect.

Going to the milieu was the only decision Tom could have taken which was more foolhardy than chancing his arm against the Greeks.

But in his new mood of optimism, as volatile as the goddess he worshipped, Tom didn't care.

If he was not a gambler, he was nothing.

A gambler without a stake is no gambler at all.

Long before Emerald had gained admittance to Peter Trevelyan's office, Tom had raised the stake he needed on the pledge of the *Dorian Gray*.

The milieu was willing to accommodate him – at a price. It was unusual, but the English milord was well known on the coast. The interest rate was a hundred per cent for twenty-four hours. An IOU would not be necessary; the milord's word was enough.

Tom was exultant. On his return to Toytown, he went straight to the roulette wheel at the far end of the Kitchen. It was his lucky wheel.

He was certain there would be a run on black. He was right. His system ran for nine spins of the wheel; the money doubled each time. Nine times the little ball flickered and danced as it rushed round the black and red whirlpool.

Sensing the drama, a crowd gathered.

'Milord?'

The croupier's rake hovered over the pile of chips, ready to push them over to the winner.

Tom smiled and shook his head.

'Laissez-le.'

He let his stake ride – even though the money he had already won was more than enough to pay off the Greeks and redeem his pledge of the *Dorian Gray*, with interest. It was not yet enought to buy Emerald a little trinket, the obligatory tribute to that other Lady whose attentions were far less constant.

He had to play by the Lady's rules. Ten spins of the wheel was the system – and there had only been nine.

The croupier shrugged. Winner or loser, it was all good for the bank. The zero, the bank's cut, saw to that.

He spun the wheel.

'Rien ne va plus.'

Then, flirtatious as a soubrette, inconstant as an expensive mistress, the little white ball tumbled on red.

Tom stared at the spinning wheel in mute horror.

He had been expecting trouble, but not on the scale that now confronted him.

The milieu would know immediately that he had lost. They had eyes and ears in every corner; he even imagined he had seen a half-familiar face among the crowd of onlookers. And once they knew he was finished.

Now at last Tom was truly frightened. The Greeks could whistle for their money; there were far bigger sharks after his blood. To the milieu, a debtor who doesn't meet his debts is a dead man.

Emerald was waiting on the steps of the bank when it opened for business. Yes, Mr Trevelyan was in his office. Yes, he could see Lady Sherwood immediately after his first appointment.

Emerald breathed a sigh of relief. If Peter was there, she was in with a chance.

'Lady Sherwood, Emerald, such a pleasure, always.'

Emerald came straight to the point. 'Peter, I need to raise money. How much can I pledge against the business?'

The banker stared at her. 'What do you mean? All of it?'

'All of it, Peter. The order book's full. We can deliver.' Emerald's gaze was level. 'What can I raise if I pledge it all?'

Peter Trevelyan smiled nervously at the young woman. He had been pleased to find her downstairs as his first visitor of the morning. Emerald Sherwood always made him feel good. Protective. Gentlemanly. Even manly. It wasn't often that Peter Trevelyan allowed himself the luxury of feeling manly.

He said: 'How much do you need?'

'Twenty thousand. Now.'

Trevelyan coughed. He said, 'You're not serious?'

He regretted his words immediately. It was as clear as daylight she was serious.

He said carefully: 'There's still leeway on the collateral. We could manage five. I could take that decision without consultation.'

'I need twenty. Today. In cash.'

'Emerald, my dear . . .'

Trevelyan leaned back. She had done well with the business, but twenty thousand – that was absurd. He had taken a personal interest in the young woman. Nursed her into profitability. It had been a real success-story. Modest in terms of the City, but solid. A balance-sheet which balanced. In a year or two, he even thought she might get a quotation. Why in the name of all that was holy did she want to throw everything away?

'Peter, I need it. For the good of Astley.'

Emerald's violet eyes were intense – giving the lie to the calm voice.

'I understand what you say. But, if I might be allowed to enquire, why?'

Emerald shook her head.

'My dear' – Trevelyan's voice was exasperated – 'I shall need to know how the repayments are to be made. It's not just a matter of the security.'

Emerald took a deep breath.

'No, I am not at liberty to tell you why I need it. Nor can I say how it'll be repaid – unless it's through the business.'

Trevelyan tried again.

'Is it Tom?'

Emerald hesitated.

'My dear, discretion is one thing. But you'll have to be specific. I can't go to my partners and pull a loan that size out of a hat.'

'I realize that, Peter, and I've brought the order-books.' Emerald spread out the papers and began to explain.

Both Bergdorf Goodman and Macey's had reordered three times in the previous month, and she had had her first orders from San Francisco. She was already supplying outlets in France and Germany, and there was a company offering to import her products in bulk into Japan. The turnover had tripled in a year, and she had expanded her packaging-rooms into the stables and taken on three extra workers to handle the demand.

As she spoke, Trevelyan's mind wandered. Once again he noted the trim figure, the glorious legs, the beauty of her. He felt protective towards her. He never understood why it was that Emerald managed to make him think such thoughts. It was not at all correct banking practice. But it happened every time.

He forced himself to concentrate on what Emerald was telling him. He knew he would have to refuse what she asked.

The prospects for the future were all very well, but the business was still in its infancy, it could not possibly afford what she said she needed.

He wasn't so naïve he could not guess who was behind the request, even if she would not be the one to tell him.

He said gently: 'I admire your loyalty, my dear. But this money isn't to expand the business, is it? It's a loan – a loan to bail out your husband.'

Emerald turned away and walked over to the window. Outside the clouds were building up for a storm.

When she turned, her face was sombre. She said: 'Of course. But what can I do, Peter? I owe Tom everything. Astley, the estate, it's all his – morally, even if not practically. This is the only way I can repay my debt. Once and for all.'

'Look, my dear. If it's blackmail—'

Emerald turned her gaze on him. 'Peter, you're the only person in the world who can help me. The only man I can ask.'

His head swam. He looked at her again. The violet eyes were filled with tears.

'There, there, my dear.' Trevelyan patted the young woman's hand in dismay. Tears, such eyes filled with such tears – and for a ne'er-do-well who had never done a day's work in his life.

'Emerald . . .' Even then he knew he was lost, knew he had made up his mind as soon she had walked through the door.

Trevelyan battled to regain his objectivity. In vain he told himself he was a banker with a reputation to protect, that he never took decisions except on strictly commercial grounds.

Then he told himself the business was in profit; it was more than possible, with the estate now running at last in the black, that Emerald Sherwood could indeed repay the debt without ruining the business.

But in his heart he knew that such reasonings were merely the excuse for what he was about to do.

For the first time in his life, Peter Trevelyan did something to put his career at risk. He took a decision which no banker should ever take.

He handed Emerald his clean white silk handkerchief, and took the young woman down to the cashier.

There he signed a personal cheque drawn on his own account, and had the money counted out. Afterwards, he thought he must have been crazy. Except that if the young Lady Sherwood was as persuasive in the market-place as she was in the banking-hall, the money would be repaid in full.

Emerald took a taxi straight to the airport. By four o'clock – with two hours to go before her rendezvous – she was driving a rented car round the hogsback of the Grande Corniche, the heavy briefcase on the passenger-seat beside her.

She did not begrudge Tom the money.

Tom had given her everything, even her beloved Jamie had Tom to thank for a future. If her dowry had been a bride-price, the bank notes she was carrying in the briefcase represented a debt discharged in full.

With half an hour to go, she took the slalom-curved road which led down into the rocky peninsula of the principality, and drove down towards the harbour where she knew Tom would be anxiously awaiting her.

On the dot of six, Emerald was there on the quayside. Tom took the briefcase from her.

'Sweetheart, you're truly wonderful.'

With a toss of the still-golden curls, a flash of the still-brilliant smile, Tom was gone.

Ignoring the coastguard's warnings, he headed out into the open sea, the hull of the boat crashing against the rising billows. The storm was blowing from the north-east, an icy blast from the Urals.

Two hundred miles across the Mediterranean lay the safe haven of the international port of Tangier. In Tangier he had friends. In Tangier he could go to ground, disappear, vanish – for good, if need be.

If Tom had a plan at all, it was to cover his tracks. He had to make it seem as if the boys from Marseilles had got to the boat first. The storm provided the perfect opportunity. Two miles out he jettisoned the boat's inflatable yellow cushions and sent out a Mayday signal. Then he swung the wheel and made for the shelter of San Remo, a little fishing harbour across the Italian border. There he intended to wait for the storm to subside before making his way calmly across to the northern shores of Africa.

All night long the storm raged. The ocean hurled itself against Nice's palm-fringed esplanade, lapping the benches which lined the Boulevard des Anglais in Cannes. The storm lashed the white beaches of Sardinia and Sicily, ripping up shanty towns on the shores of the Mediterranean, howling down the seaways from the Dardanelles to the Pillars of Hercules.

All through the night Emerald watched from her window high above the harbour, bewildered by Tom's insanity at risking his beloved boat, his very life, on the turbulent waves.

Having logged the Mayday distress call, the patrol boats of the French coastguard had to wait till the storm abated at dawn before they could leave port.

After three days' search they picked up two inflatable yellow cushions with a coronet stamped into one corner. The English milord's wife herself – distraught from the long vigil – identified them as most probably the cushions from the *Dorian Gray*.

The English milord's beautiful young wife could not be certain, of course, as she had never been on the yacht. The gendarmerie shook their heads and returned to their desks. They thought it strange that a lady so young and so beautiful should not have been her husband's first choice of companion. But, then, Englishmen were like that. Passionless. They had water in their veins instead of blood.

The search was called off. The patrol boats of the French coastguard failed to find conclusive evidence that the Fairey Huntsman had gone down. The body of the well-known Riviera gambler had not surfaced.

Or so the official files recorded. In other quarters a different story began to circulate. The men from Marseilles, it was said, had once again been obliged to teach a debtor a lesson. The milord had failed to acknowledge a debt of honour. He had paid for his carelessness with his life.

How else could his foolhardy voyage be explained, except that the devil behind him must have seemed more fearsome than the rising billows ahead?

At the very moment Tom was heading out into the open sea, Jack Sweeney was putting the finishing touches to his morning's work in New York.

As yet he knew nothing of the drama about to be played out in the Mediterranean storm. Nevertheless Emerald was on his mind. He was in the process of filing one of what he had come to see as his regular insurance payments. His little nuggets, buried among the dross of his column.

He had picked up the story of the heir ale on the wires and given it a quick reworking, telephoning around for a few quotes, and using a little creative reconstruction to fill in the gaps.

He studied the result with satisfaction.

HOW TO BE A MILLIONAIRE

Knock, knock, who's heir?

Not Tom Sherwood. Yesterday England's most exotic lord of the manor failed to pop up at the party to mark five-year-old son Jamie's 'heir ale'. No party-pooper, wife Emerald went ahead anyway. The champagne flowed as the Honourable James was declared *'heres insolitus'* to a thousand acres of England's leafy Dorset. Shake out those lovelocks, little ladies – we're talking a million dollars.

Lady Emerald flogs floral face-masks to the cream of the Chelsea set. And as an old friend of the family – Emmie and I go way back – I can confirm that the former Paradise Perfume girl is looking just peachy on her own potions.

Some smart cookie, Dorset's premier lady of the manor and business-woman of the year took advantage of the tea-party to launch her new perfume, Emerald's Secret.

Business is blooming already. Trills leader of the Manhattan frock-pack, Di Vreeland: 'Deevee – it's me.'

So what's the secret? Keep it under your floral titfer, but mother-in-law Dr Bertha Sherwood admits she slipped in the magic ingredient. And as one of Europe's leading scientists Granny ain't no slouch when it comes to brewing up a cauldron.

Well, wad'ya know? Someone has to keep the roof on the old ancestral – and it sure ain't going to be the Baron. While Daddy chances his luck at the tables, Mum prefers to back a sure-fire winner: herself.

A little bird tells me Emmie's got a few more secrets up her sleeve. Can't wait – can you?

Jack leaned back, typed in his by-line, and took the story down to the typesetters. He ran it as the second lead in *Jack's Trash,* clipped a cutting as it came off the presses, and posted it off to Lady Sherwood at Astley Keep.

The piece was nicely crafted to serve its purpose. Just to remind Her Ladyship of old times. Of the debt she owed Jack Sweeney. She'd know what he meant.

Why, she might even be secretly pleased to hear from him. Jack knew women. They never knew what they wanted till they got it. And Emerald Sherwood, for all her airs and graces, was only a woman.

73

Tangier: 1963

The storm into which the *Dorian Gray* had vanished lashed the coast of North Africa, bringing a brief respite from the violence in the streets of Tangier.

Morocco was the latest war zone. The king had declared his intention to launch an offensive against the incursions of republican Algeria, his turbulent neighbour. Those who felt the monarchy had outrun its writ took to the streets. It was expected that Tangier itself would be first victim of a strike from the sea. With ten thousand troops on their way to the border, the garrison of the port was preparing itself for Algeria's retaliation.

The press corps, the war reporters whose numbers had been swollen by the liberation struggles of the past decade, had descended like a flock of vultures. Most of them were decanted into the luxury hotels, propping up the bar along with the arms dealers and the mercenary soldiers – the jackals of the battlefields. Some of them, Callum Fergusson foremost among them, dived into the fray.

Wars sold newspapers. And it was war and the fear it engendered – the knowledge that at any moment he might meet a sniper's bullet – which kept Callum from confronting his own despair.

It had surprised those who had known him before that the former society portraitist had become a news photographer whose very presence in a war zone guaranteed a sharp increase in press interest.

The newspaper editors who admired and published Callum's work thought the young photographer was fuelled by bravery. But Callum knew it was not courage which took him into the screaming heart of the battle. Having lost Emerald, he had nothing left to lose. He had no desire to return to his homeland. He sent off his images and left it to the editors to use them as they pleased.

The young photographer showed no outward sign of his occupation as he made his way through the rain-lashed alleys. Five years in his chosen profession had taught him the value of discretion in dangerous places. The military who policed the streets did not stop and search Europeans – unless they were pointing indiscreet cameras at events or persons the military did not wish to have recorded.

Driven off the streets by the storm, Callum made his way to the Hotel Mammounia, where the splendour of the surroundings and the air-conditioning dulled the summer stench of the city.

'Hair of the dog, old buddy?'

One of the stringers for the American wire services grinned sympathetically at his colleague's bloodshot eyes.

Callum nodded. 'Might be advisable.'

The stringer shifted on his stool and thumped on the polished mahogany bar. 'Another special, Ahmed.'

'Yes, sir.' Ahmed's specials were an evil brew of yolk of egg, tomato juice and Pernod. He finished it with a shot of something scarlet and fiery from a bottle he kept under the counter.

'This one's on me.' The stringer pushed over the glass, watching as Callum lifted it to his lips. 'Got anything?'

It was the question posed automatically by all those who preferred the home comforts of the bar.

Callum shrugged. 'Bit of trouble in the docks—'

'Serious? Body-count?'

'A couple.'

'Anyone?'

Callum shook his head. 'Anyone' meant anyone newsworthy. The bodies were nameless victims of what had become an everyday occurrence. No-one and nothing which would serve more purpose than to illustrate a brief paragraph on the troubles – more troubles – in the boiling cauldron of the ex-French dependencies.

His companion grinned sympathetically. 'Do for stock. Can't win 'em all.' He stood up and stretched. 'Got to see a man in the souk. Something about a trip to the border.'

'Interesting?'

The stringer shook his head. 'All mouth and no action. Bloody darkies.'

Callum grinned. The man was a black American. 'Bit like you, Bob.'

'Yeah. Well.' The stringer patted his pocket and pulled out a roll of newsprint. 'Seen the paper? Here, I finished it already. Yesterday's. Gold dust, man. Want it?'

Callum glanced down.

He made it a rule never to read the newspapers to which he contributed. It was far less painful to bury himself in his work, using his camera as a barrier against reality, screening him from anything which might remind him of the woman he had loved and so cruelly lost. In time the pain had faded into a dull ache – rarely felt, but always there.

But this particular paper was unlikely to contain anything more personal than the baseball scores. It was a New York gossip-and-sex rag he hadn't seen before, *The Whisper*.

Idly he flicked over the pages. Suddenly he stopped, his eye caught by a familiar by-line. Jack Sweeney. Unable to resist his own curiosity, he read the opening paragraphs.

Jack hadn't changed his spots – only the jungle in which he hunted. New York society names, the doings of some Hollywood starlet and her sixth husband occupied the first few column inches. But it was the second item which reduced him first to stunned astonishment and then to a wild unreasoning joy.

Emerald. The story was about Emerald. He stared down, the words blurred into the paper.

His heart lifted with hope. Emerald. Truly and undoubtedly Emerald herself. Greedily he read on. No matter that she had made another life of which he knew nothing. It was enough that she had not perished, as he thought, in the flames of the house in Notting Hill. Enough that she was alive – alive and well.

The article – Jack's familiar mixture of malice and gossip – mentioned a son. A five-year-old son. Even if the innuendo that the child was not her husband's had not been plainly visible between the lines, Callum would have known the child was his. He felt it in his bones, in the very depth of his being.

His first thought was that he must go to her. Discover what had happened. Hold in his arms the child he was convinced must be his own.

Then, more soberly, he came to count the cost. What of Emerald herself? What of the life she had made? The picture Sweeney had painted in his column was of a woman who had made her own success. Whatever was the truth, whatever it was which had led to the choice she had made – if it was indeed a choice, and not one of Anthony Anstruther's manipulations – the consequences would not so easily be unravelled.

In the wake of hope came despair. He had nothing to give her, nothing to put in the place of the glittering life she had made for herself. Nothing except himself, and it seemed that had never been enough.

Later that evening, defying the curfew and the storm, he found his way to one of the bead-curtained, carpet-hung brothels in the port which catered to the needs of those men, armed or not, who had no home to go to.

Dawn found him in the arms of a young sloe-eyed whore who, somehow – when his perception had been sufficiently dulled by drink – by a flick of russet hair or a faint freckle on a rounded shoulder, reminded him of the woman he had lost.

The following morning, the storm had passed. The souk was crowded. There was merchandise to be bought and sold: there were deals to be concluded. On the surface, at least, it was business as usual.

It took a cameraman's eye to pick up the absences among the swirling white jellabas and clatter of commerce. Today Callum noticed that the women and children seemed to have stayed at home and there was a casualness about the discussions, a lack of concentration, as if something other than financial transactions preoccupied the participants.

Callum left the main concourse with its patrolling soldiers, and ducked under an archway which led into the scented shadows of the spice souk. Spices – freshly ground cloves and cinnamon, cardamom and coriander, were a daily requirement of every Middle Eastern housewife, and the souk was always well patronized.

Not today. In the shadowy doorways where children usually tumbled, there were only a few old men sipping mint tea and playing their endless games of chess.

The word was out that there was to be trouble. There were those who felt that the war was unjust, who saw it as an opportunity to throw off the despotic yoke of the hereditary monarchy. Those who were anxious to fan the flame of conflict into civil war.

Keeping his head well down, his powerful shoulders hunched and his camera buttoned under his loose linen jacket, Callum walked swiftly down a cobbled alleyway which opened alongside the harbour.

A stretch of quay was cordoned off around the three tall grey warships. The authorities were taking no chances. The soldiers guarding the ships

513

were unmistakable in the kepis of the élite French mercenary force, the Foreign Legion.

Callum halted and glanced up and down the quayside. There was no sign of trouble. Yet.

He turned his back to the wary garrison of legionnaires, and walked slowly away towards the string of cafés which backed the landing-pier for the fishermen. He slowed down at the corner kiosk which stocked chewing gum and cigarettes sold in singles.

He leaned casually against the kiosk, out of sight of the men with guns, and began to record the images around him.

The clicking of the shutter rattled like gunfire in that moment of silence, the familiar hush before battle when all life, even the mangy cats scuttling among the dustbins, seemed to hold its breath.

He turned the lens towards the warships, panning down the big grey wolves among the bobbing crowds of fishing boats. A sleek motor-boat rode at anchor alongside a dirty little coaster, its long lean lines battered by the recent storm. A tall young man, his blond hair ruffled by the breeze, was busying himself with the mooring-ropes.

The man on the boat was the only living creature on the harbour front who did not seem to feel the electricity of fear.

'You over there!' Callum's voice echoed loud in the silence.

The man turned, shading his eyes with his hand against sun.

Callum let his camera swing loose and windmilled his arm.

'For Christ's sake, get off and get down!'

At the sound of the voice, one of the kepi'd legionnaires swung round, pinpointing a small group of figures crouched in the shadows of one of the café doorways.

The man on the boat hesitated for an instant, then he ducked down into the cabin, re-emerging in a moment with a heavy briefcase.

At the same moment, gunshots cracked out.

For an instant the man hesitated, then leaped the gap between the deck and the lower step leading to the quayside. He covered the few yards to the protection of the kiosk in seconds.

'Jesus!' Callum could hear the breath expelled in a long sigh as the body hit the cobbles.

For the next few minutes, all hell broke loose.

The first mortar-shot was almost silent, arching within inches of the vacated deck of the boat, landing with a dull thud into the cobblestones, scattering debris and rocks which shattered those few windows which still had glass.

The second was followed by an explosion of flame, a billow of black smoke and an arc of flaming debris.

Callum felt the kick of the blast against his ribcage, the shuddering of the concrete pavement beneath his body.

The firing began again immediately, the sharp crack of bullets ricocheting off the cobblestones. Then came a sound which never failed to turn his stomach – the soft dull thud of metal tearing into flesh.

Then came the screaming. The sound of human fear was the worst of war. Worse than the blood and splintered bone, worse even than the stench of excrement which inevitably accompanied violent death.

Callum could get used to anything – no sight was too horrific to make him forget to press the shutter – but he never got used to the noise of bullets thudding into bodies.

After a moment, silence fell again. Callum raised his head cautiously, the camera at the ready.

He looked down. The square frame of the viewfinder reduced the scene to a miniature peepshow of destruction. Swinging the camera round, he chose his images. An old man crumpled over a chess game. A child running towards its mother.

It was not until he had recorded the human debris that he panned down the battleships and over the space the storm-battered boat had occupied a few moments earlier. A spreading slick of diesel fuel testified to the boat's fate.

Callum glanced down. He said. 'It's OK – all over.'

'Christ.' The man groaned and raised himself gingerly to a sitting position. His face was sheet-white with fear. He was still clutching the briefcase which had so nearly cost him his life.

Callum added. 'Seems to have done for your pretty little boat, though. You were in the nick of time.'

The man staggered to his feet, walked over to the quay, and stood staring down at the oily slick of debris which was all that was left of the beautiful boat. After a moment he swung round and stared at Callum.

'What the hell was that about?'

Callum shrugged. 'Trouble. A ton of explosive makes a mess.'

'Shit,' said the man. 'The bastards.'

Callum said quietly, 'Two dead. At least four wounded. You were lucky. We both were.'

'Sweet Jesus.'

Callum said: 'Narrow squeak.'

The Englishman held out his hand. 'I believe, sir, you saved my life.' The public-school drawl was unmistakable.

Callum accepted the proffered hand. He looked at the fingers. Long, slender and beautifully manicured. The wrist was trembling. He said: 'You OK?'

'Sure. Just not used to that kind of thing.'

Callum glanced up the now-deserted quay. Two of the legionnaires were coming over in their direction.

Callum said: 'Shit. I think we better get the hell out before anyone starts asking questions.'

The two men dived into the maze of streets, threading swiftly along the dark alleyways until the pursuing cries had faded.

Although he had initially taken the lead, Callum quickly yielded to the newcomer, aware that he clearly knew the short-cuts even better than Callum did.

Once they had joined the busy crowds in the spice souk, the man came to halt.

'We'll be OK now. Have you somewhere to go?'

'Yes, I'm here with the press corps.'

'Fine.' The man's lips curled nervously, part grimace, part smile, showing a line of perfect teeth. 'Look, I scarcely feel I should ask, but can you keep quiet about this – that you saw me, what happened about the boat? Got to lie low for a bit. You know how it is.'

Callum grinned. 'Easy. I don't even know your name.'

The man looked at Callum thoughtfully. 'Look, could I ask a favour? Could you make a private telephone call for me? Safer than if I do it myself. Just a short message to say I'm all right. No names, no geography – just that I've had a spot of bother, but I'll be in touch.'

'Sure. Who to?'

'I'll write it down.'

The man fumbled in his pocket and brought out a scrap of paper. He scribbled down a number and a name.

'Long-distance, I'm afraid. Here – a couple of dollars should cover it.'

The man held out two crumpled bills and the paper.

'Sure.'

The man hesitated again. 'Destroy the note, there's a good chap, when you've made the call. Sorry to be so cloak-and-dagger – wouldn't if it wasn't absolutely necessary. Discretion, I mean.'

Callum shrugged. 'I'm a war reporter. It's normal. You may be able to return the favour.'

'Of course. Like to buy you a drink. Any time. Several drinks, I hope. Dinner. Whatever. Eddie's will find me. Just give your name to Maman, the old dragon who guards the gate.'

Callum grinned. 'Maybe.'

'Good.' The man's face split into the nervous smile. 'Well, better get out of the firing line.'

In a moment the Englishman had vanished into the market crowd.

Eddie's, Callum had already discovered, was the nickname for one of the port's more notorious bordellos. The place also served up the best French food in Tangier.

Callum knew that Eddie's also served as a meeting place for the town's more exotic expatriates and their young friends. He speculated to himself that the Englishman might well share their tastes.

It was not until Callum made his way up to his rented room in the souk, and emptied his pockets of the exposed spools of film, that he looked at the name he had been asked to telephone.

For a long moment Callum stared down at the scribbled words.

He clenched his fists, uncertain whether to feel joy or anguish. There was no doubt at all of the identity of the man whose life he had saved.

He had really no need to check his cutting of Jack Sweeney's gossip column, but he did so just the same.

It was as if a spell had been broken – as if a window had opened, letting in the light of day.

Frantically he searched for the little bracelet which Anstruther had given him in the hospital. It was all he had to remind him of Emerald. It was safe. He stared down at the little jewelled cross which dangled from one link, turned it over and read the inscription once again, even though he knew it by heart.

The talisman clasped firmly in one hand, he went down to the public telephone exchange and dialled the number on the card.

So tightly did he clench his fist that – when he returned to his rooms after the call had been made – he found his palm had kept the print.

74

Astley Keep: 1963

The morning after the storm, Peter Trevelyan was on the telephone to Astley before breakfast. And Bertha knew she – and Emerald – had a crisis on their hands.

The estate's assets would certainly be frozen in the wake of Tom's disappearance.

The courts were quite clear in such cases. The period which had to elapse before a missing person could be declared legally of no account was seven years. Meanwhile applications could be made so that an allowance might be made for the support of the presumed widow and her children.

Could Emerald keep an appointment with him most urgently? There was the matter of an unsecured loan to be clarified. And with the likely freezing of the estate's assets, the underpinning for the business, Dr Sherwood would understand the urgency.

Bertha could not bring herself to believe that her son would not somehow manage to get himself out of whatever trouble he had landed himself in.

She did not feel it necessary to tell Emerald about Trevelyan's call when she came on the line with the news that the *Dorian Gray*'s cushions had been salvaged.

'Don't worry, my dear,' Bertha assured her distraught daughter-in-law on the telephone in the south of France, 'Tom's a survivor. Always has been.'

'The French seem convinced the boat went down. I hope to God you're right.'

'I'm sure I am.'

Nevertheless Bertha was worried. It came as a considerable relief when, late in the evening on the day after the yellow cushions had been found, with Emerald already on her way home, she received another telephone call – this time from an unfamiliar caller.

The static on the line and the connecting operator's voice confirmed it was long-distance.

'Dr Sherwood?' The voice was a young man's.

'Yes.'

'I have a message from Tom.'

'Thank heavens. Tell me.'

'He asked me to tell you he's safe, and you're not to worry.' A moment of hesitation. 'There's been a bit of trouble. He's had to disappear – go underground.'

'I won't even ask what kind of trouble he's got himself into. Just tell him I expect him to get himself out of it. With the least damage to the rest of us.'

'He'll be in touch himself; but meanwhile it's better that things remain as they seem. I wonder – could I ask you – how is Emerald? And Jamie?'

'Fine. And who, might I ask, are you?'

The man took a moment to reply. Then, cautiously: 'An old friend. An old friend of your daughter-in-law.'

'I see.' Bertha noticed the traces of a Scottish accent.

'Dr Sherwood, could you tell Emerald that I called?'

'Certainly, young man. But you have not yet told me who you are?'

The only reply was the buzz of static. The line had already gone dead.

Bertha sighed as she replaced the telephone on the hook. The news, welcome as it was, meant nothing but trouble for those who had to clear up the debris. And that, in essence, was Emerald.

'Astley Halt coming up, sir.'

The uniformed guard poked his head into the first-class compartment and nodded to the smartly dressed gentleman who had requested the optional stop on the branch line which served the hamlet of Astley.

Usually, after twenty-five years on the line, he knew most of the passengers who descended at the little unmanned station. Locals coming

519

and going from Market Bisworth just down the line, travelling salesmen in agricultural requirements, dealers in livestock, the gentry taking a few days in Town. But today's traveller, muffled up in a heavy overcoat, with dark glasses shading his eyes, was hard to place.

'You'll be for the Big House?'

The man hesitated. 'Just passing through.'

The guard peered at his passenger. One of the things he enjoyed about his job was the contact with people. Not that he was nosey, of course. Just that he liked to have a bit of a chat. It livened up the day.

Take the young lady of the manor from the Keep for instance. *She* was a pretty one – a real lady. Good manners. And she always had a moment for a chat. The disappearance of her husband had been in all the papers. The guard hoped that the news was good.

He turned his attention back to the passenger. The stranger was clearly not going to indulge the guard's curiosity about his identity.

The accent, too, was hard to place. Not quite one of the gentry – giving the lie to the expensive city clothes. Sounded a bit of a foreigner maybe. There had been a lot of them about in the war.

The guard tried again. 'There's the Pig and Whistle at the end of the village. They do rooms if you'll be needing one.'

The stranger nodded. Then he moved towards the door.

The rhythm of the train slowed.

'Coming up now, sir.'

The guard stood aside to let his passenger through.

The train swayed as the brakes were applied. The man checked his watch.

The guard wondered again what the man's business could possibly be in the little village of Astley.

'I'll get the door open, sir. Mind the step.'

The traveller pushed past the conductor and jumped down onto the platform. He gazed around, then walked over to the ticket office and asked directions to Astley Keep.

'You sure you don't want a taxi, sir?'

'No, thanks. I'd like the walk.'

'A mile up the lane and over the stile, then, sir. Follow the lake round, and take the short-cut through the gardens. You can't miss it.'

The windows of the great house blazed in the last of the evening's sun.

The man had no trouble slipping the ornate Victorian lock on the kitchen door. He paused and listened.

He had been watching the house patiently for an hour. He had powerful enough binoculars to pick out the movements of the inhabitants. He was confident that the old woman and her maidservant were tucked out of the way in the cavernous kitchens at the back.

The child's room was on the first floor. He counted the doors. The third along.

He pushed the door ajar. The hinge creaked softly. The room smelled clean and sweet and faintly of talcum powder.

There was a rustle of bedclothes. The child's voice broke the silence. 'Who's there?'

Jamie sat up sleepily. He peered through the darkness at the crack of light showing along the edge of the door.

'Piglet? Is that you, Piglet?'

Jamie had gleefully christened Mrs Piggot as soon as he had been able to get his small tongue round the word.

'Who is it?'

The child's voice was more doubtful but still unafraid.

Jamie had no reason be afraid. He had never met anyone who wished him harm. The rambling great house was his playground. There were no corners of it he had not explored, no turret-stair he had not climbed.

The crack of light was briefly obscured by a shadow.

The floorboards creaked.

Someone had slipped into the room. This time the silence triggered un-accountable waves of fear in Jamie. He wondered if he should scream.

Boys don't scream.

Bertha was working late at her desk. While Emerald was away, she had set aside her own tasks to give Jamie all her attention.

The little boy was due to go to his first real school in three weeks' time, and his grandmother was determined he would be reading and writing before his first day.

She had tried to keep everything which touched her grandson as normal as possible throughout the upheavals which surrounded Tom's disappearance. It had not been easy. Jamie was old enough to sense when things were amiss, and certainly the events of the past few days – constant badgering from the press and all the conversations behind closed doors when she took the calls from Emerald – had unsettled the household.

In Emerald's absence, Bertha had spent her mornings with Jamie at the nursery table teaching the little boy his letters – a task normally undertaken by his mother. She gave the lessons her own twist; 'A is for ant' and 'B is for bee' triggered little stories about the daily life of the insects she had spent her lifetime studying.

Jamie loved the lessons. He was a quick learner, and Bertha was delighted with his progress.

Bertha had always regretted that she had been too young and pre-occupied with her work to enjoy her own son, and as soon as Jamie was born she had resolved that with her grandson it would be different.

The afternoons were for field trips – the only knowledge she felt was truly worth acquiring. And, the day before, she had taken Jamie out at midnight to investigate the barn owls which were rearing young in one of the barns. The fluffy chicks were almost as big as their parents, and would soon be ready to hunt for themselves.

Now, as she picked up the faint sound of movement on the floor above, she thought Jamie might have decided he would check on the progress of the owl fledglings. She would have done the same thing at his age. She paused in her work and listened intently. The noise had a furtive edge to it; it was not the cheerful patter of her grandson's bare feet, nor the firm purposeful step of Mrs Piggot.

There was an intruder in the house.

Quietly Bertha moved to the foot of the wide staircase which led to the upper floors. She began to climb.

Among other things he had learned from his grandmother, Jamie had learned how to track a fox to its lair; how to tell from the gnawed bones what prey the vixen had taken home to feed her cubs.

To the little boy, half-awake and peering into the narrow beam of light from the door, the man looked like a fox. A dog-fox, come to eat him for its dinner.

Jamie remembered what the rabbits did, and burrowed down beneath the bedclothes.

The fox moved towards him.

Jamie curled himself into a little ball, and waited for the fox to go away. He wondered what the rabbits felt when the fox caught them. Once he had seen a big buck rabbit use its back legs to flip a fox cub out of the mouth of the communal burrow. It had only been a cub, but just the same the rabbit had won. Jamie had been glad.

Remembering, Jamie drew his feet up to his chest and waited for the fox to pounce. Just like the big buck rabbit, he would be ready.

The floorboards creaked again.

Jamie opened one eye and stared up.

The fox was staring right back down at him. It had sandy brows and little glittering eyes.

Jamie bunched his thigh muscles, just like the big buck rabbit, and shot his feet out with all his might. He caught the fox right off guard. He could feel his heels punching right into the soft underbelly.

'Christ, ya wee bugger . . .'

The man reeled back, temporarily winded. Then he reached forward, yanking the little boy out of bed by his pyjama collar.

'Jamie?'

Jamie, struggling frantically in the man's grip, heard his grandmother's deep voice. Her bulk was in the doorway. The light snapped on.

'What's all this?'

The intruder whirled round. He had not meant the little bastard any harm. He had only meant to get a good look at the boy, to confirm for himself what he already knew: that the child was indeed his.

'Granny . . .' Jamie wriggled out of the fox's grip.

'It's all right, Jamie. Tuck back into bed. This gentleman is just leaving.'

Bertha's voice was gentle, tranquil. Whatever the intruder had intended, there was no sense in scaring her grandson any more.

She turned her level gaze on the man. 'I don't think we have met? And you are . . . ?'

The man stared at the old woman, bewildered by her apparent calm.

He mumbled: 'Jack Sweeney, ma'am.'

'Mr Sweeney, delighted to meet you. And I am Dr Sherwood,' Bertha announced, for all the world as if they had just been introduced at a cocktail-party. 'Now, if you will follow me, Mr Sweeney, I think you have a little explaining to do.'

For an instant Jack felt like a guilty schoolboy, caught bullying a younger child in the playground.

'It's not what you think—'

'I'm sure it's not, Mr Sweeney. You can tell me all about it. Downstairs. Good night, Jamie. Tuck in now.'

Meekly Jack followed the old woman down the stairs.

As he did so, he felt his confidence returning. He had come to claim his own. He would no longer have to be content with reporting the doings of the idle rich.

He fully intended to join them.

Bertha had recognized the man's name immediately. Jack Sweeney was the author of the New York newspaper article which had arrived after the heir ale. Even though all publicity for the perfume was welcome, the item had had a sly twist to it – a thoroughly unpleasant edge. Bertha had had a premonition that the writer had an axe to grind as soon as she had read it.

As the interview had progressed, the man had done nothing to revise her opinion.

Bertha looked at him now over the top of her spectacles. She reflected she had rarely seen or heard a less appetizing specimen of humanity.

'Do I hear you right, Mr Sweeney? Are you telling me that because you had sexual relations with my daughter-in-law – and I only have your word for that – you feel you have a claim on her son? On my grandson?'

Jack grinned – a thin slash of yellowing teeth. 'Emerald and me were good friends. Very good friends. Yes, sir, we go *way* back.' Sweeney fell easily into the mid-Atlantic shorthand of his own gossip column. 'And being an intelligent woman of the world, Dr Sherwood,' Sweeney grinned, 'you know how it is. Springtime. Paris. Two young people. Heat of the moment.'

He rubbed his cheek thoughtfully. 'I'll admit I might have been a bit quick on the draw – taken the amber for the green – but that's not how it'll look in print. Passion. So easy to get carried away.'

'I think what you are describing is rape, Mr. Sweeney.'

Sweeney stared at the old woman. 'Who gives a damn what it's called? The child's mine. And I can prove it.'

'Can you, indeed? A wise man.'

Sweeney grinned. He propped his feet up on an inlaid marble-topped table which Bertha kept piled with scientific journals.

He narrowed his eyes. 'Bastards seem to run in the family, wouldn't you say, Dr Sherwood?'

'I thoroughly approve of bastards,' Bertha said quietly. 'If they are so by birth rather than by choice.'

A scavenger, thought Bertha to herself suddenly. Some men were hunters, but this man was a scavenger. A scavenging bully; and, like all bullies, he was a coward.

'In any case, I don't believe you, Mr Sweeney.'

Jack shrugged. 'Ask her.'

'I have no intention of burdening my daughter-in-law with irrelevancies, particularly at this time.'

'My feelings exactly, Your Ladyship. Which is why – to put it elegantly – I'm consulting you rather than the young lady herself. I hope we can come to an agreement without any further unpleasantness. And I can be very unpleasant – in print.'

'I've no doubt of that, Mr Sweeney.'

'Good. I felt sure we'd get on fine. I suggest we consider how best the family can recompense me if I – how shall we put it? – waive my rights to the son and heir.'

'I'm still waiting for your proof, Mr Sweeney.'

Jack rubbed his cheek again. 'Well, to put it vulgarly – and I can be a vulgar man, Your Ladyship – someone put a bun in the oven, and it certainly wasn't your son. But I'm sure I don't have to tell you that, Dr. Sherwood. Everyone knows your son's marriage is a sham – a deal rigged up between you and Billy Beaumont. The old faggot isn't above dropping a few hints when he thinks he's among friends.' Jack raised his sandy eyebrows. 'And even if Emerald herself isn't prepared to acknowledge the truth, as a scientist you know damn well there are tests.'

'I am perfectly aware of what science – or, in this case, biochemistry – can do.'

Bertha paused and examined her visitor as if he was an unsatisfactory laboratory specimen. 'I am also aware', she continued calmly, 'that as yet there is no test which can provide positive proof. The negative result merely indicates who could *not* be the parent, with various shades of likelihood in between. You'll have to do better than that, Mr Sweeney.'

Sure enough, the man's voice changed. There was a note of pleading in his voice.

'I'm a reasonable man, Dr Sherwood. Don't want to break up the happy party – get in the way of young Jamie's inheritance. Just collect what's owing to me. Reach an understanding.'

'We understand each other perfectly. You are making certain allegations about my daughter-in-law and my grandson. From this I deduce you hope for financial gain. I say you have no proof.'

The red wave washed over Jack. 'Look, old woman, I can blow your cosy family arrangement wide open. Spread Emerald's little secret all over the press. And I'm not talking about publicity for the perfume, either. I know just who and what she is – and why she's been so well protected.' He tapped his nose. 'Stinks of Establishment whitewash. And I've a shrewd idea who's holding the brush.'

Bertha's eyes met Jack's – locked and held. She thought she had never seen a face more twisted with greed. Now there was hate as well. She shook her head. Only humans were the victims of such emotions. No other mammal felt hatred for its victims. Hunger and fear – but not hatred.

'What an interesting idea, Mr Sweeney. But I'm afraid you're addressing yourself to the wrong quarter. I can in no way be considered an authority on my daughter-in-law's pedigree.'

'I have proof—'

'Young man, you are lying. If you had any such thing, you'd have used it long ago.'

'I don't think you heard me right.'

Bertha sighed. 'Many of my faculties are crumbling, but I'm happy to say that my hearing is perfect. I think you are under a misapprehension, Mr Sweeney. I could write you out a cheque here and now, but it would do you no good at all. As a result of my son's . . . unfortunate disappearance, I am informed the estate's assets are frozen for seven years. I assume you believed we'd be awash with money. But I'm afraid, sir, you couldn't be more wrong. You can naturally check the truth of what I say.'

Bertha picked up her pen. It began to move deliberately over the shiny lined paper.

'Mr Sweeney, you should have done your homework. I suggest you leave me to do mine.'

After a moment Bertha looked up. 'Still here, Mr Sweeney?'

It was a gesture Jack recognized. It was designed to humiliate him. To show him that she had much more important things on her mind. It was the same as when the schoolmistress on Eas Forse had caught him stealing sweeties from the box she kept to reward her most diligent pupils. The ones who *did* do their homework.

The memory unlocked all Jack's childhood bitterness. Once again the doors of privilege clanged shut. Once again he was left empty-bellied in the cold.

The red wave surged. Now he was leaning over her and shouting.

'I warn you, Dr Sherwood, you won't get rid of me. Ever. I shan't be cheated of what's mine. If it takes another twenty years, I'll still collect – one way or another. I'll wait my whole bloody life if need be, but I'll have it in the end. Don't any of you ever forget: Jack Sweeney will have what's owing. Now or later, you'll have to pay.'

'Goodbye, Mr Sweeney.'

Bertha rose to her feet, ambled over to the door and held it open.

'You wouldn't want to miss your train. I'm so sorry you've had to come all this way for nothing. Mrs Piggot will get you a cab.'

'Not for nothing, old woman.' The voice was low and full of menace. 'You tell your precious daughter-in-law, Jack Sweeney's still waiting for his dues. And the interest's piling up. Mark my words, sooner or later I'll teach you all a lesson you'll never forget.'

Later, when the man had gone, Bertha reflected that she had been right not even to ask the price of his silence. Even if she could have bought him off, if she had given in to every demand, she knew it would never have contented him.

What Jack Sweeney wanted was not his pound of flesh, but the blood which was shed in the cutting. And for a blood-lust there was no cure.

75

Astley Keep: 1963

As Emerald swung the car into the driveway and caught a first glimpse of the turrets of Astley, she felt a weight lift off her shoulders. After the harrowing events of the last few days, she was longing to be home.

She wound down the window and breathed deeply, soothed by the familiar scent of the beech-trees and the damp fertile earth of the woods which surrounded the house. Drifts of bronze leaves lapped the silvery trunks.

The colours of autumn always reminded her of the embers of the peat fire which warmed Margaret Mackenzie's croft.

As long as she could remember, she had loved the bonfire-bright colours of the turning year. Now the trees were flaming towards the evening sky, providing the Keep with a blazing backdrop of scarlet and gold.

Emerald slowed the vehicle as she approached the house. Bertha must have had a visitor. She pulled over to let the station taxi pass, catching a brief glimpse of the passenger in the back.

The gravel crunched under the old Daimler's wheels, warning those in the house of its approach. By the time the vehicle drew up under the Gothic porch, the heavy solid figure of Bertha Sherwood was in the doorway to greet her.

Once in Bertha's light-drenched book-lined study, Emerald pushed a sleepy collie off a cushion and sank wearily into an armchair.

'Any news, Mother-in-law?'

Bertha nodded. 'Just as I expected, I've had a telephone call.'

Emerald lifted her head eagerly. 'Tom? Is he safe?'

'Let's just say I don't think we need bother with the widow's weeds, my dear.'

'What happened?'

'Someone with a message – not Tom himself, but someone who seemed to know what he was talking about.'

Emerald frowned. 'Could've been a hoax.'

Bertha smiled. 'My dear Emerald, I know enough about my son and enough about human nature to judge such things. He was no hoaxer. In fact I quite took to him. Said he was an old friend of yours. Nice voice. Trace of a Scots accent.'

A Scots accent. Emerald's head swam. Callum's latest by-lines had been from the war zones of the north African coast – Tom's favourite stamping grounds, and the most likely place for him to go to ground.

She hesitated. 'Did he leave a name?'

'No. He seemed in a bit of a fluster. Whoever it was, he was most concerned for your welfare. And he asked after Jamie.'

Emerald's head came up. Bertha watched her daughter-in-law's expressive face. She had always been able to read Emerald like a book. Now she saw puzzlement, then hope, then something which might have been anguish.

'An old flame perhaps?'

'Something like that.' Emerald's voice was low, confronting an unspoken fear. Callum had never replied to her letters. She had been puzzled – and hurt – by his silence, not wanting to believe that he had not replied because he wanted nothing to do with his son.

Bertha's voice cut through her thoughts. 'While we're on the subject, my dear, we have just had a visitor, Jamie and I. More in the nature of an intruder. A man called Jack Sweeney.'

'Jack here? What on earth did he want?'

'Money. Perhaps you. Seemed to think he had a claim, a debt to collect, and that this was the moment to do it. And a nastier piece of work it would be hard to imagine.' Bertha looked steadily at her much-loved daughter-in-law. 'My dear, don't think it makes the slightest difference to me, but is there perhaps a possibility that that unpleasant specimen might be Jamie's father?'

For a second Emerald hesitated. She had been so sure she had known the very moment her beloved Jamie had been conceived. So sure he was the product of their love. But now, with Bertha's question echoing in her mind, she was suddenly again uncertain. What if Jamie was not Callum's son, but Jack's?

'No.' Emerald shook her head fiercely.

'Are you sure?'

'I'm sure,' she said quietly. 'But I know why he might imagine it so.'

There was bitterness in her voice as she remembered the events of that night.

'I thought as much.' Bertha's voice was tranquil, but her eyes were shrewd. 'My dear, the identity of Jamie's biological father has not concerned either of us until now. There is not the slightest reason why it should concern us in the future.'

'If I thought for a moment . . .' Emerald shook her head and buried her face in her hands. 'Oh God, Bertha. I don't know. I don't know anything any more.'

Bertha waited. When she spoke her voice was brisk, matter-of-fact.

'If you thought what? If Jamie was the product not of an act of love, but of violation? Because that was what it was, wasn't it?'

Bertha read the reply in Emerald's face.

She said gently: 'Would you love Jamie any the less? Would you deny your son? My grandson?'

Emerald stared at Bertha, her violet eyes wide with anguish. 'Of course not.'

'Quite right. My dear, in the natural world, rape is the most usual method of procreation. Brutal, nasty, but efficient. Even our own ancestors found it a convenient way of ensuring the survival of their own gene-pool. Unpalatable, unfashionable, but true. It doesn't matter a bit.'

'It matters to me, more than anyone could possibly imagine.'

'Sentimental nonsense,' Bertha said briskly. 'Fortunately our children are much too sensible to concern themselves with such trivia. Jamie is loved. And he belongs here. And there's an end of it. My dear Emerald, it matters not a jot if you know for certain who fathered your child. It's all genetic propaganda. The male of our species has engineered the most complicated of social structures to ensure that his genes enter the next generation. We women need not concern ourselves with such smalltalk. It wasn't eating the apple which was Adam's downfall; it was putting the blame on Eve.'

In spite of herself, Emerald laughed.

'That's better,' Bertha continued. 'I like to see you laugh. Anyway, it's not so bad. At least this man – what shall I call him—?'

'Bastard,' Emerald offered.

'As you know, I wouldn't use that particular description as a term of abuse. But at least this bastard has declared his hand. He clearly intended to present us with a bill. He has no interest in claiming Jamie, even if he could.'

Emerald's voice was fierce. 'No-one claims Jamie – not Tom, not even Callum.'

'Callum?'

'Callum Fergusson. The man I think you may have spoken to on the telephone. As you would have it, Jamie's biological father.' She frowned. 'Or so, at least, I have always assumed.'

'And now?'

'I think Jamie's the spitting image of his father.' Emerald shook her head unhappily. 'Oh Lord, Mother-in-law. There's no way I can be certain.'

'Good. Keep it that way. Nine months after the act, the child is born. The rest – who might or might not have posted the particular spermatozoa which fertilized that particular ovum – is entirely irrelevant. Why do you think I love Jamie? Certainly not because he may or may not carry my genes. I have long been happy to accept him for what he is. My grandson.'

'Oh, Bertha, I love you; but I think you know that.'

Bertha patted Emerald's hand. She was not only fond of her daughter-in-law, she admired her fierce independence, her disregard for convention which mirrored Bertha's own. Sometimes, as a scientist, she wondered how much was in the genes, and how much a product of Emerald's peculiar upbringing.

It went without saying that her son's wife was far more than he deserved. The old woman sighed. Whatever Tom had or hadn't done to fulfil his duty by his ancestors, he had been fortunate in his choice of wife – and through her, and none of his doing, his heir. God knows, she thought, she hadn't been much good for Tom. But with Jamie she had been surprised at how much she enjoyed his presence in the old house.

She heaved herself to her feet. From the first, she had had absolute confidence in Emerald's abilities to cope with whatever fate might throw at her.

'Don't worry about Tom. He's the least of our problems. He'll be perfectly happy wherever he's gone to ground. He never liked this place anyway. He can take care of himself. You're the one who matters now. You and Jamie.'

Emerald said wearily: 'So you think there'll be trouble over the estate?'

Bertha went over to the window and gazed across the wide lawns lapped with rose-beds, now clothed by the night. The estate was indeed in jeopardy. Trevelyan was only too anxious for Emerald's return. There was certainly trouble ahead.

But when she turned to reply, her voice was steady, conveying a confidence she desperately hoped was justified.

'Bankers have to protect themselves – and that means protecting their clients. It doesn't suit the flea to kill off the host. Peter Trevelyan knows that well enough. But he'll certainly have to make the right noises for the record. I can hear him dictating it right now. "Humble and obedient servant" – how the English do speak with forked tongues. What foreigners must think of our language, Lord only knows.'

Emerald said quietly, 'Tom cleared us out. There's not even enough in the account to pay the wages.'

'We'll manage. Somehow. Young Trevelyan usually manages to pull a rabbit out of the hat.'

'I hope to God you're right.'

'I'm quite sure I am. Now, no more of this till tomorrow, my dear. Off you go and find Jamie. He's tucked up in bed. School starts next week; we went shopping for his uniform. I know he has a million things to tell you.'

Emerald's face lit up. 'Good heavens, it quite went out of my head!'

Bertha watched Emerald head safely off upstairs.

Then she picked up the telephone, dialled a number in London, and after a brief conversation made an appointment for the following day.

Emerald had given Bertha an idea which had swiftly crystallized into a plan. Anthony Anstruther would have to bestir himself – fast. Peter Trevelyan might need a little help with the rabbit.

76

London: 1963

'Yes, Willis?'

Anstruther flicked the switch to answer the internal telephone which allowed Albany's porter to check with the residents that visitors were welcome.

'The lady you were expecting, sir.'

'Thank you, Willis. Walk her up, would you?'

After the porter had rung through, the barrister went over to the window, pulled aside the veil of net curtain and watched the burly figure bustling down the glass-canopied passageway behind the uniformed porter.

Bertha Sherwood was on the warpath. There was no doubt of that.

' 'Morning, young Anthony.'

'Dr Sherwood. Always a pleasure.'

The old woman brushed past and walked straight across to Anstruther's favourite leather chair by the window. She set herself down and put a briefcase firmly on the stool beside her.

She looked up. 'Sit down. Do.'

Anstruther perched nervously on his desk, momentarily thrown by the deprivation of his favourite vantage-spot.

'How's your mother, Anthony?'

'Fine. Bearing up, anyway.'

'Good. Best one can hope for at our age.'

Bertha Goldberg and Lady Molly had once shared a schoolroom. The social circles in which the old aristocracy moved were small and by no means exclusive. In fact, they were as tolerant of those on the way up as they were intolerant of those on the way down. The Goldberg money opened all doors, including the highest.

Bertha stared round. Then she said: 'I don't suppose you have any Turkish Delight. No? Chocolate biscuits, then.'

Anstruther went into his bachelor kitchen and began to rummage in the tins.

'Chocolate Bath Olivers?'

He came back with a plate, and set it down beside the briefcase. Bertha took one of the biscuits and bit into the thick dark chocolate, munching appreciatively.

'That's better. So fatiguing, these journeys. At my age, one is in need of regular fortification.'

Anstruther waited. Then he said: 'Any news? Of Tom?'

'That's why I'm here. I have had word from him – indirectly.'

'He's safe? That's marvellous news.'

Bertha took another bite out of the biscuit.

'So it seems. But there's a little problem. Quite apart from my own feelings of relief – and Emerald's – Tom has expressed a desire that his survival should not be made public. This is extremely inconvenient. Young Peter Trevelyan seems to think the estate's assets are about to be frozen.'

Anstruther frowned. 'It would be the usual procedure – under the circumstances.'

'Quite. To forestall any embarrassment, Tom has to be contacted as soon as possible and persuaded to sign some kind of document to prove he's in the land of the living.'

Bertha plunged her hand back into the plate of biscuits. 'I'm afraid young Tom has got himself into a little trouble with some rather unpleasant gentlemen. And, while no doubt he has no-one but himself to blame, I have no wish to see my son floating face-down in some harbour or other.'

'I can imagine.'

'So you will understand that the whole business must be handled with the utmost discretion. Unofficial channels and so forth. And you, young man, are so good at that sort of thing. I'm sure you know what I mean.'

Anstruther stared at his visitor unhappily. 'It would be very difficult—'

'But not impossible. Good. We understand each other. You are certainly the man to put the matter in hand. Naturally it must be handled with the greatest possible discretion – in both our interests.'

'Dr Sherwood – however anxious I am to be of assistance, I cannot see how I can possibly—'

'I believe you keep in touch with a certain Mr Callum Fergusson?'

Anstruther stared at his visitor. What on earth could Bertha Sherwood want with Callum?

He said carefully: 'It's possible. Why?'

'Don't beat about the bush, young man. This is a matter of extreme urgency.'

'Then, yes.'

'I was hoping you would say that. Mr Fergusson seems to be in contact with my son. It was he who made the telephone call on Tom's behalf. He also enquired after Emerald – and Jamie. Very charming, I thought.'

'Good heavens!'

Anstruther's cheeks suddenly flamed scarlet.

Bertha studied the barrister with interest. 'I gather this young man was rather fond of my daughter-in-law.'

'Yes.' Anstruther nodded unhappily.

'Don't I remember his mother? Quite a beauty. Iona Stuart, wasn't it? Knew I was right. One of those glorious Celts. I always thought they must be the lost tribe of Israel. Killed in the war, if I remember. Very unfortunate.'

Anstruther shifted uneasily on his perch. 'I've kept an eye on Callum – sorted out his affairs. I felt I owed it to his mother, in a way. One does what one can. I'll be frank, Dr Sherwood . . .' Anstruther hesitated. 'Sometimes one has to . . . not complicate decisions. How shall I put it? Be economical with the truth. I am afraid I allowed Callum to think that Emerald had met with an accident. A fatal accident.'

Bertha's mind flashed back to the telephone conversation. 'Well, he certainly doesn't think so now.'

Anstruther flushed again, like a small boy caught out in a lie. With a renewed surge of guilt, he remembered the small pile of letters which Emerald had sent to him to be forwarded to Callum. They were still in a drawer, neatly filed. It had seemed so much more . . . *prudent*. Now, it seemed, the pigeons were coming home to roost.

'I've always done the best I can . . .' His voice trailed away unhappily.

'I'm sure you have, Anthony. Just as I know you will do so now. It's merely a matter of contacting this young man. Of course, my feckless son will have to be reassured that there will be no . . . *publicity*. Tom will know that such things are well within your capacities. I'm sure you will know the proper form – how to explain the matter to Mr Fergusson. He sounded a very civil young man.'

Anstruther smiled wryly to himself. Civility was not a virtue he had particularly noted in his dealings with young Callum Fergusson.

'Emerald spoke of him – with affection,' Bertha said carefully.

'Did she?' At the mention of Emerald, Anstruther leaned forward eagerly, suddenly overcome with curiosity. 'What's she like now – Emerald?'

'Wonderful. What did you expect?'

'Ah.' The barrister's expression was almost greedy. A small sigh escaped the prim lips.

Bertha smiled. She said: 'Of course. The best thing that ever happened to Astley.'

'Ah. I haven't seen her since she was a child – in the flesh, that is. And young Jamie?'

'Perfect. Naughty, but absolutely enchanting. I am well aware I am eternally in your debt, young man – for my daughter-in-law and for my grandson.' Bertha nodded cheerfully. 'You should have got yourself a wife. Grandchildren are so good for the human male. They are thoroughly unsuitable as fathers, of course. But they make wonderful grandfathers.'

Anstruther pulled out his spectacles and began to polish them furiously. 'I shall take your word for it.'

Bertha heaved herself to her feet. 'Well. Mustn't take up any more of your time.' She reached out for the remaining chocolate biscuits, and tucked them into her pocket. 'I am content to leave the matter in your competent hands, young man. So far you have handled everything admirably. I have every confidence that you will continue to do so – for Emerald's sake. Perhaps we might see you at Astley one of these days?'

Anstruther thrust his spectacles back into his pocket. 'I don't think so, Dr Sherwood. It wouldn't be . . . *discreet*.'

Bertha threw him one last penetrating glance. 'Nevertheless I shall make sure Emerald knows of your . . . discretion in this matter.'

With that, Bertha sailed down the stairs and into the sunshine of Piccadilly.

77

Tangier: 1963

'Visitor for you, milord. He said to give the English milord his compliments, and he would be happy to accept the invitation.'

Tom looked up nervously.

He had just finished an exquisite little roasted partridge stuffed with pine-kernels and fresh dates – and was contemplating completing the evening's entertainment with an equally exquisite young shepherd boy just down from the Blue Mountains – when La Mamola came to find him. She handed him a card with a name scrawled on it. Tom breathed a sigh of relief.

'Thank you Maman; it's a friend.'

La Mamola – a massive Berber matron known to favoured customers such as Tom as 'Maman' – was the proprietress of the Bordello Edward VII. With the exception of a small but unmistakable royal coat of arms, the entrance to Eddie's was discreet. The narrow frontage led into a small café-restaurant which served the most delicate of *quenelles sauce nantua* and the best *omelette truffée* outside Périgord. The menu had made the place popular with expatriates looking for a change from the spicy native dishes of couscous and bistillas filled with honey-sweetened pigeon breasts stuffed with pine nuts.

The whorehouse itself was not officially open for business until after midnight, although the little restaurant was open all through the day and most of the night.

Those not in the know would never have guessed there was such a palace of delights through the beaded curtains which veiled the interior, or that here was the most interesting and diverse brothel in the whole of that raffish city.

Tom had always known it would be far harder to fool the men from Marseilles than it would be the authorities. The destruction of his beloved boat had provided the perfect alibi. Like a cat with nine lives, Tom had landed on his feet. As long as he lay low, the milieu would have every reason to conclude he had been killed in the explosion.

The bordello was probably the safest hideout in all Tangier. It was no-one's business who came and went – and all visitors were subjected to the scrutiny of La Mamola, perched on a barstool by the entrance. No-one got past La Mamola. She kept an eye on the customers, saw to any little problems her employees might encounter, and collected the dues. Through her specialized knowledge of her customers' little preferences, La Mamola probably wielded more power than the King of Morocco himself.

The English milord was a much-valued customer; he had only to speak for his wishes to be granted. Accommodation and discretion were what Tom had in mind. In exchange for these services, milord had something which made the old woman's eyes twinkle appreciatively: a suitcase of money.

'But of course, milord. I have just the solution.'

Tom was soon comfortably established in a little whitewashed palace on the far side of the bordello's courtyard. There was no entrance on the street. The dwelling was only accessible if you passed through the whorehouse itself. And there was no question of anyone disturbing milord's tranquillity, unless, of course, the disturbance was of his own choosing.

Most important of all, he had enough money to keep him going for as long as need be. He had felt a little guilty about landing Emerald with the price of his foolishness. But she would find some way of managing. She always did. Emerald, like him, was a survivor. It was one of the reasons he had chosen her.

Meanwhile the Bordello Edward VII would provide him with the haven he needed.

Tom had already forgotten all about his invitation to the man who had saved his skin. He was at his usual table, tucked away in the far corner. Each table was protected by high wooden screens, providing a private booth and ensuring that sworn enemies could dine in the place at the same time and never know the other had been there at all.

538

Tom watched his visitor pass through the tables. A little muscular for Tom's taste, but handsome.

Tom rose, smiling.

'My dear boy!'

Callum scarcely recognized the man who held out his hand in greeting. In the flowing midnight-blue jellaba, had it not been for the mop of golden curls Tom would have blended in perfectly in the souk.

Now he gripped Callum's hand warmly. 'Sit down, sit down. Champagne is called for – not so, Maman?' He glanced over this shoulder at the fat proprietress, and chuckled. 'And none of that rubbish you serve upstairs, either, Mamola. The proper stuff.'

La Mamola's huge shoulders shook with laughter, and she flicked her finger at one of the red-fezzed waiters.

'Dear fellow. Delighted. Have you dined? I can recommend the quail.' Tom stretched back luxuriantly. He looked as if he had quite recovered from his ordeal. 'Thought you fellows had pushed off and I had missed out on the pleasure.'

'The circus? Well, ceasefires dinna make headlines.'

'Scot, are you?'

'The Hebrides. Outer islands.'

'Ah. Never been that far north myself.'

Tom glanced up.

A beautiful young girl, gleaming henna'd hair falling in a waterfall around a perfect oval face, had appeared silently with the champagne in a bucket of ice. A thick dark silk Berber wedding gown embroidered with brilliant scarlet threads fell to small bare feet, henna'd in the traditional patterns of a desert bride. She poured the champagne with care, her little pink tongue flicking between her lips with concentration.

'Thank you, *chérie*.'

Callum was suddenly aware that Tom Sherwood was watching him with an expression of amusement.

'I see Maman has your measure. She prides herself on her ability to tell a customer's preferences at a glance. But beware – Fatima might have a surprise for you under that satin gown.'

Tom smiled and raised his glass. 'Your health, sir – and mine.'

'And yours.'

'Thanks to you. I'm afraid I was not at my best when we met. Physical violence is not much in my line.'

Callum examined the lanky Englishman now sprawled elegantly in the stiff little café chair.

To his surprise he felt no jealousy at all. Emerald's husband was

539

certainly handsome – and probably charming. But there was absolutely nothing there to like or dislike. Nothing on which to hang any emotion at all.

Tom said: 'Drink up, old comrade-in-arms. Let's talk of war and war's alarms, if you enjoy your Yeats.' He smiled and raised his glass again. 'To shared memories.'

The evening wore on, and the champagne kept coming.

Callum could feel his head growing lighter. He made up his mind. There was no sense in equivocating. Tom Sherwood would either make his task easy or he would make it hard. Either way, Callum intended to get what he wanted – what Ansthruther, in his call from London, had told him was vital.

Callum began to outline the bargain Anstruther had proposed.

Tom listened in silence, his head cocked to one side and a wry smile on his face.

But it was not until Callum explained about Jamie that Tom really came alive.

Tom's reaction to this piece of news astonished Callum. The hooded eyes lit up immediately and Tom reached over and gripped his arm.

'How marvellous. I'm delighted. I always wanted to meet you. Emerald absolutely refused even to tell me who the father was. God knows why.' He laughed. 'There was never the remotest chance I might be jealous. And there you were, saving my life – the knight on the white charger. Admit it's wonderful.' He leaned forward. 'Tell me. What did you do to her to make her run away? I mean, I'm glad you did, but it must have been something truly disgraceful.'

Callum's face clouded over and he shook his head.

'There were lies. There always seem to be lies. But something happened at the house – before the accident – between Emerald and Alison, the girl who lived in the house.' Callum glanced up. 'She was only a friend – someone who needed a place to stay. I didn't think . . .'

He hesitated. Tom grinned. 'It's a common human failing.'

Callum shook his head. 'Something must have happened – something which made Emerald run. And it's just beginning to occur to me what it might have been.' His voice was thoughtful, he was trying to work it all out for himself. 'Alison had just had an abortion – a pretty messy business. If Alison had told Emerald that I was the father of her child, and had managed to convince that her I was the reason for her getting rid of it . . .' Callum shook his head slowly. 'To Emerald it would have been a terrible betrayal – and Alison was crazy enough to say anything. Emerald would have had no choice but to believe her.'

540

'So – the poor girl ran to the safety of my arms? How *unsuitable*. Ah me! the trials of love.' Tom leaned back, his voice mocking. Then he changed his tone, his face serious. 'If you're waiting for the answer to your request. Yes. I'll do what you ask. I pay my dues. But, believe me, I wouldn't do it for anyone else.'

Tom stood up.

'It'll take an hour or so to set it up.' Tom paused. 'Apart from giving me your word that you'll never divulge to a living soul where I am – and that includes my wife and my sainted mother – you must promise me something. And not ask what it is until we have completed this transaction.'

'What if I can't deliver?'

Tom laughed. 'You can, my dear young Callum. Believe me, you can!'

Tom insisted they could only leave the shelter of the café when darkness had fallen, and then Tom was heavily muffled in a jellaba.

His face was white and his hands were once again trembling. 'You don't know the risk I'm taking to do this.'

Swiftly they slipped through the quiet streets of the European side of the town until they reached the main shopping avenue with its steel-and-plate-glass façades. Tom halted outside a branch of Switzerland's most famous export after the cuckoo clock.

The consul, who was also the bank's manager, opened the reinforced steel doors and glanced up and down the street before admitting them. He greeted Tom with polite solicitude, asked no questions, read the papers, nodded and set to work to do what was required.

Tom sprawled in the manager's chair while he went off to get an official stamp. 'Can't stand the Swiss, but they're the only bankers you can trust. They don't have the imagination to wonder where the loot comes from. See no evil, hear no evil, just bank the money. Emerald's money, I suppose, if we're being honest. And honesty is not a quality I've ever held in high esteem.' He laughed, the quick short bark of mirth which, Callum was beginning to learn, served as a punctuation mark. 'Except in other people.'

Callum grinned. There was something very endearing about Tom Sherwood. He found himself almost beginning to like the man.

When they were safely back in the white house beyond the bordello, Callum said: 'What's the promise?'

Tom tapped the document he had had notarised. 'The promise. Fair exchange. Emerald really.'

'Emerald?'

'Indeed. My wife. The love of your life, if what you tell me is true. The mother of our mutual son. Jamie's a divine little boy, although I'm not much good as a father. Didn't seem to get enough fathering myself to know what to do. Something of the sort.'

'And?'

'Such impatience. The beautiful Emerald. It wasn't a mistake, you know – her choosing me. It worked, after a fashion. I had something she needed. She had something I wanted. My mother – well, you don't know her, she was a factor. More than a factor. Emerald needed someone like her.'

He grinned. 'And my mother needed Emerald. Sounds ridiculous, doesn't it? But it was a gift – a gift of love. You may have fathered the child who bears my name. And – as my mother is so fond of pointing out – the one certainty is that Emerald gave him birth. But I gave him a lifetime.'

'Not one you had any use for.'

'He'll have the choice. That's enough for him – or me.'

'And the promise?'

'Ah, yes. The promise.' Tom's face grew thoughtful. 'I've burned my boats. In time, I may be able to come out of hiding – and, believe me, I have good reason to hide. I've made dangerous enemies. The worst. But dangerous men live dangerous lives. Much on their mind. Meanwhile I mean to make myself a new life – maybe even a new name. I don't yet know. But I shall keep in touch, at arm's length, from time to time.'

He was silent for a long moment. 'But I do love Emerald. And I want her happiness. I think you're the one who can give it to her. But it must be on my terms, because I think I now know better than you what will make her happy. Love, yes. But not imprisonment. An unquestioning loyalty – the strong arm in time of trouble. All that sort of thing. Care for her, be a father to my son.'

Tom held up his hand. 'But not betrayal. By that I mean, never try to take away what I have given – what was in my gift: Astley and the life she has built for herself. Emerald is no longer the child you remember or the young girl you loved. She is a woman – independent, strong and free.'

Callum was silent, his head bowed. What Tom had asked would not be easy. Everything in him rebelled against the danger of losing her again.

He knew he was indeed as Tom saw him, a knight on a white charger hell-bent on rescuing the damsel.

When he spoke, the words were hesitant. 'In summer, when we were children out on the hill, we would watch the blue butterflies. I never could resist chasing them. When I caught one in my hands, I'd take it to Emerald. But when I opened my fist, however gentle I had been, the wings had been destroyed.'

542

Callum closed his eyes, momentarily transported. After a moment he continued.

'But Emerald. She just sat there and held out her hand. And quite soon a butterfly would land – dance just on the tips of her fingers. It was one of the lessons she taught me. Whatever the temptation, don't close your fist. Probably that's why I chose to do what I do. Even though it's the images of war which earn my living, I don't take part in it. Sometimes, by being in the right place at the right time, I can change things for the better.'

For a moment the two men studied each other in silence.

Tom smiled. He pushed the envelope with the document Anstruther had wanted across the table.

'Take it. I'm glad Emerald chose you. If things had been different – for both of us – we might even have been friends.' Then he grinned. 'Even though you're not really my type. But, then, I suppose that's just as well. I assume I have your word?'

Callum bowed his head. After a long moment, he looked up.

'You have my word.'

'Blood brothers?'

Startled, Callum remembered the same question, so long ago, on the hillside of Eas Forse.

This time with a lighter heart, he gave the same reply.

78

London: 1963

'Pompous prick.'

Anthony Anstruther replaced the telephone on its hook, leaned back in his chair and considered the conversation which led him to make so unfavourable a judgement on the personal habits of an old friend.

Pompous prick or not, Peter Trevelyan had been in an uncharacteristic panic. Emerald Sherwood had been with him all morning, and they had been combing through the accounts of the business.

'Something has to be done, Anthony – done fast. I'm sorry I have to ask you a favour, but I really have no choice.'

What the banker meant was that he had once again promised the young woman he would move heaven and earth to help her.

Anstruther grinned to himself – until he remembered he had once again agreed to take on the consequences of Emerald's ability to make people do anything she wanted.

Emerald's business, Trevelyan explained, had been pledged against a loan which should have been secured against Astley itself. And, even though he had been relieved to hear of Anstruther's efforts to obtain the document which would unfreeze the assets, the charge had not yet been registered. Meanwhile the cash had gone. Vanished. Presumably into her wastrel husband's debts.

On its own, Emerald's business, profitable though it was, simply couldn't stand the draining of the capital.

The banker had obviously already bent over backwards to help the young woman – surprising since Anstruther knew exactly what Peter felt about what he referred to as his lady customers.

The barrister couldn't resist a quick dig. 'Looks like she's got you by the short and curlies, Peter.'

'I wouldn't say so exactly. But the situation is . . . *unclear.*'

Unclear, Anstruther knew, was a banking euphemism for a nightmare.

'You'd better tell me the truth, Peter.'

'I guaranteed the loan myself. As far as the bank's concerned, it's unsecured.'

There was genuine panic in the banker's voice.

'How on earth did that happen?'

Anstruther was startled. No banker ever got himself into a position like that. Unsecured loans were not worth a monkey's eyelash.

'Just take it from me, it happened. And Emerald – Lady Sherwood—' He took a deep breath. 'It's certainly as much my fault as it is hers. And now it's out of my hands. If we can't find an independent guarantor, I shall have to tell the other partners. My partnership's on the line. You can appreciate my position.'

Anstruther grinned. Indeed he could. Emerald had caught him with his trousers down – whether she knew it or not.

'So what do you expect me to do?'

Trevelyan told him.

It was not at all discreet that Anstruther should know all about the young woman's affairs. It was by no means acceptable banking practice to discuss clients' business with a third party. But in Emerald's case Anstruther was scarcely a third party.

And Peter Trevelyan was at his wits' end – for his own rash promises as well as for Emerald herself.

The bank handled the Duke's business as well as the Palace's. What Trevelyan suggested was by no means ethical.

'I can only assure you, Anthony, I've had three sleepless nights myself. I can think of no other solution.'

'Why did you do it, Peter?'

'Give her the money?' There was a silence. 'She – Emerald herself – I – she's an extraordinary woman. I believed—'

'You believed? A banker who believed? Credit means *he* believes.' Then he said quietly: 'I suppose we all believe.'

'She's a woman in a million.' Trevelyan's voice held a note of passion

Anstruther had never heard from him in all their years of friendship.

Anstruther smiled ruefully. It was astonishing the effect Emerald had on the most hard-headed of men.

'I know. We're both responsible, I suppose.'

'Then, you'll do it?' The banker's voice was eager.

'I can't guarantee anything, Peter. His nibs is as mean as mouse shit. You know what the pair of them are like – can't see further than the next diamond bracelet. It'll be easier if I can catch him on his own.'

'I'll have the transfer prepared and sent over to you immediately.' He could hear the relief in the banker's voice. 'Just get the signature, Anthony. That's all I ask.'

Considering the conversation again, for a moment Anstruther wondered if, should he manage to arrange that Emerald confront her father himself, whether he, too, would be captivated.

Then he shook his head. He'd know well enough the Duchess would not stand for it. Ever since Emerald might be considered safely tucked away into matrimony, there was no question of any voluntary involvement in her affairs.

Involuntary was another matter.

The barrister stood up and went over to the mahogany cabinet in the corner. He poured himself a shot of brandy. Then he put the bottle aside and spun a dial fitted to the rear of the cabinet. The back swung open to reveal the interior of the safe. He reached inside and pulled out a brown envelope. He slit it open and tipped something into his hand. He took the object over to the window and studied it. In the game he was about to play it was as well to hold an ace.

He slipped the little disc he had purchased from Jack Sweeney into his briefcase. Then he picked up the telephone again. This time the call was routed through several exchanges before it was finally connected.

A few minutes later he had the appointment he had requested. It was fortunate the Duke was over in London on one of his flying visits.

Although he was no longer the Duke's official dogsbody, he was still enough of the courtier to do small errands of a legal nature. The two men, in spite of the dispute over the Duchess's request, continued to maintain contact, even if the warmth of trust had gone. Now he was about to finish the relationship off for good and all.

Anstruther picked up his briefcase and took a taxi to Claridge's – the Duke of Windsor's home-from-home in London.

The Windsors always occupied the same suite of rooms on the second floor overlooking Brooke Street. As he had done on so many occasions in the past, Anstruther stopped outside the ornately gilded door, straightened his tie, and then knocked firmly.

'OK, Anthony, come right in.'

The American drawl was now as much a part of the Duke as the flamboyant clothes and extravagant lifestyle.

Edward Windsor was on the telephone to his wife. After all these years he was still unable to function unless he had his twice-daily fix of Wallis's conversation.

The Duke swung round and waved his hand.

'Take a seat, Anthony. Won't be a moment.'

The exchange took its course, ending in the usual syrupy endearments.

'Love to Pugsy Wugsy, sweetums. Eanum kiss. Be good. Boy loves girl.'

Anstruther suppressed a shudder. He had never got used to the sugary sweetness of his ex-employer's relationship with his wife. It seemed obscene at their age – like listening to two elderly babies blowing bubbles at each other.

'Right, Anthony, what's it about?' Edward Windsor turned his pop-eyed blue gaze back to his visitor. He glanced at his watch. 'Make it snappy, man. Got an appointment at the hatter in twenty minutes. Can't miss an appointment at the hatter's. Much as my life's worth.'

'This won't take a moment sir.'

'What? Sound like my dentist. Lying bastard.'

'I hope it won't be as painful, sir.'

Anstruther's voice was quiet. He opened his briefcase. Then he laid the little disc on the glass-topped table between them.

'What's that?'

The Duke looked down.

'Something for the Duchess, what?'

Edward Windsor was used to being asked to select trinkets for his wife. But it was not usually Anstruther who brought them. That was the business of the man from Cartier. Or Boucheron. Or Phillips.

He picked up the trinket. 'Have to find me reading specs. Can't see much without 'em these days.'

The Duke hooked a pair of glasses over his nose. He turned the disc over once. Then he laid it quietly back on the table. He peered at Anstruther.

'Not seen that before. Where'd you get it?'

Anstruther picked up the disc again and slipped it back in his pocket. He said: 'It was on the child's wrist when she was found after the shipwreck.'

'Well, get rid of it.' The Duke's voice was irritated. 'No sense in having that kind of thing lying around. Far too dangerous.'

'Yes.'

'What d'ya mean, "yes"?'

'I agree it's far too dangerous.'

'Then, get rid of it.'

'I can't do that, sir.'

'The hell's that supposed to mean?'

'It's amazing how things – people – come home to roost.' Anstruther held up the little medal and turned it in the sunlight from the window. 'The ship was officially on the way to the Bahamas, sir. It would be a little hard to explain.'

'What? Is this *blackmail*, Anthony?' The Duke's voice was sharp.

'In a manner of speaking, sir,' Anstruther said carefully.

'Good Lord.' The Duke stared at his ex-employee. Then he said, 'What the devil d'you want me to do?'

'I'd like you – that is, the bankers would like you – to sign this.'

The Duke glared down at the document Anstruther set down in front of him.

'For heaven's sake, Anthony.' The voice was petulant – the petulance of an impatient child. 'The Duchess will be most disappointed. I was thinking of having the tiara reset this year.'

'Nevertheless, sir, there's your . . .' He hesitated, and then continued. 'A grandchild to be considered.'

'So you have already informed me.'

'Perhaps the Duchess will able to survive another disappointment.'

The Duke glared at his ex-employee. 'The hell she will.'

The Duke stood up and went over to the window. When he turned back, his face was haughty, almost regal. 'I suppose I have no option?'

'I think not, sir.'

The Duke signed the papers which authorized his personal guarantee of the loan. The collateral was against holdings in an oil-rig in Texas.

As his financial adviser, Trevelyan knew the Duke had made a packet on that particular investment – and he had kept the shares well out of the way of any tax authorities, untraceable except by those in the know, as a hedge against the financial troubles he saw as a constant threat.

Anstruther bent down and picked up the signed document, blowing on the ink to dry it.

'Thank you, sir.'

Anstruther glanced up. His ex-employer's Hanoverian blue eyes were steely.

'Shut the door behind you, Anthony.'

'Yes, sir.'

The Duke watched the barrister withdraw. The royal mouth set into a thin line.

'Damn cheek,' he said, and looked at his watch. His anger was mitigated by his relief that he might just manage to keep his appointment at the hatter's.

Meanwhile, in the taxi on the way to the bank, the Duke's aide-de-camp now turned blackmailer felt not a twinge of regret.

For the first time since he had embarked on the discharging of what he saw as his responsibilities, Anstruther felt he had joined the side of the angels.

Anstruther's satisfaction with his day's work was confirmed on his return to his set of rooms in Albany, where he found Callum awaiting him with the document required for the unfreezing of the estate.

It would all need rather delicate handling, but that, after all, was second nature to Anthony Anstruther.

His discussion on the telephone with Callum had been concerned with the practicalities. Now it was clear from the young man's expression that there was going to be trouble.

'I know what you're going to say, Callum.' Anstruther held up his hand defensively. 'And I'm sorry about the past. But now is not the time—'

'The hell it isn't!'

Anstruther suddenly made up his mind. His face was scarlet. He reached behind his desk and pulled out a packet of letters. There were at least a dozen, all neatly tied together with legal tape. Silently he held them out to Callum.

'I never forwarded them. They're perfectly straightforward, as you might expect. Just news and a photograph of the boy. Emerald seems to have felt that Jamie might one day like to see his father – and this was her way of keeping in touch.'

Callum stared down at the bundle. Turned them over, once twice, and then lifted them to his cheek. He looked up at Anstruther. The tawny eyes were no longer blazing; instead, Anstruther saw with surprise, they were filled with tears.

Then, without a word, Callum turned on his heel and left the room.

Anstruther watched the young man vanish through the doorway which led into the street.

There was one more chore to be completed. He glanced at his watch, took a deep breath, and dialled Peter Trevelyan's home telephone number.

'Peter? I have a bit of good news. In the strictest confidence, of course.'

Anstruther explained – cautiously. They were not yet quite out of the wood. Chancery – the legal machinery which dealt with such matters – would have to be put in the picture. But Anstruther did not anticipate any great difficulty there. He had already put the wheels in motion, making sure that he bumped into the particular judge-in-chambers who was down to preside over the interim hearing to determine if the vanished baron's estate should be frozen.

The old boy had been at school with Anstruther's father. He knew the form. No doubt Emerald would have to make an appearance at the hearing, but Anstruther had no doubt of her ability to handle such matters.

What was less certain was Emerald's ability to handle the young man who had just left his presence so abruptly.

Women were so unpredictable when it came to matters of the heart. Or anything else, for that matter.

Anstruther did not envy Callum the task ahead of him – whatever twinges of guilt he, Anstruther, might feel about his own role in the affair.

All in all, Anstruther was grateful that he had managed to keep clear of such entanglements. Except, perhaps, there had been a moment when it might have been different. A moment when he, too, had felt the gentle warmth of something which might have been identified as love.

What was it Bertha Sherwood had said? The males of the species make wonderful grandfathers. Perhaps, after all, the old woman was right.

79

Astley Keep: 1963

'Rabbit,' said Jamie quietly to himself, just to remind himself he had an important errand to run.

He had promised Ben he would check on the rabbit snares. Now that the old man's gnarled fingers were too stiff to untie the knots, he needed Jamie's help to empty the traps.

Ben wasn't really allowed to set the snares, but he did love a rabbit pie. Ben was Jamie's friend. Friends were more important than anything.

Tonight Jamie was quite sure there would be a rabbit in the trap in the woods, and Ben would have his Sunday dinner.

So Jamie had waited, snug as a wintering hedgehog in his warm bed, until his grandmother popped her head round the door just to make sure he was sound asleep. His mummy had gone to bed quite early. She had lots to do in the morning. Something to do with the bankers, she had said.

Jamie knew that bankers were important. Jamie had a piggy bank, but that was only important at Christmas and other people's birthdays. To grown-ups, bankers seemed to be important all the time.

Jamie slipped out from beneath the bedcovers and pulled on his woolly sweater, the one with the rabbit on the front which Piglet had knitted for his last birthday. He shoved the pillow under the bedclothes to make it look as if he was still curled up safely, and tiptoed down the back stairs without making any more sound than a dormouse hurrying through a field of wheat.

He stood quite still when he reached the hall, listening. He could hear his grandmother's pen going *scratch, scratch, scratch* in the study.

Jamie hurried on. Eavesdroppers, Mrs Piggot was fond of telling him, hear no good of themselves. Piglet was full of rules like that.

Jamie found his new red gumboots in the back scullery where the coats and outdoor shoes were kept. He was quite grown-up enough to be able to tie his shoelaces, but he needed gumboots for where he was going. He pulled the boots on over his bare feet, wiggling his toes first in case there were spiders inside. Then he crept quietly through the back door which gave directly on to the kitchen garden.

Soon he was trotting through the damp meadow grass on his way to the woods by the lake. There was a bright moon, and Jamie could see everything as clearly as day.

As Ben had taught him, Jamie paused at the edge of the thicket. By day, a blackbird served sentry in the branches of a crab-apple tree in the middle of the wood, warning the wild inhabitants of approaching danger. There was a trio of notes which told of a hunting kestrel above, another to beware of egg-stealing jays. And there was a particular cry which pinpointed the presence of a prowling predator – or even a poacher.

At night the birds were safe in the branches, and there was no-one to warn him of what lay ahead.

Cautiously he crept forward.

To Jamie, reading the silent messages left by the non-human inhabitants of the estate came as easily as breathing.

Jamie knew how to recognize the pellets thrown by the tawny owls which nested in the hollow tree in the middle of the wood, and how to dissect the little bundles of fur and ivory which told him of a population of voles and shrews and field-mice in the hedgerows. He knew where and when a badger had passed through the undergrowth by the trail of bent grasses and the faint ammoniac scent.

He sniffed.

There was an old dog-fox who had learned to rob the snares. It was cunning enough to know where the wires ran, and smart enough to listen out for the squeal when a rabbit was trapped. And by the time Jamie checked the nooses there was sometimes nothing left of Ben's dinner but a hank of fur.

'Sooner or later,' said Ben, 'we'll catch the bugger.'

Today might well be the day the old dog-fox got caught.

Jamie felt his heart beating. The fox was the fiercest creature in the wood. He crept forward cautiously until he had a good view of the glade where the rabbit traps were set.

It wasn't a rabbit.

It wasn't even the old dog-fox.

Jamie eyes widened in amazement. His trap had caught a poacher.

Ben had warned Jamie about poachers.

'You see anyone creeping around as shouldn't, you come and find me.' Ben had looked very fierce when he said that.

And now Jamie would have to think what he was going to do about the poacher.

Callum had taken the short cut through the woods to Astley Keep, just as the stationmaster advised.

'A mile up the lane and over the stile, then, sir. Follow the lake round through the wood. You can't miss it.'

It was early evening, and he had been so preoccupied with his own thoughts that he had scarcely noticed where he was going. At first he had thought he had caught his leg in a bramble.

He tugged. The noose tightened. He lost his balance.

'Damn.'

Callum sat up gingerly and felt his ankle. It was a thoroughly stupid thing to do, unworthy of the countryman he was. He had been following the path through the woods without looking where he was putting his feet.

He leaned forward to examine the knot of wire. Whoever had set the snare knew exactly what they were about. The noose was not made for easy unravelling, and the flesh was already beginning to swell around it.

He felt in his pocket for his penknife. It must have fallen out as he fell. He glanced round. Then he saw it, gleaming in a pile of leaves just out his reach. The wood was full of the sounds of the night. The hoot of a hunting tawny owl. The rustle of small nocturnal creatures. And then the faint sounds of a larger animal moving through the undergrowth.

Callum called out: 'Anyone there?'

The sounds ceased abruptly. For a moment Callum thought it must be a fox, or even a deer. Whatever it was, it was a large animal.

Suddenly he guessed who it might be. 'Jamie? Is that you, Jamie?'

Jamie was startled.

He changed his mind about the man in the trap being a poacher. He thought perhaps it was the man who had come to see his grandmother before. The man who looked like a fox. It would have been perfectly right that the foxy man should have been caught in his rabbit-trap.

Then, again, the voice was different. Jamie noticed things like voices. The tone of the voice and the scent were signals which animals and small children shared.

Cautiously Jamie crept closer.

The face was different. Not all scrunched up and angry like the foxy man.

The man waited for him to come closer.

'Jamie?'

'Maybe,' Jamie said in a don't-care kind of voice. He knew he mustn't talk to strangers. Not even strangers caught in his rabbit-trap.

'Is this your rabbit trap, Jamie?'

Jamie hesitated. Then, because he didn't want to get Ben into trouble, he said: 'It might be.'

'Then, can you . . .' The man in the trap made a gesture at the wires.

'Ben said if it was a poacher to come and get him. Are you a poacher?'

'Do I look like a poacher?' The man smiled. It was a nice wide smile which made Jamie feel perhaps the man was not a poacher, after all.

'No,' said Jamie. Then he added, with five-year-old logic, 'But I've never seen a poacher.'

'Look, Jamie, whether I'm a poacher or not – can you please get me out of this trap?'

Jamie made up his mind. 'All right. If you promise not to tell about it. Granny would be really cross if she knew about Ben's traps.'

'I promise.'

The little boy bent over the wires. Patiently, his small fingers agile and neat, he unravelled the knot.

'Thanks, old fellow.' Callum rubbed his ankle. 'No bones broken.'

Jamie's eyes were bright. 'You can tell me now. Are you really a poacher?'

'No.' Callum shook his head and laughed. 'Are you disappointed, Jamie?'

'A bit. Ben says he used to be a poacher once.'

'Ben?'

'Old Ben. He's my best friend. He likes rabbit pie, so I have to empty the traps for him.'

'Well, you certainly had a catch today. I was on my way up to the house when I fell in. Just as well you came; I was beginning to give up hope.'

Jamie frowned. 'Were you coming up to see my mother? It's a bit late. She's got to go and see the bankers in the morning, you know. So she has to get up early.' Jamie considered for a moment, chewing his lip thoughtfully. 'So you couldn't see her now anyway. And she'd be really angry if she thought I'd been out in the woods on my own. No-one knows I'm here.'

'Then, we won't tell anyone.' Callum grinned at the small boy. Jamie smiled back. He liked the man's crinkly eyes. They looked kind – a bit like old Ben's. 'It's too late now to go up to the house anyway. I'll have to wait till tomorrow.'

Jamie cheered up suddenly. 'That would be best. In the morning, we could pretend you only just arrived, and no-one would know anything at all. You could sleep on the settle in old Ben's front room – Ben does, quite often. I could take you there now.'

'Wouldn't he much rather you came back with a rabbit?'

'Maybe,' Jamie giggled. 'But it'd have been even better if you'd been a poacher.'

Chattering happily, Jamie took Callum to Ben's little cottage in the garden wall. It took some time to convince the old man that Callum was indeed who he said he was: a messenger from Master Tom, and on his way to the Big House.

After that was settled, everyone agreed it was far better for Callum to stay with Ben till the morning. That way nobody would be found out at all.

Satisfied with his night's work, Jamie crept back to his own bed.

It had been a wonderful adventure. And it was Jamie's secret. Jamie's and the man with the nice eyes and the crinkly smile. He was glad the man was spending the night with Ben.

Two friends are much better than one.

80

Astley Keep: 1963

Jamie had had a wonderful day.

His mummy had left very early for London on very important business and had missed the stranger. So Jamie had had his new friend – Callum – all to himself all morning and all afternoon as well.

Callum had spent the night on old Ben's settle by the fire, just as they had arranged, and then Ben had brought him up to the house at the proper time, after breakfast, just as he had promised.

Jamie's grandmother had seemed to know all about Callum. She had been quite pleased to see him, even though she was very busy with catching up with work – his granny was always catching up with work – and she smiled a lot and made Callum sit down at the table in the kitchen and have some coffee and chocolate biscuits.

She had even offered Callum some of her Turkish Delight, and Jamie knew that was a mark of very special favour.

After the grown-ups had talked privately for a little, his grandmother had called Jamie back into the kitchen. He had been a bit worried and he hadn't gone very far away, as someone might have told about the rabbit traps and both he and Ben might get into trouble.

But nobody said anything about the rabbit traps at all.

Better still, his grandmother told him it was quite all right to take care of the visitor till his mummy came back from her business in London. And that wouldn't be until it was nearly Jamie's bedtime.

'Run along now, Jamie. I'm sure Mr Fergusson will be happy for you to show him round. Mrs Piggot will have lunch on the table sharp at twelve-thirty, mind. So don't either of you be late.'

'Of course not, Granny.'

Jamie knew immediately what Callum would most like to see. He took him to all his secret places in the wild bits of the estate. He showed him the gap in the hedge where they could watch the mother hare suckling her leverets in the form she had made for herself in the middle of the hayfield. He showed him where a goshawk had hidden her nest in the branches of the old pine-tree. They even found a little cache of nuts from the previous autumn which a squirrel must have hidden and forgotten.

After lunch, Callum said: 'My turn now, Jamie. We're going fishing.'

So they went fishing. But *such* fishing. Not the usual kind of fishing that Jamie did with Ben, when you pushed out in the punt and dropped down a line with hooks and worms wriggling on the end. It wasn't like that at all. It was proper poacher's fishing – the kind Jamie had never imagined.

First Callum walked all the way round the lake, with Jamie beside him, moving very silently, well back from the edge, and without talking at all.

Then Callum beckoned Jamie and the two of them wriggled on their tummies under the branches of a willow-tree, until they were just over the bank where Jamie knew the kingfisher liked to hunt. Then Callum showed Jamie how to put his arm quietly in the water without making any ripples, and how to move his fingers gently until he could feel a fish brushing against his fingertips. You had to be very patient. Then, when you were gently tickling the scaly tummy, and you could feel him rubbing against your nails, you suddenly grabbed – and *whoosh*! there he was, a fine fat trout flapping on the grass beside you.

It was magic. Poacher's magic.

Bertha listened out for Emerald's return. She came to greet her daughter-in-law at the door as soon as she heard the sound of the gravel.

'How was it?'

Emerald smiled. She pulled off the hat she had worn for the hearing in chambers, and hugged her mother-in-law exuberantly.

'Cross your fingers, but I think we're out of the wood.'

557

'Thank God for that. I thought young Anstruther would manage it.'

'Anstruther?' Emerald stared at her mother-in-law. 'What did he have to do with it?'

'My dear, *everything*.' Bertha returned Emerald's anguished gaze steadily. She said gently: 'I know how you feel, Emerald. But sooner or later you will have to accept that you have a past – good or bad. Sooner or later, you will have to come to terms with that reality. For your own sake – and for Jamie's.'

Emerald shook her head. 'I can see no reason—'

Bertha tucked her arm through Emerald's and led her over to the window which overlooked the lake.

'It's going to be sooner than you think. Now can you see a reason?'

Emerald gave an involuntary gasp. 'Callum!'

The shock of recognition almost took her breath away.

At the edge of the bank, two tousled heads were lowered towards the water. The twin figures were motionless, lost in their own world. With a stab of nostalgia Emerald knew exactly what engaged their rapt attention. She could feel the cool belly of a fish against the warm hand. She remembered with a blinding clarity the times when she and Callum had gone to tickle trout in the burns of Eas Forse.

'You may think what you like, my dear,' Bertha's voice continued comfortably, 'but personally I'm in no doubt at all of who is Jamie's biological father. Believe me, I have had a lot of experience observing inherited characteristics. It never fails to surprise me how strong that little cocktail of genes must be.'

She patted Emerald's hand.

'You only have to see them together. Like as two peas in a pod.'

Emerald shook her head. Callum had no right to walk back into her life, in whatever guise. He had betrayed her. She had written to him so many times, and he had never once replied. Whatever Anstruther was capable of, he would surely not have failed to forward the letters.

'You don't understand, Bertha—'

'I understand more than you think, my dear. What's done is done. You can't do anything about the past – only accept it. Get on with your life. Tom will certainly get on with his.' Her eyes twinkled. 'Anyway, as you know, I have been encouraging you for years. Callum will give you the one thing you lack.'

'For heaven's sake, Mother-in-law. I haven't seen him for five years. I can't just pick up the pieces. "Hello. Nice day. Take me, I'm yours." '

'Certainly not. It would be most improper.'

Emerald suddenly burst out laughing. 'Is that why you're suggesting it?'

'I expect so. It comes back, you know. Sex. These things do. It's like riding a bicycle. Once you've learned, you never lose it.'

'Mother-in-law, you're impossible.'

Bertha laid her hand on her daughter-in-law's arm. 'Emerald, my dear, you must forgive – yourself, as well as Callum.'

When the two fishermen return from the lake, Emerald was waiting on the lawn.

She greeted Callum politely but distantly. 'Callum. What an unexpected surprise.'

'Mummy! Mummy!'

Jamie burst in between them, clutching a large dappled fish, the gills threaded neatly on a reed.

'Look! For your supper! It's the biggest, fattest . . .'

His voice trailed away. He looked from one grown-up to the other.

Jamie was puzzled. Puzzled and a bit disappointed. He had thought his mummy would be really pleased to see Callum. Really happy to hear all the things they had done together. Yet here she was behaving as if she had hardly ever met him. Jamie knew that Callum and his mummy had gone fishing together when they were little together. Callum had told him so. Jamie was quite sure that Callum was some kind of uncle. An uncle in his life was just what Jamie needed. An uncle who could show him all sorts of marvellous things; who could share boys' interests with him.

'Callum?' Jamie looked up at Callum questioningly.

Callum glanced down. 'It's OK, Jamie. Your mother and I have lots to catch up on. We haven't seen each other since before you were born.'

'Come along, darling.' Emerald scooped Jamie up protectively in her arms, shooting Callum a fierce look.

'Let go, Mummy.'

Jamie wriggled fiercely. He didn't want his new friend thinking he was still a baby. A little baby for his mother to pick up and cuddle.

Emerald let go of the squirming body.

'Off you go, then, Jamie. Mrs Piggot's put your supper in the oven.'

Jamie looked up at his mother. He could see that her face was a little pink.

She said: 'Careful when you take it out. Don't burn your fingers.'

'Of course not,' Jamie said crossly. As if he would be so stupid. He was more than five years old, and he had had his heir ale. He had done a great many things already. He had frightened off the fox-man. He also knew how to catch poachers in a rabbit trap. And now, best of all, he knew how to tickle a trout with his bare hands. And only proper poachers knew how to do that.

He was big now, and he was going to school. Big boys like Jamie didn't really need a mother. Not really at all – except for a hug before you went to sleep.

An uncle would be nice.

His mother wasn't really interested in boys' things – the really important things.

Women were like that. Ben said so. Callum would probably say so, too, if Jamie got the chance to ask him.

Jamie had been quite hopeful, until his mother had come back.

Emerald waited until Jamie was well out of earshot. Then she swung back to face Callum, her eyes blazing.

'So what made *you* suddenly decide to turn up?'

Callum was caught momentarily off balance by her anger.

'Emerald, I didn't—'

'Didn't what?'

'For God's sake, Emerald, how could I have turned up? I thought you were dead. I thought it was you in the house. The explosion. Alison had told me she was leaving immediately. Who else could it have been but you? There was the bracelet – the one with the little cross. Anstruther let me believe—'

'Anstruther?'

Callum nodded, his eyes wary. 'He brought it to me in the hospital—'

Emerald shook her head fiercely. 'You got my letters. Why the hell didn't you answer?'

'I never got them – that is, not until yesterday.'

'The hell you didn't.'

'Emerald, here they are. They're the reason I came immediately.' He pulled the bundle out of his pocket and held it out to her.

Betrayal.

Emerald stared down, her eyes still wide with anger, filling now with tears. Sure enough, there were more than a dozen of the familiar cream envelopes, neatly tied up with tape.

'The proof. Where do you think I'd have got all that red tape?'

The ghost of a smile broke through. Emerald knew enough about the ways of lawyers to realize that was indeed a signature.

Anger surged again. 'You should have tried – again and again. Made Anstruther tell you the truth.'

'Emerald, for heaven's sake, you were the one who ran off and got yourself married to—' He waved his hand towards the towering crenellations of Astley. 'To all this. So that's thoroughly unreasonable.'

Emerald's head came up. 'Unreasonable to find myself a husband? And whose fault was that? I *had* to get married – but I suppose that was nothing to do with you, either. And I suppose it was unreasonable that I should find your poor pregnant girlfriend—'

'Emerald, she wasn't my girlfriend. She was Jack Sweeney's. I'd just given her a roof over her head.'

But Emerald forged on, the bit between her teeth now. 'And I suppose it was unreasonable that she got herself in such a state that she burned the place down – and herself with it?'

'The poor girl was out of her mind—'

'Just *why* was she out of her mind?' Emerald held up her hand. 'Let me guess. Nothing to do with you, either. "Not guilty, m'lud." '

Callum shook his head. 'It wasn't like that.'

'And afterwards – why didn't you come looking for me? Or, if not me, for Alison?'

'Be reasonable, Emerald. As far as I knew Alison had run back to Jack, and you were *dead*. I believed what Anstruther told me. What else was I to do?'

'You trusted Anstruther. I trusted you. And both of us ˅ ˑe wrong.'

'You were right to trust me. It wasn't my fault that Alison lied.'

'Don't you understand? She was desperate. She was faced with a choice – just as I was. And she made it alone, just as I did. Alison might just as well have been *me*. No difference. Even if the child she was carrying wasn't yours, she came to you for help. And you failed her.'

Suddenly the loneliness of the past was almost to much too bear. Silent tears coursed down her cheeks.

Callum waited, longing to take her in his arms, but knowing she had to face up to her demons in her own way. It was no longer Alison's battle she was fighting, but her own.

'I know and I'm sorry.' Callum's hazel eyes were steady. 'But it's over and done with now. All of five years. There's a life to be made – for all of us. I'm hoping yours will include me.'

'And now you think you can just walk in and claim me – and Jamie, too? Only one previous owner, reasonable condition? Is that what you think?'

'I think I want to look after you both – in whatever way you want. If you'll let me. I promised Tom—'

'What? To keep an eye on me? While Tom goes about his business? You're volunteering for bodyguard duty? We don't *need* to be looked after. Tom knows that. Didn't he explain that to you? Didn't either of you think what I might want? I want . . . I don't know what I want. I want Jamie – and Bertha – and Astley – and what I have made for myself. I don't know if I want you. I want to be who I am.'

'I know that, Emerald. And I wouldn't have it any other way.'

'That's kind of you. Jamie and me – we're glad to have your permission.'

Callum stared at her. Then he thrust his hand into his pocket again, pulling out the talisman bracelet.

'Here, take it. It keeps coming back – like a bad penny. I have no further use for it. It's you I want. I love you, Emerald. I've always loved you. Nothing and no-one, not even you, is going to change that.'

Emerald stared down at the little cross. Then a faint answering smile told him the storm was passing.

'Oh, Emerald, what can I do to prove I love you? Chase you up the brae?'

Callum almost laughed aloud as she wound the chain round her wrist and held it up to show him. That single gesture of acceptance told him more than any words.

'You never were much good at that, Cal.' The smile broadened. 'Anyway, here the brae's full of rabbit-traps.'

'And there's always the chance that next time Jamie might not be around to untangle me – it's a risk I'll have to take.' Callum's voice was joyful. 'But I'd settle for you to rescue me. I seem to remember you were no slouch at undoing things.'

Emerald giggled. 'True. But I'm a little out of practice. Better nowadays at doing up a small boy's shoelaces. Which reminds me – Jamie won't know what to make of all this. We'd better go and reassure him.'

His heart full of happiness, Callum followed Emerald up to the house.

'And you? Tell me.'

Long into the darkness, long after Mrs Piggot had declared the bedtime truce for Jamie, Emerald, in her turn, told Callum of the life she had chosen for herself – the battles she, too, had fought. Those she had lost and those she had won, and those she had yet to fight.

Later, after Bertha had left them alone, they sat quietly together by the fireside, taking strength and comfort from each other's presence, watching the little flames flicker and die back.

It was the comfortable intimacy of two people who share childhood memories, who know and understand the soil from which each has sprung.

After a time, they rose and went to the nursery and stood silently gazing down at the sleeping child, joined no less surely by the future than by the past.

Emerald felt her limbs melt, her body curve towards his as memory drew her into his arms. His voice was soft in her ear as he asked the question she both feared and longed to hear.

She could not answer. It had been so long.

Then, still silent and together, she led him from the shuttered room where Jamie dreamed. Together they climbed the spiral staircase to the turret room which looked over the lake.

The room was dusty, golden, filled with slanting moonlight. She drew him to her, on the bench which ran under the window-sills, trailing the air with the scent of horsehair and old beeswax polish.

Suddenly Emerald's eyes filled with tears. It had been so long – she scarcely remembered the feel of a man's arms, the taste of a man's lips, the strength of a man's body.

'Callum, I've almost forgotten what it was like . . .'

He whispered: 'Dear heart.'

Now, as before, she slipped out of her clothes and he from his, and naked she drew his body round her like a cloak, felt the silken touch of flesh to flesh.

'You remember now?'

'I remember. Oh, Callum, I remember so well.'

There was no veil between them, nothing hidden – nothing of the past to hide beneath the eaves of the old house. Only the certainty of familiarity, the pleasure of experience shared and now renewed.

The touch of fingertips, exploring gently – oh, so gently.

As his hands caressed her, Emerald felt her body stir, melting like the summer snows.

It had been so long.

At first, still uncertain of response, tentative, exploring. And then, as passion mounted, the scent of the dust in the nostrils and rough leather against soft skin.

Behind tight-pressed eyelids as she held him close, the memories of their first lovemaking bright in her heart.

As then, binding fast, and holding, and letting love take wing.

All night long she held him lightly on her fingertips, like a butterfly come to her hand.

81

Windsor: Monday 5 June 1972

The coffin was made of English oak. Heart of oak for the man who had given up an empire to win a woman's heart. On the coffin, simple and bare, lay a single sheaf of white lilies. The solitary tribute bore silent witness to an all-embracing, all-consuming, all-excluding passion.

For better, for worse, in sickness and in health, to have and to hold till death us do part. Unwavering in his devotion, with that, at least, he had kept faith.

And now, after thirty-five years in the wilderness, the man who had once been king had returned to claim his kingdom. Never mind that it was a bare six feet of earth, he had come home to rest at last.

For two days and two nights, sixty thousand of his one-time subjects paid silent tribute to the man who had given up an empire for the woman who held him in thrall.

The line of mourners snaked back a full mile from the entrance to St George's Chapel, heads bowed, remembering.

So infinitely sad, that single sheaf of white flowers. So solitary the silent witness to the love which had endured so long and so much. To that, at least, he had been true.

On the second day of the lying-in-state, Anthony Anstruther had one last duty to perform. It was a duty which was both an infinite sorrow and a happiness long delayed.

A duty to Emerald.

The happiness was the woman herself, last encountered as a vulnerable child whose beauty and spirit had even then had the power to move him.

The sorrow was at the news he had to bring.

When, five days earlier, the message had come from Paris that the Duke of Windsor had drawn his last breath, Anthony Anstruther had had no option but to take the decision to confront the woman who had never known her father in life, but who nevertheless had a right to bid him a last farewell in death.

'Is it wise, Anthony?' The Palace equerry's voice was anxious when Anstruther had telephoned to inform the Private Office of his intentions.

'My dear fellow, it may not be wise,' Anstruther snapped, 'but it's certainly proper.'

'Yes. Bit awkward, though.'

'Perhaps you'd like to check it with the boss?'

Anstruther's voice was impatient. The equerry was a new man. Nervous.

'Since it's you, Anthony, I assume you know what you're doing.'

'Naturally.'

'Your responsibility?'

'Of course.'

'That's all right, then.' The equerry coughed apologetically. 'I'll make sure you get the necessary passes.'

'Good. Drop them at the lodge, there's a good chap.'

'And, Anthony . . . ?'

'Yes?'

'She's not at all in good health – the Duchess. As you know, I picked her up from the Queen's flight yesterday and brought her to the Palace. Poor old thing seems a bit batty. She's been wandering around the corridors all night.'

'Only to be expected.'

'Yes. Just thought I'd warn you. In case you . . . hoped for anything.'

'My dear fellow, I hope for nothing. I never have – not for thirty years.'

'That's it, then. See you there.'

'Fine. Thank you – for your co-operation.'

Anstruther replaced the receiver thoughtfully. Thirty years. Emerald would now be thirty-five years old. Would be? Was.

Emerald Sherwood was very much a reality. A reality who would have to face the truth at last. And it was he who had the unenviable duty of bringing it to her.

'How did I know?'

Emerald looked at her visitor steadily. The violet eyes were wide and serious, as serious as that child had once been on the hillside.

The interview had not got off to an easy start.

Emerald had received her visitor calmly, her bearing almost regal as she made him welcome.

Anstruther's mind had been in uncharacteristic turmoil as he made the journey to the great house in Dorset from his bachelor rooms in Albany. He knew well enough what to expect – physically, at least. Emerald continued to promote her products herself. Her remarkable beauty was still the best advertisement for the philosophy which underpinned her success. The business was now international, beginning to be a powerful force in natural health care as it had been in the more restricted world of cosmetics. She gave few interviews, but when she did they were as likely to make headlines on the financial or political pages as in the women's fashion spreads.

Anstruther knew it was a powerful woman he was about to confront.

To Emerald the meeting was scarcely less daunting. Anstruther. A face now only half-remembered from that single encounter on the hills of Eas Forse. She saw in her mind's eye the little girl who raised her face, offered the parting visitor her warm cheek, a child's kiss, full of trust and hope.

Later she had feared his power. Whether the shadowy presence was for good or for evil, she never knew – and had never wanted to know. The fear had been enough. The fear of the unknown is the most terrifying fear of all.

Emerald hid her fear. Here after all was no black monster of her dreams, but flesh and blood and bone.

'Sir Anthony – please take a seat.'

Then all at once her fifteen-year-old son burst into the room. Tawny-haired and sturdy-limbed as Anstruther remembered his father in youth, he was obviously old for his years.

Emerald's sombre face changed instantly to happiness as she turned to greet him.

'Heavens, Jamie, what's happened?'

The boy – nearly a young man now – had a broad smile on his face. He was waving a document.

'I've got it, Mother!'

'Jamie, that's marvellous!'

Emerald threw her arms wide to embrace her son. He was a full head taller than she, and he had to bend his curly head so that she might kiss him.

Suddenly Emerald pulled back. She had remembered Anstruther's presence. 'We have a visitor, Jamie.'

The young man turned. 'Please forgive me, sir. I didn't see you. It was just that I've just had the news that I have won a prize which will enable me to go to my grandmother's old college. It would have given her such pleasure. Like her, I am fascinated by science.'

Emerald smiled. 'Sir Anthony, may I present my son?'

Jamie held out his hand. Anstruther took it. The grip was firm and strong. For a moment Anstruther was transported back to the moment he had greeted the young man's father. Bertha Sherwood's words echoed in his mind. This was the grandson he had never had.

'Pleased to meet you, sir.'

'And I you.'

Emerald looked up, surprised by the warmth in the barrister's voice.

Anstruther continued: 'I'm an old friend of your mother. And of your maternal grandmother – she was a wonderful woman.'

Anstruther had written a formal letter of condolence to express his sorrow at Dr Sherwood's death some five years earlier, and had received an equally formal reply from Emerald.

For a moment the man and the boy looked at each other. Anstruther could not tell whether Jamie guessed who he was, might even know of the role he had played in his mother's life.

Emerald watched them for a moment, her face calm.

'Sir Anthony's here on business, Jamie.'

'I'll leave you, then, Mother. Sir.' Jamie nodded to Anstruther and was gone.

Anstruther coughed. 'You must be proud of him.'

Pure happiness lit Emerald's face. 'I am.'

Anstruther hesitated. 'He has his mother's eyes.'

'They seem to be a strong family trait, those eyes.'

Anstruther hesitated. 'Yes.'

Emerald took a deep breath. 'I think I know why you're here, Sir Anthony. And I appreciate your courage. It's about my father, isn't it?'

'How did you know?' Anstruther's voice was almost a whisper.

Emerald gazed back at her visitor, her eyes steady.

'I read a letter. The letter Iona wrote to my real parents when she put

Callum and me on the boat. Cal thought it had been washed away in the storm, but I had hidden it in the little waterproof pocket in my life-jacket. Margaret Mackenzie hid my clothes in her treasure-chest. And on the day you came to take us away, I read it.'

Emerald shook her head. 'Then I simply tucked what I knew into the back of my mind, turned the key on it. Perhaps I believed that if I kept it locked away it would have no reality. I was only a child and, as my nan put it, fairy-touched, a changeling.'

She paused and walked over to the window, watching for a moment as the white wings flighted up from the dovecot on the lake.

After a moment she turned back to the bespectacled barrister. 'Sir Anthony, many women believe they know the moment they have conceived a child. So why should it be so strange that our own memories can reach back to that moment of first awakening? I would not have believed it myself, until I held my newborn son in my arms.'

She shook her head. How could this round-faced elderly man, so stiff and formal, so detached from the business of living and dying, possibly be expected to understand?

Bertha, now laid in her own grave in the churchyard, would have understood – and so would Margaret Mackenzie.

Quietly, almost as if she was talking to herself, she continued. 'It was my son Jamie who taught me to understand. At that moment of his birth, I knew that the long months he was growing inside me were memories we shared.'

She was silent for a moment, and then went on: 'Those memories were just as vivid as the moment of parting. Perhaps that moment of birth is so full of pain and joy that it obscures all others.'

She looked up, her eyes dark pools. 'I knew that for myself it could have been no different.'

Anstruther held his breath, fearful he might somehow break the thread which bound her to him.

'I can only tell you how it was. I can't make you understand.'

The voice reached out to him, softened by unshed tears.

'Perhaps it was that which made it so hard to accept – the loss. The realization that a love shared – that moment of conception, so brief and sweet – meant nothing to the woman who should have been my mother, the man who should have been my father.'

Anstruther raised his head and held Emerald's gaze at last. Seeing in that delicate heart-shaped face, in the sombre violet eyes, the memory of that sweet-scented night at Fort Belvedere, when the man who was already a king threw away his throne.

'I do understand,' he said quietly. 'Perhaps you, too, might understand better if you knew that, whatever else, they loved each other.'

When Emerald spoke, her voice was infinitely sad. 'I know.'

'Then, you will come?'

Emerald nodded. 'I will come.'

The chapel was crowded on that sombre morning when Emerald took her place among the throng of mourners who had gathered to bid fare-well to the man born to be king.

The Duchess herself, veiled and frail, was hidden from curious eyes behind the rood screen which divided the church – death according her that royal privilege which in life she had been so long denied.

The Garter King at Arms proclaimed the ancient titles of the one-time Defender of the Faith, King of Great Britain and Ireland, Emperor of India and all the Dominions beyond the Seas.

'Knight of the Garter, of the Thistle, of the Patrick . . .'

The voice echoed round the vaulted ceiling with the roll-call of kingdom and empire.

Gone for ever now, the earthly kingdom. Dust returned to dust. So simple and so pitiful, the final words of loss.

For a single moment, as the royal party – crowned heads and courtiers, lords temporal and spiritual – moved down the aisle in the wake of the swaying coffin, Emerald raised her head.

And then, in that single moment, eyes met, locked, saw clearly, hesitated for a single instant, and then moved on.

In that moment, for the one and only time, both recognized and ac-knowledged the relationship which, far from uniting mother and daughter, had instead served to keep them apart.

Anstruther, his hand on Emerald's arm, was the only other being who understood the significance of that hesitation. Was it simply that the Duke, as the Duchess was so fond of saying, had neither need nor desire for an heir? Or was it for another, darker purpose: that, if Wallis herself could not be queen, nor indeed would her daughter.

Six months later, the Duchess signed a document declaring that she had neither heirs nor descendants who might have a claim on her estate.

The lawyer who drew up the papers was surprised at the strength of her insistence. As far as anyone knew there were certainly no descend-ants who might bring forward a claim.

To all except those who knew the truth, the document was after all, a mere formality.

To those who knew the truth, it was an acknowledgement of that long-ago betrayal.

To Anstruther, it was no more nor less than he had expected. It was that final gesture which made him take the decision to offer himself to Emerald as – and he put it in his most detached lawyerly manner – a kind of adopted grandfather for Jamie. 'Keep a watching brief on the boy. Not quite *in loco parentis*, but you'll understand the spirit.'

And Emerald, released by that final irrevocable betrayal, found herself able to accept.

From that moment onwards, Anstruther's occasional visits to Astley, the 'watching brief' he kept on Jamie's progress through university, gave him more happiness than anything he had ever experienced in his life.

82

Geneva: Friday, 3 April 1987

It was no accident that there was more than a touch of the circus about the crowded marquee pitched on the shores of Lake Geneva.

For sale was a menagerie of barbaric jewels. The stuff of dreams was under the hammer.

'Apologies for the interruption, mesdames messieurs. We continue with the bidding for lot 160 . . .'

The auctioneer peered over his glasses at the rustling audience. There had been a brief flurry of excitement a few minutes earlier, when lot 159 had been withdrawn. The bidding between two of the participants had been so fierce that it had reduced the room to an astonished silence.

The contest – until the intervention of the elderly gentleman – had had the feel of a grudge match.

Lot 159 was a locket – by no means of any great value, unless because it was one of the few antique items in the sale. The crystal face revealed a triple curl. The strands were neatly plaited. One fair, one dark, one russet.

On the reverse was an inscription in the private language the royal lovers shared. 'EANUM WE R 3' was followed by a date.

The principal bidder, the woman with the violet eyes, followed the man who had interrupted the bidding, an English gentleman in a pin-striped suit, outside on to the lawn.

The crowd speculated on the incident. Who was she? Many in that crowd could furnish the reply. 'Emerald Sherwood. You *know*. They said she was to bid for the emerald parure. Heaven knows, she can afford it. She's on the Forbes list this year.'

But why? Why should she bid for such a small thing? Such sums for what was no more than a sentimental trinket? And who was her companion, the distinguished Englishman? Above all, who was the man who had bid against her, the man now pushing angrily towards the exit in her wake?

You could tell from the vicuña overcoat and the expensive shirting he was a wealthy man. There were those, too, in the crowd who knew his name. He was a well-known gossip columnist with his own syndicated diary. The crowd buzzed with the small drama, busy as bees about other people's business.

'Gentleman, ladies, can I have your attention, please, for lot 160?'

The crowd turned its attention back to the bidding. It had a short memory for reality tonight. Its thoughts were on the king who had surrendered his throne for his one great love, and the crowd was hungry for romance.

'Can I have your attention please? Lot 160.'

The beautiful woman and the elderly man were alone together by the shores of the lake.

Anstruther looked into the eyes of the woman who had been so long his cross and care – for whom he had risked so much.

Emerald's face was expressionless, her violet eyes dreamy. She cradled the locket in her palm, gazing down at the transparent crystal. Inside, three interlacing curls: one dark, one fair, one russet – baby-fine.

Emerald sighed. A sigh of sorrow and regret.

Anstruther said: 'You understand?'

After a long moment, Emerald held up her hand. The little bracelet on her wrist glittered in the sunshine. She turned it over, read once again the inscription.

'The date is a reference to my birth, isn't that so? And the rest?'

'The private language. *Eanum* is "little", *WE* is for "Wallis and Edward", and of course you made three.'

'That's all?'

'There's this.' Anstruther reached into his pocket. 'Perhaps it's more valuable still.'

Emerald stared at the metal disc, picked it up and held it to the light.

After a moment she said: 'I remember.'

Anstruther coughed. 'I kept it – just in case. Legally there's more than enough. There can be no doubt about your identity, or who your parents are – were. The three curls in the locket will prove it. Genetic fingerprinting is acceptable at law these days – but I would scarcely think that would be necessary. You would have a considerable claim on the estate.'

Anstruther continued, his voice as bone-dry as the skeletons whose bones he rattled.

'By claiming what is owed, you would finally lay all your ghosts,' he said.

What he meant was something different. It was his own ghosts he sought to lay.

He went on, his voice confident and lawyerly. 'We must take it straight to The Hague. No guarantee, of course, but they've a good track record – handed down favourable judgements in similar cases. Inheritance is a tricky business. No sense in wasting time around Her Majesty's High Court.'

He thought to himself: *All those years.*

He was silent.

It was as if nothing he had to say, nothing he had to offer – and it was no more than her birthright – had any relevance at all.

Emerald shook her head gently. On the manicured lawn around them, small groups of elegantly dressed men and bejewelled women stood around sipping champagne, discussing the day's prices and personalities.

For a moment Emerald scanned the crowd, her eyes anxiously quartering the knots of chattering people. Then she relaxed. Anstruther followed her gaze. Down by the water two figures were leaning over the curved balustrade, heads inclined together.

Callum's hair was no longer the barley-gold of his youth, but the set of the shoulders was still firm and strong. It seemed he would never change. He would still disappear for months at a time when all she would know of him was through the by-line on his work. Only now he came back to lie in her arms, his head, greying a little, beside hers on the pillow.

With him was Jamie, beloved Jamie, taller in adulthood than his father but with the same slender grace of his mother and his father's tawny hair. The young man inclined his head towards his father – just as she had seen them first together, by the lake at Astley. For a moment Emerald's eyes filled with tears – tears for what she herself had never known.

Behind, in the tent, the quick-fire bids – a thousand – ten thousand – twenty – rattled like the wheels of the tumbrils must have rattled on the cobbles of revolutionary Paris.

It was over at last, the long waiting.

In her ears, Anstruther's voice came and went: '. . . secured the evidence of the locket . . . prove beyond doubt . . . conclusive.'

His voice was urgent, willing Emerald to accept.

She stared down at the little pile of detritus in her palm. The glittering chain bracelet with its tiny cross, the metal disc, the locket. The proverbial three wishes, ready to be delivered.

Then, unbelievably, she shook her head. 'No.'

'But, my dear, at least take time to consider. For Jamie's sake, even if not for your own.'

Emerald studied the anxious face of the old man.

'I know, Anthony,' she said. 'But, then, I always knew. It was never meant to be any other way. I think you knew that, too.'

Her gaze was steady, her voice quiet.

Anstruther gazed back, bewildered, uncertain of what might happen now.

Even Jack Sweeney, watching eagerly from the shelter of the marquee's doorway, did not anticipate what she did then.

By the time either of them realized her intention, it was too late.

Emerald walked the few yards down to the lake's edge.

Before Anstruther could reach out to stay her hand, she swung her arm in a wide circle and opened her fist, flinging the glittering trinkets over the still water.

Arcing high over the blue mirror, they fell towards their own reflection, and then were gone.

Emerald turned away, defiant, proud. In that instant both men, unwitting allies in that last battle, knew that it was over.

Defeated at last, both men stared out into the widening ripples on the lake.

'Anthony?'

Emerald laid her hand on her grey-haired companion's arm. Once again, as on that fateful meeting on the hills of Eas Forse, her lips brushed his cheek.

When she spoke her voice was gentle, her eyes full of compassion. 'Thank you, old friend. But it could never have been otherwise.'

Compassion and pride – the certainty of a woman in the full possession of her empire, an empire she alone had earned.

'What did you expect?' There was laughter in her voice and in the violet eyes. 'After all, Sir Anthony, I am the daughter of a king.'